SWORDS &
DARK MAGIC

An Imprint of HarperCollins*Publishers*

SWORDS & DARK MAGIC

THE NEW SWORD AND SORCERY

EDITED BY

JONATHAN STRAHAN

AND

LOU ANDERS

A continuation of the copyright page appears on pages 521–522.

FIRST EDITION

Designed by Joy O'Meara

Eos is a federally registered trademark of HarperCollins Publishers.

Library of Congress Cataloging-in-Publication Data has been applied for.

ISBN 978-0-06-172381-0

10 11 12 13 14   OV/RRD   10 9 8 7 6 5 4 3 2 1

For
ROBERT E HOWARD,
FRITZ LEIBER,
and
MICHAEL MOORCOCK,
the great literary swordsmen who made it possible

ACKNOWLEDGMENTS

Thanks are due to many people for this project. Among them are Diana Gill, our editor at Harper Eos who believed in this anthology enough to make it a reality; to Benjamin Carré, for the cover; and to each of the authors involved, who contributed such wonderful stories. Thanks are also due to Lev Grossman, Tim Holman, Katie Menick, Howard Morhaim, Erik Mona, Jason M. Waltz, and Bill Schafer.

Last, and most importantly, to our wives, Xin C. Anders and Marianne Jablon, whose infinite patience and support are the key ingredient in any anthology project.

CONTENTS

CHECK YOUR DARK LORD AT THE DOOR

Sword and sorcery. The name says it all. Action meets magic. If high fantasy is about vast armies divided along the lines of obvious good versus ultimate evil, epic struggles to vanquish dark lords bent on world domination, then sword and sorcery is its antithesis. Smaller-scale character pieces, often starring morally compromised protagonists, whose heroism involves little more than trying to save their own skins from a trap they themselves blundered into in search of spoils. Sword and sorcery is where fantasy fiction meets the western, with its emphasis on traveling swordsmen wandering into an exotic setting and finding themselves thrust into unanticipated conflicts there. As high fantasy concerns itself with warring nations and final battles, sword and sorcery focuses on personal battles, fought in the back alleys of exotic cities, in the secret chambers of strange temples, in the depths of dark dungeons. If high fantasy is a child of *The Iliad*, then sword and sorcery is a product of *The Odyssey*.

J. R. R. Tolkien is the undisputed father of high, or epic, fantasy.* His *Lord of the Rings* drew on Norse mythologies, his personal experiences in World War I, and, arguably, Wagner's *The Ring of the Nibelung* (though he denied this vehemently). The story of a titanic struggle for the fate of nations, it single-handedly led to the

---

* It should be noted that William Morris, Lord Dunsany, and E. R. Eddison all preceded and influenced Tolkien.

creation of the fantasy genre *as a recognized genre,* and spawned a thousand imitators. Famous names such as Terry Brooks, Terry Goodkind, Robert Jordan, Roger Zelazny, Stephen R. Donaldson all owe an immeasurable debt to the Oxford professor. But the earlier form of sword and sorcery fantasy owes its genesis to Texan-born Robert E. Howard, who drew upon his Irish ancestry and a lifetime of tall tales of the American West to create stories of adventure that were, in contrast to his contemporaries, laced with a grim pessimism and an edge of violent realism. A boxer who stood six feet two inches, known for his stamina and for rarely losing a fight, Howard brought to his imagined conflicts a reality backed up by experience. It was in the pages of *Weird Tales* that he, a popular writer who wrote for scores of classic pulp magazines, would debut his greatest and most influential creation, Conan the Cimmerian. Like Tolkien's Middle Earth, Howard set Conan's adventures in an imagined prehistoric land, Hyperborea, which existed between the fall of Atlantis and the time of recorded history. From out of the barbaric north, Conan came, "a thief, a reaver, a slayer, with gigantic melancholies and gigantic mirth, to tread the jeweled thrones of the Earth under his sandalled feet." As he detailed Conan's exploits, Howard pioneered a new kind of fantasy, one that owed as much to the swashbuckling tales of Alexandre Dumas and Rafael Sabatini as it did to the outlaws and renegades of the American West.

Like the gunslingers whose exaggerated exploits form the bedrock of Howard's childhood entertainments, Conan was an opportunist, a self-serving fortune seeker with a fatalistic outlook, albeit a man loyal to his friends, often given to penetrating psychological insights. Between 1933 and his death in 1936, Howard placed eighteen stories of Conan in the pages of *Weird Tales*. An instant success, the character's most immediate influences were writers C. L. Moore and Fritz Leiber. The former introduced Jirel of Joiry in 1934, the year after Conan's debut. Notable for being the first female protagonist in sword and sorcery, Jirel was the monarch of an imagined medieval French province, known for relying on her wits over her fists, albeit not shy of taking up a sword and shield. Moore penned six tales between 1934 and 1939, beginning with the classic "Black God's Kiss."[†] For his part, Fritz Leiber (in conjunction with his friend Harry Otto Fischer) conceived of the first S&S buddy duo, Fafhrd the Barbarian and his friend and accomplice, the diminutive thief known as the Gray Mouser. Appearing first in 1939 in the pages of *Unknown,* Fafhrd and the Mouser are notable in that their adventures continued until 1991 and ended with the heroes settling down into married life. Unlike Howard, Tolkien, and Moore, Leiber chose to set their adventures in a purely invented, secondary world, the world of Nehwon, rather than a lost past or fantastical version of our own history. This was not fantasy's first foray into alternative constructed worlds but it was certainly one of the most influential.[‡]

Furthermore, Howard's contemporary Clark Ashton Smith is notable for his own contribution to the genre, not the least of which were his own Hyperborean tales, set, like Howard's, in a lost mythical age. In this case, though, his Hyperborea was an Arctic continent, the last gasps of a civilization facing the encroachment of an Ice Age. By peopling them with sorcerers and strange deities, Smith seemed to merge the worlds of Robert E.

[†] Paizo Publishing's Planet Stories imprint recently published all six of the Jirel of Joiry stories in one volume. *The Black God's Kiss* (2002) is notable for including "Quest of the Starstone," a story that is omitted from the two previous Jirel collections. Written with Moore's husband, Henry Kuttner, this tale features Jirel's meeting with Moore's other famous creation, spaceship pilot and smuggler Northwest Smith, direct forerunner of *Star Wars'* Hans Solo.

[‡] Many of Terry Pratchett's Discworld novels are set in a city called Ankh-Morpork, a nod to Leiber's city of Lankhmar, and the first Discworld novel features an encounter with a giant barbarian comrade "Bravd" and a swordsman-thief known as "The Weasel." Pratchett's Cohen the Barbarian is, of course, a reference to Robert E. Howard's creation as well.

Howard with that of the third great writer from this era of *Weird Tales,* their friend H. P. Lovecraft.

Come the 1960s, however, the sword and sorcery genre, with the exception of Leiber's Fafhrd and Gray Mouser tales, had waned in popularity, until writer Lin Carter crafted the first successful ongoing series in imitation of Howard's Conan. Carter's Thongor series, beginning with *The Wizard of Lemuria* in 1965, blended Howard's barbarian with the works of Edgar Rice Burroughs. Set across the lost continent of Lemuria, they featured magic, flying machines, and mankind's attempts to throw off the shackles of a serpentine race of "Dragon Kings." Carter's Thongor tales diminished, however, when he was recruited by L. Sprague de Camp to assist in a Conan revival.

De Camp had contributed his own notable sword and sorcery in the 1950s. His Pusadian series was an attempt to write in a Hyperborean setting that paid more attention to what was then known about the geology of the earth. But beginning in the 1950s, though primarily in the 1960s, de Camp began to work to republish the existing Conan tales, as well as to publish the many Howard-penned Conan stories unpublished in the author's lifetime. In the aforementioned collaboration with Lin Carter, he worked to popularize Howard and bring him back into print. Adding their own contributions to the mythos, de Camp and Carter rewrote many of Howard's unpublished non-Conan tales as new exploits of the Cimmerian. This led to a boom in Conan's popularity, with the character spilling out into new novels, comic books, and even film, though a 1983 biography of Howard, penned by de Camp and titled *Dark Valley Destiny: the Life of Robert E. Howard,* had the unintended consequence of refocusing attention on Howard's undiluted Conan, with de Camp and Carter's additions and alterations dwindling in public favor.

Sword and sorcery wouldn't officially be labeled as its own

subgenre until 1961, however, when Michael Moorcock published a letter in the fanzine *Amra,* demanding that the type of swash-buckling adventure story pioneered by Howard be given a name. Ironically, Moorcock originally proposed the term "epic fantasy," a label that has since come to be applied to the other side of the coin, that of J. R. R. Tolkien and his successors. But Fritz Leiber christened the subgenre when he wrote in the July 1961 issue of *Amra,* "I feel more certain than ever that this field should be called the sword-and-sorcery story. This accurately describes the points of culture-level and supernatural element and also immedi-ately distinguishes it from the cloak-and-sword (historical adven-ture) story—and (quite incidentally) from the cloak-and-dagger (international espionage) story too!"

In this same year, Moorcock would pen *The Dreaming City,* the first tale of his antihero Elric of Melniboné, arguably the only sword and sorcery protagonist to reach Howard's level of influence. Conceived as an anti-Conan—or, rather, Conan as an angst-ridden teenager—Elric was a sickly, drug-taking albino who relied upon an evil, soul-sucking black sword to feed him the stolen energies to both maintain his life and increase his vitality. Simply put, Moorcock's contribution to fantasy literature cannot be overstated. The New Wave movement that he later pioneered forever changed the face of science fiction, just as his concept of the "multiverse" would as well, even spilling out of the pages of imaginary tales to grace the lips of our contemporary physicists, but for our purposes here, it might be his alteration of the battle of Good versus Evil into that of Law versus Chaos (with disastrous consequences implied if either side ultimately triumphed over the other) that made the most significant contribution to fantasy literature. His heroes, whether Elric of Melniboné, or Dorian Hawkmoon, or the rock and roll assassin Jerry Cornelius, were all manifestations of the Eternal Champion, a soul doomed to forever maintain the "Cosmic Balance" by lending weight to one side of the scales or the other. Moorcock's influence is colossal, his shadow cast everywhere from role-playing games (and thus, subsequently, all third-person computer and console gaming) to rock and roll to literature. The alignment wheel of Dungeons & Dragons is nothing short of his Law vs. Chaos and Good vs. Evil plotted on an X-Y axis, and it is no surprise that Michael Chabon's foray into fantastical swashbuckling, *Gentleman of the Road,* is dedicated to the fantasy grand master. But it is Moorcock's character of Elric the Albino that came to define the sword and sorcery subgenre as much as Howard's creation.

Also of note is Andre Norton, whose long-running Witch World stories, beginning with *Witch World* in 1963 and continuing up through this century, were both seminal sword and sorcery works (albeit rather heavy on the sorcery), as well as seminal romantic fantasy works.

During the 1960s, 1970s, and 1980s, led by Lin Carter, the Swordsmen and Sorcerers' Guild of America promoted the interests of the subgenre. From 1973 to 1981, SAGA produced five anthologies, edited by Carter and featuring the contributions of their members, under the series title Flashing Swords! The year 1974 saw the debut of Charles R. Saunders's Imaro tales, which appeared first in the fanzine *Dark Fantasy* but, by way of Lin Carter's *Year's Best Fantasy Stories* (DAW Books, 1975), eventually found their way to publisher Donald A. Wolheim, who urged Saunders to publish them as a novel in 1981. *Imaro* was followed by *The Quest for Cush* (1984) and *The Trail of Bohu* (1985).[§] The stories are notable for being the first sword and sorcery penned

---

[§]   *Imaro* and *The Quest for Cush* are both currently available from Night Shade Books. *The Trail of Bohu* has recently been self-published by the author.

by a black author and starring a black protagonist. The title character, Imaro, inhabited the "black continent" of Nyumbani, an "alternate Africa" that existed thousands of years ago, perhaps contemporaneously with Robert E. Howard's Hyperborea.

Then, in 1984, Marion Zimmer Bradley made a significant contribution to the field with her Sword and Sorceress anthology series. Feeling that, C. L. Moore excepted, the subgenre was dominated by men and typified by some fairly reprehensible attitudes toward and depictions of women, she produced twenty volumes (two published posthumously) of adventure tales featuring strong female protagonists and promoting such notable authors as Bradley herself, Glen Cook, Emma Bull, Charles R. Saunders, Charles de Lint, Pat Murphy, C. J. Cherryh, Jennifer Roberson, Mercedes Lackey, and many more. After Bradley's death in 1999, the anthology series continued in a new volume edited by Diana L. Paxson (*Sword and Sorceress XXI,* DAW, 2004) and, recently, in two volumes from editor Elisabeth Waters (Norilana Books, 2007).

But, generally speaking, the last few decades was a time when sword and sorcery fiction was once again out of favor. The 1982 film *Conan the Barbarian,* which made Arnold Schwarzenegger a household name, spawned a sea of poorly executed sequels and imitations that had the effect of stigmatizing the subgenre's image. Though its practitioners never entirely went away, the fantasy genre came to be dominated by the post-Tolkien variety of epic fantasy. At the short form, sword and sorcery fiction fell out of favor with the larger magazine venues, and the type of adventure fantasy that Robert E. Howard once epitomized was relegated to the domain of the small press (most notably, *Black Gate* magazine, which has been the definitive source for sword and sorcery short-form works since its launch in 2000). But recently, sword and sorcery has been making a comeback. In the wake of George R. R. Martin, whose Song of Ice and Fire series is notable for bringing a moral ambiguity and gritty realism to the fantasy epic, a host of younger writers have emerged to bring a "sword and sorcery sensibility" back to the epic subgenre. Writers like Steven Erikson, Joe Abercrombie, Scott Lynch, Tom Lloyd, David Anthony Durham, Brian Ruckley, James Enge, Brent Weeks, and Patrick Rothfuss are pioneering a new kind of fantasy, one that blends epic struggles with a gritty realism, where good and evil mixes into realistic characters fraught with moral ambiguities, and struggles between nations are not so one-sided as they are colored by a new, politically savvy understanding. These hard-hitting tales are reinvigorating the fantasy genre, while at the same time its classic forebears are finding new readers. For the first time in many years, Robert E. Howard's and Michael Moorcock's original stories are available again, in new, lavishly illustrated editions that restore their original texts, complete with copious historical notes. Leiber's full saga of Fafhrd and the Gray Mouser is back on shelves, just as C. L. Moore's oeuvre is out in a complete collection. The MMORG *Age of Conan* is a huge success, and both Conan and Elric movies are currently in development. While Howard, sadly, left us in 1936, Moorcock has recently been writing new tales of the Melnibonéan, one of which appears in this volume. With all the excitement surrounding this new cadre of writers, combined with the recent celebration of their historic roots, there is no better time for a definitive look at the new fantasy. Here, then, are seventeen original tales of sword and sorcery, penned by masters old and new. What follows are stories of small stakes but high action, grim humor mixed with gritty violence, dry fatalism in the face of strange magics, fierce monsters and fabulous treasures, and, as ever, lots and lots of swordplay. Enjoy!

Lou Anders & Jonathan Strahan
Alabama & Australia

STEVEN ERIKSON is the pseudonym of Canadian novelist Steve Rune Lundin, best known for his ongoing fantasy series Malazan Book of the Fallen, beginning in 1999 with *Gardens of the Moon*. Trained as an archaeologist and anthropologist, Erikson is a graduate of the Iowa Writers' Workshop, and is a World Fantasy Award–nominated author. *SF Site* has called the series "the most significant work of epic fantasy since Donaldson's Chronicles of Thomas Covenant." Known for his portrayal of multidimensional characters, he said in an interview conducted by suite101.com, "It's often commented that my stuff is all shades of gray rather than black and white, but that's not the same as saying every character is similarly gray—the effect is an overall one rather than a specific one. Most of the characters I come up with have pretty fixed notions of right and wrong, they have a moral center, in other words, whether consciously recognized or not. But in coming at something from more than one side, the reader is left free to choose which one they'll favor." Erikson now lives in Cornwall, England.

GOATS OF GLORY

Steven Erikson

Five riders drew rein in the pass. Slumped in their saddles, they studied the valley sprawled out below them. A narrow river cut a jagged scar down the middle of a broad floodplain. A weathered wooden bridge sagged across the narrow span, and beyond it squatted a score of buildings, gray as the dust hovering above the dirt tracks wending between them.

A short distance upriver, on the same side as the hamlet, was a large, unnatural hill, on which stood a gray-stoned keep. The edifice looked abandoned, lifeless, no banners flying, the garden terraces ringing the hillsides overgrown with weeds, the few windows in the square towers gaping black as caves.

The riders rode battered, beaten-down horses. The beasts' heads drooped with exhaustion, their chests speckled and streaked with dried lather. The two men and three women did not look any better. Armor in tatters, blood-splashed, and all roughly bandaged here and there to mark a battle somewhere behind them. Each wore a silver brooch clasping their charcoal-gray cloaks over their hearts, a ram's head in profile.

They sat in a row, saying nothing, for some time.

And then the eldest among them, a broad-shouldered, pale-skinned woman with a flat face seamed in scars, nudged her mount down onto the stony descent. The others fell in behind their captain.

The boy came running to find Graves, chattering about strangers coming down from the border pass. Five, on horses, with sunlight glinting on chain and maybe weapons. The one in the lead had long black hair and pale skin. A foreigner for sure.

Graves finished his tankard of ale and pushed himself to his feet. He dropped two brass buttons on the counter and Swillman's crabby hand scooped them up before Graves had time to turn away. From the far end of the bar, Slim cackled, but that was a random thing with her, and she probably didn't mean anything by it. Though maybe she did. Who could know the mind of a hundred-year-old whore?

The boy, whom Graves had come to call Snotty, for his weeping nose and the smudges of dirt that collected there, led the way outside, scampering like a pup. To High Street's end, where Graves lived and where he carved the slabs he and the boy brought down from the old quarry every now and then.

Snotty went into the tiny one-stall stable and set about hitching up the mule to the cart. Graves tugged open the door to his shed, reminding himself to cut back the grass growing along the rain gutter. He stepped inside and, though his eyes had yet to adjust, he reached with overlong familiarity to the rack of long-handled shovels and picks just to the left of the door. He selected his best shovel and then the next best one for the boy, and finally his heavy pick.

Stepping outside, he glared up at the bright sun for a moment before walking to where Snotty was readying the cart. The three digging tools thumped onto the bed in a cloud of dust. "Five you say?"

"Five!"

"Bring us two casks of water."

"I will."

Graves went out back behind the shed. He eyed the heap of slabs, dragged out five—each one dressed into rough rectangular shapes, sides smoothed down, one arm's-length long and an elbow-down wide—and he squatted before them, squinting at the bare facings. "Best wait on that," he muttered, and then straightened when he heard the boy bringing the cart around.

"Watch your fingers this time," Graves warned.

"I will."

Graves moved the pick and shovels to the head of the cart bed to make room for the slabs. Working carefully, they loaded each stone onto the warped but solid planks. Then Graves went around to the mule's harness and cinched the straps tighter to ease the upward pull on the animal's chest.

"Five," said the boy.

"Heavy load."

"Heavy load. What you gonna carve on 'em?"

"We'll see."

Graves set out and Snotty led the mule and the creaking cart after him, making sure the wooden wheels fell evenly into the ruts on the road, the ruts that led to the cemetery.

When they arrived, they saw Flowers wandering the grassy humps of the burial ground, collecting blossoms, her fair hair dancing in the wind. The boy stopped and stared until Graves pushed the second-best shovel into his hands.

"Don't even think about it," Graves warned.

"I'm not," the boy lied, but some lies a man knew to just let pass. For a time.

Graves studied the misshapen lumps before them, thinking, measuring in his head. "We start a new row."

Shovels in hand, they made their way into the yard.

"Five, you said."

"Five," answered the boy.

It took most of the morning for the riders to reach the floodplain. The trail leading down into the valley was ill-frequented and there had been no work done on it in decades. Seasonal runoff had carved deep, treacherous channels around massive boulders. Snake holes gaped everywhere and the horses twitched and shied as they picked their way down the slope.

The cooler air of the pass gave way to cloying heat in the valley. Broken rock surrendered to brambles and thickets of spike-grass and sage. Upon reaching level ground, the trail opened out, flanked by tree stumps and then a thin forest of alder, aspen, and, closer to the river, cottonwoods.

The approach to the hamlet forked before reaching the bridge. The original, broader track led to a heap of tumbled blackstone, rising from the bank like the roots of shattered teeth with a similar ruin on the other side of the river. The wooden bridge at the end of the narrower path was barely wide enough to take a cart. Built of split logs and hemp rope, it promised to sway sickeningly and the riders would need to cross it one at a time.

The man who rode behind the captain was squat and wide, his broad face a collection of crooked details, from the twisted nose to the hook lifting the left side of his mouth, the dented jawline, one ear boxed and looking like a flattened cabbage, the other clipped neatly in half with top and bottom growing in opposite directions. His beard and mustache were filthy with flecks of dried spit and possibly froth. As he guided his horse over the bridge, he squinted down at the river to his left. The remnants of the stone pillars that had held up the original bridge were still visible, draped in flowing manes of algae.

Horse clumping onto solid ground once more, he drew up beside his captain and they sat watching the others cross one by one.

Captain Skint's expression was flat as her face, her eyes like scratched basalt.

"A year ago," said the man, "and it'd take half the day for alla us t'come over this bridge. A thousand Rams, hard as stone."

The third rider coming up alongside them, a tall, gangly woman with crimson glints in her black hair, snorted at the man's words. "Dreaming of the whorehouse again, Sarge?"

"What? No. Why'd ya think—"

"We ain't Rams anymore. We're goats. Fucking goats." And she spat.

Dullbreath and Huggs joined them and the five mercenaries, eager for the respite the hamlet ahead offered them—but admitting to nothing—fell into a slow canter as the track widened into something like a road.

They passed a farm: a lone log house and three stone-walled pens. The place stank of pig shit and the flies buzzed thick as black smoke. The forest came to a stumpy end beyond that. A few small fields of crops to the left, and ahead and to the right stood some kind of temple shrine, a stone edifice not much bigger than the altar stone it sheltered on three sides. Surrounding it was a burial ground.

The riders saw a man and a boy in the yard, digging pits, each one marked out with sun-bleached rags tied to trimmed saplings. A mule and cart waited motionless beneath an enormous yew tree.

"That's a few too many graves on the way," Sergeant Flapp muttered. "Plague, maybe?"

No one commented. But as they rode past, each one—barring the captain—fixed their attention on the two diggers, counting slow to reach . . . five.

"Five flags." Flapp shook his head. "That's probably half the population here."

A small girl walked the street a short distance ahead of the troop, clutching in one hand a mass of wildflowers. Honeybees spun circles around her tousled head.

The riders edged past her—she seemed oblivious to them—and cantered into the hamlet.

Slim came back from the doorway and slid along the bar rail to lurch to a halt opposite Swillman. "Give us one, then. I'll be good for it."

"Since when?"

"Them's soljers, Swilly. Come from the war—"

"What war?"

"T'other side of the mountains, o'course."

Swillman settled a gimlet regard on the ancient whore. "You hear anything about a war? From who? When?"

She shifted uneasily. "Well, you know and I know we ain't seen traffic in must be three seasons now. But they's soljers and they been chewed up bad, so there must be a war. Somewhere. And they came down from the pass, so it must be on t'other side."

"On the Demon Plain, right. Where nobody goes and nobody comes back neither. A war . . . over there. Right, Slim. Whatever you say, but I ain't giving you one unless you pay and you ain't got nothing to pay with."

"I got my ring."

He stared at her. "But that's your livelihood, Slim. You cough that up and you got nothing to offer 'em."

"You get it after they've gone, or maybe not, if I get work."

"Nobody's that desperate," Swillman said. "Seen yourself lately? Say, anytime in the last thirty years?"

"Sure. I keep that fine silver mirror all polished up, the one in my bridal suite, ya."

He grunted a laugh. "Let's see it, then, so I know you ain't up and swallowed it."

She stretched her jaw and worked with her tongue, and then hacked up something into her hand. A large rolled copper ring, tied to a string with the other end going into her mouth, wrapped around a tooth, presumably.

Swillman leaned in for a closer look. "First time I actually seen it, y'know."

"Really?"

"It's my vow of celibacy."

"Since your wife died, ya, which makes you an idiot. We could work us out a deal, y'know."

"Not a chance. It's smaller than I'd have thought."

"Most men are smaller than they think, too."

He settled back and collected a tankard.

Slim put the ring back into her mouth and watched with avid eyes the sour ale tumbling into the cup.

"Is that the tavern?" Huggs asked, eyeing the ramshackle shed with its signpost but no sign.

"If it's dry I'm going to beat on the keeper, I swear it," said Flapp, groaning as he slid down from his horse. "Beat 'im t'death, mark me." He stood for a moment, and then brushed dust from his cloak, his thighs, and his studded leather gauntlets. "No inn s'far as I can see, just a room in back. Where we gonna sleep? Put up the horses? This place is a damned pustule, is what it is."

"The old map I seen," ventured Wither, "gave this town a name."

"Town? It ain't been a town in a thousand years, if ever."

"Even so, Sarge."

"So what's it called?"

"Glory."

"You're shitting me, ain't ya?"

She shook her head, reaching over to collect the reins of the captain's horse as Skint thumped down in a plume of dust and, with a wince, walked—in her stockings as she'd lost her boots—to the tavern door.

Huggs joined Wither tying up the horses to the hitching post. "Glory, huh? Gods, I need a bath. They should call this place Dragon Mouth, it's so fucking hot. Listen, Wither, that quarrel head's still under my shoulder blade—I can't reach up and take off this cloak—I'm melting underneath—"

The taller woman turned to her, reached up, and unclasped the brooch on Huggs's cloak. "Stand still."

"It's a bit stuck on my back. Bloodglue, you know?"

"Ya. Don't move and if this hurts, I don't want to have to hear about it."

"Right. Do it."

Wither stepped around, gripping the cloak's hems, and slowly and evenly pulled the heavy wool from Huggs's narrow back. The bloodglue gave way with a sob, revealing a quilted gambeson stained black around the hole left by the quarrel. Wither studied the wound by peering through the hole. "A trickle, but not bad."

"Good. Nice. Thanks."

"I wouldn't trust the bathwater here, Huggs. That river's fulla pig shit and this place floods every spring, and I doubt the wells are dug deep."

"I know. Fucking hole."

The others had followed Captain Skint into the tavern. There was no shouting from within—a good sign.

The shorter, thinner woman—whose hips were, however, much broader than Wither's—plucked at the thongs binding the front of the gambeson. "Sweat's got me all chafed under my tits— lucky you barely got any, Withy."

"Ya. Lucky me. Like every woman says when it's hot, 'Mop 'em if you got 'em.' Let's go drink."

The soldier woman who walked into the bar didn't look like the kind to give much away. She'd be a hard drinker, though, or so Swillman judged in the single flickering glance he risked taking at her face. And things could get bad, because she didn't look like someone used to paying for what she took; and the two soldier men who clumped in behind her looked even uglier to a man like Swill—who was an honest publican just trying to do his best.

The woman wasn't wearing boots, which made her catlike as she drew up to the bar.

"Got ale," said Swillman before she could open her mouth and demand something he'd never heard of. The woman frowned, and Swill thought that maybe these people were so foreign they didn't speak the language of the land.

But she then said, in a cruel, butchered accent, "What place is this?"

"Glory."

"No." She waved one gauntleted hand. "Kingdom? Empire?"

Swillman looked over at Slim, who was watching with a hoof-stunned expression, and then he licked his lips and shrugged.

The foreign woman sighed. "Five tankards, then."

"Y'got to pay first."

To Swillman's surprise, she didn't reach across and snap his neck like a lamp taper. Instead, she tugged free a small bag looped around her throat—the bag coming up from between her breasts somewhere under that chain armor, and spilled out a half-dozen rectangular coins onto the countertop.

Swillman stared down at them. "That tin? Lead?"

"Silver."

"I can't make no give-back on silver!"

"Well, what do you use here?"

He reached down and lifted into view his wooden cash tray. Its four sculpted bowls held seven buttons in three different sizes, a few nuggets of raw copper, a polished agate, and three sticks of stale rustleaf.

"No coins?"

"Been years since I last seen one a those."

"What did it look like?"

"Oblong, not like yours at all. And they was copper."

"What was stamped on 'em?" asked the short, bearded man who'd sidled up between the woman and Slim. "Whose face, I mean? Or faces—three faces? Castle in the sky? Something like that, maybe?"

Swillman shrugged. "Don't recall."

"One of these should do us for the night, then," said the woman, nudging one of the silver coins in Swill's direction.

"A cask of ale for you and meals, too, that would be about right."

He could see that the woman knew she was being taken, but didn't seem much interested in arguing.

The bearded man was eyeing Slim, who was eyeing him back.

The other man, leaning on the rail on the other side of the stocking-footed woman, was big and stupid-looking—Swillman could hear his loud breathing and the man's mouth hung open.

Probably too dumb to understand what was going on about any-thing, from that empty look in his eyes and those snaggled teeth, yellow and dry jutting out like that.

Drawing the first three tankards, Swillman served them up. A moment later, two more women soldiers clumped in.

Slim scowled and did her usual shrink-back when people she thought of as competition ever showed up, but the bearded man just went and moved closer. "Keep," he said, "give this sweet lass another one."

Swillman gaped, and then nodded. He was already drawing two more tankards for the new women—gods, they were all cut up and bruised and knocked about, weren't they just? All five of 'em. Addled in the heads, too, he suspected. Imagine, calling Slim a sweet lass! Bastard was blind!

The loud breather startled him by speaking up. "Seen no stables—we need to put up for the night. Horses need taking care of. We want somewhere to sleep under cover. We need food for the ride, too, and clean, boiled water. Is there a drygoods here? How about a blacksmith? Anyone work leather and hide? Is there a whetstone? Anyone selling blankets?"

Swillman had begun shaking his head with the very first query, and he kept shaking it until the man ran down.

"None of that?"

"None. Sorry, we're not on, uh, any road. We see a merchant once a year, whatever he don't sell elsewhere by season's end, we can look at."

Slim drained her tankard in one long pull and then, after a gasp, she said, "Widow Bark's got some wool, I think. She spins something, anyway. Might have a blanket to sell. The stable burned down, we got no horses anyway. We got pigs, and sheep a walk south of here, near the other end of the valley, but all that wool down there goes into the next valley, to the town there—to Piety."

"How far away is Piety?" the bearded man asked.

"Four days on foot, maybe two on horseback."

"Well," the breather demanded, "where can we sleep?"

Swillman licked his lips and said, "If it's just a dry roof you're looking for, there's the old keep on the hill."

They'd dug one of the pits too close to a barrow, and from one end of the rectangular trench old bones tumbled out in lumps of yellow clay. Graves and Snotty stared down at them for a time. Splinters and shards, snapped and marrow-sucked, and then Graves scooped up most of them with his shovel.

"We'll bore a hole in the mound," he said.

Snotty wiped his running nose and nodded. "I'm thirsty."

"Let's break, then."

"They going up to the keep?"

Graves lifted the mud and bones and tipped the mess onto the ground opposite the back pile. "I expect so." He set the shovel down and clambered out, then reached back to pull the boy out of the hole.

"They was looking at us as they went past."

"I know, boy. Don't let it bother you."

"I don't. I was just noticing, that's all."

"Me too."

They went over to broach the second cask of water, shared the single tin cup back and forth a few times. "I shouldn't have had all that ale earlier," said Graves.

"You wasn't to know, though, was you?"

"That's true. Just a normal day, right?"

Snotty nodded. "A normal day in Glory."

"I'm thinking," mused Graves, "I probably shouldn't have put up the rags, though. Soldiers can count that high, mostly, if they need to. Wonder if it got them thinking."

"We could find out, when we get back to the bar."

"Might be we're not done afore dark, boy."

"They're soljers, they'll stay late, drinking and carousing."

Graves smiled. "Carousing? That's quite the imagination you got there."

"Taking turns with Slim, I mean, and getting drunk, too, and maybe getting into a few fights—"

"With who?"

"With each other, I guess, or even Swillman."

"Swillman wouldn't fight to save his life, boy. Besides, he'll be happy enough if the soldiers pay for what they take. If they don't, well, there's not much he can do about it, is there?" He paused, squinting toward town. "Taking turns with Slim. Maybe. Have to be blind drunk, though."

"She shows 'em her ring and that'll do."

Graves shot the boy a hard look. "How you know about that?"

"My birthday present, last time."

"I doubt you is—"

"That's what her tongue's for, ain't it?"

"You're too young to know anything about that. Slim—that wretched hag, what was she thinking?"

"It was the only present she had t'give me, she said."

Graves put the cup away. "Break's over. Don't want them t'drink up all the ale afore we get there, do we?"

"No, sir, that'd be bad."

The sun was down and the muggy moon yet to rise when Flapp went off with Slim into the lone back room behind the bar.

Huggs snorted. "That man's taste . . . can you believe it?"

Shrugging, Wither drained her tankard and thumped it down on the bar. "More, Swilly!" She turned to Huggs. "He's always been that way. Picks the ugliest ones or the oldest ones and if he can, the ugliest oldest ones if the two fit the same whore."

"This time he's got it all and no choice besides. Must be a happy man."

"I'd expect so."

Captain Skint had gone to one of the two tables in the bar and was working hard emptying the first cask all by herself. Dullbreath sat beside her, mouth hanging open, staring at not much. He'd taken a mace to the side of his head a week back, cracking open his helmet but not his skull. Hit that hard anywhere else and he'd be in trouble. But it was just his head, so now he was back to normal and his eyes didn't cross no more. Unless he got mad. As far as Wither could tell, there'd be no reason for Dullbreath to get mad here and on this night. This place was lively as a boy's Cut Night after three days of fasting and no booze.

She and Huggs glanced over when a man and a snot-faced boy came into the bar.

"He ain't so bad," Huggs said. "Think he's for hire?"

"Y'can ask him."

"Maybe I will. Get his face cleaned up first, though."

"Them two was the diggers."

Huggs grunted. "You're right. Could be we can find out who did all the dying."

Wither raised her voice, "You two, leave off that table and come here. We're buying."

The older man tipped his head. "Obliged. And the lad?"

"Whatever he wants."

Sure enough the boy moved up to stand close beside Huggs, wiping at his nose with a dirt-smeared forearm. His sudden smile showed a row of even white teeth. Huggs shot Wither a glance and aye, things were looking up.

A life on the march sure messed with the bent of soldiers,

Wither reflected. Camp followers were mostly people with nothing left to lose and lives going nowhere, and plenty of scrawny
orphans and bastards among 'em, and so a soldier's tastes got
twisted pretty quick. She thought the older man looked normal
enough. A grave digger like every other grave digger and she'd
met more than a few. "Swilly, more ale here."

The digger was quiet enough as he drank and he showed
plenty of practice doing that drinking.

Wither eyed him a moment and then said, "Five graves. Who
up and died?"

He glanced at her, finished his tankard, and then stepped
back. "Obliged again," he said. "Snotty, you coming?"

"I'll stay a bit, Graves."

"As you like."

The man left. Wither stared after him, and then turned to say
something to Huggs, but she had her hand down the front of the
boy's trousers and he was clearly old enough to come awake.

Sighing, Wither collected her cup and went over to join Skint
and Dullbreath. "A piss pit of a town," she pronounced as she
slumped down in a chair. "Captain, you scrape an eye o'er that
keep on the hill? Looks like it's got a walled courtyard. Stables."

Dullbreath looked at her. "It's a Jheranang motte and bailey,
Wither. That conquest was a thousand years ago. The Jheran
Concord's been dust half that long. I doubt a single inner roof's
standing. And since we're on the border to the Demon Plain, it
was probably overrun in the Birthing Wars. Probably stinks of
ghosts and murder, and that's why it stays empty."

"It stays empty because this valley's been forgotten by whoever
rules the land, and there's nothing to garrison or guard. Upkeep
on a pile like that is a pig."

Dullbreath nodded. "That too. Anyway, it should do us fine.
Nice and quiet."

"For a change."

Skint stirred. "One more round for the lot," she said, "and then we ride on up."

Wither rose. "I'll tell Huggs t'get on with it, then. Boys that age it's short but often—she'll just have to settle with that."

The Broken Moon dragged its pieces above the horizon, throwing smudged shadows on the empty street, as the troop dragged themselves back into their saddles and set off for the ruin.

Graves stood in the gloom between two gutted houses and watched them pass, his shoulders hunched against the night air. He heard a noise behind him and turned. Herribut the blind cobbler edged closer, and behind him was a half-dozen villagers—most of the population, in fact.

"Y'think?" Herribut asked.

Graves scowled. "Ya, the usual. First pick's mine, as always."

Herribut nodded. "Lots drawn on after ya. I won." He grinned toothlessly. "Imagine that! I never had a touch of luck in my whole life, not once! But I won tonight!"

"Happy for ya, cobbler. Now, alla you, go get some sleep, and be sure to stopper your ears. Nobody's fault but your own if you're all grainy-eyed and slow come the morning pickings."

They shuffled off, chattering amongst themselves.

Exciting times in Glory, and how often could anyone say that without a bitter spit into the dust and then a sour smile? Graves stepped out into the street. The soldiers had reached the base of the hill, where they had paused to stare up at the black, brooding fortification.

"Go on," Graves whispered. "It's quiet. It's perfect. Go on, damn you."

And then they did, and he sagged in relief.

Nobody invited any of this, so nobody was to blame, not for

anything. Just came down to making a living, that's all. People got the right to that, he figured. It wasn't a rule or anything like it, not some kingly law or natural truth. It was just one of those ideas people said aloud as often as they could, to make it more real and more true than it really was. When the fact was, people got no rights to anything. Not a single thing, not air to breathe, food to eat, ale to drink. Not the sweet smile between the legs, not a warm body beside you at night. Not land to own, not even a place to stand. But it made it easier, didn't it, saying that people got the right to a living, and honest hard work, like digging graves and carving capstones, well, that earned just rewards because that's how things should be.

The boy came out from the bar, weaving his way into the street. The woman had gotten him drunk besides stained in the crotch.

Graves set out to collect Snotty and take him to his solitary shack close to his own house. Couldn't be nice, he imagined, to end up just being abandoned by his ma and da when they were all passing through, and left to survive on his own. That was three years back, and Graves knew the boy had latched on to him to fill the holes in his growing up, and that was all right. To be expected. The boy would be in no shape for anything come the morning, but Graves would pluck a thing or two for him anyway. It was the least he could do.

The cobbled ramp climbed the hillside in three sharp switchbacks that would have cramped any supply wagon and likely made a mess of stocking the keep. The path was overgrown and cluttered with chunks of masonry, but otherwise picked clean.

Sergeant Flapp shifted uncomfortably in the saddle as his horse clumped up the sharp incline. That whore still had teeth, damn her, and that ring had been way too small. His snake felt strangled. He noticed, in passing, that all the anchor rings on the walls to either side had been dug out and carried off, leaving rusty-ringed holes. "They stripped this place right down," he said. "Doubt we'll find a single door, a single hinge or fitting. And now they'll probably sneak up and try and rob us tonight."

"They wouldn't be that suicidal," Wither said.

Flapp belched. "Maybe not. That Slim was one eager whore, though."

They rounded the last turn and came within sight of the gate. The portcullis was gone, as expected, all that iron, and the arched passageway yawned black as a cave mouth. Flapp followed Skint in. The drop chutes and murder holes were all plugged with muddy, guano-streaked martin nests, and they could hear the birds moving restlessly as they rode past.

The passage opened out to a yard overgrown with brambles. A stone-lined well marked the center, all its fittings removed. To the right was a low building running the length of one high wall. "Stables," Flapp said. "But we'll have to use the last of our fodder."

Skint pointed to a stone trough close to the stables. "Wither, check that, make sure it's not cracked. Huggs, collect up the water gourds and rig up a rope—let's see what we can scoop from the well. Flapp and Dullbreath, you're with me. Let's check out the main house."

That building was built to withstand its own siege. No windows on the lower floors, a narrow aperture preceding the doorway, arrow slits on the two squat towers flanking the inner facing. The slanted roof, they saw, was slate-tiled and holed through here and there.

"I'd wager the towers are solid and probably cleaner than anywhere else," said Flapp.

They dismounted. Walked toward the entrance.

• • •

The slow drumbeat of horse hoofs on the cobbles had awakened them, and now, in scores of chambers in the keep, figures stirred. Long, gnarled limbs unfolded, slitted eyes glittered as heads lifted, jaws stretching open to reveal rows of thin, vertical fangs. Twin hearts that had thumped in agonizingly slow syncopation for months now thudded faster, rushing blood and heat through tall, rope-muscled bodies. Talons clicked at the ends of unfurling hands.

The slaughterers of the garrison five hundred years ago, demons from the cursed plain beyond the mountains, awoke once more. A night of swift blood awaited them. A few soft-skinned travelers, such as haplessly sought shelter in this place every now and then. Food to share out, a mouthful of pulped meat—if that—and there would be fierce struggle over even such modest morsels. They'd eat everything but the bones and they'd split the bones and suck out the marrow and then leave the rubbish outside the gate before dawn arrived.

The imp commanding the demons ate its way out from its woven cocoon of human hair and scrambled, claws skittering, on all fours down the south tower's spiral staircase. Nostrils flaring at the sweet scent of horse and human meat, it clacked its teeth in hungry anticipation. Shin-high, the creature wore a tiny hauberk of scaled armor, a belted sword at its hip not longer than a bear's canine and nearly as dull. Its head was bare, victim to vanity, permitting its bright stiff shock of white hair to stand fully upright. Its eyes, a lurid yellow, flared with excitement.

Its fiends were awake, but the time for summoning must wait. The imp needed to see the victims with its own eyes, needed to feast on their growing fear. Needed them, indeed, trapped and then devoured by that terrifying realization. A silent command unveiled dark sorcery, swallowing the gatehouse in a swirling miasma of foul vapors, vitriolic and deadly. No, there would be no escape. There never was.

Soon, so very soon, the slaughter would begin. First the humans, and then the horses.

Dullbreath halted in the center of the broad, high-vaulted, pillar-lined hallway just inside the keep's narrow entrance. He sniffed the air. "Ghosts," he muttered. "This place was overrun, Captain. Plenty died in here."

Skint glanced back at the man, studied him for a moment, and then turned her attention once more to the far wall with its row of gaping doorways.

Flapp scanned the mosaic floor and frowned at the black, crumbly streaks all over it. He looked up to peer at the ceiling, but it was too dark to see much of anything up there—no obvious gap open to moonlight, though. "Smells kinda scaly in here."

Huggs stumped in. "Captain, we got a problem."

"What?"

"Horses getting edgy. And some kind of ward's sprung up at the gate. Stinks, burns the eyes and throat just getting close. Probably kill us if we tried to push through."

"Someone wants us to stay the night," Dullbreath said, his breathing loud and whistling in the chamber.

"Lonely ghosts?" asked Flapp.

Dullbreath shrugged. "Could be."

"All right," Skint said, "we pick us a room with one way in and one way out—"

"Ghosts go through walls, Captain—"

"Huggs, how's the wound?"

"Wither dug it out. It'll do."

Skint nodded and looked around once more. "Fuck ghosts," she said, "this ain't ghosts."

"Shit," said Huggs, and she walked back outside.

"Stay here, Dull," ordered Skint. "Sergeant, fire up that lantern and let's go find us a room."

"Never thought you cared, Captain."

The first three chambers along the row in front of them were dark, stinking hovels with passages through to secondary rooms—and those rooms opened out to both sides, their facing walls revealing the keep's heavy stones where rotted sheets of plaster had peeled away. The two mercenaries did little more than peer into those back chambers. The fourth room was an old armory, picked bare.

Flapp lifted the lantern and said, "See that? There, far corner—a trapdoor."

They walked to it. The brass ring was gone and the wood looked rotted through. "Give it a prod with your sword," Skint said.

"You sure?"

"Do it."

He handed her the lantern and withdrew his long blade of blued Aren steel. As soon as he touched the tip to the door, the planks crumpled, fell in a cloudy whoosh through the hatch. They heard sifting sounds from below.

"That ain't been used in a long time," Flapp observed.

Skint edged closer and brought the lantern over the hole. "Iron ladder, Sergeant. Looks like the looters lost their courage."

"I'm not surprised," he replied.

"Still drunk, Sergeant?"

"No. Mostly . . . no."

"We might want to take a look down there."

He nodded.

"I think," she said slowly, turning to face him, "we got ourselves a demon."

"That's the smell all right."

They heard clattering from the main hall.

Skint led the way back to the others.

Wither and Huggs had brought in the crossbows and dart-bags and were pulling and dividing up quarrels. Dullbreath was ratcheting tight the cords on the all-metal fist-punchers, smearing gobs of grease into the thick braids.

"Light the rest of the lanterns, Sergeant," said Skint, tightening the straps of her gauntlets. "Where's my helmet, Withy?"

"Behind Dullbreath, Captain."

"Everybody suit up. The night's gonna start with a bang. Then we can get some rest."

"I thought we'd left crap-face demons behind us," griped Huggs.

"One got out and squirreled up here, that's all."

"A magic-shitter, too."

"It'll show, we drive it back, corner it, and kill the fucker."

The others nodded.

High in the rafters, the imp stared down at the five fools. Soldiers! How exciting. They had managed well reining in their panic, but the imp could smell their acrid sweat, that pungent betrayal of terror. It watched as they assembled their weapons, went over each other's armor—what was left of it—and then, arranging the five lanterns in a broad circle, they donned their helmets—one of those badly cracked, the one on the taller of the two men—and, slotting quarrels into the crossbows, settled into a circle well inside the ring of fitful light.

Sound defensive positioning.

The demon they were now discussing could come from anywhere, after all, any of the doorways, including the one leading outside. Could come from the ceiling, too, for that matter. And the imp grinned with its needle teeth.

All very good, very impressive.

But there wasn't just one demon, was there?

No. There were lots. And lots. And lots.

The imp awoke sorcery again, sealing the keep's doorway. One of the women caught the stench of that and she swore. That one had a nose for magic, she did. Too bad it wasn't going to help.

Still grinning, the imp summoned its fiends.

In the stable, the horses, sensitive to such things, began shrilling and screaming.

Flapp saw the captain lift her head, as if trying to hear something behind the maddened horses. A moment later, she straightened. "Collect up the lanterns. Time to retreat to our room."

Burdened with gear, crossbows cradled, the lanterns slung by their handles over the stirrups, the group moved in a contracting circle toward a lone gaping doorway.

Flapp was the first through. A quick scan, and then a grunt. "Clear."

The others quickly filed in.

Huggs made to speak, but the captain silenced her with a gesture, and then, when Skint had everyone's attention, she hand-talked, fast, precise. Nods answered her all around. Lanterns clunked softly on the floor.

Gray-scaled, trailing cobwebs and shedding mortar dust, the demons poured like foul water down a cataract, round and round the spiral stairs of the north tower. Ten, twenty, thirty, their jaws creaking, fangs clashing, lunging on all fours, tails slithering in their wake. They spilled out onto the landing, talons screeching across the tiles as they rushed the single lit doorway two-thirds of the way down the corridor.

Cries of rising bloodlust shrilled from their throats, a frenzied chorus that could curdle a lump of lard and set it quivering. The imp dropped down from the rafters and scurried into their wake, in time to see the first of the demons plunge through the entrance.

It howled—but the cry was one of blunted frustration.

The imp slipped under, over, and around the mob clamoring at the doorway, leapt through to find itself in a room with naught but demons lashing about, gouging the walls in fury.

The lanterns had been kicked against the walls.

The five humans were gone.

Where?

Ah—the imp caught sight of a gaping hole in the floor.

With frantic screeches, it commanded the demons to pursue, and the one closest to the trapdoor slithered through, followed quickly by the others.

Clever humans! But how fast could they run?

Not fast enough!

The imp awakened the rest of its children, and curdling howls erupted from countless chambers.

The first demons swarmed down the ladder to the first sub-terranean level—there were a half-dozen such levels, a maze of narrow, low-ceilinged, crooked passageways bored in the hill's enormous mound. Storerooms, cisterns, armories, cutter sur-geries, and wards. It had been centuries since the demons last scoured these tunnels.

The imp sensed their sudden confusion—the stench of the humans went off in each of the three possible directions, and then two more at a branch ten strides along the main corridor. They had panicked! Now each fool could be hunted down, dragged to the grimy, greasy cobbles in a burst of blood and entrails.

Chittering with excitement, the imp sent demons after every one of the pathetic, wretched things.

• • •

A demon slunk noiselessly down a cramped passage, nostrils glistening, dripping in answer to the sour smell of a human hanging like mist in the dark air. Jagged black jolts ripped through its brain in waves, a jarring hunger that trembled through its elongated torso, shivering down its gnarled limbs to softly clatter its claws and talons.

The long sleep was an ugly, cruel place, and awakening was painful with savage need.

It came upon a foul woolen cloak, lost in the quarry's frantic flight. The demon crouched and breathed deep, stirring memories of centuries-old slaughter. Lifting its head, it reflexively spread wide its jaws, and crept forward.

At a sound behind it the demon spun around.

A studded, gauntleted fist smashed into the demon's face, crushing its snout, sending shards of splintered fangs into the back of its throat. The fist drove home again, snapping the demon's head against the wall. And again, and again.

Sergeant Flapp's fist was a blur, a rapid mallet that repeatedly pounded the pulped mess that was the demon's head while his other hand held the thing up by the neck. When the meaty, crunching sounds gave way to the hard impact of a skull plate driven flat against the stone of the wall, he stepped back and let the twitching fiend slide to the floor.

He could hear more coming up the corridor.

Flapp collected his cloak and set off down the narrow side passage he had been hiding in—watching the demon sidle past—only moments earlier.

Three demons skidded around at the intersection and sprinted on all fours, voicing deep growls that would shiver the hair off a pack of wolves. The lead one's head exploded in a spray of blood and bone as Wither's quarrel took it between the eyes. Sprawling, its limbs entangled the demons behind it and they howled in fury.

Ten loping strides down the passageway, Wither stepped back out of sight, into the side corridor—a narrow chute barely wide enough to let her pass. Wedging the crossbow crossways at chest height just within the entrance, she took two steps back, drawing her two longswords, and waited.

The first demon's forelimbs wrapped claws around the corner to slow it down as it lunged into the chute.

The iron crossbow brought it up short, clipping its lower jaw and snapping its head down.

Wither selected that inviting bald pate as a suitable target and swung down with both blades.

Brains splattered the walls.

The demon suddenly crowding behind it shrieked as a quarrel tore through its neck from farther up the main corridor. Gasping red froth, it staggered back and decided on a noisy death.

Wither kicked the virtually headless demon away and, sheathing one sword, wrenched loose her crossbow, and then set out down the chute.

Twenty paces along the main corridor, Huggs dropped the crossbow stirrup, set her boot toe on it, and tugged the cord into lock, wincing as the wound in her shoulder flared with pain. Slotting a new quarrel, she plunged into the gloom. Of course, demons could see in the dark, and some of them could see any hot-blooded beastie, but when hungry, they preferred to follow their noses and that was a savage yank on their leashes (not that they had leashes, not these ones anyway).

And their eyes, why, they blazed and made perfect targets.

She could hear more coming. Some would take off after Wither. The rest would latch on to her tail. She hurried off.

Crowded by four of its fellows, a demon crouched in an intersection. Human trails led into opposing corridors. It hesitated. The one behind it snarled and darted to the left, and then skidded to a halt as it stumbled on a discarded cloak. It grunted in confusion, and then whirled—

The man with the jutting yellow teeth launched himself from the corridor to the right, throwing all his weight behind a sword thrust that punched through the demon in the intersection, piercing both hearts, the hilt slamming hard against ribs. Leaving the weapon there, he ducked down, twisting to drive one scale-armored elbow into the next closest demon, caving in its forehead.

The remaining two demons collided with each other in their eagerness to reach him.

Dullbreath stepped back, and then drove a boot into the heavy balls dangling between the legs of one of the creatures. As it sank back with a grinding groan, the last demon was suddenly unimpeded and with a shriek it flung itself at the man. He caught its throat with both hands and squeezed in a single lightning-quick clench that crushed the demon's windpipe. Throwing the twitching thing aside, Dullbreath drew his hunting knife and sliced open the throat of the demon he'd kicked, since he was feeling merciful.

Sheathing the knife, he tugged loose his sword, collected up his crossbow, and set off, snagging up his cloak along the way.

One hand trailing along a wall—keeping herself straight as she ran mostly blind in the darkness—Huggs felt the sudden gap to her right. Sliding to a halt, she backed up—fighting sounds from somewhere down there. Savage-sounding stuff, maybe even desperate.

She knew she had a few and maybe more coming up behind her. Whoever she helped out might curse Huggs if she led them down after her—trapping Huggs and whomever else between two slavering mobs.

Oh well. She hefted her crossbow and darted down the side passage.

She heard a solid *thunk*—like the world's biggest crossbow—and that worried her, until she heard demonic shrieks of agony and rage.

Someone's found a new toy?

Clattering claws behind her, closing fast, and that wasn't good.

Huggs halted, crouched, raised her weapon, and waited until she saw the gleam of the first demon's eyes. Took that one down easy. Dropping the crossbow, she drew her sword into her right hand, her crack-finder into her left.

Four more sets of blazing eyes rushed upon her.

"Drop flat!"

Huggs did.

A thunderous whoosh raced over her. Sudden mayhem up the corridor, as a huge pig of a barbed quarrel ripped through three of the damned things, gouging a shoulder of the fourth one. Laughing, Huggs leapt to her feet and charged it.

With a squeal, the demon fled as fast as three working limbs could take it.

"Shit." Huggs halted, jogged back, peered in the darkness. "Who?"

"Wither—listen, found a whole storeroom of these fuckers. Siege arbalests."

"Lead the way, darling."

"Watch your step up here. Lots of bodies."

"Right."

• • •

Captain Skint shoved the faceless mess aside and pushed through the doorway, stepping clear and then turning to meet the first of the demons that lunged into view at the threshold. Her sword tip opened a wide grin in its throat. The next one, clambering over its fallen kin, lost the top of its head, bisecting its relatively small brain, which stopped working in any case.

Three more squeezed through and Skint took a step back to clear some room and let them in.

Talons slashed with murderous intent, but caught empty air. Jaws snapped on nothing. Surges to close and grapple missed again and again. The woman was a blur of motion to their eyes. A demon's head jumped free of the rest of it, and the stumpy neck poured blood everywhere. Another shrieked as something kissed its belly and it looked down to see its intestines tumbling out—withered, empty things, like starving worms. Collecting them up, it waddled to the doorway—but that was blocked as dozens of demons struggled to press through the doorway. The disemboweled demon snarled and took two fatal talons to its eyes for its ill manners.

Skint helped a demon leap into a wall, and when it fell to the floor, she stamped her heel into its throat, then jumped away to avoid its thrashing.

She cast a gauging regard upon the swarm of gleaming eyes jammed in the doorway, and then stepped forward and began hacking with her sword. Sometimes, finesse was just stupid.

Flapp balanced on the crossbeam and watched as the third and last demon passed underneath. His quarrel buried itself in the back of the thing's head, and as it fell, the sergeant flung the crossbow at the nearest beast—which had twisted around, eye flaring like coals—and saw it bounce from the demon's flat forehead even as Flapp plunged off the edge to land on the floor, two short swords snapping out but held points-down.

He rushed the demons. Blades slashed, intersecting wrists and forearms, slashed some more, cutting through hamstrings and other assorted, necessary tendons. He drove his head forward. Helmed bridge guard slammed with a happy crunch into a forehead, and then Flapp was past them both—they flopped and writhed behind him all messy with blood. He spun around and made quick work of them, and then retrieved his crossbow, only to snarl when discovering its bent arm. Flinging it away, he trundled down the corridor.

He could hear fighting.

He went to find it.

They could make out a mob of the bastards swarming a doorway, which meant someone was cornered, or, rather, had let themselves get cornered, which meant it was the captain. Grunting beneath the weight of the arbalests both women held, they sent two bolts tearing into the crowd. Torn bodies and pieces of meat flew.

And then, with a scream, Huggs charged the rest. Cursing, Wither dropped her arbalest and unsheathed her swords, setting off after her. By the time she reached the writhing mound, Huggs was buried somewhere beneath the heaving press of snarling demons.

Wither started chopping off limbs, heads.

She saw the captain's sword tip lunge from the doorway, driving deep between two widening eyes, and a moment later Skint kicked her way into view.

The demons broke, a half dozen bolting with shrieks up the corridor.

Where someone else hit them.

Wither started dragging bodies off Huggs, and found her

pounding on a knife she'd driven through the top of a demon's head, but its jaws were still clamped tight around her left thigh.

"You idiot!" snapped Wither, "get your hands away so I can pry it loose. Gods below, we could have stood back and cleared the whole mess with a couple more bolts!"

Huggs spat blood. "Why should Skint get all the fun? Get this fucking thing off my leg!"

"I'm trying—sit still!"

Sergeant Flapp arrived. "Three got away!"

"There's more," said Skint.

"You said one!" Wither hissed, finally loosening the demon's death-bite.

"So I was off by a few. Where's Dullbreath? Anyone see him?"

"Not since we split," said Flapp.

"Same here," added Wither, and Huggs nodded as she sat up.

Skint swung her sword to shed gore and blood from the blade. "They're on the run now. So we hunt."

Her soldiers checked their weapons.

Flapp saw one of the arbalest bolts and kicked at it. "Nice."

"Got a whole room of the damned things."

"I need me a replacement."

"We'll take you there, Sergeant—"

"Take us all there," said Skint. "Then we split up again. Rendezvous in the main hall up top, and don't dally. Someone's running this army, and I want it skewered."

"Follow me," said Wither.

Whimpering, the imp picked its way around yet another heap of demon corpses. Poor children! This was a slaughter, a terrible, grievous, dreadful slaughter!

And now they were hunting the survivors down—nowhere to hide!

Human stench everywhere, down every passage, every twisting, turning corridor, every cursed chamber and rank room. There was no telling where they were now, no telling what vicious ambushes they'd set up.

The imp crouched, quivering, hugging itself, and crooned its grief. Then it shook itself, drawing free its tiny sword. Enough of these evil tunnels and warrens! To the ladder! Flee this cruel place!

With renewed determination, and a healthy dose of terror, it scampered.

Breathing hard, the demon froze, nose testing the pungent, bitter air. Its eyes were wide, seeking the telltale bloom of body heat—those cursed cloaks, they'd been sopping wet, cold to the touch, blind to the demon's eyes; and the iron chain wasn't much better. Even so, there was no way a human could sneak up on it. No way.

It needed to find somewhere to hide. A privy hole, maybe. A crack in a wall. Anywhere.

The demon edged forward, and suddenly the human stench was overpowering. Mewling, it slowly straightened—and then turned around.

The bearded face hovering a hand's width in front of its snout elicited a piercing scream of horror from the demon.

"Looking for me?" And then a red-stained studded fist rammed into its face. Twice, thrice, eight, nine, twelve times.

As the demon crumpled at his feet, Flapp grunted and said, "Didn't think so."

The two demons, boon companions for centuries, clutched each other, sharing a puddle of rank piss pooling around them, as two female humans stepped into view. Ferocious barbed bolts flung the two demons apart like rag dolls.

Wither began working the crank to reload her weapon, whilst Huggs limped forward. "You see them? Fucking pathetic."

"You're getting soft, Huggs."

"Loaded?"

"Yes."

"My turn. Keep an eye peeled, Withy."

"Count on it."

The imp could hear random death-cries echoing down the corridors, each one trembling through its scrawny, puny form. Reaching the iron ladder, it clambered upward as fast as its little limbs could carry it.

Not fast enough.

"Got ya."

A mailed hand snatched the imp up, plucked it from the railing.

The imp squealed and thrashed about, but it was no use. It struggled to bring its sword to bear, but the man reached with his other hand and broke the imp's sword arm. Snap, like a twig. Broke the other one, too, and then both legs. That really hurt!

Helpless, the imp dangled limp in the man's grip. He stared down at it, breathing loud, mouth hanging open.

And then he bit down on the imp's head and held it in his mouth as he climbed the ladder.

That breath! The imp cringed, even through its agony of broken bits everywhere. That breath!

As soon as they reached the top, and the man walked out of the armory, along the corridor, and out to the main chamber, the imp sent forth a frantic cry, a sorcerous plea bristling with desperate power.

Mommy! Mommy! Help me!

None left. Of course they could not be entirely certain of that, but they'd scoured every possible hiding place, rooting out the snarling oversized rats and chopping them to pieces.

Skint led them back to the arbalest armory, where they loaded up on bolts, including the assault quarrels with their looped ends, as well as bundles of thick cables. The walk back to the ladder was slow and awkward, with all the blood, corpses, and gore cluttering the passageways. By the time they strode out into the main chamber, Dullbreath was waiting for them. He nodded to a small figure pinned by a tiny sword to the floor in the center of the room.

"Still breathing?"

"Hard to say. Hard to kill for real, those things."

"All right. Good work, Dullbreath. Let's get ready then."

The girl who walked in through the keep's doors clutched a bundle of plucked flowers, her blond hair drifting like seed fluff. Her large eyes settled on the tiny figure of the imp nailed to the floor, and she edged closer.

Her expression fell as she looked down on her dead child. Kneeling, she set aside her flowers and reached out to brush that tiny, cold forehead.

Then, as she straightened, five soldiers stepped out from behind pillars, each bearing loaded arbalests.

The girl raised her scrawny arms and vanished inside a blurry haze. Spice-laden clouds rolled from where she stood, and the soldiers stared as she awakened to her true form, burgeoning, towering at almost twice the height of an average man, and easily twice as wide. Fangs as long as short swords, a mass of muscles like bundles of rope, hands that could crush armored soldiers as if they were frail eggs.

Huggs snorted. "A demon, huh? That's not just a demon, Captain. That's a fucking Harridan!"

"Commander of a legion," added Dullbreath. "What were they thinking?"

The demon opened its maw and howled.

The sound deafened them, shook plaster loose from ceiling and walls.

The soldiers lifted their weapons. And fired.

The bolts pounded deep into the giant beast, and each dart snaked cables behind it—cables bound around the base of a pillar. The hinged barbs on the heads snagged deep in the demon's flesh. Shrieking, it sought to pull away, but the thick ropes snapped taut—to tear loose of any one of the quarrels would break bones and spill out organs and who knew what else.

"Reload," growled Skint.

And so they did.

Dawn's light slowly stole in through the entrance, crept across the floor of the main chamber.

"Last crate," said Flapp in a ragged, exhausted voice.

He went around, passing out the last of the bolts. Cranks clanked, but slowly.

Wither stepped up to squint at the pin-cushioned heap of mangled flesh huddled in the center of the chamber, and then shrugged and returned to her arbalest.

Five weapons clanged. Five bolts sank into the body.

"Quivered some," observed Flapp.

"So would you," said Huggs. "No whimpers though. Those

stopped some time ago." She turned to the captain. "Could be it's finally dead."

"Prod it with your sword," Skint commanded.

"Me and my big mouth." But Huggs drew her weapon and edged closer. She gave the thing a poke. "Nothing." She poked harder. Still no response. So she stabbed. "Hah! It's dead all right."

Arbalests dropped from exhausted arms.

"Saddle us up, Withy. Let's get the fuck out of here."

"You got it, Captain."

Graves had been up all night. No amount of beeswax could have stoppered up that seemingly endless chorus of screams and howls from the keep. It had never been so bad. Ever. Those soldiers, they'd died hard. Damned hard.

He rigged up his mule and cart and led the procession—a quiet bunch this morning, for sure—up to collect the remains and whatever loot came out with it. Work was work, wasn't it just. People did what they did to get by, and what else was life all about? Nothing. That was it. It and nothing more. But, dammit, he didn't want the boy to spend his whole cursed life here in Glory, didn't want him taking over when Graves gave it up, not stepping in when Slim finally swallowed her ring and choked to death—the gods knew she wasn't going to die naturally. Didn't want any of that, not for the boy.

After sending a few scowls at the bleary-eyed but ever-greedy faces arrayed behind him, he tugged the reluctant mule up to the first of the hillside's switchbacks.

And then stopped.

As the first clump of horse hoofs sounded up ahead.

The captain was in the lead. The others followed. Every one of them. Five, aye, five one by one by one by one by one.

Graves stared.

As she passed him, Skint flung a bloody mass of something at him. Reflexively, he caught it and looked down at the wilted remnants of flowers. Dripping red.

The sergeant was next. "Five graves? Not enough, sir, not by a long shot."

Wither added more as she rode past, "Try about ninety-five more."

Huggs snorted. "And a big one, too, and I mean big. Oh, and a tiny one, too."

Dullbreath halted opposite Graves and looked down at him with jaded eyes. "For fuck's sake, Graves, we kill those fuckers for a living."

He rode on. They all did.

Graves looked down at the flowers in his hand.

People do what they do, he reminded himself. To get by. Just that, to get by.

"Two days to Piety," said Flapp as they rode along the track on the slow climb to the distant valley mouth.

"And then—"

"Captain," called out Dullbreath from the rear.

They all reined in and turned.

Slim was riding a mule after them, the old whore rocking back and forth like she'd never learned how to ride, and that struck Flapp as damned funny. But he didn't laugh.

"We got us a camp follower," said Wither. "I don't believe it."

Flapp opened his mouth and was about to say something, and then he stopped—he'd caught a glint of metal—from way up the trail they'd come down yesterday. "Captain! I saw a flash of steel! Halfway up to the pass!"

Everyone stiffened. Stared, breaths held.

"There! You seen it?"

And the look Skint turned on him was twisted into a mask of unholy terror. "He's still after us! Ride, soldiers! To save your lives, *ride*!"

GLEN COOK grew up in northern California and served in the U.S. Navy with the Third Marine Recon Battalion, an experience that fundamentally affected his later work. Cook then attended the University of Missouri and the Clarion Writers' Workshop. His first novel, *The Heirs of Babylon,* appeared in 1972 and was followed by a broad range of fantasy and science fiction novels, including the humorous fantasy Garrett PI series and others. His most important work, though, is the gritty Black Company fantasy series, which follows a mercenary unit over several decades and which brought a whole new perspective to fantasy. Cook is currently retired and lives in St. Louis, Missouri, where he writes full-time.

TIDES ELBA

A Tale of the Black Company

Glen Cook

We were playing tonk. One-Eye was in a foul mood because he was losing. Situation normal, except nobody was trying to kill us.

Elmo dealt. One-Eye squeaked. I peeked at my cards. "Another hand so damned bad it don't qualify as a foot."

Otto said, "You're full of shit, Croaker. You won six out of the last ten hands."

Elmo said, "And bitched about the deal every time."

"I was right every time I dealt." I was right this time, too. I did not have a pair. I had no low cards and only one face card. The two in the same suit were the seven and knave of diamonds. I do not have years enough left to fill that straight. Anyway, we all knew One-Eye had one of his rare good hands.

"Then we need to make you full-time dealer."

I pushed my ante in. I drew, discarded, and tossed my cards in when it came to me.

One-Eye went down with ten. The biggest card he had was a three. His leathery old black face ripped in a grin lacking an adequate population of teeth. He raked the pot in.

Elmo asked the air, "Was that legitimate?" We had a gallery of half a dozen. We had the Dark Horse to ourselves today. It was the Company watering hole in Aloe. The owner, Markeb Zhorab, had mixed feelings. We were not the kind of guys he wanted hanging around but because we did, his business was outstanding.

Nobody indicted One-Eye. Goblin, with his butt on the table next over, reminded Elmo, "You dealt."

"Yeah, there's that."

One-Eye has been known to cheat. Hard to manage in a game as simpleminded as tonk, but there you go. He is One-Eye.

"Lucky at cards, unlucky at love," he said, which made no sense in context.

Goblin cracked, "You better hire yourself some bodyguards. Women will be tearing down doors trying to get to you."

A wisecrack from Goblin generally fires One-Eye up. He has a hair trigger. We waited for it. One-Eye just grinned and told Otto, "Deal, loser. And make it a hand like the one Elmo just gave me."

Goblin said something about Missus Hand being the only lucky lady in One-Eye's life.

One-Eye went on ignoring the bait.

I began to worry.

Otto's deal did not help.

One-Eye said, "You know how we run into weird customs wherever we go?"

Elmo glared holes through his cards. He grunted. Otto arranged and rearranged his five, meaning he had a hand so bad he did not know how to play it. One-Eye did not squeak but he kept grinning. We were on the brink of a new age, one in which he could win two hands in a row.

Everybody looked at Goblin. Goblin said, "Otto dealt."

Somebody in the gallery suggested, "Maybe he spelled the cards."

That all rolled past One-Eye. "The weirdest custom they got here is, when a girl loses her cherry, from then on she's got to keep all the hair off her body."

Otto rumbled, "That's some grade-two bullshit if I ever heard some. We been here near three months and I ain't seen a bald-headed woman yet."

Everything stopped, including One-Eye stacking his winnings.

"What?" Otto asked.

There have always been questions about Otto.

The rest of us occasionally invest a coin in a tumble with a professional comfort lady. Though the subject never came up before, I knew I had yet to see one whisker below the neckline.

"Do tell," Elmo said. "And I thought it was the luck of the draw that I wasn't seeing what ought to be there."

I said, "I figured it was how mine kept from getting the crabs."

"Nope. All tied into their weird religion."

Goblin muttered, "There's an oxymoron."

One-Eye's mood faltered.

Goblin's froglike face split in a vast grin. "I wasn't talking about you, shrimp. You're just a regular moron. I was talking about slapping the words *weird* and *religion* together."

"You guys are trying to hex my luck, aren't you?"

"Sure," Elmo said. "Talking about pussy works every time. Tell me about these bald snatches."

One-Eye restacked his winnings. He was turning surly despite his success. He had come up with some great stuff, on a subject guys can kill weeks exploring, and nobody seemed to care.

I shuffled, stacked, and dealt. One-Eye grew more glum as he picked up each card.

The last one got him. "God damn it, Croaker! You asshole! You son of a bitch!"

Elmo and Otto kept straight faces, because they did not know what was happening. Goblin tittered like a horny chickadee.

One-Eye spread his hand. He had a trey of clubs. He had a six of diamonds. He had the nine of hearts and the ace of spades. And that last card was a knave of swords.

I said, "How many times have you claimed you didn't have no two cards of the same suit? For once you won't be lying."

Now Elmo and Otto got it. They laughed harder than me or Goblin. The gallery got a good chuckle, too.

The Lieutenant stuck his head through the front door. "Anybody seen Kingpin?" The Lieutenant did not sound happy. He sounded like an executive officer who had to work on his day off.

"He skating again?" Elmo asked.

"He is. He's supposed to be on slops. He didn't show. The cooks want to chop him up for soup bones."

"I'll talk to him, sir." Though Kingpin is not one of his men. Kingpin hides out in Kragler's platoon.

"Thank you, Sergeant." Elmo does have a way of communicating with errant infantrymen. "Why are you people in here, in this gloom and stink, when you could be sucking up fresh air and sunshine?"

I said, "This is our natural habitat, sir." But the truth was, it had not occurred to anybody to take the game outside.

We gathered our cards and beer and shambled out to the street-front tables. One-Eye dealt. Talk dwelt on the hairstyles, or lack thereof, favored by Aloen ladies.

• • •

It was a grand day, cloudless, cool, air in motion but not briskly enough to disturb the game. The gallery settled in. Some just liked to watch. Some hoped a seat would open up. They joined the increasingly crude speculation, which slipped into the domain of one-upmanship.

I interjected, "How long have we been playing with these cards?" Some were so ragged you should not need to turn them over to know what they were. But my memory kept tricking me. The face sides never matched up.

Everybody looked at me funny. "Here comes something off the wall," One-Eye forecast. "Spit it out, Croaker, so we can get back to stuff that matters."

"I'm wondering if this deck hasn't been around long enough to take on a life of its own."

One-Eye opened his mouth to mock me, then his eyes glazed over as he considered the possibility. Likewise, Goblin. The pallid, ugly little man said, "Well, screw me! Croaker, you aren't half as dumb as you look. The cards have developed a mind of their own. That would explain so much."

The whole crew eyeballed One-Eye, nodding like somebody was conducting. One-Eye had insisted that the cards hated him for as long as anyone could remember.

He won again.

Three wins at one sitting should have tipped me off. Hell was on the prowl. But my mouth was off on another adventure.

"You know what? It's been eighty-seven days since somebody tried to kill me."

Elmo said, "Don't give up hope."

"Really. Think about it. Here we are, out in the damned street where anybody could take a crack. But nobody is even eyeballing us. And none of us are looking over our shoulders and whining about our ulcers."

Play stopped. Seventeen eyes glared at me. Otto said, "Croaker, you jinx it, I'll personally hold you down while somebody whittles on your favorite toy."

Goblin said, "He's right. We've been here three months. The only trouble we've seen is guys getting drunk and starting fights."

With 640 men, you know the Company has a few shitheads whose idea of a good time is to drink too much, then get in an ass-kicking contest.

One-Eye opined, "What it is is, the Lady's still got a boner for Croaker. So she stashed him someplace safe. The rest of us just live in his shadow. Watch the sky. Some night there'll be a carpet up there, Herself coming out to knock boots with her special guy."

"What's *her* hairstyle like, Croaker?"

Special treatment? Sure. We spent a year following Whisper from one blistering trouble spot to the next, fighting damned near every day.

Special treatment? Yeah. The kind you get for being competent. Whatever your racket, you do a good job, the bosses pile more work on.

"You'll be the first to know when I get a good look, Otto." I did not plow on into the kind of crudities the others found entertaining. Which they took as confirming my unabated interest in the wickedest woman in the world.

A kid named Corey said, "Speaking of hairstyles, there's one I wouldn't mind checking out."

Everybody turned to admire the young woman passing on the far side of the street. Pawnbroker congratulated Corey on his excellent taste.

She was sneaking up on twenty. She had pale red hair cut shorter than any I'd yet seen around Aloe. It fell only to her collar in back and not that far angling up the sides. She had bangs in front. I did not notice what she wore. Nothing unusual. She radiated such an intense sensuality that nothing else mattered.

Our sudden attention, heads turning like birds in a wheeling flock, startled her. She stared back for a second, trying for haughty. She failed to stick it. She took off speed-walking.

One-Eye picked up his cards. "That one is bald everywhere that matters."

Corey asked, "You know her?" Like he had found new meaning to life. He had hope. He had a mission.

"Not specifically. She's a temple girl."

The cult of Occupoa engages in holy prostitution. I hear Occupoa has some dedicated and talented daughters.

Goblin wanted to know how One-Eye could tell.

"That's the official hairstyle over there, runt." From a guy smaller than Goblin.

"And you know that because?"

"Because I've decided to enjoy the best of everything during my last few months."

We all stared. One-Eye is a notorious skinflint. And never has any money, anyway, because he is such a lousy tonk player. Not to mention that he is the next thing to immortal, having been with the Company well over a hundred years.

"What?" he demanded. "So maybe I poor-mouth more than what's the actual case. That a crime?"

No. We all do that. It is a preemptive stroke against all those good buddies who are dry and want to mooch instead of dealing with Pawn.

Somebody observed, "A lot of guys were flush when we got here. We never got no chance to get rid of our spare change before."

True. The Black Company has been good for Aloe's economy. Maybe that was why nobody was trying to kill us.

Elmo said, "I'd better round up Kingpin before the Lieutenant puts my name on the shit list, too. Silent? You want my seat? Shit! Where the hell did he go?"

I had not noticed our third minor wizard leaving. Silent is spookier than ever, these days. He is practically a ghost.

You are with the Company long enough you develop extra senses. Like for danger. Somehow, you read cues unconsciously and, suddenly, you are alert and ready. We call that smelling danger. Then there is precognition having to do with something stirring at the command level. That one warns you that your ass is about to get dumped into the shit.

Seemed like it took about fourteen electric seconds for all six hundred and some men to sense that something was up. That life was about to change. That I might not make it to a hundred days without somebody trying to kill me.

The cards had stopped moving already when Hagop loped up from the direction of the compound. "Elmo. Croaker. Goblin. One-Eye. The Old Man wants you."

One-Eye grumbled, "Goblin had to go open his big goddamn mouth."

Two minutes earlier, Goblin had muttered, "Something's up. There's something in the wind."

I kicked in, "Yeah. This is all his fault. Let's pound his ass if it turns out we have to go flush some Rebels somewhere again."

"Weak, Croaker." Elmo shoved back from the table. "But I second that emotion. I'd almost forgotten how nice it is for garrison troopers." He went on about clean clothing, ample beer, regular meals, and almost unlimited access to a soldier's favorite way of wasting time and money.

We headed down the street, leaving the cards to the others, who were already speculating. I said, "Garrison duty is all that. The hardest work I've got to do is to weasel One-Eye into using his curative on guys who come in with the clap."

One-Eye said, "I like garrison because of the financial opportunities."

He would. Put him down anywhere and give him a week, he'll be into some kind of black-market scam.

Hagop sidled close, whispered, "I need to talk to you, private." He slipped me a folded piece of parchment maybe three and a half inches to a side. It was dirty and it smelled bad. One face had a small triangular tear where it had hung up on something. Hagop looked like he might panic when I opened it.

I stopped walking. The others did, too, wondering what was up. I whispered, "Where did you get this?"

The Company maintained a compound outside the city, on a heath blasted barren back when Whisper arrived to negotiate the treaties by which Aloe gained the perquisites of participation in the Lady's empire. First among those was continued existence for Aloe and its dependent environs. The compound was nothing exciting. There was a curtain wall of dried mud brick. Everything inside was adobe, too, lightly plastered to resist the rain.

The compound was all brown. A man with a discerning eye might identify shades, but us barbarians only saw brown. Even so, I had a discerning enough eye to spot a new brown patch before Hagop pointed it out.

A flying carpet lay tucked into the shade on the eastern side of the headquarters building. My companions had equally discerning eyes but less troubled hearts.

We were part of a stream, now. Every officer and platoon sergeant had been summoned. Sometimes the Captain gets his butt hairs in a twist and pulls everybody in for an impromptu motivational speech. But there was one critical difference this time.

There was a flying carpet in the shade beside the HQ.

There are, at most, six of those in existence, and only six beings capable of using them.

We were blessed with the presence of one of the Taken.

The happy days were over. Hell had taken a nap but now it was wide awake and raring to go.

Nobody overlooked the carpet. No shoulders failed to slump.

I said, "You guys go ahead. I'll catch up in a minute. Hagop. Show me."

He headed for the shade. For the carpet. "I saw it here. I never seen a carpet up close before so I decided to check it out." He walked me through his experience. One glance at the carpet reaffirmed what I already knew. This unkempt, poorly maintained mess belonged to the Limper.

"I found that folded thing right here."

Right here would be the place where the Taken sat while the carpet was aloft. The carpet there was especially frayed, stretched, and loose.

Hagop's finger indicated a fold of material torn away from the wooden frame underneath. "It was mostly covered. It was hung up on that brad."

A small nail had worked loose maybe three-sixteenths of an inch. A wisp of parchment remained stuck to it. I removed that with my knife, careful to make no personal contact.

"I picked it up. Before I could even look at it the Captain came out and told me to go get you guys."

"All right. Stay out of sight. We'll talk later." I was going to be last inside if I did not hustle.

"It's bad, isn't it?"

"It could be bad. Scoot on into town. Don't tell anybody about this."

The mess hall was the nearest thing to an assembly hall we had. The cooks had been run off. The place reeked of unhappiness. Half the guys lived in town, now, including me. Some had women. A few even had common-law stepchildren they did not mind supporting.

Those guys would pray that carpet meant the Lady had sent somebody out with the payroll. Only, in Aloe, our pay came from gentle taxes on the people we protected. No need to fly it in from a thousand miles away.

The Captain did his trained-bear shuffle up to the half-ass stage. A creepy brown bundle of rags followed. It dragged one leg. The hall filled with a hard silence.

The Limper. The most absurdly nasty of the Taken. A dedicated enemy of the Black Company. We had screwed him over good back when he tried going against the Lady.

He was back in favor now. But so were we. He could not have his revenge just yet. But he was patient.

The Captain rumbled, "The tedium is about to end, gentlemen. We now know why the Lady put us here. We're supposed to take out a Rebel captain called Tides Elba."

I checked the spelling later. It was not a name we knew. He pronounced it "Teadace Elba."

The Captain said that Tides Elba had enjoyed some successes west of us, but none of her victories had been big enough to catch our attention.

An interesting line of bullshit, some of which might be true.

The Limper climbed up with the Captain. That was a struggle. He had that bad leg and he was a runt—in stature. In wickedness and talent for sorcery he was the baddest of the bad. A reek of dread surrounded him. So did a reek of reek. On his best day, he smelled like he had been in a grave for a long time. He considered us from behind a brown leather mask.

Folks with weaker stomachs jostled for space in the back.

The Limper said nothing. He just wanted us to know he was around. Important to remember. And something foretelling interesting times.

The Captain told the Company commanders and platoon leaders to tell their men that we might be making movement soon. Pending investigatory work here in Aloe. They should settle their debts and personal issues. Ideally, they should shut down their Aloe lives and return to the compound.

We might see some desertions.

Elmo jabbed me in the ribs. "Pay attention."

The Old Man dismissed everybody but me and the magic-users. He invoked me directly. "Croaker, stay with me." The wizards he told to stick with the Limper.

The Captain herded me over to Admin. In theory, I owned a corner space there where I was supposed to work on these Annals. I did not often take advantage.

"Sit." A command, not an invitation. I sat in one of two crude chairs facing the ragged table he uses as a bulwark against the world. "Limper is here. He hasn't said so but we know that means we're headed into the shit. He hasn't said much of anything yet, actually. That may mean he doesn't know anything himself, yet. He's following orders, too."

I nodded.

"This isn't good, Croaker. This is the Limper. There'll be more going on than what we see."

There would be. I did my best to look like a bright child awaiting ineluctable wisdom from an honored elder.

"I'd tell you you're full of shit but you don't need the special memo. You know that taste in your mouth."

He was going to come down on me for something?

"You been putting on a show of being as useless as the rest of these dicks. But when you're supposedly off whoring or getting fucked up you're usually really somewhere poking into the local history."

"A man needs to have more than one hobby."

"It's not a hobby if you can't help yourself."

"I'm a bad man. I need to understand the past. It illuminates the present."

The Captain nodded. He steepled his fingers in front of a square, strong, dimpled chin. "I got some illuminating for you to do."

He did know something about what was up.

"You could maybe fix it so the Company don't wallow in the usual cesspit."

"You sweet-talker."

"Shut the fuck up. The Lady wants Tides Elba before she turns into an eastern White Rose. Or maybe she is the Rose. I don't know. Limper, he wants to go balls to the wall so he can look good to the Lady. Hopefully getting us all killed in the process."

"You're losing me, boss."

"I doubt it. Remember, the Limper has a special hard-on for you."

He did. "All right. And?"

"Limper thinks smashing things is fun. I don't want to be remembered for wrecking Aloe on a maybe."

"Sir, you need to give me a clue. What do you want me to do? I'm not as smart as you think."

"Nor am I."

The Captain shambled out from behind his table. He paced. Then, "The Lady thinks Tides Elba was born here, has family here, and visits frequently. She wasn't born Tides Elba. Her family probably don't know what she is."

Of course this Rebel would not have been born Tides Elba. If the Lady got hold of her true name, Tides Elba would be toast before sunset.

"You've been snooping already. You know where to look. Help us lay hands on her before the Limper can catch us in a cleft stick."

"I can dig. But I can tell you now, all I'll find is holes."

"Holes tell a story, too."

They do. "Instead of worrying about this woman, how about we come up with a permanent . . ."

He made a chopping motion. I needed to shut up. "Look at you. We could put you in charge of the whole eastern campaign, you're so smart. Go away. Do what you need to do. And stay away from those moronic cards."

I thought hard. My conclusion was frightening. There was no place to conspire where the Limper could not eavesdrop if he was so inclined. So I scrounged up an extra deck, more venerable than the one usually in play, and headed for the Dark Horse. Along the way, Hagop fell in beside me. "Is it time?"

"It's time. If everybody is there." Everybody being a select few like Elmo and the wizards.

"What was the big meeting? We got to move out?"

"They don't know what they're going to do. They just want to be ready to do it."

"Same old shit."

"Pretty much."

The usual suspects were there, out front, on the fringe, waiting instead of playing. Only Silent was missing. I asked Goblin with a glance. He shrugged.

Several guys started to drift over, thinking an entertaining game might break out. I handed my deck to Corey. "You guys get a game going inside."

"Quick on the uptake," Elmo observed as they cleared off. He scooted sideways so Hagop had room to add a chair. We pretended to play a five-man game.

I asked, "You all sure you want to be here? We're going to lay our balls on the table and hope nobody hits them with a hammer."

Nobody volunteered to disappear.

I produced the parchment Hagop had found. Folded, it made a square. Opened, it was a third taller than it was wide. I spread it out. "Pass it around. Don't act like it's any big deal."

"Go teach granny to suck eggs," One-Eye grumbled. "I can't tell anything from this. It's all chicken tracks."

"Those tracks are TelleKurre." The language of the Domination. Only two native speakers remained alive. "This is an Imperial rescript, from the Lady to the Limper. The ideograph in the upper left corner tells us that. But this is a copy. The ideograph top middle tells us that, along with the fact that this is copy number two of two. The ideograph in the upper right corner is the chop of the copyist."

"Accountability," Elmo said.

"Exactly. She's big on that since the Battle at Charm."

"Uhm. So what does it say?"

"Not much, directly. But very formally. The Lady orders the Limper to come east to find and capture a woman named Tides Elba. No why, no suggestion how, just do it, then bring her back alive and undamaged."

"And there ain't nothing in there about her being some new phenom rookie Rebel captain?"

"Not a hint."

"The Limper lied."

"The Limper lied. And not just to us. He isn't dedicated to the success of his mission."

Elmo asked, "How can you tell?"

"Limper had to sign both copies, agreeing that he understood his assignment. On his keeper copy, here, he wrote, 'Up Yours, Bitch.' "

"Whoa!" Hagop barked, awed rather than surprised.

Elmo asked, "Could that be a plant?"

"You mean, did he leave it so we could find it?"

"Yeah. To let us set ourselves up."

"I've been brooding about that. I don't think so. There are a thousand ways that could go wrong. He'd have no control. We might never notice it. But, more important, there's what he wrote instead of signing."

They thought. Twice One-Eye started to say something but thought better.

We focused on clever tricks the Limper might try. Looking for deep strategies and devilish maneuvers. It took the least among us, a simple line soldier, to point out a critical fact.

Hagop asked, "If he signed it that way won't he get nervous when he realizes that it's gone?"

We all considered him with widening eyes and galloping hearts. Elmo growled, "If the little shit goes bugfuck we'll know for sure that it's real."

"Silver lining." Goblin grinned but there was sweat on his forehead.

I pushed the parchment across to One-Eye. "See if that's tagged so he can trace it. Then see if there's a way he could tell who's been handling it."

"You going to put it back?"

"Hell, no! I'm going to bury it somewhere. It could come in handy someday. The Lady wouldn't be pleased if it fell into her hands. Speaking of forgetting. Goblin, fix it so Hagop has no recollection of the parchment. The Captain saw him hanging around the Limper's carpet. Questions might be asked."

"I'll have to work on you, too, then. You were seen hanging around the carpet, too."

I expect a lot of guys took the opportunity for a close-up look. But fear streaked down my spine, reached my toes, and cramped them. "Yeah. You'd better."

Both wizards started to get out of their seats. Goblin said, "We'll need to shove those memories down so far that only the Lady's Eye could find them."

I had a thought. "Hang on. Wait a minute. Hagop, go get Zhorab."

Markeb Zhorab had been something else before he became a tavern-keeper. His face alone recalled several desperate fights. And he was a sizable man, often mistaken for the bouncer. But his past had left his courage a little sketchy.

He asked me, "You wanted me?"

"I have something I need done, not traceable to me. I'm willing to pay."

"Risky?"

"Possibly. But probably not if you do exactly what I tell you."

"I'm listening."

I showed him the rescript. "I need an exact copy calligraphed by a professional letter-writer who has no idea who you are."

"What is it?"

"A wanted poster. But the less you know the better. Can you do that?"

He could, once we finished talking money. I did not offer

enough to make it seem like I was worried. With all the practical
jokes that went on around us, I hoped he thought I was putting
something together. He asked, "How soon do you need this?"

"Right now would be especially good."

Zhorab brought my copy. And the original. "Good enough,
Croaker? He couldn't match the parchment."

"It's fine. I want it obvious that it's a copy." I paid the agreed
sum. I handed back the copy. "Hold on to this. Later on Goblin
will tell you when to give it back. There'll be another payment
then."

Elmo grumbled, "If we can ever get the self-righteous asshole
into this place." Playing to the practical-joke angle.

Puzzled, Zhorab folded the copy and went off to bite his
coins.

Elmo wondered, "Think he had more than one copy made?"

I said, "I'm counting on it. The more there are the better.
Now let's get to the forgetting."

I said, "I don't know. I forget. It must not have been important.
Look. I need you guys to help me dig for info on Tides Elba."

Grumble, grumble. Chairs pushed back grudgingly.

I said, "It has to be done."

"Yeah. Yeah."

I asked, "Hagop, do you read the local language?"

He shook his head. Once we were a few steps away, Elmo said,
"I'm not sure he can read anything."

I grunted. "One last beer."

Inside, the Dark Horse was swamped in speculation about
what might be afoot. A sizable faction did not believe that Tides
Elba existed. Old hands, who had been through the long retreat
from Oar to Charm, thought that the Limper had made it all up.

When asked my opinion, I said I never heard of Tides Elba and we had only Limper's word that she existed.

Aloe was a city-state. It was a republic, a formula common in its end of the world. It was prosperous. It had the time and money to maintain civil records, which are useful for levying taxes, calling men to the colors, or imposing a corvée.

Aloe kept those records in a small, stone-built structure. Our advent spread consternation.

Surprise arrival was of no value. Nothing jumped out. There were records aplenty, stored according to no obvious system, to keep us busy for days.

Elmo said, "I'll put out a call for men who can read this stuff." He barely managed himself, sounding out the characters.

Silent walked in. Before I could put him to work, he signed, "Wait!" and did a slow turn to make sure there were no stinky men in brown hiding in the rafters. Then he signed, "I know where to find her."

Everybody babbled questions, negating Silent's caution. He signed, "Shut up! Unless you are hungry for a taste of knuckle. Idiots."

He said the smoldering redhead from the other day was our target.

"How do you know?" I demanded. In sign.

Silent tapped the side of his head, pointed to his eyes, then his nose. Shorthand sign meaning he paid attention and he used his noggin when he smelled something a little off.

He had seen something that was not just prime split tail. So he had stalked her. To the Temple of Occupoa. And had been watching ever since.

"Predictable," I signed. Rebels everywhere hide stuff under their houses of worship. "Let's raid the place." I was unconcerned about the wrath of Occupoa. The gods seldom defend themselves. "Send her off to the Tower."

Elmo agreed. "Along with our least favorite Taken."

Elmo and I were the responsible, sensible voices. We got shouted down. Goblin jumped up and down. Every fifth sign he deployed was a vertical middle finger.

One-Eye insisted, "We'll play a riff on Roses."

"Why?"

"To gouge the Limper. Maybe frame him for something."

"Or we can just give him the girl and get him out of town."

Their enthusiasm faded as they recalled the truth of that bitter winter operation in Roses. Of circumstances that started the Limper on the road to now, notably unhappy with the Company.

Silent signed, "Croaker makes a good point. Wimpy, but solid."

One-Eye, though, being One-Eye, smelled opportunity. But One-Eye had a hundred-plus-year record of being One-Eye.

That considered, the level of enthusiasm plummeted.

I refused to go to the Captain or Limper with their idiot plan. It relied entirely on the near-immortal, almost demigod Limper being too stupid to see through them. I said, "To even start that going we'd need something magically useful from our target. You guys got some of her hair? Nail clippings? Dirty underwear? Didn't think so. Let's go dig her out and turn her over."

I did, as noted, remain deft enough to avoid being the man asked to sell the scheme. That honor went to Silent.

Silent is no bumbler but he did not close the deal. The Captain's response was, "Find the girl and bring her in. That's all. Nothing else."

Nobody wanted to hear what I thought after Silent came back. One-Eye insisted, "You worry too much, Croaker. You give the little shit too much credit. He ain't some genius. He's just an ass-hole bully whose knack for sorcery is so big he don't need to think."

"Lot of that going around."

Goblin said, "Look at all he's been through since he got out of the ground. None of it made him any smarter; it only made him more careful about what evidence he leaves behind."

Why did that make me nervous? "He can smash us like slow roaches without breaking a sweat."

One-Eye insisted, "He's as dumb-ass as you can be and survive. He's the kind of guy you can hit with the same con five times running and he still won't figure out what happened."

Idiot.

Limper might be dumb as a bushel of rocks but he was not up against the first string over here. And he had come here with a plan.

I insisted that we keep on rooting through the records. I told the others to tell me about every death of a girl child.

It was past my bedtime but I restrained my resentment when summoned by the Captain and Limper. The Old Man said, "We hear you found something."

"I did. But I think it's bogus," I reported honestly.

The Captain said, "Good work. Keep digging. But you can't use Goblin or One-Eye anymore. They're going TDA somewhere else." His glance at the Limper was so bland I knew he wanted to feed the man to the lions.

"They're useless, anyway. They can't stay focused even when they're not feuding."

The Captain said, "One more thing before you go."

My stomach sank. "Sir?"

"You were seen messing around with the lord's carpet. Why? What were you up to?"

"Messing with it? No, sir. I was talking about it to Hagop. He was all excited. He never saw a carpet up close before. He knew I had to ride carpets a couple times, back when. He wanted to know what it was like. We just talked. We never touched anything." I was babbling but that was all right. The Limper was used to terrified behavior. "Why? Is it important, sir?"

The Old Man glanced at his companion, inviting questions or comments. The old spook just stared through me.

"Apparently not. Dismissed."

I tucked my tail and ran. How did the Captain keep cool around that monster?

I fled the dread for the Dark Horse, where the useless pair and Silent waited. I passed the latest, and, in sign, added, "I don't like it, guys. The Captain thinks we're up to something. If the Limper catches on . . ."

One-Eye cursed, said something about my damned defeatist attitude, but then gave up. Even he is only blind in one eye.

Goblin acquiesced, too. Both had, at last, grasped the magnitude of the overreach they yearned to indulge. Well-founded terror settled into their hearts.

Despite all, we did not go get the girl. Goblin and One-Eye disappeared with the Limper. Silent evaded that fate by being impossible to find. I assumed he was eyes on the target.

Neither Elmo, Candy, nor the Lieutenant would let us make the catch without a full complement of supporting wizards.

Silent was supposed to keep hiding in her shadow.

Elmo's call for men able to read the local language produced three and a half men, the half being a lost-cause half-ass apprentice shared by Goblin and One-Eye who called himself the Third. The Third because his father and grandfather had worn the same

name. I never understood how he survived in the murky weirdness between his teachers.

The Third came by my town place. He looked less a sorcerer
than did One-Eye or Goblin—and was bigger than those two
squished together.

He made me wish they were. "They're going to raid the Temple of Occupoa tonight. One-Eye wants your help."

The terror had not taken deep enough root. A sanctioned operation was planned for the next morning.

"One-Eye needs his head examined by incompetent authority.
Somebody willing to recommend decapitation therapy." But I got
armed up and put together.

The Third resembled the Captain some, though he was uglier.
He talked about as much as the Old Man, too. I asked, "Where
were One-Eye and Goblin the last couple days?"

"Doing something with the Limper. Developing new skills for
the Tides Elba hunt."

I was skeptical.

We caught up with the runts and two of the soldiers who
could read the local writing, Cornello Crat and Ladora Ans. I
started kvetching. "Where's Silent? Where's Elmo?"

"Couldn't find them," One-Eye grumbled. He pulled his
floppy rag of a hat down so the brim concealed his face. "Be
quiet. Let's go."

"No."

"What?"

"This isn't going to happen. You want to play tonk with the
Taken because you think you can scam some money. But you're
so damned blind stupid you don't see that the real stake you're
shoving into the pot is the Company. All six hundred forty lives."

Goblin looked chagrined. One-Eye, though, just wanted to be
pissed off. He started to give me a piece of his mind.

"For the last time, dumb fuck. Listen! With the kind of luck you have playing penny ante tonk you want me to help play against the Limper? I can't believe that even you are that stupid. We'll do it the way it's set. Tomorrow. And you won't hand the Limper the excuse he wants."

One-Eye said nothing. His eye did get big. Seldom had he seen me so intense and never so foul of mouth.

He would have dismissed me, even so, if Goblin had not shaken like a dog just in out of the rain. "I'm going to side with Croaker on this. On reflection. Get your greed and ego out of it. Consider it on its merits."

One-Eye launched a rant about a once-in-a-lifetime opportunity.

Goblin shook all over again, looked a little puzzled, then tied into One-Eye. "How the hell do you talk yourself into this shit? How the hell do you stay alive?"

Victory! I had turned Goblin. Crat and Ans came with him. The Third had made his position clear already by vanishing after he delivered me.

I had a horrible acid stomach. A slight but stubborn tremor kept my hands unreliable. Crat and Ans seemed just as rocky.

One-Eye realized that if he wanted to pull this off he would have to do it by himself. That startled and amazed him.

There was some low cunning under that ugly old black hat. He could back off when nobody else was greedy enough or stupid enough to let him bet their hand.

"You asshole, Croaker. You win. I hope you got guts enough to put in the Annals what a huge pussy you were when we had a chance to make the biggest score ever."

"Oh, it'll be there. Count on that. Including the fact that the Company survived despite you." I went on to point out that the Company's mission was not to make a big score for One-Eye.

It started to get heated. Then Silent and Elmo turned up. They, in essence, took our little black brother into protective custody, to protect him from himself.

I consulted Elmo. Elmo consulted Candy. Candy consulted the Lieutenant. When even the gods were not looking, the Lieutenant may have consulted the Captain.

Word rolled down. Make the move, though Silent's girl was, likely, not really Tides Elba.

Elmo was in charge. Goblin and Silent would supply sorcery support. One-Eye and the Third were assigned a critically important secondary mission: a census of goats in Utbank parish. The Lady needed to know.

The Captain overlooks a lot. A good officer knows when not to see. But that blindness has limits.

Being me, I found the dark side before the action began. "We took care of One-Eye's run for the crazy prize but we didn't get out of the cleft stick."

Goblin said, "Humor him. It'll take less time. And we won't have to listen to him grumble from now till we lay him down with a stone on top to keep him from getting back up. Speak, Wise One." He went right on getting ready. So did the others. They would hear me out but did not plan to *listen*.

"The Old Man figures that this probably isn't Tides Elba. So how will the locals respond when we break into a holy place and drag off a temple girl who hasn't done anything but catch Silent's eye?"

Elmo told me, "The same orders said go get her, Croaker. That's our problem. Not what comes after. We got people who get paid to worry about what comes after. You aren't one of them.

Your job is to come along behind and plug up the holes in any of these dickheads who forget to duck."

He was right. "I don't know what's gotten into me lately." And, honestly, I did not.

A platoon on the move scattered the locals, but then they followed at a distance, moved by boneheaded nosiness.

I fell in beside Goblin. "Where did you and One-Eye go those two days with the Limper? What did you do?"

His broad, pallid face slowly collapsed into a deep frown. "With the Limper? We didn't go anywhere with the Limper."

"You didn't? But the Old Man told me you were going TDA with the spook. Who was right there when he said it. You were gone two days. Then you came back all determined to do stuff that we already decided would be suicidal."

"Two days? You're sure?"

"Two. Ask Elmo."

He turned contemplative. After maybe fifty yards he asked, "What does the Captain say?"

"Nothing. He isn't talking much these days. He has the foulest Taken of them all homesteading in his right front pocket."

A hundred yards of silence. The big ugly dome of the Temple of Occupoa now loomed over the tenements surrounding it. It had some claim to minor-wonder-of-the-world status because that huge beehive shape, over eighty feet high, was made entirely of concrete. For those interested in engineering, the temple must be fascinating. Building it had taken a generation.

The people of Aloe did not give a bat's ass.

Goblin said nothing more but did look like a man who had just enjoyed some surprisingly unpleasant revelations.

There are steps up to the entrance of Occupoa's temple, two tiers, the lower of seven steps and the upper of six. Those numbers are almost certainly significant. They were granite that mixed grays with a bit of white. The columns and walls were a native greenish-gray limestone, easy to work but susceptible to weathering. Scaffolding masked the west face.

It was not a holy day. It was too early for traffic related to Occupoa's fund-raising efforts. It was quiet.

I climbed the thirteen steps still wondering why we were doing this. Still worrying about the whole Tides Elba puzzle. I had questioned every Aloen I knew. They insisted the name was unknown, that there was no Rebel leader by that name. I believed them. That many people could not all be fine enough actors to appear so honestly baffled.

On the other hand, one did wonder how they could be so sure there was no Rebel named Tides Elba.

We paused at the temple entrance. Silent and Goblin conjured several spectral entities to go in first, to trigger ambushes or booby traps.

They were not needed. Temple defense consisted of one ancient beadle asleep on a chair just inside the entrance. His mission appeared to be to discourage unauthorized withdrawals from a nearby poor box.

Goblin did something to deepen his sleep.

One squad moved in and spread out. The rest stayed outside and surrounded the temple. We ran into a whole lot of nothing happening on the inside. The main place of worship was round, with the altar on a short dais in the middle. That was black stone without a single bloodstain. Occupoa had a more enlightened attitude toward the disposal of virgins. Instead, the altar boasted racks of votive candles, only a handful of which were burning.

The whole place seemed a little shabby.

I had my teeth clamped so tight my jaw began to ache. This was no Rebel stronghold. Had we been scammed after all? Why did I keep recalling the Limper's evil way of laughing when things were going his way?

I had a powerful urge to turn back. I did not.

Elmo asked, "Which way, Goblin? Silent?" He sounded uneasy. That would be because we had run into no one but the beadle.

I flashed a nervous grin, certain One-Eye would have tried to plunder that poor box had he been along instead of handling critical empire business in Utbank.

"Straight ahead. If you didn't have a dozen guys clanking and whispering you could hear the people up there."

I started to worry about One-Eye and Goblin again. What had been done to them while they were out of touch? Maybe Limper brainwashed them. Which could only be for the better in One-Eye's case.

Could this raid be part of Limper's grand scheme to discredit the Company?

Elmo prodded me. "Move along. What's with you, anyway? You're turning into the worst daydreamer."

Sounds of surprised excitement broke out ahead.

The excitement was not the run-for-it kind. It was the what-the-hell-is-going-on kind. It took place in a combination kitchen and dining hall where sixteen women, of a vast range of ages, had been sharing a late breakfast. The older women asked the questions. Elmo ignored them. He asked, "Silent? Which one?"

Silent pointed.

The girl from the street shared a table with five others who might have been her sisters. An effort had been made to make them look alike, but our target stood out once you spotted her. She had an aura, a magnetism that marked her as extremely special.

Maybe our employer *had* taken a gander into the future and had seen what the girl might become.

Elmo said, "Silent, get her. Tuco, Reams, help him. Goblin, cover. No weapons." All stated in a language not spoken in Aloe.

There was no resistance. The old women stopped protesting and demanding, started asking why we were doing this.

Silent stood the girl up, bound her wrists behind her. I noted that he wore gloves and was careful to make no skin-to-skin contact. She asked what was going on, once, then succumbed to fear. Which made me feel so awful I just wanted to help her. I could imagine the horrors she expected at our hands.

"Wow," Elmo said, very softly.

"Indeed," Goblin agreed. "Potent. Maybe she *is* something special."

We went back out the way we had come in, Goblin and I doing rearguard duty. Elmo, in the lead and in a hurry, caught a kid in the process of robbing the poor box. Elmo responded harshly.

The would-be thief was unconscious when I settled down to treat his broken arm. Elmo had avoided shedding too much blood.

Goblin stuck with me. Elmo collected the platoon and, with Silent valiantly negating whatever it was the girl gave off under stress, headed for the compound. Scores of baffled Aloens watched. Some tagged along after Elmo.

Goblin studied the locals for signs of belligerence. Preoccupied, he did not hear what I thought I heard from the shadows inside the temple. If it was not my frightened imagination running away with me.

It was a *drag-scrape,* sudden *clop!* then another *drag-scrape.* Like somebody with a bad leg having a hard time keeping quiet while crossing a wide stone floor.

• • •

"How come you think I imagined it?" I demanded. Goblin and I were approaching the Dark Horse. Our presence was not necessary at the compound. Elmo could handle all that. And, when the temple girl proved not to be Tides Elba, he could be the man who got in there and did some serious planning on how to track and catch the real thing.

"Because I got a great view of the southern sky." He pointed.

From out of the distance, unhurried, a flying carpet headed across town, no more than fifty feet above the rooftops. Two people were visible on the side toward us, one wearing a filthy, floppy black hat.

So. The Limper had gone to Utbank parish to find out what One-Eye was up to. And had decided to bring him and the Third back, not entirely convinced that the Old Man had sent them out there because One-Eye's greed was complicating matters.

"All right. It must have been my guilty conscience. Let's reward ourselves for work well done with some of Master Zhorab's fine ale."

Goblin said, "It's earlier than is my custom but in honor of our success I will join you, sir."

We entered. The interior of the Dark Horse exactly reflected its exterior. There were no Company brothers out there, drinking and playing tonk. There were none inside, either.

In fact, there was no one behind the bar.

Goblin rectified that by observing, "Nobody's home. Let's get back there and . . ."

Markeb Zhorab materialized. Goblin said, "Hello, magic man. We've done a hard day's work. Beer is in order."

Zhorab drew two mugs while eyeing us with unnerving intensity. "Did you catch who you were after?"

The man was incredibly tense. "Yes. Why does that mean so much to you?"

Zhorab raised a finger in a "wait one" gesture. He dug out the hidden cash box he thought was secret but was not to any sharp-eyed regular. He looked around furtively while fumbling it open. He produced a ragged deck.

"My cards." Last seen in the hands of Corey and his pals. "Where did you get those?"

"Goblin said to hang on to them till you arrested the person the Taken is here to collect."

The little wizard and I exchanged puzzled looks.

"Oh. It's not really the cards." He spread the deck across the bar, hand shaking. He watched the door like he expected doom to thunder through any second.

Goblin asked, "You haven't sold us out to somebody, have you?"

"Huh? Oh! No! Never!"

"Then how come this place is so empty? How come you're so nervous?"

I said, "The place is empty because everybody is back at the compound. Hello." I plucked a piece of parchment from amongst the scattered cards.

I unfolded it.

I stared.

I started shaking. Memories buried monstrously deep gurgled to the surface. "Goblin. Check this out."

Goblin started shaking, too.

Zhorab asked, "I did it right?"

I pushed a silver piece across. "You did it perfectly." I had found the copy now, too. "Just one more step. You had the letter writer make an extra copy. We'll want that one, too."

Zhorab wanted to lie but desisted after a look into Goblin's eyes. "It will take a few minutes."

I put another coin on the bar, with an ugly black knife for a companion. The knife was not special but looked like it ought to be.

Zhorab gulped, nodded, vanished.

Goblin observed, "He gave that up pretty easy."

"Probably has more than one copy."

"You want them all?"

"I don't mind there being a few extras floating around, maybe getting back to the Tower someday."

"Your honey would run our smelly friend through the reeducation process again."

I shuddered. I had had my own brush with the Eye. Everything inside me had been exposed had the Lady cared to look. It had been her way of getting to know me. What the Limper would endure would be a hundred times worse, but not fatal. He was much too useful—when he confined himself to being an extension of the Lady's will.

Zhorab returned. He gave me another folded parchment. I sheathed my knife. "We have to go. Be ready for a big rush later on."

We encountered Hagop halfway to the compound. "There you are. The Captain sent me to get you guys. He wants Goblin to connect with the Tower so the Lady will know we got the girl, in perfect shape, before the Limper takes her and heads out."

"Shit." Goblin looked back, considering making a run for it.

It had been a while since he had made direct contact. He did not want to endure that again. Not voluntarily.

I said, "It must be damned important if he's willing to put you through that."

Hagop said, "He really wants to make sure she knows. He doesn't trust the Limper."

"Who would?" And, "The temple girl really is Tides Elba?"

"Yes. She doesn't deny it. She claims she's no Rebel or Resurrectionist, either. But she's got some girl magic."

Goblin asked, "Croaker, it ever feel like everybody knows more than you do?"

"Every damned day since I joined this chicken-shit outfit. Hagop. Take this. First chance you get, plant it right back where you found it."

He took the folded parchment. "This isn't the one I gave you."

The Captain was behind his table. Tides Elba sat on one of his rude chairs, wrists and ankles in light fetters. She looked to have gone numb, emotionally beyond the point where she could not believe this was happening. A torc had been placed around her neck, the sort used to manage captured sorcerers. If she tried to use sorcery, it would deliver terrible pain.

The Lady must have probed far into the future. The child was sitting on the only magic she controlled right now.

The Captain scowled. "You've been drinking."

"One mug, in celebration of a job well done," Goblin replied.

"It's not done yet. Contact the Lady. Let her know. Before the Limper finds out we have her."

Goblin told me, "Welcome to the mushroom club."

The Captain said, "I don't need you here, Croaker."

"Of course you do. How else am I going to get it into the Annals right?"

He shrugged. "Move it, Goblin. You're wasting valuable time."

Goblin could make contact on the spur of the moment because he had made the connection so often before. But familiarity did not ease the pain. He shrieked. He fell down, gripped by a seizure. Startled, concerned, the Captain came out from behind his table, dropped to a knee beside Goblin, back to the girl. "Will he be all right?"

"Make sure he doesn't swallow his tongue." I took the opportunity to cop a feel of a firm, fresh breast and to slip a square of parchment in with the sweet young jubblies. The girl met my eye but said nothing. "My guess is, he's having trouble getting through."

The Lady heard Goblin but chose another means of response. Just as the Limper burst in through an exploding door.

A circle of embers two feet across appeared above Goblin, almost tangled in the Captain's hair. The Lady's beautiful face came into focus inside. Her gaze met mine. She smiled. My legs turned to gelatin.

Goblin's seizure ended. As did the Limper's charge.

A voice like a whisper from everywhere asked, "Is this her?"

The Captain said, "So we believe, ma'am. She fits all the particulars."

The Lady winked at me. We were old campaign buddies. We had hunted down and killed her sister during the fighting at Charm.

The whisper from everywhere said, "She's striking, isn't she?"

I nodded. Goblin and the Captain nodded. The Limper, oozing closer behind his miasmic stench, dipped his masked face in agreement. Tides Elba was indeed striking, and growing more so by the minute—employing an unconscious sorcery to which her torc did not respond.

"Every bit as much as my sister was. This one's remote grandmother, to whom she bears an uncanny resemblance."

Different sister, I presumed. Tides Elba bore only a passing resemblance to the one I helped kill. I started to ask a question. Needlessly. Our employer was in an expansive mood.

"Her male ancestor was my husband. He futtered anything that moved, including all my sisters and all the female Taken. Enough. She was about to mate with another of his descendants. Their child would become a vessel into which the old bastard could project his soul."

The Limper might have considered all that in whatever he had planned. The rest of us gaped. Excepting the girl. She did not understand a word. The language the Lady spoke was unknown to her.

Her whole being was focused on what hung in the air, there, though.

She voided herself. She knew where she was bound.

Something passed between the Lady and the Limper. The stinky little sorcerer bowed deeply. He moved in on the girl, took hold of her arm, forced her to her feet. He pushed her toward the door he had wrecked.

The rest of us watched, every man wishing he had the power to stop them, every man knowing that, if the Lady had spoken truly, Tides Elba was a threat to the entire world. She could become the port through which the hideous shadow known as the Dominator could make his return. No doubt she was sought by and beloved of every Resurrectionist cult hoping to free the old evil from his grave. No doubt she was a prophesied messiah of darkness.

I glanced back. The Lady was gone. The end, here, was almost an anticlimax. But that was because we were out there on the margins, able to see only the local surface of the story. For the Company, the central fact would be we had survived.

We all went out and watched the Limper get ready to go.

He seemed nervous and unhappy. He shoved the girl into a sack. He sewed that shut, then secured it to his carpet with cording. Tides Elba would not evade her fate by rolling off the carpet while it was in flight. His liftoff into the late-afternoon light seemed erratic. He wobbled as he headed west.

I found Hagop in the shadows near where the Limper's carpet had lain. He gave me a big grin and a thumbs-up. "He spotted it right away. Took it out, looked at it, and jumped like somebody just hit him with a shovel."

"He got the message, then."

Goblin stared westward, eyes still haunted, but said only, "What a waste of delicious girl flesh." And then, "Let's round up Elmo and One-Eye and go tip a few at the Dark Horse. Elmo has got the cards, don't he?"

GENE WOLFE worked as an engineer, before becoming editor of trade journal *Plant Engineering*. He came to prominence as a writer in the late 1960s with a sequence of short stories in Damon Knight's *Orbit* anthologies. His early major novels were *The Fifth Head of Cerberus* and *Peace,* but he established his reputation with a sequence of three long, multivolume novels—*The Book of the New Sun, The Book of the Long Sun,* and *The Book of the Short Sun.* His short fiction has been collected in *The Island of Doctor Death and Other Stories, Endangered Species, Strange Travelers,* and, most recently, *The Best of Gene Wolfe.* He is the recipient of the Nebula, World Fantasy, Locus, John W. Campbell Memorial, British Fantasy, British SF, and World Fantasy Lifetime Achievement Awards. Wolfe's most recent book is the novel *An Evil Guest.* Upcoming is his new novel *The Sorcerer's House.*

BLOODSPORT

Gene Wolfe

Sit down and I'll tell you.

I was but a youth when I was offered for the Game. I would have refused had that been possible; it was not—those offered were made to play. As I was already large and strong, I became a knight. Our training was arduous; two of my fellows died as a result, and one was crippled for life. I had known and liked him, drank with him, and fought him once. Seeing him leave the school in a little cart drawn by his brothers, I did not envy him.

After two years, I was knighted. I had feared that I would rank no higher than bowman; so it was a glad day for me. Later that same day I was given three stallions, the finest horses ever seen—swift golden chargers with manes and tails dark as the darkest shadows. Many an hour I spent tending and training them; and I stalled them apart, never letting them graze in the same meadow or even an adjoining meadow, lest they war. If I were refused that many meadows on a given day, one remained in his stall while the other two grazed; but I was never refused after my first Game.

Now the Game is no longer played. Perhaps you have forgot-

ten it, or perhaps you never had the ill fortune to see it. The rules
are complex—I shall not explain them.

But I shall say here and say plainly that it was never my intention to slay my opponent. Never, or at least very seldom. It was
my task to defeat my opponent—if I could. And his to defeat
me. Well do I recall my first fight. It was with another knight,
and those engagements are rarest of all. I had been ordered to a
position in which a moon knight might attack me. It seemed safe
enough, since our own dear queen would be sure to attack him if
he triumphed. Yet attack he did.

Under the rules, the attacker runs or rides to the defender's
position, a great advantage. I had been taught that; but never
so well as I learned it then, when I did not know I was to be attacked until I heard the thunder of his charger's hooves. That
white charger cleared the lists with a leap that might have made
mock of two, and he was upon me. The ax was his weapon, mine
the mace. We fought furiously until some blow of mine struck
the helm from his head and left him—still in the saddle—half-
stunned. To yield, one must drop one's weapon; so long as the
weapon remains in hand, the fight continues. His eyes were
empty, his flaccid hand scarce able to grasp his ax.

Yet he did not drop it. I might have slain him then and there;
I struck his gauntlet instead. A spike breached the steel, nailing
his hand—for a moment only—to the haft of his ax. I jerked my
mace away and watched him fall slowly from his game saddle. His
head struck the wretched stony soil of the black square first, and I
feared a broken neck. Yet he lived, and was mewing and moving
when they bore him away. The spectators were not pleased with
me, but I was pleased with myself; it is winning that matters, not
slaying.

My next was with a pawn. She was huge, as they all are; bred
like chargers, some say. Others declare that it is only a thing the

mages do to baby girls. As you are doubtless aware, pawn's arms
are the simplest of all: a long sword and a shield nearly as tall
as the pawn herself, and wider. Other than those, sandals and a
loincloth, for pawns wear no armor. I thought to ride her down,
or else to slay her readily with my sword. One always employs the
sword against pawns.

It was not to be. She sprang to my left, my stroke came too
late, and she stripped me from the saddle. A moment more and
I lay upon the fair green grass of a sun square, with her sword's
point tickling my throat. "I yield!" I cried, and she grinned her
triumph.

I was taken from the game, and Dhorie, my trainer, found me
sitting alone, my head in my hands. He slapped my back and told
me he was proud of me.

"I charged a pawn," I mumbled.

"Who bested you."

I nodded.

"Could happen to anybody. Lurn is the best of the moon
pawns, and you had been charged by a knight scarcely a hundred
breaths before." (This last was an exaggeration.) "You had given
mighty blows and received them. Two moves and you were sent
again. Do you know how often a knight is charged by another,
but defeats him? The stands are still abuzz with your name."

I did not believe him but was comforted nonetheless. Soon I
learned that he had been correct, for my bruises had not yet faded
when I was put forward in a new game. That game I shall not
describe. Nor the others.

We do not mix, yet I saw the pawn who had bested me twice
more. Once we occupied adjacent squares, and though speaking
is forbidden, her face told me she knew me just as I knew her.
She spun her sword, grinning, and I raised my own and pointed
at the sun. Her hair was black as night, her shoulders broad, and

her waist small. Her muscles slid beneath her moon-white skin like so many dragons, and I knew I could scarcely have lifted the crescent moon-sword that danced for her.

The Hunas swept down upon us, and the games were ended. There was talk of employing us in battle; and I believe—yes, I believe still—that we might have turned them back. Before it could be done, they rushed upon the city by night. We fought and fled as best we could, I on Flare, my finest charger. For four days and three nights he and I hid in the hills, where I bandaged our wounds and applied poultices of borage and the purple-flowered high-heal that none but a seventh son may find.

The city had been put to the torch, but we returned to it. My father had been a mage of power, I knew, and I felt that his house might somehow have survived. In that I was mistaken; yet it had not been destroyed wholly. The south wing stood whole, and thus I was able to return to the very chamber I had called my own as a boy. My bed was there and waiting, and I felt an attraction to it by no means strange in a weary, wounded man. I saw to Flare as well as I could—water, a roof, and a little stale bread I found in the larder—and slept where I had slept for nights that had seemed endless so long ago. In the hills I had not dreamt; the imps and fiends that sought me out there had been those of waking. Returned to my own bed in the bedchamber that had been my own, I dreamt indeed.

In dream, my father sat before me, his head cloven to the jaw. He could not speak, but wrote upon the ground for me to read: *I blessed and I cursed you, Valorius, and my blessing and my curse are the same. You will inherit.*

I woke with his words ringing in through my thoughts, and I have never forgotten them. Whether they be so or no, who is to say? Perhaps I have inherited already, and know not of it. Perhaps they are as false as most dreams—false as most words, I ought to have said. For it is only those words that hold power over the thing they represent that are not false, and they are few and seldom found.

A league beyond the Gate of Exile, I saw Lurn sleeping in the shade of a spreading chestnut. Dismounting, I went to her; I cannot say why. Seeing that she slept soundly and was not liable to waken soon, I unsaddled Flare and let him graze, which he was eager to do. After that I sat near her, my back propped by the bole of the tree, and thought upon many things.

"What puzzles you so?"

Hearing her voice for the first time, I knew it was hers, deeper than my own yet a woman's. I smiled, I hope not impudently, and said, "Gaining your friendship. I fear that you will wish to engage, and that would be but folly as the world stands today."

"Folly indeed, for it stands not but circles the moon as both swim among stars." She laughed like a river over stones. "As for engaging, Valorius, why, I bested you. I choose to stand upon my victory, for you might die were we to engage again."

"You would not see me dead."

"No," she said; and when I did not speak, she said, "Would you see me so? You might have killed me while I slept."

"You would have sprung up and wrested the sword from my hand."

"Yes! Let us say that." The river flowed again. "Let us say it, that I may be joyful."

"You would not see me dead," I repeated, "and you troubled to learn my name, Lurn."

"And you mine." She sat up.

"I have seen sun and moon in the same sky," I told her. "They did not engage."

"They do but rarely." She smiled as she spoke, and there was something in her smile of the maid no man has bussed. "When they do she bests him, as is only to be expected. Bests him, and brings darkness over the earth."

"Is that true?"

"It is. She bests him, but having bested him she bids him rise. Someday—do you credit prophesy?"

I do not, but said I did.

"Someday he will best her and, besting her, take her life. So is it written. When the evil day comes, you men will walk in blind dark from twilight to dawn and much harm come of it."

"And what of women?"

"Women will have no warning, so that they bleed in the market. Will you come and sit by me, Valorius?"

"Gladly," I said. I rose and did so.

"Have the Hunas killed everyone save you and me?"

"They have slain many," I said, "but they can scarcely have slain everyone."

"When they have looted the towns and burned them, not many will remain. Those of our people who can still hold the hilt might be rallied to resist."

"Are they really our people?" I inquired.

"I was born among them. So were you, I think. I took shelter in this deep shade because my skin can't bear your noonday sun. When your sun is low, I'll walk again. Then we'll see what a lone woman can accomplish."

I shrugged. "Much, perhaps, with a knight to assist her. We must get you a wide hat, however, and a gown with long sleeves."

When the sun declined, we journeyed on together, and very pleasant journeying it was, for her head was level with my own when I rode Flare. We chattered and joked, and in time—not that day, I think, but the next—I beheld something in Lurn's eyes that I had never seen in the eyes of any woman.

That day we discovered a crone who knew the weaving of

hats; she made such hat as Lurn required, a hat woven of straw, with a crown like a sugar loaf and brim wide as a shield. She sent us to a little man with a crooked back, who for a silver piece made Lurn not one long gown but three, all of coarse white cloth. Of our rallying of the people, I shall say little or nothing. We armed them with whatever could be made or found, and ere long enlisted a forester. Bradan knew the longbow, and taught some youths how to make and use war-arrows, bows, bowcases, bracers, quivers, and all such things—a great blessing.

The Hunas fight on horseback, and are quick to flee when they fear they may lose the fight. To defeat them, one lays an ambush that shall catch them as they flee. Or else one must block the point of flight; we did both at one time or another. It is not the Game, yet it is a game of the same sort. We played it well, Lurn and I.

A mountain town called Scarp was besieged, and we marched to its relief. It lay in the valley of the Bright, and while one may go up that valley, or down it, a mounted man may not leave it for many a long league. Lurn and I flipped a crown; I lost and took two hundred or so of the rabble we tried to make foot soldiers, seventeen archers, and twenty-five horsemen upstream, skirting the town by night. Ere the sun was high, we found a place where the mountains pressed in on either side and the land on both sides of the road was rough and thickly wooded. I set out sentries, stationed my horsemen a thousand paces higher to prevent desertion, ordered the rest to get some sleep, and led by example.

Flare stamped to wake me. When I sat up, I could hear, though but faintly, the sounds he had heard more clearly—our trumpets, the drums of the Hunas, and the shouts, clashing blades, and screams of war. Then I could picture Lurn as I had seen her so often, leading the half-armed men she alone made bold. She had held her attack until the sun declined. Now her wide hat and white gown had been laid aside, and she would be fighting in sandals and a loincloth as she had as a pawn, a woman who towered above every man as those men towered above children, and the target of every Hunas horse-bow.

I knew the Hunas had broken when their drums fell silent. Lurn's trumpets shrilled orders, call after call: "Form up!" "Give way for the horse!" "Canter!" And again, "Canter!"

The Hunas had turned and fled. Our archers had the best of targets then, the riders' backs. We wanted to capture uninjured horses almost as much as we wanted to slay Hunas. And that moment—the moment when they turned and fled—would be the best of all moments to do it. If our horsemen galloped after them, they would flee the faster, which we did not want. Besides, our horsemen would soon break up, the best mounted outdistancing the rest. Then the Hunas might rally and charge, and our best mounted would go down. We did not want that, either.

"Here they come!"

It was a sentry upon a rocky outcrop. He waved and yelled, and soon another was waving and yelling, too. I formed up my men, halberds in front and pikes behind the halberds. Archers on the flanks, half-protected by trees and stones.

"I'll be in front. Stand firm behind me when I stand. Advance behind me when I advance. I'll not retreat. Come forward to take the place of those who fall. If the Hunas get past us, we've lost. If they don't, we've won. Do we mean to win?"

They shouted their determination; and not long after, when the first Hunas rode into sight, someone struck up the battle hymn. They were farmers and farriers, tinkers, tailors, and tradesmen, not soldiers and certainly not Game pieces. Would they run? They will not run, I told myself, if I do not run.

Not all the Hunas carry lances, but a good many do. Their lances are shorter than ours, thus easier to control. Lighter, too, and thus quick to aim. Now they positioned five lancers in front—enough to fill the road side-to-side. There were more behind, and I was glad to see them there, sensing that if the first were stopped (and I meant to stop them) they might be ridden down by those pressing forward.

The drums boomed like thunder, and the first five clapped spurs to their chargers.

My shield slipped the too-high lance-head, sending it over my left shoulder, and my point took his knee. Perhaps he yowled; if so, it could not be heard above the thudding drums and thundering hooves.

No more could the singing of our bows, but I saw the lancer next to him fall with an arrow in his throat. I had warned our pikemen to spare the horses. A horse screamed nonetheless, screamed and reared with the pike still in his vitals.

Then all was silence.

Though I did not dare look behind me, I glanced to right and left and counted the five—five lancers and one charger. Four lay still. One lancer writhed until a halberd-blade split his skull. The charger struggled to regain its feet; it would never succeed, but it would not cease to try until it died.

I waited for the next five lancers, but they did not charge. They must have known, as I did, that Lurn was behind them, strengthened by whatever troops had joined her from the town. And knowing that, known that they were caught between jaws. But they did not charge. We received a shower of arrows from their horse-bows; a few men cried out, and it may be that some died. Still, they did not charge.

Our battle hymn had ceased. I waved my sword above my head and began the hymn again myself. When I advanced, I heard the rest behind me, advancing as I did.

The road was no wider here, but its shoulders were clearer.

More Hunas could front us now. They were more likely to attack, and we more likely to scatter. I wanted the first, and felt sure the last was little risk enough. They dismounted and came for us on foot; I knew the gods fought beside us then.

They had light horse-axes and serpent swords. Both were more dangerous than they appeared. They had helmets, too, and seeing them I hoped my own men would have sense enough to strip them from the dead Hunas—and wear them. There were pikes to either side of me; those Hunas who came straight at me died, unable to parry my thrusts. Again and again I stepped forward over the bodies of our foes. In a hundred Games, no knight would ever slay half so many. It ought to have sickened me. It did not because I thought only of Lurn; each Hunas who fell to me was one who would never shed her blood.

I have never liked slaying men, and slaying women—I have done that, too—is worse. No doubt slaying children would be worse still. I have never done it and am glad, though I have met children who should be slain. Slaying animals is, for me, the worst of all. A stag fell to my bow yesterday; and I was glad, for I (I had almost said "we") needed the meat. That stag has haunted me ever since. What a fine, bold beast he was! It was not until now, when I have already told so much, that I kenned why I feel as I do.

Animals have no evil in them. Men have much, women (I think) half as much or less. Children have still less. Yet all humanity is touched by evil. Possibly there are men who have never been cruel. I have tried to be such a man, but is there a man above grass who would say I have succeeded? Certainly I will not say it.

Yonder stands my stag. I see him each time I look up, standing motionless where the shadows are thickest. He watches me with innocent eyes. There are always ghosts in a forest. My father taught me that a year, perhaps, before he gave me over to the games. Ghosts in forests, and few demons. In a desert, he said, that situation is reversed. Deserts call to demons and not to ghosts. (Yet not to demons only.) Among hills and mountains, their numbers are about equal—but who shall count them?

Can you see my stag? He is there beside Lurn, who stands beside him as a woman of ordinary size may stand beside a dog.

Let me gather more wood.

When we were no longer wanted, Lurn and I passed through this forest, which covers the hills at the feet of the mountains. She pressed forward eagerly and I hurried because she did. It was no easy thing for me to keep pace with her long strides, though most of my armor had been cast away.

It was these mountains, she assured me, that had given rise to the Game. The little mounds upon which we stand at the beginning of each playing of the Game are but the toys men have fashioned in imitation of these works of the gods. "It will mean nothing to you," she told me, "but it will mean the world and more to me." As I have said, I do not credit prophesy. Gods can prophesy, perhaps. No woman can, and no man.

If I recalled more of our journey, I would tell it now. I remember only hunger and cold, for it grew colder and colder as the land rose. There was less game, too. The mountain sheep are very wise, dwelling where the land lies open to their gaze. To hunt them, one must climb behind them, disturbing not one stone. They leap at the sound of the bow, though by then it is too late—leap and fall, always breaking the arrow and too often falling into bottomless clefts where they are devoured by demons.

Oh, yes! They eat as men do, and more. They cannot starve, though they grow lean; yet they eat nevertheless. The flesh of infants is what they like best. Witches offer it to them to gain their favor. We do not do that.

In time, I gave up all hope of finding one of the forty palaces of which she spoke. I only knew that if we went far enough, the mountains would cease their climb to the clouds and diminish again. Lurn would want to turn back; I would insist that we press forward, and we would see who would prevail.

It rained and we took shelter. A day exhausted the little food we had. Famished, we waited for a second day. On the third we went forth to hunt, knowing that we must hunt or starve. I knowing, too, that I dared not use my bow lest the string be wetted. Toward afternoon we flushed a flight of deer. Lurn could run more swiftly than they, they turn more sharply than she. She turned them and turned them until at last I was able to dash among them like a wolf, stabbing and slashing. I have no doubt that some escaped us, and that some of those who thus escaped soon perished of their wounds. We got three, even so, and chewed raw meat that night, and roasted meat the night following when we were able at last to kindle a fire, and so hungry as to abide the smoke of the twigs and fallen branches we collected.

We slept long that night. Day had come when we awoke, the clouds had lifted, and far away—yet not so distant as to be beyond our sight—we beheld a white palace on the side of the mountain looming before us. "There will be a garden!" Lurn's left hand closed on my shoulder with such strength that I nearly cried out.

"I see none," I told her.

"That green . . ."

"A mountain meadow. We've seen many."

"There must be a garden!" She spun me around. "A coronation garden for me. There must be!"

There was none, but we went there even so, a half-starved journey of two days through a forest filled with birdsong. There had been a wall about the palace, a low stone wall that might readily have been stormed. In many places it had fallen, and the gate of twisted bars had fallen into rust.

The rich chambers of centuries past had been looted, and here and there defiled. Their carpets were gone, and their hangings likewise. In many chambers we saw where fires of broken furniture had once blazed. Their ashes had been cold for heaped years no man could count, and their half-burned ends of wood, their strong square nails, and their skillfully wrought bronze screws had been scattered long ago, perhaps by the feet of the great-grandsons of those who had kindled them.

"This is a palace of ghosts," I told Lurn.

"I see none."

"I have seen many, and heard them, too. If we stay the night here . . ." I let the matter drop.

"Then we will go." She shrugged. "This was an error, and an error of my doing. We must first find food, and afterward another."

"No. We must go into the vaults." My own words surprised me.

She looked incredulous, but the ghost in the dark passage ahead nodded and smiled; it seemed almost a living man, though its eyes were the eyes of death.

"What's gotten into you?"

"I must go, and you with me," I told her. "I must go and bring you. You are afraid. I—"

"You lie!"

"Fear better suits a woman than a man. Even so, I am the more frightened. Yet I will go, and you will come with me." I set off, following the ghost, and very soon I heard Lurn's heavy tread behind me.

The corridor we traversed was dark as pitch. I slung my shield over my back, traced the damp stone walls with my left hand, and groped the dark before me with my sword point, testing the flag-stones with every step. None of which mattered in the least. The ghost led me, and there was no treachery.

We descended a stair, narrow and steep, and I saw light below. Here was a cresset, filled with blazing wood and dripping embers. The ghost, which ought to have dimmed in the firelight, seemed almost a living man, a man young and nearly as tall as I, in livery of grey and crimson.

"Who is that?" Lurn's voice came from behind me, but not far behind.

I did not speak, but followed our guide.

He led us to a second stair, a winding stair that seemed at first to plunge into darkness. We had descended this for many steps when I took notice of a faint, pale light below.

"Where are we going?" Lurn asked.

I was harkening to a nightingale. It was our guide who answered her: "Where you wished to go, O pawn."

"Why are you talking to me like that, Valorius?"

I shrugged, and followed our guide into a garden lit by stars and the waning moon. He led us over smooth lawns and past tin-kling fountains. The statues we saw were of pieces, of kings and queens, of slingers and spearmen, of knights such as I and pawns like Lurn. Winged figures stood among them, figures whiter than they and equally motionless; though these did not move or appear to breathe, it seemed to me they were not statues. They might have moved, I thought, this though they did not live.

"There can be no such place underground!" Lurn exclaimed.

I turned to face her. "We are not there. Surely you can see that. We entered into the stone of the mountain, and emerged here."

"It was broad day!"

"And is now night. Be silent."

That last I said because our guide stood behind her, his finger to his lips. He pointed, but I saw only a thick growth of cypress. I went to it, nonetheless; and when I stood before it I heard a muted creaking and squeaking, as though some portal long closed were opening. I pushed aside the boughs to look. There my eyes saw nothing. My father (who seemed to sit before me, his head cloven by the ax) had entered my mind and let me see him there.

I knelt.

He took his mantle from his shoulders and fastened it about mine. For a moment only I knew the freezing cold of the gold brooch that had held it. I reached for it. My fingers found nothing, yet I knew then (as I know now) where that mantle rests.

"What's in there?" Lurn asked.

"A tomb," I told her. "You did not come here to see a tomb, but to become a queen. See you the moon?"

"My lady? Yes, of course I see her."

"She rises to behold your coronation, and is already near the zenith. There is a circle of white stones, just there." I pointed. "Do you see it?"

It appeared as I spoke.

"No—yes. Yes, I see it now."

"Stand there—and wait. When the moon-shadows are short and every copse and course is bathed in moonlight, you will become a queen."

She went gladly. I stood before her; the distance was half as far, perhaps, as a boy might fling a stone.

I recall that she said this: "Won't you sit, Valorius? You must be tired."

"Are you not?"

"I? When I am to become a queen? No, never!"

That was all. That, and this: "Why do you rub your head?"

"It is where the ax went in. I rub it because the place is healed and my father at rest."

The moon rose higher yet, and one of the white figures came to kneel before me. She held a pillow of white silk; upon it lay a great visored helm white as any pearl, and upon that a silver crown.

I accepted it and rose. Six more were arming Lurn, armor of proof that no sword could cleave: breastplate and gorget, tasset and tace. As earth circles moon, I circled her; and when her arming was complete save for the helm, poised that as high as I might. "From the goddess whom you serve, receive the crown that is your due." Standing, her head was higher than my upstretched arms; but she knelt before me to receive helm and crown, and I set them upon her head. They felt no heavier than their own pale plumes.

Rising, she pulled down the visor to try it; and I saw that there was a white face graven upon the visor now—and that white face was her own.

"I am a queen!" It might have been ten-score trumpets speaking.

I nodded.

"We will restore the kingdom, Valorius!"

I nodded as before. It had been my own thought.

"I shall restore the kingdom, and the Game will be played again. The Game, Valorius, and I a queen!"

I knew then that she whom I had kissed so often must die. Men have said my sword springs to my hand. That is not so, yet few draw more swiftly. She parried my first thrust with her gauntlet and sought to seize the blade; it escaped her—thus I lived.

Of our fight in that moonlit garden I will say little. She could parry my blows, and did. I could not parry hers; she was too strong for it. I dodged and ducked and was knocked sprawling again and again. I hoped for help, and received none. If longing could foal a horse from air, I would have had two score. No horse appeared.

What came at last was Our Lord the Sun, and that was better. I turned her until she faced it and put my point through her eye-slot. The steel that went in was not so long as my hand and less wide than two fingers together, yet it was enough. It sufficed.

Now?

Now I wander the land. Asked to prophesy, I say we shall overthrow the tyrants and make a new nation for ourselves and our children. Should our folk require a sword, I am the sword that springs to their hands. Asked to heal, I cure their sick—when I can. If they bring food, I eat it. If they do not, I fast or find my own. And that is all, save that from time to time I entertain a lost traveler, such as yourself. East lies the past, west the future. Go north to find the gods, south to find the blessed. Above stands the All High, and below lies Pandemonium. Choose your road and keep to it, for if you stray from it, you may encounter such as I. Fare you well! We shall not meet again.

JAMES ENGE has been developing his stories of Morlock Ambrosius for years, but had to wait for the pendulum to swing back in favor of sword and sorcery before he made a splash. Appearing only recently in the pages of *Black Gate, Flashing Swords,* and everyday fiction.com, his tales of a wandering wizard and swordsman built up a loyal following in a very short time, before leaping into novel form with the books *Blood of Ambrose, This Crooked Way,* and *The Wolf Age. Strange Horizon* writes of him: "There's a kind of literately sensuous pleasure in Enge's writing . . . the pleasure of an intelligent, skillful writer amusing himself and us." Little surprise then that Enge is an instructor of classical languages at a Midwestern university. Speaking to *Fantasy Book Critic,* he said, "The modern realistic novel, increasingly in the twentieth century, concerned itself with character above all else: what the character felt and perceived. I'm not knocking this: realistic fiction has some triumphant achievements in this line . . . But I think it's an approach that is susceptible to diminishing returns. Genre fiction, like medieval and classical traditions of storytelling, tends to concentrate much more on what people do and the context in which they do it. I love this concentration on conduct, on action (but not necessarily in the car-chases-and-gunfights sense) and on the world . . . I find it in the older narrative traditions; I find it in genre fiction; and I think it's the reason that twenty-first-century literary fiction is looking to refresh itself at the wells of genre."

THE SINGING SPEAR

James Enge

To drink until you vomit and then drink again is dull work. It requires no talent and won't gain you fame or fortune. It's usually followed by a deep dark stretch of unconsciousness, though, so it had become Morlock Ambrosius' favorite pastime.

In a brief lapse from chronic drunkenness he had invented a device which intensified the potency of wine many times. Because he had no use for gold (he could make it by the cartful if he needed it), he gave the device to Leen, the owner of the Broken Fist tavern. Leen proceeded to make gold by the cartful, through the more mundane method of selling distilled liquor. By his order, Morlock's cup was never to be left empty when he entered the Broken Fist. Morlock entered the Broken Fist on a daily basis thereafter and stayed until the disgusted potboys tossed him, snoring, into the street. In another time and place, Morlock might have been called an alcoholic. In the masterless lands east of the Narrow Sea, he was simply a man drinking himself to death—and not quickly enough for those few who had to deal with him.

One evening, as Morlock was just settling down to work, a man came up to him and asked, "Is it true that you're Morlock the Maker?"

If Morlock had been a little more sober, he would have just denied it. If he'd been a little drunker, he would have embarked on an elaborate series of lies to make the questioner suspect that he himself might be Morlock the Maker. And if Morlock had been very much drunker, he wouldn't have been able to answer at all. But, as it happens, he was at that precise state when he was able to know the truth and not care. Apart from actual oblivion, it was the state of mind he enjoyed the most.

"I'm Morlock," he said, lifting his slightly crooked shoulders in a shrug. "What's your poison? They have to serve you for free if you drink with me, you know. Drink with me, get served for free—that's practically a song, isn't it?"

"I don't want a drink," the questioner said, sitting down at Morlock's table. "I want help."

"I'm not in the help business. I'm in the drinking business."

"That's not a business."

"Not with your lacka— lacka— lackadaisical attitude, no. But I take these things more seriously."

Morlock drank several cups of distilled wine while the other told him a long, involved story and then concluded, "So you see, don't you, that you have to help?"

"I might, if I'd been listening," Morlock admitted. "Thank God Avenger, I wasn't."

"You useless bucket of snot!" the other shouted. "Didn't you hear me tell you that Viklorn has the Singing Spear?"

"I heard you that time. Who's Viklorn—some juggler or carnival dancer?" Morlock could see how a singing spear might be useful in a carnival act. Almost involuntarily, his mind began to envision various ways to make a spear sing on cue.

"Viklorn!" shouted the other man. "The pirate and robber! He's been using the singing spear to kill and rob all along the coast of the Narrow Sea. And now they say he's killed his own crew with it and is coming inland with Andhrakar."

"Wait a moment."

"And you sit there sucking down that swill—"

"You're telling me that this 'singing spear' is the weapon called Andhrakar?"

"Yes. And if you—"

"Just who was stupid enough to take the spear and start using it?"

The other looked at Morlock almost pityingly. "Viklorn. A pirate and robber."

"Moron, you mean. Well, it's no skin off my walrus."

"You mean you won't help?"

"I knew you'd catch up eventually. Drink? No? Mind if I do?"

"You made the damned thing! It's your responsibility to do something about it!"

"I made the weapon called Andhrakar," Morlock admitted. "Arguably, I also damned it. I didn't make Viklorn, though. Perhaps you'll have better luck if you consult *his* creator."

The other stared at Morlock for a while, then got up and walked off without a word. He rode away west that night to fight Viklorn, and was killed by the weapon called Andhrakar. It was also called "the singing spear" because, before it killed someone, it began to emit a faint musical tone, which grew louder and deeper until it sank into a human body and was satisfied with blood and life.

That's how it was with Morlock's questioner. He came upon Viklorn in the night, hoping to surprise him. But Viklorn did not sleep, could not sleep, remembering the things he had seen and done, and watching the visions that Andhrakar put in his head. He heard the man approaching stealthily through the brush and leapt up from his bedroll. Andhrakar, the singing spear, was ready in his hand—in fact, he could not let go of it now. Through Andhrakar's magic, his fingers were oak-hard, growing into the wooden shaft of the spear, bound in an unbreakable grip on the damned weapon he had chosen to wield.

Viklorn fought the man who longed to kill him, silently in the dark, until both men heard the spear begin to sing (faint and high at first, but then stronger, deeper, louder), and both men groaned (the one with fear, the other with anticipation). Soon Andhrakar split the attacker's torso and grew still. Viklorn left the corpse unburied in the dark and lay back down on his bedroll, next to the spreading pool of blood. Thus died the man Morlock would not help, a brave man but not very shrewd. No one remembers his name.

Morlock was shrewd, on occasion, but he didn't think of himself as brave. Some drunks, perhaps, display courage, but Morlock wasn't that type. He drank because he was afraid, of life and of death. It hadn't always been that way. Once Morlock had been a hero, at least in the eyes of some—in any case, he'd been a more useful sort of person than he was now. But that part of him was used up. So he jeered at himself: only a coward would drink and drink because he was afraid of the pain life held.

Viklorn continued to rob and kill throughout the region. You had to call it robbery, for he took stuff and destroyed what he couldn't take. But he was likely to leave what he took by the roadside or in an open field. He stole because part of him was still Viklorn, a robber. But there was not enough of the man left to remember what robbers robbed for, what use they made of the things they took. Increasingly, he simply killed and killed, destroying with fire what he could not kill with Andhrakar.

"Why did you make that damn spear?" the barkeep asked Morlock one night, before he was too drunk to answer sensibly.

"I had my reasons," Morlock answered sensibly.

Later that night, Leen, the owner of the Broken Fist and the man to whom Morlock had entrusted the invention of the still, sat down beside him. Now that Leen was wealthy, he never stood behind the bar himself; he was so short that he had trouble seeing over it. Back in the days when he couldn't afford to hire help, he'd kept a series of boxes behind the bar, and it had been fun to watch him deftly leaping from box to box. And if he ever needed to climb over the bar to take care of an unruly customer, he saw to it that the customer would never be a problem again. Morlock rather liked him, although he understood that to Leen he was just another gullible drunk.

"Morlock," Leen began.

"Leen."

"Morlock, what do you think you can do about Viklorn and Andhrakar?"

"Leen," Morlock answered sensibly (but just barely), "what do *you* think I can do about Viklorn and Andhrakar?"

Leen stood up and walked away. The faces scattered around the barroom, never friendly, turned to Morlock afterward with especial distaste. Morlock, never sensitive, was uncomfortable enough to leave while he was still conscious, an unusual event.

He was back at the usual time the next day, but the Broken Fist was closed. Closed permanently: the door and window-shutters of the inn were nailed shut. He asked a passing towns-woman, who told him that Leen had packed up in the night.

"People say he's moved north to Sarkunden," she said. "I'm going south, myself. People say Viklorn's already been there: why would he go back?"

Morlock brushed aside people and their concerns and stuck

to the essential point. "Leen went to Sarkunden—a *thousand* miles away?" he shouted. "Is he insane? What am I supposed to drink?"

The townswoman made a suggestion. Morlock declined (the fluid she mentioned was not an intoxicant), and went back to his cave.

For a day or so, Morlock suffered the delirium that comes sometimes at the end of a drunken binge. Finally he fell asleep and dreamt a prophetic dream. (Among his other wasted talents, Morlock was a seer.)

In the dream, Morlock saw himself confronting Viklorn and Andhrakar. Viklorn was a tall pirate with eyes as red as a weasel's. He wore dirty, pale, untanned leather with golden fittings, and a gold clip kept his shaggy blond hair out of his face. He said nothing; they fought silently, except for the sound of Andhrakar's deadly unbreakable blade clashing against Morlock's sword. Andhrakar dripped with fresh blood, but it was still hungry for life, and soon it began to sing, faintly at first, but then louder and louder. Viklorn laughed, excited and pleased, and Morlock awoke with a curse in his mouth.

This was bad, he thought, sitting up. Never in a thousand years would he have chosen to fight someone armed with Andhrakar. But, although he might be *not especially brave* (a phrase Morlock preferred, when sober, to the franker *coward*), he wasn't stupid. He would fight Viklorn: so the vision told him. He needed to act swiftly if the meeting was to be on his own terms.

He consulted a crow he knew in the neighborhood, who promised to locate Viklorn for him. He spent that day and the next doing exercises to bring his agility and wind closer to what they once had been. When the crow came and told him that Viklorn was at Dhalion, a day's walk north and west, he thanked it and fed it some grain. Then he threw his backpack on his shoulders, belted on his sword, and started loping with a long, uneven stride northeast on the old Imperial Road. The chances were he would run into Viklorn, if Viklorn was moving eastward from the Narrow Sea.

The road was bad. The old Empire of Ontil had been out of business for centuries, and its roads were returning to nature. Often Morlock walked next to the "pavement" of shattered rocks, dense with tree-roots and overgrowth. But he made pretty good time going on foot. He had a serenely unpleasant feeling he was headed straight for his destined meeting with Viklorn, and it turned out he was right.

It happened this way. Morlock topped a ridge and, looking downward, he saw a wagon overturned beside the road. This was not uncommon. The road was the only route through the masterless lands, but it was terrible for carting goods. Morlock found with surprise, though, that he recognized the man standing beside the cart: it was Leen. He'd had at least three days' head start on Morlock, but his property must have slowed him down. Morlock saw some people running away from the cart, farther up the road. Perhaps they were going for help, although there was little help to find along this road. Then Morlock saw a man approaching Leen. Morlock knew this man also, but not from seeing him in his waking life. It was the hulking blond man in his dream, the man who carried Andhrakar: Viklorn the killer.

"Leen!" shouted Morlock, lifting his leaden feet and running down the hill. "Run away, you fool! Leave your stuff! I'll make you a new still! I'll make you new gold! Run like hell!"

But Leen didn't run. He turned to face Viklorn the killer, with a piece of wood in his hand and no hope in his face. Against Viklorn, he was like a squat mountain peak, impinging on the great golden face of a rising moon. He didn't seem to hear Morlock, and as Morlock ran closer he heard what Leen must have heard before: the sweet musical tone of the singing spear, growing deeper and stronger as the foredestined moment of death approached.

Leen had stayed behind intentionally, Morlock realized—stayed to confront Viklorn, knowing he would die, giving the others a chance to run for their lives. Leen struck out at Viklorn with his makeshift club. The killer easily evaded his blow; Andhrakar slashed twice and Leen fell in three pieces on the ground. Viklorn laughed a high-pitched, weary, hysterical laugh. So Leen died—a shrewd man and brave, though that didn't save him.

"You son of a bitch!" Morlock shouted, tears stinging his eyes. "You've killed my bartender!"

Viklorn turned to face him. His eyes were red as a weasel's—as red as the fresh blood dripping from the spear. He pointed at Morlock with the dark blade—crystalline, unbreakable, fashioned by the greatest magical craftsman the world had ever known—and smiled.

Morlock shrugged his backpack off onto the broken road behind him and drew his sword. Viklorn's smile dimmed as he saw the blade, kin to the spearhead on his own weapon: dark, crystalline, unbreakable. Morlock demonstrated the latter fact by passing the sword through a broken pillar beside the road. It fell obligingly to pieces, raising a great cloud of dust. Morlock leapt through the cloud, lunging at Viklorn.

If the fight had been between Morlock and Viklorn, Morlock would have won easily. True, Morlock was a drunk rather badly in need of a drink, not at all the man he had been. But Viklorn was not well either: his face was the face of a dying man; God Sustainer knew when he had last slept, or if he ever ate or drank.

But the fight was really between Andhrakar and Morlock. Viklorn looked on in bemusement as his dark blade feinted and lunged at the man who had made it. Andhrakar didn't need sleep, or food, or water, or air. All it needed was human life; all it hungered for was the savor of dying men and women. Though it still dripped with fresh blood, it was clearly thirsty for more; it began to sing, faintly at first, but then louder and louder. Viklorn laughed, excited and pleased, and Morlock cursed. The singing tone rose and fell and rose again, like a bell, like the baying of a dog. Andhrakar would kill again, and soon.

The spear lashed out. Morlock ducked away from the spearhead and grabbed the shaft just above Viklorn's lifeless hand. Morlock brought down his dark blade and slashed off Viklorn's spear-hand at the wrist. The severed hand still clutched the shaft of the spear in an unbreakable grip. The spear still sang, louder than ever now, drowning all other noises. Morlock spun the business end of the spear about. As Viklorn stood there, blinking at the gushing stump of his arm, Morlock buried the dark shining spearhead in his neck. Viklorn fell backward to the ground and the singing spear fell silent, slaked by his death.

Morlock! The voice of the demon Andhrakar sounded in his head. *Will you free me now from this prison you made for me?*

Morlock laughed harshly as he cleaned and sheathed his dark blade. "Hope springs eternal in the demonic breast. Learn despair, Andhrakar: I won't free you to hunt human souls. I can't understand how you caught this one. I bound you in the spearhead, then buried you in a crypt full of traps, and then posted a warning outside the crypt. How did you get free?"

Warning—or advertising? the demon whispered in his mind. *Generations of heroes died seeking the lost treasure left by Morlock the Maker. Finally one succeeded. His people would be making songs about him now—if I hadn't persuaded him to kill them all.*

Morlock scowled and turned away to bury Leen. He laid him in the ground and put the still and a few gold pieces beside the butchered corpse, then covered him up. He broke some boards from the wagon and made a grave-sign for the dead innkeeper. He supposed the people that Leen had died to save would come back eventually, so he wrote the grave-message to them, in the great, sprawling runes of Ontil: LEEN DIED HERE. WHERE WERE YOU?

He returned to the dead body of Viklorn. He kicked it furiously several times, then grabbed the shaft of Andhrakar and drew it from the wound. Morlock let the dead pirate's hand stay where it was, gripping the shaft, as he carried the spear away. He looked back once from the ridge: a few carrion birds were already circling the pirate's unburied body.

Will you at least keep me and use me? the demon whispered. *I am a powerful weapon. If you feed me human lives, I can give you vengeance on your enemies.*

Morlock said nothing, but carried Andhrakar back to the village where the Broken Fist stood. He found the town abandoned: everyone had fled to escape Viklorn and Andhrakar. Morlock broke into the blacksmith's shop, kindled a fire in the forge, and assembled a set of tools at the anvil.

You cannot destroy my prison in a primitive smithy like this, the demon said, sounding somewhat uneasy.

"You don't know what I can do," Morlock disagreed. "Nor have you guessed what I'm going to do."

He fashioned a spearhead, exactly like Andhrakar in form. He even managed to give its surface a glassy basaltic glaze, something like the dark crystalline surface of Andhrakar. He tempered it, hammered it, let it cool, and polished it. He unfixed Andhrakar from its shaft and put the new spearhead on the shaft, with Viklorn's severed hand still attached. Then he took the greatest hammer in the smithy and he struck the new spearhead until it lay in fragments.

Morlock took a chisel and carved on the side of the anvil:

HERE I, WHO MADE ANDHRAKAR, DESTROYED IT,
BECAUSE IT KILLED MY FRIEND LEEN. FORGIVE ME
AND REMEMBER ME: MORLOCK AMBROSIUS.

Liar! the demon screamed inside his mind.

Morlock shrugged. "The world thinks I made you, which is
a lie. I only imprisoned you. If I could have imprisoned you in
a spittoon, or a wooden doorstop, or something not obviously
deadly I would have done so. The magical laws which govern
imprisoning demons limited me. But I can negate one lie with
another. These fragments of the accursed spear Andhrakar will
become cherished heirlooms, perhaps to be reforged as a new
weapon someday—"

They'll know! They'll know it's not me!

"—not as effective as the old weapon, of course, but they don't
make anything like they used to. And no one will go looking for
Andhrakar, since everyone knows where it is. There will be no
advertising for your new resting place. You will wither and die in
the dark and you will eat no more human souls."

I am immortal.

"You say so, but I never believed it. You eat things; I think
you'll starve to death if you never eat again. Anyway, we'll try the
experiment. I'll stop by in a few hundred years to see how you're
doing."

He threw the accursed spear-blade imprisoning the demon
Andhrakar into the pit under an outhouse. Then he shoveled a
hundredweight of soil atop it.

At last, he wanted a drink rather badly. He broke into the Broken Fist and availed himself of Leen's left-behind stock. At least,
he poured himself a cup of wine and stood at the bar, preparing
to drink it. He stood there for a moment, watching his distorted
reflection in the smooth, dark surface of the wine.

• • •

When people returned to the town, they found the inscription on the anvil, and the fragments of the spearhead, and they reacted much as Morlock had anticipated. They also found the broken door of the Broken Fist, and they saw the wine cup, full to the brim, standing untouched on the bar. But they did not see Morlock, then or ever again.

C. J. CHERRYH began writing stories at the age of ten, when she became frustrated with the cancellation of her favorite TV show, *Flash Gordon.* She has a Master of Arts degree in classics from Johns Hopkins University, where she was a Woodrow Wilson fellow, and taught Latin, Ancient Greek, the classics, and ancient history in Oklahoma. Cherryh wrote novels in her spare time when not teaching, and in 1975 sold her first novels *Gate of Ivrel* and *Brothers of Earth* to Donald A. Wollheim at DAW Books. The books won her immediate recognition and the John W. Campbell Award for Best New Writer in 1977. In 1979, her short story "Cassandra" won the Best Short Story Hugo, and she quit teaching to write full-time. She has since won the Hugo Award for Best Novel twice, first for *Downbelow Station* in 1982 and then again for *Cyteen* in 1989. In addition to developing her own fictional universes, Cherryh has contributed to several shared world anthologies, including *Thieves' World, Heroes in Hell,* and the Merovingen Nights series, which she edited. Her most recent novels are major new Alliance novel, *Regenesis,* and new Foreigner novel, *Conspirator.* She lives near Spokane, Washington, and enjoys skating and traveling. She regularly makes appearances at science fiction conventions.

A WIZARD IN WISCEZAN

C. J. Cherryh

It was an old city up an old river, Wiscezan-on-Eld.

The sea had used to be closer.

The trade had used to be more profitable.

The city had sold its timber off the heights, and the streams had poured silt down to the wharves where the big boats loaded. The silt had made little shallows, and then little channels, and then a bog around the edges. That let in the smallest enemies: buzzing swarms in summer that brought fever and unhealth.

The timber was gone. The soft hills grew lower by the year, the silt grew deeper, the bog thicker and now overgrown with substantial trees, and the little trading outpost southward on the coast, on the little Yliz River, Korianth, built wharves to take the trade. They dealt in dried fish, in carpets and dyed goods, in hammered bronze and leather, amulets, wines, and grain and beer from the sunny east.

Korianth prospered. It got itself a king, and ruled up and down the coast. It traded that king for a better one and lately thrived.

Wiscezan still, stubborn in its ways, traded a few cypress logs down its river and down the coast. It traded pottery, and furs, and building stone from the hard heart of the hills, but it was no longer what it had been.

Its last duchess of the old blood died. The last nobles lived in fair luxury, still. But Korianth under King Osric was too occupied with its own difficulties, its troublesome gods and ambitious allies, to trouble itself when Jindus ait Auzem moved in, bringing his mercenaries with him.

Jindus married a third cousin of the last duchess, a vain and silly, though noble, girl, who within three months died of a dish of mushrooms—leaving Jindus widowed and ennobled, so far as inheritance went.

Wiscezan therefore had a new duke, one with ambitions far exceeding Wiscezan's humbled circumstances. He collected taxes. He hired mercenaries, he hired a wizard of dark reputation, and he married several more wives, soon deceased, their noble names linking Jindus deeper and deeper into the ancient lineages of the Eld.

Were the nobles of Wiscezan alarmed? That they were. Even the related houses off in Korianth were alarmed at the state of affairs and appealed to King Osric to do something. But in a very little time Duke Jindus had become a potent threat beyond this fever-ridden city. Nobles in several cities prayed the right mosquito would find the duke . . . and a few tried, with small spells, to assure that happened.

But the spells went amiss. Grievously amiss. Not many knew it.

But old Cazimir did.

And took himself and his few students deeper into the alleyways and shadows of Wiscezan.

He was not what he had been, was Cazimir Eisal.

He had been a great teacher when the duchess was alive. He had had his academy and students who came even from Korianth and distant ports to study under his guidance. He had had a library and a fine house and apprentices to do the grinding of herbs and the jotting-down of his great thoughts, so that Cazimir the Wise had very little to do but teach the most advanced of his students, who taught the rest.

But on the waft of a night wind and a stray curtain and the aged duchess's bare shoulder, fever had arrived . . . and not all Cazimir's wizardry had cured it.

He had suspected then, had Cazimir, that there was another Agency at work.

He had seen that Agency when Jindus hired it . . . seen that Agency for a lean and hungry man standing always near the warlord, and he had said to himself it was not Jindus they had to fear.

But the duchess had already died, and the power had come into the heart of the new authority in Wiscezan, and Cazimir had had a grave, cold feeling that nothing now would go well for the city, or for him. The times had turned, and new omens were in the ascendant.

Accordingly, Cazimir left his house and took up residence in the lower town. His well-born disciples and apprentices, having a place to go, went to their well-born relatives, or set up shop in other places, scattered about the coast.

He still taught. He protected the Talented, the few he could find.

But age was on him, and his fortunes declined.

Oh, Miphrynes—that being the name of the Agency behind the duke—was sure Cazimir was still out there, but Miphrynes knew the nature of white wizards, that taking them on could provoke unexpected backlashes of magic, and so long as Cazimir stuck to the lower town, and until Miphrynes could get a wedge inside his defenses—well, Miphrynes found it convenient to sit in the ducal palace, enjoying the luxury in the confidence that a black wizard's citadel was no easier to crack.

And his was a great deal more comfortable.

Take students? Not Miphrynes. He held power. He didn't share it.

He got power. He obtained it from the depths of hell.

And hell was what was seeping out of Jindus's palace these days, quiet as yet, and very subtle, but it knew what it wanted. It had failed in Korianth. Now it had a new foothold.

Master had not been well the last week. Master had not made a charm in a month . . . which left the students to do the spellcraft, and to sell it in the form of bits of paper, easy to carry, that did useful things.

Healing was beyond them. But papers that could light a fire, or chill water, those they had.

And Willem Asusse was in a position. He was the senior of the three of them, but almost as useless as ten-year-old Jezzy, who could only bespell cats, and then only when the cat was in a receptive mood. It was Almore who could light fires and Almore who could freeze water or boil it. So it was Almore's charms, except one bit of paper, which offered to attract a mouser at least to some loyalty, if fed.

And it was Willem's job to sell them around and about the Alley, which was *his* Talent.

Well, more, his talent was illusion, like Master's, and he did one very important job, helping Master keep the Alley secret and shut off from the rest of Wiscezan.

But he couldn't so much as light a candle, not like Almore, so it was Almore who kept them fed in Master's little lapses, and it was Willem's art of illusion and flummery that convinced house-holders they were not scared to buy from him.

It had gotten him, thus far today, a loaf of stale bread, which he had broken in half and tucked under his jerkin. It was no small trophy, good, dark bread that had a lot of substance, even if it was burned half-black and full of hollow bubbles—young goodwife Melenne was not the best cook, but she was scatter-witted and a good customer for the fire-starting spells.

And the tavern was a safe bet. The freezing-charm improved its beer to drinkability.

It was an old contact. A safe one. They took a risk taking on any new customer these days: they daren't advertise. But the tavern relied on them, and the tavern had a back side well planted in Wink Alley.

It was a mazy sort of confusing place to begin with, the Alley: if you didn't know to take the slit of a passage at Blind Gaijer the Smith's house, and then to take the next branch to the left, you were going to wander a bit, and you could end up right over in the netherside of Beggars' Row, where the beggars didn't like you to be.

So even without a little illusion, the Alley was a maze, and dangerous. It had a few inhabitants, merchants semi-associated with the wizard, who were its outward face, a potter, and a couple of enterprising pickpockets that never worked inside the Alley. And with the illusions—you didn't see the other doors. You just thought the Merry Ox was the way out, and it was, and that was that. You never saw the other back doors, just that one . . . no matter where you wandered in Wink Alley.

But illusions were beginning to weaken—Master's, and his; and though he'd used to go outside the Alley now and again to peddle his wares, he stuck close these days.

Possibly Master's intent was weakening. Possibly Master could grow more forgetful, and a stray apprentice could end up on the streetside—forever, or at least until Master missed him. Master's hovel, unlike the commercial establishments, had no streetside door.

At any event, Willem was anxious to be home, and there was no trouble, despite the other confusion in the Alley, in his finding the Merry Ox. Getting the best deal from the innkeep—it was well not to sell him too many spells at a time, lest he get the notion they were easy-made. And it was a good hour for bargaining, the lull in the afternoon, between noon and the siesta hour.

So, turning around three times, and blinking twice, which was guaranteed to find the Merry Ox, Willem skipped up the back steps, went down the unlighted little hall to the dim bar where Wiggy Brewer ran his business. The place smelled of pork pie, of spilled beer, mildew—and Wiggy, whose contribution was sweat and garlic. There was no spell to mask Wiggy, who sold baths but never took one.

It wasn't Willem's favorite stop. Goodwife Melenne was that. But he could deal with Wiggy's daughter, who generally knew what the price ought to be, and was going to be, so it was usually short, sensible dealing and straightforward, Wiggy's daughter having no designs on him at all—there *was* a use for illusion in his trade.

But Wiggy's daughter—her name was Hersey—came flying toward him. "Willem!" said she. "Willem!" grabbing the front of his jerkin, leaning across the bar with a huge expanse of bosom flowing into his view. "There's trouble here. There's the duke's men on the prowl. Go! We c'n talk in th' alley!"

Willem needed no second hint. He broke free and headed right back down the dark back hallway, with Wiggy's ample daughter right behind him.

The Alley was safe, untenanted except by old jars and trash bins. Willem caught his breath there in the uncertain pale light, on the gritty back step of the Merry Ox, and, drawing a breath, swung around to ask Wiggy's daughter what she had seen—

—When a large man in leather armor and a steel helmet came out of that dark hall, knocking Hersey right off the step and into Willem's arms. Willem staggered backward, steadied the girl on her step, and, still holding on to her, heard a thunderous charge toward the door, from out of that dim hall.

Black-caps. The duke's men, with swords drawn, and meaning business . . . but not aimed at them. Willem cast a fast one: *I'm not here, she's not here.* And then because he didn't want trouble in the Alley, he threw another one after it: *Nobody's here.*

The guards stopped. Looked around them. Looked at the steps, and the doorway where Willem stood with Hersey, balanced on the edge of the steps. The spell was shredding. Willem held it up, and carefully stepped down to the cobbles of the Alley, keeping the illusion around him, moving slowly—you could break an illusion if you moved too fast, or let fear get into it.

He kept moving. He saw the guards look confused, and then charge back up the steps past Hersey, who delayed a moment, looking just as confused.

Then came the sounds of Wiggy's bull voice from inside, and furniture being shoved about, and Hersey whirled around and ran back inside in a hurry.

"Here, you!" Wiggy was shouting, and "Where is he?" a foreign voice yelled . . .

. . . reminding Willem he wasn't alone in the Alley. He *hadn't* seen the fugitive, who had dived for cover somewhere.

I'm not here, he sent out, and turned around and found himself facing a leather-armored chest and a drawn sword and the fugitive looking straight at him.

I'm really *not here,* he sent, heart pounding. But a hand snaked out and grabbed the front of his shirt.

"Magician," the fugitive said.

"Not me!" Willem protested, and backed up, pulling his shirt and himself and the loaf of day-old bread free of that grip. He sent very, very hard: *I was never here!*

The man looked confused for a moment, and that was enough. Willem ran for it, clutching the loaf of bread and feeling in his belt-pouch for one of the paper freeze-spells, in case.

The man was following him. But the Alley had twists, and out of sight was enough. Willem stopped with his back against grimy stone, and his feet amid blown debris, next to the potter's steps.

Lost him. By now the only doorway the man would see was the one that had let him into the alley, and that was Wiggy's place, where the guards were. So the man would stay there a while, and then go back up into the Merry Ox, and presumably get out and away for good.

It was a narrow escape. Really narrow. And going back to the Merry Ox right now to finish up business for the day was not a good idea. Hersey was going to be upset, Wiggy was, and they wouldn't be in a bargaining mood, especially if the duke's men had broken up the furniture.

And especially if the stranger came traipsing back through the bar wanting to be served.

No, it was a good time to be home, and home was two more bends down the Alley.

It was a relief, the solid sound of the door and the bar dropped— thunk!—into its slot. Willem drew his first whole breath.

But looking around at the occupants of the little house, all sitting by the fire, with its scant pot of yesterday's beans—

Willem raked a hand through his hair. He was sweating. He

had run the last block, to make sure there was no way the man could have overtaken him to spot another hole in his defense. And the faces arrayed around that waiting fireside mirrored his, in his disarray.

"Nobody followed me," he said, first off, with a wave of his hand. "I didn't lose the spells." That was second. "Trouble got into the Alley and I'm sure it's out again, by now." Unless the duke's men had stayed to swill down Wiggy's warm beer and stranded the armored fellow out in the Alley for an hour or two. Neither side was going to be happy in that transaction.

"I brought bread," he said, and admitted the truth. "I didn't get down to trading with Hersey." The usual pay was the butt end and bones of whatever roast or fowl Wiggy had been parsing out to his customers. And it made a big difference in supper. "And Melenne, well, this isn't one of her best, but it's solid." A lot of flour was in that loaf. He took the two pieces of it out of his shirt, which it had blacked with its charred end, and it weighed like two bricks. "We might want to just add that to the beans."

Two glum faces—Almore and Jezzy—greeted that suggestion; and one kind forgiveness—that was Master Cazimir, who tolerated everything.

"We can toast it, at least," Jezzy said.

"Looks as if it's *been* toasted," Almore said glumly. "Twice."

"Now, now," Master said. "With the beans and all, it should be substantial, and maybe we can conjure up a taste of butter."

Conjure was it, for sure: a taste, but no substance. Master could still do the butter trick, and occasionally toasted cheese. But Master wasn't himself lately. He looked weary, and he forgot things, and occasionally his spells went astray . . . it was no sure thing that the taste Master conjured would be butter, but no one mentioned the last time.

Nobody said *anything* about the last time.

"I didn't lose the papers," Willem said. "I'll go out early, before daylight. I'll go back to the tavern. They'll buy. And I'll bring back breakfast, with maybe a bit of coin."

"Coin!"

"Well, maybe a pot I can turn for coin. Ratty's going to fire the kilns this week. That's a long firing, for sure. That's worth a pot." He took the big knife from the cutting board—cook had run off with Master's silver, but left the cutlery—and Master, being the kind heart he was, hadn't cursed it, just contented himself with the knives, which were useful.

A little silver would have been useful, long since. But things were as they were. They survived, in their little pocket of an Alley. Things had nearly gone wrong today, but they'd toast the bread, Master would conjure butter, and they'd have beans to fill out the corners, with water to drink. There was always that.

And after dinner there were lessons. The day was long and they worked at whatever there was to do, carrying wood and water, selling spells where it was safe—a narrow, risky market, that, since spells could give them away: the duke's wizard, for one, was always sniffing about—

But in the late evening, after dinner, Master would get into his Book, and read to the three of them, and tell them about philosophy and spells and charms. Master lately never remembered where he had stopped—reading the Book was less about reading words than about the symbols in it, and Master explaining how they fit together—but they could scratch a meaning out of it, and Almore in particular kept asking about the fire mark and how to make it longer and longer and steady, and the last three evenings Master had been mostly on topic, which had Almore in a froth of earnestness on fire signs.

"If I can get a fire to hold on," Almore had said to Willem, "and keep being just as hot, and quit exactly when you want—"

"Ratty's kiln," Willem had said, figuring that. Every potter, every cook, every smith in town would want *that* one . . .

Which argued that nobody had ever been able to make a charm like that, or it would already be in the Book, wouldn't it?

But Almore had his dreams, and he was going to get Fire and Time to behave themselves, and they were all going to be rich. If they were rich, they could smuggle Master out of this city and get over to Korianth, where there *wasn't* a duke and a wizard trying to find Master and kill him.

Well, it was worth wishing for. But illusions didn't do any good at making things happen; and of Master's three students, the only one who could call himself a journeyman magician was him.

Which meant the best of Master's students could just barely make the duke's men think they were in a narrow alley with no other doors.

It was important when you had to do it, but it didn't put bread on the table. Only the two apprentices could do that.

The secrets of the Fire and the Time sigils didn't appear this night. Master nodded off in the middle of the explication of first binding marks, and didn't even finish his bread, which was the best end of the loaf, to boot.

Master's three students sat there eyeing the half-eaten piece of bread, and thinking unworthy thoughts that maybe Master wouldn't miss it, except Jezzy, who was goodhearted, got up and wrapped the heel of bread in a cloth and put it away in the cupboard for Master's breakfast.

And it stayed there. Willem was sure of that. He would have known if Almore had gotten up in the night. Nobody did, but he got up before daylight, put his clothes to rights, put on his boots, checked the little pouch of papers that was his stock in trade, and nudged up the bar on the door, so that it would fall down and lock the door behind him. He held it, slipped past the door edge, and was just halfway out the door and into the Alley . . .

A shadow rose up right next to him, and a hard hand seized his arm.

"Got you!" a man's voice said.

He struggled. He struggled at first to get back inside and then fought to get outside and let the door shut, but first he couldn't break the grip and then his struggling made him let go the bar, so when the door swung to, the bar stopped it from closing.

A second iron grip seized the front of his jerkin and shoved him against the wall beside the door as, inside, Jezzy called out:

"What's going on?"

"Shut the door!" Willem yelled. He never shouted in the Alley. But the man who had hold of him shoved him toward the door and must have hooked the door edge with his foot, because he shoved him right in, where it was dark, and where there was only an old man and two boys holding the place.

"Magician," the stranger said, letting go Willem's arm, but keeping a grip on Willem's throat. "I'm looking for Cazimir Eisal."

"I'm the one," Master said, out of the dark. "Light a lamp, boy. And let go of my student."

"Thought so," the stranger said, and didn't let go. Willem took hold of a hand like iron—used both his hands, trying to disengage that grip, and had no luck.

Almore had a straw and a lamp down by the banked fire in the hearth. That took, and a faint, single wick gave them more light than they'd had. Two wicks, and three—it was a three-sided lamp, and Willem saw the face that stared straight at Master—*he* seemed forgotten, merely a thing the stranger was determined to hold on to.

But the stranger didn't have a weapon drawn. He had several—a dagger in his belt, with knuckle-loops, for infighting; and a longsword, and well-worn armor, and the glimmer of chain at the sleeves. The man smelled of sweat and woodsmoke and all outdoors—not a city smell.

"Master Cazimir," the man said quietly, respectfully, while still close to strangling Willem. "It is you."

"Certainly it is," Master said. "It has been. It will be."

"Tewkmannon. Fyllia's son."

"Fyllia," Cazimir said. That was the old duchess's name. And he was much too young, a fool could see that, even while he was strangling. "Fyllia's dead."

"The *other* Fyllia," the man said, this Tewkmannon. "Duchess Fyllia's niece. She's dead, too. I'm here for Jindus. Grey Raisses said you were the one to talk to."

"Raisses. Raisses." Master looked overwhelmed, and gripped the table edge and sank onto the bench. He was in his nightdress, his gray beard was straggling, his hair was on end, and he didn't have the belt that kept the robes in order.

"Please," Willem said, prying at the hand that held him, and this Tewkmannon looked at him as if he'd just remembered he had something he didn't need, and then let him go.

Willem straightened his shirt and went and got Master his staff: it was Master's one weapon, and Willem put it next to his hand and stood there. He had a knife in his boot. That was all. And the two boys had the ladle and the cooking pot, such weapons as they were. But they were nothing against this man, if Master and he came at odds.

"I'm here for Jindus," Tewkmannon said. "The bastard."

He didn't like Jindus. That was good. But *here for Jindus*? That didn't sound good at all.

"All we have is water," Master said in a thin, faint voice. "Not a crust of bread, else."

"There's a heel left," Jezzy said, not too brightly.

"I don't think he'd want it," Willem muttered. "Master's an old man, sir. M'lord." They'd been talking about the old duchess, and kinship, and maybe that was due. "He's sick."

"Done for," Master said.

Tewkmannon asked: "Is it Miphrynes?"

"We don't mention that name here," Willem said in a voice he'd hoped would come out strong and forbidding.

"Miphrynes," Tewkmannon said again. "That black crow."

"Vulture's more apt," Master said under his breath. "I can't hold him. He won't come in here. Knows I'm here. I'm sure he knows I'm here. I'm not worth it to him. He knows I can't do anything. And I *can't*. He's got all the upper town."

They'd never heard Master talk this way. They didn't talk about the duke's wizard. They didn't talk about the things he did in the high town. But they knew as an article of faith that Master didn't let him come into the lower town. Miphrynes was *afraid* of Master. Left him alone.

While Master got older, and sicker, by the year.

"It's too late. You're too late . . . *What's* your name?"

"Tewk." Tewkmannon sank down on the bench at the opposite corner of the table, one hand resting on the scarred tabletop. "Tewk will do. Fyllia's son." Now Tewkmannon sounded as if he'd run out of breath in a long, long climb. "It's that bad, is it?"

"My rival," Master said, "probably guesses this place exists— in some form. But my students are gone, all but these three. This is all there are."

For the first time Tewkmannon looked directly at Willem, and then at Almore and Jezzy, and Willem stood there in the realization he was a disappointment to Master and to everybody else in some way he'd never even guessed existed.

It hurt. He didn't know who Tewkmannon was to make him

feel like that. But he wished he could do things he didn't even guess the name of. And knew he couldn't.

"The kid can throw an illusion," Tewkmannon said. "He's pretty good."

"He is," Master said. "Almore's a pyromant and Jezzy's a beast-talker—if they live to grow up. If you can wait that long. Who sent you?"

A moment of silence followed. Then Tewk said: "Korianth." With a directional nod, as if he was talking about the potter's down the block. "King Osric's got the force now. Got an army ready to move."

"Folly, at this point," Master said. "Jindus isn't your problem. His hire-ons—they suck up the gold his tax collector bleeds out of the town—and when the town stops bleeding, Jindus as he is will be done. He's not the problem."

"This wizard of his."

"He's the problem. Jindus is just a convenience, while our enemy gathers the real power." Master coughed, and went on coughing for a moment. Jezzy moved fast and got him a cup of water. Master drank it.

"What real power?" Tewk asked.

"Demon," Master said, on his first good breath, and that word spread a chill through the air. Tewk sat back. And Master just shook his head wearily. "Soon enough, it won't be just gold this town bleeds. It's here. It's already *here*."

Tewk drew back and sat up. "We've got a problem."

"Oh, a big problem," Master said, and tapped the scarred table with a long, gnarled finger, making little sounds that was Master trying not to cough. "You're here to kill Jindus. Good luck. But it won't solve your problem. These youngsters . . . they can't. I don't know if I can. But here's what I know. It's not manifested. It's *here*, up in the fortress, but it's not here, down in the town, you understand me. I don't think it can hear us. I'm betting heavily it can't. He's containing it, mostly, but it sends fingers out, sometimes a lot more of itself. I think—I'm not sure—" Another fit of coughing and a sip of water. "I'm betting Miphrynes is aiming it right for Jindus when it manifests. Big man. Strong. Attractive. Virile, frankly, capable of siring descendants, and that particular demon is a prolific bastard."

"If we get him—"

"There's a thing about demons. Hurt them and they don't think. They don't think. They'll go for any port in a storm and it'll be dangerous as hell."

Tewk leaned onto the table. "I'll tell you. Korianth is poised to come in here. King Osric has his army in the field . . . waiting. A fire in the tower. That's the signal. I'm to take out Jindus. Light the fire. It's a simple job. And you have an army at your gates."

"Demon fodder, if you don't get Miphrynes *with* Jindus."

Tewk's head dropped a moment.

Then he looked up, and looked around, and looked straight at Willem. "How's your nerve, kid?"

"Master!" Willem said, but Master was looking at him the same way.

"The students," Master said, "are all I've got. All the town's got, between them and *that*. Willem's baffled the thing. He doesn't know it. But he has."

"*Me?*"

The word just fell out. Willem had time to draw a breath, and then Tewk's hand shot out and grabbed him by the wrist.

"Master!"

"I'll be borrowing him," Tewk said. "I've got an army on the march and a cousin I already thought was a damned fool, but maybe he knows something. If what you describe gets Jindus— Korianth isn't safe, either."

"It won't be," Master said, not even mentioning what Tewk said about borrowing, or cousins. Willem tried to pry one of Tewk's fingers loose—which he couldn't do.

"Sorry," Tewk said, and let go, then reached up and clapped Willem on the shoulder. "You're smart and you're fast. I tracked your footprints. Didn't think to cloud them up, did you?"

"No," Willem admitted faintly. He hadn't had time. He'd been scared. He'd gotten in that door and he hadn't even thought somebody who could tell he was doing magic could also find his way through the Alley and wouldn't fall into the trick of wanting a door. Tewk hadn't *wanted* a door, so he didn't see one, or didn't pay attention to it when he did. What Tewk had wanted was a magic-worker, and that was what he'd tracked—here. Right to Master and all of them.

And now Master as good as agreed with this man.

His stomach had turned queasy. And it was a very empty stomach.

And this was a rich man. By the standards of the Alley, this was a rich man, and talked about armies and the king.

"We'd like breakfast," Willem said. "We'd like a good breakfast. And you can tell me what kind of spell you want, and I'll write it. I'll make it a good one."

Tewk shook his head. "Breakfast, yes. But writing won't do it. *You* have to fix whatever comes up."

"I can't."

"You've been doing it, the wizard says."

"Not— I didn't, really. *You* saw through it. You tracked me."

"A little Talent. A very little Talent. It's useful, sometimes. But it gets me into messes like this. You'll get your breakfast." He fished his purse loose and turned it out on the table. Gold shone among the coins. Heavy gold. One piece could buy every shop on the Alley. There was silver, winking pale and bright. There were all sorts of coppers, clipped and not.

Tewk used his fingers to rake out most of the coppers, and shoved them across the table to Master. And pushed over several silvers and one of the bright new golds. "For the boy's services," he said. "And your silence. You can take the kids and get out of Wiscezan. Get over to the coast, set up in style . . . supposing the boy and I can slow Jindus down." He looked straight at Willem then. "We take Jindus. That's all you have to do. One, get me near him. Two, get me cover to light the signal fire. Then keep us hidden while my lazy cousin twice removed gets his army over here and gets the gates open. I'd recommend you keep the kids here, Master Wizard. You know magic, but I know armies. It's not going to be good out there for a few days."

"Understood," Master said, and picked up the coins. He handed one to Jezzy. "Go down to the Ox and get us breakfast. This gentleman's business can wait that long. Hot bread. Fresh bread. Butter. Fish. For this man, too. Go."

Breakfast. Things rare in their lives. Jezzy scampered for the door with the coin and Willem just sank down on his heels where he stood, because he wasn't there. He didn't want to be there. He told the world so.

"Pretty damn good," Tewk said, and nudged him with his boot. "I know you're there. Can you get us both through the palace gate?"

"Maybe," he said. "Maybe I can."

"Willem," Master said, and Willem got up, not feeling well at all. "Fetch me a scrap of paper, and a pen," Master said, and Willem did that, one of the little pieces they used for spells.

"Bigger than that," Master said, so Willem brought that, and Master uncapped the inkwell, dipped the quill, and wrote symbols on the scrap of paper. "That's an unlock," Master said.

"Thank you, sir," Willem said. He could see how that was going to be useful.

Master used the larger piece of paper and wrote something long and elaborate, in the twisty way Willem had never yet been able to master. When Master finished, he held up the paper, not quite giving it to him.

"This," Master said, "is a master's paper. It ends your journey-man's restrictions. You *will* be able to do a master's spells if you take this. But if you take it, it will mark you as mine, and you will shine like a bonfire, once you leave the Alley, if you don't take the Alley with you."

"Maybe I should just be quiet, Master."

"And what when you do get there? What will you do?"

"I'd hope you'd tell me, Master."

A shake of Master's head. "I can't imagine what you'll do. But you'll smell like me. And you won't *be* me. Do you understand?"

He was a journeyman of Illusion. He understood instantly how that helped. "And the— the *problem* we don't talk about . . . can it tell?"

"Oh, maybe. Maybe it'll know who's really been holding the Alley together. It'll know who could have brought it across town. But it's not altogether *here,* with all that means. It has its limita-tions."

An illusionist understood that, too.

"Don't kill," Master said. "Look at me. Don't *intend* to kill. Especially not by magic. That takes you down a path you don't ever want to set foot on. Do you understand me?"

He did. He nodded toward Tewk. "That's his job."

"Good lad. Just do what you know how to do. Take this. I ad-vise you take it. You've earned it. Gods willing, you *will* earn it."

He reached and took it from Master's hand, and a tingle went through his hand and up his arm and to his heart. He couldn't breathe for a moment. He wasn't scared. He wasn't anything. He *really* wasn't anything. He looked at his *own hand* and couldn't see it.

I want me back! he thought, and there he was.

"That was *good*," Tewk said.

"He needs to think," Master said. "Go sit down in the corner, Willem, and think a while."

Just like with important lessons. Go think. He did. And he tried not to think about demons. That was how they got in, if you started thinking about them. He thought about the whole Alley not being there, but that wasn't too bright: if Wiggy or Hersey stepped out back and missed the steps they'd be mad. Really mad.

He marshaled his thoughts in a parade through what he had to do. Master had taught him how to do that. And everything was there. If nobody startled him, he felt stronger than he ever had.

Fool, maybe.

But a wizard couldn't doubt. Every illusion came apart when you started doubting. He sat there concentrating on believing he could do most anything, but not being specific about what he could do, until Jezzy tapped at the door and brought in the biggest breakfast anybody had ever seen: Jezzy was sweating from just carrying it.

They ate. They had a good breakfast, and water—there was beer, too, but Master said they should save that until later, and Tewk said that was a good idea. Maybe he'd had Wiggy's beer.

Master clapped Willem on the shoulder as he stood in the doorway, and Willem took one scared look back, afraid it was going to break his concentration. He looked at Almore and Jezzy, and the little room with all its shelves and books and papers, and their little table and benches and their pallets, and the faded red curtain—Master had a bed beyond that, in a little nook.

It was home.

Last, he looked Master in the eyes. They were gray and watery but they were still sharp enough to see all the way inside him, he was very sure of that.

"Yes, sir," he said, and went out into the Alley. His Alley. With Tewk striding along with him.

"You lead," Tewk said, which didn't make him feel that much better.

"Mmm," he said, trying not to talk. He was thinking hard, exactly how the Alley was, how there was just one door, to the Ox, and that was just a little blind pocket of an Alley, nothing interesting at all. He wasn't interesting. He was just a kid in un-dyed linsey-woolsey, which mostly ended up gray or nondescript brown, a kid with brown hair, a nondescript face, maybe acne—nobody would look twice; and Tewk was just a workman with a hat, just a skullcap, and needed a shave, and carried a sack lunch and a hammer, which wasn't against the law. They immediately found the Ox in front of them, and went in by the back door.

"Say, here!" Hersey said. "You think you can just walk through wi' them dusty boots? We're not the public walk, here! I just swept that floor!"

Hersey didn't recognize them. Not at all.

"Sorry," Willem said in a different voice, and he and Tewk walked out through the front door and kept going, up the street where he had never gone.

But he didn't let himself think that. He came up this way a lot. So did Tewk. They were father and son, well, maybe a youngish uncle, and he was learning stonemasonry, and there was something—a cracked stone—wanting repairing up the hill.

Maybe it was inside the palace gate, that stone. Stones cracked in summer heat, just now and again, especially along old cracks, and they might want that fixed. They did. They'd be taking the measure for it and matching some chips for the color: he knew about stonemasons. His father had been—

His *uncle* was. Uncle Tewk. They were guild folk, and important in their own way, and gate guards were going to remember them when they saw them, that they had been coming and going through that gate for days.

He couldn't sweat. It was a warm day, but he couldn't sweat. They were going to do this in broad daylight, he and Tewk, and he didn't think about what came next, just getting themselves and their business through that gate.

He'd never been near this place, not even before the duchess died. The gates loomed up, tall, with the figures of two lions on painted leather, red and brown. The guards looked at them in complete boredom. They were supposed to be here. They were a little late. The guards opened the gates for them, and they walked through, under the second gate, which could be slammed down in a hurry.

"Signal tower's to the right," Tewk muttered, which shook Willem's concentration, scarily so.

"Shhsh," Willem said fiercely, and Tewk shut up.

But saying that about the signal tower had made him think about the signal, and the army, and—

He had to stop it. Uncle Tewk. They had stone chips to compare. Had to fix the tower, was what. Broken stone. They could chisel it out and slip a new one in, cut to perfection.

"Broken stone," he said. "That's why we're here."

"I wondered," Tewk said.

It got them across the cobbled inner courtyard and over toward the tower, at least. Steps went up the side of the wall at that point.

But—

"You!" someone yelled.

I can't, Willem thought, turning on his heel. It was one of the black-caps, with a sword out, with an angry look on his face. *I can't, I can't, I can't . . .*

Steel whispered beside him. Tewk had a dagger out. A *dagger,* for the gods' sake—it wasn't enough.

Was a *big* sword. Tewk . . .

Tewk was a black-cap officer.

The man stopped dead and looked confused. And saluted.

Tewk didn't move.

"Sorry, sir," the man said. "Sorry."

"Good you are," Tewk said. "Get up there and lay a fire. Big one." This with a nod to the looming tower. "Put a squad on it."

"Yes, sir."

The man sheathed his sword and went running.

Tewk wasn't stupid. Willem was sure of that, now. He stood there shaking in the knees, and Tewk stood there solid as the stone tower itself.

"Pretty good," Tewk said. "Pretty *damned* good. You don't even write 'em down. Never saw that before."

"Who was I?" Willem remembered including himself in the disguise, and now it was coming unraveled.

"An old man. Pretty scary old man at that."

"That's good." He'd broken out in sweat. They had to get out of here. There were gates and walls between them and freedom, and Master had said he had to bring the Alley with him, but he didn't see the Alley anymore. Here was the palace grounds, a huge stone courtyard, towering stone walls, slit windows, and massive doors. They were in this place, and there was something dark inside, and there was no leaving until they'd done something he didn't want to think about—

Which was bad, because he had to think about it and get them in deeper before he could get them out again.

Who'd get to the duke? Who'd be safe going through those doors? Soldiers.

Maybe.

They're all mercs. Nobody wants the black-caps traipsing through, not even Wiggy.

Servants. He saw two men in livery crossing the yard. Which he didn't see well enough. He needed to see it to cast it.

"Come on," he said to Tewk, suddenly in a fever to get through this, get Tewk where he needed to go—not to think beyond that. Not to think about that dark thing. He knew what that was. He didn't want to know. He didn't think on it. He thought just about those two servants, and the closer he got, the better he knew what he had to cast. Only fancier. Fancy clothes gave orders. Plain clothes took them.

The two servants were headed in the door. Merc guards there opened it and let them through.

Let them through, too, Willem thought. Beyond was dark, dark. He didn't know if Tewk could see it, but he *felt* it crawling through the hallways, as if all the fortress was one great beast.

The door boomed shut. There was spotty lighting, a couple of lamps. The dark was real. It was around them.

Stone steps ahead of them led up. It hadn't been a main door. Stone steps at the right led down and a smell of cooking wafted up. Meat roasting. Bread baking. That was the kitchens.

Where did dukes live, anyway?

This time it was Tewk who said, "Come on. This way."

He climbed, keeping up with Tewk. They were two fancy-dressed servants on a mission.

They were two fancy-dressed servants. Tewk was the senior. It was all right. Everything was all right.

They reached an upstairs hall, and it was amazing. Tapestries. Oil lamps. Slit windows that let in white daylight. A carpet on the wooden floor, and then, around a left-hand corner, a bigger room and a stone floor past open doors, and huge hangings and a number of people standing around a man at a little table, who was writing.

But it wasn't the man who was writing that was best-dressed. It was the dark-haired, glowering man in the middle of the bystanders. That man was dressed in brocade and velvet and chainmail and he wore a sword low-slung at his hip. He was as big as Tewk, and his glance swept toward them like the look of the biggest, meanest dog in town.

Scary man. Scary. Willem stopped. Tewk didn't. Tewk kept right on going.

He's a servant, Willam thought about Tewk. *He's supposed to be there.*

Something slithered across the floor. It was black and it was like fog and wasn't just on the floor. It was on eye level and it was fast and it wrapped around the man in brocade as his sword came out.

Tewk looks like that, Willem thought, and instantly honed that thought like a knife: *Tewk looks* just *like that!*

Tewk did. There were two of them, and the man at the table grabbed papers and scrambled and the men around their duke drew swords as Jindus did, as Tewk did—with all that black swirling around and around like smoke in a chimney. The two swordsmen went at it, circling like the smoke, swords grating and ringing—but all the bystanders just stood, swords drawn, but nobody moving, nobody able to see anything but Jindus, twice.

Except Tewk's better, Willem thought. *Tewk's stronger. Scarier.*

A sword swung and one of the two went down, blood spurting clear across the room, spattering the men, the pillars, everything. And one Jindus stood there, spattered, too, sword lifted . . .

And all that smoke whirled around and around and *magic* hit like a hammer, magic aimed at magic. Willem staggered where he stood, and didn't see what had hit him, just felt it, and shoved *back*. The Alley was where he was. The Alley was here, and men yelled and swore, voices echoing off what wasn't here at all.

The magic lashed at him like a whip. It was dark, it was angry, and it was scared, and it came from one old man, one old man who stood over in the shadows, over beyond Tewk, who was backing up from the advance of three of Jindus's men.

Snakes, Willem thought, and there were all of a sudden snakes in their way.

But that left him open, and the magic that hit made his heart jump, and he was on his hands and knees, trying to get up, trying to defend himself from that old man, from that *thing* that wasn't here, but almost was. It was hungry for the blood. It drank it. It grew stronger. And stronger.

But it was crazy, too. Crazy, and mean, and mad.

I'm not here, Willem thought. And that left the old man. *Miphrynes is. He's right—*

An arm like iron snatched him right off the floor, up to his feet, and a length of sword was out in front of him in Tewk's strong hand, between him and that old man.

We're not here, he thought, fast.

The dark reared up above all the room like an angry horse, and then plunged down at the floor, spreading in all directions at once. It broke like a wave against the walls, and crested over, and flowed backward, all the waves headed at each other, with a shriek that racketed through Willem's bones. The men went down. Only the old man, Miphrynes, was on his feet, lifting a staff that glowed with light the color of which had never been, not in the whole world. The eyes didn't want to see it. The heart didn't want to remember it. The ears didn't want to hear the sound that racketed through the room, and the palace, and the walls.

Tewk's arm tightened until it all but cut off Willem's wind.

"Demon," Tewk yelled in his ear.

It was. And there was one man in the middle of that roiling smoke, and Miphrynes began to scream, and to scream, and to scream.

I don't hear it, Willem said to himself. But he couldn't shut it all out. *Tewk doesn't hear it. We're not here.*

It stopped finally. The smoke went away. And there were just bones, and black robes, and a charred stick across them. There was a scatter of armed dead men. There was Jindus, staring rigidly at the ceiling, pale as parchment.

There was a great, deep silence—in this room.

Outside, far away, out in the courtyard, maybe, men were shouting. People outside were still alive.

"I take it that was the wizard," Tewk said, letting up on his grip. "Are you all right, boy?"

It took three tries to say yes.

"Jindus was easier than I thought," Tewk said, and nodded toward the pile of fresh bones. "That one—that one put up a hell of a fight."

"Did," Willem said. He was on his own feet, now, and there was something over there in that pile of bones, something dangerous that as good as glowed when he thought about it. He took a deep breath and went over and got it, a small book on a chain, which came loose from the bones when he pulled on it. He didn't want to look at it. He knew better. He went over to the fireplace and threw it in.

"Ugh," he said. And watched it burn.

"That's not all that's got to burn," Tewk said, from where he stood. "Boy. Look at me."

He wasn't a boy. Not now. Wanted to be, but even magic

couldn't manage that. Tewk looked at him and something changed in Tewk's expression, something serious and sober.

"We've got to get out of here," Tewk said. "Have you got one more trick in you, son? Can you get us over to that signal tower?"

Willem thought about it. A thick fog seemed to have settled in his brain. They were in a safe place at the moment, because everybody was dead. Demons were like that. That was what Master had told him: you could control them by giving them what they wanted, which wasn't any sort of control at all—it was still what *they* wanted, after all, since they were still in *their* Place. And if you were going to bring a demon all the way into your Place so you could control it, you still had a problem, because you had to give them a shape to live in and if you wanted it to do something for you, you had to find something else it wanted. That meant you had to be stronger than that body was—Miphrynes hadn't been stronger than Jindus—or smart enough to keep outsmarting the demon.

And Miphrynes might not have been smarter than this particular demon, after all. It had gotten its blood. A lot of it. And a few souls. And it was back in its safe Place. Wherever that was. One hoped it was back in its Place.

He wanted out of here. Right now. But wishing wouldn't do it. Feet had to.

"Willem!" Tewk caught up at the door, and grabbed his arm. "The place is crawling with mercs. They don't know Jindus is dead. They might've *heard* something going on. But can you—"

"You're Jindus," he said, and Tewk was. It wasn't even a hard piece of illusion.

Tewk looked down at his hand, which was browner, and scarred, just like that of Jindus, who was dead back there on the floor.

Tewk looked a little uneasy.

"You can do it," Willem said. "We go down there and you tell them to light the fire."

"Works if nobody got out of that room," Tewk said. "Where's the old man? The scribe?"

The old man at the table. The table was overturned. The papers were scattered, the inkpot spilled on the stone floor.

But the old man was *gone*.

The upper halls were deserted. The Jindus illusion was worth holding on to, Willem thought, because not everybody might believe the duke was dead. He half-ran, being a merc, just a plain black-cap, beside Tewk, and they went rattling and thumping down the little side steps that had gotten them into the upstairs in the first place.

They passed the kitchen stairs. They descended as far as the closed outside door and Tewk drew his sword. "Open it," he said, and Willem drew the latch back and swung it inward.

The guards were gone. Mercs were all over the courtyard, opening storerooms, carrying stuff, like an overturned anthill.

"They know," Tewk said. "They know he's dead. The town's going to be next. Probably they've already started looting down there, but the gold's up here. We've got to get Osric's army in here. Got to get to the signal tower. Fast."

They tried. But about then some of the looting mercs spotted them and dropped what they were carrying on the spot. One drew a sword, clearly not even trying to explain what they were doing. Jindus was dead. Jindus was alive but his authority was in shambles. And that was trouble the mercs now wanted to solve at sword's point.

They *needed* Osric's army. They needed to see Osric's army coming through that gate.

And Willem did. He *saw* it. *The men on the other side of the courtyard were Osric's men, all in shining armor and with the king's dragon on their coats . . .*

He pointed. Even Tewk had stopped dead, sword in hand, looking in that direction. And a couple of the mercs that had been stalking them cast a half-glance over their shoulders and then turned that way, frozen in a moment's confusion.

The others turned that way, and charged what they saw— startled men, who drew their swords. A battle broke out, one band against the other.

We're mercs, Willem thought. *We're just mercs, standing here.*

Tewk shook the illusion, grabbing him by the arm, hard. It hurt, and he almost lost all of it, except there were more mercs charging into the yard with the racket going up. *They* were Osric's men, too. Willem had no idea what Osric's men looked like but he knew it was a green banner and a gold dragon, and he put good armor and red hair on all of them.

"Got to get to the tower!" Tewk shouted at him. "Come on!"

Mercs and Osric's men were dropping wherever the fighting went on. Dead ones just looked like mercs. And he had enough to do just keeping the illusion hopping from one group to the next—whoever won became Osric's men.

But he couldn't keep dicing the groups finer and finer for- ever, with Tewk pulling at him and insisting he get moving. He couldn't do both. He couldn't go with Tewk to light the signal and keep the whole lot of mercs in the courtyard from running out of Osric's men and coming after them. It was the fastest, quickest- changing illusion he'd ever cast, and he was sweating, running out of breath, and Tewk jerked him loose from it and yelled:

"The fire, damn it! They're getting out the gate—they'll be sacking the town, next!"

Then he thought: *I want that fire burning. The fire's burning up there.*

And all of a sudden Tewk stopped pulling at him. Tewk was looking up, and there was a fire, a huge fire, for everybody to see. It was the *biggest* illusion he'd ever cast, and he just stood there, as Tewk stood there, both of them being themselves, while the fire roared away on the height of the tower and sent up black smoke to the heavens.

Could Osric's men see it? Willem wondered. Could it carry that far?

Sword rang against sword. Thunked into flesh, and a dying man fell at Willem's feet. Tewk flung an arm around him and shoved him into motion, running, running, while Tewk turned and hacked another man down.

If he were Master . . . if he were even *Almore,* he would have a chance. But he didn't know where a torch was. He didn't know what he was going to do. He reached the steps. He climbed for all he was worth, and Tewk stayed behind him, but attackers were trying to come up after them and Tewk stopped to hew away at the men on the steps.

On hands and knees, Willem made it over the crest, made it as far as the top of the wall, and he could see into the signal tower, where wood was piled, and oil jars, but it wasn't lit, and there was a merc there, the same they'd told to lay the fire. That man drew his sword, and Willem's mind went momentarily blank. No fire. No torch. No way to light it.

He *wanted* it. Or everybody in the town was going to be dead and King Osric was going to be outside the walls and the mercs in charge of the town, and Master, and Almore, and Jezzy—

He dodged a sword blow. The man saw Tewk as the threat: it was Tewk he was going for, right past him.

Which left him the stack of wood in the stone fire-pit. And the oil, which was still in the jars.

And fire didn't obey illusion magic. Heat wouldn't come.

He heard swords meet behind him. Twice. Blows like a black-smith's hammer.

Sparks flying. Little sparks.

Be! he thought.

And the fire came.

The fire took the wood. It blazed up. It broke the jars, which spread fire along the wall, and the great fire roared like a living thing.

Heat flared out. He wasn't thinking it. It *was*.

A master wizard—a *real* master wizard—

Hadn't Master taught Almore? *And* taught him?

He *felt* that piece of paper he had tucked in his shirt. The one that Master had written, naming *him* master.

He stood there with the smoke going up to the sky, and the heat baking his front and calling up more sweat, and then a hand landed on his shoulder, and squeezed.

"Good job," Tewk panted. "*Good* job, boy."

"Master Willem," he said, not prideful, not arrogant, just numb. Down below the wall he could see mercs running for it, some with loot, some not, and doors pouring out men who headed for the open courtyard gate. They weren't slowing down.

"*Master* Willem," Tewk said, and squeezed a second time. "There's still work to do, for you and me. Your Talent can hound those bastards all the way to the gates. I'll mop up any that get behind us. All right? Got the strength for it?"

"People won't get killed," he said, remembering Master's injunction. He hadn't killed anybody. He hadn't tried to kill anybody. If their own inclinations were to kill people—he hadn't stopped it, but he hadn't made them do anything they wouldn't like to do. He turned, a little wobbly, and a little dizzied by the downward view of the steep and narrow stairs, and Tewk kept a firm grip on him. "I'll do it."

"Until you can magic yourself wings," Tewk said, "I'm keeping hold of you. Not losing you, no."

"Thanks," he said, and started down the steps, with Tewk's hand firmly clenching his collar, all the way down.

King Osric was holding court uptown. Master was packing, down here in the Alley. Master was going back to his house higher on the hill, and Master was going to work for Tewk's cousin, twice removed, who was going to be the new duke in Wiscezan.

"He's a little lazy," Tewk said about his cousin. "You'll notice he sat safe in Korianth. But he's a scholar, not a fighter. You'll like him," he said to Master, and Master nodded.

Almore and Jezzy were already packed, since Master said they would have real beds, and each their own room, and six changes of clothes, and servants.

Willem supposed he would have a room, too. He had new clothes—his old ones he didn't even want to remember. He'd had a bath at the Ox, he'd changed into clothes all the same color—gray—with new boots from the boot-seller, and a gray cloak he liked just to stroke, because it felt as smooth and soft as one of Jezzy's cats.

But he didn't know, now that Master and everybody called him Master Willem, exactly where he would be. He didn't have anything to pack, either, except an old knife he liked, and a few pages Master had given him, which he was going to bind into the start of a book. So he had those lying on the table, and Master and Tewk talked for a while.

King Osric had gotten into the town and into the fortress without even a fight: and it wasn't as bad as a sack, but Wiggy's place had lost furniture and tankards—and was getting new ones: King Osric had ordered damages paid, so Wiggy and his daughter were happy, and feeling rich.

Most every damage had gotten fixed. Master had fixed a few.

Master was feeling a lot better now that the demon was out of town, and was getting visibly a little younger, which was not an illusion; Willem was fairly sure of it.

So everybody had a prospect, and he was fairly sure his was bright. He just didn't know what it was.

Until Tewk walked up as he was standing, looking out the open door of their little house, and laid a hand on his shoulder.

"You're pretty good," Tewk said. "The world's wider than Wiscezan, you know. I've got a cousin up in Peghary who wants a little advice. Ever ridden?"

He hadn't. If he were Jezzy, with Jezzy's talent, he wouldn't worry about it; but horses scared him. They were tall. They had intentions of their own.

Tewk was asking him to go on the road with him. And see places. Peghary. He'd only heard of that place.

"Master might need me," he said. He still had that duty. Master had leaned on him for a long time.

"I'm doing very well," Master said. "I can spare you a few months. I'll be busy with these two. They're getting old enough. They'll take care of things."

Master never had said anything about *his* room in the house. And with Tewk—

He'd gotten used to Tewk. Tewk was smart in different ways than Master. There were things still to learn.

Places to go.

He nodded, looking out on the dust of the Alley.

Fact was, Tewk needed him. He wasn't the only one who put illusions on things. Cousin in Peghary, hell.

Maybe there even was a cousin.

"Sure," he said. "All right. I can ride."

Raised in rural Vermont, K. J. PARKER is part of the new generation of fantasy writers who, over the past ten years, has been publishing work that has been redefining sword and sorcery. Parker's first novel, *Colors in the Steel,* appeared in 1998 and was followed by two further volumes in the Fencer trilogy, the Scavenger trilogy, and the critically acclaimed Engineer trilogy. Parker's most recent books are novels *The Company* and *The Folding Knife,* and novella "Purple and Black." Having worked in law, journalism, and numismatics, Parker is married to a solicitor, lives in southern England, and, when not writing, likes to make things out of wood and metal.

A RICH FULL WEEK

K. J. Parker

He looked at me the way they all do. "You're him, then."

"Yes," I said.

"This way."

Across the square. A cart, tied up to a hitching post. One thin horse. Not so very long ago, he'd used the cart for shifting dung. I sat next to him, my bag on my knees, tucking my feet in close, and laid a bet with myself as to what he'd say next.

"You don't look like a wizard," he said.

I owed myself two nomismata. "I'm not a wizard," I said.

I always say that.

"But we sent to the Fathers for a—"

"I'm not a wizard," I repeated, "I'm a philosopher. There's no such thing as wizards."

He frowned. "We sent to the Fathers for a wizard," he said.

I have this little speech. I can say it with my eyes shut, or thinking about something else. It comes out better if I'm not thinking about what I'm saying. I tell them, we're not wizards, we don't do magic, there's no such thing as magic. Rather, we're

students of natural philosophy, specializing in mental energies, te-
lepathy, telekinesis, indirect vision. Not magic; just science where
we haven't quite figured out how it works yet. I looked at him.
His hood and coat were homespun—that open, rather scratchy
weave you get with moorland wool. The patches were a slightly
different color; I guessed they'd been salvaged from an even older
coat that had finally reached the point where there was nothing
left to sew onto. The boots had a military look. There had been
battles in these parts, thirty years ago, in the civil war. The boots
looked to be about that sort of vintage. Waste not, want not.

"I'm kidding," I said. "I'm a wizard."

He looked at me, then back at the road. I hadn't risen in his
estimation, but I hadn't sunk any lower, probably because that
wasn't possible. I waited for him to broach the subject.

By my reckoning, three miles out of town, I said, "So tell me
what's been happening."

He had big hands; too big for his wrists, which looked like
bones painted flesh-color. "The Brother wrote you a letter," he
said.

"Yes," I replied brightly. "But I want you to tell me."

The silence that followed was thought rather than rudeness or
sulking. Then he said, "No good asking me. I don't know about
that stuff."

They never want to talk to me. I have to conclude that it's my
fault. I've tried all sorts of different approaches. I've tried being
friendly, which gets you nowhere. I've tried keeping my face shut
until someone volunteers information, which gets you peace and
quiet. I've read books about agriculture, so I can talk intelligently
about the state of the crops, milk yields, prices at market, and the
weather. When I do that, of course, I end up talking to myself.
Actually, I have no problem with talking to myself. In the country, it's the only way I ever get an intelligent conversation.

"The dead man," I prompted him. I never say *the deceased*.

He shrugged. "Died about three months ago. Never had any bother till just after lambing."

"I see. And then?"

"It was sheep to begin with," he said. "The old ram, with its neck broke, and then four ewes. They all reckoned it was wolves, but I said to them, wolves don't break necks, it was something with hands did that."

I nodded. I knew all this. "And then?"

"More sheep," he said, "and the dog, and then an old man, used to go round all the farms selling stuff, buttons and needles and things he made out of old bones; and when we found him, we reckoned we'd best tell the boss up at the grange, and he sent down two of his men to look out at night, and then the same thing happened to them. I said, that's no wolf. Knew all along, see. Seen it before."

That hadn't been in the letter. "Is that right?" I said.

"When I was a kid," the man said (and now I knew the problem would be getting him to shut up). "Same thing exactly: sheep, then travelers, then three of the duke's men. My grandad, he knew what it was, but they wouldn't listen. He knew a lot of stuff, Grandad."

"What happened?" I asked.

"Him and me and my cousin from out over, we got a couple of shovels and a pick and an ax, and we went and dug up this old boy who'd died. And he was all swelled up, like he'd got the gout all over, and he was *purple*, like a grape. So we cut off his head and shoveled all the dirt back, and we dropped the head down an old well, and that was the end of that. No more bother. Didn't say what we'd done, mind. The Brother wouldn't have liked it. Funny bugger, he was."

Well, I thought. "You did the right thing," I said. "Your grandfather was a clever man, obviously."

"That's right," he said. "He knew a lot of stuff."

I was doing my mental arithmetic. *When I was a kid*—so, anything from fifty-five to sixty years ago. Rather a long interval, but not unheard of. I was about to ask if anything like it had happened before then, but I figured it out just in time. If wise old Grandfather had known exactly what to do, it stood to reason he'd learned it the old-fashioned way: watching or helping, quite possibly more than once.

"The man who died," I said.

"Him." A cartload of significance crammed into that word. "Offcomer," he explained.

"Ah," I said.

"Schoolteacher, he called himself," he went on. "Dunno about that. Him and the Brother, they tried to get a school going, to teach the boys their letters and figuring and all, but I told them, waste of time in these parts, you can't spare a boy in summer, and winter, it's too dark and cold to be walking five miles there and five miles back, just to learn stuff out of a book. And they wanted paying, two pence twice a year. People around here can't afford that for a parcel of old nonsense."

I thought of my own childhood, and said nothing. "Where did he come from?"

"Down south." Well, of course he did. "I said to him, you're a long way from home. He didn't deny it. Said it was his calling, whatever that's supposed to mean."

It was dark by the time we reached the farm. It was exactly what I'd been expecting: long and low, with turf eaves a foot off the ground, turf walls over a light timber frame. No trees this high up, so lumber had to come up the coast on a big shallow-draught freighter as far as Holy Trinity, then road haulage the rest of the way. I spent the first fifteen years of my life sleeping under turf, and I still get nightmares.

Mercifully, the Brother was there waiting for me. He was younger than I'd anticipated—you always think of village Brothers as craggy old fat men, or thin and brittle, like dried twigs with papery bark. Brother Stauracius couldn't have been much over thirty; a tall, broad-shouldered man with an almost perfectly square head, hair cropped short like winter pasture, and pale blue eyes. Even without the habit, nobody could have taken him for a farmer.

"I'm so glad you could come," he said, town voice, educated, rather high for such a big man. He sounded like he meant it. "Such a very long way. I hope the journey wasn't too dreadful."

I wondered what he'd done wrong, to have ended up here. "Thank you for your letter," I said.

He nodded, genuinely pleased. "I was worried, I didn't know what to put in and leave out. I'm afraid I've had no experience with this sort of thing, none at all. I'm sure there must be a great deal more you need to know."

I shook my head. "It sounds like a textbook case," I said.

"Really." He nodded several times, quickly. "I looked it up in *Statutes and Procedures,* naturally, but the information was very sparse, very sparse indeed. Well, of course. Obviously, this sort of thing has to be left to the experts. Further detail would only encourage the ignorant to meddle."

I thought about Grandfather: two shovels and an ax, job done. But not quite, or else I wouldn't be here. "Fine," I said. "Now, you're sure there were no other deaths within six months of the first attack."

"Quite sure," he said, as though his life depended on it. "Nobody but poor Anthemius."

Nobody had asked me to sit down, let alone take my wet boots off. The hell with it. I sat down on the end of a bench. "You didn't say what he died of."

"Exposure." Brother Stauracius looked very sad. "He was caught out in a snowstorm and froze to death, poor man."

"Near here?"

"Actually, no." A slight frown, like a crack in a wall. "We found him about two miles from here, as it happens, on the big pasture between the mountains and the river. A long way from anywhere, so presumably he lost his way in the snow and wandered about aimlessly until the cold got to him."

I thought about that. "On his way back home, then."

"I suppose so, yes."

I needed a map. You almost always need a map, and there never is one. If ever I'm emperor, I'll have the entire country surveyed and mapped, and copies of each parish hung up in the temple vestries. "I don't suppose it matters," I lied. "You'll take me to see the grave."

A faint glow of alarm in those watered-down eyes. "In the morning."

"Of course in the morning," I said.

He relaxed just a little. "You'll stay here tonight, naturally. I'm afraid the arrangements are a bit—"

"I was brought up on a farm," I said.

Unlike him. "That's all right, then," he said. "Now I suppose we should join our hosts. The evening meal is served rather early in these parts."

"Good," I said.

Sleeping under turf is like being in your grave. Of course, there's rafters. That's what you see when you look up, lying wide-awake in the dark. Your eyes get the hang of it quite soon, diluting the black into gray into a palette of pale grays; you see rafters, not the underside of turf. And the smoke hardens it off, so it doesn't crumble. You don't get worms dropping on your face. But it's unavoidable, no matter how long you do it, no matter how used you are to it. You lie there, and the thought crosses your mind as you stare at the underside of grass; is this what it'll be like?

The answer is, of course, no. First, the roof will be considerably lower; it'll be the lid of a box, if you're lucky enough to have one, or else no roof at all, just dirt chucked on your face. Second, you won't be able to see it because you'll be dead.

But you can't help wondering. For a start, there's temperature. Turf is a wonderful insulator: keeps out the cold in winter and the heat in summer. What it doesn't keep out is the damp. It occurs to you as you lie on your back there: so long as they bury me in a thick shirt, won't have to worry about being cold, or too hot in summer, but the damp could be a problem. Gets into your bones. A man could catch his death.

It's while you're lying there—everybody else is fast asleep; no imagination, no curiosity, or they've been working so hard all day they just sleep, no matter what—that you start hearing the noises. Actually, turf's pretty quiet. Doesn't creak like wood, gradually settling, and you don't get drips from leaks. What you get is the thumping noises over your head. Clump, clump, clump, then a pause, then clump, clump, clump.

They tell you, when you're a kid and you ask, that it's the sound of dead men riding the roof-tree. They tell you that dead men get up out of the ground, climb up on the roof, sit astride the peak, and jiggle about, walloping their heels into the turf like a man kicking on a horse. You believe them; I never was quite sure whether they believed it themselves. When you're older, of course, and you've left the farm and gone somewhere civilized, where it doesn't happen, you finally figure it out: what you hear is sheep, hopping up onto the roof in the night, wandering about grazing the fine sweet grass that grows there, picking out the wild leeks, of which they're particularly fond. Sheep, for crying out loud, not dead men at all. I guess they knew really, all along, and the stuff about dead men was to keep you indoors at night, keep you from wandering out under the stars (though why you should want to I couldn't begin to imagine). Or at least, at some point, way back in the dim past, some smartass with a particularly warped imagination made up the story about dead men, to scare his kids; and the kids believed, and never figured it was sheep, and they told their kids, and so on down the generations. Maybe you never figure it out unless you leave the farm, which nobody ever does, except me.

As a matter of fact, I was just beginning to drift off into a doze when the thumping started. Clump, clump, clump; pause; clump, clump, clump. I was not amused. I was bone-tired and I really wanted to get some sleep, and here were these fucking sheep walking about over my head. The hell with that, I thought, and got up.

I opened the door as quietly as I could, not wanting to wake up the household, and I stood in the doorway for a little while, letting my eyes get used to the dark. Someone had left a stick leaning against the doorframe. I picked it up, on the off chance that there might be a sheep close enough to hit.

Something was moving about again. I walked away from the house until I could see up top.

It wasn't sheep. It was a dead man.

He was sitting astride the roof, his legs drooping down either side, like a farmer on his way back from the market. His hands were on his hips and he was looking away to the east. He was just a dark shape against the sky, but there was something about the way he sat there: peaceful. I didn't think he'd seen me, and I felt no great inclination to advertise my presence. If I say I wasn't scared, I wouldn't expect to be believed; but fear wasn't uppermost in my mind. Mostly, I was *interested*.

No idea how long I stood and he sat. It occurred to me that I was just assuming he was a dead man. Looked at logically, far more likely that he was alive, and had reasons of his own for climbing up on a roof in the middle of the night. Well, there's a time and a place for logic.

He turned his head, looking down the line of the roof-tree, and lifted his heels, and dug them into the turf three times: clump, clump, clump. (And that was when I realized the flaw in my earlier rationalization. Three clumps; always three, ever since I was a kid. How many three-legged sheep do you see?) At that moment, the moon came out from behind the clouds, and suddenly we were looking at each other, me and him.

My host had been right: he was purple, like a grape. Or a bruise; the whole body one enormous bruise. Swollen, he'd said; either that or he was an enormous man, arms and legs twice as thick as normal. His eyes were white; no pupils.

"Hello," I said.

He leaned forward just a little and cupped his hand behind his left ear. "You'll have to speak up," he said.

Words from a dead man; a purple, swollen man sitting astride a roof. "Tell me," I said, raising my voice. "Why do you do that?"

He looked at me, or a little bit past me. I couldn't tell if his mouth moved, but there was a deep, gurgling noise that could only have been laughter. "Do what?"

"Ride on the roof like it's a horse," I said.

His shoulders lifted; a slow, exaggerated shrug, like he didn't know what a shrug was but was copying one he'd seen many years ago. "I'm not sure," he said. "I feel the urge to do it, so I do it."

Well, I thought. One of the great abiding mysteries of my childhood not quite cleared up. "Are you Anthemius?" I asked. "The schoolmaster?"

Again the laugh. "That's a very good question," he said. "Tell you what," he went on, "come up here and sit with me, so we can talk without yelling."

In the moonlight, I could make out the huge hands, with their monstrous overripe fingers. How tight the skin would have to be, with all that pressure against it from the inside. Breaking a neck would be like snapping a pear off a tree.

"Let me rephrase that," I said. "Were you Anthemius? When you were—"

"Yes," he said, speaking quickly to cut off a word he didn't want to hear. "I think I was. Thank you," he added. "I've been trying to remember. It's been on the tip of my tongue, but somehow I can't seem to think of any names."

The approved procedure for coping with the restless dead is, essentially, what Grandfather did; though of course we make rather more of a fuss about it. The approved procedure should, needless to say, be carried out in daylight; noon is recommended. Should you chance to encounter a specimen during the night, there are two courses of action, both recommended rather than approved. One, you draw your sword and cut its head off. Two, you challenge it to the riddle game and keep it talking all night, until dawn comes up unexpectedly and strands it like a beached whale in the cruel light.

Commentary on that. I am not a man of action. I don't vault onto roofs, I don't carry weapons. One of the reasons I left the farm in the first place was I have trouble lifting even moderate loads. So much for option one; and as for option two—

Also, I was curious. Interested.

"What happened to you?" I said.

"You know, I'm really not sure," he replied; and the voice was starting to sound like a man's voice, my ears were getting the hang of it, the way my eyes had got used to the dark. "I know I was out in the snow and I'd lost my way. I got terribly cold, so that every bit of me hurt. Then the pain started to ease up, and I sort of fell asleep."

"You died," I said.

He didn't like me saying that, but I guess he forgave me. "I remember waking up," he said, "and it was pitch dark and terribly quiet, and I couldn't move. I was very scared. And then it occurred to me, I wasn't breathing. I don't mean I was holding my breath. I wasn't breathing at all, and it didn't matter. So then I knew."

I waited, but I hadn't got all night. "And then?"

He turned his head away. No hair, just a bulging purple scalp. A head like a plum. "I was terrified," he said. "I mean, I had no way of knowing." He paused, and I have no idea what was passing through his mind. "After a long time, I found I could move after all. I got my hands up against the lid, and I pushed, and I could feel the wood burst apart. That scared me even more, I thought the roof, I mean all the earth on top of me, I thought it'd cave in and bury me." He paused again. "I was always frightened of tight places," he said. "You know."

I nodded. Me too, as it happens.

"I guess I panicked," he went on, "because I kept pushing, and I somehow knew that I was incredibly strong, much stronger than I'd ever been before, so I thought, if I push hard enough. I wasn't thinking straight, of course."

"And then?" I asked.

"Pushed right up through the dirt and into the moonlight," he said. "Amazing feeling. The first thing I wanted to do was run to the nearest farm and tell them, look, I'm not dead after all." He stopped; he'd said the word without thinking. "But then I thought about it; and I still wasn't breathing, and I couldn't actually *feel* anything. I could move my hands and feet, I could stand upright and balance, all that, but—you know when you've been sitting a long time and your feet go numb. It was like that, all over. It felt so strange."

"Go on," I said.

He didn't, not for a long time. "I think I sat down," he said. "I don't know why I'd have done that; standing up didn't make me tired or anything. I don't feel tired, ever. But I was so confused, I didn't know what I was supposed to do. It all felt wrong." He lifted his heels slowly and let them drop; clump, clump, clump. "And while I was there the sun started to come up, and the light just sort of flooded into my head and bleached everything away, so I couldn't think at all. I guess you could say I passed out. Anyway, when I opened my eyes I was back where I'd started from, lying in the dark."

I frowned. "How did you get back there?"

"I just don't know," he said. "Still don't. It always happens, that's all I know. When the sun comes up, my mind washes away. If I've gone any distance, I know I have to get back. I run. I can run really fast. I know I've got to be back—home," he said, with a sort of breaking-up laugh, "before the sun comes up. I've learned to be careful, to give myself plenty of time."

He was still and quiet for a while. I asked, "Why do you kill things?"

"No idea." He sounded distressed. "If something comes close enough, I grab it and twist it till it's dead. Like a cat lashing out at a bit of string. Reflex. I just know it's something I have to do."

I nodded. "Do you go looking—?"

"Yes." He mumbled the word, like a kid admitting a crime. "Yes, I do. I do my best to keep away from where there might be people. It's all the same to me: sheep, foxes, men. I'd go a long way away, into the mountains, if I could. But I have to stay close, so I can get back in time."

I'd been debating with myself, and I knew I had to ask. "What were you?" I said. "What did you do?"

He didn't answer. I repeated the question.

"Like you said," he replied. "I was a schoolteacher."

"Before that."

When he answered, it was against his will. The words came out slow, flat; he spoke because he had to. "I was a Brother," he said. "When I was thirty, they said I should apply to the Order, they thought I had the gift, and the brains, and the application and the self-discipline. I passed the exam and I was at the Studium for five years. Like you," he added.

I let that go. "You joined the Order."

"No." The flat voice had gone; there was a flare of anger. "No, I failed matriculation. I retook it the next year, but I failed again. They sent me back to my parish, but by then they'd got someone else. So I ended up wandering about, looking for teaching work, letter-writing, anything I could do to earn a living. There's not a lot you can do, of course."

Suddenly I felt bitter cold, right through. Took me a moment to realize it was fear. "So you came here," I said, just to keep him talking.

"Eventually. A lot of other places first, but here's where I ended up." He lifted his head abruptly. "They sent you here to deal with me, am I right?"

I didn't reply.

"Of course they did," he said. "Of course. I'm a nuisance, a pest, a menace to agriculture. You came here to dig me up and cut my head off."

This time, I was the one who had to speak against my will. "Yes."

"Of course," he said. "But I can't let you do that. It's my—"

He'd been about to say *life*. Presumably, he tried to find another way of phrasing it, then gave up. We both knew what he meant.

"You passed the exams, then," he said.

"Barely," I replied. "Two hundred seventh out of two hundred twenty."

"Which is why you're here."

His white eyes in the ash-white moonlight. "That's right," I said. "They don't give out research posts if you come two hundred seventh."

He nodded gravely. "Commercial work," he said.

"When I can get it," I replied. "Which isn't often. Others far more qualified than me."

He grunted. It could have been sympathy. "Public service work."

"Afraid so," I replied.

"Which is why you're here." He lifted his head and rolled it around on his shoulders, like someone waking up after sleeping in a chair. "Because—well, because you aren't much good. Well?"

I resented that, even though it was true. "It's not that I'm not good," I said. "It's just that everyone in my year was better than me."

"Of course." He leaned forward, his hands braced on his knees. "The question is," he said, "do I still have the gift, after what happened to me. If I've still got it, your job is going to be difficult."

"If not," I said.

"Well," he replied, "I suppose we're about to find out."

"Indeed," I said. "There could be a paper for the journals in this."

"Your chance to escape from obscurity," he said solemnly. "Under different circumstances, I'd wish you well. Unfortunately, I really don't want you cutting off my head. It's a miserable existence, but—"

I could see his point. His voice was quite human now; if I'd known him before, I'd have recognized him. He had his back to the moon, so I couldn't see the features of his face.

"What I'm trying to say is, you don't have to do it," he said. "Go away. Go home. Nobody knows you came out here tonight. I promise I'll stay away until you've gone. If I don't show up, you can report that there was no direct evidence of an infestation, and therefore you didn't feel justified in desecrating what was probably an innocent grave."

"But you'll be back," I said.

"Yes, and no doubt they'll send someone else," he said. "But it won't be you."

I was tempted. Of course I was tempted. For one thing, he was a rational creature; with my eyes shut, if I hadn't known better, I'd have said he was a natural man with a heavy cold. And what if the gift did survive death? He'd kill me. I had to admit it to myself: the thought that I could get killed doing this job hadn't occurred to me. I'd anticipated a quick, grisly hour's work in broad daylight; no risk.

I'm not a coward, but I appreciate the value of fear, the way I appreciate the value of money. I'm most definitely not brave.

I saw something in the moonlight, and said (trying not to talk quickly or raise my voice): "I could go back to bed, and then come back in the morning and dig you up."

"You could," he said.

"You don't think I would."

"Not if we'd made an agreement."

"You could be right," I said. "But what about the farmers? You've got to admit—"

At which moment, the Brother (who'd come out of the back door, crawled up on the roof behind him, and edged down the roof-tree toward him until he was close enough to reach his neck with the ax he'd brought with him) raised his arms high and swung. No sound at all; but at the last moment, the dead man leaned his head to one side, just enough, and the ax-blade swept past, cutting air. I heard the Brother grunt, shocked and panicky. I saw the dead man—eyes still fixed on me—reach behind him with his left hand and catch the swinging ax just below the head, and hold it perfectly still. The Brother gasped, but didn't let go; he was pulling with all his strength, like a little dog tugging on a belt. All his efforts couldn't move the dead man's arm the thickness of a fingernail.

"Now," the dead man said. "Let's see."

The delay on my part was unforgivable, completely unprofessional. I knew I had to do something, but my mind had gone completely blank. I couldn't remember any procedures, let alone any words. *Think,* a tiny voice was yelling inside my head, but I couldn't. I heard the Brother whimper, as he applied every scrap of strength in a tendon-ripping, joint-tearing last desperate jerk on the ax-handle, which had no effect whatsoever. The dead man was looking straight at me. His lips began to move.

Pro nobis peccatoribus—not the obvious choice, not even on the same page of the book, but it was the only procedure I could think of. Unfortunately, it's one I've always had real difficulties with. You reach out with your hand that is not a hand, extend the fingers that aren't fingers; I'm all right as far as that, and then I tend to come unstuck.

(What I was thinking was: so he failed the exam, and I passed. Yes, but maybe the reason he failed was he didn't read the questions through properly, or he spent so long on Part One that he didn't leave himself enough time for Two and Three. Maybe he's really good, just unlucky in exams.)

I was mumbling: *Sol invicte, ora pro nobis peccatoribus in die periculi.* Of course, there's a school of thought that says the magic words have no real effect whatsoever, they're just a way of concentrating the mind. I tend to agree. Why should an archaic prayer in a dead language to a god nobody's believed in for six hundred years have any effect on anything at all? *Ora pro nobis peccatoribus,* I repeated urgently, *nobis peccatoribus in die periculi.*

It worked. It can't have been the words, of course, but it felt like it was the words. I was in, I was through. I was inside his head.

There was nothing there.

Believe me, it's true. Nothing at all; like walking into a house where someone's died, and the family have been in and cleared out all the furniture. Nothing there, because I was inside the head of a dead man; albeit a dead man who was looking at me reproachfully out of blank white eyes while holding an ax absolutely still.

Fine; all the easier, if it's empty. I looked for the controls. You have to visualize them, of course. I see them as the handwheels of a lathe. It's because I had a holiday job in a foundry in Second Year. I don't know how to use a lathe. What I mostly did was sweep up piles of swarf off the floor.

Here is the handwheel that controls the arms. I reached out with the hand that is not a hand, grabbed it and tried to turn it. Stuck. I tried harder. Stuck. I tried really hard, and the bloody thing came away in my hand.

It's not supposed to do that.

I re-visualized. I saw the controls as the reins of a cart, the footbrake under my boot that was not a boot. I stamped on the brake and hauled back hard on the reins.

I haven't got around to writing that paper for the journals, so here it is for the first time anywhere. The gift does not survive death. Nothing survives. The room was empty. And the handwheel only broke off because I'm clumsy and cack-handed, the sort of person who trips over cats and breaks the nibs of pens by pressing too hard.

I heard the Brother gasp, as he jerked the ax out of the dead man's grip. The dead man didn't move. His eyes were still fixed on mine, right up to the moment when the ax sheared through his neck and his head wobbled and fell, bounced off his knee and tumbled off the roof into the short grass below. The body didn't move.

I know why. It took ten of us, with an improvised crane made of twelve-foot-three-inch fir poles, to get the body down off the roof. It must've weighed half a ton. The head alone was two hundredweight. Two men couldn't lift it; they had to use levers to roll it along the ground. There was no blood, but the neck started to ooze a milky white juice that smelt worse than anything you could possibly imagine.

We burnt the body. We drenched it in pine-pitch, and it caught quite easily and burnt down to nothing; not even any recognizable bits of bone. The white juice flared up like oil. They rolled the head over to the slurry-pond and pitched it in. It went down with a gurgle and a burp.

"I heard you talking to it," the Brother told me. For some reason, the word *it* offended me. "I guessed you were using a variation on the riddle game, to keep it distracted till the sun came up."

"Something like that," I said.

He nodded. "I shouldn't have interfered, I'm sorry," he said. "You had the situation under control, and I could have ruined everything."

"That's all right," I said.

He smiled, as if to say, it wasn't all right but thanks for forgiving me. "I guess I panicked," he said. Then he frowned. "No, I didn't. I saw a chance of getting in on the act. It was stupid and selfish of me. You'll have to write to the prebendary."

"I don't see why," I said mildly. "The way I see it, your actions were open to several different interpretations. I choose to interpret them as courage and resourcefulness. I could put that in a letter, if you like."

"Would you?" In his face, I saw all the desperation and cruelty of sudden, unexpected hope. "I mean, seriously?"

"Of course," I said.

"That'd be—" He stopped. He couldn't think of a big enough word. "You've got no idea what it's like," he said all in a rush, like diarrhea. "Being stuck here, in this miserable place with these appalling people. If I can't get back to a town, I swear I'll go mad. And it's so cold in winter. I hate the cold."

You can sleep in the coach, Father Prior said when I tried to make a fuss about the timetable. I didn't say to him, have you ever been on a provincial mail-coach, on country roads, at this time of year? A dead man couldn't sleep on a mail-coach.

I slept, nearly all the way; on account, I guess, of not having had much sleep the night before. Woke up just as we were crossing the Fulvens bridge; I looked out of the window, and all I could see was water, moonlight reflected on water. Couldn't get back to sleep after that. Too dark to read the case notes, which I'd neglected to do back at the farm. But I remembered the basic facts from the briefing. These jobs are all the same, anyhow. Piece of cake.

The coach threw me out just after dawn, at a crossroads in the middle of nowhere. Somewhere up on the moors; I'm a valley boy myself. We had cousins up on the moor. I hated it when they came to visit. The old man was deaf as a post, and the three boys (mid- to late thirties, but they were always *the boys*) just sat there, not saying a word. The mother died young, and I can't say I blame her.

They were supposed to be meeting the coach, but there was no one there. I stood for a while, then I sat on my bag, then I sat on the ground, which was damp. I heard an owl, and a fox, or at least I hope it was a fox. If not, it was something we never got around to covering in Third Year, and I'm very glad I didn't see it.

They arrived eventually, in a little dog-cart thing; an old man driving, a younger man and the Brother. One small pony, furry like a bear.

The Brother did the talking, for which I was quite grateful. He was one of the better sort of country Brothers: short man, somewhere between fifty and sixty, a distinct burr to his voice but he spoke clearly and used proper words. The boy was the younger man's son, the older man's grandson. He'd been fooling about in a big oak tree, slipped, fell; broken arm and a hideous bash on the head. He hadn't come around, and it had been a week now. They had to prize his mouth open with the back of a horn spoon to get food and water in; he swallowed all right, but that was all he did. You could stick a needle in his foot half an inch and he wouldn't even twitch. The swelling on the back of his head had gone down—the Brother disclaimed any medical knowledge, but he was lying—and they'd set the arm and splinted it, for what that was worth.

I thought, better than killing the restless dead. One of my best subjects at the Studium, though of course we did all our practicals on conscious minds, with a Father sitting a few feet away, watching like a hawk. I'd done one about eighteen months earlier, and it went off just fine; in, found her, straight out again. She followed me like a dog. I'd been relieved when Father Prior told me; it could've been something awkward and fiddly, like auspices, or horrible and scary, like a possession. Just in case, I'd brought the book. I'd meant to mug up the relevant chapter, either at the farm or on the coach, but I hadn't got around to it. Anyway, it had to be better than that empty place.

It was quite a big house, for a hill farm; sitting in the well of a valley, with a dense copper-beech hedge on all four sides, as a windbreak. Just the five of them in the house, the Brother said: grandfather, father, mother, the boy, and a hired man who slept in the hayloft. The boy was nine years old. The Brother told me his name, but I'm hopeless with names.

They asked me, did I want to rest after the journey, wash and brush up, something to eat? The correct answer was, of course, no, so I gave it.

"He's in here," the Brother said.

Big for a hill farm, but still oppressively small. Downstairs, the big kitchen, with a huge table, fireplace, two hams swinging like dead men on gibbets. A parlor, tiny and dusty and cold. Dairy, scullery, store; doorway through to the cow stalls. Upstairs, one big room and a sort of oversized cupboard, where the boy was. I could just about kneel beside the bed, if I didn't mind the windowsill digging in the small of my back.

The hell with that, I thought, I'm a qualified man, a professional, a Father; a wizard. I shouldn't have to work in conditions you wouldn't keep pigs in. "Take him downstairs," I said. "Put him on the kitchen table."

They had a job. The stairs in that house were like a bell tower, tightly coiled and cramped. Father and grandfather did the heavy lifting, while I watched. It's an odd thing about me. Sometimes, the more compassion is called for the less capable I am of feeling it. I offer no explanation or excuse.

"He shouldn't have been moved," the Brother hissed in my ear, just loud enough so that everyone could hear. "In his condition—"

"Yes, thank you," I said, in my best arrogant-city-bastard voice. I couldn't say why I was behaving like this. Sometimes I do. "Now, if you'll all stay well back, I'll see what I can do."

I looked at the boy, and I could remember the theory perfectly, every last detail, every last lecture note. His eyes were closed; he had a stupid face, fat girly lips, fat cheeks. If he lived, he'd grow up tall, solid, double-chinned, gormless; the son of the farm. Pork fat and home-brewed beer; he'd be spherical by the time he was forty, strong enough to wrestle a bullock to its knees, slow and tireless, infuriatingly calm, a man of few words; respected at the market, shrewd and fat, his bald patch hidden under a hat that would never come off, probably not even in bed. A solid, productive life, which it was my duty to save. Lucky me.

Theory; theory is your lifeline, they used to tell me, your driftwood in a shipwreck. I reminded myself of the basic propositions.

To recover a lost mind, first make an entrance. This is usually done by visualizing yourself as a penetrating object: a drill bit, a woodpecker's beak, a maggot. The drill bit works for me, though for some reason I tend to be a carpenter's auger, wound in with a brace. I go in through the spiral flakes of waste bone thrown clear by the wide grooves of the cutter. I assume it's from some childhood memory, watching Grandad at work in the barn. You're not really supposed to use personal memories, but it's easier, for someone with my limited imagination.

Once you're in, first ward, immediately, because you never know what might be waiting for you in there. I raised first ward as soon as I felt myself go through. I use *scutum fidei*, visualize a shield. Mine's round, with a hole in it at twelve o'clock so I can see what's going on.

I peered through the hole. No nasty creatures with dripping fangs crouched to pounce, which was nice. Count to ten and lower the shield slowly.

I looked around. This is the crucial bit, and you mustn't rush. How long it takes depends on the strength of your gift, so naturally I take ages. The light gradually increases. First things first; get your bearings. Orientate yourself, taking special care to get a fix on the point you came in by. Well, obviously. If you lose your entry point, you're stuck in someone else's head forever. You really don't want that.

I lined up on the corners of a ceiling, drawing diagonal lines and fixing on their point of origin, measuring the angles with my imaginary protractor (it's brass, with numbers in gothic italic). One-oh-five, seventy-five; repeat the numbers four times out loud, to make sure they're loaded into memory. Fine. Now I know where I am and how to get out again. One-oh-five, seventy-five. Now, then. Let the dog see the rabbit.

I was in a room. It's nearly always an interior; with kids, practically guaranteed it's their bedroom, or the room they sleep in, depending on social class and domestic arrangements. In all relevant essentials, it was the room upstairs I had him carried down from. Excellent; nice and small, not many places to hide anything. So much easier when you're dealing with a subject of limited intelligence.

I visualized a body for myself. I tend not to be me. With children, it's usually best to be a nice lady; the kid's mother, if possible. I'm not good enough to do specific people, and I have real problems being women. So I was a nice old man instead.

Hello, I said. Where are you?

Don't worry if they don't answer. Sometimes they do, sometimes they don't. I walked around the bed, knelt down, looked under it. There was a cupboard; one of those triangular jobs, wedged in a corner. I opened that. For some reason, it was full of the skins and bones of dead animals. None of my business; I closed it. I pulled the covers off the bed, and lifted the pillow.

Odd, I thought, and touched base with theory. The boy must still be alive, or else there would be no room. If he's alive, he must be in here somewhere. He can't be invisible, not inside his own head. He can, of course, be anything he likes, so long as it's animate and alive. A cockroach, for example, or a flea. I sighed. I get all the rotten jobs.

I adjusted the scale, making the room five times bigger. Go up in easy stages. If he was being a cockroach, he'd now be a rat-sized cockroach. If he was being a rat, of course, he'd be cat-sized and capable of giving me a nasty bite. I used *lorica,* just in case. I looked under the bed again.

I visualized a clock, in the middle of the wall opposite the door. It told me I'd been inside for ten minutes. The recommended maximum is thirty. Really first-rate practitioners have been known to stay in for an hour and still come out more or less in one piece; that's material for a leading article in the journals. I searched again, this time paying more attention to the contents of the cupboard. Dried, desiccated animal skins: squirrels, rabbits, rats. No fleas, mites, or ticks. So much for that theory.

I visualized a glass jug, to represent my energy level. You can use yourself up surprisingly quickly and not know it. Just as well I did. My jug was a third empty. You want to save at least a fifth just to get out again. I visualized calibrations, so as to be sure.

Quick think. The recommended course of action would be to visualize a tracking agent (spaniel, terrier, ferret), but that takes a fair chunk of your resources; also, it burns energy while it's in use, and getting rid of it takes energy, too. I drew a distinct red line on my measuring jug, and a blue line just above it. The alternative to a tracker is to increase the scale still further; twenty times, say, in which case your cockroach will be a wolf-sized monster that could jump you and bite your head off. I was still running *lorica,* but any effective ward burns energy. If I found myself with a fight on my hands, I could dip below that essential red line in a fraction of a second. No, the hell with that.

I visualized a terrier. I'm not a dog person, so my terrier was a bit odd; very short, stumpy legs and a rectangular head. Still, it went at it with great enthusiasm, wagging its imaginary tail and making little yapping noises. All around the room, nose into everything. Then it sat on the floor and looked at me, as if to say, Well?

Not looking good. My jug was half-empty, I'd used up my repertoire of approved techniques, and found nothing. Just my luck to get a special case, a real collector's item. Senior research fellows would be fighting each other for the chance of a go at this one, but I just wanted to get the job done and clear out. Wasted on me, you might say.

I vanished the dog. Quick think. There had to be something else I could try, but nothing occurred to me. Didn't make sense; he had to be in here somewhere, or there'd be no room. He couldn't be invisible. He could only turn himself into something he could imagine—and it had to be real; no fantasy creatures the size of a pin-head. At five times magnification, a red mite would be plainly visible; also, the dog would've found it. Tracking agents, even inferior ones visualized by me, smell life. If he was in here, the dog would've found him.

So—

As required by procedure, I considered abandoning the attempt and getting out. This would, of course, mean the boy would die; you can't go back in twice, that's an absolute. I'd be within my rights, faced with an enigma on this scale. The failure would be noted on my record, of course, but there'd be an annotation, *no blame attaches,* and it wouldn't be the first time, not by a long way. The kid would die; not my problem. I'd have done my best, and that's all you have to do.

Or I could think of something. Such as what?

They tell you: be wise, don't improvise. If in doubt, get out.

Making stuff up as you go along is mightily frowned on, in much the same way as you're not encouraged to fry eggs in a fireworks factory. There's no knowing what you might invent, and outside controlled conditions, invention could lead to the Cartographic Commission having to redraw the maps for a whole county. Or you could make a hole in a wall, which is the worst thing anybody can do. At the very least, I'd be sure to end up in front of the Board, facing charges of unauthorized innovation and divergence. Saving the life of some farm kid would be an excuse, but not a very good one.

I could think of something. Such as—

There's no such thing as magic. Instead, there's the science we don't properly understand, not yet. There are effects that work, and we have no idea why. One of these is *spes aeternitatis*, a wretchedly inconsistent, entirely inexplicable conjuring trick that no self-respecting Father would condescend to use. That's because they can't get it to work reliably.

I can.

Spes aeternitatis is an appearances-adjuster. You can use it to find hidden objects, or translate lies, or tell if a slice of cake or a glass of wine's got poison in it. I do it by visualizing everything that's wrong in light blue. It's a tiny little scrap of talent that I've got and practically everybody else hasn't; it's like being double-jointed, or wiggling your nostrils like a rabbit.

I closed my eyes and opened them again, and saw a light blue room. Everything light blue. Everything false.

Oh, I thought; then, one-oh-five, seventy-five, and I started lining up diagonals for my escape. But that wasn't to be, unfortunately. The room blurred and reappeared, and it was all different. It was my room; the room I slept in until I was fifteen years old.

He was sitting on the end of the bed; a slight man, almost completely bald, with a small nose and a soft chin, small hands, short, thin legs. I'd put him at about fifty years old. His skin was purple, like a grape.

"You were wrong," he said, looking up at me. "The talent survives death."

"That's interesting," I said. "How did you get in here?"

He smiled. "You practically invited me in," he said. "When I heard that fool behind me, with the ax, I looked at you. You felt sorry for me. You thought: is he not a man and a Brother, or words to that effect. I used Stilicho's transport, and here I am."

I nodded. "I should've put up wards."

"You should. Careless. Attention to detail isn't your strongest suit."

"The boy," I said.

He shrugged. "In there somewhere, I dare say. But we aren't in his head, we're in yours. I've made myself at home, as you can see."

I looked around quickly. The apple box with the bottom knocked out, where I used to keep my books; it was where it should be, but the books were different. They were new and beautifully bound in tooled calf, and the alphabet their titles were written in was strange to me.

"My memories," I said.

He waved his hand. "Well rid of them," he said. "Misery and failure, a life wasted, a talent dissipated. You'll be better off."

I nodded. "With yours."

"Quite. Oh, they're not pleasant reading," he said, with a scowl. "Bitter, angry; memories of bigotry and spite, relentless bad luck, a life of constant setbacks and reverses, a talent misunderstood. You'll see that I failed the exam the second time because, sitting there in Great School, I suddenly hit on a much better way of achieving *unam sanctam;* quicker, safer, ruthlessly efficient. I tried it out as soon as the exam was over, and it worked. But I got no marks, so they failed me. I ask you, where's the sense in that?"

"You failed the retake," I said. "What about the first time?"

He laughed. "I had the flu," he said. "I was practically delirious, could barely remember my name. Would they listen? No. Rules. You see what I mean. Bad luck and spite at every turn."

I nodded. "What happens to me?"

He looked at me. "You'll be better off," he repeated.

"I'll stop existing. I'll be dead."

"Not physically," he said mildly. "Your body, my mind. Your fully qualified licensed-practitioner's body, and a mind that saw how to improve *unam sanctam* in a half-second flash of intuition."

It says a lot about my self-esteem that I actually considered it, though not for very long. Half a second, maybe. "What happens now?" I asked. "Do we fight, or—?"

He shrugged. "If you like," he said, and extended his arm. It was ten feet long, thick as a gatepost. He gripped my throat like a man holding a mouse, and crushed me.

I guess I was about 70 percent dead when I remembered: I know what to do. I drew a rather shaky second ward; he closed his fingers on thin air, and I was standing behind him.

He swung around, roaring like a bull. He had bull's horns sticking out of his forehead. I tried second ward again, but he got there before I did, grabbed my head, and smashed my face into the wall.

Just in time, I remembered: there is no pain. I used Small Mercies, softening the wall into felt, and slipped through his fingers. I was smoke. I hung above him in a cloud. He laughed, and fetched me back with *vis mentis*. The back of my head hit the floor, which gave way like a mattress. I became a spear, and buried myself in his chest. He used second ward and was on the other side of the room.

"You fight like a first-year," he said.

Which was true. I clenched my mind like a fist; the walls closed in on him, squashing him like a spider under a boot. I felt him, like a nail right through the sole. Back to first ward, and we stood glowering at each other, in opposite corners of the room.

"You can't beat me," he said. "I'll wear you down and you'll simply fade away. Face it, what the hell have you got to live for?"

Valid point. "All right, then," I said.

His eyes opened wide. "I win?"

"You win," I said.

He was pleased; very pleased. He grinned at me and raised his hand, just as I got my fingers around the handle of the door and twisted as hard as I could.

He saw that and opened his mouth to scream. But the door flew open, knocking me back. I closed my eyes. The door was, of course, the intersection of two lines drawn diagonally across the room, at 105 and 75 degrees precisely.

I opened my eyes. He'd gone. I was in the boy's room, the room upstairs. The boy was sitting on the floor, legs crossed, hands under his chin. He looked up at me.

"Well, come on," I snapped at him. "I haven't got all day."

They were pathetically grateful. Mother in floods of tears, father clinging to my arm, how can we ever thank you, it's a miracle, you're a miracle-worker. I wasn't in the mood. The boy, lying on the kitchen table under a pile of blankets, looked up at me and frowned, as though something about me wasn't quite right. A quiet, analytical stare; it bothered the hell out of me. I refused food and drink and made father get out the pony and trap and take me out to the crossroads. But the mail won't be arriving for six hours, he objected; it's cold and dark, you'll catch your death.

I didn't feel cold.

At the crossroads, huddling under the smelly old hat father

insisted on giving me, I tried to search my mind, to see if he'd really gone. There was, of course, no way he could have survived. I'd opened the door (Rule One: never open the door) and he'd been sucked out of my head out into the open, where there was no talented mind to receive him. Even if he was as strong as he'd claimed to be, there was no way he could have lasted more than three seconds before he broke up and dissipated into the air. There was absolutely nothing he could have done, no way he could have survived.

The coach arrived. I got on it, and slept all the way. At the inn, I got a lamp and a mirror, and examined myself all over. Just when I thought I was all clear, I found a patch of purple skin, about the size of a crab apple, on the calf of my left leg. I told myself it was just a bruise.

(That was a year ago. It's still there.)

The rest of the round was just straightforward stuff: a possession, a small rift, a couple of incursions, which I sealed with a strong closure and duly reported when I got back. Since then, I've volunteered for a screening, been to see a couple of counselors, bought a pair of full-length mirrors. And I've been promoted; field officer, superior grade. They're quite pleased with me, and no wonder. I seem to be getting better at the job all the time. And I'm writing a paper, would you believe: modifications to *unam sanctam*. Quicker, safer, much more efficient. So blindingly obvious, I'm surprised no one's ever thought of it before.

Father Prior is surprised but pleased. I don't know what's got into you, he said.

GARTH NIX grew up in Canberra, Australia. When he turned nineteen, he left to drive around the United Kingdom in a beat-up Austin with a boot full of books and a Silver-Reed typewriter. Despite a wheel literally falling off the car, he survived to return to Australia and study at the University of Canberra. He has since worked in a bookshop, as a book publicist, a publisher's sales representative, an editor, a literary agent, and as a public relations and marketing consultant. His first story was published in 1984 and was followed by novels *The Ragwitch, Sabriel, Shade's Children, Lirael, Abhorsen,* the six-book YA fantasy series the Seventh Tower, and, most recently, the seven-book the Keys to the Kingdom series. He lives in Sydney with his wife and their two children.

A SUITABLE PRESENT
FOR A SORCEROUS PUPPET

Garth Nix

Sir Hereward licked his finger and turned the page of the enormous tome that was perched precariously on a metal frame next to his sickbed. It was not a book he would have chosen to read—or rather to fossick through like a rook searching for seed in a new-sown field—but as it was the only book in the lonely tower by the sea, he had little choice. Having broken two small but important bones in his left foot, he could not range farther afield for other amusements, so reading it had to be. This particular book was entitled *The Compendium of Commonplaces* and presented itself as a collection of knowledge that should be at the command of every reasonably educated gentleman of Jerreke, a country that had ceased to exist some thousand years before, shortly after the book was printed.

The demise of Jerreke and the publication of the book were not likely to be connected, though Sir Hereward did notice that the pages were often bound out of order, or the folios were incorrect, and that there was a general carelessness with numbers.

Together, these might be symptomatic of the somewhat unusual end of Jerreke, a city-state which had defaulted on its debts so enormously that its entire population had to be sold into slavery.

The finger-licking was required by the book's long, dark hibernation inside a chest up in the attic of the tower. A thoroughly damp finger was a necessary aid to the separation of the sadly gummed-together pages.

Sir Hereward sighed as he turned another page. His enthusiasm for reading had diminished in the turning of several hundred pages, with its concomitant several hundred finger-lickings, for he had found only two entries worth reading: one on how to cheat at a board game that had changed its name but was still widely played in the known world; and another on the multiplicity of uses of the root spice cabizend, some surprising number of which fell into Hereward's professional area of expertise as an artillerist and maker of incendiaries.

In fact, Hereward was about to give up and bellow to the housekeeper who kept the tower to bring him some ale, when the title of the next commonplace caught his eye. It was called "On the Propitiation of Sorcerous Puppets."

As Sir Hereward's constant companion, comrade-in-arms, and onetime nanny was a sorcerous puppet known as Mister Fitz, this was very much of interest to the injured knight. He eagerly read on, and though the piece was short and referred solely to the more usual kind of sorcerous puppet—one made to sing, dance, and entertain—he did learn something new.

According to Doctor Professor Laxelender Prouzin, the author of this particular, far-from-commonplace entry, all sorcerous puppets shared a common birthday, much in the manner of the priests of a number of particularly jealous godlets, who allowed no individuality among their chosen servants (some of them even going as far as the Xarwashian god of bookkeeping and warehouses, who not only refused his servants individual birthdays but referred to them all by the same name).

Sir Hereward quickly calculated this shared birthday of the puppets, transposing the Tramontic calendar that had been used in Jerreke with the more modern Adjusted Celestial, and discovered that it would occur in a matter of days, depending on whether it was currently the first or the second day of what the Adjusted Celestial calendar prosaically called "Second Month" and the Tramontics had termed "Expialomon."

As Sir Hereward had been laid up for a week already, and had no urgent matters to attend to, he had rather lost track of the date.

"Sister Gobbe!" called out Sir Hereward. "Sister Gobbe!"

Sister Gobbe was the priestess-housekeeper who looked after the tower and its guests as a representative of the Cloister of Narhalet-Narhalit. Colloquially known as Nar-Nar, it was a gentle and kindly deity whose slow but healing powers had aided tens of thousands of petitioners over the last several millennia. This particular tower was one of the more remote bastions of Nar-Nar's presence upon the earth, and likely to be abandoned in the not too distant future. Hence it was staffed only by Sister Gobbe and an as yet unseen novice Sir Hereward believed might be called "Sisterling Lallit"—a name he had overheard being hissed by Sister Gobbe outside his door the previous evening. There was also a guard, a small but broad-shouldered fellow with a very large ax, who doubtless could call upon Nar-Nar's rather less well-known powers to open wounds that hadn't even happened yet, rather than heal ones that had.

Fortunately for all concerned, Narhalet-Narhalit was far from a proscribed entity, but a welcome extrusion into the world, so the god and its followers were not an item of business for Sir Hereward and Mister Fitz. Consequently, their discovery of the tower en route from Tar's End to Bazynghame had been a welcome opportunity for the lame and hobbling knight to rest up and let the bones in his foot knit faster than they would anywhere else.

Mister Fitz had also taken their forced rest as an opportunity to engage in some activity that he said had hitherto been impracticable on their travels, though Sir Hereward was not entirely sure what that meant. The sorcerous puppet was up to something. He had taken to exploring the sea caves that ate into the cliffs near the tower, and he returned each evening covered in a layer of what looked like salt, suggesting immersion in the ocean and subsequent drying. This was odd in a creature who usually avoided complete submersion, being made of papier-mâché and carved timber, albeit sorcerously altered, but Sir Hereward had not made enquiry. He knew that Mister Fitz would tell him of his activities in due course, if there was any need for Sir Hereward to know.

"Sir?"

It was not Sister Gobbe who appeared in the doorway, red-faced and puffing as she always was from the tightly spiraling stair, but a considerably younger and far more attractive attendant, who might have wafted her way upstairs on a beam of sunlight, for she was neither out of breath, nor was her habit or broad-brimmed hat in any disarray.

"I am Sisterling Lallit," said the vision. "Sister Gobbe has had to go into the village, to speak to Boll about the veal to go with the crayfish sauce for Your Honor's dinner. Is there anything you need?"

Sir Hereward continued to stare and failed to answer. It had been some months since he had even the slightest conversation with a beautiful woman, and he was both surprised and sadly out of practice. But as she continued to stand in the door, with her head down and her face shadowed by her hat, he recovered himself.

"My companion, Mister Fitz," he began. "The puppet, you know . . ."

"Yes, sir," said Sisterling Lallit. "A most wondrous puppet, and so wise."

"Yes . . . just so," said Sir Hereward. He wondered what Mister Fitz had been talking about with Sisterling Lallit, but pressed on. "It is his birthday on the fourth of Second Month—"

"Tomorrow!" exclaimed Lallit, proving Sir Hereward had been even more careless about the passage of time than he'd thought. She raised her hands and inadvertently looked up, to show Hereward a face of great charm and liveliness, though sadly marred by the lack of the old and faded facial scars he had been brought up to regard as necessary to true beauty. "You should have said! It will be a doing to manage a feast—"

"Mister Fitz does not eat, so a feast is superfluous," said Sir Hereward, with a dismissive wave of his hand. "However, I wish to give him a present. Given that we are leagues from any shop or merchant, and in any case, I cannot for the moment leave my bed . . . I wondered if there might be something suitable in the tower that I might purchase for Mister Fitz."

"Something suitable?" asked Lallit. She tugged her earlobe and frowned, a gesture Sir Hereward found irresistible. "I don't know . . ."

"Come and sit by me," said Sir Hereward. He slid over and patted the mattress by his side. "To begin with, you can tell me what is in the attic above. Most particularly, a musical instrument would meet the need."

Doctor Professor Laxelender Prouzin had written that musical instruments were the usual gift to an entertainer puppet, and Sir Hereward supposed that one might be of interest to Mister Fitz, who was quite capable of appearing to be an entertainer puppet. He could sing most sweetly and seemingly play any musical

instrument, and dance fascinatingly as well. But Mister Fitz was
not an entertainer puppet, and usually only deployed these talents
as a ruse or deception, shortly before unleashing his other, even
more greatly developed skills as a practitioner of arcane arts that
were not generally the province of puppets. Or of people, for that
matter.

"Oh, I'm not allowed to come into your room, sir," exclaimed
Lallit. "Sister Gobbe is most strict about who may handle pa-
tients, and Mister Fitz told me of your vow, and I would not wish
to accidentally—"

"My vow?" asked Sir Hereward suspiciously. He thought for a
moment, then asked, "Ah, which one? I have . . . made several."

"To not share the breath of a woman, by intent or accident—
save a consecrated priestess of course—till you have finished your
pilgrimage to the Rood of Bazynghame," said Lallit innocently.
"Don't worry, I shall breathe ever so softly, and stay in the doorway."

"I am grateful," said Sir Hereward, though he felt quite the
opposite emotion.

"About this present for Mister Fitz . . ."

"Perhaps it is all too difficult," said Sir Hereward, whose affection for the puppet had encountered a sudden reverse. He turned
his head to the side and sighed heavily. "I shall simply wish him a
happy birthday and leave it at that."

"But there is an instrument in the attic," said Lallit. "In the
same chest your book came from, there is a mandora . . . or a
gallichon . . . of five strings, such as my uncle plays. Though it is
perhaps too large and heavy for Mister Fitz."

Sir Hereward thought of several occasions when Mister Fitz
had shown his true strength. He remembered those spindly
wooden puppet arms inside Mister Fitz's thin coat, the cuffs
sliding back as he lifted the Arch-Priest of Larruk-Agre above

his bulbous head and threw him into the mouth of the volcano; or the time when Fitz had beheaded a slave gladiator below the arena pits of Yarken. The look of surprise on the fellow's face had matched Sir Hereward's own expression, for Mister Fitz had been standing on the gladiator's head at the time, and had pulled the tip of the man's own blade back . . .

"I can fetch it down," said Lallit, interrupting his reminiscences. "Sister Gobbe would set a fair price, I'm sure."

"Very well," said Hereward. "A fine mandora might be the very thing. If it is not too much trouble, I would like to see it. When is Sister Gobbe returning?"

"Oh, I will fetch it for you now," said Lallit. "Sister Gobbe won't be back for hours yet."

"My thanks," said Sir Hereward. "But how will you hand it to me, if we must not share our breath?"

"Oh, I can hold my breath for ages," said Lallit innocently. She demonstrated, taking a deep breath that thrust out her chest. Sir Hereward watched in admiration, tempered by his annoyance at Mister Fitz. It was uncharacteristic of the puppet to preemptively meddle in Hereward's amorous affairs, and it galled no less to know it was almost certainly for a good reason.

Lallit held her breath for quite some time, before suddenly exhaling, turning her head so her breath went up the stairs. She smiled and followed it up to the attic. A minute later, Hereward heard her footsteps as she looked around, the oak-planked floor of the attic being the ceiling of his room.

The novice returned a few minutes later, carrying a stringed instrument that looked to Sir Hereward like an oversize lute. He could play the lute somewhat, and sing passably, as Mister Fitz graded his voice, but the knight had done neither for some years.

Lallit paused for an intake of breath and the resultant inflation of her habit at the door, then nimbly crossed the room, deposited the mandora on the end of Hereward's bed, and retreated as swiftly back to the stair.

Hereward leaned forward and took up the instrument. The mandora was made of ash with an open rose of ebony inlaid around the sound hole. It was still strung, which surprised him, for it had presumably been there for some lengthy time, and the strings were of a material other than gut, one that he could not immediately recognize.

He was about to pluck a note when he saw that the sound hole was obstructed, and that there was something inside the body of the mandora. Closer investigation revealed it to be a parchment folded into a triangle, which was sealed with wax at each corner. It could not be removed without de-stringing the instrument, which meant that it had been put there on purpose, and the mandora strung thereafter.

"Aha," said Sir Hereward. "A mystery within the mandora."

"What is it?" asked Lallit. The novice stood on tiptoe, craned her elegant neck, and took several steps closer.

"A parchment," said Sir Hereward. He held the mandora up to the nearer window, so the light fell more clearly through the sound hole. "Sealed three ways, and stuck to the body with a red tape and three further seals . . . I think perhaps this is a matter for . . ."

He had been going to say "Mister Fitz," for the sealed parchment smacked of sorcery, but as the true nature of the puppet was best not revealed even to the servants of friendly gods, he fell silent.

"Oh, it is exciting!" said Lallit. She clapped her hands together and took a further step toward him. "What is written on the parchment?"

Sir Hereward carefully rested the mandora across his knees, and thought. There was something not quite right about Lallit's enthusiasm, the parchment, and the mandora. He noticed that the instrument's strings were humming slightly, though he had not struck them. They appeared to be aping Lallit's enthusiasm, and Sir Hereward did not like this at all.

Nor on closer examination was he sure that it was the same Lallit who had returned from the attic. She looked a little taller, and thinner, and now that he studied her, he could see that her eyes were too far apart, and her hat was on backward.

"I shall have to remove the strings," said Sir Hereward. "To get the parchment out. I believe there is a spanner in my saddlebag . . . I shall just fetch it."

Sir Hereward's saddlebags were propped against the far wall, under the shuttered window on that side, as were his saber and two holstered wheel-lock pistols, though unfortunately these were neither primed nor loaded.

"Allow me," said Lallit.

Sir Hereward held up his hand as he swung his legs off the bed. "No, no, remember my vow."

He hopped over on his right foot, and caught hold of the shutter bolt.

"Might as well have a little more sunshine, while the weather holds," said Sir Hereward. He did not think that the thing that had assumed the shape of Lallit would be deterred by sunlight, given that the other window was already open, but more might help. He opened the shutter, knelt down by his saddlebag, and cast a smiling glance back over his shoulder.

The light from the second window had no visible effect upon his visitor, but it did allow him to see very clearly that the woman in the door was neither Lallit, nor actually a woman. It was some kind of other-dimensional entity that had assumed the shape of Lallit, and stolen her clothes. Hereward hoped Lallit was still alive in the attic, just as he hoped he would live through whatever was about to occur.

"It's very good of your god Narhalet-Narhalit to look after me so well," added Sir Hereward. He leaned into the window alcove, and looked out as if idly surveying the ground beneath. Saying the god's name might help bring its attention to this intruder in its temple. "Narhalet-Narhalit is good to look after my companion, Mister Fitz, as well."

He said "Mister Fitz" quite loudly, for the puppet's senses were extraordinarily sharp. If he was anywhere nearby, he would be alerted. But he was probably off in his sea cave, which meant Sir Hereward must manage on his own.

"The spanner," said Lallit. The thing was having trouble keeping its voice human. "The strings. The parchment."

"Ah yes," said Sir Hereward. He bent down to his saddlebag, and began to rummage through it, removing items as he went, as if to make it easier.

"Let me see. A dagger, needs a bit of sharpening . . . another dagger, this one's not too bad . . . where is that—"

He sensed a sudden movement behind him, and spun about on his good foot, the daggers in his hands. The thing was in front of him, losing its human form as it moved, its claws reaching for his arms. Hereward parried with the daggers, felt the shock of impact, and was borne back to the window and almost thrown out of it.

"You will get the parchment for me!" shrieked the thing. Flesh was melting off it, revealing the scaly, skeletal beast within, a creature not wholly present on the earth, for Hereward's daggers, ensorcelled as they were, were slowly sinking through its wrists, the scales reforming behind the passage of the steel.

"Never!" shouted Hereward, quickly followed by, "Mister Fitz! To me! Narhalet-Narhalit, aid me!"

"You will obey!" shrieked the beast, and bit at Hereward's

shoulder. He twisted away, but its teeth raked through his night-shirt and tore flesh. At the same time, his daggers lost all purchase on the creature's wrists. Instantly, it went for him again, and he only managed to avoid its grasp by suddenly slipping down the wall and sliding between the creature's legs. He was attempting to roll away when it latched on to his back, dragged him up, and threw him on the bed.

"Remove the strings and open the parchment," it instructed him. "Or you shall be hurt, and hurt again, until you obey!"

Hereward gaped. It was not in response to the creature's command, but an inadvertent reaction to the sudden arrival of a completely naked yet literally radiant Lallit. Surrounded by a nimbus of the violet hue favored by her god, she burst into the room and made a swatting motion in the air, as if crushing a mosquito.

A hole appeared in the creature's chest, followed by a geyser of greenish ichor that splashed the end of Sir Hereward's bed, the stained linen immediately beginning to send up small tendrils of evil-smelling smoke.

Despite what would be a mortal injury to a human, the beast was not distressed. It turned away from Sir Hereward and tensed to spring at Lallit.

Before it could do so, Hereward jumped up and smashed it on the head with *The Compendium of Commonplaces,* it being the only makeshift weapon close at hand. The huge, brass-and-leather-bound book boomed like a gong as it struck the monster, and most of the tome turned to ash in Hereward's hands, leaving him clutching a ragged folio of loosely bound pages, without any binding or brass accoutrements.

Hereward dropped the newly slim volume and dove for his saber. He drew it and spun about, ready to slash, but there was nothing there to hit. The creature had also turned to ash, had been picked up by a doubtlessly divine wind, and was being carried out the closest window, to be spread to the four corners of the earth.

The nimbus around Lallit faded, her knees buckled, and Hereward was just able to hop forward and catch her as she fell. However, he could not hold her weight with his injured foot, so both of them toppled back into the bed, just as Mister Fitz peered cautiously around the doorway, a sorcerous needle held in his cupped hand, its inhuman brilliance quickly dulled as he took in the situation.

But as the puppet replaced the needle inside his pointy hat, the small guard with the large ax leapt up the last step, his weapon held ready to use on anyone who violated the purity of the temple's novices.

"But I haven't . . ." protested Sir Hereward. He reluctantly released Lallit, and started patting out the incipient fire at the end of the bed. "We didn't . . ."

"What am I doing here?" asked Lallit wonderingly. She had the look of someone still waking from a dream. "I felt the god . . ."

"Narhalet-Narhalit has been here," confirmed Mister Fitz. He looked at the guard, his little blue-painted eyes sharp on his papier-mâché head. "This is the god's business, Jabek, however it may appear."

"Aye, I feel it so," said Jabek. He smiled, and added, "But I'll ask you to explain it to Sister Gobbe."

"Oh, the mandora is broken!" exclaimed Lallit. She picked up the instrument, whose neck was broken, and cradled it to her. "Sir Hereward wanted to give it to you for your birthday, Mister Fitz."

"A birthday present?" asked Mister Fitz. "For me?"

"According to the book I was reading, sorcerous puppets have a common birthday," said Sir Hereward. "The fourth day of the Second Month."

"But I am not a common puppet," said Mister Fitz. "Nor can it be said that I was born on any particular day, given my gradual ascent to full sentience over the course of my making. Besides, those other puppets have their birthday on the fifth day of the Second Month."

Hereward shrugged, grimacing as he felt a pang from the wound in his shoulder and a renewed ache in his foot.

"I appreciate the thought," said Mister Fitz. "Now, tell me. This broken mandora doubtless figures in the strange events that have just come to pass?"

"There is a triangle-folded thrice-sealed missive inside," said Hereward. "Which is strange enough, and stranger still when you consider yonder book, which until I hit that shade-walker, or whatever it was, was a much larger volume."

"I remember opening the chest to pick up the mandora, and nothing since," said Lallit. "Perhaps I may take your second blanket for a robe, Sir Hereward?"

"Pray do not cloak your beauty on my account . . ." began Sir Hereward, then, as Jabek of the Ax shifted noisily behind him, hastily added, "I mean, please do."

Mister Fitz crouched over the remnants of the book, flipping the pages with one of Sir Hereward's daggers. He then examined the mandora.

"It is simple enough," he said. "The book—which I am surprised you did not note is set in that type called Sorcery and thus highly suspect—is part of the revenge upon their creditors set in play by the sorcerer-merchants of Jerreke. Forced into slavery by their own economic ineptitude, they contrived to bind twinned otherworldly entities to their service. One would be constrained within a book or some such household item, the other in an instrument, or perhaps a game set. The items would be sent separately to the chosen target, in the hope that this would enable them to bypass any sorcerous protections. When both were in proximity, the bonds would release the entities, who would slay everyone within reach."

"But only one entity came forth," said Sir Hereward. "And it didn't try to kill me, at least not at first. It wanted me to open the parchment that was inside the mandora."

"The sorcerer-merchants of Jerreke were famous as inept merchants and ineffective sorcerers," sniffed Mister Fitz. "In this case, the spell was set off long ago, but due to the botched execution, only one entity was released. Realizing its twin was still entrapped within the mandora, it had to wait inside the chest for the opportunity to make someone else release its companion. Neither Sister Gobbe, who initially brought you the book, nor Lallit, both being in the eye of her god, would be suitable persons to release the twin, so it came down to you. However, by breaking the item that had once held it in bond—the book, or rather the outer pages bound around these remains—you immediately banished it."

"But the twin is still trapped inside the mandora?" asked Sir Hereward.

"Indeed," said Mister Fitz. "And as, of course, it is a listed entity, albeit a minor one . . ."

"Yes," said Sir Hereward. "Lallit, Jabek, if you would excuse us for a few minutes?"

"Certainly, Sir Hereward," said Jabek. He turned and left at once. Hereward helped Lallit to stand, holding her perhaps a little closer than was necessary. She looked him in the eye as she stood up, and smiled.

"I am sorry about your vow, Sir Hereward," she said. Her breath was very sweet, and the blanket very loose upon her body. "I have a vow also, as do all the novices of Narhalet-Narhalit . . . that until we are consecrated, we shall not . . ."

"I know," said Sir Hereward, with a glance at Mister Fitz. "I mean, I know now. Best you be going, Lallit."

"If it were not for the god's presence, reminding me of what I will become, I might have forgotten that vow," whispered Lallit. Then she was gone, wafting past him.

Hereward sighed, hopped over to his saddlebag, and got out a silk armband, a brassard embroidered with sorcerous symbols that shone with their own light, though this was faint under the sun's bright shaft that came in through the northern window.

"Should I fix your shoulder first?" asked Mister Fitz, as he took his own brassard out from under his hat, and slid it up his arm.

"It's only a trifle. I think that Nar-Nar has already stopped it bleeding," said Sir Hereward. He gave a grunt of pain that lessened the effect of this statement, twitching his shoulder as he settled the brassard above his elbow. "I may well get another wound in the next few minutes, to keep you busy. Now, will you open the parchment and I shall strike it on the head with the mandora?"

"Yes," said Mister Fitz, his slim puppet fingers reaching in through the now-slack strings to pull out the sealed triangle. He held it ready, and looked at Sir Hereward. "But first . . ."

"I know, I know," grumbled Sir Hereward. "What's the thing's name? Or do I just say 'Summoned Antagonist'?"

Mister Fitz looked at the parchment for a long second. His painted eyes could see many more things than any human gaze, both in and beyond the ordinary world.

"Hypgrix the Second."

"Right."

Sir Hereward picked up his saber and set it ready on the bed, just in case, before holding the mandora high above the parchment. Then he spoke, the words coming as they always did, familiar and strong, the symbols on his and Mister Fitz's brassards growing brighter with every word.

"In the name of the Council of the Treaty for the Safety of the World, acting under the authority granted by the Three Empires, the Seven Kingdoms, the Palatine Regency, the Jessar Republic, and the Forty Lesser Realms, we declare ourselves agents of the Council. We identify the godlet manifested in this parchment of Jerreke, as Hypgrix the Second, a listed entity under the Treaty. Consequently, the said godlet and all those who assist it are deemed to be enemies of the World and the Council authorizes us to pursue any and all actions necessary to banish, repel, or exterminate the said godlet."

Mister Fitz broke the seals on the parchment of "godlet," and even as the creature within boiled up like smoke and began to coalesce into something resembling flesh, Sir Hereward brought the mandora down upon it. Both beast and instrument immediately turned to dust, Mister Fitz gestured, and the dust blew out the window and was gone.

Sir Hereward winced as he sat back down on the bed, and looked at Mister Fitz.

"Now, tell me," he said. "Why are you covered in salt?"

"Salt?" asked Mister Fitz. "It is not salt, but powdered bone and chalk. I have been digging in the tomb of some ancient, vasty creatures. It has been most interesting. Though not, it is clear, as exciting as your reading."

"Perhaps not," said Sir Hereward. He lay back on the bed, and pointed at a long wooden case that lay on the floor near his saddlebag. "If you can spare yourself from your digging, what say you to a game of kings and fools?"

Mister Fitz's pumpkin-size head slowly rotated on his ridiculously thin neck, and his blue eyes peered at Sir Hereward's face.

"So soon after your last defeat? You are transparent, Hereward, but I doubt you have found some real advantage. The better player always wins."

"We shall see," said Sir Hereward. "Please lay out the set, and if you would be so kind, call down for ale."

"Oh, and put this back in its place," said Sir Hereward, stripping the brassard from his arm. "I trust that I will not need it, at least until we reach Bazynghame?"

"Best keep it near," said Mister Fitz, as he picked up the game box. "There is the small matter of what I was digging for—and what I have found . . ."

MICHAEL MOORCOCK was born in London, England. At the age of sixteen, he became editor of *Tarzan Adventures,* and later, *Sexton Black Library.* But it was his editorship of *New Worlds* magazine, from May 1964 to March 1971, during which he fostered the "New Wave," perhaps the most important movement in the history of science fiction. Moorcock is best known, however, for his creation of the Multiverse and his influence on sword and sorcery (a subgenre he helped name, together with Fritz Leiber). His character, Elric of Melniboné, is one of the most influential fantasy antiheroes the genre has ever produced. Not only have the novels been in continuous print since the 1970s, but Elric has crossed over into comics, role-playing games, and rock and roll. Moorcock's influence on sword and sorcery fiction is colossal and no anthology of same could hope to be complete without him. He and his wife, Linda, currently divide their time between Texas, France, and California.

RED PEARLS

An Elric Story

Michael Moorcock

For George Mann and G. H. Teed

Over the Edge

The sun, rimmed in copper now and bloated as if with blood, settled upon the horizon, casting long black shadows across the strangely made ship, the *Silela Li*. On deck, two priestesses of Xiombarg, in their elaborate quilted habits and glinting bronze crowns, stood at the ship's rail, considering the view and listening to the distant hungry roar which greeted the coming of darkness with godlike glee. The women began to chant, performing their evening prayers, and it seemed to them that a great shadow in the form of a woman, the shape preferred by their deity, appeared in the sky overhead. As they completed their ritual, two men came up from the passenger quarters below. One was short, with a shock of startling red hair, a ruddy complexion, large blue eyes, and a wide, smiling mouth. He wore a thick padded jacket and deerskin britches tucked into soft boots. His tall companion was clad in black, silk and leather, hair the colour of milk, skin pale as the thinnest bleached linen. His long head with its tapering ears and slightly slanting brows was as remarkable as his sharp, glittering ruby-coloured eyes. Like his companion, he was unarmed. The women, lowering their hands, completed their ceremonies and turned, surprised to see the men, who bowed politely. The priestesses acknowledged the two and passed down the companionway, returning to their cabin below decks. The men replaced the women at the rail of the *Silela Li*. The disc of the sun was halfway below the water now, its light cutting a red road across the sea.

The tall man was well known in the North and West. He was Elric, sometimes called Kinslayer, former emperor of Melniboné, until lately the dominant power in the world; the short man was Moonglum of Elwher in the so-called unmapp'd East. They had been travelling companions for some time and had shared several adventures. Most recently, they had come from Nassea-Tikri, where they had found two more people who had complicated reasons for joining them but this evening had elected to stay below.

Moonglum grinned after the disappearing priestesses. "Xiombarg's worshippers seem a little more comely in this part of the world. I'm beginning to regret that decision I made in the tavern."

A faint smile from his friend. "I'm too closely bound to Xiombarg's fellow Chaos Lord to wish any further entanglement with the Dukes and Duchesses of Entropy. And, if my knowledge of their beliefs is correct, I think you'll find those two aren't interested in sharing themselves with anyone but their patron and each other."

"Ah." Moonglum regarded the empty companionway with disappointment. "Elric, my friend, sometimes I wish you would not share your knowledge so freely with me."

"I assure you, I'm sharing very little." The albino dropped his gaze to inspect the lapping waters below.

Now the sun was almost gone, but the distant roar was somewhat louder, as if in triumph. And then the sun went down, leaving the ship in a grey-gold twilight. A strong wind blew suddenly, filling the ship's enormous blue sails, and the oarsmen below rested their long oars. Unusually, they took the oars fully into the body of the ship. The two men heard the sound of wood banging against wood, of metal being drawn against metal as the rowlocks were firmly shut.

At this, both men reluctantly left the deck and descended the companionway to where their cabins were located. In the gangway they met the captain's first officer, Ghatan, who saluted politely. "Make sure all's watertight within your cabins, masters. We'll be going over a couple of hours after moonrise. A bell will be sounded in the morning, when it's safe to unbatten."

"If we still live," Moonglum muttered cheerfully.

The mate grinned back at him. "Indeed! Good night, masters. With luck you'll wake in the World Above."

Wishing them both good night, Elric entered his quarters. From overhead came a series of heavy thumps and the sound of rattling chains as the ship was tightened against the water.

His cabin was filled with a deep orange light emanating from a lantern hanging from the centre of the low ceiling. It showed a seated woman frowning over a small scroll. She looked up and smiled as the albino entered. Extremely beautiful, she was the black-haired Princess Nauhaduar of Uyt, who, these days, called herself simply Nauha. Her large, dark eyes reflected the light. Her lips were slightly parted in an intelligent smile. "So we have passed the point of no return, my lord."

"It seems so." Elric began to strip off his shirt, moving towards their wide bunk piled with quilts and furs. "Perhaps we'd do well to sleep now, before the real noise begins. Too late for you to consider returning to Uyt."

She shrugged, replacing the scroll in its tubular case. "Never would I wish to miss this experience, my lord. After all, until you convinced me otherwise I shared the common view of our world as dish-shaped. I believed all other descriptions to be mere fool's tales."

"Aye. It's as well so few believe the truth, for the reality would surely confuse them." He spoke a little abstractedly, his mind on other matters.

"I am," she said, "still confused."

"The actuality will be demonstrated anon." He was naked now, slim and muscular in all his strange, pale beauty. He picked up a pitcher and poured water into a bowl, washing languidly.

She, too, began to prepare for bed. Since she had thrown in her fate with Elric's, the ennui to which she had become reconciled had disappeared. She felt it could never return now. Elric's dreams rarely gave him a full night's sleep, but even if the albino were to abandon her, she would never regret knowing him or, as she suspected, loving him. Kinslayer and traitor he might be, it had never mattered to her what he was or what she risked. Dark and light were inextricably combined in this strange half-human creature whose ancestors had ruled the world before her own race emerged from the mud of creation, whose terrible sword, now rolled in rough cloth and skin and stowed in the lower locker, seemed possessed of its own dark intelligence. She knew she should be afraid of it, as of him, and part of her reexperienced the horror she had already witnessed once, there in the forests of mysterious Soom, but the rest of her was drawn by curiosity to know more about the sword's properties and the moody prince who carried it. He had warned her what kind of creature he was, yet she had insisted she come with him, leaving her own father and twin sister in Nassea-Tikri to accompany him, even though she abandoned all that was familiar and dear to her. Lying beside that hard, wonderful pale and vibrant body which already slept, she listened intently to the sounds of the ship and the sea. Timbers creaked and the thunder from the horizon grew louder. She sensed the galleon's speed increasing, evidently borne on a rapid current. She had some notion of what to expect but longed to wake and question the albino. He continued to sleep, murmuring a little yet apparently at peace, and she could not rouse him. But was his apparent lack of concern feigned?

Faintly, from above, a deep-voiced bell sounded. The albino shivered, as if in response, still unwaking. The ship reared, rolling her against his body, reared once more, sending a vibrant shock through her. The *Silela Li* rocked, shuddered, her timbers moaning and straining as her hull dipped one way and then another, rolling from side to side so wildly that Nauha was forced to wrap her arms around her lover to steady herself. Elric moved as if to resist her, then woke for a moment. "Are we over?"

"Not yet."

He closed his crimson eyes again. For a while they slept. Perhaps for hours, she could not tell.

Nauha awoke to a sense of the ship's speed increasing. "Elric?"

She gasped as they were tossed cruelly about as if in a vast maelstrom. "Elric!"

Still he made no response. She wondered if he had died or lay in an enchantment, while, from the locker below, came a deep complaint from her lover's sentient blade. The noise of the water grew into a deafening roar, drowning the grumblings of the black sword as the ship was borne at a steeper and steeper angle of descent:

Towards the edge of the world.

Strangers at Sea

Earlier, when Elric had told her where he was going and assured her he would leave her at the port from which she could return home, Nauha had asked him levelly if he were tired of her. "No," he had said. "But I would not wish to put you at peril."

She had no intention of parting from him. She had always wondered at the rumours concerning the doomed prince of ruins. Now she had the chance to discover at least a little of the truth. Moved as much by curiosity as by attraction to him, she gave herself up to the adventure as readily as she had given herself up to his urgent, alien body. Now she was ready to risk her life and her sanity, as she had been warned she must, to discover whatever lay beyond the edge of the world. The albino sorcerer had told her of the dangers, from which few voyagers ever returned. He had spoken quietly of all they might face. And then she had replied to him.

"While I care for life, my lord, I care not for life without risk or excitement." She had laughed at his serious expression. Did she regret her decision now?

Still the ship gathered speed, trembling urgently from side to side. Every timber protesting, it dipped at an even steeper angle, rocking horribly, threatening to throw Nauha from the bunk. Again she clung to the albino. He murmured, "Cymoril," and held her in those white arms with gentle strength. How could one so apparently sickly own such power? She moved against him. This was not the first time he had cried out the name of his betrothed, slain, albeit accidentally, by his own hand. In his sleep, he steadied her.

The ship bucked again. Now, suddenly, there was the sensation of falling, falling as the ship plunged over the edge, falling forever, it seemed, until with a massive crash, which made her feel every bone in her was smashed, the *Silela Li* struck an unyielding mass.

Nauha bit her lip. They had hit a reef. There could be no other explanation. The ship was breaking apart. The *Silela Li* moved rhythmically up and down as if in the grip of a monster. Nauha could no longer silence the long, full-throated scream which burst from her body. Certain that they were destroyed and were rapidly sinking, she reconciled herself for death, but Elric's arms tightened a little more and, when she opened her eyes, she could see through the gloom that he was amused. Was this how he accepted their fate? Why was she reassured?

Then the water became strangely quiet. Were they sinking? The ship gentled into an easy forward motion. Elric closed his eyes. A faint smile touched his lips, as if he'd read her thoughts. Overhead she heard men's urgent voices, full of relief, calling orders and responses. Suddenly Elric swung out of the bunk and began to unscrew the covers over the cabin's only porthole, letting in silver light which made his body almost invisible to her. Cool, sweet air crept through the ship. Did she hear a seabird?

"Where are we?" Then she secretly cursed herself for her inanity. He did not answer but moved away from the porthole, becoming a shadow. Eventually he spoke. His voice was soft, his tone almost formally polite.

"We're where you did not expect to be. On the underside of the world. Which the people who dwell here call the World Above. I'm not greatly experienced in this, but I think we had an easy transition. There are still several hours to dawn. Best sleep some more." He touched her face, perhaps making a small spell, and she obeyed.

Later, dozing, she heard a tap at the cabin door and Moonglum called from the other side. Elric rose to answer, letting her cover herself before opening the door to the redheaded Elwherite, who stood there grinning, his arm around Cita Tine. She was pretty, with steady, daring eyes and a firm mouth. Moonglum had met her in the Steel Womb the night before they embarked. Cita Tine was short and sturdy, with a dancer's figure and muscles. She had black hair and eyes, a dark skin typical of her people. She seemed most relieved of all. No doubt she too had expected to die as the ship fell. Now she breathed in the sweet, cool air blowing through the ship and she cocked her head merrily, hearing the oars being unshipped and thrust into choppy water. There came a snap as the wind took a sail. From somewhere came the smell of frying meat. Overhead a dozen voices called at once. Everyone aboard had an air of astonishment, of disbelief that they survived. Even Nauha's moody lover was apparently more light-headed than usual as he made his excuses and called for warm water.

When they had bathed and dressed, Elric and Nauha joined the others in the big public gallery where passengers and ship's officers took their meals. Besides the two priestesses and Elric's party, there were six more passengers of the merchant class, more than a little shaken by their recent experience, exchanging excited descriptions of their night. Only one other was not evidently a merchant, for he sat a little apart from the rest, wrapped up in a dark red sea-cloak, as if against a cold only he experienced. Saturnine, incommunicative, he showed only a passing interest in his fellow passengers. Like most of the others, he was bound for fabled Hizss. The previous night, he had eaten quickly and retired. Moonglum had glanced at him once or twice, but Elric's interest in mortals and their affairs was casual at best. He ignored the passenger as thoroughly as he did the rest, giving his attention only to Moonglum, who had a trick of amusing him, and to Princess Nauha, for whom he had an unusual regard.

"And so here we are!" Moonglum munched on his bread, looking out of the nearest porthole at the calm sea. "I owe you an apology, Prince Elric, for I did not wholly believe your assertions of another world beneath our own. But now it is demonstrated! Our plane is not flat but egg-shaped. And here we are alive to prove it! While I do not understand by what supernatural agency the ocean remains upon the surface of the egg, I have to accept that it does . . ."

A deep-throated laugh from one of the merchants. "And do your folk believe, as some of mine do, that there are other eggs, scattered across the ether, of all sizes, some of which resemble our own, Master Melnibonéan? With people dwelling on them, of commensurate dimensions, perhaps existing within other eggs, those eggs contained within still more eggs and so on?"

"Or perhaps," smiled another, "you do not believe any of our worlds to be egg-shaped, and think they are instead round, like the nuts of the omerhav tree?"

Elric shrugged, sipping his own yellow breakfast wine and refusing to be drawn into their conversation. As usual, Moonglum was more gregarious and curious. "So some philosophers are convinced, I understand, amongst the intellectuals of my own country. Yet none has yet explained how the waters remain spread upon the surface of these worlds, nor indeed how ships sail on them or how we are able to stand upon the decks and not float like pollen into the air."

The saturnine man raised his head, suddenly alert, but when neither Moonglum nor Elric elaborated, returned his attention to his food.

Cita Tine, the tavern girl, giggled. "My people have known of the sea passage between the two worlds for centuries. Our young men come to seek their fortunes here. We grew wealthy as a result of that knowledge and learned to build ships like this one, able to withstand the massive pressures on their hulls, and so we came to negotiate the passage."

The captain, seated at the far end of the table, put a caution-
ary finger to his lips. "Best say no more, girl, or our secrets become common property. We're rich only while most folk believe
this side of the world to be legend."

"But my companion here has been this way before," declared
Moonglum. "Which is why I was ready to take the risk of it. And
swear that oath of silence, of course, before we set sail."

"I was not aware, sir . . ." The captain raised an enquiring
eyebrow at Elric. But the albino did not respond, merely dropping his gaze to look at his own pale hand gripping his wine cup.
"What proposed your first visit, sir, if I might ask?" The captain
made cheerful, casual conversation. "Trade? Curiosity?"

For the sake of his companions, Elric made some effort. "I
have relatives here."

He had, he thought, been unusually loquacious and egalitar-
ian. The captain did not pursue his theme.

Later, as they took the fine air on deck, staring out over what
seemed an infinity of rolling blue white-tipped water, Princess
Nauha said to him: "I shall be curious to meet these relations.
I had no idea Melnibonéans lived elsewhere than the Dragon
Isle."

"They are relatives," he told her, "but they are not of Melniboné and never were. Nor wished to be."

The ship sailed smoothly on, through unchanging weather,
across that undisturbed ocean, beneath strange stars, and Elric,
in the days that followed, grew increasingly taciturn. Even his
friends, save Nauha, took to avoiding him.

On the fifth day of wide water, the focs'l lookout vigorously
cried, "Land! Land ho!" bringing all the passengers but the
saturnine merchant up on deck to follow the pointing hand
to where a long shoreline was visible through light mist, soon
more clearly revealing a series of deep, sandy beaches on which

white waves broke. Behind the beaches rose dark green foliage, a dense forest, but no sign of settlements of any kind.

Moonglum speculated that possibly these woods were an extension of that jungle which they had lately left, wrapping itself across the world, but this was ignored, so he fell silent as the ship changed course to follow the new coast as she had followed the other.

"Shug Banatt," replied one of the merchants when Moonglum asked what their first port of call would be. "A grim city where the captain has business. We should be there within a day. If of course the pirate slavers spare us."

Moonglum had heard no previous talk of pirates or slavers. "Eh?"

The merchant was pleased with his affect. "They watch for ships coming in from the edge and prey on them. Some vessels are here by accident and make perfect victims. Because we anticipate attack, they are therefore unlikely to attack us."

"Why do the folk of your home port say nothing of this?"

The merchant shrugged and grinned. "We can't drive off trade, Sir Moonglum, can we? The captain's share comes from the fees we charge passengers like yourself. But fear not. We watch for them and are prepared. We carry comparatively little cargo, mostly goods the slavers have no use for, while our money's only of use to merchants like ourselves. They place no value on minted silver. Some say they find it unlucky."

For the rest of the day, the ship held a steady course, following the coast. There was little wind but the water was calm, giving good purchase to their oars, allowing the rowers, all freemen, to keep steady time. Moonglum and his lady friend went below, as usual, while Elric and the princess remained on deck. She was grateful for the sweetness of the air, asking if he smelled the forest.

Elric smiled at this. "I have my own theory. This second world has fewer inhabitants. Therefore they expel less foul air . . ." He was not entirely serious. She left his side and went to stand on the foredeck, raising her head against the breeze, letting it lift her dark hair and sending it streaming behind her.

The albino stared landward, his thoughts in his past when, on a dreamquest, he had first found this world and a city and a people which welcomed him. Would he be welcomed again? he wondered. He could not recall whether he had originally come to this world in his past or his future. He stared at his bone-white hand. But his skin offered no clue to his age, then or now. He sighed, glad to be alone.

A great yell from above. Still on the foredeck, Princess Nauha echoed the lookout's voice from the crow's nest. Swiftly, over the horizon came a great, grey square sail. Two more. A fourth. But Elric's interest was claimed by a lower, darker hull in the water, the other ships following it in rough formation. The hull had no sails, no oars, yet it slipped through the waves like a killer whale, a triangular shape rising from its slender deck like a dorsal fin. The long, sharp prow, crimson as blood, split the light waves, and several men stood leaning forward as it sped towards them. Never had Elric seen a ship move so quickly, darting like a fish.

"What kind of ship is that, captain? She moves like a living thing."

The captain kept his eyes on the ships, answering from the corner of his mouth, his body tense as he readied himself to give orders. "First they had the dragons, two centuries or more ago, who raided with them and made them invulnerable. Then the dragons slowly disappeared and these strange, supernatural vessels replaced them. Now there is only one left, but so great is their power and so impregnable their White Fort, deep in that forest, that we cannot ever hope to resist them. We can only negotiate and pray they find it wasteful of their lives to fight us."

Archers were already running to their positions around Elric. Others pulled canvas from the oiled wood of catapults. The stink of Chaos Fire filled his nostrils as braziers were lit. Black smoke gusted. From below, Moonglum, his twin swords sheathed on his hips, came running up the companionway. He carried something large and thoroughly wrapped in his hands and threw it towards Elric, glad to be rid of it. Elric caught it easily, stripping away the cloth and leather wrapping to reveal a heavy scabbard, a hilt with a pulsing dark jewel embedded in it. He attached the long sword to his belt. The sword moaned for a moment, perhaps anticipating a bloodletting, and then was silent.

"Pirates with a supernatural ship?" Moonglum murmured. "Will they attack, my lord?"

"Perhaps." Elric glanced to where the princess, tying back her hair, approached. "My lady. You had best arm yourself." She had her own blades below.

"They'll fight?" she asked, turning to follow his suggestion.

"Best be ready for the worst." He indicated the crew. "Just as they are."

She went below and reappeared with slender sword and poignard.

A kind of gasp from the strange leading ship.

Followed by a loud hissing.

A cloud rose from around the central greyish dorsal. Clad in armour the colour of amber, pirate warriors crowded forward. Their long features, slightly slanted eyes peered out of their helmets. Moonglum gave a grunt of surprise.

"Melnibonéans!"

Elric said nothing but his left hand tightened on Stormbringer's hilt.

The ship, still moving towards them without evident propulsion, was clearly visible to them now. With its high triple prow, its long, sleek decks and elaborately carved rails, it had only seemed smaller than the surrounding ships because it sat so low in the water. One tall man stood on the massive upper deck, his armour more intricate than the rest. His features declared his race, but the ship and armour, even the look of his weapons, had little in common with familiar Melnibonéan artefacts.

Slowly, the red hull hove to. The tall captain called out from his poop-deck. "Who are you and where are you bound?" Another great hissing sigh came from the oddly shaped dorsal, ribbed and faintly rosy with reflected light, in the middle-deck. "Quickly now!"

"We're the *Silela Li* bound for Hizss, Selwing Aftra, and ports beyond," replied the captain. "Carrying trade goods and passengers from the World Below."

But the strange ship's captain barely acknowledged him, staring straight at Elric and frowning. Elric stared back with equal hauteur.

Then, to Moonglum's astonishment, the pirate captain spoke in High Melnibonéan, addressing the albino. Moonglum understood enough to recognise a different accent.

"You have come from Below? Where do you journey?"

Elric did not reply directly. "You must answer me first. Do you mean this ship harm?"

The amber-armoured captain shook his head slowly. "Not if you mean to sail on." But he remained curious. He switched to Common Tongue, addressing the captain of the *Silela Li*. "We're no threat to you or your ship. You're bound for Apho and Selwing Aftra?"

"We are, my lord. And Shugg Banat before that. Then Hizss, where we shall take on provisions, make repairs, and give our men some rest before going on to the Snow Islands and sampling the warm water via the Silver Coast, then home again, with our gods' will."

"And stop at no other ports between Shugg Banat and Hizss?"

"We do not."

"Then go in peace." The pirate frowned, placing slender hands on his railing. He seemed strangely unsettled about his decision.

Moonglum was staring at the tall, pale triangle in the centre of the ship. Under his breath, he said: "I'll swear that's flesh . . . Those are scales. Some reptile. A harnessed monster." Then the ship was backing, clouded air still hissing, obscuring the dorsal, giving out a not-unpleasant stink.

There was a dreadful, heavy stillness in the air, as if an attack might yet still come. All that could be heard was a creaking of timbers, the heavy slap of fabric in the wind, the sound of water lapping against oars. Moonglum thought he could just hear the sound of breathing.

"They believe our side to be the netherworld," said the first mate, keeping his lips from moving too much. "But I believe that this place is Hell and we have just met one of Hell's aristocrats."

Elric and the pirate captain continued to stare at each other in fixed fascination until the two ships were far apart. Then, without comment, Elric returned to his cabin, leaving his companions on the upper deck.

"My lord has more relations here than he previously owned," observed the princess dryly. "Has he spoken of that captain to you, Master Moonglum?"

Moonglum shook his head slowly.

"Is that why he is here?" she wondered.

"I think not." Moonglum watched the archers unstringing

their bows and replacing them, together with long quivers of arrows, in their oiled wooden cases.

Then, unbuckling his swords, he followed his friend below.

Ancestral Memories

Moonglum had not expected to find such subtle beauty in the port of Hizss. Until now, the ports on this side of the world had been somewhat gloomy, massive fortifications as if they had once fought long battles. But not Hizss. Her pastel terraces formed slender ziggurats over which poured all manner of flowers. On her terraces lounged brightly dressed, brown-skinned citizens, lazing in the warm, easy air, cupping their hands to call down into her streets to vendors and messengers or merchants on their way to inspect the broad-beamed galleon's cargo and greet her traders. Artefacts which were common on his side of the world, the captain had warned them, might be highly valuable to people on this side, and so, should he be offered something for, say, his belt buckle, he should be prepared to spend some time bartering. The tavern girl, Cita Tine, had brought a whole sack of goods she planned to trade. To his chagrin, Moonglum understood that it was not wholly out of blind passion that she had decided to accompany him to the World Below (or, as the locals preferred, Above). Indeed, almost as soon as they had berthed, Cita had raced down the gangplank to the quay, telling him she would see him back at the ship around suppertime. The last he glimpsed of her was, sack over her shoulder, her pushing through a crowd of men and women and entering a narrow side street between two warehouses. Clearly, she knew exactly where she wanted to go. Moonglum rather resented the fact that she had not thought to include him in her confidence. Once again, they were running out of money. Elric disdained such considerations, but they needed treasure, not close encounters with pirates. Moonglum watched the group of merchants as they made for a couple of dockside inns, saw the priestesses met by two of their own in a canvas-covered carriage, and the saturnine trader sign for a rickshaw to take him up the hill into the city's centre. Then Moonglum glanced at Elric and followed his friend's gaze down to the quay.

Separated from the others, hanging back somewhat in the shadows, stood a tall woman. She was dressed in several shades of green silk, a wide-brimmed green hat hiding the upper part of her face. A small slave boy held a long-handled parasol to protect her from the noonday heat and she rested one slender hand on his shoulder. That hand attracted the Eastlander's attention most. There was a familiar pallor to it. He knew at once that, like his friend, the woman was an albino; and, when she turned to avoid a lumbering merchant anxious to reach the ship ahead of his fellows, the Eastlander's observation was confirmed. Her face was as white as Elric's, her eyes protected by a mask of fine gauze through which, no doubt, she could see, but through which the sun's rays could not entirely penetrate. She had the same languid insouciance in her manner. She could be the albino's sister. Was this Elric's motive for being here? Was Moonglum the only one risking the voyage from simple curiosity? He sighed and began to wonder about the quality of the local wine.

But when Elric, guiding his princess towards the gangplank, indicated that he would be glad of Moonglum's presence, the little Elwherite hitched his two swords about his waist and went with them, glad, after a moment, to feel solid land beneath his feet, even if he had some slight difficulty in standing upright.

"Another of your Melnibonéan relatives," murmured Nauha, as they approached the green-clad woman. "Is she blind?"

"I don't think so. And she is not Melnibonéan."

The princess frowned, looking up into his face in the hope of learning something more from his expression. "Then—what—?"

Elric might have shrugged, even smiled, as he said: "She's Phoorn."

"Phoorn?"

"At any rate more Phoorn than I am."

"But what is Phoorn?"

For the first time since she had known him, the albino seemed ill at ease. "Oh, we are closely related. But I'm not sure. I don't . . ." Now he recalled that this was not the kind of thing his people discussed too frequently, and probably never with humans.

"You don't remember . . ." She was sceptical.

"I remember her. She might not know me."

He had told her enough about the nature of his dreamquests for her to understand at least the gist of what he said. He might have met this particular woman before or after that moment. She might not even be the same woman Elric remembered. Dreamquests usually took place in his plane's past or in utterly alien periods of time; but in the other worlds, where his quests had taken him as a youth, lying on the dream-couches of Melniboné, time became more flexible, more chaotic even. Drawing closer, however, it was obvious that this woman knew Elric. She looked up expectantly as he approached. And began to smile.

"Lady—Fernrath?" To Nauha's surprise, his voice was again a little hesitant. But the woman smiled and held her hand to be touched in that odd way Melnibonéans used for greeting. "Prince Elric," she said. Her voice was unlike Elric's, somewhat sibilant and strangely accented, as if she used an unfamiliar language.

Pushing back his long white hair, he offered her a short bow. "At your service, my lady." He introduced the others. Princess Nauha was a little overenthusiastic in her response while Moonglum's bow was swaggering and deep.

"You knew we were coming?" asked the albino, while her slave struck at the oncoming crowd with his rolled parasol. She led the little party to where a carriage, drawn by two lively but unhappy striped horses, waited for her at the top of the quay.

She answered: "How could I have known? I always meet such ships."

He helped first Fernrath, then Nauha into the carriage. Moonglum, comparing his traveller's cloak to the fine linen and silk, chose to join the driver on his seat. This clearly gave the driver no particular pleasure.

"You used your magic, perhaps?" he answered Lady Fernrath, challenging her apparent innocence.

She smiled back, but was silent on the subject. "Such a crowd today. Ships from your world are so rare." She lifted an elegant cane and tapped the driver on the shoulder.

The narrow streets, crowded with merchants' stalls, led away into less busy thoroughfares, becoming roads, which eventually passed between slender pines and cypresses, giving glimpses of the port below and the glittering sea beyond.

"Your city is lovely," said Princess Nauha, by way of small talk.

"Oh, it is not *mine*!" Lady Fernrath laughed. "In fact I have very little communication with it at all. But I suppose it is prettier than most hereabouts."

Thereafter they travelled mostly in silence, the visitors occasionally remarking on aspects of the city or the bay, which Lady Fernrath, as if remembering her manners, acknowledged gracefully enough. At last, they followed a white wall to tall twin pillars. Between the pillars were great bronze gates inscribed in a language they could not read but which resembled Melnibonéan. At a cry from the driver, the gates opened and they entered a long drive, which took them to the steps of a low, rather simple house, built in marble and glittering quartz.

While a servant indicated the house's appointments, Lady Fernrath led them through high, cool rooms, sparsely decorated and furnished, to the far side of the house and a well-landscaped garden surrounded on three sides by a tall wall, offering a view directly ahead. The garden smelled sweetly of flowers and gorgeous shrubs. Summer insects flew from one to another. On the lawn, a low table and couches had been arranged, ready for a meal. The view was superb, looking out for miles over rolling, wooded hills, all the way to the indigo sea.

The architecture and design of the place was thoroughly unlike anything Moonglum remembered from Elric's Imrryr, the Dreaming City. The capital of Melniboné had been designed, through her ten thousand years of evolution, to impress with her aesthetic magnificence, her overwhelming power. In contrast, this house and its garden were meant to soothe and welcome and afford privacy.

Almost immediately, Lady Fernrath's servants, all of ordinary human appearance, emerged, taking their outer garments, showing them to guest rooms, helping them to bathe and put on slightly scented fresh, cool robes. Each guest was assigned at least one servant. Only Moonglum was not used to this and took considerable pleasure in the luxury.

Nauha remarked that the fountains and the walls felt to her, though she could not be sure why, like the work of a desert people. "You must think me naïve!"

Lady Fernrath bowed her head, denying this. "I believe they were from some desert place, yes." She spoke vaguely.

It was not long, as they took wine prior to dinner, before Moonglum raised the question of the pirates and in particular their king. He laughed. "He did not make his business clear, though at first we thought he might attack and prepared for the worst."

"You were wise to do so, Master Moonglum. Your instincts did not betray you. Oh, it's clear enough, I would guess, what Addric Heed does for a living." She laughed, perhaps bitterly. "He is a pirate and a slaver. A tradesman! A creature born to the highest blood of all—of *all*—reducing himself to such filthy work!" Her mood changed as she glared into the middle distance. Dark green-gold stars flickered in the depths of her pale eyes. "A thief; corrupt as any human you'll find here. A betrayer and destroyer of his own kin! A *slaver*! A *tradesman*!" She spoke as a woman obsessed. "And his crew is worse. Why even that remaining ship of his is an act of cruel betrayal . . ."

She lifted her long head like an angry beast. Her robes seemed independently agitated. She broke off, remembering her manners. "He is— he has—" She drew a long, slow breath. "It's said he has pacts with the Lords of the Balance. Yet why they would trust him or use him I have no idea!" Her voice took on a light, dismissive tone. She clapped her hands and ordered another decanter of wine. "Here's one from our own vineyards I hope you'll find palatable."

Moonglum would have asked more about Addric Heed if he could, but no further opportunity came. Then a little later, their hostess saw him yawn discretely behind his hand. "You'll be my guests here, I hope, while you stay in Hizss? I should have mentioned it sooner how welcome you are at my house."

"You are kind, madam." Before either of the others could answer, Elric accepted for them all.

"I have my lady friend," Moonglum murmured, a little embarrassed.

"Then, of course, she must be sent for, too. It is so rare for me to receive guests at the best of times. And such rare guests! From so far away. From the exotic World Below!" She gave the servants appropriate orders. They should go with the driver to the ship and bring all their things, as well as Moonglum's lady, back with them.

But when the servants returned with their luggage and Elric's light armour, it was to report that the wench had indeed been waiting on the ship for Moonglum, but she had chosen to remain on board ship. She sent a message to Moonglum, saying that she was happier there and likely to remain so.

On hearing this, Moonglum flushed and turned away for a moment. Then, bowing to Lady Fernrath, he said that while he appreciated her invitation he felt he should return to the ship and see to the well-being of his friend.

"I understand," said Lady Fernrath. "I do hope she finds our air more agreeable in the morning."

The sun was setting now and Moonglum thought he saw a hint of pale scales under her neck, but it was surely no more than a trick of the light. Somewhat subdued and doing all he could to hide his emotion, the Eastlander climbed into the carriage and left again for the ship he'd hoped not to see for another few days at least. That his wench should take to pouting now was not to be tolerated. He decided to give her a piece of his mind. And he could not be wholly certain she wouldn't try to steal something of local value from his luggage. He was in such poor temper that he almost forgot the swords he had left in his chamber above.

With Moonglum's absence, the Princess of Uyt felt a little removed from the company, though Lady Fernrath did all that should be expected to put her at her ease.

"And how fares my brother Sadric?" asked their hostess when they were settled on the couches again. "Has his temper or his attitude towards you improved, my lord?"

Elric shook his head briefly. "The Emperor died still voicing disappointment at my failings of moral courage." His voice held a trace of irony, but was without emotion. "The succession lay between myself and my cousin, you'll recall. How we behaved upon our respective dreamquests would determine who ascended the throne of the Dragon Empire. I believe I was chosen not from any sense of fitness but because I made fewer mistakes—in Sadric's eyes, at least!" Another faint, sardonic smile.

As the sun came closer to the horizon, the woman removed the gauze visor to reveal eyes of pale green-gold, but, when her milk-white hair fell from below her scarf, it was clear she was also an albino. She noticed Nauha's look of surprise and laughed. Nauha blurted: "Forgive me, my lady, I had not realised you were related. You are the Emperor Sadric's sister?"

"My sister married him," she answered softly, while Elric frowned at his lover's rather sudden interruption.

Lady Fernrath waved away any imagined rudeness but leaned towards the albino. "So, Elric, is Yyrkoon emperor now?"

"I killed him. My father named me his successor but Yyrkoon was uneasy with the decision. And he disapproved of my betrothal."

"Your betrothed was not high-born?"

"She was his sister. I killed her also."

"You loved her?"

"After a fashion." His expression became unreadable. "I am surprised you had not heard. Most of my world knows the story so well . . ."

"I had not understood you to be such close relatives." There was some relief in Nauha's voice.

"Aye," said Lady Fernrath, sipping with relish a glass of grey-green wine. "None closer. Blood relatives."

On hearing this, a mysterious expression passed across Princess Nauha's face but was quickly controlled. Elric, noticing this, seemed for a moment amused.

Then suddenly the princess felt as if a gate had shut against her. She followed them up onto the terrace to dine as the moon came out. The marble and alabaster took on a greenish tinge, touched with gold, and even Lady Fernrath's features offered a faint reflection of colour, but not, Princess Nauha noticed, Elric's.

As soon as Nauha was able, she blamed the change of environment for her tiredness. Then she, too, graciously begged their pardon, saying she was poor company and could see they had much to talk about on family matters. She did not add how the fact that they had increasingly dropped into High Melnibonéan speech as the evening grew older had decidedly helped give that impression.

All went according to the best protocol, but afterwards, in her room, the Uyt princess allowed herself one small growl of rage until her maid had gone and, weeping, she took hopelessly to her bed and lay upon it, staring at the oddly ornamented ceiling, trying to control her wounded feelings. She knew he would not even consider explaining himself when he joined her. She would be lucky, she thought, if she ever saw him again. This took her mind from her own anger and made her recall that she also feared for him.

Princess Nauha had studied the occult under Uyt's wisest scholars and knew a witch when she smelt one. She was very glad she had brought her swords with her and that they were with her armour in her luggage. She might at least save her own life, she thought, but she was not sure she would be needed to save the albino's. Did the fool understand he was in danger? Or—realisation came suddenly—was she the only visitor in danger here?

Was it coincidence that Elric had brought her with him to

Hizss? He had told her nothing of this relative—if relative was all she was—had told her of no plans to visit. Clearly, he had known she would be here. He had hinted at something only a short time before they reached the port. Had he some disgusting plan for the three of them? Or did the sorceress mean to bewitch them both? Or had Elric been bewitched since the moment he had decided to take ship for the edge of the world?

Nauha carefully inspected the room and the garden beyond for ways out of the grounds. Then she took out her armour and laid it upon the floor. Then she polished her sword and dagger, ensuring they would slip easily from their scabbards.

Then she lay down again. She controlled her breathing, forcing herself to think as coolly as she could. A little more relaxed, she next began to wonder if the wine had not been over-strong. There was nothing sinister about the night, after all. Indeed it was beautiful, as were the city and the house. Yet why had all the ports they had seen, she wondered, been so heavily fortified? But not this one?

She drew a long, deep breath. It was stupid to brood on all this, particularly now her swords were stowed close to hand. She was perfectly well prepared to take on any danger that might present itself. She was certain that clean steel could cope with any ordinary foreign witchery.

The Phoorn's Bargain

"I heard you had found the White Sword," Elric said to Lady Fernrath as soon as they were alone together.

She laughed easily, with genuine humour. "And that's why you are here?"

He saw no purpose in lying. "You have it? Oh, I see from your eyes that you do. Or know where it is, at least." He spoke with quiet humour. But he could feel intimations of what he feared, his energy slipping slowly away and little to replenish it, save Storm-bringer.

This time she made no reply. She lay back on her couch and stared up at the stars. Then, after a while, she said: "You have heard of the Eyes of Hemric, otherwise known as the Eyes of the Skaradin?"

"An even vaguer legend than that of the White Sword. Hem-ric? Skaradin? Some serpent from your world's hinterland?"

"I know where they can be found. I do not need to search for them, young prince. They are, however, the blade's price." She turned in the moonlight and looked at him, suddenly hungry for something. Her eyes had taken on a deeper, harder green, even her voice had changed timbre, was oddly accented. "Red pearls. But you need not win them for me, my lord. They are, however, the price of the blade." She moved restlessly on her couch. "Blood pearls, they call them . . . There are two. I desire them . . . I de-sire . . . Do you remember when we first met, Prince Elric?"

"I remember my dreamquest. I was scarcely more than a boy. My father sent me to seek you and bring back my mother's jade dagger."

"Oh, Elric, you were a comely lad when I saw you surrounded by three of those golden warriors from another plane entirely, who used to inhabit these parts. We drew so much more energy from those alien places. So much *material* . . . You had no famous sword at that time. I gave you the jade dagger . . ."

"You did not ask me then to pay you for it."

She smiled reminiscently. "Oh, you paid me. Did your father ever tell you why he wanted it?"

"Never. I think he sought it simply because it had belonged to my mother. But you saved my life."

"You were ever to my taste." Her mouth seemed to have widened now, revealing rather too many teeth. They were sharper, too, while her tongue—that tongue . . .

He roused himself. "So you will sell me the White Sword for those red pearls? Nothing else? You know what that sword means to me. It could free me from my dependency . . ."

"Just so. Nothing else. I possess the Sword of Law. And I know where to find the pearls."

"Lady Fernrath, I did not travel this far to bargain. What do you take me for? Like you, I despise merchants. Besides, I know nothing of this world. How could I begin to look for what you want?" Was there, he wondered, some way he could get to Stormbringer? He had come here following a legend, a memory, something he had heard of long before the Black Sword was his. He remembered one of his first dreamquests and the woman he had met here on the other side of the world, whom he remembered as a friend. Since then, Lady Fernrath had changed or, perhaps he had been naïve, too inexperienced to see her for what she was. Now his desire to be independent of Stormbringer could be further destroying his judgement. With that blade he had killed the only other creature he had ever truly loved. A wave of profound regret swept over him. He sighed, turning away from Fernrath. "My lady . . ."

She rose from the couch and, as she did so, she seemed to grow larger, her gown taking on greater substance. A heat—or it might have been an intense cold—came out of her, strong enough to burn him if he touched her. He remembered those nights. Those terrifying, fascinating nights, when she had introduced him to all the secrets of his ancestors—the real reason, he guessed, why his father had sent him upon his dreamquest. Or so she had told him. Now she said otherwise. He frowned. Why did she lie to him now? Or had she lied to him then? "Madam. I must go. I can't do what you desire of me."

That great, reptilian face glared down at him. "You are my sister's son. Your blood demands you help me! You come here seeking the White Sword when you already possess the Black. And you did not know there would be a price? Have you forgotten all loyalty to your own, Prince Elric?"

"I did not know what you would demand." He sounded feeble to his own ears.

She drew a strong breath and seemed to grow again.

Elric moved nervously on his couch, wishing he had his sword with him now. He was becoming alarmed. Somehow he needed to renew his energy. He had so few resources left. Lady Fernrath's skin was no longer white but had taken on a gold-green sheen, while her hair moved under its own volition. He feared her in a way he had not when he first came to Hizss, existing in two worlds at the same time, visiting as a courtesy, he thought, the sister of his mother, whom Sadric had loved to distraction. Elric had learned more than he had wished to know. Of his ancestry. Of the people called the Phoorn, who even now lived on in Melniboné, who had not been scattered as the others had been scattered, or killed as his cousins and his other relatives had almost all been killed, after he had brought the sea reavers to destroy Imrryr.

Then he had loved the Phoorn as he loved them still. They had made alliances when they first discovered this world, coming as exiles to found a civilisation which would be based on notions of justice until then unknown to most gods or mortals. They had, by some vast supernatural alchemy, interbred, though their offspring usually took one form or the other, not both. It was not always possible to predict what would emerge from a Phoorn egg or, indeed, a human womb. Yet, Lady Fernrath had told him of the shape-changers, those few who could be what they willed themselves to be and who had, for centuries, continued their race. He owed much to her. He was wrong to begin fearing her now.

"My lady, I would help you if I could, not because you would strike a bargain with me, but for the sake of our old alliances. I came here, after all, to ask a favour. And I would gladly do you a favour in return."

Her great Phoorn eyes softened. Her speech changed. She sounded affectionate again. "I should not have tried to bargain with you, Elric. But life here has changed a great deal since we last met. Though you never met them, I had a brother, a father, other kin. Over many centuries our world has grown corrupt. Wars were fought. You saw those fortified ports. Monstrous treacheries were conceived. Such appalling treachery . . ." Her tone became sad, reminiscent. "I need your help, Elric. There is something I have to do. One task before I die. A duty . . ." Perhaps she cast an enchantment on him, but he found himself sympathizing with her.

Yet he was still wary, still unsure. "No need to bargain with me, my lady. We have an ancient blood pact. I would help you without reward if I could. But could you not have found a warrior here to help you?"

"No. For none possesses what you own."

"You mean Stormbringer? I will fetch it from the ship. And my armour. I will tell Princess Nauha where I am going—"

"My servant has already brought both sword and armour. No need to disturb the Princess of Uyt."

A darkness was filling the sky as deep clouds sailed in from the south. The night grew colder and the albino shivered, fearing further for Nauha's safety.

"Nobody here will harm her," said the Phoorn. "But now I must venture into—take more substance—from—the—nether-world . . ." A noise like a whirlpool, running fast in high seas.

He had difficulty seeing her now. His mind was less clear than before. The table seemed to have disappeared. The house was a black shadow, unlit.

The sounds of the night had faded when her voice came again. He turned, peering into a void. Above him were two green-gold staring stars: passionless, cold. Her voice was still recognisable, yet hissed like waves on shingle:

"Are you ready to go with me, Elric?"

"You have my word."

Something fell at his feet then. He knew what it was and bent to pick it up. He buckled on his breastplate and greaves, settled his helmet on his head, attached the scabbard to his belt. When he straightened, scaled flesh, long and sinuous, stretched down out of the sky and he looked deeper into those green-gold eyes, knowing them for what and whose they were. At the base of her long, reptilian neck was a natural indentation in which a man might sit. It had not been long since, in the great Dragon Caves of his people, he had taken a carved Vilmirian saddle and placed it in just such an indentation. The Lady Fernrath, a shape-changer of a very specific kind, touched him affectionately with her long claw. While Elric had experienced her strange powers before, reliving the first coming together of their related races, he had never seen her change so rapidly. Nor, in all his adventures and his dreams, had he seen movement so rapid in any shape-changer from mammal to reptile, though the Phoorn were not true reptiles, any more than Melnibonéans were true humans. Both had come into being in other worlds under different gods and philosophies. Both had learned the virtues of the other. And then, at last, they had mated, though still in many ways alien one to the other. And these were the folk whom the Dragon Kings of Melniboné claimed as their ancestors. This was not the first time he had seen why in his world dragons were called "brother" or "sister" and treated with such complete respect, each conversing with the other, when they lived on altered time, so that it seemed to Melnibonéans that their dragons slept for years or decades.

There were no further traces of the human about the Lady Fernrath. She was completely Phoorn, speaking in the ancient language used between Phoorn and Melnibonéan. Completely Phoorn as she bent that beautiful serrated neck to let him mount, turning her head so that residues of fiery venom from her mouth-sacs fell bursting upon the tiled terrace and did not harm him.

As if suspicious of pursuit, the lady firedrake peered this way and that into the night, her great claws clattering on the terra cotta, her wings stretching, wide, wide as she prepared to lift into the darkness of the night, giving voice with wild, beautiful music to the Phoorn's ancient Song of Flight. Springing off the terrace, she began to gallop across the lawn, her sharp senses noting the obstacles as she approached that obsidian sea.

And then she was aloft.

And Elric, seated astride her gigantic, exquisite body, found himself flinging back his head, letting the cool air stream through his long white hair as he lifted his own voice to join in harmony with that complex melody, as natural to him and his kind as when the Phoorn and his own people first came to this sweet, glorious world and determined to take stewardship of it in the name of their ideals.

What had gone wrong between the time when he had enjoyed a long idyll with her and fallen in love in a new way? Then their faith in the Great Balance translated into so many practical notions of order and justice. Now? Now he had become used to lies, secrecies, political and other bargains. The whole world was a darker, more threatening place. If he had known how the changes in the World Below were mirrored in the World Above, he would not have had his friends come with him.

But all such thoughts were dissipating, for he rode a dragon again, bonding, as his genes remembered, with that monstrous, thumping heart, the deep, slow pulse, the beating of vast wings and the sweeping from side to side of that long, muscular tail. He relished the comfort of his heavy black armour but missed his great dragon spear, through which his thoughts were transmitted back and forth.

Now all he could tell was that he was heading west and inland. As dawn sunlight streaked the blue-black horizon, they flew over a forest, spired by great pines, towards a turreted fortress of gold-veined white marble, woven in a way to show both artistic elegance and sturdy practicality—and also, somehow, a faint sense of menace.

Fernrath dived into the depth of the forest, wings close together, claws extended, and neck hunched. She landed perfectly in a glade through which light had yet to penetrate. She allowed him to descend, then spoke to him in Phoorn. "Now we must roost until this afternoon when they begin their tournament. The targets have yet to be chosen and assembled in the castle grounds, within the central bailiwick." And, cocooning him in her folded wings, she perched on a massive lower branch of one of the tallest trees, and went to sleep.

A Question of Ancestry

That evening, when the sun was still high enough in the sky to burn a bright orange, and she told him of her plans, Prince Elric and Lady Fernrath made their way along a hard-beaten red earthen road towards the unsuspected magnificence of the White Fort, which rose like a fantastic cloud of clear-edged smoke from the sharp green of the almost impenetrable forest.

Reaching the six-foot-thick ironbound timber of the white-painted gates, she called out with such authority that the gates swung open at once, the huge iron bars rising on balancing machinery. They were recognised by their race and this gave them unquestioned admission.

The fort was formed as a series of large towers, one inside the other, to be defended to the death. Each tower had land, which could, if necessary, grow its own food. Elric realised it existed on the same principles as Imrryr, built to impress and to be impregnable at the same time. His people had used an island and an ocean for this. Addric Heed used a trackless forest.

She led him through one walled area after another, through towers and halls and finally up a flight of steps to a short gallery and out into the upper tiers of an amphitheatre, the stone seats arranged to look down onto a long oval green where targets had been arranged for an archery contest. Elric recognised this as something his own ancestors used to play. At Fernrath's signal, he sat down with her well above the occupied tiers. She began to tell him again what she planned and what he must do. From the archery green, drifting in on the light, late-morning air, came the distant screams of the targets, the heavy *thunk* of arrows into bodies, and the applause as an archer made a good score in one of the marked parts of the slave's upper body.

Sitting in a tall, carved chair was the slender pirate slaver Addric Heed, clad in light-yellow robes, an orange scarf swathing his head and shoulders. Surrounded by his captains, of his own kind as well as human, and by others, lightly armed or bearing no weapons at all, he was unmistakeably Elric's and Fernrath's kin. Elric recognized one of the men as the saturnine trader on the ship. Fernrath nodded when he murmured this information to her. "He raids up and down this coast, as he has done for two centuries. The slaves will be sold in Hizss, which depends upon the trade for her subsistence. Those traders inspect the stock here and know roughly what they'll bid when they return to Hizss. They keep their own bands of soldiers in Hizss. You know the place of which I told you?"

"Aye. On the far side and in the furthest tower."

"He'll expect no attack if I work my Phoorn sorcery, but you must hurry, Nephew, for it will be hard for me to keep so many engaged."

Then, as a lull came in the tournament, Lady Fernrath rose in her seat and called: "How goes the game, Brother?"

And saw Addric Heed's head come up in astonishment as he stopped halfway through a joke with his human visitors. He controlled his features, though a question still hovered in his eyes. "Sister! You should have warned me. I'll have rooms prepared! Your entourage is below?"

"Beyond the gates," she said. "I did not know if I'd be welcome." She swayed a little, the outline of her human shape flickering like a mirage, just enough for the onlookers to narrow their eyes, wondering at their own untrustworthy perceptions. A light mist seemed to escape from her mouth and nostrils.

Addric Heed frowned. "Are you well, Sister?"

"Oh, well enough, Brother. Well enough." A strange scent drifted upon the air. "Prince Elric and myself have been travelling through a night and a day to find you. He is here to recruit your help, as I understand it. I agreed to bring him to you."

Addric Heed relaxed a little now he had an explanation he could believe. She made a movement with her hands. Her watchers found it hard to take their attention off her. "Can you help me, Brother? Can you help me, Brother? Can you help our cousin?"

"Gladly, dear Sister." His words were quite as formal and without warmth, but there was no animosity in them. Elric guessed that both had grown used to keeping secrets, even from themselves. Evidently, Addric Heed had no notion of how disgusting his sister found his trade and why, for other reasons, she should hate him when she and her adopted city did so well from the wealth he brought in. Equally, who knew the resentments and greed her brother fostered in his own soul?

Elric hung back as if in discretion or embarrassment, for Addric Heed had forgotten his manners, his whole attention upon his sister. Elric nodded to his nearest kinfolk and typically ignored the humans, even the one he knew from the ship. He went to loll in a seat some distance away, as if to enjoy on his own the meeting of brother and sister. None offered him any attention.

All eyes but Elric's were now on the were-dragon as she continued to mesmerise them, her body swaying almost imperceptibly. After some minutes, he rose and slipped away. None noticed when he was no longer in his seat. He crossed an expanse of marble and, lifting a metal bar, stepped swiftly into the doorway she had told him to find.

Within the tower room, the only light came from what stood on a small table. This rosy radiance drew Elric to it immediately. He blinked, holding his hand before his eyes.

At first it seemed the room and its treasure were unguarded. No need for guards when the whole fort was occupied by one's own men, thought the albino, stepping towards a beautifully carved pedestal. He responded audibly to their beauty. They were just as she had described them on the road to the fort. This was Addric Heed's most valuable treasure indeed. With these in his possession, he controlled his ship, and with his unique ship, he dominated the seaways. Elric had seen many extraordinary gems in his life and his dreamquests, yet still he was astonished. The bloody light pulsed from two perfect crimson-coloured pearls of magnificent size, depth, and luster, each as large as his fist. Was Addric Heed so certain of his power that he could leave such remarkable gems where anyone might come upon them? The albino reached towards them. He had understood that more than men protected the red pearls.

As he moved to pluck them from the pedestal, there came a movement from the corner of the room. A sound. Something

chuckled. Then a voice dry as summer corn spoke. "Good afternoon, stranger. You are an optimist, I see. For all your appearance, no doubt you are another would-be thief who supposes my
master grows careless as he watches the competition. Well, Lord
Addric Heed might not give his treasure the attention it deserves,
but I value it if anything too much." The unseen guardian uttered a small, squeaking sound, like a mouse. "Oh, I do. I do. But
then it's easier for me, eh?" Squeak, squeak. "For you see I have
only one task to perform, after all. And I take much pleasure in
performing that task." Squeak. "While Addric Heed has many
things on his mind. Do you fear me yet, mortal?"

At this question, Elric laughed, knowing a sudden exhilaration as his hand flew to his left hip. He seized the hilt of his sword
and began slowly to slide it from its scabbard.

A responding chuckle from the darkness, almost good-
humoured and lazy. "My dear mortal, you had best hear who I
am before you waste your time drawing a weapon. You still have
time to open that door and leave. Who knows? Perhaps Lord Addric Heed will not notice your visit and you can escape with your
life. See? I give you time to turn and just possibly reach the door
before I catch you." Another squeak was followed by a series of
little wet ticking noises, as if from tiny rodent lips.

Elric sighed. He continued to unscabbard his great black
battle blade, standing his ground, peering into the roseate darkness in the hope of seeing his antagonist. "You are a very assured
guard," he said.

"I would perhaps be more modest had I not caught and punished every thief who ever sought to steal those beautiful pearls.
They are living things, you know, the Eyes of Hemric. I have
guarded them for the past hundred and fifty years, ever since my
master, Lord Addric Heed, brought me up from Hell for the purpose and placed them in my safekeeping."

Then something large began to rise from the flagstone floor to hover over the crimson pearls. The gems glittered and winked in their own light and Elric had the uncanny sense that they watched him. In that, at least, they certainly resembled eyes. The albino permitted himself a shudder as he continued to draw his sword. What was it that guarded the Eyes of Hemric so confidently?

Then Stormbringer was free at last of the scabbard and writhing like a living thing in its master's two hands and howling with a profound and horrible hunger. And then Elric let his laughter roar from his throat as all the old lust for death filled him.

Overhead, two black wings spread with a brittle, whispering sound and fluttered up towards the tower room's roof. Squeak. A kind of invitation.

"Coward," said Elric. "Do you know who I am now? Do you fear for your life? For your soul, if you have one? Come down and engage me if you dare, for it would give me pleasure. I look forward to the novelty. I have never fought one of your race before."

From above, there came a further series of squeaks and smackings. "No mortal has ever fought an Asquinux and succeeded in defeating one." The flying thing opened huge blue eyes, glaring into Elric's face. "You are dead," it said. "I have your life now, for I know your secret. You have failed to restore Law to your dissipating world."

"No doubt you are confusing me with another, Sir Monster, for when I die it will not be in the cause of Law, but in my own cause, or that of Chaos." With casual familiarity, Elric swung the howling blade this way and that. Its black radiance met the red and flowed into it, throbbing. "But all that will depend on my luck and the Duke of Hell I serve. For my patron is Arioch of Chaos, one of Entropy's great generals."

"That hero died in another world. He has no power here."

There was puzzlement in the half-seen creature's blue eyes. It's black, flat muzzle twitched. Then it opened a scarlet mouth, glittering with luminous teeth, each sharp as a dagger. Languidly, it licked its oddly shaped lips with a long blue tongue.

"I know not by what crude sorcery your master brought you out of the Far Hell and kept you here, but I warn you, petty demon, to avoid me if you can. I am Elric and the sword I hold was forged in the flames of the burning damned to serve Chaos as I serve Duke Arioch. This blade is called Stormbringer and is quite as hungry as you are. I am very hungry, too."

The demon squeaked again. Each time the sound grew less audible yet somehow more ominous. It flapped up towards the roof again and hung there for a moment, its dark blue frowning eyes regarding Elric's own glittering red orbs. It shifted its gaze from Elric's eyes to the pearls it guarded and it made a small, puzzled sound. Again it opened its mouth and licked its teeth with its blue tongue, one by one, as if counting them. Then, with a high, whistling sound, its long white fangs clashing, its eyes glaring, the thing dropped upon him. Elric whirled, trying to engage the Asquinux face-to-face, but it would not let him. Its slender claws dug through his armoured back, making it impossible for him to stab with any precision.

Eyes blazing with battle hunger, Elric lifted his head and howled.

"Arioch! Arioch! Aid me!"

Roaring the name of his patron, Elric swung the blade back over his left shoulder and there was a crack as it connected with the demon's bones.

The Asquinux shouted suddenly, shockingly, red mouth widening, the noise filling the tower. One claw came free. A swinging cut over his head and Elric's blade bit into the monster's knotted flesh. There came a terrible shrieking sound as the demon dragged those claws from the metal protecting Elric's shoulder. It flapped back into the shadows. Its white mouth was panting now and it turned its head, lapping its own foaming wounds, its blood dripping like rain.

"You are more powerful than I, it is true," said the demon in a quiet, deadly voice. "But I must try to kill you or break my compact with Addric Heed, in which case I should perish all the more painfully. Soon his army will come and you will perish on the points of a thousand swords."

With evident reluctance, the demon flapped down, attempting again to get purchase with its claws in Elric's body. This time, however, Elric understood its intent and ducked, throwing up Stormbringer so that the demon fell back, yelling curses in its own tongue. Then Elric leapt forwards, stabbing, and the thing flapped further up the tower, trying to work its way around so that it could make another attack on the albino's back, clearly its only manoeuvre. So Elric deliberately turned his back until he heard the demon begin to drop down, then whirled, swinging the great blade with all its wild momentum and striking the demon in its hip, which cracked and made the Asquinux scream and keep screaming. A flood of ichor gushed from its wound as it wheeled, its wings smacking at the crimson air.

Again Elric ducked and threw himself to one side, dodging the attack. The thing's fluids splashed on the floor, narrowly missing the albino. He leapt this time, stabbing. The blade slipped through flesh and met bone. Now a foul stench began to fill the tower room, and black blood boiled as the demon gave its sudden attention to the two great pearls, its claws reaching for them desperately.

"You'll not save them from me, little monster!"

Elric swung Stormbringer again. The sword wailed with pleasure as its hunger began to be satiated. Elric felt the dark, supernatural energy flowing into him. He shuddered, for the stuff made every nerve tense, every muscle threaten to cramp. Savagely, he swung at one of the grasping claws and sliced it off.

The claw began to inch by its own volition towards the pulsing red pearls. The demon shouted and its teeth clashed in fury. Elric grinned and swept the claw into a corner. Then he stabbed once more.

The Asquinux whimpered, understanding its defeat as Stormbringer purred to itself, like a satisfied cat, feasting. The albino drew a deep, shuddering breath. Now the wounded Asquinux flapped about in the air just above the pearls, still struggling to fulfill the duty of its compact, knowing that the penalty of failure was worse than death. Something like a plea for mercy filled those huge blue eyes. But Elric was never merciful. The notion was alien to him and his kind.

Elric chopped off the demon's other grasping claw. Raging, it span in the air overhead, its teeth clashing, the ichor spraying. "You are a poor wretch of a guardian," he said, "but you are doubtless all that Addric Heed could afford."

And when the creature turned its blue, despairing eyes upon him, the long teeth shuddering and clashing in its mouth, the red tongue flicking up and down, it said: "My weird said I could never be slain by a living mortal. But I did not know I could be killed by a dead man, nor by one as powerful as the thing dwelling in your blade." The last of its energy throbbed out of it, pulsing through the sword, which took its due and passed the rest of the foul stuff on to its wielder. "Which is the master? You or the blade?"

The wounds from the demon's claws had burned into him and though he now had extra energy, he was losing blood. He stumbled to the table and picked up first one heavy pearl and then another, slipping them into his shirt beneath his breastplate and tightening the laces with one hand.

It was as well that Stormbringer remained unsheathed. Next moment, the door had burst open and there stood the saturnine man from the ship with about a dozen of his fellow slave-traders. All of them were fully armed with a miscellaneous collection of weapons. They had not expected to find Elric standing, let alone observe him delivering a death blow to the still-writhing body of the guardian Asquinux.

If the doorway had not been so narrow, they would have backed off, but that was not easily done. Warily, they edged towards the albino, beginning to form a half-circle, closing in on him. He smiled at them as if in welcome, holding Stormbringer almost lazily. He was breathing heavily from his exertions but otherwise the creature's own tainted energy still sustained him. He was vaguely aware of the blood running down inside his armour from his wounded back.

"I am glad to see you gentlemen." The albino offered them a brief bow. "I cannot tell you how famished I have been."

With rather less confidence than they had shown on first entering, their boots slipping in the demon's dark, stinking blood, they began to close in.

Elric was laughing easily now, enjoying their dismay. He mocked them, feinting with his growling, insatiable blade. The men's eyes narrowed as they pressed in. Then the albino reached out, almost elegantly, and took the head off the nearest soldier. They backed away, pushing one another aside in their panic. All they wanted to do now was escape, but Elric moved quickly so that he was between them and the dying demon. He reached behind him and drew the door as shut as possible. The severed head had rolled into the aperture and stopped the door from closing completely. From outside, a single bar of light entered the tower room. He feinted again, moving like a herdsman gathering his flock. Then, when the men were grouped together in the light,

he swung the great, moaning broadsword so that its blade sliced
into one, cutting him so deeply in the torso that half his body fell
backwards while the other half fell forwards.

Elric yelled with battle joy as the slaver's energy filled him. He
struck again and two arms flopped in the mess made by the demon's dying. He stabbed, drawing that man's life-force deep into
himself, and then, when only the saturnine slave-trader was left,
he took his sword and slipped it delicately into the man's chest so
that instantly the pumping heart sent energy into the sword and
from Stormbringer into Elric's own glowing body. His white skin
blazed like silver and his red eyes glared in triumph. He lifted his
head, surrounded by its halo of milk-white hair, and laughed—a
sound which filled the tower with anguished triumph and which
keened and echoed through all the countless worlds of the multiverse.

When Elric had drawn a quick breath, he stepped through the
door and saw the amphitheatre filled with startled faces. Addric
Heed and his slavers stared up at him in baffled astonishment and
Lady Fernrath ran like the wind towards him, shouting, "The
slave quarters! Follow me!"

"The slave quarters? Would you free the slaves?"

"That, too, if we can. It might buy us time."

Then, while Addric Heed and his baffled warriors began to
absorb what had happened, the two albinos dashed down the
outer steps of the tower. Panting, she led Elric into the bowels of
the White Fort. She had armed herself with a massive, beautifully
balanced battle-axe, which she handled with considerable expertise. Together they cut down any who sought to stop them while
Stormbringer sang its bloodthirsty song.

Then, at last, they stood in long corridors stinking of human
waste and putrifying flesh. There, shackled in every available
space, were the choice men, women, and children whom Addric

Heed had taken from all the cities and ships of the coast to be sold at the slave markets of Hizss in the coming days. These were the healthiest. The rest had failed to survive. Some corpses still hung in their shackles beside the living. Some slaves raised their heads, hopelessly curious. They were reconciled to their future.

Lady Fernrath did not listen to their questions or answer their hope. She was headed for a large marble enclosure at the far end of the corridor, whose bars were set further apart and were four times the thickness of any others. She dropped the axe, her eyes fixed on that great cage. But, while she ran on, Elric spared time to strike through chains wherever he could and release as many slaves as possible, especially the men. He anticipated rapid pursuit from Addric Heed and his slavers and wanted as many people fighting for their own interests as possible.

By the time he reached her, she had drawn back heavy bolts from the gigantic cage. Within, its empty sockets staring into space, its wings crumpled and awkwardly set, its claws clipped and bound with brass, sat a frail old Phoorn seemingly on the point of death.

Lady Fernrath approached the creature and placed gentle hands upon it, stroking its grey-white leathery scales and crooning to it in the ancient language of her people.

"Father, it is I, your daughter Fernrath. Here to free you."

"Oh, child, you know I cannot be free. I cannot see to be gone from here. I cannot fly. Your brother will always keep me prisoner. There is no hope, daughter. You should not have risked Addric discovering the truth, of knowing what only we two know."

"It is different now, Father."

From the far end of the slave quarters, there came shouts and the noise of fighting. Clearly, now they were free, the slaves were not readily going to lose their liberty again. They understood that this was their last chance. This knowledge gave them the power to fight, even though few of them were professional soldiers. Clashing metal told Elric that some had already seized weapons. But he knew only a miracle would allow them to prevail for long against Addric Heed's trained warriors.

With a deep, not-unhappy sigh, Elric prepared to do battle with an army.

The Advantages of Supernatural Compacts

The old Phoorn was called Hemric and he was, of course, Lady Fernrath's father. "He has been here for over two centuries," she told the albino, "dying to serve my brother's despicable descent into trade."

"Your brother is a poor specimen of our race," said Elric in distaste. "And he has held his own father with human slaves?" Elric frowned. "Bad form at best, madam. If one would blind and imprison a relative, it should be with its own kind."

She was too hurried to answer. "Quickly, the pearls. Give me the pearls!"

He slipped them from his shirt, already half-guessing what she meant to do. Stroking her father's long snout, she persuaded the old Phoorn to lower his head, then, taking the glowing crimson pearls from Elric's hands, she placed them one by one carefully and delicately into the long-healed sockets where his eyes had been, all the time crooning a long, melodic spell. Elric watched, fascinated, as the flesh began to form around the orbs and suddenly the Phoorn blinked. He blinked again. He could see.

And then, as there came a shout from up ahead and the battling slaves, protecting their children, began to fall back before Addric Heed's well-armed warriors, the twin crimson pearls glowed and pulsed. Intelligence came into them and with intelligence came anger. The old Phoorn's venom had long since dried up, but the long, beautiful snout twitched and snorted as fury filled him.

A deep, distant boom rose from somewhere within the old Phoorn's huge chest. He lifted his head, and the quills—each the height of a tall man—rattled on his chest, while all along his tessellated tail the huge combs rose and stood proud. Even Elric found the transformation astonishing. The booming grew deeper and louder. He raised himself up on his muscular legs and blinked. From each eye now fell a drop of blood. The face, which regarded first his daughter and then Elric, was benign and profoundly sad, full of bitter wisdom. "With vision comes power," he said in Phoorn. And blinked again. This time it was a gigantic salt tear which fell.

Elric realised that the slaves had fallen back, were running past him, seeking the freedom of the forest. Addric Heed was there, riding astride a massive battle horse, blond and armoured. Behind him were massed more cavalry and fresh infantry. The slaves had, for the most part, dropped their weapons, taken up their children, and ran out into the light, only to stagger back in, pierced by the arrows of Addric Heed's waiting archers. "Like all others, save Hizss, this place was designed for warfare," she said, "no matter what the occasion." She watched as her father flexed wings long unused.

From directly above, came a thunderous excitement of yelling, terrified voices, a clashing of metal.

"Some fresh sorcery of Addric Heed's no doubt," she said. "It was through his magic that he first learned to make slaves of his ancestors and use them to build his power."

"Aye," agreed Hemric, seeking her out with his unfamiliar sight and looking down on her with a benign expression never seen any longer on the faces of his Melnibonéan kin. "We were unsuspecting. When he could not make us fly for him, he took out our eyes and made us swim. I would like to kill my son if I could."

"You shall, Father, when we find him," she promised. But it was a promise she would not keep.

Another roll of thunder. Did it come from the sky? Addric Heed lifted his handsome, arrogant head, surprised by it. He reined in his pale stallion, looking upwards, staring about him. Having no other plan, the slaves had returned to mass around Elric. They had reached a sudden impasse. Even with the black sword, the albino knew they could not defeat such numbers.

Elric considered a parlay with Addric Heed, but the power in him, which filled his mind, his body, and his soul, was not a compromising power; it did not apologise for itself, for it had no conscience. His unnatural empathy for humans had drawn him to the Young Kingdoms and beyond, to learn of their morality and humility, their curiosity, all that his people had lost, for he had realised instinctively that only with these qualities restored could his own folk survive.

Then Elric's cruel Melnibonéan pride had brought him home and achieved all he had desired to avert. He had assured the destruction of his people, the burning of their towers, and the end of a power they had taken for granted. The only power he had now was from Melniboné; his family's sorcery and its history, the pacts which it had, in its moments of crisis, been forced to make with Chaos, where once, long, long ago, it had leaned towards Law. His dreamquests into other planes, including his own family's past and present, had taught him all this; but he had learned only to a degree how to harness and control such power, to restore his vitality with the life-stuff of living, sentient things.

Addric's army advanced through the echoing galleries towards Elric, that panting, unthinking creature bearing a pulsing, moaning sword in which red runes writhed, who was the last emperor of a dying race, a ragged horde of slaves at his back, together with an albino woman and her enfeebled father. At the pirate chief's command, the archers began assembling before him. But then the thunder came again. This time Elric saw a messenger riding through the ranks to address Addric Heed. Fernrath's brother lifted his hand to halt his men, turning in his saddle to speak, but not all had heard and some continued to advance. Elric watched as the pirate slaver led his men back through the prison quarters and up into the main fortress. The stairways were wide enough to allow the cavalry to remain mounted through several of the upper galleries.

Soon the advancing soldiers began to realise they had been deserted. Some turned to follow. Others called out, warning that the fewer their numbers the worse their plight.

Wearily, the slaves bent again to pick up abandoned weapons.

This was an opportunity Elric had not anticipated and, trained strategist that he was, he at once shouted to the rabble army to follow, leading a charge that almost immediately broke Addric Heed's forces, sending them running behind their master, convinced they were already defeated.

The warriors were brave and experienced, but they were completely demoralised from the moment Elric struck them—a ghost from their own pasts—a whirlwind of black, vampiric death, its howling rune-blade an image of their own legends, its blazing crimson eyes haunting all their nightmares. And with their leader gone, and in the certain presence of their own Prince of Chaos, the demon lord Arioch, who was one of their shared pantheon, they had no stomach for fighting their kind. It took the Lady Fernrath to speak to Elric in the High Tongue of the Phoorn, reminding him of who and where he was, to urge him to lower his sword and look wonderingly around him at the piled corpses, the bodies of all those who had gone to feed himself and

Stormbringer. So many damned souls! And then the albino knew a kind of grief. But it was not for the dead slavers that he wept.

While Elric wept, there came another wave of amber-armoured soldiers. At first it seemed they had rallied, but they were in obvious disarray. Many had lost their weapons and, seeing that their comrades were captured, threw themselves on the mercy of their former booty, who promptly stripped them of their arms and put them in chains. For the moment, the air was free of arrows. Clearly, the archers had been called to another part of the fort to reinforce Addric Heed's army. But who could be attacking?

Suddenly Elric looked up to hear the constant rolling thunder moving first towards them, then away again, while the alabaster walls shook and shivered, and small showers of stone and plaster fell from ceilings and walls.

Leaving the others behind to guard the ancient Phoorn and to organise themselves and their prisoners, Elric and Lady Fernrath stalked warily to the nearest stair and began to climb. As they reached galleries with windows which looked out on other windowed galleries, they could see that all the way to the top of the great fort, a terrible fight had been taking place and dead soldiers in amber armour lay everywhere. The sound of thunder was beginning to subside. The sky was clearing and the sun turned clouds to pale gold. From above, Elric heard his name being called.

"Elric! My lord! We thought you dead!"

The albino stopped and looked up. At length, he saw through a smashed window in the gallery above a broad, redheaded face grinning down. The face was Moonglum's.

Slowly, the madness deserted Elric and in something close to joy he ran through the galleries until he found his friend. Princess Nauha stood with Moonglum and also Cita Tine, the tavern wench. All were armed with bloody swords and bore the familiar look of war-wolves who had fought a long, exhilarating fight. And then, as if Insensate Fate could not contain this level of coincidence but must burst and spread it across the multiverse, there appeared the nuns of Xiombarg, smug as nuns are who have pleased themselves by some deed of virtue, to report that all was settled as justice demanded.

"Our lady answered us and we reached an agreement," declared one as she straightened her unwieldy crown.

"Agreement?" Elric knew that the Gods of the Balance rarely made bargains not to their advantage.

Then Cita Tine was calling out. "Where? The slaves? Are they still in the pens?"

Elric shrugged. "Some are. Others set off through the forest." He was puzzled by her interest.

She sheathed her blades and peered down. Then she moved away in the direction from which Elric and the Lady Fernrath had come.

Elric turned enquiring eyes on his friend. Moonglum sighed and scratched his head. "That's why she came with us. Her plan all along was to sell valuables here and use the money to buy her husband back from the traders. He was taken a voyage ago."

Elric frowned. "So—?"

"Aye. She used me and now she's off to see if her spouse survived." Moonglum sighed. "Still, for a few weeks, I have to say, she was happy to have me as his substitute." He cast a hopeful eye upon one of the acolytes, who moved closer to her colleague. And he sighed again.

"So Xiombarg's the cause of all this destruction?" Elric wiped other men's life-stuff from his face.

"We fought hard and well, but we could not have succeeded without her ghastly help." Nauha stepped closer, "We certainly enjoyed a little sword work of our own." She noticed that blood was crusting on both her blades and, glancing around her, saw a useful cloak. Bending, she ripped the garment away from its former owner and began to wipe first one sword and then the other.

"Addric Heed?" asked Fernrath, looking about her at the devastation. "Does he live?"

"After a fashion," said the Princess of Uyt. "Knowing your relationship, I begged him spared. But I was almost too late. Xiombarg—"

"Where is he?"

Nauha frowned, thinking. "Two floors below and . . ." She shook her head. "Two to the left. His banners and his horse are there. He barely lives, however. Xiombarg was eating him."

Lady Fernrath was already running from the hall seeking the downward staircase and calling her father's and her brother's names.

"There has been a feasting here today." From curiosity, Elric followed her, the others coming in his wake. "Was this Xiombarg's only payment?" He indicated the mounded dead.

Nauha laughed. "I think not. I recruited the priestesses when it became clear the supernatural was involved. Moonglum and the girl came up from the town, ready to defend you, but Fernrath had already—already transformed herself. And carried you off."

"You knew where we went?" He moved down a staircase covered in corpses. "How so?"

"We were in time to see you leave. Cita Tine knew of the White Fort and how to get there."

"But you arrived so swiftly!"

"Xiombarg was enlisted for that, too. The priestesses summoned their goddess and she transported us here."

"Yet no sacrifice was made?"

"Oh, she feasted very well. And there was some trinket at

Fernrath's house, which Xiombarg valued. All she did, she did for that."

They came upon Fernrath then, amongst all the blood and dismembered bodies, amber-coloured armour discarded like the remains of shrimp sucked clean of their shells. She crouched on the marble floor, her shoulders shaking in grief. In her arms, she held something ragged and red. Elric saw that it was all that was left of a man. Addric Heed, proud pirate prince and dealer in slaves lay there, taking great gasps, his lifeblood bubbling from his chest. Little was left of his face. His legs and an arm were missing. One side of him looked as if it had been gnawed upon. Xiombarg had been interrupted in her feasting. He tried to speak, but failed.

Suddenly a bulky form appeared in the nearest window. It clung uncertainly to the sill, then flapped awkwardly into the gallery, its huge wings slapping and snapping in the sunlight, its bulk vast and white as it turned, its massive tail swinging, its long, pale neck stretched out and topped by a massive reptilian head from which blazed two eyes as brilliant and crimson as Elric's own. The so-called red pearls, now animated with a new life-force, gazed up into the pale gold clouds passing high above. The Eyes of Hemric had returned to the possession of he from whom Addric Heed had stolen them.

The old Phoorn's red eyes blazed for a moment and his long, wizened snout grunted as he made his way forwards on stiff legs. At last, he stood over the body of the son who had enslaved him and suddenly all the anger left him. His great, pale wings folded themselves around his son's remains and he lifted the dying thing in his foreclaws, a strange, soft keening coming from somewhere deep in his chest.

"I cannot," murmured Hemric. "I cannot." Then he moved towards the window, still carrying what was left of Addric Heed.

With considerable difficulty, he hopped again onto the sill and then he had flapped into the air, the long keening note rising as he flew low over the far forest, making a peace with himself and his kin which the onlookers honoured but could scarcely understand.

When Elric next looked at Fernrath, he saw that she wept silently, her eyes following her father, her head on one side, the better to hear that melancholy music. Then she turned, straightening herself. She saw Elric but walked away from him, to stare through one of the tall, broken windows at her disappearing father and what was left of her wretched brother.

When, after some moments, she looked back to glare at the albino, her eyes blazed green and the tongue, which flickered across her teeth, was not human. "He has paid a fair price for what he did. His blood and the blood of his followers shall feed the forest and soon nothing will be seen of the White Fort. It is all he deserves. But now I am the last of my kind, at least on this side of the world." She let out a deep, hissing breath.

"Anywhere," said Elric. "There are none of us who are fully Phoorn and non-Phoorn at once. None who bridge the history of both races. None, save your father."

She sighed. All the anger was gone from her. "And now we are both avenged."

Hemric, most ancient of the Phoorn race; father to both Lady Fernrath and the renegade Addric Heed, who had blinded him and forced him under water to drive the last of the slaver's ships, flew against the golden horizon, his voice still keening, deep-throated and full of the joy of flight, the anguish of death.

"Addric Heed was ever jealous of his father," murmured Lady Fernrath. "For years he and his fellow Dukes of the Blood plotted to enslave the true Phoorn who were not Halflings like me. And when the time came, and their eyes were stolen, I lacked the courage or the character to resist. I saw the great runes cast and the great sorcery made and then the Phoorn were robbed of their eyes and forced into servitude. First they were harnessed to the ships and made to fly just above the water, guided by sharp goads. As they grew old and too feeble for that task, Addric Heed determined how he might have ships built around them, using their wings to drive those vessels at enormous speeds, terrifying and mystifying all they claimed as prey. I could do nothing but help my brother. He swore that if I did not, then he would torture my father to death. Thus I acted between him and the slave merchants of Hizss."

"That is why Hizss is the only unfortified city along this coast," murmured Elric in clear understanding. "Hizss did not defend herself because Addric Heed never attacked there. Indeed, he preferred only to prey on ships and left the well-armed cities alone as his dragon allies died, one by one. But his own father!" He spoke almost in admiration. "This is treachery even I could not match . . ."

Her smile was tragic, her voice sardonic. "Few could," she said.

Elric watched the albino dragon as he returned, no longer bearing his son's remains. He saw Hemric twisting and turning high above them, then diving to sail across the tops of the trees, and for a moment he envied the creature, his own ancestor, who had existed for as long as the bright empire of Melniboné, who had seen its birth and lived to learn of its end.

He looked around. The two priestesses stood a few steps back behind Elric and the others. They watched the old Phoorn's flight in disbelieving wonder.

"We have to thank you, ladies, for your intervention," said Elric. "But might I ask what price your patron asked for her help?"

The acolytes of Xiombarg exchanged glances. "It was something not strictly our right to offer her," said one.

"But the needs of the moment seemed to dictate our agreement with her bargain." Nauha stepped forward, the better to watch the wheeling dragon. "She knew it was in your house, Lady Fernrath. I knew it was your property . . ."

"It was all she would accept in exchange." The other priestess seemed a little embarrassed. "That said, the Balance has been restored and Chaos brought to her rightful place in this plane's grand cosmology! That was the will of Xiombarg. For as you serve Duke Arioch, my lord Elric, so we serve his cousin, his rival and his ally."

"Ah," said Lady Fernrath in quick understanding. "But it was already promised, I think. By me."

"We had no choice."

"It was, I take it, a white sword." Suddenly weary, Fernrath glanced round her at all the destruction.

"Aye." Moonglum was surprised she had guessed so easily. "There was nothing else Xiombarg would accept and time was pressing."

They all seemed stunned by the next sound.

Even when Stormbringer was drawn and he was engaged upon his joyful work of destruction, Elric had never been heard to laugh in that particular way before.

TIM LEBBON was born in London and lived in Devon until the age of eight. His first short story was published in 1994 in the indie magazine *Psychotrope*, and his first novel, *Mesmer,* appeared three years later, in 1997. Since then he has published over thirty books, including 2009's *The Island* and *The Map of Moments* (with Christopher Golden). His dark fantasy novel, *Dusk,* which came out in 2007, won the August Derleth Award from the British Fantasy Society, and his novelization of the film *30 Days of Night* was a *New York Times* bestseller. His new novel, *Echo City Falls,* is due out in 2010. A full-time writer since 2006, he now lives in Goytre, Monmouthshire, with his wife and two children.

THE DEIFICATION OF DAL BAMORE

A Tale from Echo City

Tim Lebbon

Jan Ray Marcellan wished they could just nail the bastard to the Wall. She hated venturing beyond Marcellan Canton and into Course, where the people were rougher, less educated, poorer, harsher, and more likely to aim abuse at a Hanharan priestess. It was outside the norm, and even the complement of thirty Scarlet Blades could not make her feel completely safe. She thought the air smelled different out here, though of course that was a foolish notion. It was simply her discomfort getting the better of her.

But Dal Bamore had to be transported to Gaol Ten prior to his trial, even though his death sentence was a foregone conclusion. And she had chosen to accompany him.

She parted the curtains on the front of her carriage, looking between the driver's feet and the bobbing heads of the four tusked swine hauling it, and saw Dal Bamore staked naked on his rack. Six Scarlet Blades pulled the rack, Bamore's heels dragging across the cobbles and leaving bloody streaks, and now that they were outside the wall, the crowds were throwing rotten fruit and stones. The Blades raised their hoods and hunkered down, though few missiles struck them. Marcellan soldiers were greatly feared. Fruit exploded across the condemned man's body, stones struck with meaty or sharp impacts, and he barely moved his head.

Jan Ray smiled thinly. With everything they had done to Bamore to extract his confession, she'd be surprised if he opened his eyes even when they drove in the first nail. She dropped the curtains back into place and settled into her cushions, sucked on her slash pipe, and sighed.

A scream came from outside, and the thud of something hitting the ground. She froze, fingers touching the curtains again but not quite opening them.

The crowd, blood-hungry, frenzied, Blades on edge, and that's Bamore out there, Bamore, *one of the most dangerous—*

The curtain was tugged aside and Jave's face appeared. Her most trusted Blade captain. And he had fresh blood splashed across his cape.

"Wreckers. Stay here."

As Jave disappeared and more screams rose up, Jan Ray lay back and wished they'd finished Bamore down in the Dungeons.

She only ever visits the deep dungeons if it's something important. And right from the very beginning, she's suspected that they have never tortured anyone as important as Dal Bamore.

He has already been in his cell for three days by the time she goes down to question him. The chief torturer has been instructed to loosen his tongue, but not to risk his life. Anything he says must be taken down—there is a scribe beside the prisoner every moment of the day and night—but he must remain lucid and conscious for whenever the Marcellans decide to question him themselves.

Jan Ray is always eager for this sort of duty. It gets her away from the daily grind of running the city as part of the Council, and the way she spends most of her waking time as a Hanharan priestess is dictated by generations of tradition and protocol. She understands its importance, but sometimes it becomes tiresome.

Down here in the Dungeons, she can be herself, just for a while.

There are no screams as she approaches. No sighs or grunts, no pleas for mercy. She is almost concerned, but when she reaches the door and the Scarlet Blade on guard opens it for her, those concerns evaporate immediately.

Bamore is hanging upside down from the ceiling. He is streaked with blood and feces. Beneath him, there is a large bowl collecting all the fluids that leak from him. She can tell that it has already been emptied over him more than once. A thin gray man sits on a chair some distance away, an open book propped on his knees, a pen in his hand. The pages appear completely blank.

"Trivner," she says, and the fat man in the corner hauls himself upright. Rolls of flab sway beneath his loose robe.

"Priestess!" he says, bowing low. "An honor to see you down here with us lowlifes." She can hear the smile in his voice, but forgives him that. He's their head torturer, and it takes someone of particular skills and tendencies to perform the job competently. He has been employed down here for longer than she has been a priestess, over forty years. Some say he has never seen the sky.

"So tell me what he has to say."

"Nothing, Priestess," Trivner says.

Jan Ray raises her eyebrows in surprise. Bamore seems to be looking at her, but she cannot be sure. The light is poor down here, his eyes swollen almost shut.

"Nothing?" she asks, glancing at the thin scribe. He shakes his head.

"I started with air shards," Trivner says, and she knows what is coming. Many times she has heard his delighted recitation of the tortures he has performed. It's like listening to a poet's expression of love for the one thing in life he can never let go. "Into his knees and elbows, then both shins. The first I slipped only into the flesh, but the last selection I pushed through his bones. They'll never come out. Any movement is agony."

"Delightful," Jan Ray says. "Hurry with this, Trivner. And then perhaps I can get some answers from him where you've failed."

The torturer blusters for a moment, but then breathes deeply, calming himself. *Remember who you're talking to,* Jan Ray thinks. His voice becomes more businesslike.

"After the air shards, some more basic forms of persuasion. Fingernails extracted. Cuts filled with powdered swine-horn. Fire ants into every body opening." Trivner's confidence seems to falter, and the lilt drops from his voice. "No one ever gets past the fire ants."

"But still nothing," Jan Ray muses. Bamore turns slightly on the rope and it creaks, wet from his blood. He coughs and vomits something black.

"Leave me with him, both of you." Trivner goes to protest but she holds up one hand, eyes closed. He knows better than to argue with a priestess.

"I'll wait right outside," Trivner says, as if that will be a comfort.

"By Hanharan's will, he will tell me what I need to know," Jan Ray says. But as the fat torturer and the thin scribe leave the stinking chamber, she feels a slight shiver of something she does not quite understand.

Soon, she will know it as fear.

∙ ∙ ∙

Stay here, Jave had told her. Like talking to a child. He had been her most trusted captain for some years, and they had developed a rapport that bordered on friendship, though any hint of closeness between priestess and soldier was vehemently discouraged. But still she felt a tingle of anger at his brusqueness.

"He's concerned, you fool," she murmured, and the sounds from outside grew more startling. Shouted orders and screams of pain; panicked cries from the people who had been lining the street; the whip of arrows and impacts of cruel metal tips on stone, wood, and flesh. *They've come for him.* She shivered and leaned forward, pulling the curtain aside.

She had been involved in trouble like this several times before. Eighteen years ago, when Willem Marcellan was assassinated by a breakaway Watcher sect, she had been at his side in the carriage when the murderer climbed in and stabbed him to death. The killer had been moving across to her when a Blade's sword pinned him to the carriage floor and gutted him before her. More recently, she and several other Hanharan priests had been trapped in a blood-feud riot between two powerful families from Mino Mont Canton, a skirmish that had resulted in the Marcellan Wall running red with the blood of fourteen executions over the space of three moons. Brutal, shocking, but necessary. So she was no stranger to bloodshed and the shock of violence, and fear was tempered by her faith. The spirit of Hanharan, the originator of Echo City, would welcome her down into the One Echo should she die here today.

But her concern was not for herself.

If they take Bamore and hide him away . . .

That could not happen. He knew too much—he *was* too much—and the city was nowhere near ready for him and his kind. If Hanharan chose to smile upon her today, it would never need to be.

It took her a few moments to assess exactly what was happening. The Wreckers must have been waiting among the crowd and in some of the buildings they passed by, because the carriage and its escort appeared to be surrounded. Arrows arced in from several directions, and she could hear the vicious *thunk* of crossbows being fired. Three Blades were already down, writhing on the ground and flailing for the arrows or bolts piercing them. One of them screamed. *How unbecoming,* Jan Ray thought. It seemed not even Scarlet Blade training was perfect.

The four tusked swine were also down, their tough hides spiked with many arrows and bolts. Two of them still moved, kicking feebly, the network of ropes and timber supports tethering them to the carriage twisted and useless. The first thing the attackers had done was to make sure they couldn't move.

The crowd was panicking and trying to retreat from the scene, but others behind them pushed forward to see what was happening. The resultant crush denied them any hope of escape, and she saw very quickly that this ambush must be fought and won here. Gaol Ten was two miles away, but might as well have been twenty.

Buildings lined both sides of the street—taverns, a chocolate shop, a street café where several jugglers cowered in colorful terror among scattered tables and chairs. Some of the upper windows were open, and she saw movement here and there as Wreckers inside aimed and fired at the Blades pinned down in the street below. Over the rooftops to Jan Ray's right rose the looming mass of the Marcellan Wall, and she so wished she were back behind it now.

But Jave had acted quickly, and their position was far from hopeless. A dozen Blades surrounded Dal Bamore where he bled on his rack, their billowing wire-rich capes pulled before them to divert incoming arrows. Their archers fired back, and she knew that they were the finest in the city. Even as she watched, she heard a scream from the upstairs window of a tavern, and a shadow fell away inside. Several Blades were lowering the wooden shutters around her carriage, striving to lock her in and protect her from danger. Jave was one of them, and he glared angrily when he saw her peering from the carriage window.

"Inside!" he shouted.

"Have you sent—"

"Of course!" There would already be several pairs of Scarlet Blades infiltrating the surrounding buildings, working their way toward concealed attackers. And there were also several combats occurring in the street, Wreckers clashing swords with Blade soldiers whom they had very little hope of defeating in one-on-one combat, and that confused Jan Ray. Wreckers were far from suicidal. Resorting to this strategy so early in the ambush meant that they were desperate, or . . .

"Jave, they shouldn't have come forward so soon," she said.

He dropped the final wooden shutter, trapping it with one hand just before it cracked into the priestess's head. "I know that," he said impatiently. "They're stalling for something. We'll be ready."

"Make sure they don't get him, Jave," Jan Ray said, and even she was shocked by the tremor in her voice.

Despite the shouts, screams, and smells of battle, he paused and gave her a questioning stare. "Who *is* he?" he asked.

"Someone who must be seen to die on the Wall." She ducked back into the carriage and let him shut her in, and the sudden darkness was terrifying. Closing her eyes, Jan Ray prayed to the spirit of Hanharan, but not for herself. She asked that Dal Bamore be spared so that he could be crucified.

· · ·

"That's no way for a man to die," Jan Ray says, "covered in his own shit and piss." She pulls a small curved knife from her sleeve and steps toward the hanging man.

"Don't pity me," Dal Bamore says. His voice has changed. Last time, as he stood before the Council four days earlier, there had been humor to his tone, and insolence in the way he formed his words. Now he sounds defeated. But she will not let him fool her.

It takes several slices at the rope to cut it through. As the last strands strain and part, she steps back quickly. He falls into the large bowl and tips it over, spilling the disgusting mess across the stone floor. Jan Ray wrinkles her nose in revulsion.

"Look at you," she says. "The big revolutionary, the idealist, the heathen."

"I'm no heathen," he says. He manages to sit up, though his hands are still tied, and she can see that he's woozy. She wonders how long Trivner has had him hanging upside down. His face is red beneath the streaks of muck. There's blood all over his body, dried and still running. He appears unabashed at his nakedness, and Jan Ray glances away uncomfortably. From the corner of her eye she sees him shifting one leg aside.

"I'll have Scrivner cut it off," she says. "He's done it to others, many times."

Bamore chuckles and brings his knees up to rest his chin. He groans, but looks almost contemplative as he stares past her into the shadows.

"Give yourself to Hanharan," she says. "It'll make everything easier on you."

"This is where we have a problem," he says. He spits blood, closes his eyes, breathing heavily. *He's almost passing out,* she thinks. *We've almost broken him, and—*

But he is not broken. Far from it. And as he starts talking,

Jan Ray realizes that he has spent these last three days growing stronger.

"And the problem is need. You want me to give myself to Hanharan, because that will satisfy this curious need you Marcellans have to gather everyone to your flock. You need to hear acceptance from my mouth, because the idea that I don't require Hanharan to make my life worthwhile scares you."

"No," Jan Ray says.

"It *terrifies* you. And I don't need any of that at all."

"If it means so little to you, accept Him and have done with it."

"And then you win."

"We win anyway. Tomorrow we take you to Gaol Ten. Three days later you go on trial for heresy, for which you *will* be sentenced to death. You'll be taken to the Wall, nails hammered into your wrists and ankles. We'll pierce you with thirteen mepple shoots to attract the lizards, and leave you to die. And after you die you rot, in sight of anyone who cares to look. I've heard of people staying up there for thirty days before they decay enough to rip free of the nails and fall."

"I'll be dead. It doesn't matter."

"If you accept Him, I can arrange for the executioner to stick you with a poisoned knife. You'll be dead before he descends the ladder."

"Where's the fun in that?" He grins at her. It is a grotesque expression, his startling white teeth glaring from a mask of blood and excrement.

Jan Ray turns and walks to the far end of the chamber. Trivner has his tools of torture set out here, an array of metal, stone, leather, paper, wood, bone, and jars containing living creatures, that is in itself enough to give anyone nightmares for life. The tools are exquisitely clean, the insects well-kept, and the thought of someone tending lovingly to such things is horrific. She wonders if Trivner has a wife and children, and hopes not.

"So why you?" she asks, picking up a long, pointed bone. It's hollow, and dozens of small holes give it barbs.

"Why me what?"

"Why have the Wreckers become organized under you?"

"Have they?" he asks, and for the first time she hears doubt. She remains facing away from him, putting down the hollowed bone in favor of a clawed glove. Each flapping finger is tipped with a razor-sharp hook. She can barely imagine the damage this would do to a human body.

She slips her hand inside and grimaces at the slick, oiled feel.

"Of course they have. And they're little more than gangsters calling themselves terrorists. The name they choose for themselves says it all. They want anarchy, but for their own ends. They spout secularism, but only if it means they line their pockets, get all the slash they want. They claim to shun false gods—"

"All gods are false," Bamore says, "and the Wreckers—"

"No!" Jan Ray shouts. She turns and advances on the bloodied man, and as she swings her gloved hand she sees something in his eyes that confuses her. The hooks bite in and she uses her weight to tear them through his skin. He screams—

He screams but he's laughing *at me.*

—and the hooks open him across the chest. Blood flows. Dal Bamore falls onto his side, and Jan Ray steps back and drops the glove. She has lowered herself to this out of anger and rage, but also because she has feared this man ever since he stood before the Council and said, *If Hanharan is a raindrop, I am the storm; if Hanharan is a fly, I am the spider. Now take me and make me God.*

"How can you be a god hanging from that Wall?" she shouts, and his cries fade away into a chuckle.

As he sits up, the wounds across his chest cease bleeding.

"No," she says, backing away. She starts hammering on the door, screaming for Trivner, feeling her old heart fluttering in her chest like a bird trapped in a clenching. "No!"

Bamore stops laughing, closes his eyes, and grimaces, and the cuts heal, leaving only pale streaks beneath the dried blood flaked across his body.

"Whatever you do, they'll remember me," he says. As the door behind her opens and she falls out into the unlit hallway beyond, Jan Ray thinks, *There's no way that can happen.*

The last time there was a sorcerer in Echo City was almost four hundred years before.

More screams, more shouts, and being blind was driving her mad. Jan Ray poked at knotholes in the wooden shutters with her ceremonial knife, popping out one knot large enough for her to see through. It afforded her a view of the street ahead of them, the dead tusked swine, the Blades gathered around Bamore's rack, and the facade of one row of buildings. But she only had eyes for Bamore.

Don't let him wake, she thought. *I had no idea how much to give him, or how little; no inkling of how effective it would be. I was flailing in the dark even before this, and now . . .*

If the Wreckers achieved the unbelievable and managed to take him away, there was no telling what Bamore would do. He had come to them supercilious and aloof, welcoming the tortures because they would allow for a miraculous recovery. But he had not expected what had happened *after* the torture. If he gained time to let it wear off, then perhaps his air of superiority would transform into a need for revenge. And powerful though the Marcellan family was, sorcery was anathema to them, evil and unknown.

One of the buildings to their left was on fire. Screams originated within, and a flaming shape burst from a window and fell into the street. Two Blades shoved their way past a scatter of café tables and approached, and when they confirmed it was a Wrecker and not one of their own, they retreated and left them to burn. The cries soon bubbled to nothing, but the dying person continued moving for some time.

Her soldiers seemed to have taken control. Though surrounded and besieged, they were fighting with calm determination, archers picking their targets, swordsmen allowing Wrecker attackers to approach them, picking their own places to fight. She could see two dead Blades close to the carriage, and further away were six dead Wreckers.

Several arrows struck the carriage. It was too dark inside to see properly, but moving back from the knothole, she saw the gleam of one arrowhead protruding through the shutter. It was likely that they were using poisoned tips; she would have to be careful.

She widened the knothole with her knife, peeling out slivers of wood to afford a better view. When she looked again, it was just in time to see a dozen Wreckers charge into view from the other direction.

Where did they *come from?* she thought. She almost shouted a warning, but Jave appeared from where he'd been protecting the carriage, rushing across the street toward the enemy. Four Blades went with him, swords drawn, and clashed with the Wreckers close to where Bamore was being shielded.

Jave's first sword swipe cut across the throat of one shrieking woman, and a spray of blood misted the air. *It won't be long now,* Jan Ray thought. Reinforcements would be on their way—the moment the ambush fell, a messenger bat would have been sent back to the barracks at the gate they'd passed through—and she could already see the fight swinging their way. Besieged they might be, but the Blades were far superior fighters.

But then something began to change. The Wreckers engaged by Jave and the others stepped back slightly, swords held before them, and something about their faces was different. It took Jan Ray a moment to discern just what it was, and she squinted through the knothole, wondering whether her poor view was distorting her vision. But no. One Wrecker screamed as his head began to shake, and before he even drew a breath for another shout, he was raving. He leapt forward onto an outstretched sword, his own slashing at the air, other hand clawing for the Blade he'd gone for . . . and then he grabbed the sword piercing his stomach and pulled himself closer.

The Blade stepped back, forgetting for a moment that she was drawing the impaled man with her. In that moment of confusion, the bleeding, screaming man fisted her across the face. Her head flipped around, and he swung his other hand and buried his sword in her skull.

Other Wreckers had charged, shifting from angry to raving, and they swept across the Scarlet Blades. Blood splashed, but wounds seemed not to hinder them. Blades parried and fought bravely, but they were not used to enemies with slashed throats coming at them still, screams faded but rage just as rich.

"Jave," Jan Ray said, partly in fear for her captain, partly terror at what she realized had happened. Whatever blasphemous sorceries Dal Bamore had been practicing were employed here to rescue him from certain death.

Jave fell back and hacked at a man slashing at his arms and face. He kicked the man from him, stood, and stabbed him, again and again until he seemed to die at last. Glancing at the carriage, he shouted some order that Jan Ray could not hear, then pointed. *Sending them back to protect me!* she realized, and six soldiers from around Bamore moved past the dead swine to surround the carriage.

"No!" she cried, because this could not be allowed. "No! Protect Bamore, save the prisoner! He cannot be taken!" But whether the soldiers failed to hear, or chose to obey their captain's orders over her own, they remained close, leaving Bamore protected only by four remaining Blades.

More fell, bodies lay strewn across the street. And she saw something terrible. The Blades who had been cut or clawed down were almost all dead, yet some of the Wreckers that lay there still moved, hauling themselves toward the soldiers even if limbs were missing, guts trailing . . . and, in one case, a head was severed.

Sorcery, Jan Ray thought. *Sorcery, on the streets of Echo City!*

She reached out and opened the carriage door, lifting a wooden shutter aside. She had to speak to Jave. The most important person here now was their prisoner, and if she lost her own life preventing him from being rescued by the Wreckers, so be it.

A soldier glanced back and saw her, and his eyes went wide.

Something struck her in the shoulder, something else fell on her and crushed her to the ground.

She saw red.

Jan Ray has to go deep. With the blood of the tortured man still on her hands, she leaves the dungeon levels, heading first up a slowly curving staircase with over a hundred steps that leads eventually to a lush courtyard deep in Hanharan Heights. She passes huge oxomanlia bushes, waving away tame red sparrows that flutter around her head in case she has seed for them, and everything here is beautiful, brought into being by Hanharan countless years ago and uncorrupted by the stain of sorcery. That's what makes her most upset: not the fear of what Bamore could mean but the sadness at what his talents might bring. Echo City is miraculous and amazing enough without a monster like him using magic to twist its many meanings.

An aide approaches and she waves him away, not even catching his eyes. *And now he knows that something is amiss,* she thinks, but that does not matter. She should go to the Council with this, but that does not matter either—they would brood and muse, discuss options and argue alternatives, and all the while he would be down in the Dungeons deciding when to escape.

One chance, she thinks. *There's only one, and it all hinges on whether he knows of it or not.* Dal Bamore has the talent, but he looks young. Where he had acquired it she cannot tell, and she knows for sure he will never reveal the source to her. So she must use his ego against him. He welcomed capture and torture, and now he plans the miraculous escape and recovery that will draw the wonder of the masses. She has to ensure the escape fails, and that he dies up on the Wall.

In the corner of the courtyard, she unlocks a heavy wooden door with a key around her neck. Every priest or priestess carries such a key, but none of them has yet found cause to use it. Being the first gives her a flush of pride.

"In Hanharan I find my strength," she says as she closes the door behind her. There is a rack of oil lamps fixed to the wall and she lights one, watching shadows scamper out of sight. Spiders and ghourt lizards. They'll leave her alone if she shows no fear. She draws in a deep breath and starts down. "In you I seek my truth, and to you I promise my best. In your words I hear the history of Echo City, and I vow to listen, adding my own life to the history you impart."

The staircase curves onto landings, doors lure her in, tunnels are swallowed in darkness. Eventually she crosses a street of the most recent Echo, built upon several hundred years before and preserved down here like a painting of older times. What she sees of the buildings' facades resembles those above, except deserted. There are shadows that move the wrong way, and whispers, but she recites the route aloud, remembering which way to go, feeling the importance of what she is doing pressing heavily upon her like the weight of the city itself. She has no wish to see or hear phantoms.

Several times her oil lamp almost goes out when a sudden breeze whistles in from the darkness, and she tries to ignore the smells.

Reaching the hidden place, she uses her key again to unlock another heavy wooden door.

Inside, the room is small and sparse. Its corners and junctions are blurred by dust and sand-spider structures. There is a table at one end, upon which sit several books, and three shelves on the left wall that hold two storage jars each. Dust on the floor is thick and undisturbed, and the books appear to have settled into place. No one has been here for a very long time.

There is a mummified corpse curled beneath the table, wrapped in heavy chains.

She feels a flush of terror, and for a moment she cannot believe in this place. What it contains goes against everything she holds true: the last sorcerer, trapped down here with the things that put him down . . .

"I only hope it's still here," she says, reaching for a jar.

The torture's over," she says later, holding the back of Bamore's head and offering him the mug. "I've consulted with the Council. Your lack of confession means that you'll be sent to trial, and you'll be crucified in three days."

"Won't that depend upon the verdict?"

"The verdict is a formality."

"So predictable," he says, trying to grin through his broken face. "But I won't die up there." Why he has not chosen to mend the damage as he healed those cuts she does not know. Perhaps it's a sort of perverted vanity. Or, more likely, he wants people to see what has been done to him.

"Drink, in the name of Hanharan. He will watch over your final days."

"Your god?" Bamore sips, swallows, sighs. He has not been given a drink in days. "Hanharan can suck my cock." He stares up at her, his one good eye twinkling as he awaits her reaction to such blasphemy.

But she only smiles, and, behind his ruined face, Dal Bamore's smugness turns to confusion.

Jan Ray tried not to scream. It felt as if her whole shoulder and arm had been dipped in molten metal and then solidified, locking all the pain inside. She kept her eyes open, because she needed to see, and when she lifted the knife still in her hand, someone pressed down on her wound.

"Priestess!" a voice hissed. It was a Scarlet Blade, splayed across her body to protect her from any more woundings. But the fool was young, and scared, and with every movement he nudged the bolt protruding from her shoulder.

"Get . . . off . . ." she managed, and then the soldier was lifted away from her. Jave's face came close, and he even smiled.

"Jan Ray, I'll give you a sword if you're so eager to fight." He helped her sit up, glancing around all the time, watching for danger.

She grimaced through the agony, then looked around. The raving Wreckers had been cut down, and there were three Blades hacking at their still-twitching bodies. They appeared shocked and terrified, but beneath that was a professionalism that shone through. They'd have a story for their barracks tonight, that was for sure.

"What are you doing out?" Jave said.

"Going for Bamore. He can't be taken by them, Jave."

"I'm ready to slit his throat myself," the tall captain said.

"No!" She stood, holding on to his arm and blinking away dizziness. More arrows flickered in, their energy expended in Blades' robes. Blood soaked the street, filling the spaces between cobbles. The crowds had drawn back now, but further along the street, close to a fountain, she could still see a few curious onlookers. She knew what some people thought of the Blades, and she hated the smiles she saw.

"Is he still alive?" she asked, a tremor in her voice.

"My Blades have him surrounded," Jave replied, nodding along the road. "I don't think an errant arrow has killed him yet."

"It can't. And neither can your blade. Jave, I have a secret, and if I speak it to you, you'll be only the second person to know." She let go of his arm and leaned against the carriage.

"You!" Jave said, nodding at the two Blades who had been guarding her. "Help them protect the prisoner." They left Jave and Jan Ray alone.

"Bamore is a sorcerer," Jan Ray said. Jave smiled.

"A sorcerer? What, like magic?"

"Magic," she said. She nodded at the quivering body parts strewn across the street, all that remained of those strange, raving Wreckers. One severed head seemed to tilt this way and that, and she saw the moist pinkness of its tongue licking its lips. "They're his."

"I've seen worse on bad slash," he said.

"Really?"

Jave frowned, and she knew that he believed. *Any other soldier would think me a fool,* she thought.

"So let me kill him."

"He has to die on the Wall!" she said. "Anything else—anything unseen—and he'll become a martyr, and they'll follow him as a god. There's one chance to rid ourselves of him, and I've taken it."

Someone shouted, a man charged from the shadows beneath a shop awning, and his sword met a Blade's. He was a Wrecker, tattoos and heavy piercings giving him a threatening countenance, but he looked terrified. He seemed to be looking *past* the soldier as he fought, striving to see his master. The Blade gutted him in the street, stepping back to avoid getting more blood on his boots.

"They still have us pinned down," Jave said hesitantly.

"Get him in the carriage with me."

"Are you mad?"

"You dare to talk to a Hanharan priestess like that, soldier?" she asked softly. Jave nodded slowly, and something about his face changed. *Did I just spoil something special?* she wondered. She could not care.

"Bring the prisoner here!" Jave shouted. The Blades dragged Bamore's rack a dozen steps to the carriage, skirting around bodies, using the fallen tusked swine as cover. Five archers providing covering fire all the way. Now that the hand-to-hand fighting had died down, the ongoing battle had taken on an almost peaceful air. Arrows whipped at the air, feet scraped on ground muddied with blood, and occasionally someone grunted when an arrow found home. From along the street some people started to cheer, but a Blade fired an arrow their way. Shapes shuffled away and hid.

"I mean it, Jave," she whispered as she climbed steps into the carriage. "His life is more important than yours, and mine. If he's killed here, his death will be denied. If they take him, he heals himself of those wounds and becomes a god. Our only hope to rid ourselves of him is public trial and crucifixion." The carriage's inside was stuffy, and light slanted across from several places where arrows had struck.

"Get him in," Jave instructed. A Blade slashed Bamore's bonds and two of them threw his loose body into the carriage.

Jan Ray pressed herself back into one corner. She saw Jave looking, and knew that he believed.

Then he shut the door and locked the sorcerer in there with her, and the tortured man said, "What have you done to me, bitch?"

He shouts and rages as she turns to leave the torture chamber. She sees him bringing his hands up, forming shapes, whispering strange words, coughing phrases she cannot understand, casting sigils into the floor that glare briefly before fading away. The shapes his hands make remain silhouetted on the wall for a moment, but then they too fade, shriveling to nothing when he had expected them to grow.

"What have you done to me, bitch?" he shouts. She's surprised that he can even speak that loud; one of Trivner's favorite tortures is fire ants down the throat.

She slams the cell door behind her, and his shouts become distant. In three days he will be dead. And if all goes to plan, she'll never have to tell a soul.

They were concentrating on the carriage now. Arrow after arrow struck the wooden shutters enclosing it, and as the timber splintered, so more light came in. Jan Ray was huddled down in one corner away from the raving sorcerer, knife in her hand even though she could never use it, and she was beginning to fear how this would end.

They're not afraid of hurting him, she thought. *They know what he can do—he's united the Wreckers, after all. They know if an arrow hits him he'll get better, that his powers will protect him . . .*

But they don't know what I've done to him.

If Bamore did die now, the Wreckers would turn their sorcerer into a god and await his triumphant return. News of his powers would spread, rumors of magic would filter through the city, and Hanharan might not look so appealing with Bamore offering such romantic notions. The only thing that ever kept peace in the city was the Order of Hanharan, and those who preached and policed it.

"I made you normal," she said. "For long enough to hang on the Wall, at least. You bloody fool, Bamore. You bloody, stupid fool, you think you pluck up a bit of knowledge from some slummy side-street and make yourself a god?"

"Gods don't make themselves." He spat, groaned as he rolled onto his side. "Their followers do it for them."

"How did it happen? The magic, the sorcery . . . where did you *find* it?"

"Why should I tell you?"

"Because your people are going to kill me," she said.

He watched her with his one good eye, smiling slightly, glancing away, listening to the sounds of battle from outside. The fight was louder again now, closer, and Jan Ray imagined her soldiers surrounding the carriage and holding off a sustained attack. If there were more Wreckers like those ravers . . . if there was something else they were hiding . . .

But reinforcements would be with them soon.

"Fair enough," he said. And Jan Ray thought, *It's always in a madman's nature to gloat.*

"It's Deathtouch, not magic. Stronger than the older magics. More specific. I bestow death, or take it back. You saw those rav-

ing bloody monsters out there? Mine. As for where I found it . . ."
He started laughing. It was a horrible sound, rising from a chest
half-flooded with blood and passing through a throat damaged
by Trivner's awful tortures. But Jan Ray thought that even were
he fit and whole, Bamore's laughter would have been dreadful.
They'd failed to discover what he had been before he took the
name Bamore; now she was glad.

"What?" she asked. "Where?"

"Under your very noses," he said. "Not all Marcellans are as
pure as you wish to imagine." He pressed his hands together and
grunted, trying another Deathtouch spell but failing.

"And without it, you're just swine shit on my shoe," she said.

Something struck the carriage. It rocked on its axles, wood
creaking and cracking, and another hail of arrows struck the left
side, the impacts continuing for some time as if the shooters were
reloading again and again.

"They'll have me soon," Bamore said. "I'll be unconscious
from your tortures, of course. And once whatever you've done to
me lifts, I'll wake, and heal. As a victim of your cruelties, my followers will increase tenfold overnight."

"You're going to die on the Wall."

He groaned and sat up, and she pressed back into the corner.
He's weak, but if he comes at me now . . . ? I'm just an old woman.
And she was injured. The bolt in her shoulder seemed to be super-
heated, and she feared she might have been poisoned. An insidi-
ous infection, perhaps, that would kill her in days, not moments.
She would not put such a cruel death past Dal Bamore.

More shouts came from outside, and then a terrible scream,
loud and long, that seemed to come from many voices.

"Ahh," Bamore said, "more of my children."

Jan Ray heard Jave shouting to his remaining soldiers, and
then his voice was snapped off, and the sound of chaos took over.

Screams and shouts, the hacking of metal into flesh, and then the door of the carriage was ripped open.

Jave's face appeared, and for a moment Jan Ray almost went to him, mouth opening to ask if it was over. But then she saw that below his face was nothing, only the spewing, ragged mess of his severed neck.

"Time to leave you, I think," Bamore said. "But first, I'll have one of my creations service your dry—"

An arrow struck him in the right cheek. His right eye flushed red, mouth opened, and he raised one hand and pointed at Jan Ray.

A Wrecker climbed into the carriage and glared at the priestess. The man's throat had been torn out, half of his scalp ripped off, and yet he did not bleed.

Dead, Jan Ray thought. She lifted her knife and pressed it to her own throat.

She does not sleep that night. To defeat a sorcerer she has used magic herself, a remnant from an ancient conflict that the Hanharans have kept in their possession simply because they cannot let it go. She did not *perform* a spell, but *administered* it, and yet . . .

She has betrayed Hanharan, who said that the only magic is in him. She has denied his status as the one true god. Confused, angry, terrified, empowered, Jan Ray cries and smiles her way through the night.

They killed Bamore. The dead man went first, falling on the tortured sorcerer and hacking away with his short sword. Jan Ray watched with her breath held, trying to understand, wondering if they really thought their god could come back from this, refreshed and renewed. Then the dead man fell to the side, and someone else entered the carriage.

It was a tall man, with heavy piercings and tattoos displaying some high rank in the Wrecker gang. He glanced at Jan Ray, looked down at his bloody sword, then took turn hacking at Bamore's corpse.

The sorcerer was meat. The man took his head and threw it from the carriage.

"Stamp on it!" he shouted. "Crush it, and grind his brains into the dust. There can be nothing left."

Jan Ray lowered her knife and waited for the man to turn around and kill her. But when he did turn, he merely looked, fascination and disgust mingling in his eyes.

"So you're a Hanharan Priestess," he said. "Well . . . you're not much to look at. And I thought suicide was forbidden under Hanharan's word." The man's voice was empty, as if he cared about nothing at all.

"You just killed . . ."

"The man who would be god." He dragged one foot through Bamore's grisly remains. "He was a monster. What he did to my brother . . . what he put our people through, in the name of his damned Deathtouch . . ." The man shook his head, and Jan Ray wondered whether the other body in the carriage—still now, given itself over to death at last—was someone he had known.

She leaned to one side and looked out into the street. There were no Scarlet Blades left standing. A group of men and women squatted in the middle of the road, blood on their chins and painting their grins, and in their vacant eyes she saw a reflection of the dead man on the floor.

"So you'll kill me now?" she asked softly.

"*He's* dead. That's all that matters. We couldn't risk you letting him live. And I . . . for me it was only revenge." The man was crying. Tears coursed a path down his tattooed cheeks, and he did nothing to hide them. It was as if Jan Ray were not there at all.

"He destroyed us *all*," he said. He dropped his sword and climbed from the carriage, slipping in blood and sprawling to the ground. No one came to help. She saw them dispersing, the surviving Wreckers and those raving people who'd finished their fight, and who perhaps now would find some sort of peace in death.

The carriage stank, so she slowly climbed out, wincing at the pain in her shoulder. *Under your very noses,* Bamore had said when she'd asked him where the Deathtouch had originated. She wondered if she could ever trust another Hanharan ever again.

The street was red, and it grew redder as a flood of Scarlet Blade reinforcements arrived to fight in a battle already lost. Or won. Jan Ray wasn't quite sure.

It would be some time before she could make up her mind.

ROBERT SILVERBERG, born in New York City, is a science fiction Grand Master, and a multiple Hugo and Nebula Award–winning author. He published his first novel, the children's book *Revolt on Alpha C,* in 1955. Silverberg won his first Hugo Award for Best New Writer the following year, 1956, the same year he completed an AB in English Literature from Columbia University. A prolific author, he contributed to the genre such classics as *Dying Inside, Nightwings,* and *Downward to the Earth.* In 1980 he published *Lord Valentine's Castle,* the first book in his landmark sci-fantasy Majipoor series. He currently resides in the San Francisco Bay Area with his wife, author and editor Karen Haber.

DARK TIMES AT THE MIDNIGHT MARKET

Robert Silverberg

Business was slow nowadays for the spellmongers of Bombifale's famed Midnight Market, and getting slower all the time. No one regretted that more than Ghambivole Zwoll, licensed dealer in potions and spells: a person of the Vroonish race, a small many-tentacled creature with a jutting beak and fiery yellow eyes, who represented the fourth generation of his line to hold the fifth stall in the leftmost rank of the back room of the Midnight Market of Bombifale.

Oh, the glorious times he could remember! The crowds of eager buyers for the wizardry he had for sale! The challenges triumphantly met, the wonders of conjuring that he had performed! In those great days of yore he had moved without fear through the strangest of realms, journeying among the cockatrices and gorgons, the flame-spitting basilisks and winged serpents, the universes beyond the universe, to bring back the secrets needed to meet the demands of his insatiable clients.

But now— but now—!

Popular interest in the various thaumaturgic arts, which had

begun to sprout on Majipoor in the reign of the Coronal Lord
Prankipin, had grown into a wild planetwide craze in the days
of his glorious successor, Lord Confalume. That king's personal
dabblings in sorcery had done much to spur the mode for it. But
it had been gradually waning during the reigns of the more skeptical monarchs who had followed him, Lord Prestimion and then
Lord Dekkeret, and now, a century and more after Dekkeret's
time, sorcery had become a mere minor commodity, neither
more nor less in demand than pepper, wine, dishware, or any
other commonly used good. When one had need, one consulted
the appropriate sort of wizard; but the era when a magus would
be besieged by importunate patrons all through the hours of the
clock was long over.

In those days the sorcerers' section of the market was open
only on the first and third Seadays of the month, creating pent-
up demand that helped to spur a sense of urgency among the
purchasers. But for the past decade the wizards had, of necessity,
kept their shops open night after night to make themselves readily
available to such few customers as did appear, and even so their
trade seemed to be waning steadily year after year.

Even a dozen years ago Ghambivole Zwoll had had more work
than he could handle. But two years back he had been forced to
take in a partner, Shostik-Willeron of the Su-Suheris race, and
together they barely managed to eke out a modest living in this
era of diminishing fascination with all forms of magecraft. Their
coffers were dipping ever lower, their debts were mounting to an
uncomfortable level, and they were near the point where they
might have to discharge their one employee, the stolid, husky
Skandar woman who swept and tidied for them every evening
before the shop opened. So it was a matter of some excitement one
night, three hours past midnight, when a tall, swaggering young
man clad in the flamboyant garb of an aristocrat—close-fitting

blue coat with ruffled sleeves trimmed with gold, flaring skirts, wide-brimmed hat trimmed with leather of some costly sort—came sweeping into their shop.

He was red-haired, blue-eyed, handsome, energetic. He had the look of wealth about him. But there was something else about him, or so it seemed to Ghambivole Zwoll: the smirking set of his mouth, the overly rakish slant of his hat that cried *scoundrel, wastrel, idler.*

No matter. Ghambivole Zwoll had dealt with plenty of those in his time. So long as they paid their bills on time, Ghambivole Zwoll had no concern with his clients' moral failings.

The proud lordling struck a lofty pose, his hand resting on the gleaming hilt of the sword that hung from a broad beribboned baldric at his side, and boomed, "I will have a love potion, if you please. To snare the heart of a lady of the highest birth! And I mean to spare no expense."

Ghambivole Zwoll masked his joy with a calm, businesslike demeanor. He stared up—and up and up and up, for the new client was very tall indeed and Vroons are diminutive beings, knee-high at best to humans—and said judiciously, "Yes, yes, of course. We offer such compounds at every level of efficacy and potency." He reached for a writing tablet. "Your name, please?"

He expected some fanciful pseudonym. Instead his visitor said grandly, "I am the Marquis Mirl Meldelleran, fourth son of the third son of the Count of Canzilaine."

"Indeed," said Ghambivole Zwoll, a little stunned, for the Count of Canzilaine was one of the wealthiest and most influential men of Castle Mount. He looked across the room toward the towering figure of Shostik-Willeron, standing against the far wall. The Su-Suheris appeared to be displaying mixed emotions, his optimistic right-hand head glittering with pleasure at the prospect of a hefty fee but the left-hand head, which disliked such high-born fops as this, glowering in distaste. The Vroon shot him a quick, bright-eyed glance to let him know that he would handle this client without interference. "I'll need to know the details of your requirements, of course."

"Details?"

"The goal you hope to achieve—whether it be only a seduction and light romance, or something deeper, leading, even, perhaps to a marriage. And some information about the lady's age and physical appearance, her approximate height and weight, you understand, so that we may calculate the proper dosage." He risked letting the intense blaze of his yellow eyes meet the blander gaze of the marquis. As tactfully as he could he said, "You will, I hope, be forthcoming about these matters, or it may be difficult to fulfill your needs. She is young, I take it?"

"Of course. Eighteen."

"Ah. Eighteen." The Vroon delicately looked away. "And of limited sexual experience, perhaps?—I have no wish to pry, you understand, but in order to calculate—"

"Yes," said the Marquis Mirl Meldelleran. "I hold nothing back from you. She is a virgin of the purest purity."

"Ah," said Ghambivole Zwoll.

"And moves in the highest circles at court. She is in fact the Lady Alesarda of Muldemar, of whose beauty and wit you undoubtedly have heard report."

That was jolting news. Ghambivole Zwoll fought to hide any show of the concern that that lady's name had awakened in him, but he was unable to fight back a complex, anguished writhing of his innumerable tentacles. "The Lady—Alesarda—of Muldemar," the Vroon said slowly. "Ah. Ah." His partner was glaring furiously at him now from his station in the corner shadows, the wary left-hand head glowering with wrath and even the normally cheerful right one showing alarm. "I have heard the name—she is, I believe, of royal lineage?"

"Sixth in descent from the Pontifex Prestimion himself."

"Ah. Ah. Ah." Ghambivole Zwoll saw that they were getting into exceedingly deep waters. He wished the marquis had kept the lady's identity to himself. But business was business, and the shop's exchequer was distressingly low. To mask his uncertainties he scribbled notes for quite some time; and then, looking up at last, said with a cheeriness he certainly did not feel, "We will have what you need in one week's time. The fee will be— ah—"

Quickly, almost desperately, he reckoned the highest price he thought the traffic would bear, and then doubled it, expecting to be haggled with. "Twenty royals."

"Twenty," said the marquis impassively. "So be it."

Ghambivole wondered what the response would have been if he had said thirty. Or fifty. It had been so long since he had had a client of the marquis's station that he had forgotten that such people were utterly indifferent to cost. Well, too late now.

"Will a deposit of five cause any difficulties, do you think?"

"Hardly." Mirl Meldelleran drew a thick, glossy coin from his purse and dropped it on Ghambivole Zwoll's desk. The Vroon swept it quickly toward him with a trembling tentacle. "One week," said the Marquis Mirl Meldelleran. "The results, I assume, are guaranteed?"

"Of course," said Ghambivole Zwoll.

"This is madness," said Shostik-Willeron, the moment the door of the stall had closed behind the Marquis Mirl Meldelleran and they were alone again. "We will be ruined! A virgin princess of Prestimion's line, one who moves in the highest circles at court, and you propose to fling her into the bed of the fourth son of a third son?"

"Twenty royals," Ghambivole Zwoll said. "Do you know what our gross revenue for the past three months has been? Hardly one third as much. I expected him to bargain me down, and I would have settled for ten, or even five. Or three or two. But twenty— *twenty!*—"

"The risk is tremendous. The sellers of the potion will be traced."

"What of it? We are not the ones who will debauch the young princess."

"But it's an abomination, Ghambivole!" The words were coming from the right-hand head, and that gave Ghambivole Zwoll pause, for the right-hand head always brimmed with enthusiasm and exuberance, while it was the other, the dominant left head, that was ever urging caution. "We'll be whipped! We'll be flayed!"

"We are only purveyors, nothing more. We are protected by the mercantile laws. What we sell is legal, and what he plans to use it for is legal too, however deplorable. The girl is of age."

"So he says."

"If he's lied to me about it, the sin is his. Do you think I would dare to ask the grandson of the Count of Canzilaine for an affidavit?"

"But even so, Ghambivole—"

"Twenty royals, Shostik-Willeron."

They argued over it another fifteen minutes. But in the end the Vroon won, as he knew he would. He was the senior partner; this was his shop, and had been in his family four generations; and he was the only one of the two who had any real skill at wizardry. Shostik-Willeron's sole contribution to the partnership had been capital, not any great knowledge of the art; and if the shop failed, the Su-Suheris would lose that capital. They were in no position to turn away such lucrative business, chancy though it might be.

The partners were an oddly assorted pair. Like all the Su-Suheris race, Shostik-Willeron was tall and slender, with a pallid body tapering upward to a narrow forking neck a foot in length, atop which sprouted a pair of hairless, vastly elongated heads, each of which had an independent mind and identity. Gham-bivole Zwoll could hardly have looked more different: a tiny person, barely reaching as high as his partner's shins, fragile and insubstantial of body, with a host of flexible rubbery limbs and a small head, out of which jutted a sharp hook of a beak, above which were two huge yellow eyes with horizontal black stripes to serve as pupils. There were times when the Vroon barely avoided being trampled by Shostik-Willeron as they moved about their cramped little emporium.

But Ghambivole Zwoll was accustomed to moving in a world of oversized creatures. Vroons were the dominant beings on their own home planet, but giant Majipoor was Ghambivole Zwoll's native world, his ancestors having arrived in the great wave of Vroon immigration during the reign of Lord Prankipin, and like all his kind, he wove his way easily and lithely through throngs of heedless entities of much greater size than he, three and four and even five times his height, not only humans but also the reptilian Ghayrogs and the lofty Su-Suheris and the various other peoples of Majipoor, going on up to the gigantic shaggy four-armed Skan-dars, who stood eight feet tall and taller. Not even the presence of the ponderous, slow-witted Skandar cleaning-woman, Hendaya Zanzan, who moved slowly and clumsily about the shop as she dusted and fussed with its displays, intimidated him with her dangerous bulk.

"A love potion," Ghambivole Zwoll said, setting about his task. "One that is suitable to win the heart of a highborn maiden, slender, delicate—"

The job called for no little forethought. At Ghambivole

Zwoll's request, the Su-Suheris began taking books of reference down from the high shelves, the reliable old book of incantations that Ghambivole Zwoll had kept by his side since his student days in the sorcerers' city of Triggoin, and the ever-useful *Great Grimoire of Hadin Vakkimorin,* and *Thalimiod Gur's Book of Specifics,* and many another volume—more, in fact, than would possibly be needed. Ghambivole Zwoll suspected that he could compound the potion that the marquis had commissioned out of his own fund of accumulated skills, without recourse to any of these books. But he wanted to take no unnecessary risks; he had a whole week to complete what he could probably deal with in a morning, but any miscalculation due to overconfidence would surely have ugly consequences, and that stupefying fee of twenty royals more than amply compensated him for any unnecessary time that he expended on the task. It was not as though he had a great many other things to do this week, after all.

Besides, he loved to burrow in the great array of wizardly materials with which his forefathers had crammed the small shop. These two centuries of professional magicking had made the place a virtual museum of the magus's art. It was not an easy shop to find, tucked away as it was in a far back corner of the huge marketplace, but in happier days it had enjoyed great acclaim, and throngs of impatient clients had jostled elbow-to-elbow in the hall just outside, peering in at the racks of arcane powders and oils, bearing the awesome labels *Scamion* and *Thekka Ammoniaca* and *Elecamp* and *Golden Rue,* and the rows of leather-bound books of great antiquity, and the mysterious devices that sorcerers used, the ammatepilas and rohillas, the ambivials and verilistias, and much more apparatus of that sort, impressive to laymen and useful to practitioners. Even now, in this dreary materialistic era, the patrons of the Midnight Market who had come there to purchase such ordinary things as brooms and baskets, bangles and beads, spices, dried meats, cheese, and wine and honey, often took the trouble to wend their way this deep into the building—for the Midnight Market was a huge subterranean vault, long and low, divided into a myriad narrow aisles, with the sorcerers' booths tucked away in the hindmost quarter—to stare through the dusty window of Ghambivole Zwoll's shop. That was all that most of them did, though: stare. The Marquis Mirl Meldelleran had been the first patron to step through the doorway in many days.

Ghambivole Zwoll drew the work out for nearly the full week, sequestered in the constricted little Vroon-sized laboratory behind the main showroom, jotting recipes, calculating quantities, measuring, weighing, mixing: the fine brandy of Gimkandale as a base, and then dried ghumba root, and a pinch of fermented hingamort, and some drops of tincture of vejloo, and just a bit of powdered sea-dragon hide, not strictly necessary, but always useful in speeding the effects of such potions. Allow it all to set a little while; then would come the heating, the cooling, the filtering, the titration, the spectral analysis. Meanwhile Shostik-Willeron remained out front, handling a surprising amount of walk-in trade: a Ghayrog who stopped by for a couple of amulets, two tourists from Ni-moya who came in out of nothing more than curiosity and stayed long enough to purchase a dozen of the black candles of divination, and a grain merchant from one of the downslope cities who sought a spell that would cast a blight on the fields of a supplier whom he had come to loathe. Three sales the same week, and also the potion for the marquis!

Ghambivole Zwoll allowed himself to think that perhaps a return to the prosperity of old might be in its early stages.

By the end of the week the job was done. There was one moment of near catastrophe on the evening when Ghambivole Zwoll arrived to begin his night's work and found the massive Skandar charwoman Hendaya Zanzan bashing around with her mop in his rear workroom, where he had left the vials of ingredients that would go into the marquis's potion sitting atop his desk in a carefully arranged row. In disbelief, he watched the gigantic woman, who was far too large actually to enter the room, standing at the entrance energetically swinging the mop from side to side and thereby placing everything within in great jeopardy.

"No!" he cried. "What are you doing, idiot? How many times have I told you— Stop! Stop!"

She halted and swung about uncertainly, looming above him like a mountain as she shifted the handle of the mop from one to another of her four hands. "But it has been so many weeks, master, since I last cleaned that room—"

"I've told you *never* to clean that room. Never! Never! And especially not now, when I have work in progress."

"Never, master?"

"Oh, what a great stupid thing you are. Never: it means Not Ever. Not at any time. Keep your big idiotic mop out of there! Do you understand me, Hendaya Zanzan?"

It seemed to take her quite a while to process the instruction.

She stood with all four burly arms drooping, the slow workings of her mind manifesting themselves meanwhile by a series of odd twitchings and clampings of her lips. Ghambivole Zwoll waited, struggling with his temper. He knew it did very little good to get angry with Hendaya Zanzan. The woman was a moron, a great furry clod of a moron, a dull-witted shaggy mass of a creature eight feet high and nearly as wide, hardly more than an animal. Not only stupid but ugly besides, even as Skandars went, flat-faced, empty-eyed, slack-jawed, covered from head to toe with a bestial coarse gray pelt that had the stale stink of some dead creature's hide left too long to fester in the sun. He had no idea why he had hired her—out of pity, probably—nor why he had kept her on so long. The shop did need to be cleaned once in a while, he supposed, but it had been madness to hire anyone as bulky as a Skandar to do the sweeping in such a small, cluttered space, and in any case Shostik-Willeron had little enough to occupy his time and could easily take care of the chore. But for the grace of the Marquis Mirl Meldelleran's twenty-royal job Ghambivole Zwoll would have let her go in another week or two. Now it seemed that he could afford to keep her on a little longer, and he would, for discharging her would be an unpleasant task and he tended to postpone all such things; but if business were to slacken once again—

"I am never to go into this little room," she said finally. "Is that so, master?"

"Very good, Hendaya Zanzan! Very good. Say it once again! Never. Never."

"Never to go into. The little room. Never."

"And never means—?"

"Not ever?"

He didn't care for the interrogative tone of her reply; but he saw that it was the best he was going to get out of the poor thing, and, sending her on her way, he went into his workshop and closed the door behind him. It took him no more than an hour to complete the final titration for the marquis's potion. While he worked he heard the Su-Suheris moving about in the outer room, talking to someone, then pointlessly shifting furniture about, then whistling to himself in that maddening double-headed counterpoint his species so greatly cherished. What a useless fool the man was! Not a dolt like the Skandar woman, of course, but certainly he had little of the clear-eyed wisdom and cunning that the Su-Suheris, with the benefit of their double brain, were reputed to possess. Ghambivole Zwoll had badly needed an injection of fresh capital to meet the ongoing expenses of his shop or he would never have taken him on as a partner, an act that unquestionably would have brought fiery condemnation upon him from his fore-bears. If only business would pick up a little, he would surely buy Shostik-Willeron out and return to running the place as a sole proprietorship. But he knew what a futile fantasy that was.

Scowling in annoyance, Ghambivole Zwoll poured his com-pleted potion into an elegant flask worthy of the twenty-royal price, inscribed the accompanying spell on a sheet of vellum. On the appointed day the Marquis Mirl Meldelleran returned, clad even more grandly than before—high-waisted doublet of orange velvet, long-legged golden breeches bedecked with loops of braid and buttons, slender dress sword fastened to a wide silk sash tied in a huge bow. "Is this it?" he asked, holding the flask up to a glowglobe above his head and studying it intently.

"Be certain that you are the object of her gaze when she drinks it," said the Vroon. "And here," he said, handing him the vellum scroll, "are the words you must speak as she consumes the po-tion."

The marquis's brow furrowed. "*Sathis pephoouth mouraph anour?* What nonsense is this?"

"Not nonsense at all. It is a powerful spell. The meaning is, 'Let her be well disposed to me, let her fall in love with me, let her yield to me.' And the third word is pronounced *mouroph;* take care that you get it right, or the effect may be lost. Even worse: you may achieve the opposite of what you desire. Again: *Sathis pephoouth mouroph anour.*"

"*Sathis pephoouth mouroph anour.*"

"Excellent! But rehearse it many times before you approach her. She will fall helplessly into your arms. I guarantee it, your grace."

"Well, then. *Sathis pephoouth mouraph anour.*"

"*Mouroph,* your grace."

"Mouroph. Sathis pephoouth mouroph anour."

"She is yours, your grace."

"Let us hope so. And this is yours." The marquis produced his bulging purse and casually tossed two coins, a fine fat ten-royal piece and a glossy fiver, onto Ghambivole Zwoll's desk. "Good day to you. And may the Divine protect you if you have played me false! *Sathis pephoouth mouraph anour. Mouroph. Mouroph.*" He spun neatly on his heel and was gone.

Three days passed quietly. Ghambivole Zwoll made two small sales, one for one crown fifty weights, one for slightly less. Otherwise the shop did no business. Creditors devoured most of the Marquis Mirl Meldelleran's twenty royals almost at once. The Vroon returned to the state of gloom that had occupied him before the arrival of his aristocratic client.

On the second of those three evenings Shostik-Willeron was late coming to the shop; and when he did, both his long, pallid faces were tightly drawn in the Su-Suheris expression of uneasiness verging on despair.

"I warned you we were making a great mistake," he said at once. "And now I'm sure of it!" It was the right-hand head that spoke: the cheerful, optimistic one, usually.

Ghambivole Zwoll sighed. "What now, Shostik-Willeron?"

"I have been speaking with my kinsman Sagamorn-Endik, who is in service at the Castle. Do you know that the Lady Alesarda of Muldemar, whom you have delivered so blithely into the clutches of that ridiculous dandy with your drug, is spoken of widely at court as the promised bride of the Coronal's son? That by interfering in those nuptials, by despoiling this precious princess, your marquis runs perilously close to treason? And you and I, as abettors of his crime—"

"It is no crime."

"To sleep with a simple scullery maid or some illiterate juggler girl, no. But for the fourth son of the third son of a provincial count to seduce a noblewoman destined for a royal marriage, to interpose his sweaty lusts in such high and delicate negotiations, or simply to be the ones who enable him to carry out such a thing, to be the agents who help him to have his way with her—oh, Ghambivole Zwoll, Ghambivole Zwoll, let us hope that that little potion of yours was a worthless draught! Otherwise your marquis is destroyed, and we are destroyed with him."

"If the potion worked," said the Vroon in the calmest tone he was capable of mustering, "there is no certainty that what took place between the marquis and the princess will become known to anyone else. And if it does, the marquis will have to look to the consequences of his deed on his own. We are mere merchants, protected by law. But if the potion has failed—and how can it have failed, unless he blundered with the spell?—we owe him twenty royals, to fulfill my guarantee. Where will we get twenty royals, Shostik-Willeron? Conjure them out of the air? Look here." He opened the cash drawer of his desk. "This is what's left of it. Three royals, two crowns, and sixty—no, seventy weights. The rest is gone. Let us pray that the potion has done its work, for our own sakes, if nothing else."

"A princess of Muldemar—a descendant of the great Prestimion—a beautiful lass, innocent, pure, betrothed to the son of the Coronal—"

"Stop it, Shostik-Willeron. For all we know, she's no more innocent and pure than that ox of a Skandar who works for us, and everybody at the Castle from the Coronal on down knows it and doesn't care. And even if this tale of royal betrothals should be true—but do we know that it is? Only this kinsman of yours says so—we are in no danger ourselves. We are here to serve the public by making use of our skills, and so we have. We bear no responsibility for our client's interference in other people's arrangements. In any case, this blubbering of yours achieves nothing. What's done is done." Ghambivole Zwoll made shooing gestures with his outermost ring of tentacles. "Go. Go. If you keep this up you will jangle my nerves tonight to no useful purpose."

The Vroon's nerves were indeed already thoroughly jangled, however much he tried to put a good face on the matter. He wished most profoundly that Mirl Meldelleran had never shared with him the identity of his inamorata. It would have been sufficient to know her age, her approximate height and weight, and, perhaps, some inkling of her degree of experience in the wars of love. But no, no, the braggart Mirl Meldelleran had had to go and name her, besides; and if this rumor of a royal marriage truly had any substance to it, and the marquis's seduction of the princess caused any disruption of that marriage, and the tale of how the marquis had managed to achieve his triumph came out, Shostik-Willeron quite possibly was correct: the magus who had compounded the dastardly potion might very well be made a scapegoat in the hubbub that ensued. Ghambivole Zwoll felt sure that the law would be on his side in any action against him, but a lawyer's fee for defending him against an outraged Prince of Muldemar or, even worse, the Coronal's son would be something more than trifling pocket-change, and he was on the verge of bankruptcy as it was.

Still, there was nothing he could do about any of this now. The potion had been made and delivered and, in all likelihood, used, and, as he had said, whatever had happened after that had happened, and he could only wait and see what consequences befell. He mixed himself a mild calming elixir, and after a time it took effect, and he went about his business without giving the matter further thought.

The next evening, half an hour or so before the official opening time of the Midnight Market, Ghambivole Zwoll was moodily going over his accounts when he heard a disturbance in the hall outside, shouting and clatter, and then came the hammering of a fist on the door of his shop; and, looking up, he beheld the gaudy figure of the Marquis Mirl Meldelleran gesturing at him through the time-dimmed glass.

The marquis looked furious, and he was brandishing his bared sword in his right hand, swishing it angrily back and forth. Ghambivole Zwoll had never seen anyone brandishing a drawn sword before, let alone one that was being waved threateningly in front of his own beak. It was a dress sword, ornate and absurd, intended only as an ornamental appurtenance—the fad for swordplay in daily life had long ago ended on Majipoor—but its edge looked quite keen, all the same, and Ghambivole Zwoll had no doubt of the damage it could work on the frail tissues of his small body.

He was alone in the shop. The Skandar woman had already finished her nightly chores and gone, and Shostik-Willeron had not yet arrived. What to do? Darken the room, hide under the desk? No. The marquis had already seen him. He would only smash his way in. That would entail even more expense.

"We are not yet open for business, your grace," said the Vroon through the closed door.

"I know that. I have no time to wait! Let me in."

Sadly Ghambivole Zwoll said, "As you wish, sir."

The Marquis Mirl Meldelleran strode into the shop and took up a stance just inside the door. Everything about him radiated anger, anger, anger. The Vroon looked upward at the figure that rose high above him, and made a mild gesture to indicate that he found the bared sword disconcerting.

"The potion," he said mildly. "It was satisfactory, I trust?"

"Up to a point, yes. But only up to a point."

The tale came spilling out quickly enough. The lady had trustingly sipped the drink the marquis had put before her, and the marquis had managed even to recite the spell in proper fashion, and the potion had performed its function most admirably: the Lady Alesarda had instantly fallen into a heated passion, the Marquis Mirl Meldelleran had swept her off to bed, and they had passed such a night together as the marquis had never imagined in his most torrid dreams.

Ghambivole Zwoll sensed that there had to be more to the story than that, and indeed there was; for the next night the marquis had returned to Muldemar House, anticipating a renewal of the erotic joys so gloriously inaugurated the night before, only to find himself abruptly, coolly dismissed. The Lady Alesarda had no wish to see him again, not this evening, not the next evening, not any evening at all between now and the end of the universe. The Lady Alesarda requested, via an intermediary, that the Marquis Mirl Meldelleran never so much as look in her direction, should they find themselves ever again in the same social gathering, which was, unfortunately for her, all too likely, considering that they both moved in the same lofty circles among the younger nobility of Castle Mount.

"It was," said the marquis, smoldering with barely suppressed rage, "the most humiliating experience of my life!"

Ghambivole Zwoll said mildly, "But you came to me seeking, so you said, a night of pleasure with the woman you most desired in all the world. By your own account, my skills have provided you with exactly that."

"I sought a continuing relationship. I certainly didn't seek to be spurned after a single night. What am I to think: that when she looked back on our night together, she thought of my embrace as something vile, something loathsome, something that had left her with nothing but black memories that she longed to purge from her mind?"

"I have heard tell that the lady is betrothed to a great prince of Castle Mount," said the Vroon. "Can it be that when she returned to her proper senses she was smitten by a sense of obligation to her prince? By guilt, by shame, by terrible remorse?"

"I had hoped that her night with me would leave her with no further interest in that other person."

"As well you might, your grace. But the potion was specifically designed to obtain her surrender on that one occasion when it was administered, and so it did. It would not necessarily have a lingering effect after it had left her body."

As he spoke the door opened behind the marquis and Shostik-Willeron, arriving for the night, stepped into the shop. The eyes of the Su-Suheris flickered quickly from Ghambivole Zwoll to the Marquis Mirl Meldelleran to the marquis's unsheathed sword, and a look of terrible dismay crossed his faces. The Vroon signaled to him to be still.

"Literature is full of examples of similar cases," Ghambivole Zwoll said. "The tale of Lisinamond and Prince Ghorn, for example, in which the prince, after at long last consummating the great desire of his life, discovers that she—"

"Spare me the poetic quotations," the marquis said. "I don't regard a single night's success, followed by icy repudiation the next day, as in any way a fulfillment of your guarantee. I require fuller satisfaction."

Satisfaction? What did he mean by that? A duel, perhaps? Ghambivole Zwoll, appalled, did not immediately reply. In that moment of silence, Shostik-Willeron stepped forward. "If you will pardon me, your grace," said the Su-Suheris, "I must point out to you that my partner did not stipulate anything more than the assurance that the potion would secure you the lady's favors, and it does appear that this was—"

The Marquis Mirl Meldelleran whirled to face him and flicked his sword savagely through the air from side to side before him. "Be quiet, monster, or I'll cut off your head. Just *one* of them, you understand. As a special favor I'll allow you the choice of which it is to be."

Shostik-Willeron moved into the shadows and said nothing further.

The marquis went on, "To continue: I regard the terms of our agreement as having been breached."

"A refund, milord, would be very difficult for us to—"

"I'm not interested in a refund. Make me a second potion. A stronger one, much stronger, one that will obliterate all other affections from her mind and bind her to me forever. You make it and I'll find some way to get it to her and all will be well, and my account with you will be quits. What do you say, wizard? Can you do that?"

The Vroon pondered the question a moment. Shostik-Willeron was right, he knew: Shostik-Willeron had been right all along. They never should have had anything to do with this grimy business. And they should refuse now to continue with it. Like all his kind, he had some slight power of foretelling the future, and the images that came to him by way of such second sight were not encouraging ones. Whether or not the law was on their side, the great lords of Castle Mount certainly were unlikely to be, and if this slippery marquis continued his pursuit of the Lady Alesarda, he would sooner or later bring down the vengeance of those mighty ones not only upon him but upon those who had aided and abetted him in his quest.

On the other hand, that consideration was a relatively abstract one, at least when compared with the sharp and gleaming reality of the sword in the Marquis Mirl Meldelleran's hand. The great lords of Castle Mount were far away; the sword of the marquis was right here and very close. That alone was incentive enough for the Vroon to plunge ahead with this new task that the marquis required of him, regardless of the obvious riskiness of it.

The hard blue eyes were bright with menace. "Well, little magus? Will you do it or won't you?"

In a low, weak voice, the Vroon said, "I suppose so, your grace."

"Good. How soon?"

Again, Ghambivole Zwoll hesitated. "Eight days? Perhaps nine? The task will not be an easy one, and I realize that you will accept nothing less than complete success. I'll need to consult many sources. And beyond doubt a great many rare ingredients must be obtained, which will take some little while."

"Eight days," said the Marquis Mirl Meldelleran. "Not an hour more."

Compounding such a powerful potion, far more intense than the one he had given the marquis, would be perfectly feasible, of course. It was years since he had made such a thing, but he had not forgotten the art of it. It would call for the utmost in technical skill, Ghambivole Zwoll knew, and would require, just as he had asserted, some rare and costly ingredients: they would have to go back to the moneylenders once again to cover the expense.

But he had no choice. Doubtless Shostik-Willeron was right that there was great peril in meddling in the romantic affairs of the aristocracy; the marriage of a Coronal's son to a princess of Muldemar must surely be a matter not just of romance but of high political intrigue, and woe betide anyone who sought to undo such a match for his own sordid purposes. Still, Ghambivole Zwoll wanted to believe, even now, that whatever consequences might befall such meddling would fall upon the Marquis Mirl Meldelleran, not on the lowly proprietors of some unimportant sorcerers' shop in the Midnight Market. The real peril he and

Shostik-Willeron faced, he told himself again and again, was not from so remote a thing as the displeasure of the great lords of the Castle but rather from the uncontrolled anger of the rash, reckless, and frustrated marquis.

Gloomily Shostik-Willeron concurred in this reasoning. And so they floated a new loan, which left them almost as deep in debt as they had been before the marquis and his twenty-royal commission had come to plague their lives. Ghambivole Zwoll sent orders far and wide to suppliers of precious herbs and elixirs and powders, the bone of this creature and the blood of that one, the sap of this tree, the seed of another, potations of a dozen sort, galliuc and ravenswort, spider lettuce and bloodleaf, wolf-parsley and viperbane and black fennel, and waited, fidgeting, until they began to arrive, and commenced, once the proper ingredients for the basis of the drug were in his hands, to mix and measure and weigh and test. He doubted very much that he would have the stuff ready by the eighth day, and in truth he had never regarded that as a realistic goal; but the marquis had insisted. The Vroon hoped that when the marquis did return on the eighth day and found the potion still incomplete, he would see that the magus was toiling in good faith and did indeed hope to have the job done in another day or two, or three, and would be patient until then.

The eighth day came and midnight tolled, and the market was thrown open for business. As Ghambivole Zwoll had expected, the drug was not quite ready. But, to his surprise, the Marquis Mirl Meldelleran did not appear to claim it. He was hardly likely to have forgotten; but something pressing must have cropped up to keep him from making the short journey downslope to Bombifale to pick up his merchandise tonight. Just as well, the Vroon thought.

Nor did the marquis show up on the ninth night either, though Ghambivole Zwoll had brought the stuff to the verge of completion by then. The following afternoon, by dint of having worked all through a difficult sleepless day, the Vroon tipped a few drops of the final reagent into the flask, saw the mixture turn a rewarding amber hue shimmering with highlights of scarlet and green, and knew that the job was finished. If the marquis came here at last this evening to claim his potion, Ghambivole Zwoll would be ready to make delivery. And the marquis would have no complaints this time. The new potion did not even require the recitation of a spell, so powerful was its effect. So the poor high-born simpleton would be spared the effort of memorizing five or six strange words. Ghambivole Zwoll hoped he would be grateful for that.

With midnight still a few hours away, the market had not yet opened for business. Ghambivole Zwoll waited, alone in the shop, tense, eager to have this hazardous transaction done with at last.

A little while later he heard the sounds of some commotion in the hall: an outcry from the warders, someone's angry response, a further protest from one of the warders. In all likelihood, the Vroon thought, the Marquis Mirl Meldelleran had finally come, and in his usual blustering way was trying to force his way into the market before regular hours.

But the noise outside was none of the marquis's doing this time. Abruptly, the door of Ghambivole Zwoll's shop burst open and two sturdy-looking men in fine velvet livery brightly embla-zoned across the left shoulder with the image of the Muldemar Ruby, the huge red stone that was the well-known emblem of that great princely house, came thundering in. They were armed with formidable swords: no foppish dress swords these, but great, gleaming, grim-looking military sabers.

Ghambivole Zwoll understood at once what must have hap-pened. Some Muldemar House maid had confessed, or had been made to confess, that her lady had had an illicit nocturnal visitation. One question had led to another, the whole story had come out, the identity of the sorcerer in question had somehow been revealed, and now these thugs had come on their princely master's behalf to take revenge.

The way they were glaring at him seemed to leave no doubt of that. But from the manner in which they held themselves, not merely threatening but at the same time wary, ill at ease, it appeared likely that they feared he would use some dark mantic power against them. As if he could! He cursed them for their stupidity, their great useless height and bulk, their mere presence in his shop. What madness it had been, Ghambivole Zwoll thought, for his forebears to have settled on this world of oafish, oversized clods!

"Are you the magus Ghambivole Zwoll?" the bigger of the two demanded, in a voice like rolling boulders. And he slid his great sword a short way into view.

Ghambivole Zwoll, swept now with a terror greater than any he had ever known in his life, shrank back against his desk. If only he could have used some magical power to thrust them out the door, he would have done so. If only. But his powers were gentle ones, and these two were huge, bulky ruffians, and he did not dare make even the slightest move.

"I am," he murmured, and did what he could to prepare himself for death.

"The Prince of Muldemar will speak with you," the big man said ominously.

The Prince of Muldemar? Here in the marketplace, in Ghambivole Zwoll's own shop? The fifth or sixth highest noble of the realm?

Incredible. Unthinkable. The man might just as well have said, *The Coronal is here to see you. The Pontifex. The Lady of the Isle.*

The two huge footmen stepped aside. Into the shop came now a golden-haired man of fifty or so, short of stature and slender but broad-shouldered and regal of bearing. His lips were thin and tightly compressed, his face was narrow. It could almost have been the face Ghambivole Zwoll had often seen on coins of long ago, the face of this prince's royal ancestor five generations removed, the great monarch Prestimion.

There was no mistaking the searing anger in the prince's keen, intense greenish-blue eyes.

"You have supplied a potion to a certain unimportant lordling of Castle Mount," the prince said.

Not a question. A statement of fact.

Ghambivole Zwoll's vision wavered. His tentacles trembled.

"I am licensed, sir, to provide my services to the public as they may be required."

"Within discretion. Are you aware that you went far beyond the bounds of discretion?"

"I was asked to fulfill a need. The Marquis Mirl Meldelleran requested—"

"You will not name him. Speak of him only as your client. You should know that your client, who committed a foul act with the aid of your skills, has taken himself at our request this very day into exile in Suvrael."

Ghambivole Zwoll shivered. Suvrael? That terrible place, the sun-blasted, demon-haunted desert continent far to the south? Death would be a more desirable punishment than exile to Suvrael.

In a hoarse croak Ghambivole Zwoll said, "My client asked me to fulfill a need, your grace. I did not think it was my responsibility to—"

"You did not think. You did not think."

"No, your grace. I did not think."

There was no possibility of success in disputing the matter with the Prince of Muldemar. Ghambivole Zwoll bowed his head and waited to hear his sentence.

The prince said sternly, "You will forget that you ever had dealings with that client. You will forget his very name. You will forget the purpose for which he came to you. You will forget everything connected with him and with the task you carried out on his behalf. Your client has ceased to exist on Castle Mount. If you keep records, Vroon, you will expunge from them all indication of the so-called service you performed for him. Is that understood?"

Seeing that he evidently was going to be allowed to live, Ghambivole Zwoll bowed his head and said in a husky whisper, "I understand and obey, your grace."

"Good."

Was that all? So it seemed. The Vroon gave inward thanks to the half-forgotten gods of his forefathers' ancestral world.

But then the prince, turning, took a long glance around the cluttered shop. His gaze came to rest on the handsome flask on Ghambivole Zwoll's desk, the flask containing the new and potent elixir that the Vroon had prepared for the Marquis Mirl Meldelleran.

"What is that?"

"A potion, your grace."

"Another love potion, is it?"

"Merely a potion, sir." Then, in agony, when the prince gave him a terrible glare: "Yes. One could call it a love potion."

"For the same client as before? So that he might compound the damage he has already done?"

"I must reply that I am bound by the laws of confidentiality, sir, not to reveal—"

The Prince of Muldemar responded with a somber laugh.

"Yes. Yes! Of course. What a law-abiding thing you are, wizard! Very well. Pick up the flask and drink the stuff yourself."

"Sir?"

"Drink it!"

Aghast, Ghambivole Zwoll cried, "Sir, I must object!"

The prince nodded to one of the footmen. From the corner of his eye Ghambivole Zwoll saw the ugly glint of a saber's blade coming once more into view.

"Sir?" he murmured. "Sir?"

"Drink it, or you'll join your former client in Suvrael, and you'll count yourself lucky that your fate is no worse."

"Yes. Yes. I understand and obey."

There could be no refusing the prince's command. Ghambivole Zwoll reached for the flask and shakily lifted it to his beak.

Dimly the Vroon watched the Prince of Muldemar and his two footmen leaving the shop, a moment later, slamming the door behind them. It was all he could do to cling to consciousness. His head was spinning. A bright crimson haze whirled about him. He was scarcely able to think coherently.

Then through the fog that engulfed his brain he saw the shop door open again, and the huge Skandar woman Hendaya Zanzan entered to begin her evening's work of tidying and sweeping. Ghambivole Zwoll stared at her in awe and wonder. Instantly a sudden all-consuming passion overwhelmed him. She was radiant; she was glorious; she glowed before him like a dazzling flame. He had never seen anyone more beautiful.

He ran to her, reached up, clasped his tentacles tightly around her enormous calf. His heart pounded with a great surge of desperate love. His vision blurred as tears of joy dimmed his blazing yellow eyes.

"Oh, beloved— beloved—!"

GREG KEYES, who also writes under the names Gregory Keyes and J. Gregory Keyes, was born in Meridian, Mississippi, to a large, diverse, storytelling family. He received degrees in anthropology from Mississippi State and the University of Georgia before becoming a full-time writer. He is the author of *The Waterborn*, *The Blackgod*, the Age of Unreason tetralogy, and the Star Wars: New Jedi Order novels *Edge of Victory I: Conquest*, *Edge of Victory II: Rebirth*, and *The Final Prophecy*. In 2003, he began his fantasy quartet called the Kingdoms of Thorn and Bone, which began with *The Briar King* and continued with *The Charnel*, *The Blood Knight*, and *The Born Queen*. He lives with his family in Savannah, Georgia, where he is also the head coach of the Savannah College of Art and Design's fencing club.

THE UNDEFILED

Greg Keyes

Fool Wolf woke slicked in blood and surrounded by corpses. Again.

The first time he'd been sixteen, and there had only been one casualty—a woman he had kissed, stroked, made love to, planned to have children with. He'd watched as the same hands and lips and body that once brought her pleasure took her to heights of sustained agony with such skill that she remained alive to experience it long after her heart should have stopped. When her eyes finally went hollow, he had heard his voice croon in disappointment.

There were many, many more bodies this time, all as ruined as hers had been. They looked small, as if he were high above them, gazing down.

She twisted in him, not quiescent yet, and he felt her stroke his flesh from the inside, smelled snake and lightning smoke.

Beautiful, she purred.

Trying not to retch, he pushed himself up to standing on limbs trembling with fatigue.

Chugaachik made sure he recalled every detail of that first

death, but since then he sometimes had the good fortune to not remember the details of what he did under her influence.

Not this time, Chugaachik whispered mockingly.

"You should have freed her," Inah pouted from the cell across from his, her usually jade eyes more like obsidian in the torchlight, the lithe curves of her body no more than shadow.

He rested his forehead against the heavy bars.

"You know better than that."

"Do I? She's saved us in the past."

"She saved *me.* If she ever got my hands on you, she would rape and eviscerate you—not in that order."

She has godblood, the spirit caged in his bones murmured. *She could survive our games for a long while, my sweet. She might even enjoy them. Remember, she is something of a sister to me.*

Inah couldn't hear her, of course.

"I can take care of myself," she said.

Fool Wolf grated out a harsh chuckle. "You still don't understand? If I ever unleash her again, the only thing you can do is run."

Yes, why not? A chase is always fun.

"I do understand," she replied. "I would have escaped her—the river was right there. In the river, even she couldn't harm me. Not using *your* body."

"That might have worked," he admitted. "But then she would have just turned on random people."

Never random. I have my tastes, as well you know.

"So?" said Inah.

Good girl.

"Then you really don't understand," he replied, summoning his will to push Chugaachik down, away, to silence her if for only a little while.

He managed it, but realized he'd missed something Inah was saying.

"What?" he asked.

"I said, will you still feel this way when they take us to be executed?"

"We'll see," Fool Wolf replied. "We'll see how I feel then."

She was silent for a moment, then laughed lightly.

"You love me, don't you? That's why you keep her in."

"Darken your mouth," he said. "You don't even know what that means."

Men came for them sometime later, young men with pale, almost blue skin, dressed in brown sarongs and shirts batiked with turtles, snakes, and scorpions.

"This would be a good time," Inah pointed out, in her native tongue. "There are only eight of them."

He didn't answer.

Presently, they were brought into the light and hustled into an enormous cedar house roofed in greenish slate. A narrow entrance hall brought them into a large room with high benches rising in tiers on three sides. Seated on the benches were men—he didn't have time to count them, but there were more than twenty. They were of the same unfortunate paleness as the guards who had escorted them there, and they were all quite young—some looked no older than sixteen. They wore quilted coats that left their arms free, and all were armed, variously, with swords or spears. Some had shields resting against their knees.

One fellow sat alone, directly before them, in a chair with armrests. While the others wore their hair long, in complicated braids, his head was shorn.

He looked down at them for a moment, then spoke, in a language similar enough to that of Nah that Fool Wolf understood it.

"I am Hesqel, the Voice. What is your business in QashQul, other than petty thievery?"

"We have no other business here," Fool Wolf replied. "We were only trying to procure enough food to be on our way. We would be happy to provide some service for what we took—"

"Your crime isn't theft," Hesqel replied. "Your crime is in coming here. Didn't the Urled tribes tell you this valley is forbidden?"

Fool Wolf decided it was probably best not to point out that the Urled tribes had chased Inah and him into the valley, following another disagreement over property.

"They neglected to tell us that," he said.

"Well. Normally this would be a clear case, and you would be executed, but at the moment we have need of an outlander, someone unhampered by the curse. And so your offer of service is accepted."

This isn't going to be good, Fool Wolf thought.

"Curse?" he asked.

Hesqel's tone changed a bit, became a bit more like singing.

"In the ancient times, our people were lost in these mountains, starving and freezing. Then we came to this valley and found it fertile. But the gods here were wild, having never known men before. Many sacrifices were made, but all ignored. The goddess in the uplands, Qul, and Qash—the god of the river and its lands—were bitter enemies, and neither would allow the smaller gods to deal with our ancestors. But at last a sacrifice was found that appeased Qash, and through it gave him the power to subjugate Qul, and they became one—QashQul. We—those of us in this room—descend from him, and thus share his need for the same sacrifice that won him to sustain us."

This could be very, very bad, Fool Wolf thought.

"So the curse is your need for this . . . sacrifice?"

Hesqel blinked and looked as if the question didn't make any sense. Low laughter rippled through the benches.

"No," Hesqel said, now speaking as if to a child. "We are the Sons of Qash, the Undefiled. The sacrifice is part of our nature and is our honor to perform. If we fail to keep the ritual, we wither with time and Qash himself will starve. The curse lies in the schism. QashQul was broken again with the aid of the sorceress Ruwhere. Qul reclaimed her ancient domain, and no descendant of Qash may step there." He leaned forward. "Our curse is that our sacred sword rests in Qul's domain. And it is also to her realm that Ruwhere has taken our rightful sacrifices."

"Ah," Fool Wolf said, relieved. "And you want me—"

"You will recover our sword," Hesqel said.

That seemed straightforward enough.

He didn't believe it.

"I'll be glad to help," he replied.

And like that, he was free, dressed in quilted armor and armed with a short, double-edged sword. He was smiling as he left the walls of QashQul behind him. His step felt light, the future replete with possibility. Of course, they'd kept Inah to ensure he would return, which only proved they didn't know him very well. Oh, he might come back for her, one way or another—he was, after all, fond of her. But given her own powers—which the QashQulites seemed blissfully unaware of—she would probably find her own escape. The point was, he had choices.

The trail went by a clear pool, where he bathed and dallied, watching dragonflies dance in the warm sun. A bit after noon he dressed and—after some hesitation—continued to follow the directions he'd been given. He might as well see what the situation was. Perhaps the sorceress could be bargained with, if she seemed dangerous. Of course, he didn't have much to negotiate with . . .

It's best this way, just you and me, Chugaachik said.

"Best if it was just me," he said.

You know better than that by now, sweet thing. Don't you?

Fool Wolf slowed his step. Yes, a sorceress powerful enough to split a god in half bore talking to.

"This god they're talking about," he mused. "I'm curious. Let's have a look at him, under the lake."

Deep in his mansion of bone, she stirred. His skin felt like flint, his teeth like knives. He smelled blood all around him, practically tasted it.

Then he sank beneath the lake, what his people called the upper skin of the world that most people never saw beyond. The trees and mountains faded to shadow, and the light bled through them. The gods appeared.

He'd seen his first god when he was thirteen. It had been the god of a white juniper tree, a minor spirit, and yet the sight of it had driven him into madness and fever that nearly killed him, for Human Beings were not meant to look directly at gods. Only a few, born to be shamans, could see unmanifested spirits—and unless they became shamans by taking a helping spirit into themselves, they went mad.

His father found him such a spirit, believing her to be that of a lion goddess.

He'd been wrong.

But now, with Chugaachik to open his eyes, he could see beneath the lake and not lose his mind. Usually.

He distinguished the little gods first, those that belonged to things—trees, stones, the pool he had bathed in. Like most gods, their forms were not set; they played at many shapes. He wondered at how few they were; there should have been hundreds, but instead he saw only dozens, and all appeared somehow ill.

Qash was everywhere; he was a god of land, of place. Beneath the lake, these usually had no form either.

But Qash did. He appeared as an obscene, naked older version of the white-skinned men who held Inah, and he sat crouched upon the land, hands shifting aimlessly as if searching for something. His eyes were mirrors of insanity and his drool dripped upward into the streams and pools of his country. Veins erupted from his flesh and went out to connect him to the little gods, to the men in the city—and one sickly yellow quivering string went off ahead, in the direction Fool Wolf was supposed to travel. He could not see where it went; something blocked him there.

Something to bargain with, he thought.

He reached, and with Chugaachik's power he plucked at one of the strands, pulled a new one from it and tied it to a nearby grapevine.

Then he came back up through the surface of the lake. He sat down, feeling dizzy and ill but that passed after a few moments. He rose, cut the grapevine, and wove it into a small hoop about the diameter of his forearm. Then he continued on.

The ground sloped up sharply into a forest of odd, twisting oaks, star pine, and juniper. The resinous scent of the last made the damp air fragrant, and for a moment he felt as if he was far away, on the windswept Steppes of the Mang, where he had been born, where his people still made their annual rounds, hunted grass bears and bison, raided Stone-Leggings and Cattle People.

How far was he from there? If he ever made it north out of these mountains, he ought to be somewhere near Lhe, and from there he could take one of the old, faded roads that ran up through the Sherirut chiefdoms. If he had horses, he might do it in a year, or better. It would be good to eat dube stew again, see Ch'ebegau, the White Spruce Mountain. Feel like a Mang once more, like he belonged. His mother—was she still alive? His sisters and cousins?

He tried to picture his mother's face, but found only a blur.

He'd searched the world from the Northern Forests of the Giants to the ancient, decaying cities and febrile islands of the south for a way to be rid of Chugaachik, to have his life back. He hadn't found any answers there. Maybe they lay back where it had all begun, where his father had first introduced him to Chugaachik.

But he didn't belong there, now. He had never really belonged there.

So he continued on, and soon found the shrine that had been described to him: a building with walls of natural stone fitted without mortar, a roof of cedar shingles in need of repair. The door was open.

On the steps leading up to the shrine sat a woman.

Her hair was white and pulled back in a long braid. The face beneath was seamed by years of laughter, sorrow, and pain. Her blue-eyed gaze stayed on him, a bit curious, a bit accusing.

"I wasn't sure what to imagine," she said. "I see desert and red stone," she said. "Scrubby trees in the sand and tall white ones in the mountains. Where are you from?"

"Mangangan."

"I've not heard of it, but it hangs on you. You've been thinking about it."

"It's north, a long ways." Feeling uncomfortable: "If I had been thinking about sex, would you be asking about my women now?"

She smiled. "I see her, too. From very far away, surrounded by water—not your place."

"No."

"Is she why you've come here, to do this thing? Do they have her captive?"

Fool Wolf shrugged. "They have her, yes. But I've yet to decide what I'm going to do."

"I see," she replied. "That's good, to have an open mind."

"Are you Ruwhere?"

"They told you about me, then. And about the freeing of Qul?"

"Yes, although they didn't put it that way. They sent me after a sword."

"Why do you suppose I'm here?" Ruwhere asked.

"To keep me from the sword."

She nodded. "You really don't want it, trust me. Did they tell you why they wanted it back?"

"No. Something about a curse and sacrifices."

"You weren't curious?"

"Whatever they told me, I would have to waste my time trying to figure out what was true and what wasn't. It was easier to just come here and find out."

"I might have chosen to kill you without speaking to you," she pointed out.

"You might have. And yet they seemed pretty confident sending me up here."

"That's what the last three they sent thought," she replied. "It's not confidence—they're just not very bright. They get stupider and weaker every day, without their sustenance. If you wait long enough, they will die, and you will have your woman back."

"How long?"

"Without their ritual, they will age like men. A few decades, at most."

"I don't really have that much time on my hands," Fool Wolf said.

"I suppose not," she replied.

"What happens if I give them their sword?"

She shook her head. "You should put that thought out of your head. First of all, I won't let you touch it. But even if you did—

the fact is, they don't want their sword. None of them can wield it without their lives draining back into Qash. What they want is some idiot who doesn't know better to pick it up."

"Why?"

"Well, to take it you would have to slay me, and they want that. And once you held the sword, Qash would possess you and send you after the virgins."

Fool Wolf suddenly felt completely lost.

Virgins? Chugaachik hissed. *This gets better and better.*

Fool Wolf did his best to ignore her, but she was aroused, and he felt warm behind his ears, as if someone were kissing him there.

"I don't understand," he told Ruwhere.

"The sword is part of Qash," she replied. "And Qash is quite mad. Our people drove him mad a thousand years ago when they sacrificed a virgin to him."

"Ah," Fool Wolf said, "and since they are his descendants, they also require virgin sacrifices."

"Yes, you see that do you? But their union was unnatural, evil. Qul always strained to be free and finally—after centuries, with my help—Qul managed to break away and take her daughters with her."

"The virgins are Qul's daughters?"

"The men who sent you here are the sons of Qash. It is from the daughters of Qul that they must have their sacrifices. I brought the daughters here, the ones who remain virgin, to keep them safe."

"I can think of better ways to save a virgin," Fool Wolf said. "The problem is in being virgin, yes? If only virgins are fit for sacrifice—"

The air suddenly crackled with force, and his sight opened as he was yanked beneath the lake. Ruwhere was a burning brand, the knot in the heartstrings of a god, and the god was all around them, a half-formed woman, naked, mutilated. Her gaze was all deranged fury.

Ruwhere's calm exterior broke, and that rage rushed through her.

"Wait—"

"You're like them," Ruwhere said, in a low, flat tone. The reasonable old woman was nowhere in that voice. "They don't *kill* them. They *rape* them, just as they taught Qash to rape Qul, just as they now must rape to keep their youth."

"I didn't understand that," Fool Wolf said, backing away. "I was only joking. I wouldn't . . ."

It's too late, Chugaachik snarled. *Qul has her.*

"You have!" Ruwhere screamed. "The things you've done, I see them now, the things . . ." She choked off, and her eyes rolled back.

He did the only thing he could do. He tossed the grapevine ring so that it landed about Ruwhere's neck. Her eyes went wide with shock as Qash entered her by his vein, seeking through to Qul. Mad or not, Qul understood the danger, and in an instant severed the conduit. But by then, Fool Wolf had lunged past the sorceress and taken grip on the sword.

He turned and found Ruwhere blazing with godforce and knew that if it weren't for Chugaachik, he would already be dead. Gasping as his bones began to burn, he threw himself at her, plunging the weapon in deep just below her breastbone. Ruwhere hung on the blade, her eyes gradually calming.

"You've done it," she gasped. "You monster. You don't understand what . . ."

But she fell away, and the presence of Qul diminished and then fled from the sword.

"It was only a joke." Fool Wolf sighed.

He tried to drop the blade, but his head seemed to fill with locusts and his legs began jerking without his permission.

And he knew Ruwhere had been right, and Qash was in him.

He's trying to make you walk, Chugaachik said. She seemed weak, far away.

"I'm not walking," he noticed.

Because I'm fighting him. He's trying to drive me out.

Fool Wolf considered that for a moment. "Can he?"

No. But this is taxing, and I cannot help you like this.

"That's interesting," he said. "I wonder if you're lying. If he might rid me of you, given time."

He would have you then, always. Do you want that?

"I could drop the sword."

Not if I'm gone. But you can drop it now. You should *drop it now.*

Fool Wolf looked at the weapon, considering, seeing possibilities. If Qash forced her out, and he managed to leave the valley, wouldn't he be free? Qash was a god of place—he would stay. It might be a chance worth taking.

But he didn't know enough yet.

"Let's not be in a hurry about this," Fool Wolf said. "I think I'll go have a look at those virgins, first."

Ruwhere hadn't made any effort to hide her trail, and even without his senses heightened by Chugaachik Fool Wolf was a good tracker. Her path carried him higher up the steepening valley wall, through rattling stands of bamboo and graceful tree ferns, and finally to a series of broad terraces planted in crops that Fool Wolf didn't recognize. A few men and women working in the fields gave him odd glances, but no one spoke to him.

Above the fields he came to the village, if it could be called that. Tents, lean-tos, and a few crude houses—all clearly recent—

clustered thickly around an older, much more solid building, an enormous longhouse of cedar raised up on twelve thick stone pedestals. A lot of people were watching him now, but he didn't see any with weapons. He strolled toward one of the long ladders that led up to the house as if he belonged there. He almost made it before a young woman stepped in front of him. She was pretty, with a round face and pink cheeks, probably no more than sixteen.

"Who are you?" she demanded. She seemed frightened, but determined.

"My name is Fool Wolf," he said. "Ruwhere sent me to make sure the virgins are safe."

"They are," she said.

He put on his most winning smile. "Might you be one of them?"

She laughed bitterly. "Not for a while," she said. "You're a foreigner aren't you? You don't know much about this place." She looked him up and down. "But you wear their armor," she said.

"I took this from one of them," he lied. "After I killed him."

"Maybe you did," she said. "If so, thank you. But if you serve them, I will find a way to kill you."

"I take it . . ." he trailed off.

"We all were," she said shortly.

He noticed that a crowd had gathered now, mostly women.

"I'll never bear children," she said. "That's how badly they hurt me—and I was lucky. I used to think that was for the best, because I would never have my daughter taken for the ritual. But then Ruwhere freed Qul, and everything has changed." She lifted her chin defiantly. "You'll have to kill me if you want them."

"I don't want . . ." he stopped. "How old were you?"

"Older than most. The younger we are, the more we sustain them. Or so they think, anyway."

Fool Wolf looked up the ladder. He heard a long, piercing wail.

He shoved the girl out of the way, rushed up the bamboo steps. He heard her screaming and felt her weight join his on the ladder.

The longhouse was one vast empty space. A few older people looked up as he entered, but besides them, of the more than a hundred inhabitants of the building, none looked to be over the age of four. Most were infants.

The girl hit him in the back. He ignored her as the sword in his hand hummed in hunger and Chugaachik howled with lust. A wind came through the house, and he smelled juniper.

Hesqel looked down at Fool Wolf from his high seat and smiled.

"You've done it," he said. "You have the sword."

"That I do," he replied. "And so where is my companion?"

"She is safe, in the prison. But you've only performed half of your task."

"You sent me to get the sword, nothing more."

"Something's wrong," one of the others said. "He should be—"

"Yes, he should," Hesqel said. "He who bears the sword should be host to Qash."

"Oh, he's here," Fool Wolf said, raising the blade.

Hesqel sneered. "I don't know what witchery prevents his incorporation, but that weapon cannot harm any of us."

"I believe you," Fool Wolf said.

He dropped the sword.

Godblood, Chugaachik sighed as he stepped over the dead. *Almost as good as babies. Release me again—we'll go back up there, find out what Qash sees in virgins.*

He didn't even bother to answer her, but just shook his head wearily.

You've never been like that before, sweet thing. That was more you than me.

"I know."

Why?

"You wouldn't understand," he said.

We've killed children before. We've done things these pathetic half-men never dreamed of.

"That's right," Fool Wolf replied. "Now, sleep."

It was easy, because she was sated. As she slunk away, he could still feel her genuine confusion.

He had to kill a guard to free Inah. She looked at the yellowish blood that soaked his clothes and coated his face and shook her head,

"You let her out," she said. "After all that talk."

"I did it to save you, of course," he replied.

"That's a lie," she said, "but I like it." She leaned up and kissed him.

He bathed in the same pool as he had earlier, then donned some clothes they had taken from a line on the outskirts of the city. By nightfall they were at the rim of the valley. Unfamiliar dales and peaks walked off north, east, and west.

"Which way?" Inah asked.

In the darkening sky, Fool Wolf picked out the constellation his people called the Twins, used that to find the star called the Yekt Kben, the Hearth, the one that never moved. Then he pointed a bit to its right.

"What's there?" she asked.

"Home," he replied.

MICHAEL SHEA was born to Irish parents in Los Angeles, California, where he frequented Venice Beach and the Baldwin Hills for their wildlife. After attending UCLA on the advance-placement program while still in the tenth grade, he made his way to UC Berkeley for the wildlife there during the Time of Troubles. He hitchhiked across America and Canada twice, and at a hotel in Juneau, Alaska, chanced on a battered book from the lobby shelves: *The Eyes of the Overworld,* by Jack Vance. It led to his first Vancean novel, *A Quest for Simbilis,* which was published in 1974. Shea followed that with several novellas, some horrific, some comic, in the *Magazine of Fantasy and Science Fiction,* including the Nebula Finalist, "The Autopsy." He published *Nifft the Lean* in 1982. A classic of the genre, it won the World Fantasy Award and was followed by *The Mines of Behemoth* and *The A'rak.* Other work includes novels *The Color Out of Time; In Yana, the Touch of Undying;* and collections *Polyphemus* and *The Autopsy and Other Stories.*

HEW THE TINTMASTER

Michael Shea

Ah, colorful Helix! It's a rainbow whirligig, a bright coil of bustling streets and painted structures that spirals up the little mountain—or grand hill—of the same name. It lies a few miles inland from Karkmahn-Ra, Earth's most seething port, and the hub of trade for the whole Sea of Agon.

Every ridgeline of Helix's slopes is crusted with proud halls and domiciles, and their burnished roof-tiles and gaudy walls flash like the jumbled facets of a grand jewel extruded from the plain. For color's the thing in Helix. True, the whole Ephesion Island Chain boasts a culture of panache and proud display—the Bazaar of the Southern Hemisphere it's called—but in Helix, pigmentation borders on obsession, on delirium. Mounted as the city is on the rough cone of its eminence, every structure's on exhibit, and an ethos of self-proclamation prevails. It is a chromatic carnival.

This was the city Bront the Inexorable beheld one autumn morning, wending his way up its spiral streets, threading among the drays and freight-wagons, the wains and rickshaws. From the

Jarkeladd Tundras, a man raised to raiding and war, Bront viewed dazzling Helix with an uneasy sense of excess. Look where he would, he saw no cornice not surmounted by frieze work, no window not lavishly mullioned, nor doorway undadoed and unpilastered . . . and every one of these embellishments painstakingly traced in its own tint.

Color was a constant rumor in his ears as well—the tale on every tongue. Bront heard from the jostling throng such shards of talk as: " . . . the lintels *puce,* you understand, the dadoes *apricot,* and all the panels *mauve!*"

"*Mauve?* Do you trifle with me?"

"The grim truth, nothing less!"

"*Mauve* . . . ! You tax belief!"

Bront's shoulders were as muscled as a titanoplod's thigh. He wore his broadsword's hilt thrust up behind his head, and in the matter of decoration of any kind, he was an ascetic. His bronze cuirass, a scarred and dented veteran of many a subarctic skirmish, bore only the severest touch of embellishment: an embossed severed head between his pectorals. It was a crudely executed piece at that, done by a Tundra tinker on a little anvil mounted on the tail of his cart. Not surprisingly, the warrior overheard such aesthetic cavils with a mounting exasperation.

Bront, it must be said, was no dunce, nor was he utterly dead to the aesthetic joys. One's senses were windows to the divine, and excellence must be sought through all the senses' apertures. What man with a soul in him did not thrill to a plangent paean at the close of slaughter? To the architecture of an houri's haunch, or the succulence of snow-chilled wine? To the heft of specie nested in a pouch? Or, indeed, to that specie's glint of buttery gold?

But how many colors did a sane man need? What color, by the Black Crack, *was* mauve? What color was *puce*?

His errand irked him, and that was half his trouble. He had to

fetch his employer a tintwright—for which, in terms less pretentious, read housepainter. People didn't paint things at all in Bront's
native tundras, but he had mercenaried for years in the Great
Shallows, along whose timbered coasts the cities were all plank
and beam, all of which were protected by whitewashes, serviceable
varnishes, and paint of sober hues. And he knew that there, a wall-
smearer ranked about with a mill-hand—was a cut above an ostler,
for the minor heights he climbed, and well below a tree-jack, who
truly climbed. But *here* housepainters would be made much of, and
doubtless whatever scaffold-monkey he engaged would put on airs.

Only the ample advance his employer disbursed to him secured Bront's compliance with this menial errand—that, and
the necromantic aura that haloed his employer's name. Eldest
Kadaster had met him at the dock in Karkmahn-Ra, and proved
to be gaunt and white-haired, his eyebrows brambly and luxuri-
ant, his beard thin and sere, converging to a wispy point below
his chin. He wore a black leathern gown that was scuffed and
scorched here and there—it struck you as some tradesman's
garment, till you looked into the remote serenity of his eyes
and remembered who he was. Eldest Kadaster's name moved in
murmurs throughout the Ephesion Isles, and Bront knuckled his
forehead at their meeting, a northern gesture of respect.

The mage conducted him to a tavern and a corner-table
conference—asked preferences and graciously ordered for him.
Though gratified by the sorcerer's affability, Bront was troubled
when Kadaster explained his first errand.

"But you see, sir," said Bront, "I don't know the first thing
about housepainters . . . How am I to choose one?"

"It doesn't matter. Indeed, the randomness of your choice is
itself the point. A natural conjunction is required between you.
Just go looking, and when the conjunction occurs, you need not
seek me. I'll be with you."

The last promise gave Bront just the faintest tingle down his spine.

Thus it was he now wended his way toward the peak of Helix—and amid an embarrassment of riches, housepainter-wise. Had passed a score and more of them already, glimpsed at work in open-doored interiors, or up on scaffolds anchored to facades. But knowing his choice must be random didn't help Bront. Quite the reverse. How could he know he was making the *right* random choice in so important a matter?

Doing what clearly must be done was the essence of Bront's trade. Here a parry, there a thrust—in a fight to the death, taken moment by moment, there was little ambiguity. How, on what *basis,* was he supposed to pick a particular wall-smearer? All were equally ignoble, all comically daubed with the tints of their trade . . .

On his left now rose a wide web of iron and wood fully eight stories high, with seven stories of gaudily painted windows peeping out of the scaffold's frame, and work still in progress up on the eighth. He studied the man toiling up there—too much un-dignified climbing to reach *that* smearer . . .

As he idly scanned those heights, he saw a blip of motion in the sky. No . . . *out* of the sky, something plummeting right for him. He moved aside, but a beat too late, and felt a weighty im-pact on his shoulder, and a drenching splash covering the whole left side of his head.

Though Bront couldn't have named it, the object that struck him was a half-round paint mop: a large wad of sheep's wool af-fixed to a short pole, its fleece charged with a good half-gallon of bright-blue paint.

It was not so much *laughter* that filled the street around him, as it was a shocked and commiserating exclamation *laced* with laughter from those startled witnesses who couldn't help it.

A voice, reedy with distance and concern, came down to him from the scaffold's crest. "I'm terribly terribly sorry, sir! It slipped my grip! Unforgivable clumsiness! I beg you to accept a reparation! May I toss you down twenty gold lictors?"

As Bront peered upward for the speaker, blue paint dripped down his brow from his drenched hair, like rain from an eave. He slashed with one hand the gaudy pollution from his face, and beheld, leaning out solicitously far from the scaffold's highest railing, a smallish figure with spiky red hair. Even at a distance of over eighty feet, smears of color could be detected on this figure's cheek, his chin . . .

Twenty lictors was a princely sum. These wall-smearers seemed to be obscenely well-paid—thoughts which came to him as from a great distance, for at his core, Bront was molten with wrath. The smearer's proposition, declaimed as it seemed to half the city, perfected that wrath. To be painted half-blue, like a harlequin, in full public view! And then to be tossed down a *tip,* and sent on his way, still half-blue!

Bront roared, throat veins bulging, "You will come *down* here, and clean me *off,* and then I will *kill* you!"

The figure up on the scaffold neither moved nor answered for a moment. The whole street, rapt, harkened as one for his reply.

"Honored sir! So unjustly and undeservedly spattered sir! With the deepest, most abject and heartfelt apologies, I would prefer to throw you down some towels, and perhaps twenty-*five* lictors!"

"Throw me a *tip,* will you? I'll bring a *sword-tip* up to you!" His rage tore his throat, shouting this. He leapt atop one of the great paint-casks arrayed on the pavement below a dangling block and tackle, and seized the scaffold. Up the outer frame he swarmed—having mounted, under fire, many a battlement as vertiginous as this.

"I must regretfully, deeply regretfully, insist that you do not climb my scaffold, sir!" Shouting this, the housepainter vanished from view. Bront felt the far, hasty tread of the man through the frame he climbed—running along the crest to intersect Bront's line of ascent. His smudged face thrust out from the top tier directly overhead now. Bront, already three tiers up and moving fast, could see his face much plainer—ferrety cheekbones, small-ish nose and jaw.

"Don't climb your scaffold you say?" shrieked Bront, and climbed faster. The smearer ducked out of sight, and then reappeared with a long, heavy foot-plank hugged around its middle—leaning out again with this in arms. The vile ferret was stronger than he looked.

"*Please* stop climbing! I entreat you! My apologies are beyond expression!"

Just two tiers below the wretch, Bront climbed with reckless speed. In three more lunges he would have his hands around the smearer's throat.

But suddenly, the plank came down dropping crosswise across his arms. Like a sidewise battering ram, it broke the grip of both his hands, and he pitched backward from the scaffold.

Throughout this whole encounter, it seemed that Bront's reflexes had been just one beat late—and late they were again, for he was thirty feet into his fall before he began a backward somersault, to bring his feet down first on impact.

He might just have made it, but for a huge paint-cask standing on a trestle. The cask intercepted his somersault, so that the back of his neck and shoulders punched through its heading. Bront was swallowed upside down to his knees in a geyser of pigment, spreading a corona of color from which the throng simultaneously—but not all successfully—recoiled.

Despite the crowd's besmirchment, the spectacular quality of this brief transaction between swordsman and painter left them almost mute with awe. The loudest sound in the whole street was that of the painter hastily descending the scaffold along its outer frame.

"Friends! Neighbors! Your help! Please! He might drown!" He called this from a monkey's perch just above the ruptured cask.

"He's drowned already!" someone shouted. "Look!"

And just below the painter, Bront's sandaled feet and greaved shins pedaled spasmodically against the air, and then were still, like two grotesque blossoms protruding from a mauve pond.

"Friends!" said the painter. "You saw it all! Surely you do not blame me?"

"No one blames you, sir." The voice startled everyone. The speaker had not been noticed in their midst—a thin, white-bearded man in a shabby leather gown. "Dear citizens! This was a tragic mishap from first to last! Not least tragic is the defacement of your street, your garments! I am moved by civic feeling to re-pair the damage."

It seemed, for just a pulse or two, that the day grew dimmer. The sunlight turned from gold to dark honey, and an early-evening feeling filled the street, like the hour of lamps a-lighting. The painter, still clinging to the scaffold above the cask, blinked, and shook his head.

And then it was broad noon again, people were dispersing, the soft roar of their varied discourse rising as if never interrupted. The painter saw not one spot of mauve on any garment in the crowd—nor anywhere on the pavement. The stranger smiled up at him. "Will you come down? May I know your name? I am Elder Kadaster, of Karkmahn-Ra, and I am wholly at your ser-vice."

"I am Dapplehew, tintmaster, at *your* service. Please call me Hew." The man jumped to the street. While not large, he seemed

of a dense and springy construction. He wore an affable, courteous expression. The orbits of his blue eyes were crinkly and sun-
burned—far-squinting eyes they seemed, that had long studied
great facades, and imagined their new coloring.

"Hew, if you would help me, I would like to put this unfortunate gentleman to rest. I knew him, you see, and no one else
hereabouts does. He was a decent fellow in his way, but tragically
inclined to passion."

"You are a remarkable, generous gentleman! I am *so* sorry to
have unwittingly—"

Hew's new friend turned away and graciously detained the
driver of a passing wain, the vehicle empty and loud on steel-shod
wheels. He murmured earnestly to the driver, a massive dolt with
hayrick hair. Amazement slowly dawned on the fellow's face.
Receiving from the mage a weighty pouch, the man dismounted,
unhitched his little 'plod, and led the beast away. Kadaster beckoned the painter.

"Now, Hew, perhaps we can use your tackle to place the cask,
and poor Bront, in the wain?"

This transfer accomplished, Kadaster reached up, affectionately patted one of Bront's protruding calves, and said in elegy,
"He was, within his limits, a decent man. Who of us, after all,
lacks *some* defect? And now, shall we take him to my domicile?"
And the mage gestured toward the entry of the very structure
whose topmost floor Hew had just been painting.

The tintmaster stood astonished. He knew the structure—all
Helix did—to be the Seigneurial, a luxurious residential club,
second home to Old Money rentiers and retired notables. And
he knew the doors Kadaster indicated opened on an elegantly
carpeted lobby, spacious to be sure, but as unable to receive the
bulky wagon as the doorframe was too narrow to admit it.

"Pull the wain in *there,* sir?"

"Well, let's start by pulling just the traces through, and see how we fare from that point. Shall we?"

They pulled the traces over the threshold—scarcely pulled, the wheels seemed to roll of themselves—and entered, not the well-known lobby of the Seigneurial Club but a high passage of hewn stone, dark above but yellowishly lit below, as if from a subtle lambency of the flagstones they trod. The wain rolled softly after them, tragic Bront's sandaled feet nodding with its movement like two funeral lilies in their pool of mauve.

"I will confess to you, Hew," said Kadaster as they walked, "that I sent Bront here in search of a man of your trade. The mode of your meeting I perforce left to chance. I grieve that it proved . . . stressful for you both. But now that we are all together, I would like to engage your services, yours and Bront's here, for what I hope you'll consider a handsome emolument in fine-gold specie: fifty thousand lictors each."

Hew's mouth opened, without at first producing speech. At length, he said, "I am deeply honored that you should consider my services worth such a sum, and I am of course keen to learn what you have in view. Still, though I would rather die than offend you," he added, "I must ask if Master Bront's being, ah, dead, isn't an obstacle to this project of yours."

"Ah!" cried Kadaster. "Here's the terrace—I'll pour us all some refreshment!"

And indeed, just ahead of them, the tunnel ended at a blaze of sunlight. They stepped out onto the magnificent terrace of a manse that clung to a great gray mountain's shoulder. Hew stood gazing out into the yawning gulfs of blue air. He realized, finding himself so distant from where he had been mere minutes before, that he was already hired. "Have we come so far? Is that Helix there, barely visible upon the plain? Are we up in the Siderions?"

"Yes, yes, and yes."

Hew gazed at Helix, a little cone of brightness on the distant plain that swept down from these mountains' feet. "Well, great Kadaster, I'm stunned to be so . . . honored."

"The honor is mine. But help me with Bront."

He opened the wain's tailgate. They hoisted the traces high, and the paint cask toppled, releasing the dead mauve Bront. His corpse was slick as an otter, except for his calves and his feet.

Kadaster made a gesture and the wain sprang off the terrace and tumbled away into the mountain gulfs. He seized up a bucket from somewhere and made an emptying gesture with it at the flood of pigment, and every scrap of color peeled off of the terrace and the corpse and cohered in the bucket, which Kadaster tossed, in its turn, out into the abyss.

Now he produced a second bucket, gripping the perfectly clean Bront by the back of his neck, and tucking the bucket under his face. "Bront," he said. "Come back."

Upheaval shook the mighty frame. His head came up and he began to puke mightily. Endless this disgorging seemed, yet when he was done, the bucket was precisely filled with pigment, and there was not an iota of spillage. Hew had taken up one of his host's flasks of wine, and now gently offered it to the warrior, whose eyes seemed to be clearing.

"Perhaps you'd like a cleansing draught?" he said.

Disbelief, then outrage entered Bront's unfocused eyes as he recognized the two solicitous faces gazing down at him. The proffered flask was something he could grasp—he did so, and drank it off. Rose unsteadily and stood swaying, gaping dazedly upon the mountain peaks that marched away from this fastness on every side.

"Drop that over the railing, would you Bront?" the sorcerer pleasantly suggested, indicating the bucket which the warrior had spewed full. The swordsman stiffly picked it up, and carried it to the balcony's edge as if it weighed a thousand stone. Then set it down and stood gripping the balustrade, and gazing out wild-eyed into the gulf.

"I was *dead*!" It was a hoarse shout of protest addressed to the universe. Hew came cautiously to his side.

"I can't tell you how I rejoice in your . . . recovery."

"You *killed* me!"

"No! I prevented you from killing *me*, and it resulted in your death! Surely you'll acknowledge there's an important differ-ence?"

But the gulf distracted Bront's wild eye. He had, it was appar-ent, no thought to spare for quibbles over cause and effect. Again he announced to the vast, limpid mountain air: "I was *dead*!"—wonder now equaled the note of protest in his voice.

"Come, my dear, respected Bront," urged Kadaster, "drop the bucket off the balcony, and let us take more wine together."

As the warrior held the bucket poised to drop, he slanted a question to the tintmaster. "What color would you call this here that I drowned in?"

"Mauve."

Bront released it as he might a striking snake, and shuddered as he watched it—his death there plummeting into the void, dwindling away . . .

In easy chairs, gazing over the gulf, the three of them drank wine. Bront between swallows sometimes seemed to marvel at the flask itself, and at his own hand that held it, but soon enough he drained the wine, and poured himself some more.

"Gentlemen," Kadaster said, "your commission is of the high-est importance. To understand where I mean to send you, you must first consider that no light is ever lost, or ever *will be* lost. Second, you must grasp that time *is* light. No light is ever lost, and every eon's glow, each intricate detail, is still fleeing through the universe, radiating outward from its moment of origin. Your destination will lie within this swelling sphere of light."

"Will lie," Hew added carefully, "within this sphere of time."

"Precisely. And precisely what you are to deliver is a bit of light. You, estimable Hew, will shortly be given an insight into the details of this delivery, which it falls to you particularly to execute."

The wizard paused, and seemed to muse. Bront cleared his throat. "What you need done, this man here, this execrable scaffold-monkey, can do. But you've gone to the trouble of painting me mauve before the eyes of the town, *drowning* me in it, and resurrecting me up here, all because I *too* have some part in this wall-smearing commission?"

"Your assumption is absolutely correct, good Bront, and I sincerely grieve at the understandable pique your words express. We had, perforce, to rely on chance, and chance was dreadfully unkind to you.

"And I fear the same element of chance will govern your execution of our aim where I will shortly send you. We may rejoice, at least, that this mission of yours lies near at hand." He rose, and invited them back to the parapet. "It lies, indeed, not thirty leagues due south of here. You'll be there in scarce three days' march."

Hew and Bront viewed the Siderion Mountains on whose spine they were perched. It was an awesome range of sharp, snow-crowned peaks which they knew to stretch a hundred leagues due south.

"Thirty leagues as the crow flies?" Hew was amazed. "Scarce three days? You mean a month's trek, surely."

Bront's thoughts seemed to have wandered. "Resurrection . . ." he murmured. "How strange it feels, this . . . reacquaintance with the world . . ."

The wizard smiled his sympathy. To Hew's question, he said, "You misconceive the mission. When, in an hour or so, you set out yonder, these mountains will be utterly worn away. A gently rolling high plateau—all that will be left of them—is what you'll tread. But come now, both of you, to my storerooms to be armed and clad."

Returning alone to the balcony, Bront did not disdain the wine—nor had he refused from Kadaster's stores a trail cloak and stout new buskins. While the sorcerer's golden advance had not erased, it had surely moderated his indignation at his sufferings in that cask of paint.

It irked him that the wall-smearer was still closeted with the mage in private conference . . . Still, his curiosity was undeniably piqued: the distant future was to be their destination.

When the sorcerer and Hew returned, the tintmaster wore a leathern harness which wrapped a row of cylinders across his chest. A jar of pigment was socketed in each of these lidded cylinders, and each jar sprouted the handle of what looked to be a remarkably small brush.

"My friends . . ." The mage was pouring a round into their cups. " . . . Forgive me now if my parting injunctions seem spare to you. This is the mage's hardest task—to stint direction when chance is the magic's key additive. I must, perforce, describe your task elliptically.

"At the distance I have named due south of here, lies Minion. It is a bustling place, a gamester's hive of sleepless carnival. Your task lies in the Crystal Combs, a few leagues eastward, but your preparation must commence in Minion. There you will procure the materials good Hew has determined. Engage a jack-haul—a spry one who can run and fight as well as carry—and make up his load with all you will need inside the Combs.

"At some point prior to your departure from Minion, you will have met your third man, precisely how I cannot say. You will know him for your own because he too will be bound for the Combs. These are reached via tunnels beneath them, and in these, you will certainly encounter conflict with the men who sap and chip from below at the crystals. Your third man will know a way into the tunnels.

"Here, Bront, the combative skills that so distinguish you will come into play. But please note that yours is, in essence, a beneficent mission. Where a solid clubbing will suffice, you are not to spill avoidable blood. When you are up in the Combs themselves, you must take particular care not to harm the denizens there, the Slymires, though I am afraid they are dangerous in the extreme, and may be fiercely aggressive.

"When you have reached the primitive Archive of the Slymires—their grotto of runes—you will have a final and most vital task. Hew will need a great deal of help in constructing the scaffolding he needs to ascend the walls of those colossal vaults, and execute that last, most vital act."

" . . . I am to help him construct his . . . *scaffold*?"

"Yes."

Bront shuddered violently. He seemed to be having a full-body memory of his most recent experience on a scaffold. He touched, beneath his cuirass, a pouch of golden lictors—Kadaster's advance. Registering some comfort from this contact, he shuddered again, more softly.

"Now gentlemen," smiled the mage. "Please stand with your toes touching the parapet. I wish you godspeed, and ask you to take one step forward."

"The parapet impedes all forward motion," protested Bront, but in reflexively pushing his right foot against the wall, he felt it swing effortlessly forward, and come to rest on level rock, and found himself standing on a vast, rolling plateau, beneath the rosy light of a far redder sun, at high noon . . .

Early on their third day's march, the weary Bront fell back a bit, and watched Hew's progress on ahead. The scaffold-monkey, though smallish and squarish, was very tight-knit and nimble. He'd evolved a steady, dancing kind of gait to deal with the terrain, and while Bront had scorned the indignity of it from the first, he'd been forced, at length, to imitate—in a more ponderous way, to be sure—that same half-dancing progress.

The endless plateau received—as they quickly learned—recurrent rains, and this red sun's more feeble light yet had power to nourish a lush growth of lichens and algaes on the fissured granite. This tough greenish-purplish growth flourished in a springy-clingy carpet, which cushioned one's boot-soles yet constantly tripped them if they dragged.

Bront disliked this world, the rubescent gloom that was its daylight. What had happened to the sun? Where was its golden fire and fierceness? The landscape seemed not over-populous. They'd seen distant caravans—what looked like men on tall, spindle-legged mounts—seen other solitary journeyers, pairs and trios too. Human-seeming, a good half of these transients. Occasionally, across the furry turf, far flocks of rock-toads moved, batrachian shapes the size of horses grazing the lichens, then drifting on in a lurching, wriggling way to farther pasture. None of these other beings showed any wish to intercept their path. All seemed bent on their own business here on this later Earth, and Bront was vexed that he could not imagine that business. What was everyone *doing* here?

Irksome too, he found Hew's endless silence. He had at the outset, of course, told Hew he did not wish to speak to him. But the man might have tried to talk him out of this once or twice! Instead he had marched perfectly mute for more than two days now—save for the exchange of some polite syllables, during the business of making each night's camp.

"Very well!" Bront at last erupted. Hew turned to face him.

Entering the last quarter of its transit of this endless terrain, the sun's red grew purplish, while the east took on shades of maroon. It gave one an underwater feeling, to move through air so richly hued. "I wish to know," he told Hew stiffly, "all that *you* know of this task we're at. Mere civility, I'd think, would have prompted you to share that by now!"

"Permit me to ask," replied Hew. "Is it your wish that we should speak to one another now?"

"Have I not just said so?"

"And that we should speak to one another henceforth?"

"Yes."

"I'm delighted. I will tell you as clearly as I can what we are enjoined to do. Much is unknown, and much else unclear to me, so . . . we must have patience."

"Of course we must! Do you take me for a lout?"

"Certainly not! But you exerted yourself furiously to kill me for a minor clumsiness! It's only natural I should ask."

"Well then."

"Well then. Our mission is for me to make a delivery to the Slymires. A delivery of light. This will take the form of certain colors I will apply to a nook high in their dwelling place within the Crystal Combs. Hence my bandolier of tints."

A gesture here at his harness, which Bront had noted he never took off till just before sleep, taking it then inside his cloak with him when he lay down.

"And what colors are you to apply?"

"I don't yet know the colors I shall use. I'll only know them when I see where they are to go. The site always tells me the color it requires."

"So, in a subterraneous, and, I take it, vertiginous place, we are to construct scaffolding while under heavy assault, so that you can apply some colors you have not yet identified."

"Just so."

"May one ask"—Bront struggled to frame his question in a civil tone—"if this bizarre and difficult exploit has some purpose, beyond driving us to grotesque extremes of effort?"

"Kadaster said—not very comprehensibly to me—that the purpose of this work was to, in his words, *save* this world."

"To save this world. To save *our* world's future."

"Well, yes, I suppose so."

Bront resettled his cuirass, and re-draped his cloak. This seemed a task not entirely unworthy of a man of his stature.

"What else can you tell me of what we are to encounter?"

"I know as little as you of this. Look southeastward there. Do you note a kind of glow?"

A plum-hued gloom had settled on that horizon. Against its backdrop, a frail blossom of golden light—just a smudge as fine as pollen dusting a fingertip—seemed to unfold from a distant hollow in the plateau.

"It must be Minion," Bront said. "Let's press on. We might make up our load of . . . *scaffolding* before we sleep."

Full dark drew down as they reached the broad depression where Minion lay like a nest of jewels. For some time they'd been hearing the noise of it across the plateau, a faint exhalation which was now resolved into a tumult of music, laughter, exclamation, and the rattle of myriad wheel-rims on flagstones and cobbles. Before them, an inland sea of lamps and lanterns, tapers, torches, beacons, cressets, and flambeaux—a lake of light and uproar.

Descending into its purlieus, they encountered a vigorous

trafficking, even in these more sparsely built-up industrial fringes. Here were dray-beast stables, wagon-wrights, caravan chandlers, brickyards and masonries, and the isolate but boisterous taverns that enliven all such workmen's districts.

Clearly, commerce flourished by day and by dark, while, amidst the commercial bustle, not a few barouches of more mon-eyed revelers—blazing with lanterns and rocking with song—rocketed among the crowd: top-pocket gamesters rollicking through their eccentric orbits.

Hew thought a wagon-wright might have spoke-staves that would answer their need. "We want stout rungs not too wide, and then thumb-thick whipcord to ladder them on."

"Some drovers' provisioner might be the place for the whip-cord," suggested Bront.

"That's well bethought! Look there—is that not a wheel-wright?"

The wright, his hair in a high comb dyed silver, was at his cups in the saw-shed with two burly mates.

"Hmmm," he replied. "I have three-quarter cubit stock that I might sell in bulk. What footage need you?"

"Well," said Hew, thoughtful at this moment of choice, " . . . I need no less than five hundred cubits of reach for the lad-der work. Eight hundred staves should do."

"By the Crack," muttered Bront. "Is it so much weight we'll be carrying?"

"The bulk," said Hew regretfully, "will be substantial. Yet the scaffold will be—comparatively—of gossamer thinness for the span it must cross and my weight, which it must bear."

"Then I'd best engage the jack-haul now. He'll need time to make up such a load."

Bront, stoically sidestepping careening carriages of yodeling revelers, found a dray stable nearby. The stable neighbored a very active tavern, and within the yard it took some halooing to find a jack-haul to serve him. This one lay in clean straw on his stomach, his chin resting on his huge crossed arms. "How may we help you?" he rumbled.

"I need to engage one of your brotherhood for strenuous drayage through tunnels and up into the Crystal Combs, the said drayage involving self-defense against violent armed assault."

"You seek considerable services beyond drayage."

"That is correct. I'd very much like a jack who can fight."

"Well. We all can, when assaulted." It struck Bront as an odd and reckless notion, to assault a jack-haul. This one's legs, shorter than his arms, were just as massive, jointed for maximum thrust. His fists were as broad as bucklers. "But I must say the work you propose outgoes my own appetite for strife. To enter the Chippers' tunnels alone I would engage, with adequate recompense—"

"We are instructed that you shall name your price."

The jack gave this declaration a long moment of thought, as anyone would. " . . . Even so. The tunnels, yes. But to climb up into the Combs! Well. But there is one of my colleagues whose present circumstances incline him to be much moved by gold."

This second jack Bront found curled on his side in his straw, snoring peacefully. The warrior was surprised. He'd assumed he'd find a younger, more combative jack. This one's fur was in its autumn—he was almost a silver-back.

Salutations failing, Bront had to give him a careful nudge. He woke at once, and on Bront's self-introduction, equably proposed a stroll through the yards to wake him more fully. They passed the pens of other sleeping jacks, and the hay barn, while Bront stated his needs.

The jack paused, and placed his hindquarters on a bale of hay. He stroked his beard, and even against that massive jaw, his fingertips looked shockingly large.

"Well. I can see a way we might make the tunnels. An implement must be improvised which I would wield. But within the Combs . . . imagination fails me. I can climb, but not as you must climb at the last inside the comb. Nor would your scaffold bear me. I will fight to the last to defend our lives against the Slymires, but I cannot yet see how that might be done."

"Nor can I. And . . . I fear that we are not to kill any of these Slymires."

"Oh! Assuming I could do it, I would never kill one!"

"Why not?"

The jack smiled thinly. "Call it . . . an intractable preference of my own, that all of them should live. Now. Forgive my reversion to contractual considerations. Am I, freely and absolutely, to name my own price?"

"That is correct."

The jack promptly named a sum that staggered Bront. He worked his mouth, but naught came out. Yet even as he did, he felt something growing, swelling against his ribs. It was a pouch Kadaster had given him to tuck behind his cuirass. He had to unbuckle the cuirass to extract the suddenly engorged poke, and hand it over to the jack.

"Well then. I am Bront, and my partner is Hew."

"I am Jacques."

Against the great wedge of his back, Jacques put on his load-bed, inserting arms and legs into its massive harness, massively buckled. At the wheelwrights', they found Hew and the others hard at work. The whipcord had been procured, and they were tying fifty-cubit lengths of ladder, and rolling these in bundles. Jacques shucked his load-bed, and they began to lash the ladder-rolls upon it.

An uproar and a commotion of boot soles came surging into the wheelwrights' yard. A tall, lean figure, pursued by the rest, dodged narrowly past Bront, but then tripped over Hew and went sprawling, while the rout of his pursuers, so close upon him, collided outright with the expeditioners.

This rout, some dozen men much in their liquor but rapt in their onrush of outrage, began at once to ply their staves and knouts on the jack-haul, the wheelwrights, and their employers alike. Bonneted and glad-ragged in a way that suggested moneyed revelers from the gaming halls, they fought with a furious tenacity, even against the wakened wrath of Jacques and Bront, and the spirited counterattack of Hew and the wrights and the lanky stranger they'd pursued here.

The turmoil was but briefly intense, the larger, more practiced bruisers soon enough laying the whole gaggle of gamblers on the ground. The object of their pursuit professed his gratitude, as well as his utter puzzlement as to his pursuers' motives. His bows of acknowledgment showed a sinewy strength, as had his fighting. His profile in the torchlight was sharp-jawed, with a nose most aquiline, and there was something droll, and instantly untrustworthy, in his face.

Bront set to dragging the pummeled gamblers out into the public lane, while the rest of his party continued loading and lashing Jacques's back-bed.

The stranger lent Bront a hand. They dropped a pair of his stunned persecutors onto the cobbles, and he bowed graciously.

"Sir. I ducked your way merely seeking some obscurity in which to evade my attackers. I am Cugel, a name not unadorned with my sobriquet—the, ahem, Clever. I am an itinerant entrepreneur, and most grateful for your help."

"Think nothing of it. I am Bront, a stranger to these parts."

"Tell me, good Brunt—"

"Bront, the Inexorable."

"Tell me, esteemed Bront. Have you come here seeking personal enrichment?"

"Alas." They were dragging out a second pair of groggy gamblers in their mud-spotted finery. "We have a mission of our own."

"May I just breathe you a notion? A single thought? The Chippers' tunnels, underneath the Crystal Combs. A wealth of gems and lenses."

"You can find these tunnels? Find your way into them?"

"Nothing easier!—nothing easier for *me,* I mean," he added solemnly. Bront knew him then for their third man, chance-met and similarly bound, but he recoiled from the carte blanche he was instructed to offer. Plainly a rogue and a ready felon, this man, if paid his own price in advance, would vanish at once. "I sense, good Cugel, that you seek allies within the Combs."

"No! Within the tunnels below them."

"Of course, of course." Bront cursed his near-betrayal of their own objective, and struck a note of innocent enthusiasm. "It is a wonderful coincidence, our meeting thus, for we share your goal of penetrating the Chippers' tunnels! The more hands for defense there, the better."

"My own view precisely! Crystal is my very purpose here. I was in a den of chance, financing my expedition, when these ruffians assaulted me."

They were now dragging out the last pair of the groggy gamesters. "Indeed!" Bront commiserated, repressing a sardonic smile. "You mean to say they burst into your place of recreation?"

"No! They were seated at my table! Who would have imagined?"

"Shocking!"

When Jacques's bed was loaded with the rolls of laddering,

and balanced and lashed to his satisfaction, he led their party to a
sawyer, and then a joiner, where he presided over the manufacture
of a large wooden piston with a shaft to fit his huge hands—for
"tunnel clearing," he said. Cugel completed his own preparations
by the simple acquisition of a stout, commodious knapsack. They
repaired to Jacques's stables with a demi-amphora of tart Skaldish
wine. Seated on hay bales, the three men wielded the jacks' big
goblets two-handed.

The coincidence of Cugel's destination with their own caused
Hew to nod to Bront, as if to say, here was their liaison foretold.
"I regret," he told Cugel, "that we are sworn not to speak of our
own errand in the mines, but we must—forgive us—know yours,
lest it impede our own."

Cugel drank off his goblet with evident relish. "My venture
involves a lovely commercial arrangement which I do not blush
to boast of. I've made a colleague among the Chippers who has
sequestered for me a load of prime dodecas! Naturally, with such
precious contraband at issue, my rendezvous within the mines
must be discreetly made."

"It may be," Jacques growled thoughtfully, "that our aims will
hinder yours, for we foresee our entry as arousing something of a
stir."

"Too truly said," conceded Cugel. "My hope is to assist your
struggles to the point where I may . . . branch off to my quieter
work. There is much traffic in the shafts, and the adits, where
gantries tunnel upward toward the Combs, are busy zones, where
one can slip betimes away."

The jack-haul's great sable eyes sought Hew's and Bront's. "Do
you object to having his help until he leaves us?"

Bront said, "We rejoice that our enterprise will, as it seems,
offer protection to yours. May we know a bit more? What, for
instance, *are* dodecas?"

"I can answer you with perfect candor. They are twelve-faceted crystals, fractible into lenses for heat-cannons, intensifiers of the sunlight. I can even openly avow the prospective purchasers of my dodecas: the Biblionites, who presently besiege the Museum of Man, to despoil Guyal the Curator and distribute the museum's numberless gnomens to the world at large. It is only by these sun-cannons' use that the besiegers have damaged those mighty walls even the little that they have."

The jack nodded his huge head, and took a pensive draft. "I, for one, have always doubted the sincerity of the Biblionites. Do they truly intend a philanthropic flooding of the earth with all their plundered texts? Nonetheless . . . en route to our divergent goals, I am inclined to welcome your knout and your blade. Gentlemen?" This last to his employers.

A wind blew through the yard, icy and intimate, rifling their garments with pickpocket fingers. This wind's scent and haunting whisper were unearthly—or rather, seemed to breathe from the entire earth at once—the tang of midnight ocean, the sear of arctic tundra, the green humidity of endless jungle were in it, and every note of restless atmosphere, and a hint of cold like the absolute cold between the stars . . . Along the street—empty some long while now—a figure came gliding, and turned in at the gate.

Caped and hooded in black, both tall and wide this figure was, advancing on them. No gait was evident in its going, no rhythm of legs, but a smooth drifting which, though it never paused at all, seemed forever in arriving, its approach unending, never done. And the four of them, bound in one rapture, watched it come, and felt that, suddenly, this was a different world they sat in.

The visitant towered before them. Lifted ragged hands of smoke, and drew back the hood. What she uncowled—within an undulant mane of tendriling black smoke—was a globe of eyes, eyes only and uncountable, for each eye focused on resolved into a globular cluster of eyes more myriad, and each of these distinctly brimming with memories and meaning . . .

And all at once, the four dumbfounded entrepreneurs *knew* those memories. It smote them down into a reeling madness, this storm of beauties recollected in those eyes. Their minds were blown beneath skies paved with starfire, or flotillaed with sun-struck cumuli sailing, were chased along shores and valleys and mountains, rode prairie gales flattening the earth's deep golden fur, crossed red-and-cerulean deserts where cactus armies stood swollen with green fire, saw carpentered villages bobbing on the swell of forested foothills—all while their hearts were shown nearer things, shown, from a mother's nearness, radiant infants laid in cradles, or in graves, shown the long-beloved, white-haired, kissed farewell, shown the dying eyes of an enemy stabbed amid tumult and dire extremity, shown the devout eyes that guide the laying of the capstone on a temple of prayer . . .

Torn in this storm of multi-mindedness, they toppled from their seats and groveled in the straw, groped for their sanity in a maelstrom of worlds and of hearts' upheaval, and as they crouched in this gale, their visitant spoke within them.

"Go no further in your wicked work. I am this world's future and its destined end. I am this world's witness at its dying, carrying within me the centuries whose terminus I am. Fecund with their whole remembered span, I will embrace eternity. I am this world's future, and you shall not unmake me."

It came to them, after a long, dazed time, that they were alone. They rose to their feet, and stood on solid ground again. They searched one another's eyes, and each learned that he had not dreamed. Jacques withdrew from his doublet the swollen pouch of Kadaster's gold, and tendered it to Bront.

"My profound apologies. I have not strength to *move* against such power."

"Do not apologize," said Hew, and cleared his throat. "Hold fast to your stipend. We have been provided with a means . . . to shield our wits and wills from Her. Forgive me, I was taken unawares. For our next encounter we will be prepared."

They drank, and mused. "A ghost of the yet-to-be," muttered Bront. "*Are* we slayers of an entire future?"

"Indeed we are," Hew said gravely, "if we save this earth from its predestined end."

They all took more wine, sorting silently through their thoughts. Cugel, who had been in the gaming dens for three straight days and nights, made his pallet on the straw and fell asleep. The other three, in lower tones, tried to collect some clearer notion of the work that lay ahead of them, and of the Combs' denizens, the Slymires.

Bront, at length, summarized their meager certainties. "So. The Chippers will do their best to kill us every step of the way. They mine the veins of crystal that run below the Combs, but, high though they follow these veins, they have never dared to enter the Combs themselves, for awe of the Slymires. As to the nature of those dread beings, so wildly different are our notions of them that we seem to concur on only one point: that it is at least uncertain whether or not they eat the bodies of the human intruders they kill."

"And that is because," rumbled Jacques, "we have no notion of what they do eat. Penetration of the Combs has never been thought of by even the most rapacious Chipper . . . Well. It seems we had all best take some sleep, don't you think so, gentlemen?"

In the magenta dawn, they shouldered their gear, and stepped out into heavy rain. Up from Minion's hollow, and out onto the sodden plateau they climbed, and thereafter, for two leagues, they marched through an unremitting, drenching downpour so loud that it impeded speech. Approaching the immemorial antiquity of the Crystal Combs, Hew felt himself—felt all four of them to be the merest ephemera, as brief and slight as dead leaves. Surely this deluge would erase them long before they ever reached those ancient eminences . . .

But the storm-rack thinned as the land rose, the rain broke into brief soakings now and then, and murky amber morning filtered down on the rising terrain. Ahead, rocky knolls and fold-ings of the earth formed a kind of corolla encircling much taller shapes: the towering warped domes and wrenched hogbacks of a smoother, blacker stone. These dusky megaliths overtopped by some three hundred cubits their jumbled piedmont: the Combs—all their crystal immured within those huge shells of black basalt.

Across the plateau, other people, here and there, converged toward the same place. "These you see," said Cugel, "the various mines' agents, assayers, bookkeepers, commissaries—all use the main entries. These are far too heavily guarded for us. But all the big mines have quite a few secondary entries. These can be hard to find in that jumbled terrain—the trick is to look for their sen-tries. These, though they also lie hid, can be spotted."

And so it proved. They'd searched the piedmont's knolls and gullies through but one rain-squall more, when Bront detected, just beyond a hillside boulder, the movement of a hand resetting a rain hood on a briefly exposed head.

Storm-rack, red-shot by a sun now nearer zenith, still paved the sky, and wraiths of mist surrounded them. Yet the expedi-tioners suddenly lost the feeling that they were enveloped in this weather's embrace. A sense of overarching space, of a gulf above them, prickled their napes. They all looked up.

The wraith of the future hung over them, itself like storm-

rack now, four hundred cubits' span, swirling in its corona of
black smoke, which seemed to rise from its galaxy of eyes as from
blazing white coals.

But though it roofed them with terror, it could not unseat
their minds. For all four expeditioners, upon first rising from
their pallets in the stable yard, had dashed a few drops in both
eyes from a tiny flask that Hew had produced from his bandolier.
This effusion had, throughout their morning's trek, produced no
alteration of their sight.

Only now did its effect appear, when the mighty ghost unleashed her sleet of madness. Now the riots of memory could not
engulf them, were a translucence which enshrouded them like a
cyclone but did not touch them within the sorcerous envelope.

And so, from grandeurs and glories, the imagery changed
character, became a homicidal tapestry of war and murder—
every kind of dying ever done tornadoed about them. Ravaged
populations struck with plague died as they dropped their dead
in burial pits, and fell in after. Conflagrations chewed cities to
cascades of red-hot coals, in which whole shoals of humankind
were shrunk to blackened sticks. Cataclysmic floods slid tidal
tongues through thickly peopled valleys, and swept their populations streaming over their sunken towns, their struggles like some
strange spasmodic flight, until these struggles slowed, and they
sank down with dreaming eyes.

But finding the four untouched, again she spoke within
them.

"Your world-killing work here will never be done. I nullify
your dark transaction before it can begin."

And she poured, in her tempest of homicide, up toward the
ragged terrain whose sentries the party had detected. Her undu-
lous, all-seeing smoke flowed into the gullied knolls, and gathered
there like an earth-gripping storm, during which time a dozen

men, in dun capes and strapped with weaponry, erupted from their coverts emitting hoarse cries and unhinged screeches, and fled scrambling away across the gaunt bluffs.

But then all the jeweled smoke of her bannered up, and her whole mass drained into one deep gully, and vanished. In the ensuing silence, Hew cleared his throat. "We can only hope. We can only follow her in."

They clambered down into the network of gullies, and threaded toward that fold in the bluff they had marked. Long before they reached it, hoarse echoes—as from a tunnel—erupted, and wild-eyed miners fled toward them, colliding, stumbling, fleeing past.

By the time they reached the shaft-mouth, Jacques was using his wooden piston to deflect a veritable river of fleeing, maddened miners the ghost had stampeded.

The party paused outside the stonework portal. Still the miners poured out from an echosome clamor that seemed to branch deep in the earth. "In there," Hew told them, "we are seeking a vertical shaft high enough to enter the Combs themselves. The bigger the gantry, the higher we'll know they have tunneled. Some of these adits reach natural fissures up into the crystal lodes, and into one of these, we climb."

Into the tunnel's long, lanterned demi-gloom they ran, ran amidst mayhem, the three men clustered in Jacques's wake, plying their staves to either side. Many were the dead and wounded that they overleapt, miners mutually battered in their frenzy. Jacques's piston proved an excellent defensive weapon—the madmen it shouldered aside were instantly locked in combat with those they were thrown against.

The shaft broadened: an adit ahead, where a wide-legged derrick of timber thrust straight up into the basal stone of the Comb. Heavily lanterned, this was a populous site, accommodating assayers' benches, storage bins, ore-cracking mills. Here, locked in epidemic frenzy, the miners toiled, battering and bludgeoning each other as diligently as ever they had mined crystal. The derrick, well strung with lights, showed eighty cubits of vertical shaft, and though its higher faces gleamed with seams of crystal, it dead-ended in the matrix stone.

On they charged, shouldering, heaving, clubbing. They ran and fought, ran and fought past weariness, and in this delirium, three other adits they encountered—all too shallow. Meanwhile, the shafts had grown less populous, those miners not stricken down having fled away.

The fifth adit was the largest yet encountered. Though all the miners here lay stunned or dead, the howl of farther echoes in the mine bespoke more distant reaches still in uproar, where the ghost's madness was still reaping new victims.

A far more massive gantry was this one, and, though it was all strung with lamps, it had a very different light pouring down it. Through the lanterns' saffron glow there wove a silvery spiderweb-light of ricocheting filaments, a little labyrinth of transecting beams.

Jacques, Bront, and Hew went to the gantry and gazed up it. "Does the Comb's black shell," mused Jacques, "let filter through itself some exiguous remnant of the sun? Or do those crystals in the Comb *breed* light from the darkness?"

Cugel, unmoved by this kind of speculation, was drawn elsewhere: to an assayer's bench heaped with field-cut crystals, a wealth of lenses. He slipped off his knapsack, began to fill it, and then looked back at the trio. He viewed their rapture, gazing up the gantry. He hesitated, harking uneasily to the hellish echoes branching through the tunnels . . . and then he rejoined his fellows. The derrick rose 120 cubits up—not to a cap of stone but to a faceted aperture, a crooked chimney of crystals whence poured the web-work of icy light.

"That is your destination?" Cugel asked. "Is it truly up into the Combs themselves?"

Their only answer was to begin climbing the derrick, and after a moment, Cugel began climbing after, disbelieving his own action at first, until, climbing, he grew wholly absorbed in the great size and perfection of the crystals they climbed toward.

Jacques entered the aperture first, testing the crystals' strength to bear his great weight. His hugeness dwindled into the high, diamond-white radiance that leaked from the Comb above. He passed a turning, out of view. And some time after . . . "Ye gods!" they heard him rumble. "Come up! Come up!"

They ascended the faceted throat that narrowed, narrowed . . . and then it widened, and then they climbed into the Combs . . . and stood in awe.

In darkness visible, the colossal caverns loomed away: barrel vaults, groined domes, crooked steeplings, raftered transepts— clustered polyhedra clad each surface, their intersecting beams of such coherence that all this light was matrixed in deep night. Their dizzied eyes climbed the networked rays like spiders. And then, a stir in the high vaults. It was soft, but vast, like a whisper of breeze across acres of grass. The Slymires? But nothing of them was yet to be seen.

"I must be quick," said Hew. He drew from his bandolier a little placket of smoothed bone, which the others saw to be inscribed with a black sketch of cursives, diagonals, and polygons, creating a curious little maze of voids. He plucked out a brush from one of his pigments, studied its color in this alien light, and began to fill in the pattern's voids, plucking brush after brush in turn with quick intuition. Then he gazed at the finished pattern.

"What is it?" asked Bront.

"It is our passport."

"What does it mean?"

"I don't know."

"There!" barked Bront. "What's that which rises from the shaft?"

An ocular tentacle coronaed in smoke came pythoning up into the Comb. It seemed to writhe in that crystalline gloom. Hew held the passport aloft, but it was not from this the ghost recoiled. Her eyes seemed to scan something higher in the vertical abyss. She beheld it in multiplex horror for a long moment, and then crumbled into smoke entire, shrank to an inky fume that drained back down the crystal sinus . . . and was gone.

"She did not know of the Slymires," said Hew. "Until this moment they have never intersected with the world's affairs. *From* this moment, our world has a different future . . . and She is no more. A different future . . . and here it comes."

Standing on their diamond knoll, the four intruders saw, high up the nearest wall, that converging shadows were blotting out the jewels. Big, quick shadows they were, trickling together, and branching downward toward them. Cugel hefted his staff, but Hew touched his arm, and stepped before him.

Down they came, twice man-sized, sinewy-limbed, their hind legs high-jutting, batrachian, and all their four paws splay-fingered and knuckly and suction-padded. Terrifying was the utter fluid ease, the dire prehensile strength with which they descended the faceted steeps . . .

Much nearer now, their long skulls proved frontally dished, and in these broad concavities gleamed five great opalescent eyes, pentagonally arrayed.

"What can they eat," rumbled Bront, "with such tiny mouths?"

Their muscled limbs and torsos now showed clearer too, seemed densely furred—or feathered, rather, with a short, foliate plumage that rippled as they moved, restlessly, like breeze-stirred leaves.

"See!" murmured Hew in awe. "See how their plumage seems to . . . lick each beam of light they move through. Perhaps they feed on light, like plants . . ." He held aloft his little painted plaque, for the mute host was not two rods distant now.

The Slymires froze. Their supple unison was uncanny, as if they shared a single mind. Their little mouths began to whisper, and a vast, low susurration spread through the host. After a long pause, their phalanx parted, and one of their number, larger than the rest, came stealing forward, something like wonder in its hesitance. So near to Hew, at the last, it crouched, that Hew could see a narrow iris, white as frost, around each of its huge black pupils.

The beast slowly reached forth its huge hand, each exquisitely articulated digit like a muscled frond. It touched—so tenderly—the tintmaster's colored rune, and a whisper came from its little lips. Hew gestured the plaque, and pointed aloft to the Comb's highest vault. The Slymire gazed, then nodded, and raised its palms in offering, in acquiescence.

Jacques shed his cargo bed, and unlashed the first rolled length of ladder, while such a whispering spread among the alien multitude that it seemed the tides of a ghostly sea echoed within those mighty vaults. Hew pantomimed the ladder's unscrolling up to the heights, and Cugel and Bront displayed the mallets and pitons, and their use in anchoring it.

The elder nodded, and his companions swarmed to the task. They ran the ladder up the dizzy slope and spiked it down, while others tucked the rest of the rolls under their arms and ran them higher still . . .

"Ye powers!" growled Jacques. "Do our labors end so easily?"

"All but mine, I think," said Hew, gazing up into those dizzy jeweled heights.

"How think you it will go with you, on such a height?" Bront softly asked him.

"Good Bront." Hew faintly smiled. "I'm trying not to think about that particular aspect of my task." And tightening his harness of tints, Hew began his climb.

Zig and zag, the Slymires strung it higher, and zig and zag he climbed. His nerve for heights was firm enough, but four hundred cubits aloft wildly outwent the worst he'd ever faced. Yet his fear, though great, was strangely dwarfed by the radiance he ascended. The crystals he touched woke odd imaginings within his very flesh. He saw—remembered, it almost seemed—terrains he'd never dreamed of, sweeping planet-scapes of barbarous beauty, suns gilding seas on worlds he never knew, in hues unviewed by any human eye . . .

And he came, almost before he knew it, into an apex of the Comb where, on a stretch of naked stone, abstract patterns were arrayed. Belting himself to the ladder, he gazed a moment at the first of these runes . . . and plucked out a brush.

At what behest he chose a hue, and applied it, then chose again—at what prompting he worked, he never knew. It was his nerves that did the work, his spine, which coruscated with strange fear, strange joy. At one point, almost unknown to himself, he murmured, "I am in the very hand of time, painting the future . . ."

After an unmeasurable interval, Hew socketed his final brush, and, with a strange reluctance, began his descent of the slender ladder's vertiginous zigzag. He was exhausted to the very bone, but there was exaltation in his heart. And as he inched downward, a tide of Slymires poured past him, surging up to view his work.

Throughout his descent, still they rivered up to the runic grotto, seething there to see, and see again, while the vast whisper raged throughout the Comb, a troubled breeze of rumor and report. Denial and doubt, alarm and disbelief hissed everywhere, while urgent crosswinds swept the swarming shadows, awed rebuttals breathing possibility . . . amazement . . . revelation.

Hew found his comrades girt for their return, and Jacques *un*girt. "Do you leave your cargo bed here, Jacques?" he asked.

"Indeed I do! I therewith solemnize my retirement from my trade, thanks to your bounty, good Bront. Also, the Chippers stir below—" and indeed there was a rumble and clatter, a noise of returning forces filling the shaft far below, "—and I'll fight better disencumbered . . . Where has friend Cugel gone?"

"Why," marveled Bront, "he was here not a moment past!"

Movement rippled above them, and their eyes went aloft. Here came a sinuous cascade of Slymires converging toward them. Their silver-backed elder led them. They converged around the artist and his crew. But as the elder beamed his clustered eyes upon them, a whisper of alarm was heard, and here came a pair of the beasts, bearing between them the powerfully pinioned Cugel, whose rock hammer and half-filled knapsack of crystals were still incriminatingly clenched in his hands.

Brought near the elder, Cugel prepared to vent words of reproof and expostulation for his unjust seizure, yet his voice died in his throat as he beheld the labyrinthine luster of the elder's gaze. Such . . . *reverence* he saw there. It could be called nothing else.

Cugel stood gaping when they tenderly set him down, and the elder loomed over him, and spread his marvelous long, supple fingers at all the cold fire of the Crystal Combs around them, and with a second ineffable gesture, laid it all at Cugel's feet.

Then Cugel stood bemused as the elder's fleet, surgical fingers danced across the crystals of the wall, and snapped off now here, now there, huge, flawless dodecas, swiftly filling his rucksack with a fortune.

When Cugel had bowed his acknowledgment, the elder gathered all four of the intruders in his gaze. Long and long he whispered to them. The four interlopers received this intricate

communication almost comprehendingly. When they saw the
tremors of this host around them, the coruscations of their countless eyes like living gems, and felt the longing in this inhuman
multitude, they thought they understood. This race had never
been outside the Combs. Now that they were convinced there
was an Outside, and that they must see it, it was their purpose to
emerge . . .

The three men and the jack—with gracious gestures—stood
aside. The elder led the supple Slymires down, through the crystal
sinus, down the drain-hole human enterprise had dug into their
Comb, flooding over the gantry.

"We are done, my friends," said Bront. "Let's after them."

Below in the adit, they found a few more lifeless forms than
they had left there, for a resurgence of the miners—commenc-
ing with the ghost's death—could now be heard fleeing before
the Slymires' onrush. Outcry and tumult echoed as the creatures
swept onward, outward. Jacques in the van, the men ran after
them.

At length, the mine's mouth opened before them, and the sky
beyond where broken clouds, red-litten, drifted through a purple
sky. Like a liquid, the Slymires' legions flooded out, coursed
through gullies, surged up bluffs, to fill, with their fluid concourse, a broad plateau dispread a little ways below the Combs.

What a host they were, the Slymires crouched on this plain,
their gorgeous eyes abrim with the never-known sky, and its
never-known sun sinking swollen to the western horizon!

"They've never even dreamed of it before . . . the sun," murmured Hew. "I think there was a vague rumor of it, recorded
in their runes. It seems, by augmenting these, that we have . . .
awakened their minds."

"And how will this . . ." Bront's voice trailed off, so strange the
rapture of that monstrous throng, their fellows joining them in

a steady stream still issuing out of the earth, all of them settling down into the same mute awe of the dying sun.

" . . . how will this save this world?" finished Bront in Hew's ear.

"I have no idea," said Hew.

The Slymires sat under the darkening wine of the sky, feeling the breeze which they had never known, watching the sun's carmine eye slowly lidded by the black horizon. Their own eyes were unearthly gems, entranced in wild surmise. Their foliate plumage bristled and stirred insatiably.

The four stole away from that devout concourse with a courteous, embarrassed stealth, like that of folk who leave a church before the service ends. They picked their way back down to the lichened plain, just as dark began to settle down.

"Gentlemen," said Hew, "we must make north. I cannot express my gratitude for your stalwart spirits, for your help."

Cugel resettled his knapsack of crystal. "My friends. I can't recall a more astonishing or more profitable venture than this we have just shared. I must ask you, without prying I hope, what you gain by what you've done. You've taken no crystal."

"Our aim was, ah, altruistic," Hew answered. "It was, in some way we do not understand, to save this world."

"You quite astonish me!" said Cugel. "And yet perhaps I am not too amazed, for have not I gained a prize that works a great philanthropy? I bring more power to the Biblionites' sun-cannons, and haste the selfish Guyal's fall, and the Biblionites, when they have spread the museum's gnomens far and wide, will have worked a great service to the world."

"If indeed they prove the pious altruists they claim to be," rumbled Jacques.

"Ah well!" Cugel smiled. "Who can see the future?" (Bront and Hew here exchanged a glance.) "I would like to stand you to a fine refreshment back in Minion, and perhaps a bracing little game of chance . . . but laden with wealth as I now am, night and haste must hide my passage from the common eye. Gentlemen, it has been a privilege, an honor, and an amazement to have made one with you!"

Laden with their warm acknowledgments, Cugel turned away into the dark and made light-foot back toward Minion.

Bront turned to Jacques. "Permit me to say, good sir . . . that you were worth every lictor of your hire."

The jack-haul laughed. "Dear Bront—I like you too, and I think you a most excellent fellow. Adieu." The gloom concealed Bront's blush, but he was not displeased by the jack-haul's declaration. As Jacques moved off, Bront cleared his throat in some discomfort.

"Esteemed Hew . . ."

"Please, most excellent Bront. You are my friend, and I am yours. And I am now, and shall henceforward be, most delighted in our friendship."

Bront smiled gratefully. "Well then."

"Well then."

They turned northward, and at their second stride, found themselves standing on Kadaster's balcony, the grand sharp peaks of the Siderions marching snow-capped past the edge of sight, splendid beneath a golden sun.

Broadly smiling, Kadaster gestured them toward a table, whereon stood three goblets and a pitcher of wine, and beside which sat two obese pouches of gold specie.

"Hew! Bront! You have done well! You have far exceeded my most sanguine hopes. Sit, and be refreshed!"

"Then your aim has been fulfilled?" asked Hew.

"Oh, yes indeed. Or, technically, it will be."

They drank, and rested for a space, though the expeditioners eyed the mage aslant, now and again. Bront, at last, could not forbear to ask, "May we know, Kadaster, just how we have helped to . . ."

"How you have helped to save this world? Why, of course you may! How stupid of me not to explain it at once, now that its eventuation is assured! Now that *you* have assured it!

"The Slymires, you see, will, not too long after you have visited them, build an array of huge reflecting mirrors of amplificatory crystal. With these they will return to the sun its own tremendously augmented light. I must spare you the rather intricate technical paradoxes—all of them mutually contradictory—involved in this transaction, but by so doing, they will rekindle it."

Hew blinked. "They will rekindle . . . the sun?"

"Rekindle the sun. Just so! Another flagon, my dear friends?"

SCOTT LYNCH was born in Saint Paul, Minnesota. He worked a variety of jobs, including as a dishwasher, waiter, Web designer, free-lance writer, and office manager, before publishing his first novel, *The Lies of Locke Lamora,* in 2006. Part of the Gentleman Bastard Sequence, concerned with the life of thief and con man Locke Lamora, and set in the world of the shattered Therin Throne Empire, the series is projected to run to seven books. In addition to being a 2007 John W. Campbell Award, William L. Crawford Award, and Locus Award finalist, Scott is a volunteer firefighter, certified in both Minnesota and Wisconsin. He lives with his wife, Jenny, in the city of New Richmond, Wisconsin.

IN THE STACKS

Scott Lynch

Laszlo Jazera, aspirant wizard of the High University of Hazar, spent a long hour on the morning of his fifth-year exam worming his way into an uncomfortable suit of leather armor. A late growth spurt had ambushed Laszlo that spring, and the cuirass, once form-fitted, was now tight across the shoulders despite every adjustment of the buckles and straps. As for the groin guard, well, the less said the better. Damn, but he'd been an idiot, putting off a test-fit of his old personal gear until it was much too late for a trip to the armory.

"Still trying to suck it in?" Casimir Vrana, his chambers-mate, strolled in already fully armored, not merely with physical gear but with his usual air of total ease. In truth, he'd spent even less time in fighting leathers than Laszlo had in their half-decade at school together. He simply had the curious power of total, improbable deportment. Every inch the patrician, commanding and comely, he could have feigned relaxation even while standing in fire up to his privates. "You're embarrassing me, Laszlo. And you with all your dueling society ribbons."

"We wear silks," huffed Laszlo, buckling on his stiff leather neck-guard. "So we can damn well move when we have to. This creaking heap of boiled pigskin, I've hardly worn it since Archaic Homicide Theory—"

"Forgot to go to the armory for a refit, eh?"

"Well, I've been busy as all hells, hardly sleeping—"

"A fifth-year aspirant, busy and confused at finals time? What an unprecedented misfortune. A unique tale of woe." Casimir moved around Laszlo and began adjusting what he could. "Let's skip our exam. You need warm milk and cuddles."

"I swear on my mother, Caz, I'll set fire to your cryptomancy dissertation."

"Can't. Turned it in two hours ago. And why are you still dicking around with purely physical means here?" Casimir muttered something, and Laszlo yelped in surprise as the heat of spontaneous magic ran up and down his back—but a moment later, the armor felt looser. Still not a good fit, but at least not tight enough to hobble his every movement. "Better?"

"Moderately."

"I don't mean to lecture, *magician,* but sooner or later you should probably start using, you know, *magic* to smooth out your little inconveniences."

"You're a lot more confident with practical use than I am."

"Theory's a wading pool, Laz. You've got to come out into deep water sooner or later." Casimir grinned, and slapped Laszlo on the back. "You're gonna see that today, I promise. Let's get your kit together so they don't start without us."

Laszlo pulled on a pair of fingerless leather gauntlets, the sort peculiar to the profession of magicians intending to go in harm's way. With Casimir's oversight, he filled the sheathes on his belt and boots with half a dozen stilettos, then strapped or tied on no fewer than fourteen auspicious charms and protective wards.

Some of these he'd crafted himself; the rest had been begged or temporarily stolen from friends. His sable cloak and mantle, lined in aspirant gray, settled lastly and awkwardly over the creaking, clinking mass he'd become.

"Oh damn," Laszlo muttered after he'd adjusted his cloak, "where did I set my—"

"Sword," said Casimir, holding it out in both hands. Laszlo's wire-hilted rapier was his pride and joy, an elegant old thing held together by mage-smithery through three centuries of duties not always ceremonial. It was an heirloom of his diminished family, the only valuable item his parents had been able to bequeath him when his mild sorcerous aptitude had won him a standard nine-year scholarship to the university. "Checked it myself."

Laszlo buckled the scabbard into his belt and covered it with his cloak. The armor still left him feeling vaguely ridiculous, but at least he trusted his steel. Thus protected, layered head-to-toe in leather, enchantments, and weapons, he was at last ready for the final challenge each fifth-year student faced if they wanted to return for a sixth.

Today, Laszlo Jazera would return a library book.

The Living Library of Hazar was visible from anywhere in the city, a vast onyx cube that hung in the sky like a square moon, directly over the towers of the university's western campus. Laszlo and Casimir hurried out of their dorm and into the actual shadow of the library, a darkness that bisected Hazar as the sun rose to-ward noon and was eclipsed by the cube.

There was no teleportation between campuses for students. Few creatures in the universe are lazier than magicians with stud-ies to keep them busy indoors, and the masters of the university ensured that aspirants would preserve at least some measure of physical virtue by forcing them to scuttle around like ordinary folk. Scuttle was precisely what Laszlo and Casimir needed to do, in undignified haste, in order to reach the library for their noon appointment. Across the heart of Hazar they sped.

Hazar! The City of Distractions, the most perfect mechanism ever evolved for snaring the attention of young people like the two cloaked aspirants! The High University, a power beyond governments, sat at the nexus of gates to fifty known worlds, and took in the students of eight thinking species. Hazar existed not just to serve the university's practical needs, but to sift heroic quantities of valuables out of the student body by catering to its less practical desires.

Laszlo and Casimir passed whorehouses, gambling dens, fighting pits, freak shows, pet shops, concert halls, and private clubs. There were restaurants serving a hundred cuisines, and bars serving a thousand liquors, teas, dusts, smokes, and spells. Bars more than anything—bars on top of bars, bars next to bars, bars within bars. A bar for every student, a different bar for every day of the nine years most would spend in Hazar, yet Laszlo and Casimir somehow managed to ignore them all. On any other day, that would have required heroic effort, but it was exams week, and the dread magic of the last minute was in the air.

At the center of the eastern university campus, five hundred feet beneath the dark cube, was a tiny green bordered with waterfalls. No direct physical access to the Living Library was allowed, for several reasons. Instead, a single tall silver pillar stood in the middle of the grass. Without stopping to catch his breath after arrival, Laszlo placed the bare fingers of his right hand against the pillar and muttered, "Laszlo Jazera, fifth year, reporting to Master Molnar of the—"

Between blinks it was done. The grass beneath his boots became hard tile, the waterfalls became dark wood paneling on high walls and ceilings. He was in a lobby the size of a manor house, and the cool, dry air was rich with the musty scent of library stacks. There was daylight shining in from above, but it was tamed by enchanted glass and fell on the hall with the gentle amber color of a good ale. Laszlo shook his head to clear a momentary sensation of vertigo, and an instant later Casimir appeared just beside him.

"Ha! Not late yet," said Casimir, pointing to a tasteful wall clock where tiny blue spheres of light floated over the symbols that indicated seven minutes to noon. "We won't be early enough to shove our noses up old Molnar's ass like eager little slaves, but we won't technically be tardy. Come on. Which gate?"

"Ahhh, Manticore."

Casimir all but dragged Laszlo to the right, down the long circular hallway that ringed the innards of the library. Past the Wyvern Gate they hurried, past the Chimaera Gate, past the reading rooms, past a steady stream of fellow aspirants, many of them armed and girded for the very same errand they were on. Laszlo picked up instantly on the general atmosphere of nervous tension, as sensitive as a prey animal in the middle of a spooked herd. Final exams were out there, prowling, waiting to tear the weak and sickly out of the mass.

On the clock outside the gate to the Manticore Wing of the library, the little blue flame was just floating past the symbol for high noon when Laszlo and Casimir skidded to a halt before a single tall figure.

"I see you two aspirants have chosen to favor us with a dramatic last-minute arrival," said the man. "I was not aware this was to be a drama exam."

"Yes, Master Molnar. Apologies, Master Molnar," said Laszlo and Casimir in unison.

Hargus Molnar, Master Librarian, had a face that would have been at home in a gallery of military statues, among dead conquerors casting their permanent scowls down across the centuries. Lean and sinewy, with close-cropped gray hair and a dozen visible scars, he wore a use-seasoned suit of black leather and silvery mail. Etched on his cuirass was a stylized scroll, symbol of the Living Library, surmounted by the phrase *Auvidestes, Gerani, Molokare.* The words were Alaurin, the formal language of scholars, and they formed the motto of the Librarians:

RETRIEVE. RETURN. SURVIVE.

"May I presume," said Molnar, sparing neither aspirant the very excellent disdainful stare he'd cultivated over decades of practice, "that you have familiarized yourselves with the introductory materials that were provided to you last month?"

"Yes, Master Molnar. Both of us," said Casimir. Laszlo was pleased to see that Casimir's swagger had prudently evaporated for the moment.

"Good." Molnar spread his fingers and words of white fire appeared in the air before him, neatly organized paragraphs floating vertically in the space between Laszlo's forehead and navel. "This is your Statement of Intent; namely, that you wish to enter the Living Library directly as part of an academic requirement. I'll need your sorcerer's marks *here.*"

Laszlo reached out to touch the letters where Molnar indicated, feeling a warm tingle on his fingertips. He closed his eyes and visualized his First Secret Name, part of his private identity as a wizard, a word-symbol that could leave an indelible imprint of his personality without actually revealing itself to anyone else. This might seem like a neat trick, but when all was said and done, it was mostly used for occasional bits of magical paperwork and for bar tabs.

"And here," said Molnar, moving his own finger. "This is a Statement of Informed Acceptance of Risk . . . and here, this absolves the custodial staff of any liability should you injure yourself by being irretrievably stupid . . . and this one, which certifies that you are armed and equipped according to your own comfort."

Laszlo hesitated for a second, bit the inside of his left cheek, and gave his assent. When Casimir had done the same, Molnar snapped his fingers and the letters of fire vanished. At the same instant, the polished wooden doors of the Manticore Gate rumbled apart. Laszlo glanced at the inner edges of the doors and saw that, beneath the wooden veneer, each had a core of some dark metal a foot thick. He'd never once been past that gate, or any like it—aspirants were usually confined to the reading rooms, where their requests for materials were passed to the library staff.

"Come then," said Molnar, striding through the gate. "You'll be going in with two other students, already waiting inside. Until I escort you back out this gate, you may consider your exam to be in progress."

Past the Manticore Gate lay a long, vault-ceilinged room in which Indexers toiled amongst thousands of scrolls and card-files. Unlike the Librarians, the Indexers preferred comfortable blue robes to armor, but they were all visibly armed with daggers and hatchets. Furthermore, in niches along the walls, Laszlo could see spears, truncheons, mail vests, and helmets readily accessible on racks.

"I envy your precision, friend Laszlo."

The gravelly voice that spoke those words was familiar, and Laszlo turned to the left to find himself staring up into the gold-flecked eyes of a lizard about seven feet tall. The creature had a chest as broad as a doorway under shoulders to match, and his gleaming scales were the red of a desert sunset. He wore a sort of thin quilted armor over everything but his muscular legs and feet, which ended in sickle-shaped claws the size of Laszlo's stilettos. The reptile's cloak was specially tailored to part over his long, sinuous tail and hang with dignity.

"Lev," said Laszlo. "Hi! What precision?"

"Your ability to sleep late and still arrive within a hair's breadth of accruing penalties for your tardiness. Your laziness is . . . artistic."

"The administration rarely agrees." Laszlo was deeply pleased to see Inappropriate Levity Bronzeclaw, "Lev" to everyone at the university. Lev's people, dour and dutiful, gave their adolescents names based on perceived character flaws, so the wayward youths would supposedly dwell upon their correction until granted more honorable adult names. Lev was a mediocre sorcerer, very much of Laszlo's stripe, but his natural weaponry was one hell of an asset when hungry weirdness might be trying to bite your head off.

"Oh, I doubt they were *sleeping*." Another new voice, female, smooth and lovely. It belonged to Yvette d'Courin, who'd been hidden from Laszlo's view behind Lev, and could have remained hidden behind a creature half the lizard's size. Yvette's skin was darker than the armor she wore, a more petite version of Laszlo's and Casimir's gear, and her ribbon-threaded hair was as black as her aspirant's cloak. "Not Laz and Caz. Boys of such a *sensitive* disposition, why, we all know they were probably tending to certain . . . extracurricular activities." She made a strangely demure series of sucking sounds, and some gestures with her hands that were not demure at all.

"Yvette, you gorgeous little menace to my academic rank," said Casimir, "that is most assuredly not true. However, if it were, I reckon that would make Laszlo and myself the only humans present to have ever seen a grown man with his clothes off."

Laszlo felt a warm, unexpected sensation in the pit of his stomach, and it took him a moment of confusion to identify it. Great gods, was that relief? Hope, even? Yvette d'Courin was a gifted aspirant, Casimir's match at the very least. Whatever might be waiting inside the Living Library, some bureaucratic stroke of luck had put him on a team with two natural magicians and a lizard that could kick a hole through a brick wall. All he had to do to earn a sixth year was stay out of their way and try to look busy!

Yvette retaliated at Casimir with another series of gestures, some of which might have been the beginning of a minor spell, but she snapped to attention as Master Molnar loudly cleared his throat.

"When you're all *ready,* of course," he drawled. "I do so hate to burden you with anything so tedious as the future of your thaumaturgical careers—"

"Yes, Master Molnar. Sorry, Master Molnar," said the students, now a perfectly harmonized quartet of apology.

"This is the Manticore Index," said Molnar, spreading his arms. "One of eleven such indices serving to catalog, however incompletely, the contents of the Living Library. Take a good look around. Unless you choose to join the ranks of the Librarians after surviving your nine years, you will never be allowed into this area again. Now, Aspirant Jazera, can you tell me how many cataloged items the Living Library is believed to contain?"

"Uh," said Laszlo, who'd wisely refreshed his limited knowledge of the library's innards the previous night, "about 10 million, I think?"

"You think?" said Molnar. "I'll believe that when further evidence is presented, but you are nearly correct. At a minimum, this collection consists of some 10 million scrolls and bound volumes. The majority of which, Aspirant Bronzeclaw, are what?"

"Grimoires," hissed the lizard.

"Correct. Grimoires, the personal references and notebooks of magicians from across all the known worlds, some more than four thousand years old. Some of them quite famous . . . or infamous. When the High University of Hazar was founded, a grimoire collection project was undertaken. An effort to create the great-est magical library in existence, to unearth literally every scrap of arcane knowledge that could be retrieved from the places where those scraps had been abandoned, forgotten, or deliberately hid-den. It took centuries. It was largely successful."

Molnar turned and began moving down the central aisle between the tables and shelves where Indexers worked, politely ignoring him. No doubt they'd heard this same lecture many times already.

"Largely successful," Molnar continued, "at creating one hell of a mess! Aspirant d'Courin, what is a grimoire?"

"Well," she began, seemingly taken aback by the simplicity of the question. "As you said, a magician's personal reference. De-tails of spells, and experiments—"

"A catalog of a magician's private *obsessions*," said Molnar.

"I suppose, sir."

"More private than any diary, every page stained with a sor-cerer's hidden character, his private demons, his wildest ambi-tions. Some magicians produce collections, others produce only a single book, but nearly all of them produce *something* before they die. Chances are the four of you will produce *something*, in your time. Some of you have certainly begun them by now."

Laszlo glanced around at the others, wondering. He had a few basic project journals, notes on the simple magics he'd been able to grasp. Nothing that could yet be accused of showing any ambi-tion. But Casimir, or Yvette? Who could know?

"Grimoires," continued Molnar, "are firsthand witnesses to every triumph and every shame of their creators. They are left in laboratories, stored haphazardly next to untold powers, exposed to magical materials and energies for years. Their pages are saturated with arcane dust and residue, as well as deliberate sorceries. They are magical artifacts, uniquely infused with what can only be called the divine madness of individuals such as yourselves. They evolve, as many magical artifacts do, a faint quasi-intelligence. A distinct sort of low cunning that your run-of-the mill chair or rock or library book does not possess.

"Individually, this characteristic is harmless. But when you take grimoires . . . powerful grimoires, from the hands and minds of powerful magicians, and you store them together by the hundreds, by the thousands, by the tens of thousands, by the *millions* . . ."

This last word was almost shouted, and Molnar's arms were raised to the ceiling again, for dramatic effect. This speech had lost the dry tones of lecture and acquired the dark passion of theatrical oration. Whatever Master Molnar might have thought of the aspirants entrusted to his care, he was clearly a believer in his work.

"You need thick walls," he said, slowly, with a thin smile on his lips. "Thick walls, and rough Librarians to guard them. Millions of grimoires, locked away together. Each one is a mote of quasi-intelligence, a speck of possibility, a particle of magic. Bring them together in a teeming library, in the stacks, and you have . . ."

"What?" said Laszlo, buying into the drama despite himself.

"Not a mind," said Molnar, meeting his eyes like a carnival fortune-teller making a sales pitch. "Not quite a mind, not a focused intelligence. But a jungle! A jungle that *dreams,* and those dreams are currents of deadly strangeness. A Living Library . . . within our power to contain, but well beyond our power to control."

Molnar stopped beside a low table, on which were four reinforced leather satchels, each containing a single large book. Pinned to each satchel was a small pile of handwritten notes.

"A collection of thaumaturgical knowledge so vast and so

deep," said Molnar, "is far, far too useful a thing to give up merely because it has become a magical *disaster area* perfectly capable of killing anyone who enters it unprepared!"

Laszlo felt his sudden good cheer slinking away. All of this, in a much less explicit form, was common knowledge among the aspirants of the High University. The Living Library was a place of weirdness, of mild dangers, sure, but to hear Molnar speak of it . . .

"You aspirants have reaped the benefit of the library for several years now." Molnar smiled and brushed a speck of imaginary dust from the cuirass of his Librarian's armor. "You have filed your requests for certain volumes, and waited the days or weeks required for the library staff to fetch them out. And, in the reading rooms, you have studied them in perfect comfort, because a grimoire safely removed from the Living Library is just another book.

"The masters of the university, as one of their more commendable policies, have decreed that all aspirant magicians need to learn to *appreciate* the sacrifices of the library staff that make this singular resource available. Before you can proceed to the more advanced studies of your final years, you are required to enter the Living Library, just once, to assist us in the return of a volume to its rightful place in the collection. That is all. That is the extent of your fifth-year exam. On the table beside me you will see four books in protective satchels. Take one, and handle it with care. Until those satchels are empty, your careers at the High University are in the balance."

Lev passed the satchels out one by one. Laszlo received his and examined the little bundle of notes that came with it. Written in several different hands, they named the borrower of the grimoire as a third-year aspirant he didn't know, and described the process of hunting the book down, with references to library sections, code phrases, and number sequences that Laszlo couldn't understand.

"The library is so complex," said Molnar, "and has grown so strange in its ways that physical surveillance of the collection has been impractical for centuries. We rely on the index enchantments, powerful processes of our most orderly sorcery, to give us the information that the Indexers maintain here. From that information, we plan our expeditions, and map the best ways to go about fetching an item from the stacks, or returning one."

"Master Molnar, sir, forgive me," said Casimir. "Is that a focus for the index enchantments over there?"

Laszlo followed Casimir's pointing hand, and in a deeper niche behind one of the little armories along the walls, he saw a recessed column of black glass, behind which soft pulses of blue light rose and fell.

"Just so," said Molnar. "Either you've made pleasing use of the introductory materials, or that was a good guess."

"It's, ah, a sort of personal interest." Casimir reached inside a belt pouch and took out a thick hunk of triangular crystal, like a prism with a milky-white center. "May I leave this next to the focus while we're in the stacks? It's just an impression device. It'll give me a basic idea of how the index enchantments function. My family has a huge library, not magical, of course, but if I could create spells to organize it—"

"Ambition wedded to sloth," said Molnar. "Let no one say you don't think like a true magician, Aspirant Vrana."

"I won't even have to think about it while we're inside, sir. It would just mind itself, and I could pick it up on the way out." Casimir was laying it on, Laszlo saw, every ounce of obsequiousness he could conjure.

But what was he talking about? Personal project? Family library? Caz had never breathed a word of any such thing to him. While they came from very different worlds, they'd always gotten along excellently as chambers-mates, and Laszlo had thought there were no real secrets between them. Where had this sprung from?

"Of course, Vrana," said Master Molnar. "We go to some trouble to maintain those enchantments, after all, and today is *all about* appreciating our work."

While Casimir hurried to emplace his little device near the glass column, Molnar beckoned the rest of them on toward another gate at the inner end of the Manticore Index. It was as tall and wide as the door they'd entered, but even more grimly functional—cold, dark metal inscribed with geometric patterns and runes of warding.

"A gateway to the stacks," said Molnar, "can only be opened by the personal keys of two Librarians. I'll be one of your guides today, and the other . . . the other should have been here by—"

"I'm here, Master Librarian."

In the popular imagination (which had, to this point, included Laszlo's), female Librarians were lithe, comely warrior maidens out of some barbarian legend. The woman now hurrying toward them through the Manticore Index was short, barely taller than Yvette, and she was as sturdy as a concrete teapot, with broad hips and arms like a blacksmith's. Her honey-colored hair was tied back in a short tail, and over her black Librarian's armor she wore an unusual harness that carried a pair of swords crossed over her back. Her plump face was as heavily scarred as Molnar's, and Laszlo had learned just enough in his hobby duels to see that she was no one he would ever want to annoy.

"Aspirants," said Molnar, "allow me to present Sword-Librarian Astriza Mezaros."

As she moved past him, Laszlo noticed two things. First, the curious harness held not just her swords but a large book, buckled securely over her lower back beneath her scabbards. Second, she had a large quantity of fresh blood soaking the gauntlet on her left hand.

"Sorry to be late," said Mezaros. "Came from the infirmary."

"Indeed," said Molnar, "and are you—"

"Oh, I'm fine. I'm not the one that got hit. It was that boy Selucas, from the morning group."

"Ahhhh. And will he recover?"

"Given a few weeks." Mezaros grinned as she ran her eyes across the four aspirants. "Earned his passing grade the hard way, that's for sure."

"Well, I've given them the lecture," said Molnar. "Let's proceed."

"On it." Mezaros reached down the front of her cuirass and drew out a key hanging on a chain. Molnar did the same, and each Librarian took up a position beside the inner door. The walls before them rippled, and small keyholes appeared where blank stone had been a moment before.

"Opening," yelled Master Molnar.

"Opening," chorused the Indexers. Each of them dropped whatever they were working on and turned to face the inner door. One blue-robed woman hurried to the hallway door, checked it, and shouted, "Manticore Gate secure!"

"Opening," repeated Molnar. "On three. One, two—"

The two Librarians inserted their keys and turned them in unison. The inner door slid open, just as the outer one had, revealing an empty, metal-walled room lit by amber lanterns set in heavy iron cages.

Mezaros was the first one into the metal-walled chamber, holding up a hand to keep the aspirants back. She glanced around quickly, surveying every inch of the walls, floors, and ceiling, and then she nodded.

"In," said Molnar, herding the aspirants forward. He snapped his fingers, and with a flash of light he conjured a walking staff, a tall object of polished dark wood. It had few ornaments, but it was shod at both ends with iron, and that iron looked well-dented to Laszlo's eyes.

Once the six of them were inside the metal-walled chamber, Molnar waved a hand over some innocuous portion of the wall, and the door behind them rumbled shut. Locking mechanisms engaged with an ominous series of echoing clicks.

"Begging your pardon, Master Molnar," said Lev, "not to seem irresolute, for I am firmly committed to any course of action that will prevent me from having to return to my clan's ancestral trade of scale-grooming, but merely as a point of personal curiosity, exactly how much danger are we reckoned to be in?"

"A good question," said Molnar slyly. "We Librarians have been asking it daily for more than a thousand years. Astriza, what can you tell the good aspirant?"

"I guard aspirants about a dozen times each year," said Mezaros. "The fastest trip I can remember was about two hours. The longest took a day and a half. You have the distinct disadvantage of not being trained Librarians, and the dubious advantage of sheer numbers. Most books are returned by experienced professionals operating in pairs."

"Librarian Mezaros," said Lev, "I am fully prepared to spend a week here if required, but I was more concerned with the, ah, chance of ending the exam with a visit to the infirmary."

"Aspirant Inappropriate Levity Bronzeclaw," said Mezaros, "in here, I prefer to be called Astriza. Do me that favor, and I won't use your full name every time I need to tell you to duck."

"Ah, of course. Astriza."

"As for what's going to happen, well, it might be nothing. It might be pretty brutal. I've never had anyone get killed under my watch, but it's been a near thing. Look, I've spent months in the infirmary myself. Had my right leg broken twice, right arm twice, left arm once, nose more times than I can count."

"This is our routine," said Molnar with grim pride. "I've been in a coma twice. Both of my legs have been broken. I was blind for four months—"

"I was there for that," said Astriza.

"She carried me out on her shoulders." Molnar was beaming. "Only her second year as a Librarian. Yes, this place has done its very best to kill the pair of us. *But the books were returned to the shelves.*"

"Damn straight," said Astriza. "Librarians always get the books back to the shelves. *Always.* And that's what you *browsers* are here to learn by firsthand experience. If you listen to the Master Librarian and myself at all times, your chances of a happy return will be greatly improved. No other promises."

"Past the inner door," said Molnar, "your ordinary perceptions of time and distance will be taxed. Don't trust them. Follow our lead, and for the love of all gods everywhere, stay close."

Laszlo, who'd spent his years at the university comfortably surrounded by books of all sorts, now found himself staring down at his satchel-clad grimoire with a sense of real unease. He was knocked out of his reverie when Astriza set a hand on the satchel and gently pushed it down.

"That's just one grimoire, Laszlo. Nothing to fear in a single drop of water, right?" She was grinning again. "It takes an ocean to drown yourself."

Another series of clicks echoed throughout the chamber, and with a rumbling hiss the final door to the library stacks slid open before them.

• • •

"It doesn't seem possible," said Yvette, taking the words right out of Laszlo's mouth.

Row upon row of tall bookcases stretched away into the distance, but the farther Laszlo strained to see down the aisles between those shelves, the more they seemed to curve, to turn upon themselves, to become a knotted labyrinth leading away into darkness. And gods, the place was vast, the ceiling was hundreds of feet above them, the outer walls were so distant they faded into mist . . .

"This place has weather!" said Laszlo.

"All kinds," said Astriza, peering around. Once all six of them were through the door, she used her key to lock it shut behind them.

"And it doesn't fit," said Yvette. "Inside the cube, I mean. This place is much too big. Or is that just—"

"No, it's not just an illusion. At least not as we understand the term," said Molnar. "This place was orderly once. Pure, sane geometries. But after the collection was installed, the change began . . . by the time the old Librarians tried to do something, it was too late. Individual books are happy to come and go, but when they tried to remove large numbers at once, the library got angry."

"What happened?" said Casimir.

"Suffice to say that in the thousand years since, it has been our strictest policy to never, *ever* make the library angry again."

As Laszlo's senses adjusted to the place, more and more details leapt out at him. It really was a jungle, a tangled forest of shelves and drawers and columns and railed balconies, as though the Living Library had somehow reached out across time and space, and raided other buildings for components that suited its whims. Dark galleries branched off like caves, baroque structures grew out of the mists and shadows, a sort of cancer-architecture that had no business standing upright. Yet it did, under gray clouds that occasionally pulsed with faint eldritch light. The cool air was ripe with the thousand odors of old books and preservatives, and other things—hot metal, musty earth, wet fur, old blood. Ever so faint, ever so unnerving.

The two Librarians pulled a pair of small lanterns from a locker beside the gate, and tossed them into the air after muttering brief incantations. The lanterns glowed a soft red, and hovered unobtrusively just above the party.

"Ground rules," said Astriza. "Nothing in here is friendly. If any sort of *something* should try any sort of *anything,* defend yourself and your classmates. However, you *must* avoid damaging the books."

"I can only wonder," said Lev, "does the library not realize that we are returning books to their proper places? Should that not buy us some measure of safety?"

"We believe it understands what we're doing, on some level," said Molnar. "And we're quite certain that, regardless of what it understands, it simply can't help itself. Now, let's start with your book, Aspirant D'Courin. Hand me the notes."

Molnar and Astriza read the notes, muttering together, while the aspirants kept an uneasy lookout. After a few moments, Molnar raised his hand and sketched an ideogram of red light in the air. Strange sparks moved within the glowing lines, and the two Librarians studied these intently.

"Take heed, aspirants," muttered Molnar, absorbed in his work. "This journey has been loosely planned, but only inside the library itself can the index enchantments give more precise and reliable . . . ah. Case in point. This book has moved itself."

"Twenty-eight Manticore East," said Astriza. "Border of the Chimaera stacks, near the Tree of Knives."

"The tree's gone," said Molnar. "Vanished yesterday, could be anywhere."

"Oh *piss*," said Astriza. "I really hate hunting that thing."

"Map," said Molnar. Astriza dropped to one knee, presenting her back to Molnar. The Master Librarian knelt and unbuckled the heavy volume that she wore as a sort of backpack, and by the red light of the floating lanterns he skimmed the pages, nodding to himself. After a few moments, he resecured the book and rose to his feet.

"Yvette's book," he said, "isn't actually a proper grimoire, it's more of a philosophical treatise. Adrilankha's *Discourse on Necessary Thaumaturgical Irresponsibilities*. However, it keeps some peculiar company, so we've got a long walk ahead of us. Be on your guard."

They moved into the stacks in a column, with Astriza leading and Molnar guarding the rear. The red lanterns drifted along just above them. As they took their first steps into the actual shadows of the shelves, Laszlo bit back the urge to draw his sword and keep it waiting for whatever might be out there.

"What do you think of the place?" Casimir, walking just in front of Laszlo, was staring around as though in a pleasant dream, and he spoke softly.

"I'm going to kiss the floor wherever we get out. Yourself?"

"It's marvelous. It's everything I ever hoped it would be."

"Interested in becoming a Librarian?" said Yvette.

"Oh no," said Casimir. "Not that. But all this power . . . half-awake, just as Master Molnar said, flowing in currents without any conscious force behind it. It's astonishing. Can't you feel it?"

"I can," said Yvette. "It scares the hell out of me."

Laszlo could feel the power they spoke of, but only faintly, as a sort of icy tickle on the back of his neck. He knew he was a great deal less sensitive than Yvette or Casimir, and he wondered if experiencing the place through an intuition as heightened as theirs would help him check his fears, or make him soil his trousers.

Through the dark aisles they walked, eyes wide and searching, between the high walls of book spines. Tendrils of mist curled around Laszlo's feet, and from time to time he heard sounds in the distance—faint echoes of movement, of rustling pages, of soft, sighing winds. Astriza turned right, then right again, choosing new directions at aisle junctions according to the unknowable spells she and Molnar had cast earlier. Half an hour passed uneasily, and it seemed to Laszlo that they should have doubled back on their own trail several times, but they were undeniably pressing steadily onward into deeper, stranger territory.

"Laszlo," muttered Casimir.

"What?"

"Just tell me what you want, quit poking me."

"I haven't touched you."

Astriza raised a hand, and their little column halted in its tracks. Casimir whirled on Laszlo, rubbing the back of his neck. "That wasn't you?"

"Hells, no!"

The first attack of the journey came then, from the shadowy canyon-walls of the bookcases around them, a pelting rain of dark objects. Laszlo yelped and put up his arms to protect his eyes. Astriza had her swords out in the time it took him to flinch, and Yvette, moving not much slower, thrust out her hands and conjured some sort of rippling barrier in the air above them. Peering up at it, Laszlo realized that the objects bouncing off it were all but harmless—crumpled paper, fragments of wood, chunks of broken plaster, dark dried things that looked like . . . gods, small animal turds! Bless Yvette and her shield.

In the hazy red light of the hovering lanterns he could see

the things responsible for this disrespectful cascade—dozens of spindly-limbed, flabby gray creatures the rough size and shape of stillborn infants. Their eyes were hollow dark pits and their mouths were thin slits, as though cut into their flesh with one quick slash of a blade. They were scampering out from behind books and perching atop the shelves, and launching their rain of junk from there.

Casimir laughed, gestured, and spoke a low, sharp word of command that stung Laszlo's ears. One of the little creatures dropped whatever it was about to throw, moaned, and flashed into a cloud of greasy, red-hot ash that dispersed like steam. Its nearby companions scattered, screeching.

"You can't tell me we're in any actual danger from these," said Casimir.

"We're tell me can't," whispered a harsh voice from somewhere in the shelves, "known, known!"

"Any actual you, known, *from these in danger,"* came a screeching answer. "Known, known, known!"

"Oh, hell," shouted Astriza, "shut up, everyone shut up! Say nothing!"

"Known, known, known," came another whispered chorus, and then a dozen voices repeating her words in a dozen babbled variations. "Known, known, known!"

"They're vocabuvores," whispered Master Molnar. "Just keep moving out of their territory. Stay silent."

"Known," hissed one of the creatures from somewhere above. "All known! New words. GIVE NEW WORDS!"

Molnar prodded Lev, who occupied the penultimate spot in their column, forward with the butt of his staff. Lev pushed Laszlo, who passed the courtesy on. Stumbling and slipping, the aspirants and their guides moved haltingly, for the annoying rain of junk persisted and Yvette's barrier was limited in size. Something soft and wet smacked the ground just in front of Laszlo, and in an uncharacteristic moment of pure clumsiness he set foot on it and went sprawling. His jaw rattled on the cold, hard tiles of the floor, and without thinking he yelped, "Shit!"

"Known!" screeched a chorus of the little creatures.

"NEW!" cried a triumphant voice, directly above him. "New! NEW!"

There was a new sound, a sickly crackling noise. Laszlo gaped as one of the little dark shapes on the shelves far above swelled, doubling in size in seconds, its grotesque flesh bubbling and rising like some unholy dough. The little claws and limbs, previously smaller than a cat's, took on a more menacing heft. "More," it croaked in a deeper voice. "Give more new words!" And with that, it flung itself down at him, wider mouth open to display a fresh set of sharp teeth.

Astriza's sword hit the thing before Laszlo could choke out a scream, rupturing it like a lanced boil and spattering a goodly radius with hot, vomit-scented ichor. Laszlo gagged, stumbled to his feet, and hurriedly wiped the awful stuff away from his eyes. Astriza spared him a furious glare, then pulled him forward by the mantle of his cloak.

Silently enduring the rain of junk and the screeching calls for new words, the party stumbled on through aisles and junctions until the last of the hooting, scrabbling, missile-flinging multitude was lost in the misty darkness behind them.

"Vocabuvores," said Master Molnar when they had stopped in a place of apparent safety, "goblin-like creatures that feed on any new words they learn from human speech. Their metabolisms turn vocabulary into body mass. They're like insects at birth, but a few careless sentences and they can grow to human size, and beyond."

"Do they eat people, too?" said Laszlo, shuddering.

"They'd cripple us," said Astriza, wiping vocabuvore slop

from her sword. "And torture us as long as they could, until we screamed every word we knew for them."

"We don't have time to wipe that colony out today," said Molnar. "Fortunately, vocabuvores are extremely territorial. And totally illiterate. Their nests are surrounded by enough books to feed their little minds forever, but they can't read a word."

"How can such things have stolen in, past your gates and sorcery?" asked Lev.

"It's the books again," said Molnar. "Their power sometimes snatches the damnedest things away from distant worlds. The stacks are filled with living and quasi-living dwellers, of two general types."

"The first sort we call *externals*," said Astriza. "Anything recently dumped or summoned here. Animals, spirits, even the occasional sentient being. Most of them don't last long. Either we deal with them, or they become prey for the other sort of dweller."

"Bibliofauna," said Molnar. "Creatures created by the actions of the books themselves, or somehow dependent upon them. A stranger sort of being, twisted by the environment and more suited to survive in it. Vocabuvores certainly didn't spawn anywhere else."

"Well," said Astriza, "we're a bit smellier, but we all seem to be in one piece. We're not far now from twenty-eight Manticore East. Keep moving, and the next time I tell you to shut up, Laszlo, please shut up."

"Apologies, Librarian Mezar—"

"Titles are for outside the library," she growled. "In here, you can best apologize by not getting killed."

"Ahhh," said Molnar, gazing down at his guiding ideogram. The lights within the red lines had turned green. "Bang-on. Anywhere on the third shelf will do. Aspirant D'Courin, let Astriza handle the actual placement."

Yvette seemed only too happy to pass her satchel off to the sturdy Librarian. "Cover me," said Astriza as she moved carefully toward the bookcase indicated by Molnar's spells. It was about twelve feet high, and while the dark wood of its exterior was warped and weathered, the volumes tucked onto its shelves looked pristine. Astriza settled Yvette's book into an empty spot, then leapt backward, both of her swords flashing out. She had the fastest over-shoulder draw Laszlo had ever seen.

"What is it?" said Molnar, rushing forward to place himself between the shelf and the four aspirants.

"Fifth shelf," said Astriza. She gestured, and one of the hovering lanterns moved in, throwing its scarlet light into the dark recesses of the shelves. Something long and dark and cylindrical was lying across the books on that shelf, and as the lantern moved, Laszlo caught a glimpse of scales.

"I think—" said Astriza, lowering one of her swords, "I think it's dead." She stabbed carefully with her other blade, several times, then nodded. She and Molnar reached in gingerly and heaved the thing out onto the floor, where it landed with a heavy smack.

It was a serpent of some sort, with a green body as thick as Laszlo's arm. It was about ten feet long, and it had three flat, triangular heads with beady eyes, now glassy in death. Crescent-shaped bite marks marred most of its length, as though something had worked its way up and down the body, chewing at leisure.

"External," said Astriza.

"A swamp hydra," said Lev, prodding the body with one of his clawed feet. "From my home world . . . very dangerous. I had night terrors of them when I was newly hatched. What killed it?"

"Too many possible culprits to name," said Molnar. He

touched the serpent's body with the butt of his staff and uttered a spell. The dead flesh lurched, smoked, and split apart, turning gray before their eyes. In seconds, it had begun to shrink, until at last it was nothing more than a smear of charcoal-colored ash on the floor. "The Tree of Knives used to scare predators away from this section, but it's uprooted itself. Anything could have moved in. Aspirant Bronzeclaw, give me the notes for your book."

"*Private Reflections of Grand Necrosophist Jaklur the Unendurable*," said Astriza as Molnar shared the notes with her. "Charming." The two Librarians performed their divinations once again, with more urgency than before. After a few moments, Astriza looked up, pointed somewhere off to Laszlo's left, and said: "Fifty-five Manticore Northwest. Another hell of a walk. Let's get moving."

The second stage of their journey was longer than the first. The other aspirants looked anxious, all except Casimir, who continued to stroll while others crept cautiously. Caz seemed to have a limitless reserve of enchantment with the place. As for Laszlo, well, before another hour had passed, the last reeking traces of the vocabuvore's gore had been washed from his face and neck by streams of nervous sweat. He was acutely aware, as they moved on through the dark canyons and grottos of the stacks, that unseen things in every direction were scuttling, growling, and hissing.

At one point, he heard a high-pitched giggling from the darkness, and stopped to listen more closely. Master Molnar, not missing a step, grabbed him firmly by his shoulders, spun him around, and pushed him onward.

They came at last to one of the outer walls of the library, where the air was clammy with a mist that swirled more thickly than ever before. Railed galleries loomed above them, utterly lightless, and Astriza waved the party far clear of the spiral stair-cases and ladders that led up into those silent spaces.

"Not much farther," she said. "And Casimir's book goes some-where pretty close after this. If we get lucky, we might just—"

"Get down," hissed Molnar.

Astriza was down on one knee in a flash, swords out, and the aspirants followed her example. Laszlo knelt and drew his sword. Only Molnar remained on his feet.

The quality of the mist had changed. A breeze was stirring, growing more and more powerful as Laszlo watched. Down the long, dark aisle before them the skin-chilling current came, and with it a fluttering, rustling sound, like clothes rippling on a drying line. A swirling, nebulous shape appeared, and the mist surged and parted before it. As it came nearer, Laszlo saw that it was a mass of papers, a column of book pages, hundreds of them, whirling on a tight axis like a tornado.

"No," shouted Molnar as Casimir raised his hands to begin a spell. "Don't harm it! Protect yourselves, but don't fight back or the library will—"

His words were drowned out as the tumbling mass of pages washed over them and its sound increased tenfold. Laszlo was buffeted with winds like a dozen invisible fists—his cloak streamed out behind him as though he were in free-fall, and a cloud of dust and grime torn from the surfaces nearby filled the air as a stinging miasma. He barely managed to fumble his sword safely back into his scabbard as he sought the floor. Just above him, the red lanterns were slammed against a stone balcony and shattered to fragments.

From out of the wailing wind there came a screech like knives drawn over slate. Through slitted eyes, Laszlo saw that Lev was losing his balance and sliding backward. Laszlo realized that Lev's torso, wider than any human's, was catching the wind like a sail despite the lizard's efforts to sink his claws into the tile floor.

Laszlo threw himself at Lev's back and strained against the lizard's overpowering bulk and momentum for a few desperate seconds. Just as he realized that he was about to get bowled over, Casimir appeared out of the whirling confusion and added his weight to Laszlo's. Heaving with all their might, the two human aspirants managed to help Lev finally force himself flat to the ground, where they sprawled on top of him.

Actinic light flared. Molnar and Astriza, leaning into the terrible wind together, had placed their hands on Molnar's staff and wrought some sort of spell. The brutal gray cyclone parted before them like the bow-shock of a swift-sailing ship, and the dazed aspirants behind them were released from the choking grip of the page-storm. Not a moment too soon, in fact, for the storm had caught up the jagged copper and glass fragments of the broken lanterns, sharper claws than any it had possessed before. Once, twice, three times it lashed out with these new weapons, rattling against the invisible barrier, but the sorcery of the Librarians held firm. It seemed to Laszlo that a note of frustration entered the wail of the thing around them.

Tense moments passed. The papers continued to snap and twirl above them, and the winds still wailed madly, but after a short while the worst of the page-storm seemed to be spent. Glass and metal fragments rained around them like discarded toys, and the whole screaming mess fluttered on down the aisle, leaving a slowly falling haze of upflung dust in its wake. Coughing and sneezing, Laszlo and his companions stumbled shakily to their feet, while the noise and chaos of the indoor cyclone faded into the distant mist and darkness.

"My thanks, humans," said Lev hoarsely. "My clan's ancestral trade of scale-grooming is beginning to acquire a certain tint of nostalgia in my thoughts."

"Don't mention it," coughed Laszlo. "What the hell was that?"

"Believe it or not, that was a book," said Astriza.

"A forcibly unbound grimoire," said Molnar, dusting off his armor. "The creatures and forces in here occasionally destroy books by accident. And sometimes, when a truly ancient grimoire bound with particularly powerful spells is torn apart, it doesn't want to *stop* being a book. It becomes a focus for the library's unconscious anger. A book without spine or covers is like an unquiet spirit without mortal form. Whatever's left of it holds itself together out of sheer resentment, roaming without purpose, lashing out at whatever crosses its path."

"Like my face," said Laszlo, suddenly aware of hot, stinging pains across his cheeks and forehead. "Ow, gods."

"Paper cuts," said Casimir, grinning. "Won't be impressing any beautiful women with those scars, I'm afraid."

"Oh, I'm impressed," muttered Yvette, pressing her fingertips gingerly against her own face. "You just let those things whirl around as they please, Master Molnar?"

"They never attack other books. And they uproot or destroy a number of the library's smaller vermin. You might compare them to forest fires in the outside world—ugly, but perhaps ultimately beneficial to the cycle of existence."

"Pity about the lamps, though," said Yvette.

"Ah. Yes," said Molnar. He tapped the head of his staff, and a ball of flickering red light sprang from it, fainter than that of the lost lamps but adequate to dispel the gloom. "Aspirants, use the empty book satchel. Pick up all the lantern fragments you can see. The library has a sufficient quantity of disorder that we need not import any."

While the aspirants tended their cuts and scoured the vicinity for lantern parts, Astriza glanced around, consulted some sort of amulet chained around her wrist, and whistled appreciatively. "Hey, here's a stroke of luck." She moved over to a bookcase nestled against the outer library wall, slid Lev's grimoire into an empty spot, and backed away cautiously. "Two down. You four are halfway to your sixth year."

"Aspirant Vrana," said Molnar, "I believe we'll find a home for your book not a stone's throw along the outer wall, at sixty-one Manticore Northwest. And then we'll have just one more delivery before we can speed the four of you on your way, back to the carefree world of making requests from the comfort of the reading rooms."

"No need to hurry on my account," said Casimir, stretching lazily. His cloak and armor were back in near perfect order. "I'm having a lovely time. And I'm sure the best is yet to come."

It was a bit more than a stone's throw, thought Laszlo, unless you discarded the human arm as a reference and went in for something like a trebuchet. Along the aisle they moved, past section after section of books that were, as Master Molnar had promised, completely unharmed by the passage of the unbound grimoire. The mist crept back in around them, and the two Librarians fussed and muttered over their guidance spells as they walked. Eventually, they arrived at what Molnar claimed was sixty-one Manticore Northwest, a cluster of shelves under a particularly heavy overhanging stone balcony.

"Ta-daaaaaa," cried Astriza as she backed away from the shelf once she had successfully replaced Casimir's book. "You see, children, some returns are boring. And in here, boring is beautiful."

"Help me!" cried a faint voice from somewhere off to Laszlo's right, in the dark forest of bookcases leading away to the unseen heart of the library.

"Not to mention damned rare." Astriza moved out into the aisle with Molnar, scanning the shelves and shadows surrounding the party. "Who's out there?"

"Help me!" The voice was soft and hoarse. There was no telling whether or not it came from the throat of a thinking creature.

"Someone from another book-return team?" asked Yvette.

"I'd know," said Molnar. "More likely it's a trick. We'll investigate, but very, very cautiously."

As though it were a response to the Master Librarian's words, a book came sailing out of the darkened stacks. The two Librarians ducked, and, after bouncing off the floor once, the book wound up at Yvette's feet. She nudged it with the tip of a boot and then, satisfied that it was genuine, picked it up and examined the cover.

"What is it?" said Molnar.

"*Annotated Commentaries on the Mysteries of the Worm,*" said Yvette. "I don't know if that means anything special—"

"An-no-tated," hissed a voice from the darkness. There was a strange snort of satisfaction. "New!"

"Commentaries," hissed another. "New, new!"

"Hells!" Molnar turned to the aspirants and lowered his voice to a whisper. "A trick, after all! Vocabuvores again. Keep your voices down, use simple words. We've just given them food. Could be a group as large as the last one."

"Mysteries," groaned one of the creatures. "New!" A series of wet snapping and bubbling noises followed. Laszlo shuddered, remembering the rapid growth of the thing that had tried to jump him earlier, and his sword was in his hand in an instant.

"New words," chanted a chorus of voices that deepened even

as they spoke. "New words, new words!" It sounded like at least a dozen of the things were out there, and beneath their voices was the crackling and bubbling, as though cauldrons of fat were on the boil . . . many cauldrons.

"All you, give new words." A deeper, harsher voice than the others, more commanding. "All you, except BOY. Boy that KILL with spell! Him we kill! Others give new words!"

"Him we kill," chanted the chorus. "Others give new words!"

"No way," whispered Astriza. "No gods-damned way!"

"It's the same band of vocabuvores," whispered Molnar. "They've actually followed us. Merciful gods, they're learning to overcome their instincts. We've *got* to destroy them!"

"We sure as hell can't let them pass this behavior on to others," whispered Astriza, nodding grimly. "Just as Master Molnar said, clamp your mouths shut. Let your swords and spells do the talking. If—"

Whatever she was about to say, Laszlo never found out. Growling, panting, gibbering, screeching, the vocabuvores surged out of the darkness, over bookcases and out of aisles, into the wan circle of red light cast by Molnar's staff. Nor were they the small-framed creatures of the previous attack—most had grown to the size of wolves. Their bodies had elongated, their limbs had knotted with thick strands of ropy muscle, and their claws had become slaughterhouse implements. Some had acquired plates of chitinous armor, while others had sacks of flab hanging off them like pendulous tumors. They came by the dozens, in an arc that closed on Laszlo and his companions like a set of jaws.

The first to strike on either side was Casimir, who uttered a syllable so harsh that Laszlo reeled just to hear it. His ears rang, and a bitter metallic taste filled his mouth. It was a death-weaving, true dread sorcery, the sort of thing that Laszlo had never imagined himself even daring to study, and the closest of the vocabuvores paid for its enthusiasm by receiving the full brunt of the spell. Its skin literally peeled itself from the bones and muscles beneath, a ragged wet leathery flower tearing open and blowing away. And, an instant later, the muscles followed, then the bones and the glistening internal organs; the creature exploded layer by layer. But there were many more behind it, and as the fight began in earnest, Laszlo found himself praying silently that words of command, which were so much babble to non-magicians, couldn't nourish the creatures.

Snarling they came, eyes like black hollows, mouths like gaping pits, and in an instant Laszlo's awareness of the battle narrowed to those claws that were meant to shred his armor, those fangs that were meant to sink into his flesh. Darting and dodging, he fought the wildest duel of his career, his centuries-old steel punching through quivering vocabuvore flesh. They died, sure enough, but there were many to replace the dead, rank on writhing rank, pushing forward to grasp and tear at him.

"New words," the creatures croaked, as he slashed at bulging throats and slammed his heavy hilt down on monstrous skulls. The things vomited fountains of reeking gore when they died, soaking his cloak and breeches, but he barely noticed as he gave ground step by step, backing away from the press of falling bodies as new combatants continually scrambled to take their places.

As Laszlo fought on, he managed to catch glimpses of what was happening around him. Molnar and Astriza fought back to back, the Master Librarian's staff sweeping before him in powerful arcs. As for Astriza, her curved blades were broader and heavier than Laszlo's—no stabbing and dancing for her. When she swung, limbs flew, and vocabuvores were laid open guts to groins. He admired her power, and that admiration nearly became a fatal distraction.

"NEW WORD!" screeched one of the vocabuvores, seizing

him by his mantle and forcing him down to his knees. It pried and scraped at his leather neck-guard, salivating. The thing's breath was unbelievable, like a dead animal soaked in sewage and garlic wine. Was that what the digestion of words smelled like? "NEW WORD!"

"Die," Laszlo muttered, swatting the thing's hands away just long enough to drive his sword up and into the orbless pit of its left eye. It demonstrated immediate comprehension of the new word by sliding down the front of his armor, claws scrabbling at him in a useless final reflex. Laszlo stumbled up, kicked the corpse away, and freed his blade to face the next one . . . and the next one . . .

Working in a similar vein was Lev Bronzeclaw, forgoing his mediocre magic in order to leap about and bring his natural weaponry into play just a few feet to Laszlo's left. Some foes he lashed with his heavy tail, sending them sprawling. Others he seized with his upper limbs and held firmly while his blindingly fast kicks sunk claws into guts. Furious, inexorable, he scythed vocabuvores in half and spilled their steaming bowels as though the creatures were fruits in the grasp of some devilish mechanical pulping machine.

Casimir and Yvette, meanwhile, had put their backs to a bookshelf and were plying their sorceries in tandem against a chaotic, flailing press of attackers. Yvette had conjured another one of her invisible barriers and was moving it back and forth like a tower shield, absorbing vocabuvore attacks with it and then slamming them backward. Casimir, grinning wildly, was methodically unleashing his killing spells at the creatures Yvette knocked off-balance, consuming them in flashing pillars of blue flame. The oily black smoke from these fires swirled across the battle and made Laszlo gag.

Still, they seemed to be making progress—there could only be so many vocabuvores, and Laszlo began to feel a curious exaltation as the ranks of their brutish foes thinned. Just a few more for him, a few more for the Librarians, a few more for Lev, and the fight was all but—

"KILL BOY," roared the commanding vocabuvore, the deep-voiced one that had launched the attack moments earlier. At last it joined the fight proper, bounding out of the bookcases, twice the size of any of its brethren, more like a pallid gray bear than anything else. *"Kill boy with spells! Kill girl!"*

Heeding the call, the surviving vocabuvores abandoned all other opponents and dove toward Casimir and Yvette, forcing the two aspirants back against the shelf under the desperate press of their new surge. Laszlo and Lev, caught off guard by the instant withdrawal of their remaining foes, stumbled clumsily into one another.

The huge vocabuvore charged across the aisle, and Astriza and Molnar moved to intercept it. Laszlo watched in disbelief as they were simply shoved over by stiff smacks from the creature's massive forelimbs. It even carried one of Astriza's blades away with it, embedded in a sack of oozing gristle along its right side, without visible effect. It dove into the bookcases behind the one Casimir and Yvette were standing against, and disappeared momentarily from sight.

The smaller survivors had pinned Yvette between the shelf and her shield; like an insect under glass, she was being crushed behind her own magic. Having neutralized her protection, they finally seized Casmir's arms, interfering with his ability to cast spells. Pushing frantically past the smoldering shells of their dead comrades, they seemed to have abandoned any hope of new words in exchange for a last act of vengeance against Casimir.

But there were only a bare dozen left, and Laszlo and Lev had regained their balance. Moving in unison, they charged through the smoke and blood to fall on the rear of the pack of surviving vocabuvores. There they slew unopposed, and if only they could slay fast enough . . . claws and sword sang out together, *ten*. And again, *eight,* and again, *six* . . .

Yvette's shield buckled at last, and she and Casimir slid sideways with vocabuvore claws at their throats. But now there were only half a dozen, and then there were four, then two. A triumphant moment later, Laszlo, gasping for breath, grabbed the last of the creatures by the back of its leathery neck and hauled it off his chambers-mate. Laszlo drove his sword into the vocabuvore's back, transfixing it through whatever approximation of a heart it possessed, and flung it down to join the rest of its dead brood.

"Thanks," coughed Casimir, reaching over to help Yvette sit up. Other than a near-total drenching with the nauseating contents of dead vocabuvores, the two of them seemed to have escaped the worst possibilities.

"Big one," gasped Yvette. "Find the big one, kill it quickly—"

At that precise instant, the big one struck the bookcase from behind, heaving it over directly on top of them, a sudden rain of books followed by a heavy dark blur that slammed Casimir and Yvette out of sight beneath it. Laszlo stumbled back in shock as the huge vocabuvore stepped onto the tumbled bookcase, stomping its feet like a jungle predator gloating over a fresh kill.

"Casimir," Laszlo screamed. "Yvette!"

"No," cried Master Molnar, lurching back to his feet. "No! Proper nouns are the most powerful words of all!"

Alas, what was said could not be unsaid. The flesh of the last vocabuvore rippled as though a hundred burrowing things were about to erupt from within, but the expression on its baleful face was sheer ecstasy. New masses of flesh billowed forth, new cords of muscle and sinew wormed their way out of thin air, new rows of shark-like teeth rose gleaming in the black pit of the thing's mouth. In a moment, it had gained several feet of height and girth, and the top of its head was now not far below the stones that floored the gallery above.

With a foot far weightier than before, the thing stomped the bookcase again, splintering the ancient wood. Lev flung his mighty scarlet-scaled bulk against the creature without hesitation, but it had already eclipsed his strength. It caught him in midair, turned, and flung him spinning head-over-tail into Molnar and Astriza. Still dull from their earlier clubbing, the two librarians failed spectacularly to duck, and four hundred pounds of whirling reptilian aspirant took them down hard.

That left Laszlo, facing the creature all alone, gore-slick sword shaking in his hand, with sorcerous powers about adequate, on his best day, to heat a cup of tea.

"Oh, *shit*," he muttered.

"Known," chuckled the creature. Its voice was now a bass rumble, deep as oncoming thunder. "Now will kill boy. Now EASY."

"Uh," said Laszlo, scanning the smoke-swirled area for any surprise, any advantage, any unused weapon. While it was flattering to imagine himself charging in and dispatching the thing with his sword, the treatment it had given Lev was not at all encouraging in that respect. He flicked his gaze from the bookshelves to the ceiling—and then it hit him, a sensation that would have been familiar to any aspirant ever graduated from the High University. The inherent magic of all undergraduates—the magic of the last minute. The power to embrace any solution, no matter how insane or desperate.

"No," he yelled. "No! Spare boy!"

"Kill boy," roared the creature, no more scintillating a conversationalist for all its physical changes.

"No." Laszlo tossed his sword aside and beckoned to the vocabuvore. "Spare boy. I will give new words!"

"I kill boy, *then* you give new words!"

"No. Spare boy. I will give many new words. I will give *all* my words."

"No," howled Lev. "No, you can't—"

"Trust me," said Laszlo. He picked a book out of the mess at his feet and waved it at the vocabuvore. "Come here. I'll *read* to you!"

"Book of words . . ." the creature hissed. It took a step forward.

"Yes. Many books, new words. Come to me, and they're yours."

"New words!" Another step. The creature was off the bookcase now, towering over him. Ropy strands of hot saliva tumbled from the corners of its mouth . . . good gods, Laszlo thought, he'd really made it hungry.

"Occultation!" he said, by way of a test.

The creature growled with pleasure, shuddering, and more mass boiled out of its grotesque frame. The change was not as severe as that caused by proper nouns, but it was still obvious. The vocabuvore's head moved an inch closer to the ceiling. Laszlo took a deep breath, and then began shouting as rapidly as he could:

"Fuliginous! Occluded! Uh, canticle! Portmanteau! Tea cozy!" He racked his mind. He needed obscure words, complex words, words unlikely to have been uttered by cautious librarians prowling the stacks. "Indeterminate! Mendacious! Vestibule! Tits, testicles, aluminum, heliotrope, *narcolepsy*!"

The vocabuvore panted in pleasure, gorging itself on the stream of fresh words. Its stomach doubled in size, tripled, becoming a sack of flab that could have supplied fat for ten thousand candles. Inch by inch, it surged outward and upward. Its head bumped into the stone ceiling and it glanced up, as though realizing for the first time just how cramped its quarters were.

"Adamant," cried Laszlo, backing away from the creature's limbs, now as thick as tree trunks. "Resolute, unyielding, unwavering, reckless, irresponsible, foolhardy!"

"Noooo," yowled the creature, clearly recognizing its predicament and struggling to fight down the throes of ecstasy from its unprecedented feast. Its unfolding masses of new flesh were wedging it more and more firmly in place between the floor and the heavy stones of the overhead gallery, sorcery-laid stones that had stood fast for more than a thousand years. "Stop, stop, stop!"

"Engorgement," shouted Laszlo, almost dancing with excitement. "Avarice! Rapaciousness! Corpulence! Superabundance! *Comeuppance!*"

"Ngggggh," the vocabuvore, now elephant-sized, shrieked in a deafening voice. It pushed against the overhead surface with hands six or seven feet across. To no avail— its head bent sideways at an unnatural angle until its spine, still growing, finally snapped against the terrible pressure of floor and ceiling. The huge arms fell to the ground with a thud that jarred Laszlo's teeth, and a veritable waterfall of dark blood began to pour from the corner of the thing's slack mouth.

Not stopping to admire this still-twitching flesh edifice, Laszlo ran around it, reaching the collapsed bookcase just as Lev did. Working together, they managed to heave it up, disgorging a flow of books that slid out around their ankles. Laszlo grinned uncontrollably when Casimir and Yvette pushed themselves shakily up to their hands and knees. Lev pulled Yvette off the ground and she tumbled into his arms, laughing, while Laszlo heaved Casimir up.

"I apologize," said Caz, "for every word I've ever criticized in every dissertation you've ever scribbled."

"Tonight we will get drunk," yelled Lev. The big lizard's friendly slap between Laszlo's shoulder blades almost knocked him into the spot previously occupied by Yvette. "In your human fashion, without forethought, in strange neighborhoods that will yield anecdotes for future mortification—"

"Master Molnar!" said Yvette. In an instant, the four aspirants had turned and come to attention like nervous students of arms.

Molnar and Astriza were supporting each other gingerly, sharing Molnar's staff as a sort of fifth leg. Each had received a thoroughly bloody nose, and Molnar's left eye was swelling shut under livid bruises.

"My deepest apologies," hissed Lev. "I fear that I have done you some injury—"

"Hardly your fault, Aspirant Bronzeclaw," said Molnar. "You merely served as an involuntary projectile."

Laszlo felt the exhilaration of the fight draining from him, and the familiar sensations of tired limbs and fresh bruises took its place. Everyone seemed able to stand on their own two feet, and everyone was a mess. Torn cloaks, slashed armor, bent scabbards, myriad cuts and welts—all of it under a thorough coating of black vocabuvore blood, still warm and sopping. Even Casimir— No, thought Laszlo, the bastard had done it again. He was as disgusting as anyone, but somewhere, between blinks, he'd reassumed his mantle of sly contentment.

"Nicely done, Laszlo," said Astriza. "Personally, I'm glad Lev bowled me over. If I'd been on my feet when you offered to feed that thing new words, I'd have tried to punch your lights out. My compliments on fast thinking."

"Agreed," said Molnar. "That was the most singular entanglement I've seen in all my years of minding student book-return expeditions. All of you did fine work, fine work putting down a real threat."

"And importing a fair amount of new disorder to the stacks," said Yvette. Laszlo followed her gaze around the site of the battle.

Between the sprawled tribe of slain vocabuvores, the rivers of blood, the haze of thaumaturgical smoke, and the smashed shelf, sixty-one Manticore Northwest looked worse than all of them put together.

"My report will describe the carnage as 'regretfully unavoidable,'" said Master Molnar with a smile. "Besides, we've cleaned up messes before. Everything here will be back in place before the end of the day."

Laszlo imagined that he could actually feel his spirits sag. Spend all day in here, cleaning up? Even with magic, it would take hours, and gods knew what else might jump them while they worked. Evidently, his face betrayed his feelings, for Molnar and Astriza laughed in unison.

"Though not because of anything *you* four will be doing," said Molnar. "Putting a section back into operation after a major incident is Librarian's work. You four are finished here. I believe you get the idea, and I'm passing you all."

"But my book," said Laszlo. "It—"

"There'll be more aspirants tomorrow, and the next day, and the day after that. You've done your part," said Molnar. "Aspirant Bronzeclaw's suggestion is a sensible one, and I believe you deserve to carry it out as soon as possible. Retrieve your personal equipment, and let's get back to daylight."

If the blue-robed functionaries in the Manticore Index were alarmed to see the six of them return drenched in gore, they certainly didn't show it. The aspirants tossed their book-satchels and lantern fragments aside, and began to loosen or remove gloves, neck-guards, cloaks, and amulets. Laszlo released some of the buckles on his cuirass and sighed with pleasure.

"Shall we meet in an hour?" said Lev. "At the eastern commons, after we've had a chance to, ah, thoroughly bathe?"

"Make it two," said Yvette. "Your people don't have any hair to deal with."

"We were in there for four hours," said Casimir, glancing at a wall clock. "I scarcely believe it."

"Well, time slows down when everything around you is trying to kill you," said Astriza. "Master Molnar, do you want me to put together a team to work on the mess in Manticore Northwest?"

"Yes, notify all the night staff. I'll be back to lead it myself. I should only require a few hours." He gestured at his left eye, now swollen shut. "I'll be at the infirmary."

"Of course. And the, ah . . ."

"Indeed." Molnar sighed. "You don't mind taking care of it, if—"

"Yes, if," said Astriza. "I'll take care of all the details. Get that eye looked at, sir."

"We all leaving together?" said Yvette.

"I need to grab my impression device," said Casimir, pointing to the glass niche that housed a focus for the index enchantments. "And, ah, study it for a few moments. You don't need to wait around for my sake. I'll meet you later."

"Farewell, then," said Lev. He and Yvette left the Manticore Index together.

"Well, my boys, you did some bold work in there," said Molnar, staring at Laszlo and Casimir with his good eye. Suddenly he seemed much older to Laszlo, old and tired. "I would hope . . . that boldness and wisdom will always go hand in hand for the pair of you."

"Thank you, Master Molnar," said Casimir. "That's very kind of you."

Molnar seemed to wait an uncommon length of time before he nodded, but nod he did, and then he walked out of the room after Lev and Yvette.

"You staying too, Laz?" Casimir had peeled off his bloody gauntlets and rubbed his hands clean. "You don't need to, really."

"It's okay," said Laszlo, curious once again about Casimir's pet project. "I can stand to be a reeking mess for a few extra minutes."

"Suit yourself."

While Casimir began to fiddle with his white crystal, Astriza conjured several documents out of letters that floated in the air before her. "You two take as long as you need," she said distractedly. "I've got a pile of work orders to put together."

Casimir reached into a belt pouch, drew out a small container of greasy white paint, and began to quickly sketch designs on the floor in front of the pulsing glass column. Laszlo frowned as he studied the symbols—he recognized some of them, variations on warding and focusing sigils that any first-year aspirant could use to contain or redirect magical energy. But these were far more complex, like combinations of notes that any student could puzzle out but only a virtuoso could actually play. Compared to Laszlo, Casimir was such a virtuoso.

"Caz," said Laszlo, "what exactly are you doing?"

"Graduating early." Casimir finished his design at last, a lattice of arcane symbols so advanced and tight-woven that Laszlo's eyes crossed as he tried to puzzle it out. As a final touch, Casimir drew a simple white circle around himself—the traditional basis for any protective magical ward.

"What the hell are you talking about?"

"I'm sorry, Laszlo. You've been a good chambers-mate. I wish you'd just left with the rest." Casimir smiled at him sadly, and there was something new and alien in his manner—condescension. Dismissal. He'd always been pompous and cocksure, but gods, he'd never looked at Laszlo like *this*. With pity, as though he were a favorite pet about to be thrown out of the house.

"Caz, this isn't funny."

"If you were more sensitive, I think you'd have already understood. But I know you can't feel it like I do. *Yvette* felt it. But she's like the rest of you, sewn up in all the little damn rules you make for yourselves to paint timidity as a virtue."

"Felt *what*—"

"The magic in this place. The currents. Hell, an ocean of power, fermenting for a thousand years, lashing out at random like some headless animal. And all they can do with it is keep it bottled up and hope it doesn't bite them too sharply. It needs a *will*, Laszlo! It needs a mind to guide it, to wrestle it down, to put it to constructive use."

"You're kidding." Laszlo's mouth was suddenly dry. "This is a finals-week joke, Caz. You're kidding."

"No." Casimir gestured at the glass focus. "It's all here already, everything necessary. If you'd had any ambition at all you would have seen the hints in the introductory materials. The index enchantments are like a nervous system, in touch with everything, and they can be used to communicate with everything. I'm going to bend this place, Laz. Bend it around my finger and make it something new."

"It'll kill you!"

"It could win." Casimir flashed his teeth, a grin as predatory as any worn by the vocabuvores that had tried to devour him less than an hour before. "But so what? I graduate with honors, I go back to my people, and what then? Fighting demons, writing books, advising ministers? To hell with it. In the long run I'm still a footnote. But if I can seize *this*, rule *this*, that's more power than ten thousand lifetimes of dutiful slavery."

"Aspirant Vrana," said Astriza. She had come up behind Laszlo, so quietly that he hadn't heard her approach. "Casimir. Is something the matter?"

"On the contrary, Librarian Mezaros. Everything is better than ever."

"Casimir," she said, "I've been listening. I strongly urge you to reconsider this course of action, before—"

"Before *what*? Before I do what you people should have done a thousand years ago when this place bucked the harness? Stay back, Librarian, or I'll weave a death for you before your spells can touch me. Look on the bright side . . . anything is possible once this is done. The University and I will have to reach . . . an accommodation."

"What about me, Caz?" Laszlo threw his tattered cloak aside and placed a hand on the hilt of his sword. "Would you slay me, too?"

"Interesting question, Laszlo. Would you really pull that thing on me?"

"Five years! I thought we were friends!" The sword came out in a silver blur, and Laszlo shook with fury.

"You could have gone on thinking that if you'd just left me alone for a few minutes. I already said I was sorry."

"Step out of the circle, Casimir. Step out, or decide which one of us you have time to kill before we can reach you."

"Laszlo, even for someone as mildly magical as yourself, you disappoint me. I said I checked your sword personally this morning, didn't I?"

Casimir snapped his fingers, and Laszlo's sword wrenched itself from his grasp so quickly that it scraped the skin from most of his knuckles. Animated by magical force, it whirled in the air and thrust itself firmly against Laszlo's throat. He gasped—the razor-edge that had slashed vocabuvore flesh like wet parchment was pressed firmly against his windpipe, and a modicum of added pressure would drive it in.

"Now," shouted Casimir, "Indexers, *out*! If anyone else comes in, if I am interfered with, or knocked unconscious or by any means further *annoyed*, my enchantment on that sword will slice this aspirant's head off."

The blue-robed Indexers withdrew from the room hastily, and the heavy door clanged shut behind them.

"Astriza," said Casimir, "somewhere in this room is the master index book, the one updated by the enchantments. Bring it to me now."

"Casimir," said the Librarian, "it's still not too late for you to—"

"How will you write up Laszlo's death in your report? 'Regretfully unavoidable'? Bring me the damn book."

"As you wish," she said coldly. She moved to a nearby table, and returned with a thick volume, two feet high and nearly as wide.

"Simply hand it over," said Casimir. "Don't touch the warding paint."

She complied, and Casimir ran his right hand over the cover of the awkwardly large volume, cradling it against his chest with his left arm.

"Well, then, Laszlo," he said. "This is it. All the information collected by the index enchantments is sorted in the master books like this one. My little alterations will reverse the process, making this a focus for me to reshape all this chaos to my own liking."

"Casimir," said Laszlo, "please—"

"Hoist a few for me tonight if you live through whatever happens next. I'm moving past such things."

He flipped the book open, and a pale silvery glow rippled up from the pages he selected. Casimir took a deep breath, raised his right hand, and began to intone the words of a spell.

Things happened very fast then. Astriza moved, but not against Casimir—instead she hit Laszlo, taking him completely by surprise with an elbow to the chest. As he toppled backward, she darted her right arm past his face, slamming her leather-armored limb against Laszlo's blade before it could shift positions to follow him. The sword fought furiously, but Astriza caught the hilt in her other hand, and with all of her strength managed to lever it into a stack of encyclopedias, where it stuck, quivering furiously.

At the same instant, Casimir started screaming.

Laszlo sat up, rubbing his chest, shocked to find his throat uncut, and he was just in time to see the *thing* that erupted out of the master index book, though it took his mind a moment to properly assemble the details. The silvery glow of the pages brightened and flickered, like a magical portal opening, for that was exactly what it was—a portal opening horizontally like a hatch rather than vertically like a door.

Through it came a gleaming, segmented black thing nearly as wide as the book itself, something like a man-sized centipede, and uncannily fast. In an instant it had sunk half a dozen hooked foreclaws into Casimir's neck and cheeks, and then came the screams, the most horrible Laszlo had ever heard. Casimir lost his grip on the book, but it didn't matter—the massive volume floated in midair of its own accord while the new arrival did its gruesome work.

With Casimir's head gripped firmly in its larger claws, it extended dozens of narrower pink appendages from its underside, a writhing carpet of hollow, fleshy needles. These plunged into Casimir's eyes, his face, his mouth and neck, and only bare trickles of blood slid from the holes they bored, for the thing began to pulse and buzz rhythmically, sucking fluid and soft tissue from the body of the once-handsome aspirant. The screams choked to a halt, for Casimir had nothing left to scream with.

Laszlo whirled away from this and lost what was left of his

long-ago breakfast. By the time he managed to wipe his mouth and stumble to his feet at last, the affair was finished. The book creature released Casimir's desiccated corpse, its features utterly destroyed, a weirdly sagging and empty thing that hung nearly hollow on its bones and crumpled to the ground. The segmented monster withdrew, and the book slammed shut with a sound like a thunderclap.

"Caz," whispered Laszlo, astonished to find his eyes moistening. "Gods, Caz, why?"

"Master Molnar hoped he wouldn't try it," said Astriza. She scuffed the white circle with the tip of a boot and reached out to grab the master index book from where it floated in midair. "I said he showed all the classic signs. It's not always pleasant being right."

"The book was a trap," said Laszlo.

"Well, the whole thing was a trap, Laszlo. We know perfectly well what sort of hints we drop in the introductory materials, and what a powerful sorcerer could theoretically attempt to do with the index enchantments."

"I never even saw it," muttered Laszlo.

"And you think that makes you some sort of failure? Grow up, Laszlo. It just makes you well-adjusted. Not likely to spend weeks of your life planning a way to seize more power than any mortal can sanely command. Look, every once in a while, a place like the High College is bound to get a student with excessive competence and no scruples, right?"

"I suppose it must," said Laszlo. "I just . . . I never would have guessed my own chambers-mate . . ."

"The most dangerous sort. The ones that make themselves obvious can be dealt with almost at leisure. It's the ones that can disguise their true nature, get along socially, feign friendships . . . those are much, much worse. The only real way to catch them is to leave rope lying around and let them knot their own nooses."

"Merciful gods." Laszlo retrieved his sword and slid it into the scabbard for what he hoped would be the last time that day. "What about the body?"

"Library property. Some of the grimoires in here are bound in human skin, and occasionally need repair."

"Are you *kidding*?"

"Waste not, want not."

"But his family—"

"Won't get to know. Because he vanished in an unfortunate magical accident just after you turned and left him in here, didn't he?"

"I . . . damn. I don't know if I can—"

"The alternative is disgrace for him, disgrace for his family, and a major headache for everyone who knew him, especially his chambers-mate for the last five years."

"The Indexers will just play along?"

"The Indexers see what they're told to see. I sign their pay chits."

"It just seems incredible," said Laszlo. "To stand here and hide everything about his real fate, as casually as you'd shelve a book."

"Who around here *casually* shelves a book?"

"Good point." Laszlo sighed and held his hand out to Astriza. "I suppose, then, that Casimir vanished in a magical accident just after I turned and left him in here."

"Rely on us to handle the details, Laszlo." She gave his hand a firm, friendly shake. "After all, what better place than a library for keeping things hushed?"

TANITH LEE became a freelance writer in 1975, and has been one ever since. Her first published books were children's fantasies *The Dragon Hoard* and *Animal Castle*. Her first adult fantasy novel, *The Birthgrave,* was the start of a long association with DAW, which published more than twenty of her works of fantasy, SF, and horror in the 1970s and 1980s. She received the British Fantasy Society's August Derleth Award in 1980 for *Death's Master,* World Fantasy Awards for Best Short Story in 1983 (for "The Gorgon") and 1984 (for "Elle est Trois (La Mort)"). Enormously prolific, Lee has recently published a trilogy of pirate novels for young adults (*Piratica* and sequels), a science fiction novel for adults (*Mortal Suns*), an adult fantasy trilogy (Lionwolf), a young adult fantasy trilogy (*Claidi* and sequels), and the first of two retrospective short story collections (*Tempting the Gods*). Upcoming are new books in the Flat Earth series. In 2009 she was made a Grand Master of Horror. Tanith Lee lives with her husband, the writer and artist John Kaiine, on the southeast coast of England

TWO LIONS, A WITCH, AND THE WAR-ROBE

Tanith Lee

To come on the apparently unguarded forest city of Cashloria was often a surprise, since it lay, as its name implied, deep in one of the vast ancient forests of Trosp. Enormous pines, cedars, beeches, oaks, poplars, and other trees towered up, for hundreds of miles. A single wide road, in places rather overgrown, eccentrically bisected the area. Once night began, the city was quite arresting. Then its thousands of lamp-lit windows, many with stained glass, blazed in slices between the trunks. Huge old stone mansions, public halls, and various fortresses appeared, but all smothered in among the forest, with trees growing everywhere about them, in some cases out of the stonework itself. In the narrow central valley to which the road eventually descended, where lay the city's hub, ran the thrashing River Ca, along which only the most courageous water-traffic ventured, and that in the calm of summer.

It was now fall. The forest had clothed itself in scarlet, copper, magenta, black, and gold. Audible from a day's ride away, the Ca roared angrily with pre-freeze melt-snow from distant mountains. Sunset dropped screaming red on the horizon and went out, and utter darkness closed its wings.

Zire the Scholar had been traveling a long while. He was weary and aggrieved. Yesterday, forest brigands had set on him and stolen his horse. Though naturally he had tracked and tricked them and stolen it back, the horse next cast a shoe, so now both of them must plod.

As night gathered and he spotted the lights of Cashloria, Zire gave a grunt of relief. He had read of the city over a year before, and set out to see it along with others, but during the last hour doubted he would find it at all. Benign unhuman guardians were supposed to take care of the conurbation, for example by protecting it with sorcery rather than city walls. This evening Zire had begun to think they had also rendered the place invisible. But lights shone. Here he was.

Zire was young and tall, and well-made. His hair was, where light revealed it, the rich somber red of the dying beech leaves. His eyes were the cold gray of approaching winter skies. His spirit was not dissimilar: fires vied with melancholy, exuberance with introversion.

Presently, the young man reached a promontory, thick with trees and pillared buildings. Below, the landscape tumbled down, still clad in darkling foliage, roofs, and windows of ruby and jade, to a coil of the angry river. A few lights also marked the river's course, but mainly it was made obvious by its uproar. They said, in Cashloria—or so Zire had read—"The Ca is foul-mouthed and always shouting."

Nevertheless, here was an inn, by name the Plucked Dragon.

Lanterns burned, and Zire, having tethered his horse, and maneuvered through a hedge of willows, thrust in at the door.

At once a loud outcry resounded, after which total silence

enveloped the smoky yellow-lit room beyond. It was not that the several customers had reacted in astonishment on seeing a newcomer; they were reasonably used to visitors in Cashloria. It was simply that, during the exact moment Zire stepped into the inn, a man standing at the long counter had swung about and plunged his knife between the ribs of another. Everyone, Zire included, watched in inevitable awe as the knife's unlucky recipient dropped dead on the ground.

The murderer, however, only wiped his blade on a sleeve, sheathed the weapon, and turned to regard the landlord. "Fetch me another jug, you pig. Then clear that up," jerking his thumb over-shoulder to indicate the corpse.

He was, the murderer, a burly fellow, with dark locks hanging over a flat low brow. He wore a guardsman's uniform of leather and studs, with a gaudy insignia of two crossed swords surmounted by a diadem. Certainly no one argued with him. Here rushed an inn-boy with a brimming jug, and there went the landlord himself with another inn-boy, hauling the dead body off along the floor and out the back. Even the third man, on whose sleeve the murderer had wiped his knife—not, presumably, wishing to soil his own—made no complaint.

"Cheers and a hale life!" cried the killer, and downed a large cupful in one gulp.

All present, with the exception of Zire, echoed the toast in fast fellowship. And some of them added, for good measure, "And hale life to you, *too*, Razibond!" "Yes, long life. That dolt had it coming to him."

Razibond, satisfied, belched. Then his small eyes slid straight to Zire, still poised in the doorway. Those little eyes might just as well have been two more greasy blades. If looks could kill, they might.

"And *you*," said Razibond. "What do *you* say, Copper-Nod?"

"I?" Zire smiled and shrugged. "About what?"

"Oh, you're blind then, as well as carrot-mopped. Come, let's have your opinion. You saw I slew him."

"That? True, I did see."

"You seem offended," said Razibond, ugly voice now sinking to an uglier growl. "Want to make something of it, eh?"

If Zire had been in any doubt as to what Razibond meant, further evidence was instantly supplied, as all the other drinkers withdrew in haste, plastering themselves to the walls, some even crawling beneath the long tables. Even the fire crouched down abruptly on the wide hearth, while the girl who had been tending a roast there sprinted up the inn stair with a flash of bare white feet.

"Well?" bellowed ugly Razibond, seemingly further incensed by Zire's speechlessness.

"Really," said Zire, "what you do is your own affair. After all, perhaps the man you stabbed had done you some terrible wrong."

"He had," Razibond declared. "He refused me use of his wife and daughter."

"Or, on the other hand," continued Zire smoothly, "you are, as I suspected, merely a drunken thug who throws his weight about, that being considerable since he is now running to podge, and slaughters at random. One day you will answer in the afterlife, to an uproar of furious ghosts. Don't think I joke there, friend Razi. Another life exists than this one, and we pay our dues once we are in it. I imagine your reckoning will be both long and tedious, not to mention painful."

Razibond's face was now a marvelous study for any student of the human mood. It had passed through the blank pink of shock to the crimson of wrath, sunk a second in superstitious, uneasy yellow, before escalating into an extraordinary puce—a hue that would have assured any dye-maker a fortune, had he been able to reproduce it. More than this, Razibond had swollen up like a toad. He cast his wine cup to the ground, where it shattered, being unwisely made of clay, and, disdaining his knife, heaved out a cleaverish blade some four feet long.

Zire raised his eyes to heaven, or the ceiling. Next instant, he, too, had drawn a sword, this one fine almost as a wand, and going by the name of Scribe. As Razibond lumbered at him, Zire moved, easy as smoke, from his path, extending as he did so a booted foot. This brief gesture sent the homicidal guardsman crashing, at which Zire leapt onto his back, landing with deliberate heaviness and knocking the breath right out of him. Then, with a casualness truly awful to behold, Zire drove his own bright sword straight in, through Razibond's leathers, skin, flesh, muscle, and heart. Blood spurted like a fountain, and decorated the blackened beam above.

At the inn once more, only silence held sway. Zire did not wipe the sword, he kept it ready in one hand. He looked contritely about at the stricken faces.

"My apologies," said Zire. "But I object to dying at this late hour. I would prefer supper. Oh, and my horse needs shoeing. Otherwise, if you want, we can continue the violence."

No one answered. None moved. The landlord himself, who had ducked below his counter then reemerged to witness the short fight's climax, stared with mouth agape.

Then there came the sound of bare feet, and down the stair hurried the inn-girl. She alone seemed able to move, and now, too, proved capable of speech, although it came out in a sort of a quavering shriek.

"Rash sir, you know not what you've done!"

"But I do know," said Zire. "Let me see, killed a killer. Maybe all you here loved him, and now wish to attack me. If so, let's get on. As I said, I'm hungry."

"*Love* him?" wailed the girl. "*Razibond?* He was a fiend."

At this, the strange inertia that had held the room broke in pieces. Voices from all sides honked and whispered: "He was a monster—" "A bully—no woman left alone, no man of honor safe—" "May he rot in the swampmost belly of the worst-devisable hell—"

"But," yelled the girl on the stair, "he was one of the False Prince's guardsmen. None must harm *them* no matter what their crimes. Or the False Prince will seek obscene vengeances. He is in league with dark magic, too, and will already know you have trespassed against his soldiers."

"This inn," intoned the landlord, gripping the counter white-knuckled, "may be burned to the earth, and all of us whipped. As for you, sir, he will hang you by your feet above a pit of snakes, whose poison dispatches in the slowest, most heinous stages—"

"Or else—" vocalized another, "he will sentence you to the death of two hundred hornets, each the size of a rat—"

"Or the live burial amid fractious scorpions—"

"Or—"

"Yes, very well," interrupted Zire, apparently tired. "I have inferred the correct sting-laden picture of my proposed fate."

"Run—" shrilled the pale girl from the stair. "It's your only chance! We dare not shield you."

Zire grimaced. He sat down on a bench. "First serve me some dinner," he said. "Also my poor starved horse must eat. Both he and I refuse to run on an empty stomach."

Silence once more submerged the room. The noise of the river, always angrier after moonrise, filled it instead.

Some half-mile below, at a second inn, whose name was the Quiet Night, and which directly adjoined the thunderous River Ca, Bretilf the Artisan sat over the remainder of his dinner, thoughtfully slicing the last roast meat from a bone. Beside him rested a jug of Cashloria's black ale. His tankard stayed full. He was concentrating equally on the bone and on a shape he could detect in the bone's surface. Once all the meat was gone, he intended to carve the figure free, but an interruption came.

Two drunken bravos, belonging—judging by their cross-swords-and-diadem insignia and studded-leather garments—to some guard militia of the city, had begun to quarrel.

Bretilf watched them sidelong through narrowed, tawny-amber eyes. His hair was of a similar shade, a type of ginger-amber, marking him out through the gilding of a stray lamp. He was otherwise young, tall, and well-made, and, had he but known it, bore a definite resemblance to another man, who only some minutes earlier, and half a mile above on the promontory, had stuck a sword straight through the heart of space-wasty Razibond.

"Damn it all, Kange," ranted the bigger of the quarrelers, "I say we *shall*."

"I don't deny we have a perfect *right*. But the house walls are high and she is protected by loyal servants and hounds, the latter of which will snap off a man's leg soon as make water on it." This was the retort of the smaller though no less repulsive Kange.

Bretilf could hear all clearly, even through the general din. He suspected others in the room heard the dialogue, too, but pretended deafness.

"Pahf!" went on the first guard. "No need for that. We'll knock at the gate and remind the girl the False Prince has given us permission to delve any wench we fancy. Besides, when she sees our beauty, how can she not succumb? Failing that we'll poison both servants and dogs, and burn the house to show we called."

"True, you're wise, Ovrisd," relented Kange. "But before we set forth on our mission, let's see what money we can squeeze out of that foreigner over there, with the pumpkin-colored mane."

Bretilf put down the meat bone.

The guardsmen were advancing, smiling winningly upon him, carefully ignored on every side by the rest of the inn.

"Greetings, stranger," said the unpresentable Kange.

"Welcome, stranger," added the revolting Ovrisd.

"To you also," replied Bretilf, rising. "I believe you wish me to render you something," he presumed.

"Oh, indeed! How perceptive. We would like all of it!"

"And pretty fast."

"Perhaps not all, but certainly a great deal. All that you deserve," said Bretilf. He finished mildly, "Nevertheless, once is enough. To seek me later for more will not be to your liking." And, leaning forward, he grasped both their unlovely necks and, in one sleek, quick movement, smashed their heads together. Like two halves of a severed pear, each guardsman fell, thumpingly senseless, to the floor.

Instantly, every person in the inn, including the landlord, his slim wife, and large cat, fled the premises.

Bretilf placed coins in generous amount on the counter, and toting the jug and the sculptable bone, walked off into the riverine night.

A golden moon howled radiance like wild music in the sky. The insane river answered. Bretilf sat awhile on the bank and started the carving of the bone. But his own bones guessed the night's difficulties were not done.

Sure enough, about an hour later, two sore-headed and bleary-eyed guardsmen came staggering to the bank with drawn blades and antisocial motives.

"I said," gently reminded Bretilf, as once again he rose to his feet, "it was not advisable that you ask for more."

Seething and blathering, Kange and Ovrisd leapt ungainly at him. Bretilf flipped back his cloak. The moon splashed like hot lava on a sudden broadsword, that had the name Second Thoughts. *Swish, swish* went the two severed heads of Kange and Ovrisd, plunging off the land's edge into the hungry river. Their now leaderless bodies slumped, this time conclusively, to the earth.

Bretilf strode away into the slinks of Cashloria. It was his creed never to kill, if at all possible, at an initial encounter. But so many people were determined to try his patience. Reticence and extremity coexisted always with him. Presently, he found a much less clean, and more secluded, inn where he might spend the night in peace asleep, or carving the figure of a militant stag.

Bretilf awoke to find, with some bemusement, he was staring at himself in a mirror. Zire awoke to find exactly the same thing.

Neither man recalled a mirror placed before him, in either of the inns they had last night occupied. In fact, Zire had fallen asleep at the table in the Plucked Dragon, after his first cup of wine. Bretilf had done much the same in his own inn, the Affectionate Flea. Besides, the mirrors were unreliable. Bretilf immediately noted that his own reflection rubbed its eyes, which Bretilf had not done and was not doing. Zire noted that, though he had rubbed his eyes, his reflection refused to copy him. In any case, said reflection's eyes, in both instances, were the wrong color.

"Oh," said Zire then, boredly, "are you some sorcerous fetch summoned up to haunt me?"

"No," returned Bretilf. "I think rather your—or possibly my own—father played his flute away from home. And I, and you therefore, are half-brothers."

"Hmn," said Zire. "You may be correct. We're certainly nearly doubles."

Then each got up, conscious as they did so of three further things. First, that in height and build they were also neatly matched. Second, that the faint bee-ish buzzing in their skulls, and taste of dry wool in their mouths, was very likely the result of their having been drugged. The third revelation was that, rather than remaining at an inn, whether wholesome or squalid, they were now in a cramped stone room with iron bars across the window.

Glancing at each other, they observed as one: "Dead guards. Royal disapproval. The False Prince."

A moment later, the door was opened, and several more guards, these ones with whom Zire and Bretilf were unacquainted, bundled into the space. They seized, then dragged Bretilf and Zire, the foray ornamented by a selection of punches and kicks, up many stairs and into another cell, plain but less prisonlike.

"Lie there, you scum," the guards instructed. "And prepare for horrors. The prince will arrive soon to judge you." They departed, slamming the door.

"Do you have a knife or sword?" inquired Bretilf.

"Yes, my knife. And Scribe is still with me."

"My Second Thoughts, also," said Bretilf. "And with my knife, the carving even that I was fashioning with it."

"Not disarmed then."

"Nor bound."

"It would seem," said Zire, "this prince has enough magical power to deal with us, whatever we try. A great shame," he added. "I had hoped to visit Traze next, over the river. And then the Red Desert."

"And I to finish my carving."

A spinning began in one of the cell walls. The two men watched attentively as it grew black, then electric, and roiled away, leaving an opening into a vast white marble chamber, its ceiling high as a full-grown oak. This was easily gauged, too, since live oak trees formed a colonnade along it. But they had trunks and boughs like twisted ebony, and blue leaves that quivered on their own, filling the air with a serpentine rustling.

At the room's far end rose a tall black chair upholstered in violet velvet. On either side of this squatted a fearsome beast, something like a wolf crossed with a raccoon. In the chair sat a stooped, thin man. He was a young man, but with an old man's face, and weaves of gray and white ran through his own light-colored hair. His eyes were like shards chipped from something blue and long-dead. But he wore fine clothes, and on his head a silver circlet. He pointed with a long, thin finger.

"You are here for punishment. You have slain my men, my chosen guards. For this, only the worst deaths are given. What do you say?"

"Oh, dear," said Zire.

Bretilf added, "Since Your Highness has already decided, what point for us to say anything?"

"I will have you speak."

Zire said, "It would be redundant to attempt to placate, please, or obey you. We're dead. We can be as rude as we like."

"Yet," said Bretilf, however, "why are you called the *False* Prince? Or is that only because all Cashlorians hate you? Just as they hate your guards, who seem, all told, a pack of cowards, rapists, thieves, and cutthroats."

The elderly young man cursed. He reached up and pulled at the silver circlet, next sending it bowling along the floor, until it fell over into a rug. The two monsters by the chair snarled.

"Hush," said the prince to them. "I am called False because, although I rule here, by right of direct descent, I have never in-herited the one artifact that would ensure my rule, and my power. It was stolen, during the last years of my father, the Old Prince's, reign—due to some foolishness of his. At once the Benign Guardians, said to protect the city, left us. Efforts to recover the sacred item failed. They fail always—for several have gone to reclaim it for me. All here know where it is interred. But that counts for naught. None can master the resident magics that hold it in. And all who try perish on the quest. Perish *horribly,* I have been led to believe, and have indeed witnessed.

"For example," said the prince, settling himself in a doleful mimicry of some storyteller, "there was the famous hero Drod Laphel. It was well known that he alone had, twice or thrice, bested five or six men together in a sword fight—"

"Only five or six?" grunted Bretilf sotto voce.

"My revered granny," hissed Zire, "could beat off eight at least at a go. Albeit with a special cloak-pin she possessed and not—"

"You would do well to attend," coldly broke in the prince. "It is an option I have, to torture you a little, before sentence. This can be waived or not, as you like."

Zire and Bretilf composed themselves meekly.

"Drod Laphel," went on the prince, "was also handy with spear and throwing ax, and had besides learnt certain charms that enabled him to bewitch serpents. When pausing in this city, he soon fell afoul of my guardsmen. Ten set on him, and accordingly he slew them single-handedly, if admittedly in two batches of five. Following the episode, I had him dispatched to thieve back the vital article I miss. I even had, numbskull that I was, some faith that *he,* of all men, might succeed where no other ever had. But no. Drod Laphel, the snake-charmer, athlete, and magician of swords, returned empty-handed. Quite literally, since he lacked both of them. And he was deader than a coffin nail, besides being the awful shade of rotted plums."

Zire cleared his throat. Bretilf regarded his boots, as if counting the cracks in their leather.

"Are we then to conclude," said Zire, "our punishment for

culling your degenerate guards is, personally, to be forced to undertake the self-same quest?"

"You are brave men," said the False Prince with dreary jealousy.
"Bold and reckless as lions. Yes, you will be made to go. That
much sorcery I can command. Understand this, too. If I were able
to reclaim the needed object, and my rightful power given to me, I
would not require a single human guard. I would throw the degen-
erates out, nor would they dare return here. Additionally, though
it hardly merits saying, as you will never succeed at this challenge,
whoever *is* successful will find his reward proportionate. Rather
than death, riches beyond comprehension would be rendered you."
Sourly, he recapped: "But best not to dwell on futile daydreams.
Nor have I any pity for you. Why should I pity others when my
own lot is so cruel? The supernatural agencies that should guard
Cashloria are gone, or in hiding. The heart of the city itself refuses
to acknowledge me, and conversely does me ill-turns. Only those
guards, and these two creatures here, stand between me and the
vengeance of a rioting populace. Were all my weakness known, I
should not last a minute. But my days are scarce enough. Cashloria's thwarted energies are already killing me. Can you see? How
old would you say I am?"

Neither Bretilf nor Zire replied.

"Fifteen," said the False Prince, lowering his blue, dead eyes.
"I am fifteen. And if I leave Cashloria, its stony atoms will tear
me in pieces. While if I remain, they will drain me of all life
in another year. Yes, you shall go and try to snatch back for
me the sacred artifact, the Garment of Winning, as it is called.
Why should I spare you? Who, in the name of any god, has ever
spared *me*?"

"So, tell me of your father," said Zire, as they rode over the long
stone bridge above the Ca.

"A minor lordlet, killed by assassins before my birth. My mother and grandsire raised me in the irksome shadow of his death. At eleven I broke free."

"Then I believe your father died too young to have coined *me*."

"Who was your own?"

"A chalk merchant. I grew up white as a sheep, till at seventeen some foe threw me down a well. Crawling out, no one recognized the red-headed youth who then stole the local grandee's horse, and pelted for freedom. I doubt my father, either, sired you. He was less white than uncouth and uncomely. No elegant lady, wed to—or widowed of—a lordlet would have let him touch her maid, let alone herself."

After this they rode awhile unspeaking. The river gushed green below, and on the farther bank the daytime forest was massed like a russet storm cloud.

They had no choice but to undertake the lethal task, so much had been made clear to them, not least by the False Prince's wizards, whose spokesman was a man in unfriendly middle age. "You are already under Cashloria's *geas*," he had told them. "It will avail you nothing to essay escape. You must travel to the place of dread, there enter in, and do whatever you're able to retrieve the Garment of Princedom—which is otherwise known as *The Robe Which Wins All Wars*."

At this news, Zire had yawned convulsively and Bretilf's hungry stomach grumbled. They had been from the start well aware some coercive spell was on them. They were its captives until either they had gained the trophy—or died, "horribly," in the attempt.

During the breakfast that was eventually served them, and that might have been enjoyable, including platters of fresh-baked shrimp, clam, and prawn, good ham, and eggs curdled with white wine, the indefatigable wizard informed them of all the conditions of their unwanted and unavoidable quest.

The original thief of the Winning Robe was allegedly a mischievously malignant elemental of the forest. It had next created a bizarre castle in which to hide the Robe, ringing it prudently with a labyrinth, unknown yet frightful safeguards, and energizing all with a sorcery so strident none had ever survived it. More than fifty men, all intelligent, cunning, and courageous, and well-versed in the use of stealth and weaponry, had been sent to the castle. And all had returned—but in disturbingly dead states: headless, footless, heartless; lurid with alien venom, rigid with stings of weird sort, skinned, scalped, or dissected. This multitude of squeam-making ends were duly attributed to the prince himself, in order the citizens might fear him and be kept down. "Hence the tales of scorpions and snakes," Zire had muttered.

"It seems a perfect genius is needed," said Bretilf, "if mere cleverness, cunning, and all other skills are no use."

"Well, whatever we have to our credit, there being two of us, it's doubled," hazarded Zire.

They were awarded two horses, a bay gelding for Bretilf, Zire's horse being his own gray, nicely reshod. Both animals were well fed, saddled, and burnished.

Now on the bridge over the Ca, the farther bank having become the nearer one, Zire abruptly drew rein. Bretilf copied him. "What?"

"Let us," said Zire, "see if we're able, after all, to turn back and make off."

Bretilf looked once over his shoulder. "Each of us is aware he can't. The *geas* prevents it. Or else we would still be escorted. We can only go forward to the goal of the castle. We were told we did not even need a map, the compulsion on us being so strong we can only follow the compulsory direction.

"Perhaps, however," suggested Zire, "the *horses* can carry us in the opposite one, despite whatever spell binds *us*."

They turned the horses' heads. Grimly, Zire and Bretilf faced back down the bridge to the city, gripped the reins, and kicked both mounts lightly in the side.

The horses instantly reared as if confronted by flailing flames or slavering demons. Jumping about in a shriek of metal hooves on stone paving, they reversed themselves with such enthusiasm their riders were nearly unseated. Both mounts then tore the last quarter of a mile along the bridge in the unwanted direction, and plunged off into the forest beyond.

Only with great awkwardness and noise were they persuaded to calm down and stop. They were deep into the trees—bridge, river, and city out of sight. Bretilf and Zire scowled about at the red-leafed gloom, to which they were so well matched.

"So much for that, then."

The morning waxed through the coppery forest canopy toward noon. Glumly, Zire and Bretilf rode along the track the *geas* had selected. Birds sang, and once a deer broke across the path. A pair of squirrels mocked them from a tall black pine.

Not long after, something appeared ahead at the roadside. At first, both men took it for a marker of some sort. It stayed completely still. But, presently, Zire exclaimed, "Look there. It's a young woman. Why, it's the inn-girl from the Plucked Dragon, who was so full of warnings."

Bretilf added, "I seem to know her, too. Either she served me at the first inn, or the second."

The girl, drably clad, and with a tattered white shawl over hair greasy from constant nearness to roast meat, just then raised her hand—not in greeting, but to beckon.

"Perhaps she was thrown out of work because of us," said Zire.

"I can spare her a coin," said Bretilf.

The riders reached the girl and halted. She gazed into their faces with dull eyes. She spoke:

"Alas! The False Prince has ensorcelled and sent you to your dooms. Oh, you'll be done for like all the others. The Robe That Wins is untakable. Poor souls, poor lost souls!"

"Exactly," said Zire.

Bretilf remarked, "But it's kind of you to wish us luck so encouragingly."

The girl took no notice either of pragmatics or sarcasm. Solemnly, she cried, in a high, self-important voice, "My name is Loë, and I am of no account. But seek the house of Ysmarel Star that lies along this very track. There only may you find assistance."

"What is Ysmarel Star?"

"Seek the house and learn!" melodramatically declaimed the rather aggravating Loë. "You can hardly miss the mansion. White roses crowd the walls and white owls flit around it, while a huge diamond star hangs low above."

"Not modestly self-effacing then, as are you," said Zire.

"I am nothing. I am only *Loë*."

And the girl ran suddenly off the track and in among the copper-gold patchwork of the trees. Bretilf and Zire stared after her thoughtfully.

"It seemed to me . . ." Bretilf murmured after a second or so.

" . . . also to me . . ." agreed Zire.

" . . . that where the shadow of that cedar falls . . ."

" . . . girl ceased to be girl . . ."

"and became instead . . . ?"

" . . . a weasel," concluded Zire. "Perhaps," he added, "we hallucinate from hunger. Let's enjoy a brief rest, and dine on the provisions in the saddlebags."

• • •

During the afternoon, the autumnal forest changed from metals to wines, and so to lilacs. That evening the track, now very overgrown, and interrupted by the strong claws of neighboring trees, meandered out into a series of clearings. Here dusk filtered, littered by tiny bats.

A sweep of land was rising upward on their left, the trees thinly scattered about on it. Then a hill was to be seen, clear on the mauve-glowing sky. One star had risen there of unusual size and brilliance, and beneath lay a dark, rambling house, here and there pierced by the needles of lamps.

"Ysmarel's mansion?"

"So it seems," affirmed Zire.

"Do we visit?"

"Why not? The track winds close, and the *geas* allows intervals."

"And anyway, to the doomed," Bretilf appended, "all delays are *good*."

The gray and bay climbed the hill.

High stone barricades appeared, smothered with moon-pale flowers, whose scent seemed enhanced by darkness. Above, six or seven gigantic bats flew about. But the low-strung star illuminated their wings, which were white. They were owls.

Purple glass and glass like saffron was in the lighted windows. A bell hung over the gate.

The two men observed the bell, but before they could decide to ring it, it pealingly rang of itself. At this, the owls descended together, and perched along the tops of the walls, looking at Zire and Bretilf through the stained glass of their eyes.

Some moments later, the gate swung wide, and inside was framed a dark garden, full of white roses that caught the starshine and ghostly shone. About twenty paces on, a broad door stood open and, even as they watched, soft lamps bloomed there. It was all most enticing. So much so that neither man advanced. They sat their horses, and the owls sat on the walls, and not a sound was to be heard, as if time had grown cautious, too, and stood still.

After a while, Bretilf stirred. "Do we go in? Or retreat?"

"All's lost, it seems, whatever we do." They dismounted, tethered the horses among the roses, and walked straight in at the soft-lighted door.

They were at once in a charmingly informal hall, lit by depending lamps of fretted bronze and lavender glass. Luxurious rugs clothed a floor of delicate rainbow tiling.

A long table had been loaded with tall gilded flagons individually filled with black ale, red wine, blue spirit, or honeyed beer. A selection of pies, smoking roasts, cheeses, dewy salads, fruits, and sweets of many kinds waited on plates of gold or in dishes of silver decorated with pearls and zircons.

"Do you trust this feast?" asked Zire.

"Less than I'd trust a starving thief who jumped in the window."

"My own thought. Shall we dine?"

"Let's do so."

But even as they pulled out the gilded chairs to sit, a curtain across the length of the room blew back, and out stepped a vision that stopped them, once more, in their tracks.

A young woman, again, but this time of surpassing attractions. The undeniable beauty of her face was made yet more marvelous by two large eyes of velvet darkness. From her lovely head cascaded darkly shining hair in loose curls, that each took a chestnut highlight from the lamps. Her slim but voluptuous figure had been clad in a filmy gown of amethyst silk, caught at the waist by serpentine twists of white gold.

"How rewarding that you should call on me," said this apparition, in a musical voice that suggested the color of smoky peach mixed with platinum. "Pray sit."

Bretilf the Artisan and Zire the Scholar—sat.

Instantly, some bowls of scented water were brought to them, by a pair of white rabbits. Without comment, each man rinsed his hands, at which two black rabbits appeared to offer linen towels. All four rabbits had come from under the table draperies, to which area they next withdrew. But, unceremoniously yanking up the drapery, Zire and Bretilf peered beneath—to find no sign of rabbits, bowls, towels, nor any hatch that might afford entry and exit.

Reemerging from under the cloth, the two found instead their beautiful hostess had herself sat down at the table's central position. Her serenity was exquisite.

"Brave sirs, do choose whatever you wish to eat. Munch and Janthon there will serve you."

Anticipating further rabbits, Bretilf and Zire were startled when a handsome, long-haired white cat appeared, walking upright out of a bouquet of pale flowers at the table's southern end. In another breath, a larger, but also handsome, short-haired black dog manifested at the table's northern end. This being stood on the floor by Zire's chair. The dog, too, walked upright, which meant its head was level with Zire's own—it was a large canine indeed.

Zire pulled himself around with a little effort. "Good evening, Janthon," said Zire. "If you'll be so kind, I will have—"

"No trouble, sir," replied the dog with faultless articulation. "Your mind is read." And, taking the proper implements from the board, dexterously began to slice for Zire the very cooked fowl he had been intent on. That done, Janthon stalked to Bretilf's place and, unasked, extended agile front paws and carved up for him a paté and a pie. Munch the cat meanwhile filled Bretilf's crystal glass of spirit, and now came to Zire to pour his silver tankard of beer.

Unnoted during these operations, three white owls had entered through a high window. Perching upon golden stands, they now began to sing a quiet but melodious trio, to the accompaniment of three black, crow-like birds, which seemed to have arrived via the mansion's open door. One beat a drum with its claws, another performed on a small harp, which it struck tunefully with one wing. The third whistled through its beak.

Zire and Bretilf ate and drank some while without a word exchanged.

At last, Bretilf spoke levelly to Zire. "Have we gone mad?"

"I think so," answered Zire in an offhand way. "Probably some effect of the *geas,* or else too strong a drug used to subdue us in the city."

"Or, alternatively, perhaps it's a dream." Bretilf turned to their delicious female companion, who sat quietly sipping a goblet of sherbet laced with wine. "Would you say so, madam?"

"All life is a dream," she replied, smiling. "Or so it is said."

"You are then a philosopher, lady," said Zire.

"No. I am a witch. Whose name is Ysmarel Star."

Zire and Bretilf put down their silver knives and drinking vessels. Each man rose.

"A witch. What else? I fear," said Zire, "we must be on our way."

"Urgent business at a castle," elaborated Bretilf, "involving doom and horrible death."

Ysmarel Star nodded. "So many have passed by, en route to such a fate. Few ever listened to my messenger, Loë."

"Perhaps, unlike ourselves, they knew your true vocation—witchcraft—and were too . . . respectful to call. There is sorcery enough in the city and the forest, surely. It tends to make even

desperate men—among whom we must be counted—reluctant."
This, from Zire.

"We trust not to offend by such frankness," finished Bretilf.

But Ysmarel paid no attention. She went on as if neither of her
guests had spoken a word.

"Of the few who did heed Loë, none before, suspecting a trap,
dared enter my house. There were others who, having seen Loë,
failed to see my gate, or anything else. It takes, gentlemen, a particular type of acuteness and sparkle, to note such things. Even
that a rabbit, cat, or dog waits on them at table. That owls make
music. Let alone the presence of my humble self."

"Any man who missed seeing *you,* fair lady," said Zire, "would
need to be blind, and other things besides, perhaps more personally unhappy in his lower regions."

Bretilf said, "Any man who failed at seeing you, Ysmarel,
would need to be *dead.*"

"However," continued Zire, "we must get on."

"To be late for a doom is the worst bad manners," augmented
Bretilf.

Ysmarel still gave no heed.

"I have known for long months the imposed task which the
False Prince of Cashloria sets any transgressor: to steal back the
Robe of War-Winning. It is a hopeless venture. Men of great
courage and genius have gone to the doom you refer to. Even
thirteen women of unusual battle-skills and wisdom. But all perished, male and female alike. And each, it's true, ended horribly.

"For example," continued Ysmarel Star, modifying her stance
rather in the manner of certain feminine storytellers, "the glamor-
ous and gifted sword-mistress, Shaiy of the Red Desert, having
killed two guards who attempted unwanted affection, was sentenced to seek the Robe.

"Shaiy was well known for her varied warrior talents, not to mention her learning and quick wit. It's said she could compose an ode worthy of the greatest poets in twice ten minutes. Or a bawdy song inside three slow heartbeats. Riddles she could answer while asleep. She was a notoriously sage robber, said to have stolen the Great Emerald of Gullo. Though she then kindly gave it away to a destitute lover. But even Shaiy only returned from the evil castle dead, and *minced small,* everything of her in a tiny box, all but her dainty white ears—which were pinned on the lid in the exact form of a butterfly."

Zire studied his boots; Bretilf cleared his throat.

Ysmarel simply clapped her slender hands. At the signal, every light in the mansion died, every waft of perfume, tasty dinner, or music—fled. A dog barked once, a rabbit squeaked, and a cat spat. A rattle of wings and clatter of discarded perches and instruments revealed where crows and owls beat it at top speed through a window and a door. The room had become black as tar. Only the star gleamed on the garden outside.

Male voices uttered.

"Are you able, Bretilf, to move at all?"

"Not I. And you, Zire?"

"Neither."

"Rest, my friends," murmured the seductive tones of the witch. "I have concocted, for your intelligence and reckless natures, another destiny than you predict."

"A witch, what else? That food," said Bretilf next, now in a slurred and impersonal way.

"Or that witchy bloody beer," grumbled Zire. "To the lowest hell with it, we have yet again—"

"—been drugged and enspelled," explained Bretilf.

In the darkness, there now sounded a discordant slumping couple of thuds, as of two muscular young men dropping on a tiled floor, amid their boots, garments, a part-sculpted stag, swords, and other accessories.

There followed a woman's provocative laugh. And night extinguished the scene both inside and out, as the low diamond of the abnormal star capsized in clouds.

In sleep, there was no respite either. Each man dreamed a selection of episodes concerning those luckless heroes—and heroines—who had entered the infamous castle.

Bretilf beheld Drod Laphel, tall and powerful, with golden locks, striding through an enormous sable building, sword ready, while a huge serpent oozed toward him. It was scaled like an alligator, yet black-blue as midnight. It opened its scarlet jaws and made a noise as of steam rising from a hot spring. At that, Drod chanted some spell so hypnotic even the actually ensorcelled and drugged and anyway non-serpentine Bretilf grew helpless. Surprisingly, the serpent did not. It surged forward, a scaly wave from a midnight ocean, and the golden swordsman vanished in its coils.

Zire, too, dreamed, but his surreality concerned the beautiful Shaiy. She was a lightly sturdy young woman, with skin of cream and eyes like green embers. Now, standing inside a huge vaulted hall, she confronted a sort of puma, with the head of a falcon and falcon wings. The falcon-puma had challenged her, it seemed, to solve some conundrum, and to sing her reply. This Shaiy proceeded to do. But no sooner did her excellent mezzo-soprano fill the space than the echo of her voice itself became a living entity, which boomed and howled like thunder. Blocks of masonry started to fall. And both Shaiy and the cat-bird-sphinx were lost to view.

Thereafter there were endless such dreams. Maybe even fifty

or more of those condemned to seek the Robe appeared before
Bretilf and Zire. All foundered. In each case, definite clues were
given as to the vile methods of their ending.

Then at last Bretilf dreamed, and Zire, too, that they themselves—each solo—entered the same lapideous building. Their
names had altered, for some reason. Zire was called Izer, Bretilf—
Ibfrelt. Knowing this was less than useful to them.

Upon Zire, from the shadowy architecture rushed flapping
creatures, most like colossal books, and he, spinning and leaping, wielding Scribe to parry and slash and pierce, the knife to
stab and slice, still battled them in vain. They closed on him, and
slammed him shut inside their covers.

Bretilf found that he had tried to draw, or carve out on the
walls, talismans of beneficent gods. But they erupted like boiling
black milk, grew solid, ripped away his weapons from his grip.
After which a giant stag rose out of the floor and tore at him, and
stove in his ribs, with antlers and feet.

Slaughtered personally over and over in their dreams, Izer-Zire
and Ibfrelt-Bretilf longed for day and awakening, whether in a
hell or heaven, or—the favorite choice—the world.

Dawn though, as was its habit, took its own time.

A century later, perhaps, it seemed, the metal-leafed forest
flooded pink as a blush. The sun rose. The things of darkness . . .
fled?

The mansion of the witch was somber and deserted-looking in
the morning. No owls, or any birds, were evident. The white roses
had folded tight as buds, as if only after sunset could they open.

Even so, the door to the mansion remained wide. As did the
outer gate.

In a while, something might be seen to be moving through
the garden.

If the sun watched for Zire and Bretilf, the sun was due for a disappointment, since what presently padded through the gates on to the hillside, though two in number, were a pair of young lions. Once outside, both paused to sniff the gate-posts, the air. One growled, the other lashed its tail. Roughly of an age, and having the same lean girth and obvious male stamina, tawny and limber, white-fanged, and tail tufted and maned—one dark red, the other more a tangerine shade—they might have been brothers of a single pride.

A look of slight unease was swiftly concealed by them, in the way of animals. They turned and cuffed each other, and rolled about play-fighting—until suddenly rolling right across on to the track. Here they got up, shook themselves, touched noses, and glanced around, one with topaz eyes, the other with eyes of shined silver.

To anyone who knew no better than to credit all sorcery, they would be taken for Bretilf the Artisan and Zire the Scholar magicked into feline beasts.

Both lions, anyway, now raced off along the track, perhaps coincidentally in the very direction the *geas* prescribed.

A lion knows it is a lion, even if it has no occasion to tell itself so. Had it found occasion, it would, and using whatever words make up the lionesque language. All animals, naturally, employ language. Human ignorance of this results from the fact most humans have never understood most of the animal tongues. The reason being perhaps because, beyond the very obvious, animal language is formulated to convey states, ideas, and principles of conduct quite out of the range of human grasp. Certain schools of thought even maintain that what man sees in himself as "acting like an animal," rather than a sign of degeneracy, is a sadly inadequate effort on mankind's part to copy the philosophical intellectual animal technique in the mastery of life, love, and death.

Zire, then, knew himself a lion. And Bretilf likewise knew himself a lion. That they were brothers was undeniable, fundamental, and largely irrelevant. As for a strange jumble each vaguely noticed as being a name, and a *distorted* name, neither bothered with it.

Nevertheless, both lions were slightly conscious of bizarre concepts, which sometimes swirled about in their maned and noble heads. To these also they paid little attention. What they knew was this: the day was warm, the earth and trees smelled good, and everywhere blew the scents of interesting things both to experience and to eat. Something excited and pushed them on in a particular direction. It went without saying therefore this direction was desirable, and promised much. To resist the tug of it was not even considered.

For hours the lions bounded through the forest. By now verdure was thick, and the track less than a thread between the roots of trees and laceries of fern. Now and then they paused to investigate some interesting odor, sight, or noise, rested in shade under the sun-flamed canopy, drank from a streamlet dark as malachite. All was as it should be.

Noon filled the sky and so the forest. From safe tree-tents, squirrels, chipmunks, possums, and wood pigeons watched the lions, most respectfully.

To a man, the scene that now appeared between the trees was that of a huge clearing. For almost a mile all vegetation had been mown down or dredged up, and then a floor laid there, made of odd triangular flagstones, which seemed of polished basalt. In this surface the unhidden sky reflected, so it glimmered like a black lake. At its center rose a building. To a man, again, or a woman, it was instantly apparent this structure had been formed from the trunks and heavy summer crowns of many living trees. Yet they had also been deformed. Some leaned askew, some were warped in unnerving hoops, and some forced together at their tops to provide a roof with branches, boughs, and foliage. After that, sorcery had struck them. They had turned to stone—not the smooth basalt of the paving, but petrified coal of dense, ashen black.

As no men were in the clearing, but rather lions, that analysis did not occur. The lions saw a cave-like mass, cool in the day's heat, and having to it an olfactory tang of human flesh and blood. In other words, recent fresh corpses.

Pausing only to dip cautious paws into the lake which surrounded the caves, and so learn it was solid, they sprang forward, and vanished through the entrance.

Izer, the lion who had been Zire, darted through a succession of lowering, gaping, all-black vistas. Space led into space, some more narrow, others wider or more winding. Izer galloped blithely through them all. Their enormity, and cranky arboreal sculpting, did not faze him. He did not feel made small and vulnerable, as a man might. Instead, curious as a young cat, he climbed where able up the malformed sides of the stone trees, and stuck his long, big nose into holes and fissures. He raised his paw and scraped the petrified material with a single claw. At which blue sparks flew and he veered away.

From the guts of this inert yet nastily intestine-suggestive labyrinth, came the most insidious wavering drone of sound. It was the sound of utter *soundlessness,* disturbed only in the ear of the listener by the tempo of pulse and heart. Izer paid it little attention. *His* hearing was honed for more informative noises. Of these there seemed to be none.

Then with no warning, something rushed sharply through the air, about three lion-lengths above him. Izer raised his head.

It was a bird. But a bird Izer had never seen, nor been self-trained to expect. It had no beak, nor even a head. Its outflung, fluttering wings were dark above, with complex paler featherings below, but they supported nothing. The bird had no body either.

Izer did not identify the flying object as a book, which, to a human, it would appear to be. For him it was only logical to classify it as a bird. And as lions are generally a match for most birds, save those of supernatural size, such as a roc, he leapt straight at it, bore it to the earth and smashed it there. The book's spine broke. Izer tore at its feather pages, champed and spat them out. The bird was not good eating, good for nothing, aside from a bit of swift exercise. When the next one came flapping at him, Izer took this in sporting spirit, sprang at it and batted it about a while, before destroying it on the ground. Other books followed in streamers, though not very many. Izer danced about with them, enjoying himself. When the last was felled, he noted tiny scurrying things that were spilling from the carcasses. He put his paws on them, bit and squashed them. They were written words, yet Izer did not know this. They meant nothing at all to him beyond a playful moment or two. They tasted only of ink anyway. He also spat their shredded bodies forth, rolled on his back, shook his henna mane, and trotted off deeper into the petrified maze.

Elsewhere, Ibfrelt, the lion who had been Bretilf, was nosing around some knots in the floor that might, once, have been edible fungi. He, too, was uninterested in the persistent yodel of the silence. However, presently he heard a curious scraping noise, and looking around saw some sharp implements worming out of a wall. No sooner were they ejected than they began to crawl over the floor, scratching irritatingly as they did so. Ibfrelt went to examine them, batting at them rather as Izer had at the books. Their steel edges made no impression on his well-toughened lion pads. In the end, he became bored with the things and loped off. He did not actually realize that they then pursued him in a highly sinister manner. To Ibfrelt, there could be nothing sinister about them. Nor did he see when, by then some way behind him, they lost momentum, rusted, flaked, and fell apart.

Wandering on into another chamber of the building, Ibfrelt paused only when a sudden form reared up from the floor. A man would have known this figure at once for a fellow man—a sword fighter for a fellow swordsman, and a dangerous one. He was tall, and laden with muscle, clad in mail, and armed both with a broadsword of considerable size and a dagger of extraordinary length. At Ibfrelt, he glared with flashing, maniacal eyes, and from a sneering gob let out a challenge: "Match me then, you damnable nonentity!"

But Ibfrelt evidently only knew men—when he *had* known them—as menu-worthy pieces of prey. Shows of weapons, of aggression, protective armorings—they meant nothing at all, to a lion. Ibfrelt smelled live meat, and he gave a snarl of appetite, then launched himself, like a vast ginger firework, at the threatening hulk.

Over went the hulk, amid a resounding bash and clamor, sword flying one way, and dagger doing no more damage than to shave four of Ibfrelt's impressive whiskers, before a couple of jaws, equally impressively toothed, met in his esophageal tract.

Ibfrelt was already feeding greedily when, to his disgust, his kill dissolved like a mist and faded into thin air.

Some snaggle of labyrinthine turns away, Izer was just undergoing a similar disillusion. *His* adversary had been a rapier-brandishing swordsman, with a back-up ax. But Izer had simply jumped on him in the midst of the fellow's posturing, fangs seeing to the rest. When this nice hot meal vanished, Izer let out a complaint so loud even Ibfrelt paid attention, and rumbled back.

Rising from the teasing absent carcass, Izer padded through the maze and, with leonine instincts of scent, vision, hearing, and *sub*thought, located Ibfrelt inside two minutes.

The lions commiserated with each other. This was a poor place after all. It would be better to depart instantly.

It was then that a blazing light flared up in the next cave or chamber. They were lions; they took it for the undoing of an exit into the afternoon forest. Shoulder to shoulder, they flung themselves toward it—

They found themselves contrastingly inside a gargantuan inner region of the complex. The compartment would have evoked, to most human eyes, a colossal temple hall. To the lions, it was just an especially oversized cavern. Yet light from some invisible source filled it full.

In the very middle of the space stood a solitary *living* tree, or so it appeared. The tree was a sort of maple, but of absurd dimensions, and with autumnal leaves colored raspberry, orange, and ripe prune. From the boughs hung a dowdy banner—or a garment? It seemed stranded there, whatever it was, by mistake, shoddy and threadbare, stained, and itself the hue of over-cooked porridge.

Neither lion glanced at it. A spectacle of greater fascination pended. The living trunk was slowly splitting along a hinge of softer, more elusive light. When the gap was wide enough, a form burst from within. It cantered into the cavern, a sight to render any warrior numb with astonished horror.

Directly before the lions epically bulged a stag of unusual size. It was almost spotless white, its antlers like boughs, its eyes glittering like fires. It snorted, and from its nostrils black smolders gushed out.

Lions do not shake hands, or smite paws together to announce brotherhood. If they did, these two would have done.

Without preamble, both vaulted headfirst at the stag. They hit it square, one to each side of the breast. Fearful splinterings, jangles, cracks, and clangs engulfed the air. In a thousand shards, the stag, which seemed fashioned from one house-huge bone, collapsed. The giant maple shook at the detonation. Leaves rained like—*rain*. One other item was dislodged and drifted foolishly down, like dirty washing. Izer and Ibfrelt, Ibfrelt and Izer, ignored this. They were busy. The bone of which the monster stag had been constructed had once belonged to some improbably prodigious roast. They were engaged in extracting the marrow, any shreds of meat, savoring the cooked tastes, finding every splinter on the ground.

In this way, they missed the dim phantasmal wailing of something, which, seeing all its ploys, even those untried, would never work, lamented in the stony masonry. They missed the dislodgement of the building, too, and how its walls and halls, openings and enclosures, came apart and smeared into nothing. They even missed the last descent of the unappealing porridge-colored garment, until it fell over both their heads.

"So, what do you make of it?"

Trudging back through the forest, stark naked, and with the fall weather turning a touch more chilly, Bretilf put this question to the matchingly unclothed and chilled Zire.

Zire said, "It seems, now, perfectly obvious."

"To me also. Yet maybe we've drawn two different conclusions."

Bretilf carried the item from the cave-labyrinth, bundled up and tied tight with grasses.

From the trees, which overnight seemed themselves partly to have disrobed, leaving great swathes of cold and unclad sky and blowing wind, birds and squirrels threw nutshells at them. Foxes and wild pig distantly passed, snorting as if with scornful laughter. Snakes seemed embarrassed by the stupidity of men and slipped down holes.

Bretilf and Zire had not decided what they *made* of anything, despite their exchange. And some hours on, when they reached the mansion of the witch Ysmarel Star, and found only the hill— they made not much of that, either. The gray and the bay horses were tethered nearby, however, and adjacent were neatly folded clothes, swords, and so on. Bretilf examined the part-finished carving he had begun of a stag.

"Just as I thought," said Bretilf.

"Oh, indeed," concurred Zire.

There followed a short conversation then, on whether it was worse to eat men or words, not mentioning meat bones. The consensus on this was that probably none of those items had been strictly real, more elemental, if potentially fatal, and so no moral issue was involved.

They rode the rest of the way to the city of Cashloria. Zire had taken his turn at carrying the rolled-up wretched rag from the maple. Neither man had wished to try it on, not even when naked in the woods. Just the first swipe of it across their heads had changed them back into men. That was enough.

Even so, sitting once more above the crazy River Ca, they held their horses in check and stared at nothing.

"It seems to me," said Bretilf, "the witch Ysmarel—"

"Yes?"

"Ensorcelled us into animal shape less to cause us trouble in the manner of ancient legends—"

"—than in order we might survive the maze and regain the Robe. Any intelligent or gifted man or woman who intruded on that spot," Zire went on, "was seemingly destroyed by demons conjured from their own abilities."

"The singer found her song turned against her in so dreadful a way, it tore the ears from her lovely head."

"The charmer of snakes found a snake he could not charm, which poisoned him."

The horses cropped the grass. Both men digested the effect of the beautiful witch's spell. By making them beasts, she had released them from any true engagement with their everyday beliefs. Though ghosts of their human preoccupations were yet accessible to the sorcery in the labyrinth, when presented with nightmare elements of them, as lions, they had either had no interest, or made short work and dined.

The humanly superior had perished in that place. But they, as lions, had had another agenda, *another* superiority. Which was why, too, they had gained the Winning-of-War-Robe. It had meant nothing to them; they had only run out growling with it tangled in their manes—then hair.

Modestly, Zire and Bretilf reentered the city. Yet on the streets people swarmed to gape and cheer. At the False Prince's villa, they were admitted after a wait of only an hour.

The prince lay on a couch like one almost dead. He gazed up with weary dislike. "Who are these ruffians?"

"Highness," said the affronted servant, "can't you hear the joyful uproar outside? These—*ruffians*—have won back the Robe—the Robe of the Winning of War With Oneself."

"Garbage," said the prince and turned over on his face.

Another hour on, when he had been, rather roughly, convinced by his attendants, Zire and Bretilf had the dubious pleasure of beholding the transformation. With some revulsion, they saw how the War-Robe, when the prince had put it on, altered from a sartorial nonevent to a glowing sumptuousness of colors and gems. The prince was also changed. In a matter of seconds, he grew young and strong, handsome and profound, pristine, pure, and kingly. And then, with pleasing open-handedness, from the coffers of the city, stunning riches were obtained and loaded on to mules, all for Bretilf and Zire.

They were by then incorrigibly drunk. They had sampled

much of the royal cellars, and also rambled about the city, where everyone was eager to stand them a drink. Sometimes they drew into corners and spoke in low tones of the anomaly of such a man as the prince, so sticky with cruelty and crime, now entirely changed into a genuine paragon, worthy only of loyalty and praise. But they heard, too, a rumor of a kitchen girl, named Loë, who had that very day ridden off in a carriage that sparkled like a diamond, and with her many animals, owls, and crows from neglected temples, rabbits kept for the pot, cats and dogs who had earned their keep in various inns. Loë, or Weasel as she was sometimes called, or Ermine, was now said to be one of the Benign Guardians of Cashloria, who had lingered on the premises in disguise during the city's troubles. The Robe's return had freed her, it seemed, to go back to her own mysterious life on a distant star.

"I could sleep a million years," said Zire. "Alas, it's farewell now between us."

"Perhaps neither, yet," said Bretilf. "I've heard another rumor—that those villainous guards the prince is about to expel have vengefully scored our names on their swords. Will we fare better alone or in tandem?"

"Where are the horses and mules?" asked Zire, with respectable common sense.

"Below," said Bretilf, ditto.

As they jumped from the window to the backs of bay and gray, they picked up the nearby threatening roar composed of rejoicing, rage, and river. But soon the happy pounce of hooves, blissful jingle of coins and jewels, rumble of determined mules and carts, muffled all else. Heed this, then. The more noisily and threateningly the torrent bellows below and around, the louder make your song.

CAITLÍN R. KIERNAN was born in Skerries, Dublin, Ireland, but grew up in Leeds, Alabama. As a teenager, she worked as a volunteer in Birmingham, Alabama's, Red Mountain Museum, and later studied geology and vertebrate paleontology at the University of Alabama at Birmingham and the University of Colorado at Boulder. She has coauthored several scientific publications, beginning in 1988, the latest published in the *Journal of Vertebrate Paleontology* in 2002. Her first novel, *Silk,* was published in 1998, and she has written eight novels to date, the most recent being *The Red Tree*. A multiple International Horror Guild Award–winning author, she has also been nominated for the World Fantasy Award, the British Fantasy Award, the Bram Stoker Award, and the Gay & Lesbian Alliance Against Defamation Award. Kiernan has also written for DC Comics. She lives with her partner in Providence, Rhode Island.

THE SEA TROLL'S DAUGHTER

Caitlín R. Kiernan

It had been three days since the stranger returned to Invergó, there on the muddy shores of the milky blue-green bay where the glacier met the sea. Bruised and bleeding, she'd walked out of the freezing water. Much of her armor and clothing were torn or missing, but she still had her spear and her dagger, and claimed to have slain the demon troll that had for so long plagued the people of the tiny village.

Yet, she returned to them with no proof of this mighty deed, except her word and her wounds. Many were quick to point out that the former could be lies, and that she could have come by the latter in any number of ways that did not actually involve killing the troll—or anything else, for that matter. She might have been foolhardy and wandered up onto the wide splay of the glacier, then taken a bad tumble on the ice. It might have happened just that way. Or she might have only slain a bear, or a wild boar or auroch, or a walrus, having mistaken one of these beasts for the demon. Some even suggested it may have been an honest mistake, for bears and walrus, and even boars and aurochs, can be quite fearsome when angered, and if encountered unexpectedly in the night, may have easily been confused with the troll.

Others among the villagers were much less gracious, such as the blacksmith and his one-eyed wife, who went so far as to suggest the stranger's injuries may have been self-inflicted. She had bludgeoned and battered herself, they argued, so that she might claim the reward, then flee the village before the creature showed itself again, exposing her deceit. This stranger from the south, they said, thought them all feebleminded. She intended to take their gold and leave them that much poorer and still troubled by the troll.

The elders of Invergó spoke with the stranger, and they relayed these concerns, even as her wounds were being cleaned and dressed. They'd arrived at a solution by which the matter might be settled. And it seemed fair enough, at least to them.

"Merely deliver unto us the body," they told the stranger. "Show us this irrefutable testament to your handiwork, and we will happily see that you are compensated with all that has been promised to whomsoever slays the troll. All the monies and horses and mammoth hides, for ours was not an idle offer. We would not have the world thinking we are liars, but neither would we have it thinking we can be beguiled by make-believe heroics."

But, she replied, the corpse had been snatched away from her by a treacherous current. She'd searched the murky depths, all to no avail, and had been forced to return to the village empty-handed, with nothing but the scars of a lengthy and terrible battle to attest to her victory over the monster.

The elders remained unconvinced, repeated their demand, and left the stranger to puzzle over her dilemma.

So, penniless and deemed either a fool or a charlatan, she sat in the moldering, broken-down hovel that passed for Invergó's one tavern, bandaged and staring forlornly into a smoky peat fire.

She stayed drunk on whatever mead or barley wine the curious villagers might offer to loosen her tongue, so that she'd repeat the tale of how she'd purportedly bested the demon. They came and listened and bought her drinks, almost as though they believed her story, though it was plain none among them did.

"The fiend wasn't hard to find," the stranger muttered, thoroughly dispirited, looking from the fire to her half-empty cup to the doubtful faces of her audience. "There's a sort of reef, far down at the very bottom of the bay. The troll made his home there, in a hall fashioned from the bones of great whales and other such leviathans. How did I learn this?" she asked, and when no one ventured a guess, she continued, more dispirited than before.

"Well, after dark, I lay in wait along the shore, and there I spied your monster making off with a ewe and a lamb, one tucked under each arm, and so I trailed him into the water. He was bold, and took no notice of me, and so I swam down, down, down through the tangling blades of kelp and the ruins of sunken trees and the masts of ships that have foundered—"

"Now, exactly how did you hold your breath so long?" one of the men asked, raising a skeptical eyebrow.

"And, also, how did you not succumb to the chill?" asked a woman with a fat goose in her lap. "The water is so dreadfully cold, and especially—"

"Might it be that someone here knows this tale *better* than I?" the stranger growled, and when no one admitted they did, she continued. "Now, as *I* was saying, the troll kept close to the bottom of the bay, in a hall made all of bones, and it was here that he retired with the ewe and the lamb he'd slaughtered and dragged into the water. I drew my weapon," and here she quickly slipped her dagger from its sheath for effect. The iron blade glinted dully in the firelight. Startled, the goose began honking and flapping her wings.

"I *still* don't see how you possibly held your breath so long as that," the man said, raising his voice to be heard above the noise of the frightened goose. "Not to mention the darkness. How did you see anything at all down there, it being night and the bay being so silty?"

The stranger shook her head and sighed in disgust, her face half hidden by the tangled black tresses that covered her head and hung down almost to the tavern's dirt floor. She returned the dagger to its sheath and informed the lot of them they'd hear not another word from her if they persisted with all these questions and interruptions. She also raised up her cup, and the woman with the goose nodded to the barmaid, indicating a refill was in order.

"I *found* the troll there inside its lair," the stranger continued, "feasting on the entrails and viscera of the slaughtered sheep. Inside, the walls of its lair *glowed,* and they glowed rather *brightly,* I might add, casting a ghostly phantom light all across the bottom of the bay."

"Awfully bloody convenient, that." The woman with the goose frowned, as the barmaid refilled the stranger's cup.

"*Sometimes,* the Fates, they do us a favorable turn," the stranger said, and took an especially long swallow of barley wine. She belched, then went on. "I watched the troll, I did, for a moment or two, hoping to discern any weak spots it might have in its scaly, knobby hide. That's when it espied me, and straightaway the fiend released its dinner and rushed towards me, baring a mouth filled with fangs longer even than the tusks of a bull walrus."

"Long as that?" asked the woman with the goose, stroking the bird's head.

"Longer, maybe," the stranger told her. "Of a sudden, it was upon me, all fins and claws, and there was hardly time to fix every detail in my memory. As I said, it *rushed* me, and bore me down upon the muddy belly of that accursed hall with all its weight. I thought it might crush me, stave in my skull and chest, and soon mine would count among the jumble of bleached skeletons littering that floor. There were plenty enough human bones, I *do* recall that much. Its talons sundered my armor, and sliced my flesh, and soon my blood was mingling with that of the stolen ewe and lamb. I almost despaired, then and there, and I'll admit that much freely and suffer no shame in the admission."

"Still," the woman with the goose persisted, "awfully damned convenient, all that light."

The stranger sighed and stared sullenly into the fire.

And for the people of Invergó, and also for the stranger who claimed to have done them such a service, this was the way those three days and those three nights passed. The curious came to the tavern to hear the tale, and most of them went away just as skeptical as they'd arrived. The stranger only slept when the drink overcame her, and then she sprawled on a filthy mat at one side of the hearth; at least no one saw fit to begrudge her that small luxury.

But then, late on the morning of the fourth day, the troll's mangled corpse fetched up on the tide, not far distant from the village. A clam-digger and his three sons had been working the mudflats where the narrow aquamarine bay meets the open sea, and they were the ones who discovered the creature's remains. Before midday, a group had been dispatched by the village constabulary to retrieve the body and haul it across the marshes, delivering it to Invergó, where all could see the remains and judge for themselves. Seven strong men were required to hoist the carcass onto a litter (usually reserved for transporting strips of blubber and the like), which was drawn across the mire and through the rushes by a team of six oxen. Most of the afternoon was required to cross hardly a single league. The mud was deep and the going slow, and the animals strained in their harnesses, foam flecking their lips and nostrils. One of the cattle perished from exhaustion not long after the putrefying load was finally dragged through the village gates and dumped unceremoniously upon the flagstones in the common square.

Before this day, none among them had been afforded more than the briefest, fleeting glimpse of the sea devil. And now, every man, woman, and child who'd heard the news of the recovered corpse crowded about, able to peer and gawk and prod the dead thing to their hearts' content. The mob seethed with awe and morbid curiosity, apprehension and disbelief. For their pleasure, the enormous head was raised up and an anvil slid underneath its broken jaw, and, also, a fishing gaff was inserted into the dripping mouth, that all could look upon those protruding fangs, which did, indeed, put to shame the tusks of many a bull walrus.

However, it was almost twilight before anyone thought to rouse the stranger, who was still lying unconscious on her mat in the tavern, sleeping off the proceeds of the previous evening's storytelling. She'd been dreaming of her home, which was very far to the south, beyond the raw black mountains and the glaciers, the fjords and the snow. In the dream, she'd been sitting at the edge of a wide green pool, shaded by willow boughs from the heat of the noonday sun, watching the pretty women who came to bathe there. Half a bucket of soapy, lukewarm seawater was required to wake her from this reverie, and the stranger spat and sputtered and cursed the man who'd doused her (he'd drawn the short straw). She was ready to reach for her spear when someone hastily explained that a clam-digger had come across the troll's body on the mudflats, and so the people of Invergó were now quite a bit more inclined than before to accept her tale.

"That means I'll get the reward and can be shed of this sorry one-whore piss hole of a town?" she asked. The barmaid explained how the decision was still up to the elders, but that the scales *did* seem to have tipped somewhat in her favor.

And so, with help from the barmaid and the cook, the still half-drunken stranger was led from the shadows and into what passed for bright daylight, there on the gloomy streets of Invergó. Soon, she was pushing her way roughly through the mumbling throng of bodies that had gathered about the slain sea troll, and when she saw the fruits of her battle—when she saw that everyone *else* had seen them—she smiled broadly and spat directly in the monster's face.

"Do you doubt me *still*?" she called out, and managed to climb onto the creature's back, slipping off only once before she gained secure footing on its shoulders. "Will you continue to ridicule me as a liar, when the evidence is right here before your own eyes?"

"Well, it *might* conceivably have died some other way," a peat-cutter said without looking at the stranger.

"Perhaps," suggested a cooper, "it swam too near the glacier, and was struck by a chunk of calving ice."

The stranger glared furiously and whirled about to face the elders, who were gathered together near the troll's webbed feet. "Do you truly mean to *cheat* me of the bounty?" she demanded. "Why, you ungrateful, two-faced gaggle of sheep-fuckers," she began, then almost slipped off the cadaver again.

"Now, now," one of the elders said, holding up a hand in a gesture meant to calm the stranger. "There will, of course, be an inquest. Certainly. But, be assured, my fine woman, it is only a matter of formality, you understand. I'm sure not one here among us doubts, even for a moment, it was *your* blade returned this vile, contemptible spirit to the nether pits that spawned it."

For a few tense seconds, the stranger stared warily back at the elder, for she'd never liked men, and especially not men who used many words when only a few would suffice. She then looked out over the restless crowd, silently daring anyone present to contradict him. And, when no one did, she once again turned her gaze down to the corpse, laid out below her feet.

"I cut its throat, from ear to ear," the stranger said, though she was not entirely sure the troll *had* ears. "I gouged out the left eye, and I expect you'll come across the tip end of my blade lodged somewhere in the gore. I am Malmury, daughter of My Lord Gwrtheyrn the Undefeated, and before the eyes of the gods do I so claim this as *my* kill, and I know that even *they* would not gainsay this rightful averment."

And with that, the stranger, who they at last knew was named Malmury, slid clumsily off the monster's back, her boots and breeches now stained with blood and the various excrescences leaking from the troll. She returned immediately to the tavern, as the salty evening air had made her quite thirsty. When she'd gone, the men and women and children of Invergó went back to examining the corpse, though a disquiet and guilty sort of solemnity had settled over them, and what was said was generally spoken in whispers. Overhead, a chorus of hungry gulls and ravens cawed and greedily surveyed the troll's shattered body.

"Malmury," the cooper murmured to the clam-digger who'd found the corpse (and so was, himself, enjoying some small degree of celebrity). "A *fine* name, that. And the daughter of a lord, even. Never questioned her story in the least. No, not me."

"Nor I," whispered the peat-cutter, leaning in a little closer for a better look at the creature's warty hide. "Can't imagine where she'd have gotten the notion any of us distrusted her."

Torches were lit and set up round about the troll, and much of the crowd lingered far into the night, though a few found their way back to the tavern to listen to Malmury's tale a third or fourth time, for it had grown considerably more interesting, now that it seemed to be true. A local alchemist and astrologer, rarely seen by the other inhabitants of Invergó, arrived and was permitted to take samples of the monster's flesh and saliva. It was he who located the point of the stranger's broken dagger, embedded firmly in the troll's sternum, and the artifact was duly handed over to the constabulary. A young boy in the alchemist's service made highly detailed sketches from numerous angles, and labeled anatomical features as the old man had taught him. By midnight, it became necessary to post a sentry to prevent fishermen and urchins slicing off souvenirs. Only half an hour later, a fishwife was found with a horn cut from the sea troll's cheek hidden in her bustle, and a second sentry was posted.

In the tavern, Malmury, daughter of Lord Gwrtheyrn, managed to regale her audience with increasingly fabulous variations of her battle with the demon. But no one much seemed to mind the embellishments, or that, partway through the tenth retelling of the night, it was revealed that the troll had summoned a gigantic, fire-breathing worm from the ooze that carpeted the floor of the bay, and which Malmury also claimed to have dispatched in short order.

"Sure," she said, wiping at her lips with the hem of the barmaid's skirt. "And now, there's something *else* for your clamdiggers to turn up, sooner or later."

By dawn, the stench wafting from the common was becoming unbearable, and a daunting array of dogs and cats had begun to gather round about the edges of the square, attracted by the odor, which promised a fine carrion feast. The cries of the gulls and the ravens had become a cacophony, as though all the heavens had sprouted feathers and sharp, pecking beaks and were descending upon the village. The harbormaster, two physicians, and a cadre of minor civil servants were becoming concerned about the assorted noxious fluids seeping from the rapidly decomposing carcass. This poisonous concoction oozed between the cobbles and had begun to fill gutters and strangle drains as it flowed downhill, towards both the waterfront and the village well. Though there was some talk of removing the source of the taint from the village, it was decided, rather, that a low bulwark or levee of dried peat would be stacked around the corpse.

And, true, this appeared to solve the problem of seepage, for the time being, the peat acting both as a dam and serving to absorb much of the rot. But it did nothing whatsoever to deter the cats and dogs milling about the square, or the raucous cloud of birds that had begun to swoop in, snatching mouthfuls of flesh, before they could be chased away by the two sentries, who shouted at them and brandished brooms and long wooden poles.

Inside the smoky warmth of the tavern—which, by the way, was known as the Cod's Demise, though no sign had ever born that title—Malmury knew nothing of the trouble and worry her trophy was causing in the square, or the talk of having the troll hauled back into the marshes. But neither was she any longer precisely carefree, despite her drunkenness. Even as the sun was rising over the village and peat was being stacked about the corpse, a stooped and toothless old crone of a woman had entered the Cod's Demise. All those who'd been enjoying the tale's new wrinkle of a fire-breathing worm, turned towards her. Not a few of them uttered prayers and clutched tightly to the fetishes they carried against the evil eye and all manner of sorcery and malevolent spirits. The crone stood near the doorway, and she leveled a long, crooked finger at Malmury.

"Her," she said ominously, in a voice that was not unlike low tide swishing about rocks and rubbery heaps of bladder rack. "She is the stranger? The one who has murdered the troll who for so long called the bay his home?"

There was a brief silence, as eyes drifted from the crone to Malmury, who was blinking and peering through a haze of alcohol and smoke, trying to get a better view of the frail, hunched woman.

"That I am," Malmury said at last, confused by this latest arrival and the way the people of Invergó appeared to fear her. Malmury tried to stand, then thought better of it and stayed in her seat by the hearth, where there was less chance of tipping over.

"Then she's the one I've come to see," said the crone, who seemed less like a living, breathing woman and more like something assembled from bundles of twigs and scraps of leather, sloppily held together with twine, rope, and sinew. She leaned on a gnarled cane, though it was difficult to be sure if the cane was wood or bone, or some skillful amalgam of the two. "She's the interloper who has doomed this village and all those who dwell here."

Malmury, confused and growing angry, rubbed at her eyes, starting to think this was surely nothing more than an unpleasant dream, born of too much drink and the boiled mutton and cabbage she'd eaten for dinner.

"How *dare* you stand there and speak to me this way?" she barked back at the crone, trying hard not to slur as she spoke. "Aren't I the one who, only five days ago, *delivered* this place from the depredations of that demon? Am I not the one who risked her *life* in the icy brine of the bay to keep these people safe?"

"*Oh,* she thinks much of herself," the crone cackled, slowly bobbing her head, as though in time to some music nobody else could hear. "Yes, she thinks herself gallant and brave and favored by the gods of *her* land. And who can say? Maybe she is. But she should know, this is *not* her land, and we have our *own* gods. And it is one of *their* children she has slain."

Malmury sat up as straight as she could manage, which wasn't very straight at all, and, with her sloshing cup, jabbed fiercely at the old woman. Barley wine spilled out and spattered across the toes of Malmury's boots and the hard-packed dirt floor.

"Hag," she snarled, "how dare you address me as though I'm not even present. If you have some quarrel with me, then let's hear it spoken. Else, scuttle away and bother this good house no more."

"This good *house*?" the crone asked, feigning dismay as she peered into the gloom, her stooped countenance framed by the morning light coming in through the opened door. "Beg your pardon. I thought possibly I'd wandered into a rather ambitious privy hole, but that the swine had found it first."

Malmury dropped her cup and drew her chipped dagger, which she brandished menacingly at the crone. "You *will* leave now, and without another insult passing across those withered lips, or we shall be presenting *you* to the swine for their breakfast."

At this, the barmaid, a fair woman with blondish hair, bent close to Malmury and whispered in her ear, "Worse yet than the blasted troll, this one. Be cautious, my lady."

Malmury looked away from the crone, and, for a long moment, stared, instead, at the barmaid. Malmury had the distinct sensation that she was missing some crucial bit of wisdom or history that would serve to make sense of the foul old woman's intrusion and the villagers' reactions to her. Without turning from the barmaid, Malmury furrowed her brow and again pointed at the crone with her dagger.

"This slattern?" she asked, almost laughing. "This shriveled harridan not even the most miserable of harpies would claim? I'm to *fear* her?"

"No," the crone said, coming nearer now. The crowd parted to grant her passage, one or two among them stumbling in their haste to avoid the witch. "*You* need not fear *me*, Malmury Troll-bane. Not this day. But you *would* do well to find some ounce of sobriety and fear the consequences of your actions."

"She's insane," Malmury sneered, than spat at the space of damp floor between herself and the crone. "Someone show her a mercy, and find the hag a root cellar to haunt."

The old woman stopped and stared down at the glob of spittle, then raised her head, flared her nostrils, and fixed Malmury in her gaze.

"There was a balance here, Trollbane, an equity, decreed when my great-grandmothers were still infants swaddled in their cribs. The debt paid for a grave injustice born of the arrogance of men. A tithe, if you will, and if it cost these people a few souls now and again, or thinned their bleating flocks, it also kept them safe from that greater wrath that watches us always from the Sea at the Top of the World. But this selfsame balance have *you* undone, and, foolishly, they name you a hero for that deed. For their damnation and their doom."

Malmury cursed, spat again, and tried then to rise from her chair, but was held back by her own inebriation and by the barmaid's firm hand upon her shoulder.

The crone coughed and added a portion of her own jaundiced spittle to the floor of the tavern. "They will *tell* you, Trollbane, though the tales be less than half-remembered among this misbegotten legion of cowards and imbeciles. You *ask* them, they will tell you what has not yet been spoken, what was never freely uttered for fear no hero would have accepted their blood money. Do not think *me* the villain in this ballad they are spinning around you."

"You would do well to *leave,* witch," answered Malmury, her voice grown low and throaty, as threatful as breakers before a storm tide or the grumble of a chained hound. "They might fear you, but I do not, and I'm in an ill temper to suffer your threats and intimations."

"Very well," the old woman replied, and she bowed her head

to Malmury, though it was clear to all that the crone's gesture carried not one whit of respect. "So be it. But you *ask* them, Troll-bane. You ask after the *cause* of the troll's coming, and you ask after his daughter, too."

And with that, she raised her cane, and the fumy air about her appeared to shimmer and fold back upon itself. There was a strong smell, like the scent of brimstone and of smoldering sage, and a sound, as well. Later, Malmury would not be able to decide if it was more akin to a distant thunderclap or the crackle of burning logs. And, with that, the old woman vanished, and her spit sizzled loudly upon the floor.

"Then she *is* a sorceress," Malmury said, sliding the dagger back into its sheath.

"After a fashion," the barmaid told her, and slowly removed her grip upon Malmury's shoulder. "She's the last priestess of the Old Ways, and still pays tribute to those beings who came before the gods. I've heard her called Grímhildr, and also Gunna, though none among us recall her right name. She is powerful, and treacherous, but know that she has also done great *good* for Invergó and all the people along the coast. When there was plague, she dispelled the sickness—"

"What did she *mean,* to ask after the coming of the troll and its daughter?"

"These are not questions I would answer," the barmaid replied, and turned suddenly away. "You must take them to the elders. They can tell you these things."

Malmury nodded and sipped from her cup, her eyes wandering about the tavern, which she saw was now emptying out into the morning-drenched street. The crone's warnings had left them in no mood for tales of monsters, and had ruined their appetite for the stranger's endless boasting and bluster. No matter, Malmury thought. They'd be back come nightfall, and she was weary, besides, and needed sleep. There was now a cot waiting for her upstairs, in the loft above the kitchen, a proper bed complete with mattress and pillows stuffed with the down of geese, even a white bearskin blanket to guard against the frigid air that blew in through the cracks in the walls. She considered going before the council of elders, after she was rested and only hungover, and pressing them for answers to the crone's questions. But Malmury's head was beginning to ache, and she only entertained the proposition in passing. Already, the appearance of the old woman and what she'd said was beginning to seem less like something that had actually happened, and Malmury wondered, dimly, if she was having trouble discerning where the truth ended and her own generous embroidery of the truth began. Perhaps she'd invented the hag, feeling the tale needed an appropriate epilogue, and then, in her drunkenness, forgotten that she'd invented her.

Soon, the barmaid—whose name was Dóta—returned to lead Malmury up the narrow, creaking stairs to her small room and the cot, and Malmury forgot about sea trolls and witches and even the gold she had coming. For Dóta was a comely girl, and free with her favors, and the stranger's sex mattered little to her.

The daughter of the sea troll lived among the jagged, windswept highlands that loomed above the milky blue-green bay and the village of Invergó. Here had she dwelt for almost three generations, as men reckoned the passing of time, and here did she imagine she would live until the long span of her days was at last exhausted.

Her cave lay deep within the earth, where once had been only solid basalt. But over incalculable eons, the glacier that swept down from the mountains, inching between high volcanic cliffs as it carved a wide path to the sea, had worked its way beneath the bare and stony flesh of the land. A ceaseless trickle of meltwater had carried the bedrock away, grain by igneous grain, down to the bay, as the perpetual cycle of freeze and thaw had split and shattered the stone. In time (and then, as now, the world had nothing but time), the smallest of breaches had become cracks, cracks became fissures, and intersecting labyrinths of fissures collapsed to form a cavern. And so, in this way, had the struggle between mountain and ice prepared for her a home, and she dwelt there, alone, almost beyond the memory of the village and its inhabitants, which she despised and feared and avoided when at all possible.

However, she had not always lived in the cave, nor unattended. Her mother, a child of man, had died while birthing the sea troll's daughter, and, afterwards, she'd been taken in by the widowed conjurer who would, so many years later, seek out and confront a stranger named Malmury who'd come up from the southern kingdoms. When the people of Invergó had looked upon the infant, what they'd seen was enough to guess at its parentage. And they would have put the mother to death, then and there, for her congress with the fiend, had she not been dead already. And surely, likewise, would they have murdered the baby, had the old woman not seen fit to intervene. The villagers had always feared the crone, but also they'd had cause to seek her out in times of hardship and calamity. So it gave them pause, once she'd made it known that the infant was in her care, and this knowledge stayed their hand, for a while.

In the tumbledown remains of a stone cottage, at the edge of the mudflats, the crone had raised the infant until she was old enough to care for herself. And until even the old woman's infamy, and the prospect of losing her favors, was no longer enough to protect the sea troll's daughter from the villagers. Though more human than not, she had the creature's blood in her veins. In the eyes of some, this made her a greater abomination than her father.

Finally, rumors had spread that the girl was a danger to them all, and, after an especially harsh winter, many became convinced that she could make herself into an ocean mist and pass easily through windowpanes. In this way, it was claimed, had she begun feeding on the blood of men and women while they slept. Soon, a much-prized milking cow had been found with her udders mutilated, and the farmer had been forced to put the beast out of its misery. The very next day, the elders of Invergó had sent a warning to the crone that their tolerance of the half-breed was at an end, and she was to be remanded to the constable forthwith.

But the old woman had planned against this day. She'd discovered the cave high above the bay, and she'd taught the sea troll's daughter to find auk eggs and mushrooms and to hunt the goats and such other wild things as lived among the peaks and ravines bordering the glacier. The girl was bright, and had learned to make clothing and boots from the hides of her kills, and also had been taught herb lore, and much else that would be needed to survive on her own in that forbidding, barren place.

Late one night in the summer of her fourteenth year, she'd fled Invergó, and made her way to the cave. Only one man had ever been foolish enough to go looking for her, and his body was found pinned to an iceberg floating in the bay, his own sword driven through his chest to the hilt. After that, they left her alone, and soon the daughter of the sea troll was little more than legend, and a tale to frighten children. She began to believe, and to hope, that she would never again have cause to journey down the slopes to the village.

But then, as the stranger Malmury, senseless with drink, slept in the arms of a barmaid, the crone came to the sea troll's daughter in her dreams, as the old woman had done many times before.

"Your father has been slain," she said, not bothering to temper the words. "His corpse lies desecrated and rotting in the village square, where all can come and gloat and admire the mischief of the one who killed him."

The sea troll's daughter, whom the crone had named Sæhildr, for the ocean, had been dreaming of stalking elk and a shaggy herd of mammoth across a meadow. But the crone's voice had startled her prey, and the dream animals had all fled across the tundra.

The sea troll's daughter rolled over onto her back, stared up at the grizzled face of the old woman, and asked, "Should this bring me sorrow? Should I have tears, to receive such tidings? If so, I must admit it doesn't, and I don't. Never have I seen the face of my father, not with my waking eyes, and never has he spoken unto me, nor sought me out. I was nothing more to him than a curious consequence of his indiscretions."

"You have lived always in different worlds," the old woman replied, but the one she called Sæhildr had turned back over onto her belly and was staring forlornly at the place where the elk and mammoth had been grazing only a few moments before.

"It is none of my concern," the sea troll's daughter sighed, thinking she should wake soon, that then the old woman could no longer plague her thoughts. Besides, she was hungry, and she'd killed a bear only the day before.

"Sæhildr," the crone said, "I've not come expecting you to grieve, for too well do I know your mettle. I've come with a warning, as the one who slew your father may yet come seeking you."

The sea troll's daughter smiled, baring her teeth, that effortlessly cracked bone that she might reach the rich marrow inside. With the hooked claws of a thumb and forefinger, she plucked the yellow blossom from an arctic poppy, and held it to her wide nostrils.

"Old Mother, knowing my mettle, you should know that I am

not afraid of men," she whispered, then she let the flower fall back to the ground.

"The one who slew your father was not a man, but a woman, the likes of which I've never seen," the crone replied. "She is a warrior, of noble birth, from the lands south of the mountains. She came to collect the bounty placed upon the troll's head. Sæhildr, this one is strong, and I fear for you."

In the dream, low clouds the color of steel raced by overhead, fat with snow, and the sea troll's daughter lay among the flowers of the meadow and thought about the father she'd never met. Her short tail twitched from side to side, like the tail of a lazy, contented cat, and she decapitated another poppy.

"You believe this warrior will hunt *me* now?" she asked the crone.

"What I think, Sæhildr, is that the men of Invergó have no intention of honoring their agreement to pay this woman her reward. Rather, I believe they will entice her with even greater riches, if only she will stalk and destroy the bastard daughter of their dispatched foe. The woman is greedy, and prideful, and I hold that she will hunt you, yes."

"Then let her come to me, Old Mother," the sea troll's daughter said. "There is little enough sport to be had in these hills. Let her come into the mountains and face me."

The old woman sighed and began to break apart on the wind, like sea foam before a wave. "She's not a fool," the crone said. "A braggart, yes, and a liar, but by her own strength and wits did she undo your father. I'd not see the same fate befall you, Sæhildr. She will lay a trap . . ."

"Oh, I know something of traps," the troll's daughter replied, and then the dream ended. She opened her black eyes and lay awake in her freezing den, deep within the mountains. Not far from the nest of pelts that was her bed, a lantern she'd fashioned from walrus bone and blubber burned unsteadily, casting tall, writhing shadows across the basalt walls. The sea troll's daughter lay very still, watching the flame, and praying to all the beings who'd come before the gods of men that the battle with her father's killer would not be over too quickly.

As it happened, however, the elders of Invergó were far too preoccupied with other matters to busy themselves trying to conceive of schemes by which they might cheat Malmury of her bounty. With each passing hour, the clam-digger's grisly trophy became increasingly putrid, and the decision not to remove it from the village's common square had set in motion a chain of events that would prove far more disastrous to the village than the *living* troll ever could have been. Moreover, Malmury was entirely too distracted by her own intoxication and with the pleasures visited upon her by the barmaid, Dóta, to even recollect she had the reward coming. So, while there can be hardly any doubt that the old crone who lived at the edge of the mudflats was, in fact, both wise and clever, she had little cause to fear for Sæhildr's immediate well-being.

The troll's corpse, hauled so triumphantly from the marsh, had begun to swell in the midday sun, distending magnificently as the gases of decomposition built up inside its innards. Meanwhile, the flock of gulls and ravens had been joined by countless numbers of fish crows and kittiwakes, a constantly shifting, swooping, shrieking cloud that, at last, succeeded in chasing off the two sentries who'd been charged with the task of protecting the carcass from scavengers. And, no longer dissuaded by the men and their jabbing sticks, the cats and dogs that had skulked all night about the edges of the common grew bold and joined in the banquet (though the cats proved more interested in seizing unwary birds than in the sour flesh of the troll). A terrific swarm of biting flies arrived only a short time later, and there were ants, as well, and voracious beetles the size of a grown man's thumb. Crabs and less savory things made their way up from the beach. An order was posted that the citizens of Invergó should retreat to their homes and bolt all doors and windows until such time as the pandemonium could be dealt with.

There was, briefly, talk of towing the body back to the salt marshes from whence it had come. But this proposal was soon dismissed as impractical and hazardous. Even if a determined crew of men dragging a litter or wagon, and armed with the requisite hooks and cables, the block and tackle, could fight their way through the seething, foraging mass of birds, cats, dogs, insects, and crustaceans, it seemed very unlikely that the corpse retained enough integrity that it could now be moved in a single piece. And just the thought of intentionally breaking it apart, tearing it open and thereby releasing whatever foul brew festered within, was enough to inspire the elders to seek some alternate route of ridding the village of the corruption and all its attendant chaos. To make matters worse, the peat levee that had been hastily stacked around the carcass suddenly failed partway through the day, disgorging all the oily fluid that had built up behind it. There was now talk of pestilence, and a second order was posted, advising the villagers that all water from the pumps was no longer potable, and that the bay, too, appeared to have been contaminated. The fish market was closed, and incoming ships forbidden to offload any of the day's catch.

And then, when the elders thought matters were surely at their worst, the alchemist's young apprentice arrived bearing a sheaf of equations and ascertainments based upon the samples taken from the carcass. In their chambers, the old men flipped through these pages for some considerable time, no one wanting to be the first to admit he didn't actually understand what he was reading.

Finally, the apprentice cleared his throat, which caused them to look up at him.

"It's simple, really," the boy said. "You see, the various humors of the troll's peculiar composition have been demonstrated to undergo a predictable variance during the process of putrefaction."

The elders stared back at him, seeming no less confused by his words than by the spidery handwriting on the pages spread out before them.

"To put it more plainly," the boy said, "the creature's blood is becoming volatile. Flammable. Given significant enough concentrations, which must certainly exist by now, even explosive."

Almost in unison, the faces of the elders of Invergó went pale. One of them immediately stood and ordered the boy to fetch his master forthwith, but was duly informed that the alchemist had already fled the village. He'd packed a mule and left by the winding, narrow path that led west through the marshes, into the wilderness. He hoped, the apprentice told them, to observe for posterity the grandeur of the inevitable conflagration, but from a safe distance.

At once, a proclamation went out that all flames were to be extinguished, all hearths and forges and ovens, every candle and lantern in Invergó. Not so much as a tinderbox or pipe must be left smoldering anywhere, so dire was the threat to life and property. However, most of the men dispatched to see that this proclamation was enforced, instead fled into the marshes, or towards the hills, or across the milky blue-green bay to the far shore, which was reckoned to be sufficiently remote that sanctuary could be found there. The calls that rang through the streets of the village were not so much "Douse the fires," or "Mind your stray embers," as "Flee for your lives, the troll's going to explode."

In their cot, in the small but cozy space above the Cod's Demise, Malmury and Dóta had been dozing. But the commotion from outside, both the wild ruckus from the feeding scavengers and the panic that was now sweeping through the village, woke them. Malmury cursed and groped about for the jug of apple brandy on the floor, which Dóta had pilfered from the larder. Dóta lay listening to the uproar, and, being sober, began to sense that something, somewhere, somehow had gone terribly wrong, and that they might now be in very grave danger.

Dóta handed the brandy to Malmury, who took a long pull from the jug and squinted at the barmaid.

"They have no intention of paying you," Dóta said flatly, buttoning her blouse. "We've known it all along. All of us, everyone who lives in Invergó."

Malmury blinked and rubbed at her eyes, not quite able to make sense of what she was hearing. She had another swallow from the jug, hoping the strong liquor might clear her ears.

"It was a dreadful thing we did," Dóta admitted. "I know that now. You're brave, and risked much, and—"

"I'll beat it out of them," Malmury muttered.

"That might work," Dóta said softly, nodding her head. "Only they don't have it. The elders, I mean. In all Invergó's coffers, there's not even a quarter what they offered."

Beyond the walls of the tavern, there was a terrific crash, then, and, soon thereafter, the sound of women screaming.

"Malmury, listen to me. You stay here, and have the last of the brandy. I'll be back very soon."

"I'll beat it out of them," Malmury declared again, though this time with slightly less conviction.

"Yes," Dóta told her. "I'm sure you will do just that. Only now, wait here. I'll return as quickly as I can."

"Bastards," Malmury sneered. "Bastards and ingrates."

"You finish the brandy," Dóta said, pointing at the jug

clutched in Malmury's hands. "It's excellent brandy, and very expensive. Maybe not the same as gold, but . . ." and then the barmaid trailed off, seeing that Malmury had passed out again. Dóta dressed and hurried downstairs, leaving the stranger, who no longer seemed quite so strange, alone and naked, snoring loudly on the cot.

In the street outside the Cod's Demise, the barmaid was greeted by a scene of utter pandemonium. The reek from the rotting troll, only palpable in the tavern, was now overwhelming, and she covered her mouth and tried not to gag. Men, women, and children rushed to and fro, many burdened with bundles of valuables or food, some on horseback, others trying to drive herds of pigs or sheep through the crowd. And, yet, rising above it all, was the deafening clamor of that horde of sea birds and dogs and cats squabbling amongst themselves for a share of the troll. Off towards the docks, someone was clanging the huge bronze bell reserved for naught but the direst of catastrophes. Dóta shrank back against the tavern wall, recalling the crone's warnings and admonitions, expecting to see, any moment now, the titanic form of one of those beings who came before the gods, towering over the rooftops, striding towards her through the village.

Just then, a tinker, who frequently spent his evenings and his earnings in the tavern, stopped and seized the barmaid by both shoulders, gazing directly into her eyes.

"You must *run!*" he implored. "Now, this very minute, you must get away from this place!"

"But why?" Dóta responded, trying to show as little of her terror as possible, trying to behave the way she imagined a woman like Malmury might behave. "What has happened?"

"It *burns,*" the tinker said, and before she could ask him *what* burned, he released her and vanished into the mob. But, as if in answer to that unasked question, there came a muffled crack, and then a boom that shook the very street beneath her boots. A roiling mass of charcoal-colored smoke shot through with glowing red-orange cinders billowed up from the direction of the livery, and Dóta turned and dashed back into the Cod's Demise.

Another explosion followed, and another, and by the time she reached the cot upstairs, dust was sifting down from the rafters of the tavern, and the roofing timbers had begun to creak alarmingly. Malmury was still asleep, oblivious to whatever cataclysm was befalling Invergó. The barmaid grabbed the bearskin blanket and wrapped it about Malmury's shoulders, then slapped her several times, hard, until Malmury's eyelids fluttered open partway.

"Stop that," she glowered, seeming now more like an indignant girl-child than the warrior who'd swum to the bottom of the bay and slain their sea troll.

"We have to *go*," Dóta said, almost shouting to be understood above the racket. "It's not *safe* here anymore, Malmury. We have to get out of Invergó."

"But I *killed* the poor, sorry wretch," Malmury mumbled, shivering and pulling the bearskin tighter about her. "Have you lot gone and found another?"

"Truthfully," Dóta replied, "I do not *know* what fresh devilry this is, only that we can't stay here. There is fire, and a roar like naval cannonade."

"I was sleeping," Malmury said petulantly. "I was dreaming of—"

The barmaid slapped her again, harder, and this time Malmury seized her wrist and glared blearily back at Dóta. "I *told* you not to do that."

"Aye, and I told *you* to get up off your fat ass and get moving." There was another explosion then, nearer than any of the others, and both women felt the floorboards shift and tilt below them.

Malmury nodded, some dim comprehension wriggling its way through the brandy and wine.

"My horse is in the stable," she said. "I cannot leave without my horse. She was given me by my father."

Dóta shook her head, straining to help Malmury to her feet. "I'm sorry," she said. "It's too late. The stables are all ablaze." Then neither of them said anything more, and the barmaid led the stranger down the swaying stairs and through the tavern and out into the burning village.

From a rocky crag high above Invergó, the sea troll's daughter watched as the town burned. Even at this distance and altitude, the earth shuddered with the force of each successive detonation. Loose stones were shaken free of the talus and rolled away down the steep slope. The sky was sooty with smoke, and beneath the pall, everything glowed from the hellish light of the flames.

And, too, she watched the progress of those who'd managed to escape the fire. Most fled westward, across the mudflats, but some had filled the hulls of doggers and dories and ventured out into the bay. She'd seen one of the little boats lurch to starboard and capsize, and was surprised at how many of those it spilled into the icy cove reached the other shore. But of all these refugees, only two had headed south, into the hills, choosing the treacherous pass that led up towards the glacier and the basalt mountains that flanked it. The daughter of the sea troll watched their progress with an especial fascination. One of them appeared to be unconscious and was slung across the back of a mule, and the other, a woman with hair the color of the sun, held tight to the mule's reins and urged it forward. With every new explosion, the animal bucked and brayed and struggled against her; once or twice, they almost went over the edge, all three of them. By the time they

gained the wide ledge where Sæhildr crouched, the sun was setting and nothing much remained of Invergó, nothing that hadn't
been touched by the devouring fire.

The sun-haired woman lashed the reins securely to a boulder,
then sat down in the rubble. She was trembling, and it was clear
she'd not had time to dress with an eye towards the cold breath of
the mountains. There was a heavy belt cinched about her waist,
and from it hung a sheathed dagger. The sea troll's daughter
noted the blade, then turned her attention to the mule and its
burden. She could see now that the person slung over the animal's
back was also a woman, unconscious and partially covered with
a moth-eaten bearskin. Her long black hair hung down almost to
the muddy ground.

Invisible from her hiding place in the scree, Sæhildr asked, "Is
she dead, your companion?"

Without raising her head, the sun-haired woman replied,
"Now, why would I have bothered to drag a dead woman all the
way up here?"

"Perhaps she is dear to you," the daughter of the sea troll replied. "It may be you did not wish to see her corpse go to ash with
the others."

"Well, she's *not* a corpse," the woman said. "Not yet, anyway."
And as if to corroborate the claim, the body draped across the
mule farted loudly and then muttered a few unintelligible words.

"Your sister?" the daughter of the sea troll asked, and when
the sun-haired woman told her no, Sæhildr said, "She seems far
too young to be your mother."

"She's not my mother. She's . . . a friend. More than that, she's
a hero."

The sea troll's daughter licked at her lips, then glanced back
to the inferno by the bay. "A hero," she said, almost too softly to
be heard.

"That's the way it started," the sun-haired woman said, her teeth chattering so badly she was having trouble speaking. "She came here from a kingdom beyond the mountains, and, single-handedly, she slew the fiend that haunted the bay. But—"

"Then the fire came," Sæhildr said, and, with that, she stood, revealing herself to the woman. "My *father's* fire, the wrath of the Old Ones, unleashed by the blade there on your hip."

The woman stared at the sea troll's daughter, her eyes filling with wonder and fear and confusion, with panic. Her mouth opened, as though she meant to say something or to scream, but she uttered not a sound. Her hand drifted towards the dagger's hilt.

"*That,* my lady, would be a very poor idea," Sæhildr said calmly. Taller by a head than even the tallest of tall men, she stood looking down at the shivering woman, and her skin glinted oddly in the half-light. "Why do you think I mean you harm?"

"You," the woman stammered. "You're the troll's whelp. I have heard the tales. The old witch is your mother."

Sæhildr made an ugly, derisive noise that was partly a laugh. "Is *that* how they tell it these days, that Gunna is my mother?"

The sun-haired woman only nodded once and stared at the rocks.

"*My* mother is dead," the troll's daughter said, moving nearer, causing the mule to bray and tug at its reins. "And now, it seems, my father has joined her."

"I cannot let you harm her," the woman said, risking a quick sidewise glance at Sæhildr. The daughter of the sea troll laughed again, and dipped her head, almost seeming to bow. The distant firelight reflected off the small, curved horns on either side of her head, hardly more than nubs and mostly hidden by her thick hair, and shone off the scales dappling her cheekbones and brow, as well.

"What you *mean* to say, is that you would have to *try* to prevent me from harming her."

"Yes," the sun-haired woman replied, and now she glanced nervously towards the mule and her unconscious companion.

"If, of course, I *intended* her harm."

"Are you saying that you don't?" the woman asked. "That you do not desire vengeance for your father's death?"

Sæhildr licked her lips again, then stepped past the seated woman to stand above the mule. The animal rolled its eyes, neighed horribly, and kicked at the air, almost dislodging its load. But then the sea troll's daughter gently laid a hand on its rump, and immediately the beast grew calm and silent once more. Sæhildr leaned forwards and grasped the unconscious woman's chin, lifting it, wishing to know the face of the one who'd defeated the brute who'd raped her mother and made of his daughter so shunned and misshapen a thing.

"This one is drunk," Sæhildr said, sniffing the air.

"Very much so," the sun-haired woman replied.

"A *drunkard* slew the troll?"

"She was sober that day. I think."

Sæhildr snorted and said, "Know that there was no bond but blood between my father and me. Hence, what need have I to seek vengeance upon his executioner? Though, I will confess, I'd hoped she might bring me some measure of sport. But even that seems unlikely in her current state." She released the sleeping woman's jaw, letting it bump roughly against the mule's ribs, and stood upright again. "No, I think you need not fear for your lover's life. Not this day. Besides, wouldn't the utter destruction of your village count as a more appropriate reprisal?"

The sun-haired woman blinked, and said, "Why do you say that, that she's my lover?"

"Liquor is not the only stink on her," answered the sea troll's daughter. "Now, *deny* the truth of this, my lady, and I may yet grow angry."

The woman from doomed Invergó didn't reply, but only sighed and continued staring into the gravel at her feet.

"This one is practically naked," Sæhildr said. "And you're not much better. You'll freeze, the both of you, before morning."

"There was no time to find proper clothes," the woman protested, and the wind shifted then, bringing with it the cloying reek of the burning village.

"Not very much farther along this path, you'll come to a small cave," the sea troll's daughter said. "I will find you there, tonight, and bring what furs and provisions I can spare. Enough, perhaps, that you may yet have some slim chance of making your way through the mountains."

"I don't understand," Dóta said, exhausted and near tears, and when the troll's daughter made no response, the barmaid discovered that she and the mule and Malmury were alone on the mountain ledge. She'd not heard the demon take its leave, so maybe the stories were true, and it could become a fog and float away whenever it so pleased. Dóta sat a moment longer, watching the raging fire spread out far below them. And then she got to her feet, took up the mule's reins, and began searching for the shelter that the troll's daughter had promised her she would discover. She did not spare a thought for the people of Invergó, not for her lost family, and not even for the kindly old man who'd owned the Cod's Demise and had taken her in off the streets when she was hardly more than a child. They were the past, and the past would keep neither her nor Malmury alive.

Twice, she lost her way among the boulders, and by the time Dóta stumbled upon the cave, a heavy snow had begun to fall, large wet flakes spiraling down from the darkness. But it was warm inside, out of the howling wind. And, what's more, she found bundles of wolf and bear pelts, seal skins, and mammoth hide, some sewn together into sturdy garments. And there was salted meat, a few potatoes, and a freshly killed rabbit spitted and roasting above a small cooking fire. She would never again set eyes on the sea troll's daughter, but in the long days ahead, as Dóta and the stranger named Malmury made their way through blizzards and across fields of ice, she would often sense someone nearby, watching over them. Or only watching.

BILL WILLINGHAM was born in Fort Belvoir, Virginia. He got his start as staff artist for TSR, Inc., providing illustrations for a number of its role-playing games, among them *Advanced Dungeons & Dragons* and *Gamma World*. In the 1980s, he gained attention for his comic book series *Elementals* (published by Comico), and contributed as an illustrator to such titles as DC's *Green Lantern*. Willingham created the popular DC Vertigo comic book *Fables* in 2002, about characters from folklore residing in contemporary Manhattan. To date, *Fables* is the recipient of fourteen coveted Eisner Awards. His *Jack of Fables,* created with Matthew Sturges, was chosen by *Time* magazine as number five in their Top Ten Graphic Novels of 2007. His first *Fables* prose novel, *Peter and Max*, was released in 2009, the same year that his comic book *Fables: War and Pieces* was nominated for the first Hugo Award for Best Graphic Story. One of the most popular comics writers of our time, he currently lives in the woods in Minnesota.

THIEVES OF DARING

Bill Willingham

*Septavian is 24 or 25 by this time, still adventuring in the company
of the Brothers Frogbarding. They work as mercenaries for the most
part, in the much-fragmented northern kingdoms, traveling south
on occasion to spend their pay and thieve in the large and wealthy
port cities. Though the city is not specifically named in the following tale, it is widely assumed to be Vess, which is identified in other
stories as a center for the practice of dark arts and the location of the
wizard Ulmore's winter palace.*

From *A Probable Outline of Septavian's Life and Adventures*
by Walter Marsh

Jonar Frogbarding, the giant red-bearded northlander was
dead, headless, on the upper landing, a victim of one of Ulmore's roving guards, his infamous Golems Decapitant. His
fair-haired brother Tywar was bleeding out at my feet on the
main floor. Nothing I could do would help him. Too many deep
wounds, each one a killing stroke. I watched the quickly expand-

ing red lake spread out from the disordered pieces of him to lu-
ridly paint the floor's elaborate central mosaic, hand-cut marble
tiles of every conceivable color, depicting an imaginary monster
attacking a ship at sea. Maybe not imaginary, I corrected myself,
considering the other impossible things we'd encountered today.
The blade that had dispatched Tywar lay on the floor beside him,
apparently finally drained of whatever animating force had lent
some manner of autonomous life to it.

I hadn't seen Roe Zelazar, the black-haired, black-eyed Lemurian, since the four of us had breached the estate's outer wall,
more than an hour ago. Four thieves of daring, out on a wine-
fueled lark, to make ourselves famous, at least among a select
underworld set, by looting the vacant winter palace of Ulmore,
the legendary Last Atlantean Sorcerer. As soon as we'd reached
the first inner courtyard, Roe had whispered something frantic
and unintelligible before running off in his own direction, leaving
me with the brothers.

"I think he heard something," Jonar had whispered. "Went to
investigate."

"I'm not inclined to stay here in the open, waiting for him,"
I'd said.

"Nor I," Tywar said.

So the three of us continued the raid without him, making
our way past the outbuildings, over the lawn, sewn with spike-
bottomed mantraps, among other snares and distractions, and to
the main building, a fortress disguised as a palace. Once inside,
we'd run into the real defenses, constructs of darkest sorcery, that
worried and harried at us, room by room, step by step, steadily
wearing us down, making us pay for every foot gained, until I
had to watch the brothers, my friends and companions for the
past three years, cut into lifeless bone and carcass.

Now it seemed I was on my own.

At this point, I'd forgotten any notion of robbery. I just wanted to find Roe and get free of this murder house. I didn't really know the Lemurian. He was a companion of the moment, after a long night of drinking. Not a proven friend, like the brothers had been. But he'd set out on this foolhardy raid with us, and I'm not one to leave any companion behind, if I can help it.

Retreating back to the upper landing, where we'd made our original entry, was out of the question. It had been cut off as an avenue of escape by the blade-armed golems that had arrived in force by now. They blocked both stairways. They were fast, untiring, and near impossible to harm. One of them had been enough to overmatch Jonar. Though I was faster than the northlander, and a considerably smaller target, I had no illusions that I'd be able to make it past the three dozen or more that were up there now. At least they seemed content to remain on the upper landing. Assigned territories, perhaps?

There were six doorways attached to the large room I was in, plus a winding stairway leading down into the dark. Low, rumbling growls and coughs issued up from that, as if some great unearthly creature lurked below.

Staying where I was for any length of time seemed a bad idea. The room was filled with metal statues depicting mighty armored warriors. All but one of them held swords, spears, axes, or other weapons. The sword missing from the remaining statue was the one that had come to life long enough to butcher Tywar. I didn't trust the other weapons to remain inanimate.

So which door do I try? This room seemed centrally located within the sprawling building. One door was as likely as any other to lead outside, or to a dead end.

While I was still considering my options, looking for any clue that might favor one possible exit over another, one of the doors opened and Roe Zelazar walked through it. Perhaps I shouldn't have been surprised, but I was.

"You're free to go, Septavian," he said. "I've no wish to harm you, or cause you any further distress. It was those two ruffians I was after." His gesture took in most of the room, including the two corpses. His rough brown tunic and leggings of the night before were gone, replaced by black-and-grey robes of fine linen. He'd obviously found time to bathe and perfume himself, too, while we were being hunted and cut down.

"You're the Wizard Ulmore?" I said.

"No, of course not. I'm merely one of his students. True, I'm one of his more accomplished students, whose duties happen to include looking after his winter residence when he's absent." Roe approached to just outside of a common sword range. A mistake on his part—possibly.

"And yet I seem to recall it was your idea to rob this place," I said. We were already pretty deep in our cups, and bragging rather boisterously about our intent to do some bold act of mischief, when the Lemurian had joined us.

"Since you were clearly intent on thievery, I merely suggested the target. This is my adopted home, after all, and I have a strong sense of civic duty."

"Luring unwary people into this death trap?"

"Identifying the brutes and vermin that infiltrate our community and disposing of them, before they can cause real harm."

"A good wizard? A servant to his town and country?" I didn't quite scoff at the notion—not quite.

"Exactly so. Sorcery is the foundation on which civilization is built. We devise comforts and luxuries not otherwise available through more ordinary means. Better food. Longer life. Not everyone is content to scratch out a meager existence in your wild lands, prey to anyone stronger in arm, or more savage in will.

The elegant art is the final achievement of a life spent in exacting education and study. Only men of refinement and letters succeed. Compare that to the brutish existence of these northlanders and ask yourself, which life is better?"

"Not all of us are without letters," I said.

"One of the reasons I singled you out from these others for clemency. And there was a practical consideration as well. Unless Septavian is a more common name than I'm given to understand, then you must be Septavian of the Waterhouse. If that's true, and judging by your appearance and odd weapons I believe it is, then I've no wish to incur the wrath of your secretive martial brotherhood. Your people have a nasty reputation of finding and killing those who kill your own, even those of us well practiced in the dark arts."

"I'm no longer associated with that society. I was forced to leave them under less than honorable circumstances. Kill me and I suspect the only reason they'd even think of hunting you down would be to thank you." I always correct those who believe me to still be a part of the Waterhouse Brotherhood. Always. They're more fanatic about hunting down those who pretend association with them than they are about those who kill one of their members.

"An odd moment for full candor," Roe said. He paced, circling just out of sword reach, avoiding the bloodstain on the floor, which had already begun to grow tacky. Roe's slippers whispered against the tiles. He was careful to keep his wary eyes on me. Though he might be willing to be friends, we weren't there yet.

"It doesn't matter," I said. "I can't accept your offer anyway. Tywar and Jonar were friends. I have an obligation to try to avenge them."

"They were thugs. Refined men owe nothing to such animals."

"Nevertheless."

"You won't succeed. Nor will you survive this house. I've constructed so many wonderful snares, subtle and deadly. You've already met my Golems Decapitant. They're just to ensure the mouse stays inside the trap."

"I thought they were Ulmore's creations."

"Hardly. My master is great in power, but lacking in art. He wields his power strictly in the old ways, like a blunt instrument. That monstrous thing growling and groaning downstairs is one of his creatures, summoned up from one of the many hells where the old gods were thrown down. I created the other protections, constantly improving and refining them. That's another reason why your two companions were invited to do their thieving here. My work needs frequent testing."

"So it wasn't all a selfless urge to better serve your adopted hometown."

"Try one of the doors," he said. "They all lead to freedom— eventually. But first you'll have to get through my gauntlet. Survive the wire hounds and you'll have to face the Shades Perilous, and perhaps then the fragrance room, or the black pattern, or— well, I've written a number of elegant murder stories, each one a variation on a central theme."

"Care to tell me which door leads to which trap?"

"All to each. Choosing a specific door just changes the order in which you encounter them."

"And how were you planning to let me get out alive?"

"By accompanying you. They won't activate if I'm present."

"Then I should bring you with me, shouldn't I?" For the most part, swordplay in our world is a matter of closing with an opponent and hacking at him with the broad edge of a heavy blade. Roe was still safely outside the range of that sort of business. But at the Waterhouse, we'd learned a different kind of bladework, with improved weaponry. In a single motion, I drew my long, thin, and flexible waterblade from its sheath and thrust it, point-forward, in a deep lunge that more than doubled the effective range of a sword. Roe was taken entirely by surprise. My blade plunged deep into his chest. Several inches of its tip passed out the other side.

For a second, he just stood there, looking down at the sword stuck through him, a mild look of wonder on his face. Then he crumpled, lifeless, to the floor.

I put a foot in his gut, pulled my blade out from him, and wiped it off on his robes before sheathing it. With both hands free again, I picked up his corpse and hoisted it over one shoulder.

"I hope the protection of your company still works when you're dead."

I picked a door more or less at random and started towards it. Before I'd gone a dozen steps, I felt myself losing my grip on Roe's body. It was rapidly growing lighter, and falling apart. I dropped the thing back on the floor and watched it turn to dust before my eyes. Then the dust turned into smaller specks that blew about for a bit, before disappearing entirely. Laughter echoed throughout the chamber.

"I withdraw my offer of release," the voice said, coming from everywhere, or nowhere. It was unmistakably Roe's voice. "You'll just have to win your own way out. I doubt you'll make it. No one ever has before. But I hope you do. Oddly, I've come to like you in our short acquaintance, and I'd enjoy continuing our conversation sometime."

I didn't reply. It seemed we'd said all that needed to be said. Since I was already pointed at one of the doors, I continued in that direction and opened it. There was a darkened corridor behind the door, leading only a few feet inward before it took a sharp right turn. I could smell a heavy and cloying musk from somewhere within, both attractive and repellent, fragrant decay. I also heard the distant sharpening of many knives, odd skittering sounds, and the musical notes of a thousand glass shards brushing against each other. The attractive part of the odor grew stronger, tugging at me, almost compelling me to enter.

I slammed the door and stepped back.

In the central room, the blade-armed golems had been released from whatever invisible force was confining them to the upper landing. They were shuffling down both staircases, increasing speed with each step. Swords and knives and spears were twisting and shaking in the grips of the statues, screeching, metal against metal, straining to be free of them. And the animal sounds from downstairs were growing louder, more agitated, and more proximate. Whatever it was down there was on its way up.

Okay, I may be in some trouble here.

JOE ABERCROMBIE attended Lancaster Royal Grammar School and Manchester University, where he studied psychology. He moved into television production before taking up a career as a freelance film editor. His first novel, *The Blade Itself*, was published in 2004, and was followed by two further books in the First Law trilogy, *Before They Are Hanged* and *Last Argument of Kings*. His most recent book is a stand-alone novel set in the same world, *Best Served Cold*, and he is currently at work on another, *The Heroes*. Joe now lives in Bath with his wife, Lou, and his daughters, Grace and Eve. He still occasionally edits concerts and music festivals for TV, but spends most of his time writing edgy yet humorous fantasy novels.

THE FOOL JOBS

Joe Abercrombie

Craw chewed the hard skin around his nails, just like he always did. They hurt, just like they always did. He thought to himself that he really had to stop doing that. Just like he always did.

"Why is it," he muttered under his breath, and with some bitterness too, "I always get stuck with the fool jobs?"

The village squatted in the fork of the river, a clutch of damp thatch roofs, scratty as an idiot's hair, a man-high fence of rough-cut logs ringing it. Round wattle huts and three long halls dumped in the muck, ends of the curving wooden uprights on the biggest badly carved like dragon's heads, or wolf's heads, or something that was meant to make men scared but only made Craw nostalgic for decent carpentry. Smoke limped up from chimneys in muddy smears. Half-bare trees still shook browning leaves. In the distance the reedy sunlight glimmered on the rotten fens, like a thousand mirrors stretching off to the horizon. But without the romance.

Wonderful stopped scratching at the long scar through her shaved-stubble hair long enough to make a contribution. "Looks to me," she said, "like a confirmed shit-hole."

"We're way out east of the Crinna, no?" Craw worked a speck of skin between teeth and tongue and spat it out, wincing at the pink mark left on his finger, way more painful than it had any right to be. "Nothing but hundreds of miles of shit-hole in every direction. You sure this is the place, Raubin?"

"I'm sure. She was most specifical."

Craw frowned round. He wasn't sure if he'd taken such a pronounced dislike to Raubin 'cause he was the one that brought the jobs and the jobs were usually cracked, or if he'd taken such a pronounced dislike to Raubin 'cause the man was a weasel-faced arsehole. Bit of both, maybe. "The word is 'specific,' half-head."

"Got my meaning, no? Village in a fork in the river, she said, south o' the fens, three halls, biggest one with uprights carved like fox heads."

"Aaaah." Craw snapped his fingers. "They're meant to be foxes."

"Fox Clan, these crowd."

"Are they?"

"So she said."

"And this thing we've got to bring her. What sort of a thing is it, exactly?"

"Well, it's a thing," said Raubin.

"That much we know."

"Sort of, this long, I guess. She didn't say, precisely."

"Unspecifical, was she?" asked Wonderful, grinning with every tooth.

"She said it'd have a kind of a light about it."

"A light? What? Like a magic bloody candle?"

All Raubin could do was shrug, which wasn't a scrap of use to no one. "I don't know. She said you'd know it when you saw it."

"Oh, nice." Craw hadn't thought his mood could drop much lower. Now he knew better. "That's real nice. So you want me to bet my life, and the lives o' my crew, on knowing it when I see it?" He shoved himself back off the rocks on his belly, out of sight of the village, clambered up and brushed the dirt from his coat, muttering darkly to himself, since it was a new one and he'd been taking some trouble to keep it clean. Should've known that'd be a waste of effort, what with the shitty jobs he always ended up in to his neck. He started back down the slope, shaking his head, striding through the trees towards the others. A good, confident stride. A leader's stride. It was important, Craw reckoned, for a chief to walk like he knew where he was going.

Especially when he didn't.

Raubin hurried after him, whiny voice picking at his back. "She didn't precisely say. About the thing, you know. I mean, she don't, always. She just looks at you, with those eyes . . ." He gave a shudder. "And says, get me this thing, and where from. And what with the paint, and that voice o' hers, and that sweat o' bloody fear you get when she looks at you . . ." Another shudder, hard enough to rattle his rotten teeth. "I ain't asking no questions, I can tell you that. I'm just looking to run out fast so I don't piss myself on the spot. Run out fast, and get whatever thing she's after . . ."

"Well that's real sweet for you," said Craw, "except insofar as actually getting this thing."

"As far as getting the thing goes," mused Wonderful, splashes of light and shadow swimming across her bony face as she looked up into the branches, "the lack of detail presents serious difficulties. All manner of things in a village that size. Which one, though? Which thing, is the question." Seemed she was in a thoughtful mood. "One might say the voice, and the paint, and the aura of fear are, in the present case . . . self-defeating."

"Oh no," said Craw. "Self-defeating would be if she was the

one who'd end up way out past the Crinna with her throat cut, on account of some blurry details on the minor point of the actual job we're bloody here to do." And he gave Raubin a hard glare as he strode out of the trees and into the clearing.

Scorry was sitting sharpening his knives, eight blades neatly laid out on the patchy grass in front of his crossed legs, from a little pricker no longer'n Craw's thumb to a hefty carver just this side of a short-sword. The ninth he had in his hands, whetstone working at steel, *squick, scrick,* marking the rhythm to his soft, high singing. He had a wonder of a singing voice, did Scorry Tiptoe. No doubt he would've been a bard in a happier age, but there was a steadier living in sneaking up and knifing folk these days. A sad fact, Craw reckoned, but those were the times.

Brack-i-Dayn was sat beside Scorry, lips curled back, nibbling at a stripped rabbit bone like a sheep nibbling at grass. A huge, very dangerous sheep. The little thing looked like a toothpick in his great tattooed blue lump of a fist. Jolly Yon frowned down at him as if he were a great heap of shit, which Brack might've been upset by, if it hadn't been Yon's confirmed habit to look at everything and everyone that way. He properly looked like the least jolly man in all the North at that moment. It was how he'd come by the name, after all.

Whirrun of Bligh was kneeling on his own on the other side of the clearing, in front of his great long sword, leaned up against a tree for the purpose. He had his hands clasped in front of his chin, hood drawn down over his head and with just the sharp end of his nose showing. Praying, by the look of him. Craw had always been a bit worried by men who prayed to gods, let alone swords. But those were the times, he guessed. In bloody days, swords were worth more than gods. They certainly had 'em outnumbered. Besides, Whirrun was a valley man, from way out north and west, across the mountains near the White Sea, where it snowed in summer and no one with the slightest sense would ever choose to live. Who knew how he thought?

"Told you it was a real piss-stain of a village, didn't I?" Never was in the midst of stringing his bow. He had that grin he tended to have, like he'd made a joke on everyone else and no one but him had got it. Craw would've liked to know what it was, he could've done with a laugh. The joke was on all of 'em, far as he could see.

"Reckon you had the right of it," said Wonderful as she strutted past into the clearing. "Piss. Stain."

"Well, we didn't come to settle down," said Craw, "we came to get a thing."

Jolly Yon achieved what many might've thought impossible by frowning deeper, black eyes grim as graves, dragging his thick fingers through his thick tangle of a beard. "What sort of a thing, exactly?"

Craw gave Raubin another look. "You want to dig that one over?" The fixer only spread his hands, helpless. "I hear we'll know it when we see it."

"Know it when we see it? What kind of a—"

"Tell it to the trees, Yon, the task is the task."

"And we're here now, aren't we?" said Raubin.

Craw sucked his teeth at him. "Brilliant fucking observation. Like all the best ones, it's true whenever you say it. Yes, we're here."

"We're here," sang Brack-i-Dayn in his up-and-down hillman accent, sucking the last shred o' grease from his bone and flicking it into the bushes. "East of the Crinna where the moon don't shine, a hundred miles from a clean place to shit, and with wild, crazy bastards dancing all around who think it's a good idea to put bones through their own faces." Which was a little rich, considering he was so covered in tattoos he was more blue than white.

There's no style of contempt like the stuff one kind of savage has for another, Craw guessed.

"Can't deny they've got some funny ideas east of the Crinna." Raubin shrugged. "But here's where the thing is, and here's where we are, so why don't we just get the fucking thing and go back fucking home?"

"Why don't you get the fucking thing, Raubin?" growled Jolly Yon.

" 'Cause it's my fucking job to fucking tell you to get the fucking thing is why, Yon fucking Cumber."

There was a long, ugly pause. Uglier than the child of a man and a sheep, as the hillmen have it. Then Yon talked in his quiet voice, the one that still gave Craw prickles up his arms, even after all these years. "I hope I'm wrong. By the dead, I hope I'm wrong. But I'm getting this feeling . . ." He shifted forwards, and it was awfully clear all of a sudden just how many axes he was carrying, "like I'm being disrespected."

"No, no, not at all, I didn't mean—"

"*Respect,* Raubin. That shit costs nothing, but it can spare a man from trying to hold his brains in all the way back home. Am I clear enough?"

" 'Course you are, Yon, 'course you are. I'm over the line. I'm all over it on both sides of it, and I'm sorry. Didn't mean no disrespect. Lot o' pressure, is all. Lot o' pressure for everyone. It's my neck on the block just like yours. Not down there, maybe, but back home, you can be sure o' that, if she don't get her way . . ." Raubin shuddered again, worse'n ever.

"A touch of respect don't seem too much to ask—"

"All right, all right." Craw waved the pair of 'em down. "We're all sinking on the same leaky bloody skiff, there's no help arguing about it. We need every man to a bucket, and every woman too."

"I'm always helpful," said Wonderful, all innocence.

"If only." Craw squatted, pulling out a blade and starting to scratch a map of the village in the dirt. The way Threetrees used to do a long, low time ago. "We might not know exactly what this thing is, but we know where it is, at least." Knife scraped through earth, the others all gathering around, kneeling, sitting, squatting, looking on. "A big hall, in the middle, with uprights on it carved like foxes. They look more like dragons to me, but, you know, that's another story. There's a fence around the outside, two gates, north and south. Houses and huts all around here. Looked like a pig pen there. That's a forge, maybe."

"How many do we reckon might be down there?" asked Yon.

Wonderful rubbed at the scar on her scalp, face twisted as she looked up towards the pale sky. "Could be fifty, sixty fighting men? A few elders, few dozen women and children too. Some o' those might hold a blade."

"Women fighting." Never grinned. "A disgrace, is that."

Wonderful bared her teeth back at him. "Get those bitches to the cook fire, eh?"

"Oh, the cook fire . . ." Brack stared up into the cloudy sky like it was packed with happy memories.

"Sixty warriors? And we're but seven—plus the baggage." Jolly Yon curled his tongue and blew spit over Raubin's boots in a neat arc. "Shit on that. We need more men."

"Wouldn't be enough food then." Brack-i-Dayn laid a sad hand on his belly. "There's hardly enough as it—"

Craw cut him off. "Maybe we should stick to plans using the number we've got, eh? Plain as plain, sixty's way too many to fight fair." Not that anyone had joined his crew for a fair fight, of course. "We need to draw some off."

Never winced. "Any point asking why you're looking at me?"

"Because ugly men hate nothing worse than handsome men, pretty boy."

"It's a fact I can't deny," sighed Never, flicking his long hair back. "I'm cursed with a fine face."

"Your curse, my blessing." Craw jabbed at the north end of his dirt-plan, where a wooden bridge crossed a stream. "You'll take your unmatched beauty in towards the bridge. They'll have guards posted, no doubt. Mount a diversion."

"Shoot one of 'em, you mean?"

"Shoot near 'em, maybe. Let's not kill anyone we don't have to, eh? They might be nice enough folks under different circumstances."

Never sent up a dubious eyebrow. "You reckon?"

Craw didn't, particularly, but he'd no desire to weight his conscience down any further. It didn't float too well as it was. "Just lead 'em a little dance, that's all."

Wonderful clapped a hand to her chest. "I'm so sorry I'll miss it. No one dances prettier than our Never when the music gets going."

Never grinned at her. "Don't worry, sweetness, I'll dance for you later."

"Promises, promises."

"Yes, yes." Craw shut the pair of 'em up with another wave. "You can make us all laugh when this fool job's done with, if we're still breathing."

"Maybe we'll make you laugh too, eh Whirrun?"

The valley man sat cross-legged, sword across his knees, and shrugged. "Maybe."

"We're a tight little group, us lot, we like things friendly."

Whirrun's eyes slid across to Jolly Yon's black frown, and back. "I see that."

"We're like brothers," said Brack, grinning all over his tattooed face. "We share the risks, we share the food, we share the rewards, and from time to time we even share a laugh."

"Never got on too well with my brothers," said Whirrun.

Wonderful snorted. "Well aren't you blessed, boy? You've been given a second chance at a loving family. You last long enough, you'll learn how it works."

The shadow of Whirrun's hood crept up and down his face as he slowly nodded. "Every day should be a new lesson."

"Good advice," said Craw. "Ears open, then, one and all. Once Never's drawn a few off, we creep in at the south gate." And he put a cross in the dirt to show where it was. "Two groups, one each side o' the main hall there, where the thing is. Where the thing's meant to be, leastways. Me, Yon, and Whirrun on the left." Yon spat again, Whirrun gave the slightest nod. "Wonderful, take Brack and Scorry down the right."

"Right y'are, chief," said Wonderful.

"Right for us," sang Brack.

"So, so, so," said Scorry, which Craw took for a yes.

He stabbed at each of 'em with one chewed-to-bugger fingernail. "And all on your best behaviour, you hear? Quiet as a spring breeze. No tripping over the pots this time, eh, Brack?"

"I'll mind my boots, chief."

"Good enough."

"We got a backup plan?" asked Wonderful, "in case the impossible happens and things don't work out quite according to the scheme?"

"The usual. Grab the thing if we can, then run like fuck. You," and Craw gave Raubin a look.

His eyes went wide as two cook pots. "What, me?"

"Stay here and mind the gear." Raubin gave a long sigh of relief, and Craw felt his lip curl. He didn't blame the man for being a hell of a coward, most men are. Craw was one himself. But he blamed him for letting it show. "Don't get too comfortable, though, eh? If the rest of us come to grief these Fox fuckers'll track you down before our blood's dry and more'n likely cut your fruits off." Raubin's sigh rattled to a quick stop.

"Cut your head off," whispered Never, eyes all scary-wide.

"Pull your guts out and cook 'em," growled Jolly Yon.

"Skin your face off and wear it as a mask," rumbled Brack.

"Use your cock for a spoon," said Wonderful. They all thought about that for a moment.

"Right then," said Craw. "Nice and careful, and let's get in that hall without no one noticing and get us that thing. Above all . . ." And he swept the lot of 'em with his sternest look, a half circle of dirt-smeared, scar-pocked, bright-eyed, beard-fuzzed faces. His crew. His family. "Nobody die, eh? Weapons."

Quick, sharp, and with no grumbling now the work was at their feet, Craw's crew got ready for action, each one smooth and practiced with their gear as a weaver with his loom, weapons neat as their clothes were ragged, bright and clean as their faces were dirty. Belts, straps, and bootlaces hissed tight, metal scraped, rattled, and rang, and all the while Scorry's song floated out, soft and high.

Craw's hands moved by themselves through the old routines, mind wandering back across the years to other times he'd done it, other places, other faces around him, a lot of 'em gone back to the mud long ago. A few he'd buried with his own hands. He hoped none of these folk died today, and became nothing but dirt and worn-out memories. He checked his shield, grip bound in leather all tight and sturdy, straps firm. He checked his knife, his backup knife, and his backup backup knife, all tight in their sheaths. You can never have too many knives, someone once told him, and it was solid advice, provided you were careful how you stowed 'em and didn't fall over and get your own blade in your fruits.

Everyone had their work to be about. Except Whirrun. He just bowed his head as he lifted his sword gently from the tree-trunk, holding it under the crosspiece by its stained leather scabbard, sheathed blade longer'n one of his own long legs. Then he pushed his hood back, scrubbed one hand through his flattened hair, and stood watching the others, head on one side.

"That the only blade you carry?" asked Craw as he stowed his own sword at his hip, hoping to draw the tall man in, start to build some trust with him. Tight crew like this was, a bit of trust might save your life. Might save everyone's.

Whirrun's eyes swiveled to him. "This is the Father of Swords, and men have a hundred names for it. Dawn Razor. Grave-Maker. Blood Harvest. Highest and Lowest. Scac-ang-Gaioc in the valley tongue which means the Splitting of the World, the Battle that was fought at the start of time and will be fought again at its end." For a moment he had Craw wondering if he'd list the whole bloody hundred but thankfully he stopped there, frowning at the hilt, wound with dull grey wire. "This is my reward and my punishment both. This is the only blade I need."

"Bit long for eating with, no?" asked Wonderful, strutting up from the other side.

Whirrun bared his teeth at her. "That's what these are for."

"Don't you ever sharpen it?" asked Craw.

"It sharpens me."

"Right. Right y'are." Just the style of nonsense Craw would've expected from Cracknut Leef or some other rune-tosser. He hoped Whirrun was as good with that great big blade as he was supposed to be, 'cause it seemed he brought nothing to the table as a conversationalist.

"Besides, to sharpen it you'd have to draw it," said Wonderful, winking at Craw with the eye Whirrun couldn't see.

"True." Whirrun's eyes slid up to her face. "And once the Father of Swords is drawn, it cannot be sheathed without—"

"Being blooded?" she finished for him. Didn't take skill with the runes to see that coming, Whirrun must've said the same words a dozen times since they left Carleon. Enough for everyone to get somewhat tired of it.

"Blooded," echoed Whirrun, voice full of portent.

Wonderful gave Craw a look. "You ever think, Whirrun of Bligh, you might take yourself a touch too serious?"

He tipped his head back and stared up into the sky. "I'll laugh when I hear something funny."

Craw felt Yon's hand on his shoulder. "A word, chief?"

"'Course," with a grin that took some effort.

He guided Craw away from the others a few steps, and spoke soft. The same words he always did before a fight. "If I die down there . . ."

"No one's dying today," snapped Craw, the same words he always used in reply.

"So you said last time, 'fore we buried Jutlan." That drove Craw's mood another rung down the ladder into the bog. "No one's fault, we do a dangerous style o' work, and all know it. Chances are good I'll live through, but all I'm saying is, if I don't—"

"I'll stop by your children, and take 'em your share, and tell them what you were."

"That's right. And?"

"And I won't dress it up any."

"Right, then." Jolly Yon didn't smile, of course. Craw had known him years, and hadn't seen him smile more'n a dozen times, and even then when it was least expected. But he nodded, satisfied. "Right. No man I'd rather give the task to."

Craw nodded back. "Good. Great." No task he wanted less. As Yon walked off, he muttered to himself. "Always the fool jobs . . ."

• • •

It went pretty much just like Craw planned. He wouldn't have called it the first time ever, but it was a pleasant surprise, that was sure. The six of them lay still and silent on the rise, followed the little movements of leaf and branch that marked Never creeping towards that crap-arse of a village. It looked no better the closer you got to it. Things rarely did, in Craw's experience. He chewed at his nails some more, saw Never kneel in the bushes across the stream from the north gate, nocking an arrow and drawing the string. It was hard to tell from this range, but it looked like he still had that knowing little grin even now.

He loosed his shaft and Craw thought it clicked into one of the logs that made the fence. Faint shouting drifted on the wind. A couple of arrows wobbled back the other way, vanished into the trees as Never turned and scuttled off, lost in the brush. Craw heard some kind of a drum beating, more shouting, then men started to hurry out across that bridge, weapons of rough iron clutched in their hands, some still pulling their furs or boots on. Perhaps three dozen, all told. A neat piece of work. Provided Never got away, of course.

Yon shook his head as he watched a good chunk of the Fox Clan shambling over their bridge and into the trees. "Amazing, ain't it? I never quite get used to just how fucking stupid people are."

"Always a mistake to overestimate the bastards," whispered Craw. "Good thing we're the cleverest crew in the Circle of the World, eh? So could we have no fuckups, today, if you please?"

"I won't if you won't, chief," muttered Wonderful.

"Huh." If only he'd been able to make that promise. Craw tapped Scorry on his shoulder and pointed down into the village. The little man winked back, then slid over the rise on his belly and down through the undergrowth, nimble as a tadpole through a pond.

Craw worked his dry tongue around his dry mouth. Always ran out of spit at a time like this, and however often he did it, it never got any better. He glanced out the corner of his eye at the others, none of 'em showing much sign of a weak nerve. He wondered if they were bubbling up with worry on the inside, just like he was, and putting a stern face on the wreckage, just like he was. Or if it was only him scared. But in the end it didn't seem to make much difference. The best you could do with fear was act like you had none.

He held his fist up, pleased to see his hand didn't shake, then pointed after Scorry, and they all set off. Down towards the south gate—if you could use the phrase about a gap in a rotten fence under a kind of arch made from crooked branches, skull of some animal unlucky enough to have a fearsome pair of horns mounted in the middle of it. Made Craw wonder if they had a straight piece of wood within a hundred bloody miles.

The one guard left stood under that skull, leaning on his spear, staring at nothing, tangle-haired and fur-clad. He picked his nose, and held one finger up to look at the results. He flicked it away. He stretched, and reached around to scratch his arse. Scorry's knife thudded into the side of his neck and chopped his throat out, quick and simple as a fisher gutting a salmon. Craw winced, just for a moment, but he knew there'd been no dodging it. They'd be lucky if that was the only man who lost his life so they could get this fool job done. Scorry held him a moment while blood showered from his slit neck, caught him as he fell, guided his twitching body soundless to the side of the gate, out of sight of any curious eyes inside.

No more noise than the breeze in the brush, Craw and the rest hurried up the bank, bent double, weapons ready. Scorry was waiting, knife already wiped, peering around the side of the gate post with one hand up behind him to say wait. Craw frowned down at the dead man's bloody face, mouth a bit open as though he was about to ask a question. A potter makes pots. A baker makes bread. And this is what Craw made. All he'd made all his life, pretty much.

It was hard to feel much pride at the sight, however neatly the work had been done. It was still a man murdered just for guarding his own village. Because they were men, these, with hopes and sorrows and all the rest, even if they lived out here past the Crinna and didn't wash too often. But what could one man do? Craw took a long breath in, and let it out slow. Just get the task done without any of his own people killed. In hard times, soft thoughts can kill you quicker than the plague.

He looked at Wonderful, and he jerked his head into the village, and she slid around the gate post and in, slipping across to the right-hand track, shaved head swivelling carefully left and right. Scorry followed at her heels and Brack crept after, silent for all his great bulk.

Craw took a long breath, then crept across to the left-hand track, wincing as he tried to find the hardest, quietest bits of the rutted muck to plant his feet on. He heard the hissing of Yon's careful breath behind him, knew Whirrun was there too, though he moved quiet as a cat. Craw could hear something clicking. A spinning wheel, maybe. He heard someone laugh, not sure if he was imagining it. His head was jerked this way and that to every trace of a sound, like he had a hook through his nose. The whole thing seemed horribly bright and obvious, right then. Maybe they should've waited for darkness, but Craw had never liked working at night. Not since that fucking disaster at Gurndrift where Pale-as-Snow's boys ended up fighting Littlebone's on an accident and more'n fifty men dead without an enemy within ten miles. Too much to go wrong at night.

But then Craw had seen plenty of men die in the day too.

He slid along beside a wattle wall, and he had that sweat of fear on him. That prickling sweat that comes with death right at your shoulder. Everything was picked out sharper than sharp. Every stick in the wattle, every pebble in the dirt. The way the leather binding the grip of his sword dug at his palm when he shifted his fingers. The way each in-breath gave the tiniest whistle when it got three quarters into his aching lungs. The way the sole of his foot stuck to the inside of his boot through the hole in his sock with every careful step. Stuck to it and peeled away.

He needed to get him some new socks, was what he needed. Well, first he needed to live out the day, then socks. Maybe even those ones he'd seen in Uffrith last time he was there, dyed red. They'd all laughed at that. Him, and Yon, and Wonderful, and poor dead Jutlan. Laughed at the madness of it. But afterwards, he'd thought to himself—there's luxury, that a man could afford to have his socks dyed—and cast a wistful glance over his shoulder at that fine cloth. Maybe he'd go back after this fool job was done with, and get himself a pair of red socks. Maybe he'd get himself two pairs. Wear 'em on the outside of his boots just to show folk what a big man he was. Maybe they'd take to calling him Curnden Red Socks. He felt a smile in spite of himself. Red socks, that was the first step on the road to ruin if ever he'd—

The door to a hovel on their left wobbled open and three men walked out of it, all laughing. The one at the front turned his shaggy head, big smile still plastered across his face, yellow teeth sticking out of it. He looked straight at Craw, and Yon, and Whirrun, stuck frozen against the side of a longhouse with their mouths open like three children caught nicking biscuits. Everyone stared at each other.

Craw felt time slow to a weird crawl, that way it did before blood spilled. Enough time to take in silly things. To wonder whether it was a chicken bone through one of their ears. To count the nails through one of their clubs. Eight and a half. Enough time to think it was funny he wasn't thinking something more useful. It was like he stood outside himself, wondering what he'd do but feeling it probably weren't up to him. And the oddest thing of all was that it had happened so often to him now, that feeling, he could recognise it when it came. That frozen, baffled moment before the world comes apart.

Shit. Here I am again—

He felt the cold wind kiss the side of his face as Whirrun swung his sword in a great reaping circle. The man at the front didn't even have time to duck. The flat of the sheathed blade hit him on the side of the head, whipped him off his feet, turned him head over heels in the air, and sent him crashing into the wall of the shack beside them upside down. Craw's hand lifted his sword without being told. Whirrun darted forwards, arm lancing out, smashing the pommel of his sword into the second man's mouth, sending teeth and bits of teeth flying.

While he was toppling back like a felled tree, arms spread wide, the third tried to raise a club. Craw hacked him in the side, steel biting through fur and flesh with a wet thud, spots of blood showering out of him. The man opened his mouth and gave a great high shriek, tottering forward, bent over, eyes bulging. Craw split his skull wide open, sword-grip jolting in his hand, the scream choked off in a surprised yip. The body sprawled, blood pouring from broken head and all over Craw's boots. Looked like he'd come out of this with red socks after all. So much for no more dead, and so much for quiet as a spring breeze too.

"Fuck," said Craw.

By then time was moving way too fast for comfort. The world jerked and wobbled, full of flying dirt as he ran. Screams rang and metal clashed, his own breath and his own heart roaring and surging in his ears. He snatched a glance over his shoulder, saw Yon turn a mace away with his shield and roar as he hacked a man down. As Craw turned back an arrow came from the dead knew where and clicked into the mud wall just in front of him, almost made him fall over backwards with shock. Whirrun went into his arse and knocked him sprawling, gave him a mouthful of mud. When he struggled up a man was charging right at him, a flash of screaming face and wild hair smeared across his sight. Craw was twisting around behind his shield when Scorry slid out from nowhere and knifed the running bastard in the side, made him shriek and stumble sideways, off-balance. Craw took the side of his head off, blade pinging gently as it chopped through bone, then thumped into the ground, nearly jerking from his raw fist.

"Move!" he shouted, not sure who at, trying to wrench his blade free of the earth. Jolly Yon rushed past, head of his axe dashed with red, teeth bared in a mad snarl. Craw followed, Whirrun behind him, face slack, eyes darting from one hut to another, sword still sheathed in one hand. Around the corner of a hovel and into a wide stretch of muck, scattered with ground-up straw. Pigs were honking and squirming in a pen at one side. The hall with the carved uprights stood at the other, steps up to a wide doorway, only darkness inside.

A red-haired man pounded across the ground in front of them, a wood axe in his fist. Wonderful calmly put an arrow through his cheek at six strides distant and he came up short, clapping a hand to his face, still stumbling towards her. She stepped to meet him with a fighting scream, swept her sword out and around and took his head right off. It span into the air, showering blood, and dropped in the pig pen. Craw wondered for a moment if the poor bastard still knew what was going on.

Then he saw the heavy door of the hall being swung shut, a pale face at the edge. "Door!" he bellowed, and ran for it, pounding across squelching mud and up the wooden steps, making the boards rattle. He shoved one bloody, muddy boot in the gap just as the door was slammed and gave a howl, eyes bulging, pain lancing up his leg. "My foot! Fuck!"

There were a dozen Fox Clan or more crowded around the end of the yard now, growling and grunting louder and uglier than the hogs. They waved jagged swords, axes, rough clubs in their fists, a few with shields too, one at the front with a rusted chain hauberk on, tattered around the hem, straggling hair tangled with rings of rough-forged silver.

"Back." Whirrun stood tall in front of them, holding out his sword at long arm's length, hilt up, like it was some magic charm to ward off evil. "Back, and you needn't die today."

The one in mail spat, then snarled back at him in broken Northern. "Show us your iron, thief!"

"Then I will. Look upon the Father of Swords, and look your last." And Whirrun drew it from the sheath.

Men might've had a hundred names for it—Dawn Razor, Grave-Maker, Blood Harvest, Highest and Lowest, Scac-ang-Gaioc in the valley tongue which means the Splitting of the World, and so on, and so on—but Craw had to admit it was a disappointing length of metal. There was no flame, no golden light, no distant trumpets or mirrored steel. Just the gentle scrape as long blade came free of stained leather, the flat grey of damp slate, no shine or ornament about it, except for the gleam of something engraved down near the plain, dull crosspiece.

But Craw had other worries than that Whirrun's sword wasn't worth all the songs. "Door!" he squealed at Yon, scrabbling at the edge of it with his left hand, all tangled up with his shield, shoving his sword through the gap and waving it about to no effect. "My fucking foot!"

Yon roared as he pounded up the steps and rammed into the door with his shoulder. It gave all of a sudden, tearing from its hinges and crushing some fool underneath. Him and Craw burst stumbling into the room beyond, dim as twilight, hazy with scratchy-sweet smoke. A shape came at Craw and he whipped his shield up on an instinct, felt something thud into it, splinters flying in his face. He reeled off-balance, crashed into something else, metal clattering, pottery shattering. Someone loomed up, a ghostly face, a necklace of rattling teeth. Craw lashed at him with his sword, and again, and again, and he went down, white-painted face spattered with red.

Craw coughed, retched, coughed, blinking into the reeking gloom, sword ready to swing. He heard Yon roaring, heard the thud of an axe in flesh and someone squeal. The smoke was clearing now, enough for Craw to get some sense of the hall. Coals glowed in a fire pit, lighting a spider's web of carved rafters in sooty red and orange, casting shifting shadows on each other, tricking his eyes. The place was hot as hell, and smelled like hell besides. Old hangings around the walls, tattered canvas daubed with painted marks. A block of black stone at the far end, a rough statue standing over it, and at its feet the glint of gold. A cup, Craw thought. A goblet. He took a step towards it, trying to waft the murk away from his face with his shield.

"Yon?" he shouted.

"Craw, where you at?"

Some strange kind of song was coming from somewhere, words Craw didn't know but didn't like the sound of. Not one bit. "Yon?" And a figure sprang up suddenly from behind that block of stone. Craw's eyes went wide and he almost fell in the fire pit as he stumbled back.

He wore a tattered red robe; long, sinewy arms sticking from it, spread wide, smeared with paint and beaded up with sweat, the skull of some animal drawn down over his face, black horns curling from it so he looked in the shifting light like a devil bursting straight up from hell. Craw knew it was a mask, but looming up like that out of the smoke, strange song echoing from that skull, he felt suddenly rooted to the spot with fear. So much he couldn't even lift his sword. Just stood there trembling, every muscle turned to water. He'd never been a hero, that was true, but he'd never felt fear like this. Not even at Ineward when he'd seen the Bloody-Nine coming for him, snarling madman's face all dashed with other men's blood. He stood helpless.

"Fuh . . . fuh . . . fuh . . ."

The priest came forward, lifting one long arm. He had a thing gripped in painted fingers. A twisted piece of wood, the faintest pale glow about it.

The thing. The thing they'd come for.

Light flared from it brighter and brighter, so bright it burned its twisted shape fizzing into Craw's eyes, the sound of the song filling his ears until he couldn't hear anything else, couldn't think anything else, couldn't see nothing but that thing, searing bright as the sun, stealing his breath, crushing his will, stopping his breath, cutting his—

Crack. Jolly Yon's axe split the animal skull in half and chopped into the face underneath it. Blood sprayed, hissed in the coals of the fire pit. Craw felt spots on his face, blinked, and shook his head, loosed all of a sudden from the freezing grip of fear. The priest lurched sideways, song turned to a gutturing gurgle, mask split in half and blood squirting from under it. Craw snarled as he swung his sword and it chopped into the sorcerer's chest and knocked him over on his back. The thing bounced from his hand and span away across the rough plank floor, the blinding light faded to the faintest glimmer.

"Fucking sorcerers," snarled Yon, curling his tongue and blowing spit onto the corpse. "Why do they bother? How long does it take to learn all that jabber and it never does you half the good a decent knife . . ." He frowned. "Uh-oh."

The priest had fallen in the fire pit, scattering glowing coals across the floor. A couple had spun as far as the ragged hem of one of the hangings.

"Shit." Craw took a step on shaky legs to kick it away. Before he got there, flame sputtered around the old cloth. "Shit." He tried to stamp it out, but his head was still a touch spinny and he only got embers scattered up his trouser leg, had to hop around, slapping them off. The flames spread, licking up faster'n the plague. Too much flame to put out, spurting higher than a man. "Shit!" Craw stumbled back, feeling the heat on his face, red shadows dancing among the rafters. "Get the thing and let's go!"

Yon was already fumbling with the straps on his leather pack. "Right y'are, chief, right y'are! Backup plan!"

Craw left him and hurried to the doorway, not sure who'd be alive still on the other side. He burst out into the day, light stabbing at his eyes after the gloom.

Wonderful was standing there, mouth hanging wide open. She'd an arrow nocked to her half-drawn bow, but it was pointed at the ground, hands slack. Craw couldn't remember the last time he'd seen her surprised.

"What is it?" he snapped, getting his sword tangled up on the doorframe then snarling as he wrenched it free, "you hurt?" He squinted into the sun, shading his eyes with his shield. "What's the . . ." And he stopped on the steps and stared. "By the dead."

Whirrun had hardly moved, the Father of Swords still gripped in his fist, long, dull blade pointing to the ground. Only now he was spotted and spattered head to toe in blood, and the twisted and hacked, split and ruined corpses of the dozen Fox Clan who'd faced him were scattered around his boots in a wide half-circle, a few bits that used to be attached to them scattered wider still.

"He killed the whole lot." Brack's face was all crinkled up with confusion. "Just like that. I never even lifted my hammer."

"Damndest thing," muttered Wonderful. "Damndest thing." She wrinkled her nose. "Can I smell smoke?"

Yon burst from the hall, stumbled into Craw's back, and nearly sent the pair of them tumbling down the steps. "Did you get the thing?" snapped Craw.

"I think I . . ." Yon blinked at Whirrun, stood tall in his circle of slaughter. "By the dead, though."

Whirrun started to back towards them, twisted himself sideways as an arrow looped over and stuck wobbling into the side of the hall. He waved his free hand. "Maybe we better—"

"Run!" roared Craw. Perhaps a good leader should wait until everyone else gets clear. First man to arrive in a fight and the last to leave. That was how Threetrees used to do it. But Craw wasn't Threetrees, it hardly needed to be said, and he was off like a rabbit with its tail on fire. Leading by example, he'd have called it. He heard bow strings behind him. An arrow zipped past, just wide of his flailing arm, stuck wobbling into one of the hovels. Then another. His squashed foot was aching like fury but he limped on, waving his shield arm. Pounding towards the jerking, wobbling archway with the animal's skull above it. "Go! Go!"

Wonderful tore past, feet flying, flicking mud in Craw's face. He saw Scorry flit between two huts up ahead, then swift as a lizard around one of the gateposts and out of the village. He hurled himself after, under the arch of branches. Jumped down the bank, caught his hurt foot, body jolting, teeth snapping together and catching his tongue. He took one more wobbling step, then went flying, crashed into the boggy bracken, rolled over his shield, just with enough thought to keep his sword from cutting his own nose off. He struggled to his feet, laboured on up the slope, legs burning, lungs burning, through the trees, trousers soaked to the knee with marsh-water. He could hear Brack lumbering along at his shoulder, grunting with the effort, and behind him Yon's growl, "bloody . . . shit . . . bloody . . . running . . . bloody . . . shit . . ."

He tore through the brush and wobbled into the clearing where they'd made their plans. Plans that hadn't flown too smoothly, as it went. Raubin was standing by the gear. Wonderful near him with her hands on her hips. Never was kneeling on the far side of the clearing, arrow nocked to his bow. He grinned as he saw Craw. "You made it then, chief?"

"Shit." Craw stood bent over, head spinning, dragging in air. "Shit." He straightened, staring at the sky, face on fire, not able to think of another word, and without the breath to say one if he had been.

Brack looked even more shot than Craw, if it was possible, crouched over, hands on knees and knees wobbling, big chest heaving, big face red as a slapped arse around his tattoos. Yon tottered up and leaned against a tree, cheeks puffed out, skin shining with sweat.

Wonderful was hardly out of breath. "By the dead, the state o' you fat old men." She slapped Never on the arm. "That was some nice work down there at the village. Thought they'd catch you and skin you sure."

"You hoped, you mean," said Never, "but you should've known better. I'm the best damn runner-away in the North."

"That is a fact."

"Where's Scorry?" gasped Craw, enough breath in him now to worry.

Never jerked his thumb. "Circled 'round to check no one's coming for us."

Whirrun ambled back into the clearing now, hood drawn up

again and the Father of Swords sheathed across his shoulders like a milkmaid's yoke, one hand on the grip, the other dangling over the blade.

"I take it they're not following?" asked Wonderful, one eyebrow raised.

Whirrun shook his head. "Nope."

"Can't say I blame the poor bastards. I take back what I said about you taking yourself too serious. You're one serious fucker with that sword."

"You get the thing?" asked Raubin, face all pale with worry.

"That's right, Raubin, we saved your skin." Craw wiped his mouth, blood on the back of his hand from his bitten tongue. They'd done it, and his sense of humour was starting to leak back in. "Hah. Could you imagine if we'd left the bastard thing behind?"

"Never fear," said Yon, flipping open his pack. "Jolly Yon Cumber, once more the fucking hero." And he delved his hand inside and pulled it out.

Craw blinked. Then he frowned. Then he stared. Gold glinted in the fading light, and he felt his heart sink lower than it had all day. "That ain't fucking it, Yon!"

"It's not?"

"That's a cup! It was the thing we wanted!" He stuck his sword point-down in the ground and waved one hand about. "The bloody thing with the kind of bloody light about it!"

Yon stared back at him. "No one told me it had a bloody light!"

There was silence for a moment then, while they all thought about it. No sound but the wind rustling the old leaves, making the black branches creak. Then Whirrun tipped his head back and roared with laughter. A couple of crows took off startled from a branch it was that loud, flapping up sluggish into the grey sky.

"Why the hell are you laughing?" snapped Wonderful.

Inside his hood Whirrun's twisted face was glistening with happy tears. "I told you I'd laugh when I heard something funny!" And he was off again, arching back like a full-drawn bow, whole body shaking.

"You'll have to go back," said Raubin.

"Back?" muttered Wonderful, her dirt-streaked face a picture of disbelief. "Back, you mad fucker?"

"You know the hall caught fire, don't you?" snapped Brack, one big trembling arm pointing down towards the thickening column of smoke wafting up from the village.

"It what?" asked Raubin as Whirrun blasted a fresh shriek at the sky, hacking, gurgling, only just keeping on his feet.

"Oh, aye, burned down, more'n likely with the damn thing in it."

"Well . . . I don't know . . . you'll just have to pick through the ashes!"

"How about we pick through your fucking ashes?" snarled Yon, throwing the cup down on the ground.

Craw gave a long sigh, rubbed at his eyes, then winced down towards that shit-hole of a village. Behind him, Whirrun's laughter sawed throaty at the dusk. "Always," he muttered, under his breath. "Why do I always get stuck with the fool jobs?"

ABOUT THE EDITORS

Lou Anders is the editorial director of Pyr Books, in which capacity he has been nominated three times for the Best Editor Hugo Award, twice for the Best Art Director Chesley Award (one of which he won), and once for the World Fantasy Award. He is the editor of nine critically acclaimed anthologies, one of which, *Fast Forward 2*, was itself nominated for the Philip K. Dick Award. He is the author of *The Making of Star Trek: First Contact* (Titan Books, 1996), and has published over five hundred articles in such magazines as *The Believer, Publishers Weekly, Dreamwatch, Death Ray, free inquiry, Star Trek Monthly, Star Wars Monthly, Babylon 5 Magazine, Sci Fi Universe, Doctor Who Magazine*, and *Manga Max*. His articles and stories have been translated into Danish, Greek, German, Italian, and French. He lives with his family in Alabama.

Jonathan Strahan is the two-time Hugo Award–nominated editor of the Locus Award–winning anthology *The New Space Opera*, Aurealis Award–winner *The Starry Rift*, the multiple award-winning Eclipse anthology series, and many more. He is the reviews editor for *Locus* and lives in Perth, Australia.

COPYRIGHT NOTICES

Something's wrong with Star!

"You two stay right there," the groom said, turning to point his finger at them before opening the door to the office.

"Yeah, right," Melanie muttered. "Where's Star's stall?"

"I don't know. He wasn't kept in the training barn before I left. He was turned out."

"We'll find him. You go that way." Melanie jerked her thumb to the left. "I'll look this way. He's got to be in one of these stalls."

Melanie strode off in the same direction as the office. Christina hesitated. If she wanted to keep visiting Star, she knew she shouldn't get on Dunkirk's bad side. She was aware from her previous visits that Brad's head trainer kept a close eye on everything.

"I think this is him down here!" Melanie called out.

Suddenly Christina forgot her fears. "Star!" she cried out, and hurried down the aisle. Excited, she halted in front of the colt's stall door. He was turned away from her, his head in the corner as if he were asleep. "Star, it's me."

Slowly the colt swung his head around to gaze at her. Christina gasped. His ears drooped; his eyes were dull.

Star looked so different from the feisty colt she'd seen frolicking in the field a month earlier that she almost didn't recognize him.

"Melanie," Christina whispered, her heart beginning to race, "something's wrong with Star!"

Collect all the books in the
THOROUGHBRED series

THOROUGHBRED Super Editions

ASHLEIGH'S Thoroughbred Collection

* coming soon

THOROUGHBRED

STAR IN DANGER

CREATED BY
JOANNA CAMPBELL

WRITTEN BY
ALICE LEONHARDT

HarperEntertainment
A Division of HarperCollins*Publishers*

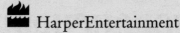

HarperEntertainment

A Division of HarperCollins*Publishers*

10 East 53rd Street, New York, NY 10022-5299

  Produced by 17th Street Productions,
a division of Daniel Weiss Associates, Inc.

HarperCollins books are available at special quantity discounts for bulk
purchases for sales promotions, premiums, or fund-raising.
For information, please call or write:
Special Markets Department, HarperCollins Publishers,
10 East 53rd Street, New York, NY 10022-5299.
Telephone: (212) 207-7528. Fax: (212) 207-7222.

ISBN 0-06-106608-7

First printing: October 1999

Printed in the United States of America

Visit HarperEntertainment on the World Wide Web at
http://www.harpercollins.com

❖ 10 9 8 7 6 5 4 3 2 1

STAR IN DANGER

"THIS NEW FOAL WATCH SYSTEM IS SO COOL!" CHRISTINA Reese exclaimed to her cousin, Melanie Graham. The two girls were kneeling on the floor of the office watching the computer monitor. On-screen, a large bay mare, heavy with foal, circled her stall restlessly.

"Shh," Melanie whispered.

Christina giggled and elbowed her cousin in the arm. Melanie sounded kind of silly telling her to be quiet when Miss America was all the way down in the barn, but Christina had to admit the system did make her feel as though they were right there by the mare's side.

Overhead, she could hear the steady rap of ice crystals hitting the roof of the farmhouse. "It's better than being outside in the freezing rain, anyway," she added.

They could see the bay mare biting at her sides and

1

swishing her tail restlessly. Christina scooted forward to get a better look. Her red-brown hair fell in her face, and she pulled it back in a loose ponytail, twisting a rubber band around it.

"It looks like she's going to foal pretty soon," Melanie said, reaching up to tap the screen. "I saw your dad check her bag today and he said it was starting to drip milk."

"Switch it to the other foaling stall," Christina said. "I want to see how Faith is doing." Melanie pressed a button, and the picture shifted to a pretty chestnut with a white blaze, who was eating her hay contentedly.

"Faith seems pretty calm for her first foal," Melanie said. A year earlier, Leap of Faith had bowed a tendon. She'd been retired after a winning racing season and bred to Whitebrook Farm's prized stallion, Jazzman.

"I'd better tell Mom that Miss America looks like she's ready to foal." Tilting her head back, Christina called out, "Mom!"

Moments later Ashleigh Griffen, Christina's mother, came to the office doorway. She was holding a racing magazine, and Christina felt a little guilty about disturbing her. It was a rare moment when Ashleigh took time to relax.

Christina's parents owned and operated Whitebrook Farm, a small Thoroughbred breeding and racing farm in Kentucky. With three barns and more than thirty horses, things were always busy—especially during foaling season.

2

"What is it?" Ashleigh asked.

"We think Miss America's ready," she told her mother. "Like, any minute now."

Ashleigh smiled tiredly. "Great. Why don't you two put on your rain gear and go out there? Jonnie's on duty."

"Hey," Melanie protested. "I thought that's why you bought this fancy system, so we didn't have to be in the barn."

Ashleigh laughed. "Your father bought the fancy system because he likes gadgets. I still think it's better to be right there with the mares when they foal."

"Good, then *you* can put on *your* rain gear," Melanie joked.

"Make that hail gear," Christina added.

Ashleigh groaned. "The mares always pick the worst nights. Anyway, she hasn't gone down yet—it looks to me like she could still be a while. Why don't you stay here and call me when she starts to really do something? I'll get your father to go out when he gets home from Louisville."

Christina nodded, but when her mother left, she frowned worriedly. Since the beginning of foaling season that year, her mother had avoided the mares and foals as much as she could. Christina knew Ashleigh was still sad about her horse Wonder, who'd died after giving birth the previous March. But a year had passed since then, and Christina had hoped that her mother would be over it by now.

Thinking about Wonder, Christina's thoughts couldn't help but jump to Wonder's Star, Wonder's orphaned foal. And suddenly Christina felt sad. After Wonder died, Ashleigh couldn't stand even to look at Star. So Christina had taken over the orphan's care, quickly falling in love with the beautiful chestnut foal. He was weak at first, and no one was sure whether he would live or die. But Christina persevered, sleeping with the foal in the barn when she could. Under her care, Star grew strong and fit. For the first six months of his life, Christina fed, played, and worked with the rambunctious colt. And now he was gone. Her mother had sent him to live at Townsend Acres, on the other side of Lexington.

"Wait, she's lying down," Melanie said excitedly.

Christina turned her attention back to the monitor. Miss America was bending her knees as if she was going to lie down. Just as abruptly, she straightened and began to pace once more.

"False alarm," Melanie said with a yawn. She rocked back on her heels and nibbled at her apple core. "This is getting kind of boring," she said with a sigh, running her fingers through her short, white-blond hair.

"Well, there's always the exciting world of homework," Christina teased her cousin. "We have a science test tomorrow, remember?"

"Yeah, yeah," Melanie grumbled.

Christina grinned at her cousin's disgruntled expression. They were both sophomores at Henry Clay High, but while Christina was always on the honor roll, Melanie did just enough work to keep from flunking out.

That was only one of the differences between the two cousins. Ever since Melanie had come to live with Christina's family at Whitebrook Farm, she'd been obsessed with racehorses and racing. Under Ashleigh's expert guidance she'd started exercise riding two years ago, and now she couldn't wait to turn sixteen so she could get her jockey's license.

But Christina didn't share her cousin's or her parents' love for racing. She loved eventing. At Christina's level of eventing, there were three phases: the dressage test, the cross-country course, and finally stadium jumping. Christina had broken down the previous summer and started exercise riding, too, but only because it would help her ride her event horse—Sterling Dream—better over cross-country. Sterling was an ex-racehorse, and often acted like one.

The past fall, Christina had hoped to qualify for a three-day event—the next step in her eventing career. But she'd been so busy taking care of Wonder's Star that she hadn't competed as much as she'd hoped.

During the winter she'd thrown herself into getting Sterling fit and ready for the spring eventing season. In April they'd be going to Meadowlark Acres for a local event. But all her training and preparation on Sterling hadn't kept her from desperately missing Star.

With a sigh, Christina leaned back on her hands and stared, unseeing, at the Foal Watch monitor.

"Hey." Melanie broke into her thoughts. "The science test can't be that bad."

"It's not that. I was thinking about Star," Christina answered.

Melanie rolled her eyes. "Come on, Chris. It's not like he moved to Alaska. He's only at Townsend Acres. You can visit him whenever you want."

Townsend Acres was an exclusive Thoroughbred breeding and training farm owned by Brad and Lavinia Townsend. Because of a deal made a long time ago between Ashleigh and Brad Townsend's father, Clay, the Townsends were half owners of all of Wonder's foals. That included Star. Christina had become so attached to the colt that she'd started harboring secret hopes that one day he would be her Olympic event horse. But now that Star had been sent to Townsend Acres, his future was clear—he was destined to become a racehorse.

"In fact, you *do* visit him all the time," Melanie added, grinning slyly. "Not that Star's the *only* reason you hang around the Townsends'."

Christina blushed. The "reason" Melanie was referring was Parker Townsend, Brad and Lavinia's son. Parker was a good friend and shared her love of eventing. He was also kind of cute.

"For your information, Star is the only reason I visit Townsend Acres," Christina replied. "Parker's never at

Townsend Acres. If I want to see him, there's always school or our lessons at Whisperwood."

"What do you mean, *if* you want to see Parker? I think you'd die if you didn't see him every day."

"I would not," Christina shot back—though she had to admit Melanie might be right. "You shouldn't talk, Melanie Graham. You and Kevin are like this." She crossed her two middle fingers.

"Yeah, right," Melanie scoffed, but she didn't deny it. Kevin McLean was the son of Whitebrook Farm's manager, Ian McLean. The McLeans had lived in a cottage at Whitebrook as long as Christina could remember. When Melanie had moved from New York to Kentucky, she and Kevin had hit it off instantly.

Christina got up and went into the family room to get her backpack, though after a grueling lesson on Sterling that afternoon, she didn't feel much like studying, either.

Her mother was settled on the sofa, reading. Her feet were propped on the coffee table, and she held a mug of tea in one hand.

"Comfy?" Christina teased.

Her mother nodded, then sneezed. "I'm trying to beat this cold. I wish spring would just hurry up and get here."

"You always say, 'In like a lion . . . ,'" Christina reminded her. She picked up her backpack. As she was turning to go, Ashleigh called out, "Chris," and Christina turned around, studying her mother with a frown.

"I know you must think I don't care about this crop of foals. . . ." Ashleigh's voice trailed off and the magazine dropped to her lap.

Christina shook her head. "I know you care. Maybe too much. But Mom, you've got to stop thinking about Wonder."

Ashleigh shook her head, her dark hair falling against her cheeks. "Wonder has been a part of my life since I was twelve. That's a long time, Chris. I won't ever forget her."

Christina watched her mother blink back tears, looking down at her magazine as if embarrassed.

"I understand," Christina said softly. And she did. She was just as bad—mooning over Star, a foal she'd cared for and loved for only six months.

Visiting Star at the Townsends' wasn't the same as having him at Whitebrook, either. Brad or his head trainer, Ralph Dunkirk, was always hanging around, watching. Fortunately, Star was thriving. All winter he'd been turned out in a big pasture with the other young colts and fillies. After Wonder died, Star had been alone except for Christina and a nanny goat for company. Being with a group of young horses was just what he'd needed.

Christina glanced over at a framed picture sitting on a lamp table by the sofa. It was a photograph of her mother and Wonder taken the day Clay Townsend had given the mare to Ashleigh.

Crossing the room, Christina picked up the photo.

"I'm glad we got a new frame for it," she said.

Vividly Christina remembered the day the photo had fallen to the floor, smashing the glass and frame. It was the day Ashleigh and Mike had decided to send Star to Townsend Acres. Christina had been furious, until she found her mother sobbing over that same photograph. Only then did she realize why her mother needed to send Star away.

"Whitebrook has never been the same," Christina murmured.

"I know." Her mother's sigh was filled with sadness. "Wonder's death left a big hole."

Except I meant since Star left, Christina wanted to tell her mother. "Melanie and I had better get our homework done," she said instead. Slinging her backpack over one shoulder, Christina headed for the office.

Melanie came racing from the room, almost crashing into her. "She's foaling!" her cousin screamed.

Christina dropped the backpack on the hall floor. "Mom! We're going out to the barn!" she called as she followed Melanie into the kitchen.

The two girls stopped in the mud room of the farmhouse and put on raincoats and boots. "Better take gloves and hats, too," Melanie said when she pushed open the back door. A cold rush of March wind blew in, and Christina could still hear the hail beating against the porch roof.

Flipping her hood over her head, Christina jogged after Melanie. The outside lights of the mare and foal barn were on, illuminating the backyard and drive. Miss America was an experienced broodmare, so no one anticipated problems. Still, there was always a chance something could go wrong.

When they reached the barn, Melanie slid back the heavy door. The lights were on at the far end of the barn. Jonnie, one of Whitebrook's grooms, was standing outside Miss America's foaling stall, a bucket of supplies at his feet.

"Is she okay?" Christina whispered when she and Melanie came down the aisle.

"More than okay." Jonnie stepped back and gestured for them to go up to the stall door. "In fact, you'd better look or you'll miss it."

Moving quietly, Christina and Melanie went up to the wire mesh door. Miss America was lying in the straw, her head turned to her flank. Under the mare's wrapped tail, Christina could see the foal's head and two front hooves.

"Cool!" Melanie gasped. Christina had to agree. Christina had helped her mother when Wonder gave birth to Star the year before. Since then, she'd helped Jonnie or her dad several times. But no matter how often she saw a foal being born, it was still an incredible experience.

Miss America groaned softly, her body tensed, and the rest of the foal slid out. Immediately the mare stood up, turned, and bent to nuzzle her new foal.

"Is it a colt or filly?" Melanie asked excitedly.

"Right now I only care that it's healthy," Jonnie said. Picking up the bucket, he opened the stall door.

"Can Melanie and I do it?" Christina asked.

Grinning, Jonnie handed Christina the bucket and Melanie the lead line. "Sure."

Christina went in, crooning softly to the mare. Melanie was right behind her, talking baby talk under her breath: "Hey, widdle foal, you're so cu-u-te and . . . slimy."

Christina laughed as Melanie clipped the lead to the mare's halter. Miss America's ears flicked anxiously, but she stood quietly. Stooping down, Christina took a soft towel and cleaned out the foal's nostrils. Then she dipped the stub of its umbilical cord in iodine. The little filly shook her head and blinked up at Christina with soft brown eyes.

"She's perfect!" Christina announced, stepping back as the filly made her first attempt to stand.

"Hmmm. Miss Perfect," Melanie said. "How's that sound for your new name, little girl?"

When the two had finished, they left the mare and her foal alone. Christina checked her watch. It was almost ten o'clock, and they still had their science test to study for. "You two go on back to the house. I'll wait and make sure she nurses," Jonnie reassured them.

"Call if you need anything," Melanie said seriously. She sounded so much like Ashleigh, Christina had to smile.

By the time the two girls headed back outside, the hail had stopped. A layer of ice was covering the fences and trees.

11

"A winter wonderland," Melanie said.

Like the night Star was born. Sadness filled Christina as she thought back to that special night, and for the thousandth time she wished with all her heart that Star were home with her.

"Whoa. That was a gloomy sigh," Melanie said, breaking into Christina's thoughts.

"I was thinking how much I miss Star."

"Again? Why don't you just ask your mom and dad to bring him home?"

Stopping in her tracks, Christina turned to face Melanie. A shower of ice from the branches above pelted the hood of her raincoat. "I can't. Mom's still so upset. She's still in mourning over Wonder."

"Just tell her you love Star as much as she loves Wonder," Melanie said. "That will convince her."

Christina eyed Melanie suspiciously. Lately her cousin had been making so much sense it worried her. Then she smiled. "You're right. I'll do it."

"Go for it." Melanie punched her playfully on the shoulder.

As they started for the house again, Christina grinned happily. Her heart felt lighter than it had all winter. When she went in the house, she hurriedly kicked off her boots and hung up her coat.

"I'm going to head upstairs and start studying," Melanie said as she passed Christina. "Good luck with your mom."

"See you in a few minutes." Christina went into the

12

family room. The magazine was on the sofa; her mother wasn't.

"Mom!" Christina called. She walked down the hall and peeked into the office. A half-empty mug of tea sat next to the monitor. On-screen, Christina could see Miss America and her new foal, who flicked her tail as she nursed.

Christina touched the mug. It was still warm. Her mother had been there, watching to make sure everything was all right. Christina heard the slam of the kitchen door. Keys jingled as someone dropped them on the table. Her dad was home.

She hurried into the kitchen. Her father stood in front of the open refrigerator door, his blond hair tousled. When he turned to look at Christina, she could see dark rings around his eyes.

"Hey there, Chris," he said, smiling tiredly.

"I'll make you a sandwich," Christina offered. "Were the roads really bad?"

"Icy. I'm glad we didn't have a van full of horses." Mike slumped into a kitchen chair, his coat still on. He and Ian had been to Louisville to look over some yearlings, but it sounded as though they hadn't brought any home. "Where's your mom?"

"In bed, I think. She's catching a cold. So—you find anything you like?"

"Nope. Some had good bloodlines, but there was something about every one that I didn't like."

Christina nodded as she pulled bread and cheese

from the fridge. Her father had been in the horse business forever. He had a good eye as well as good intuition about horses.

"That's too bad." She brought over his sandwich and a glass of milk, then slid into the chair across from him. "But I know of a really good-looking colt."

"Yeah?" Mike arched one brow. "Whose? How much?"

"Ours. And he's free." Christina held her breath.

Her father shook his head. "Don't start, Christina."

"What do you mean?"

"Don't start pestering me about bringing Star home."

"Why not?"

"You know the situation. Your mother's not ready."

Disappointment flared in Christina's chest. "But Wonder's been dead a year. If she's not ready now, she'll never be!"

Her dad gave her a stern look. "You'll just have to wait and see."

Christina blew out her breath. Her dad was usually so fair. Why was he being so stubborn? Why couldn't he see her side? "I'm tired of waiting. I want Star to come home." Before she could stop them, tears began to roll down her cheeks.

"I know it's hard, Chris . . . ," her father said.

Christina dashed the tears away with the back of her hand and hurried out of the kitchen and up the stairs, taking the steps by twos. When she reached her bedroom, she ran in and flung herself on her bed, narrowly missing Melanie, who was leaning against the head-board, a science book open on her lap.

"I take it she said no," Melanie commented, tossing her book to the side.

"*He* said no," Christina corrected, and buried her face in her pillow.

Melanie whistled. "Wow. I figured that at least your dad would be rooting for you."

"Me too."

"Hey, don't give up. We just have to come up with plan B."

"Plan B?" Christina asked. She propped herself on one elbow and looked hopefully at her cousin. Melanie was famous for her devious schemes.

Melanie frowned. "I'm still working on plan B."

Christina buried her face back into her pillow. *Then I'll just have to come up with plan B myself,* she thought.

One thing she was sure of: She wasn't going to give up. She loved Star too much.

Star didn't belong at Townsend Acres. He belonged at Whitebrook, with her.

But Christina had to think of a way to get him back.

2

"THERE YOU GO, MR. SPOILED," CHRISTINA SAID. STAR hung his head over the fence, and she fed him one more carrot. Four other Townsend Acres yearlings pushed and crowded around him. Whipping around, Star pinned his ears and cocked his hind leg menacingly, and they scattered. Then he turned back to lip the carrot gently from Christina's palm.

While the colt munched happily, Christina scratched under his forelock. When she'd visited him two days earlier, she'd curried him hard, sending clouds of fuzzy winter hair sailing into the breeze. Now there was a patch of sleek, copper-colored coat gleaming on his neck.

"I can't wait to see you when you've shedded out," Christina told him as she traced the heart-shaped star on his forehead. "I have to go ride Sterling, but I'll curry you again tomorrow, promise."

That winter, while Star's coat had grown long and shaggy, his legs had grown even longer. He was almost a hand taller than the other colts, and awkward and gangly. But as he turned and raced with the other yearlings across the field, he quickly took the lead.

Christina smiled. Just like his mother, he had the makings of a champion. When she was a three-year-old, Wonder had won the Kentucky Derby. Would Star do the same in two years?

Resting her arms on the top board of the fence, Christina stared across the rolling hills of Townsend Acres. The farm was perfectly manicured. Beds of daffodils and hyacinths were starting to bloom despite the late cold snap. In the distance, the manor house stood on a hill, a two-story brick house with stately white columns. The farm had five large barns designed to match the colonial-style house, many paddocks, fields, and sheds, and an oval training track.

The place was gorgeous but cold, and not because of the crisp wind, Christina decided. Whitebrook wasn't as lovely, but it bustled along cheerfully. The horses and the staff always seemed happy. During her visits to see Star over the winter, Christina had noticed that although the staff at Townsend Acres worked hard, there was little enthusiasm. And the head trainer, Mr. Dunkirk, did nothing to lift their spirits. He was an unpleasant man, intent only on breaking horses quickly and making them run fast at any cost.

I wish Parker would hurry, Christina thought as she turned her attention back to the frolicking colts. She'd taken the bus home with him after school, and he'd run in to change into his riding clothes while she visited Star. He was going to drop her off at Whitebrook so she could change and tack up Sterling. At five they would share a dressage lesson at Whisperwood, Samantha and Tor Nelson's farm. Parker kept his horse, Foxglove, at the Nelsons'. But Christina lived close enough to hack Sterling over to Whisperwood for lessons in the indoor arena.

"What do you think?" said a man behind Christina. "Is he a Derby winner?"

Christina swung around. Brad Townsend came up beside her and leaned one elbow on the top of the fence. Parker's father was handsome, with salt-and-pepper hair, and was immaculately dressed in pressed khakis and a navy blue jacket. He was always polite to Christina, but whenever she saw him, she had a hard time being cordial in return. She couldn't help remembering all the times he and his wife, Lavinia, had treated Parker so indifferently—all the times they'd chosen money or prestige over kindness, even when it came to their own son. Christina had decided that the only reason Parker had turned into a decent human being was his kind grandfather, Clay.

"I don't know. He might be on the next winning

Olympic eventing team, though," Christina countered. "He's got the right conformation for jumping."

Brad snorted. "Come on, Christina. You can't think for a second that one of Wonder's colts is going to do anything but race."

She shrugged. "No, I'm sure he'll race. But maybe he won't like it the way Wonder did. Maybe he'll like eventing more, like Parker and me."

"Hmpf." Brad stared out over the field, ignoring Christina's jab. Mr. Townsend was not at all enthusiastic about Parker's interest in eventing.

In the middle of the pasture, Star sparred with another colt. They reared, their long legs lashing the air.

"That colt has more energy than he knows what to do with. Tell your mother and father that we're going to begin his training next week," Brad said. "We'll start backing him at the end of the month."

Utterly shocked, Christina gasped and spun around to face him. "What? But that's crazy! He's only a yearling."

"We start all our yearlings in the spring."

"But most yearlings aren't ready! Their knees aren't closed. If you put someone on Star now, you could ruin him for good." At Whitebrook, Ashleigh and Mike never started backing a horse—putting the weight of a human on its back—until it was a good eighteen months old, and sometimes older; it depended on how quickly the colt matured and was able to handle the emotional and physical stress of training.

19

Brad's face had turned a deep, angry red. "Young lady," he snapped, "how dare you tell me how to train racehorses?"

"I've been around racehorses all my life, too," Christina retorted. "And at Whitebrook we don't start our horses until late—"

"I don't care what you do at Whitebrook," Brad cut her off. "Townsend Acres is one of the finest Thoroughbred farms on the East Coast. I don't think I need to defend our training methods to you."

"What's going on?" Parker came striding across the lawn, his brow furrowed as he glanced from his father to Christina. He wore tan riding breeches and tall black boots. His dark hair hung shaggy and soft around his neck. Christina immediately noticed how much he looked like his father.

"Nothing," Christina said quickly. She knew how volatile Brad and Parker's relationship was, and she didn't want them getting into an argument over her. "We were just discussing Star's training."

"Oh," Parker said, looking unconvinced.

"Ready to go?" Christina asked, striding toward Parker's truck. Her heart was pounding, and she needed to get away before she said something terrible to Brad Townsend in front of his son.

"Uh, bye, Dad," Parker said hastily as he hurried after Christina. "What's going on?" he asked again as he pulled his door shut and started the engine.

"Nothing." Christina pressed her lips together. More

than anything she wanted to tell Parker, but she didn't want him to get caught in the middle of a battle between her and his father. So she remained quiet as they pulled down Townsend Acres' driveway, her pulse still racing in outrage.

Townsend Acres might start all their yearlings in the early spring, but Christina knew Star wasn't ready. And she was sure that her father and mother would agree. When she told them what Brad was going to do, they would realize she was right. They'd *have* to change their minds about leaving the colt at Townsend Acres. They'd have to bring Star home.

"So nothing's wrong," Parker said, breaking into her thoughts. "You're just ignoring me completely for absolutely no reason."

Christina turned to study his profile. *What can I say?* she wondered. *Your father is going to ruin Star if I don't get him out of there—fast.* Parker had enough trouble with his parents, and she didn't want to add to it. "I'm sorry, Parker. I guess I just hate leaving Star," she answered lamely.

"Well, *I* don't mind having Star living at my place. Not if it means I get to see you more," Parker said, flashing her a sly smile.

Christina knew he was trying to be sweet, but Parker had said completely the wrong thing. She pressed her lips together and stared out the window. They were close to Whitebrook, but it was getting late— she'd have to hurry if she was going to talk to her parents about Star and still make her lesson on time.

Parker pulled over at the end of Whitebrook's driveway.

"Chris, are you *sure* there's nothing you want to tell me?" Parker tried once more as he stopped the truck, letting the engine idle.

"See you there," Christina said, hopping from the truck and slamming the door.

She could feel Parker staring after her as she jogged up the drive, but she didn't look back. She just had to hope he'd understand.

Christina found her mother in the training barn. Ashleigh was bent over in the aisle, wrapping a two-year-old colt's front leg.

"How was school?" Ashleigh asked without looking up. Christina stopped in front of the chestnut colt, who threw up his head, jingling the crossties. "Easy, Highlight," Christina crooned. After giving him a soothing pat, she replied, "It was okay. The science test was hard, but I think I did pretty well."

Ashleigh straightened. Hands on her hips, she inspected the wrapped leg.

"I saw Star this afternoon," Christina said. "And I talked to Mr. Townsend," she added, suddenly hesitant to dive right in and tell her mother everything. What if Ashleigh still insisted that Star had to stay at Townsend Acres?

"How is Brad?" her mother asked as she bent to wrap the other leg. "I haven't seen him in a while."

"He said he's going to start backing Star this spring!" Christina blurted, unable to hold it in any longer.

Ashleigh continued to wind the stretchy red wrap around Highlight's left leg. "Really?"

Openmouthed, Christina stared down at her mother. Highlight stamped his right foot impatiently.

"*Really?*" Christina repeated. "That's all you can say? Didn't you hear me? They're backing Star—*soon*. We never start our yearlings until at least August. He'll be ruined!"

Ashleigh secured the Velcro on the wrap, then stood up to face Christina. "A lot of farms start their horses in the spring," she said. "Brad knows what he's doing. I'm sure he wouldn't hurt Star. Come on, Highlight, let's put you back in your stall." Reaching up, she unsnapped the crossties.

Christina couldn't believe her mother's indifference. Her heart thumped wildly as she followed Ashleigh and Highlight down the aisle. "What about all the stories you've told me about how Brad treated Wonder?" Christina demanded. "Didn't he try to make her lose one of her races on purpose?"

"That was a long time ago," Ashleigh pointed out. "I'll admit, we've had our differences through the years, but Brad's a respected horseman and Townsend Acres has an excellent reputation."

"Okay, maybe Brad is Mr. Big-Deal Trainer, but he

doesn't know Star. Not the way I do. He's not ready. I just know it."

Ashleigh glanced at Christina with an amused expression. "Aren't you being a little melodramatic?" she asked before leading Highlight into his stall.

"No!" Christina answered angrily. "If Star wasn't Wonder's colt, you'd agree with me. I know it. You just don't want Star at Whitebrook, no matter what. It's not fair!"

Her mother came out of Highlight's stall and shut the door. Her expression was so pained that Christina instantly regretted what she had said. "I'm sorry, I didn't mean to sound so mean," she said, touching her mother's arm. "I know you still miss Wonder. But I miss Star. *A lot.* I just want you to understand."

Ashleigh's smile was thin. "And I do, Chris. I'm just not ready to have Star at Whitebrook. I know that sounds selfish, but seeing him every day would—" Raising her hand, Ashleigh pressed her fingers against her mouth as if holding back a sob.

Tears pricked Christina's own eyes. She wrapped her arm around her mother's shoulders. "No, I'm the one who's being selfish," Christina insisted. "I'm sorry." And she was. Sorry that Ashleigh was still so sad about Wonder's death. Sorry that Star was like a living reminder of Wonder.

And most of all, sorry that Star couldn't come home.

"YOU FINALLY MADE IT," PARKER CALLED WHEN CHRISTINA rode Sterling Dream into Whisperwood's indoor arena. He was already warming up Foxglove, his bay mare. The sun was low in the sky and the ground outside was muddy—it would be another month or so before they could have their dressage lessons outdoors.

"Sorry I'm late," Christina said. "Sterling took a mud bath and it took me forever to clean her." Which was true, Christina told herself. Just not the whole truth.

On the ride from Whitebrook to Whisperwood, Christina had mulled over every word she'd said to her mother. How could she have approached her differently? What could she have said that would have changed her mother's mind?

Christina halted Sterling in the center of the large indoor arena and reached down to check her girth.

Eager to get moving, Sterling stepped sideways.

"Whoa," Christina said, sitting back and tightening her hold on the reins so the mare would stand squarely in the soft footing. Turning her head, Sterling looked up at Christina with her huge brown eyes. Then she bobbed her head as if to say, *Hurry up!*

"Almost ready," Christina said, reaching up to stroke the mare's neck. She'd kept a blanket on Sterling all winter, and her dappled gray coat felt silky smooth.

Parker and Foxy trotted a circle in front of them. As Christina adjusted her helmet strap, she couldn't help watching them. Lately Foxy had been performing beautifully, and Parker looked great, too. Foxy had a wide barrel, but Parker's long legs fit perfectly around her. His hands and body were relaxed, moving rhythmically to the mare's long stride as she lengthened at the trot.

At the Meadowlark Acres event, Christina and Parker would both be competing at the preliminary level. Parker and Foxy were definitely ready. But even though the event was still seven weeks away, Christina knew she wasn't ready. She'd been spending too many afternoons that winter with Star instead of schooling and conditioning Sterling.

"Looking good!" Christina called out to her friend.

Parker grinned in reply, but he didn't break his concentration.

Christina gathered her reins, and Sterling strode off. They trotted in a large circle to warm up. As Christina

26

rode past the blue plastic mounting block, she smiled to herself. Every time she saw the block, she pictured Star and Nana, Star's baby-sitting goat, standing on a similar block in the paddock at Whitebrook. The goat had been a lot of trouble to have around, but she had done miracles for Star. Before Nana, Star had been shy, a weak shadow of the horse Christina had known he could be. Nana had brought the colt out of his shell.

With her mind on Star, the conversation with Brad came flying back. How could he think of starting Star so early? If only she could train him herself—

Suddenly Sterling ducked her head and gave a playful buck. Christina flew forward, grabbing a hunk of mane at the last second. Her feet slipped from the stirrups and she fell on the mare's neck.

Flushing hotly, she regained her balance, sat deep in the saddle, and pulled Sterling to a halt. "No bucking," she scolded.

"You can't blame her." Samantha Nelson, Ian McLean's daughter, came striding across the arena. Earmuffs held back her thick red hair, and just like father, Ian, and her brother, Kevin, she had freckles sprinkled across her nose and cheeks.

Christina blew out her breath in frustration. "I know—it's cold and she's feeling fresh," she said, making excuses for Sterling's behavior.

"That's not what I'm talking about." Samantha put a gloved hand on Sterling's neck. The gray mare rooted her head, trying to pull the reins from Christina's fingers. "She bucked because she knew she could get away with it. You weren't paying one bit of attention to her."

"Oh." Christina dropped her gaze to Sterling's mane. Samantha was right. As usual, Christina had been thinking about Star.

"You know, Chris, being able to focus is as important as being a skillful rider," Sam said seriously. "When you're riding preliminary at a three-day event, you'll be jumping complex courses of fences almost four feet high with even larger spreads. One mistake and you could have a terrible accident. You absolutely cannot get distracted."

Chris hung her head, unable to look Sam in the eye. "I know. And if I don't concentrate in dressage, Sterling will probably put a buck in every other stride."

"Right. So, what's so distracting, anyway?"

Christina shrugged. Should she tell Sam how worried she was about Star? Sam and Ashleigh were close friends. Maybe Sam could help her convince her mother to take Star back. "It's Star," she admitted.

"Wonder's foal?"

Christina nodded. On the other side of the arena, she saw Parker and Foxy slow to a walk. Parker patted Foxy, but his attention was on Christina, as if he was wondering what she and Sam were talking about.

"I just found out that Mr. Townsend is going to start backing him in a couple of weeks," Chris told her.

Sam didn't say anything. She just looked up at

Christina expectantly, as if she was waiting for her to say something else.

"Okay," Samantha said finally. "So what's the problem?"

"But that *is* the problem," Christina said impatiently. "Star's not ready."

"Brad knows what he's doing, Chris. He's trained some great horses—he's not an idiot."

Christina rolled her eyes. Samantha sounded just like her mother. "I didn't say he was. He just doesn't know Star the way I do. Star shouldn't be rushed. Look how careful you've been with your filly. Star's a lot like her."

Samantha smiled and put her hand on Christina's knee. "I'm training Sweet Dreams to be an event horse, Chris. That's completely different from training a racehorse. You know that."

Christina nodded. "Yeah, but I know I'm right. Star should be home at Whitebrook. I miss him, and we're the ones that should be training him."

"But you don't have time to miss him *or* train him," Samantha reminded her. "Remember your dream—the Young Riders program and then the Olympics? If you don't pay attention to Sterling, you're not even going to move up to three-day events this year. That means no Young Riders program."

The Young Riders was a special intensive training program for promising riders. Many of its students wound up on the Olympic team. The age limit for the

Young Riders was sixteen, so Christina had only one more year to prove that she was worthy.

"You're right." Christina agreed, and straightened in the saddle.

"Besides, Star is going to be a racehorse. You wouldn't be working with him even if he was at Whitebrook. Or are you still dreaming that he'll be your next event horse?"

Christina blew out her breath. "No," she answered, though she wasn't sure if she meant it or not.

Samantha patted Sterling's neck. "You've already got a talented horse, Chris, and you're a gifted rider. But you know it takes more than that to make it to the Olympics."

"Right. Focus. Determination. Drive." Christina repeated the mantra that Sam chanted in almost every one of her lessons.

Samantha laughed. "You've got it. Now let's see you put it into practice."

Feeling a little better, Christina steered Sterling to the outside wall. Sitting deep, she collected the mare and squeezed her into a sitting trot. Samantha was right. If she was going to do well that year and move from one-day to three-day events, she had to forget about Star and concentrate.

I won't even visit him, Christina promised herself silently. *It will be easier that way—for both of us.*

It was probably for the best. Her mother's feelings

about Star were clear, and Christina had to respect them—Star would stay at Townsend Acres. The colt's future was in racing, anyway. One day Star would be a champion racehorse like his mother, and Christina would cheer him on from the stands.

4

THE WARM WIND CARESSED CHRISTINA'S CHEEKS AS SHE trotted Rascal clockwise around the oval track. It was a beautiful morning on the last day of March, and it finally felt as if spring had arrived. At least Rascal thought it had arrived. The jet black two-year-old was in such high spirits, he wanted to run, not jog. A wind-blown leaf made him skitter sideways, and a flock of sparrows taking off from the track made him brace his legs and halt in terror.

"Those are *birds*," Chris scolded good-naturedly. She had caught spring fever, too. Easter vacation started in one week, and she couldn't wait to get out of school. Then she'd have a whole week to work with Sterling *and* exercise racehorses, every day, for as long as she wanted.

I'm sounding more and more like Melanie, Chris thought as she squeezed her legs against Rascal's sides. She really did enjoy riding the racehorses, and working with youngsters such as Rascal had helped to take her mind off Star.

Christina hadn't visited Star in four weeks. She'd convinced herself that the only way to get Star out of her mind was to stop seeing him. That way she wouldn't worry over every little thing that was happening to him at Townsend Acres. At least that had been her plan. Unfortunately, it hadn't worked. She still thought about him constantly. That day she was going to break her boycott and pay Star a visit.

On the inside rail, Melanie came galloping toward them mounted on Pride's Heart. The sight set Rascal off again. He neighed excitedly, then spun in a circle, almost slamming into the outside rail.

"Whoa," Christina called, making him halt. For a second the colt stood quietly, his nostrils flared. Then Christina sat deep and, using her body and legs, urged him forward at a trot once more. When they reached the quarter-mile pole, she urged Rascal into a gallop. She breezed him the last quarter mile, his long, smooth stride carrying him swiftly across the finish line.

"Good boy." Leaning down, she stroked his neck. Melanie and Heart, who were finished with their gallop, were walking toward them. Pride's Heart, a three-year-old chestnut filly with a large white heart on her forehead, had been laid up over the winter. Melanie was getting her fit again for the spring racing season.

"Good workout?" Christina asked.

"The best. Her first race is three weeks from today."

"But that's the same day as the Meadowlark event," Christina said.

"I know. But don't worry—I'm still going to groom for you, and Kevin's going to groom for Parker. It'll be fun," Melanie assured her.

"You don't mind missing the race?"

"Nah. Watching you and Sterling charge around knocking down fences is much more fun," Melanie teased.

Christina grinned. They were so different and their relationship had been a little rocky to start with, but she felt lucky to have her cousin for a friend.

Worn out by his workout, Rascal followed Heart calmly through the gate.

"Do you want to go over to the Townsends' after lunch?" Christina asked Melanie as they rode the horses side by side back to the barn.

"Sure," Melanie said, sounding surprised. "So you're finally breaking down. How long has it been?"

"Almost a month." Christina's shoulders slumped. "Believe me, it wasn't easy."

Melanie halted Heart outside the training barn. Ian was leading two yearlings out to the paddocks, and inside Christina could hear her father talking to one of the grooms.

"I bet when we get to Townsend Acres, you'll find out that Star's doing great," Melanie reassured her.

"I hope so," Christina said. She dismounted and quickly ran up her stirrups. Now that she'd decided to visit Star, she couldn't wait to see him.

"Doesn't this place kind of give you the creeps?" Christina asked Melanie as they hurried up Townsend Acres' driveway. Jonnie had just dropped them off, and he would be picking them up in an hour on his way back from town, so they didn't have much time. White board fence and Bradford pear trees just starting to bloom bordered both sides of the lane. In the pasture on the right were several mares with brand-new foals, and in the pasture on the left were several very pregnant broodmares.

Melanie furrowed her brow. "You mean like haunted-house creeps?" she asked Christina.

"No. Creeps as in the place is too perfect." Christina swept her arm in front of her. "Every blade of grass is the same length. There aren't any weeds. The trees are all the same size, like clones or something, and the fence is totally white. I bet when we get to the barns, there won't be a speck of dust anywhere."

Melanie nodded as she glanced around. "You're right. And I thought Ashleigh was picky."

"Not compared to Brad Townsend," Christina said.

"I don't see Star anywhere, do you?" Melanie asked.

Christina bit her lip, gazing out across the fields to the pasture where Star was usually turned out. There were two bay colts and a roan filly, but no Star.

"Maybe he's in the training barn," Christina said.

They took a shortcut across the lawn of the manor house. Melanie suddenly stooped and then held up a yellow flower. "A dandelion!" she cried in mock horror. She and Chris raced the rest of the way, giggling.

Several cars were parked outside the training barn. Chris hoped Brad wasn't home. She wanted to see Star without him watching over her.

They paused to let their eyes adjust to the darker interior of the barn. In the aisle, a young horse in crossties was being groomed. Otherwise the place was quiet.

"Hi," Christina said, walking up to the groom—a stocky blue-eyed boy who looked about eighteen. He stopped brushing the horse. "You girls want something?" he asked.

"I'm Christina Reese, from Whitebrook, and this is my cousin, Melanie. We're visiting Wonder's Star, one of the yearling colts."

"Do you have permission?"

"My family is half owner," Christina said.

"Really," Melanie said, stepping forward. "We don't need permission."

The kid made a scoffing noise in his throat. "Yeah, you do. Let me ask Mr. Dunkirk." Dropping the brush into a grooming box, he turned and walked toward the barn office.

Christina groaned. "Oh, great. Not Dunkirk. He'll tell us we have to come back when King Brad is here."

"You two stay right there," the groom said, turning to point his finger at them before opening the door to the office.

"Yeah, right," Melanie muttered. "Where's Star's stall?"

"I don't know. He wasn't kept in the training barn before I left. He was turned out."

"We'll find him. You go that way." Melanie jerked her thumb to the left. "I'll look this way. He's got to be in one of these stalls."

Melanie strode off in the same direction as the office. Christina hesitated. If she wanted to keep visiting Star, she knew she shouldn't get on Dunkirk's bad side. She was aware from her previous visits that Brad's head trainer kept a close eye on everything.

"I think this is him down here!" Melanie called out.

Suddenly Christina forgot her fears. "Star!" she cried out, and hurried down the aisle. Excited, she halted in front of the colt's stall door. He was turned away from her, his head in the corner as if he were asleep. "Star, it's me."

Slowly the colt swung his head around to gaze at her. Christina gasped. His ears drooped; his eyes were dull.

Star looked so different from the feisty colt she'd seen frolicking in the field a month earlier that she almost didn't recognize him.

"Melanie," Christina whispered, her heart beginning to race, "something's wrong with Star!"

5

"STAR? HEY, BOY." CHRISTINA THREW BACK THE LATCH AND opened the stall door. She pulled a carrot from her back pocket. Holding it in front of her, she walked around to the colt's head. "It's me, boy. See?"

When she reached out and slid the carrot under Star's muzzle, his nostrils puffed in and out as he smelled it. Then, listlessly, he took it from her palm and ate it.

"Is it him?" Melanie asked dubiously. She stood in the doorway of the stall, nervously glancing over her shoulder toward the office door.

"It's him." Christina ran her hand down his neck. His winter coat had fallen out, but his new coat seemed rough and dry—not the gleaming coppery coat he was supposed to have.

"Is he okay?" Melanie continued. "They've got him

39

down here by himself. There aren't any horses in the stalls around him. It's like he's been quarantined."

"No, he's not okay," Christina said, frowning. *How long has Star been like this?* she wondered desperately.

"Uh-oh. The watchdog's coming," Melanie suddenly warned.

"Hey, what're you girls doing in there?" Christina heard the young groom call out, striding toward them.

"Looking at our horse," Melanie hollered back. She turned to face him, planting herself in front of the open stall door.

Christina studied Star more closely. His chest was creased with dried sweat, and there was a matted saddle mark on his back, as if he hadn't been bathed or groomed since he'd been worked.

Walking around to the other side, she checked his legs. His ankles were stocked up—puffy with fluid, as if he'd been standing in the stall after hard exercise. Manure caked his hocks, and patches of dirty winter hair still covered his belly.

Christina frowned. Not only had Star's personality changed, but no one was taking care of him. Something was definitely wrong. Her heart pounded in pity and anger—who could have done this?

Suddenly Christina heard the office door slam. Then someone bellowed, "What in the devil is going on? What're you girls doing in there?"

Mr. Dunkirk. Christina gritted her teeth. Usually she steered clear of Brad's rough-talking head trainer. But not that day. She had to stand up for Star.

"We're looking at *our* horse," Christina heard Melanie say bravely.

"Look, I know you're Ashleigh and Mike's niece, but no one said you could go in there. In fact, *no one's* supposed to go in there."

Clenching her fists, Christina stepped around Star and stood beside Melanie. "Why not?" she demanded. "Is Star sick? Is he in quarantine? Why haven't you told my parents?"

Her questions stopped Dunkirk in his tracks. He was a beefy man with a belly hanging over his belt and a tan, leathery complexion from working outside year round. Christina had heard stories about Dunkirk. Some people said he was able to break even the most recalcitrant of horses.

"Star's not sick," Dunkirk said. "But if you want any other answers, you're going to have to ask Mr. Townsend."

"Where is he?"

"He and Mrs. Townsend are in Lexington for the afternoon. They'll be back later. Don't worry, I'll tell him you were here."

Stepping closer, he took hold of the stall door as if to shut it. Christina stood rooted to the spot. She didn't want to leave Star until she had some answers.

"If he's not sick, why is he all by himself?" she asked.

Dunkirk folded his arms against his chest. "You'll

have to ask Mr. Townsend," he repeated, his eyes narrowing.

"And why is he so dirty?" Christina continued. "Surely you can answer that."

Dunkirk shot the groom an annoyed look. "Weren't you supposed to clean him up?"

"Uh . . ." The groom flushed red.

Christina couldn't help noticing how tense the groom was.

"Then do it!" Dunkirk barked.

"Yes, sir." Turning on his boot heels, the groom went back to the horse still standing in crossties and unhooked him.

"Don't forget to tell Mr. Townsend we were here," Christina said to Mr. Dunkirk, her voice shaking. "And tell him my parents and I will be over tonight to check on Star."

Dunkirk grunted. "I'll do that. Now you two get going."

"Come on, Chris." Melanie linked her arm with Christina's. "Let's get out of here." Christina gave Star one last look before leaving. He hadn't moved. The poor colt was still standing quietly, his head hanging low.

When the girls got outside, they both exhaled in relief. "Whew. Am I glad to get out of there," Melanie said as they headed down the drive. "That Dunkirk is a real meathead."

"A mean and stubborn meathead," Christina grumbled. A hundred feet from the barn, she stopped in her tracks. "He was definitely keeping something from us," she told Melanie. "Something's wrong with Star. I can feel it."

"I think Dunkirk's just too scared to tell us anything without King Brad's permission."

"I guess," Christina agreed reluctantly as she followed Melanie down the drive. When they passed one of the pastures, she thought about the last time she'd seen Star. He'd been racing around the field with his friends. How could the colt have changed so much in only four weeks?

Stopping under a pear tree, Melanie turned to Christina. "Dunkirk said Star wasn't sick. Do you believe that?"

Christina shrugged. "I guess. My parents have known Dunkirk for years. They've never said anything bad about him other than that he's a little rough," she admitted. "But if Star's not sick, what could be wrong with him?"

Melanie shook her head. "I don't know. And I also wonder why Parker hasn't said anything about Star."

"Parker's hardly ever home, and when he is, he kind of stays away from the barn," Christina said.

"But didn't you ask him to keep an eye on Star?"

Christina shook her head. "No. I never really told Parker how worried I am about Star. He and his dad don't get along as it is. I didn't want to give them something more to argue about, so I just told Parker I wasn't coming over to see Star anymore because I needed to concentrate on getting ready for Meadowlark."

Melanie chewed on her lip a second, then linked her arm with Christina's. "Come on, there's Jonnie waiting for us. You promised Dunkirk your parents would be coming by later—we'd better go tell them that Star's in trouble."

Half an hour later Christina found her father in Whitebrook's breeding barn. Melanie had stopped to help Kevin bathe a feisty weanling.

Mike was standing in the aisle, talking to a well-dressed couple. George Ballard, the stallion manager, was leading Jazzman, one of Whitebrook's stallions, up and down the wide aisle. The handsome coal black stallion arched his neck and pranced sideways as if to show off for the onlookers. He was the oldest horse in the barn, but he was still sleek and fit.

"Dad, may I talk to you a minute?" Christina said in a low voice when she came up beside him.

"Hi, Chris." Mike put his arm around her shoulder. "Mr. and Mrs. Androni, I'd like you to meet my daughter, Christina. Mr. and Mrs. Androni own Mile High Acres Farm in Louisville. They have several mares they want to breed to Jazzman."

"Great. He's a terrific horse," Christina said enthusiastically. She smiled at the Andronis, then turned back to her father. "This'll just take a second," she whispered. "We need to go to Townsend Acres tonight and—"

"Christina." Ducking his head, her father spoke in a low voice. "I will talk to you as soon as the Andronis leave." Christina sighed impatiently. She could tell from her father's brusque tone of voice that she wasn't going to get anywhere with him just then. "Okay." She said good-bye to the Andronis, then headed outside to find her mother.

Tucking a stray lock of hair behind her ear, Christina scanned the barn area. Her mother could be anywhere doing anything. But that evening Christina had a lesson on Sterling. She had to get her parents to go over to the Townsends' with her *before* she left for Whisperwood.

Christina hurried toward the training barn. When she stepped inside, she spotted her mother coming out of one of the stalls with Maureen Mack, Ian's assistant trainer, followed by Samantha.

"Hey, Sam, what are you doing here?" Christina asked as she hurried down the aisle.

The worried look on Samantha's face made her slow down. When she reached them, Christina glanced into the stall the three had just left. Wind Chaser stood next to the open door. He was a gorgeous light chestnut with a blond mane and tail. Samantha and her father had bought him together two years earlier. The purchase had been a gamble—the then two-year-old had been untrained and unraced. But since then he'd proven himself on the track many times.

"What's wrong?" Christina asked, glancing from Chaser to Samantha to Maureen.

"Nothing," Maureen said. The farm's assistant trainer was petite, with short, streaked hair. "We're just discussing training strategies. Ian wants to push Chaser this spring. After all, he is four. If he does really well this year, we can retire him to stud at the end of the season."

"Sam and I aren't sure that's the way to go, though," Ashleigh said. She wore a T-shirt, jeans, and paddock boots. With her brown hair tucked under a baseball cap, she looked like a teenager.

"I just remember what happened to Wonder when we pushed her too hard in training," her mother continued. "It was heartbreaking."

"And I want Chaser to retire sound," Samantha added. Her thick red hair was held back with a horseshoe-shaped barrette. "I'd hate to see him blow a tendon or ruin his wind just so we can have a winning season."

Christina cleared her throat. This was the *perfect* time to bring up Star—while the two of them were thinking about the horses they loved. "Mom, I need to talk to you about—"

"Excuse me one second," Maureen interrupted. "I've got to find Joe and redo the feeding schedule. Ian's anxious to talk to you, Sam, so don't run off without seeing him. I'm sure you can come up with a compromise."

"I'll go talk to him now," Samantha said. "I'll see you later," she told Christina before heading out the barn door with Maureen.

"Mom, Melanie and I went to visit Star," Christina said quickly before her mother dashed off, too.

"How was he?" her mother asked distractedly as she started down the aisle. "I know you were worried about Brad starting him too early."

"He was *terrible*," Christina said, hot tears filling her eyes before she could stop them. Turning away, she wiped them away with the heel of her hand.

"Terrible?" Ashleigh repeated. "What's wrong?"

"I don't know. He was really listless, and they have him isolated at one end of the barn. Mr. Dunkirk wouldn't answer any of our questions. He practically kicked us off the farm."

Stopping, Ashleigh frowned. "Where was Brad?"

"Lexington. At least that's what Dunkirk said."

"Is Star sick?"

"Dunkirk said he wasn't, but I don't believe a word he says!" Christina blurted, her voice rising.

Ashleigh cocked her head, her eyes wide. Christina recognized her mother's expression. She was thinking that Christina was overreacting about Star—again.

"It's true," Christina declared. "You can even ask Melanie."

"Ask me what?"

Christina turned and saw Melanie coming down the aisle toward them. Her short blond hair was damp, and she had muddy streaks on her forehead and cheeks.

"What happened to you?" Ashleigh asked.

Melanie laughed. "I tried to give a weanling a bath. What did you want to ask me?" She stopped in front of them, her hands in her back pockets.

"About Star," Christina explained. "Tell my mom how sick he looked."

"Uh . . ." Melanie suddenly looked uncomfortable. "I never really got a good look at Star, remember?" she reminded Chris. "I was too busy keeping that groom out of his stall."

"What groom out of what stall?" Ashleigh repeated. "Did you two do something at Townsend Acres that you weren't supposed to?"

"Of course not!" Chris exclaimed. "Dunkirk was acting like we were trespassing. We told him that Star was our horse."

"Half our horse," Ashleigh reminded her. "And right now he's the Townsends' responsibility. I'd be mad, too, if Dunkirk or Brad came barging in here, questioning what we were doing."

"But, Mom, you don't understand," Christina continued. "They had Star isolated like he was in quarantine."

"But they told you he wasn't sick?"

"Yes, but—"

"Do you think Mr. Dunkirk was lying?"

"No, but he had sweat marks all over him and his

48

legs looked really stocked up. He—" Christina opened her mouth to say more, then realized there was no use—her mother wasn't listening anymore. Slowly she shut it.

"They *were* acting weird, Aunt Ashleigh," Melanie said. "Like they had something to hide. And Star was really quiet."

"Did you two girls ever think that maybe he'd just been longed or something?" Ashleigh asked. "Training can really take it out of a youngster, you know that. And maybe they just hadn't had a chance to bathe him yet."

"That only proves he's too young!" Chris countered, silently furious that her mother didn't believe her.

"Christina, our yearlings get tired even when we start them later."

Christina hung her head. Her mother made Star's behavior sound so logical. Maybe she *had* overreacted.

Then Ashleigh sighed, as if she was giving in. "You're really worried about him, aren't you?" she asked gently.

Christina nodded.

"Then how about after dinner we go to the Townsends' and check on him? I'd like to see—" She faltered. "I'd like to see him."

"Thank you!" Christina exclaimed, throwing her arms around her mother. She knew how hard it was for her mother to agree to see Star. "I know you think I'm overreacting. And maybe I am. I just miss Star more than anyone really knows."

Christina felt her mother's deep sigh. "Yes, I do know," Ashleigh said quietly. "I imagine it's just as much as I miss Wonder."

6

"LET US DO THE TALKING, CHRIS," CHRISTINA'S FATHER SAID AS they rolled up the Townsends' drive. "You know how Brad can be."

"Snobby, pretentious, and haughty?" Christina suggested.

Ashleigh stifled a laugh. "That's not what your father was going to say," she said, turning around to wink at Christina in the backseat of the car. "Townsend Acres has always been very competitive with Whitebrook, especially since Brad took over. We've sort of had a truce lately, but Brad's *not* going to want us to come in and tell him he's doing something wrong."

Mike gave Christina a stern look in the rearview mirror. "And we don't *know* he's doing something wrong, right, Chris? We're just here to check out one of our horses."

"Right," Christina muttered. She was glad her parents had taken her seriously enough to visit Star. They weren't going to view Star with as much sympathy as she did, but she trusted her parents' judgment. If something was wrong, they would notice and would want to do something about it.

As they drove past the Townsends' house, Christina noticed the line of cars parked in the front drive: three Mercedes, two Rolls-Royces, two Jaguars, and three limousines.

"Looks like the Townsends are having one of their little get-togethers," Mike joked. "A simple barbecue where they roast an entire pig and invite the governor of Kentucky and the mayor of Lexington."

Christina scooted closer to the window so she could see better. Women in floppy hats and long dresses strolled around the gardens, which were bursting with flowering tulips, daffodils, and azaleas. Two men in tuxedos carried trays of champagne glasses. On the side lawn a quartet played under a canopy.

"Wow," was all Christina could say.

"Don't worry, Chris, we'll do something just like this for your sweet sixteen," Ashleigh said with a chuckle.

They parked in front of the training barn. Christina leaped out and jogged down the aisle to the stall where she and Melanie had found Star earlier. The stall was empty.

The office door opened and Ralph Dunkirk came

out. He was dressed up in a tweed jacket and pressed trousers. "Hello, Miss Reese," he said. "I just called Mr. Townsend and told him you and your parents were here."

Christina noticed how polite he was acting. *Orders from Brad?* she wondered. "Where's Star?"

Dunkirk nodded down the aisle. Ashleigh and Mike were just coming in through the double doors.

"Third stall from the end," Dunkirk said.

"Star's down by you," Christina called, hurrying to join her parents. "Third stall." By the time Christina had reached them, Mike had opened the door.

"How is he?" Christina asked breathlessly. She glanced in. Mike was standing on one side of Star, his hand lightly holding the colt's halter.

Christina was surprised at the change in the yearling. His chestnut coat was clean, and his mane and tail had been combed out. Ears pricked, he looked at Christina and her parents with a curious expression. There was no sign of the saddle marks, and his legs looked tight and smooth.

"He's really filled out," Ashleigh breathed. She stood outside the stall, peering in as if afraid to get too close to the colt. Christina's heart went out to her mother—even she couldn't deny that Star looked a lot like Wonder.

"Triple Crown material, don't you agree?" a voice boomed behind Christina.

She swung around. It was Brad Townsend and two

other men, all holding glasses of champagne.

"Hello, Brad," Mike said. When he and Ashleigh came out of the stall, Christina stepped inside. She wasn't interested in Brad Townsend and his big-shot friends.

"Mike Reese and Ashleigh Griffen, I'd like to introduce you to—"

Christina tuned Brad out. Holding out her hand, she approached Star. Instantly he flattened his ears, swished his tail, and rolled his eyes menacingly. Startled, Christina stopped in her tracks. Star had always been feisty and devilish, but he'd *never* been mean, especially not to her.

Moving away from her, he stood in the corner, his expression sullen. Christina studied him carefully. Sure, he was well groomed and he wasn't listless anymore, but what had happened to the sweet colt she used to know and love?

"Christina, I think you'd better get out of there," Brad warned from the doorway. "I was just telling your parents that Star thinks he's a tough stallion, even though he's only a yearling. That's good, though. We want him to be top dog on the racetrack. He *is* going to follow in his dam's footsteps and be our next big winner, right, Ashleigh?" Brad raised his glass as if in a toast. "Still, we have to make him understand that he can't boss us around."

Brad sounds polished and knowledgeable, Christina thought. *He's thrilled to be playing the role of powerful estate owner and racehorse breeder.* She also knew something wasn't quite right. Star had changed, and not just because he was growing up.

"Mr. Townsend, when I saw Star before, he—" Christina began, but Mike shot her a stern look that clearly said, *Not now.*

Christina flushed. Weren't her parents on her side?

"Bring Wonder's Star out and show him to our guests," Brad said to Dunkirk, who was hovering in the background.

The trainer came into the stall carrying a chain lead shank. Christina moved back against the wall, feeling invisible.

When Dunkirk looped the chain over Star's nose, the colt threw his head up and tried to pull away. Dunkirk gave one yank and told him to stand.

With another yank, the trainer steered Star from the stall. The colt bolted into the aisle, scattering the guests, who laughed uncomfortably as Brad boasted, "He's a handful all right, but if we can channel that energy in the right direction, we're going to have a powerful stakes winner."

Or a mean and difficult two-year-old, Christina thought. As Dunkirk led Star up and down the aisle, the colt danced sideways. His nostrils were flared and his eyes showed white. He reminded Christina of Jazzman, showing off for the onlookers. Only there was a difference. Jazzman had pranced because he felt good. Star pranced because he was nervous. Every time Dunkirk rattled the chain or made him turn, the colt's ears flicked nervously.

He's scared of Dunkirk, Christina thought, her heart racing anxiously. She glanced at her parents, who were still talking, their attention only half on Star. *Can't they see how miserable Star is?* Christina wondered desperately. *Aren't they going to say something?*

But they didn't.

"Thank you, Ralph," Brad said finally. Coming up beside Christina, he put his arm around her shoulder. "What do you think? Are we taking good care of your baby?"

"Uh, yes," Christina said, shrinking from his touch. She didn't dare say what she really felt—her parents would be furious with her. Besides, if she wanted to keep seeing Star, she'd have to stay on the good side of both Brad and Dunkirk. "He looks great," she added, her voice flat.

"Mike, Ashleigh, won't you stay for dinner?" Brad asked. "Christina's welcome to stay as well. Parker will be home later this evening."

"No, thank you," Ashleigh said, glancing down at her jeans and tennis shoes. "I don't think we're dressed for it."

"Oh, this is just a little get-together," Brad assured them.

"Really, I'm afraid we can't," Ashleigh insisted. "We still have work to do back at the farm."

"The work of a Thoroughbred owner is never done," Brad said, sipping from his glass.

Catching Christina's eye, Mike winked at her. Remembering her father's earlier joke, Christina forced herself to smile. But it quickly faded when she watched Star dance nervously back into his stall. She hated feeling so helpless while Star was clearly suffering!

As soon as Dunkirk took the chain from around his nose, the colt practically threw himself into the corner. Christina wanted to rush forward and put her arms around his neck, but she forced herself to stay where she was.

Dunkirk closed the stall door. Christina linked her fingers through the wire mesh and stared at her colt. The trainer gave her a stern look. "Don't get too close," he warned. "He might rush at the door."

Christina nodded but didn't move. Mike and Ashleigh started down the aisle with the others. "Let's go, Chris," Ashleigh called when the group reached the barn doors.

"Good-bye, Star," she whispered, tears choking her. "Don't worry—this time I won't leave you. I'll come to see you every day. And I won't let them hurt you. I promise."

Christina was silent on the drive home. She knew there was no use talking about her concerns. In the front seat, her parents were discussing how good Star looked.

"He wasn't listless, that's for sure," Ashleigh said. "So I bet when you saw him earlier he had just been longed."

"And don't be dismayed by Dunkirk's firm treatment," Mike said, glancing at Christina in the rearview mirror. "It looks like your orphan has turned into another Terminator. And you know how firm George Ballard has to be with *him*."

Christina looked out the side window. Terminator, one of Whitebrook's stallions, was known for his aggressive temperament. George was the only one who handled him, and after many years Terminator had come to respect the stallion manager.

But that's different, Christina wanted to protest. Terminator respected George Ballard. He wasn't afraid of him.

She slumped back against the seat. How could she make them understand?

"Look, Parker's here," Ashleigh said as they drove up Whitebrook's drive.

Christina sat upright. Parker's truck was in front of their house. Her heart quickened. It was time to tell him what was going on. If anyone would understand, Parker would. He knew from experience how rigid Brad could be. Plus she needed to ask him to keep an eye on Star for her.

"Been waiting long?" Christina asked when she opened the car door and climbed out. Parker was leaning against the truck bed, his arms crossed in front of his chest. He was wearing breeches, a baggy T-shirt, and high black boots.

"About two hours," he said.

"Two hours?" Christina repeated, confused.

"Hey, Parker," Mike greeted when he and Ashleigh got out of the car. "How's that mare of yours?"

"Super. She went great at our *lesson.*"

The lesson! Christina swallowed. "Oh, no! I forgot all about it."

"You had a lesson with Sam tonight?" Ashleigh asked.

"Uh, yes, but when you said you'd go see Star with me, I totally forgot."

"That wasn't very responsible. You'd better call Sam and apologize," Ashleigh said.

Christina nodded. Her mother didn't have to tell her she'd messed up. "I know, I'm sorry. Sterling probably wonders where I was, too."

"Why don't I drive you to Whisperwood?" Parker offered. "That way you can apologize to Sam in person."

"Good idea. Is that all right?" she asked her parents. Mike and Ashleigh hadn't lost their stern expressions, but they said yes.

"What's this about going to see Star?" Parker asked when they got into the truck. "And why was it more important than the lesson? Or aren't you going to tell me what's going on?" he added, sounding annoyed.

Christina glanced sharply at him. He was frowning, but the look in his eyes was one of bewilderment. Christina realized the anger in his voice was covering up his hurt feelings. She hadn't been honest with him

59

for fear of coming between him and his father, but now she felt horrible and guilty for not sharing her concerns with her friend.

"Drive slowly, and I'll explain everything," she told him.

By the time they reached Whisperwood, Christina had confided all her fears about Star based on what she'd seen that day. Parker listened quietly. He stopped the truck in front of Whisperwood's barn and killed the motor. For a minute he sat there, staring out the windshield.

"Dunkirk's a good trainer," Parker said finally. "And even though my dad's a pompous jerk, he does know horses." Christina's heart sank. She should have guessed Parker wouldn't see anything wrong, either.

Turning in the truck seat, Parker directed his intense gaze toward Christina. "But Dunkirk can be rough and impatient. And my father sees dollar signs first, the animal second."

"So what are you saying?" Christina asked.

"Star was raised by you—a girl who loves him—and a goat. It wasn't exactly a conventional upbringing for a Thoroughbred racehorse."

"What's that supposed to mean?" Christina responded. Parker didn't sound very complimentary.

"It means Star is used to a completely different kind of treatment. You were patient with him and sweet. Neither of those adjectives describes Dunkirk or any of the workers at Townsend Acres except for my grandfather, and he's been spending so much time in England lately, he hasn't been involved with Star's training. I don't think they mean to harm him, but maybe when Star gets fresh they don't let him get away with it. Then he gets scared and reacts aggressively."

Christina stared at Parker. Though she hated to admit it, what he said made sense. "I guess I never thought of it that way," she said

"I know that doesn't make it any better," Parker went on. "Obviously their methods aren't doing Star any good. But they're not deliberately trying to hurt him—if that gives you any comfort."

It was such a relief to have finally talked to Parker about Star; she *did* feel comforted. "Oh Parker," Christina said, stifling a sob. "Thanks so much for listening." She scooted across the seat and reached out to hug him gratefully.

"You're welcome," Parker said, hugging her back. His breath was soft on Christina's cheek. "I had no idea how worried you've been—I'll keep an eye on Star for you from now on. Promise."

Christina was suddenly intensely aware of how close they were. Flushing, she pulled away and quickly slid back over to her side of the seat. Parker glanced out the window, running his fingers through his hair nervously. His cheeks were a little red, too, she noticed.

"I mean, I know Star isn't going to suddenly turn

into some kind of killer," Christina mumbled, remembering what they'd been talking about. "I just wasn't sure what was going on."

The air in the truck seemed to have heated up. Eager to make her escape before she said anything embarrassing, Christina opened the door of the truck and climbed out, hurrying up the driveway to Samantha and Tor's house.

She didn't know why one hug was making her feel so flustered. She and Parker had been friends for almost three years.

"What's your hurry?" Parker teased when he caught up to her on the front porch.

He was tall and lanky, and he towered over Christina. She looked up at him, thinking back to the day they'd first met. Even then she'd been attracted to his bold manner and quick sense of humor.

"Wait a minute before going in," Parker said, putting a hand on Christina's shoulder.

Christina swallowed hard.

"You've been kind of tense lately," Parker went on. "How about if we go on a trail ride tomorrow? We could pack a picnic lunch and ride to the river."

"Great," Christina squeaked. "I'll invite Kevin and Melanie and—"

"Why don't just the two of us go for once?" Parker interrupted. "We can work on our campaign to save Star."

Christina laughed, but her heart skipped a beat. Alone with Parker on a long trail ride?

You're just friends, remember? Christina chided herself. "It sounds great—the picnic *and* the campaign," she agreed. "Now I'd better go in and apologize to Sam and get my lecture over with."

"She's just going to say, 'If you're serious about eventing, Christina, you're going to have to work hard and *focus*,'" Parker said, mimicking Samantha.

Christina laughed again, and the tension between them was broken. "Well, she's right. I've been so worried about Star, I haven't been focusing recently. That's even more reason for us to come up with a plan to save Star!"

7

"SHRIMP, CAVIAR CANAPÉS, STRAWBERRIES DIPPED IN CHOCO-late, pâté, miniature eclairs, and crab-stuffed mush-rooms," Parker recited the next day as he handed a pic-nic basket to Christina. She had ridden over to Whisperwood and stood holding Sterling in the barn aisle.

It was early Sunday afternoon. The sun was shining, the sky was cloudless, and a light breeze rustled the high Kentucky bluegrass. It was a perfect day for a picnic.

"You bought all this stuff?" Christina asked, peek-ing inside.

"No way. They're leftovers from my parents' party last night."

"Oh, right." Christina constantly forgot that Parker was even related to Brad and Lavinia. Not only did he not spend much time with his parents, but he had none of their pretentious manners. Luckily for him, he *did* get to eat the same food, though.

"So how are we going to carry this feast on our horses?" Christina asked, closing the basket.

"Saddlebags," Parker replied as he took the basket and headed for Foxy's stall. "I've already got them on Foxy's saddle. And one bag has a blanket in it for us to sit on."

"You thought of everything," Christina said as she led Sterling down the aisle.

"*Almost* everything. I still haven't got a strategy to save Star," Parker replied. "But I did check on him this morning."

Christina's eyes widened. "And?"

"He *has* changed." Parker opened the stall door, then turned to face Christina. "I noticed it right away. When I went in the stall, he hid in the corner like a small child being punished."

Christina bit her lower lip. She was glad Parker had noticed the change, but it made her sad to be reminded of how unhappy Star was.

"Why can't my parents see?" she asked desperately. "They insist that Star has to stay at Townsend Acres, especially after Brad told them how aggressive he was."

"Your mom never spent any time with Star when he was a baby, right?" Parker asked.

"Right."

"Then she wouldn't see a change. And your dad is probably just trying to stay on her side. As far as your parents are concerned, Star's just another yearling that's being difficult."

Christina nodded. "You're right. But I've got to think of something before Star's ruined." She glanced apologetically at Parker. "Not that your dad wants to ruin him," she added quickly.

Parker snorted. "Dad still uses the same old outdated breaking techniques they used fifty years ago. He won't face the fact that things have changed. Modern trainers use natural communication methods and take training slowly. My dad's idea of communicating is a sharp yank on the lead shank."

"But what about your grandfather?" Christina asked. "He's an old-time trainer, but he's really good with horses."

"My grandfather understood about communicating with horses way before it became cool," Parker said. "And when he's around, he's able to influence the grooms and riders. But he's not very active at the farm anymore."

Christina sighed. "What am I going to do?"

"Well . . . ," Parker said, hesitating, "I did think of something, but I'm not sure you're going to like it."

"I'm listening."

"Why don't you offer to work with Star at Townsend Acres? Become his groom."

The idea took Christina so much by surprise, she

didn't know what to say. *Go to work for Brad Townsend?* Just the thought made her cringe.

"Don't say no right away," Parker said with a grin as he opened Foxy's door. "Think about it for a little while. Okay?"

Parker had caught her—Christina had been about to give him a few very good reasons why she could never work at Townsend Acres. She didn't want to take time away from Sterling, she didn't want to work with Brad and Dunkirk, and she had too much to do at Whitebrook already. But if she really thought about it, none of those things was as important to her as Star.

"I'll definitely think about it," she promised.

"Good." Parker appeared in the stall doorway with Foxy in tow. "Now let's go have a picnic."

Parker led Foxy outside, with Sterling and Christina right behind them. As Foxy walked down the aisle, she switched her tail when she felt the heavy bags against her sides.

"I'm glad you didn't try to put those on Sterling," Christina said. "She would have gone nuts."

"Foxy might not like them too well, either. She's acting like she might try a buck or two," Parker said as he mounted up. When he pressed his legs against the mare's sides, she burst forward, causing the saddlebags to flap against her sides. Tucking her tail, Foxy bucked twice, then landed on all fours and crow-hopped across the grass.

Christina watched wide-eyed, waiting for Parker to

go flying off. But he raised one hand in the air and whooped, "Ride 'em, cowboy!" as if he were on a bucking bronco.

Christina shook her head. "You're crazy!" she called to him, laughing. When Foxy finally settled into a jig, Christina mounted Sterling, who pranced off as soon as she hit the saddle. The other horse's antics had charged her up, too.

"I thought this was going to be a leisurely trail ride," Christina grumbled as she made Sterling halt.

"That would be way too dull," Parker said. Turning Foxy, he headed into the cross-country field at a trot. Sterling started after them so fast, Christina lost her balance. When she saw Parker steer Foxy toward a fence, she *knew* he was crazy.

"Oh, no, you don't, Parker," Christina called in a warning tone. "Don't you go over any jumps with those bags—"

But Parker was already cantering straight for the low end of a stack of logs. Christina sat deep, trying to hold Sterling back. The mare chewed her bit and pranced in place, eager to catch up with Foxy.

Christina made Sterling trot in circles until she quieted down. By then Parker was cantering back toward them, a roguish smile on his face.

"Whoa," Parker told Foxy, and she slid to a halt. The bay mare's nostrils were flared and her ears flicked with excitement.

"You really are nuts. Our picnic lunch is probably

gourmet mush by now," Christina joked. "And if Samantha saw you, she'd ban you from riding forever."

"Hey, all week long Foxy and I work hard on bending and lengthening and acting proper. We deserve to let loose once in a while. Right, Foxy?" Parker patted the mare's neck, and she bobbed her head as if in agreement.

Parker's enthusiasm was so contagious, Christina couldn't help smiling. She loved his ability to work so hard on his riding without losing his wild streak.

He flashed her a mischievous grin. "Race you to the woods," he challenged.

Christina opened her mouth to say no. She knew how easily Sterling could get out of control and how quickly a horse could stumble and fall on the rough ground.

But then she thought back to the previous day. Since she'd seen Star, all she'd been doing was worrying. She was beginning to feel like an old lady. Maybe she and Sterling needed to cut loose, too.

Besides, Christina reasoned, *I've been exercise-riding racehorses—Parker hasn't. Sterling's an ex-racehorse—Foxy isn't. That means if we race, we're going to win!*

"What're the stakes?" Christina asked.

"Loser treats the winner to dinner and a movie," Parker said.

Christina's heart flip-flopped. "That sounds like a date," she said without thinking.

Parker raised his eyebrows. "So? Are you afraid of a date, Reese?"

"No way," Christina said. Reaching down, she quickly shortened both stirrup leathers two holes. Then she gathered her reins. Immediately Sterling arched her neck and began to jig, her muscles bunched in anticipation.

"Eat my dust, Parker," Christina called. Nudging her heels against Sterling's sides, they took off before Parker had a chance to protest.

Sterling didn't need any more encouragement. She flew up the hill toward the woods, her hooves pounding the earth. Christina crouched on her neck, jockey style. Closing her eyes, she felt the rhythm of Sterling's gait, and instinctively she moved to the same rhythm, becoming one with her horse.

Glancing over her shoulder, she glimpsed Parker about ten feet behind and gaining.

"Go, Sterling," Christina whispered. She fed the reins up the mare's neck and hunched low over her withers.

Sterling kicked into high gear, reaching the woods so fast, Christina almost didn't stop her in time. Tugging on the right rein, she turned the mare away from the trees. Parker and Foxy were just galloping up.

Christina whooped, patting Sterling's shoulder. "We won!" she cried.

"Whoowee!" Parker crowed when he slowed Foxy to a trot. "You've missed your calling, Christina Reese. You've got racing in your blood!"

Christina shook her head. "It's Sterling. She's really fast," she explained breathlessly.

Parker gave Christina a knowing look. "No, it wasn't just Sterling," he said. "I saw you—you've got the instincts of a jockey."

Christina shrugged, but her cheeks were hot. "Let's cool these guys off," she said, changing the subject.

She let the reins slide through her fingers, and Sterling stretched out her neck at a walk. The mare's coat was dark with sweat and she was blowing. As they walked down the dirt road into the woods, Parker steered Foxy next to them. Christina noticed that Foxy had barely broken a sweat.

"Sterling may have won, but she's really winded," Christina pointed out. "I don't know if she's going to be ready for Meadowlark—she's not fit."

"Well, you've still got three weeks to train," Parker countered.

"That's not very long."

"Except Easter vacation is one of those weeks. You'll be able to work her every day."

"I guess you're right," Christina agreed. She wove her fingers through Sterling's mane, and glanced over at Parker. "About lots of things," she added. "I think I *will* ask your dad if I can groom for Star. It's worth a try. And I can tell my parents I want to learn more about racing—that way they'll have to agree."

"Great!" Parker reached out his hand to slap hers. "I don't think my dad would give up an opportunity to get some free labor. Besides, you've got just as much experience as any professional groom."

"And thanks for suggesting this picnic," Christina added, feeling as if a weight had been lifted from her shoulders. Now that she'd made the decision to work with Star, she felt a hundred times better. "I haven't had this much fun in a long time."

"Good. And I think we should top off the day with our dinner and movie."

Christina tensed. "Right. Dinner and movie, just for fun, right? It's not really a date?" she asked, a little too quickly.

Parker didn't reply. "Right. It's not a date," he said finally, looking straight ahead.

Christina turned her attention back to the trail. *Parker sounds relieved, doesn't he?* she asked herself. Of course he was relieved. Parker had never actually said—or even suggested—that they should be anything more than friends.

An unexpected lump welled up in Christina's throat as Sterling strode ahead of Foxy. She almost wished Parker had insisted that it was a date after all.

She went up the trail, posting to Sterling's jaunty trot and trying to imagine what it would be like to work at Townsend Acres. Would she have to call Brad "sir"? More important, would she have to do everything he told her to do?

No, Christina vowed to herself. *Not if it means putting Star in danger.*

8

"EASY, GIRL," CHRISTINA CALLED TO STERLING. "WE'RE JUST walking today." She reached down and patted Sterling's hindquarters.

It was Friday evening, school was out for spring break, and Christina had decided to take it easy. The Meadowlark event was in two weeks, but they'd been training hard with Samantha at Whisperwood, and both horse and rider needed a break. It was a beautiful April evening, and as Sterling ambled along the trail, Christina allowed her mind to drift.

The next day she would begin working as Star's groom at Townsend Acres. *Starting tomorrow, I'll make it up to you, Star,* Christina thought. *I'll never leave you alone again.*

As they walked on through the woods, her thoughts drifted to Parker, and she felt a pang of sadness. Ever

73

since their picnic last Sunday, Parker had seemed distant. They'd never gone out for dinner and a movie. When they'd gotten back from the picnic, Parker hadn't mentioned their "date" again, and Christina was too embarrassed to bring it up.

Why did I have to open my big mouth? Christina thought miserably.

Abruptly Sterling halted, interrupting Christina's thoughts. Ears pricked, the mare stared intently into the woods. "What do you see, silly?" Christina chided as she looked in the same direction.

Something moved deep in the brush. Christina held her breath. A doe and fawn silently wound their way through the leafy trees and brambles. They were so well camouflaged, Christina caught only a glimpse before they disappeared.

"Wow." Christina stroked Sterling's neck. "That was awesome."

"Chris!" A shrill holler rang through the woods, shattering the stillness. Christina recognized Melanie's bellow. Moments later Melanie and Tribulation, Christina's first pony, came cantering toward them on the trail.

Melanie rode bareback, her legs clasped around Trib's fat sides. Out of shape, the pinto pony puffed with each stride.

"What are you doing here?" Christina asked.

Trib stopped dead in front of Sterling. The horse and pony sniffed noses, then squealed excitedly. "Trib looked sort of bored, so I decided to take him out and catch up with you," Melanie explained. "I can't believe it's already spring break."

"Yeah, it's amazing how fast the time has gone. Meadowlark's in only two weeks," Christina said, biting her lip.

"What's wrong?"

"I don't really feel ready," Christina admitted. "Last year all I thought about was moving up to preliminary level. Now I'm riding in a preliminary-level event and I'm . . ." Christina hesitated. "Well, I'm not really into it."

"Feeling a little scared?"

Christina nodded, though that wasn't really what she meant.

"But last fall you and Sterling did great in preliminary," Melanie reminded her cousin as she nudged Trib on. The trail widened and the two horses were able to go side by side.

"Well, Sterling was fit and I was really into training. This year . . ."

"Hey, as soon as you get to the event it will all come back," Melanie reassured her. "You've been dreaming forever about moving up and getting into the Young Riders program. And you're almost there. It's just like with me and my jockey's license—I can't wait until May twenty-fifth!"

"What happens then?" Christina asked, confused.

"My birthday, dumbo," Melanie scolded her jokingly. "I'll be sixteen. I'll finally be able to get my bug license! Then I can start racing and work my way up to being a real jockey."

Christina's eyes widened. "Wow. You'll be a real apprentice jockey. I almost forgot."

"I didn't," Melanie said. "I think about it all the time."

Christina chewed on her lip again. *That's how obsessed I used to be about eventing,* she thought. *What happened?*

But she knew the answer.

Star.

"We'll have to have a big party," Christina said distractedly.

"Sounds good to me!" Melanie said. "And don't worry," she added. "You and Sterling will do great at Meadowlark."

Christina nodded, but her mind wasn't on the event. As usual, she was thinking about Star.

When Christina arrived at Townsend Acres, Brad was waiting outside the training barn. He was dressed in his usual pressed khakis and button-down shirt, and was seated behind the wheel of a brand-new pickup truck. Christina glanced down at her stained jeans and T-shirt, suddenly feeling messy.

"Hop in," Brad said. "All new employees get the grand tour."

They drove around the training barn and down a long, shaded drive. "This is the stallion area of the farm," Brad commented, pointing as the pickup truck rattled through an open gate and down the lane.

Christina blinked in amazement. The stallion barn at Townsend Acres was as big as Whitebrook's training barn. It was tucked behind the main house, separated by a grove of oaks and a lake. Ten large paddocks surrounded the barn. Christina was amazed. She couldn't remember ever visiting that part of Townsend Acres before.

Brad parked the truck in front of the stallion barn. As soon as he climbed out and slammed the truck door, a man wearing a tan shirt and matching pants came out of the barn. His name, Ed Tumi, and the words *Townsend Acres* were embroidered on his shirt pocket.

"Morning, Mr. Townsend. Ready for a tour?" Mr. Tumi asked, his tone friendly but formal.

"I think I'll show her around myself, Tumi," Brad said cheerfully, shaking the man's hand.

"All right, then," Mr. Tumi said. "I've got a few calls to make—I'll be in the office if you need me."

Christina followed Brad into the barn. "Mr. Tumi is one of our stallion managers," Brad explained. "We have twelve stallions. There are two managers and four grooms. From February through June, during breeding season, we work day shift or night shift."

"Twelve stallions?" Christina gulped. Whitebrook had only four. "No wonder you're so busy."

"That's small—some of the bigger farms have forty stallions." As they walked down the aisle, Brad named each stallion and his bloodlines and racing record. Christina peered into the stalls. Not only were the horses major stakes winners with top sires and dams, but they were perfectly groomed and handsome.

The barn was also immaculate. Each spacious, thickly bedded stall had a brass nameplate over the door, a bug mister, and a fan to stir the air. Halters and lead shanks hung on the outside walls, and labeled grooming kits and buckets stood on a low shelf under them.

Christina's gaze traveled down one side of the aisle and back. Everything, even the halters and shanks, was lined up uniformly.

"Six of the stallions are outside, grazing," Brad said when they reached the end of the barn. "We turn them out every day, even during breeding season, to keep them healthy and sane."

"How many mares do you breed a year?" Christina asked.

"Over six hundred. We get mares in from as far as Australia, so we even breed in the late summer. Their season is different from ours."

"Wow," Christina said under her breath. Compared to Whitebrook, Townsend Acres was a fantastically huge operation.

"Impressed?" Brad asked.

"Yes," Christina admitted reluctantly. She *was* impressed.

Next Brad took her to the mare and foal area. There were four barns clustered in a semicircle, all beautifully landscaped. Pastures with run-in sheds surrounded the barns.

"We have the visiting mares separated from my own stock," he explained. "My own mares are housed in five different barns. That way, if we ever have a fire, we won't lose everything."

"That makes sense," Christina said. "Your hay and straw are in separate sheds?"

"Yes. They're stored away from the animals. We haul it over daily. It's more work, but it's safer that way."

Christina nodded. With the amount of hay and straw stored at farms, a fire started by an electrical malfunction, a careless accident, or lightning was always a threat.

"You've already seen the training barn," Brad said when they walked back to the truck. "So I'll show you our other new addition—the equine swimming pool."

A swimming pool for horses? Christina bit her lip, trying not to blurt her surprise. She knew many horse farms had them. Swimming helped injured horses recover faster by providing exercise without hurting their legs.

But she hadn't known that Townsend Acres had a pool. In fact, she realized, there was a lot she didn't know about Townsend Acres. She'd known Brad, Lavinia, and Clay all her life, but mostly she'd seen them at the racetrack, where Brad and Lavinia were busy being big shots. She'd never really paid attention to the farm itself. No wonder Brad and Dunkirk had been miffed when she'd charged into the barn demanding to know what was wrong with Star.

Christina looked at Brad out of the corner of her eye. He said he gave every new employee a tour. But she wasn't exactly an employee. Was he showing her around to make a point? If so, he'd made it. He obviously knew how to run a Thoroughbred racing farm.

"We added the stallion area about four years ago, and then the pool last year," Brad said. "After we bought out the old Hanley farm."

Christina vaguely remembered her parents talking about Townsend Acres expanding, but she hadn't paid much attention. What was really odd was that Parker never talked about Townsend Acres at all. After school, he always went straight to Whisperwood. About all he did at his parents' was sleep.

Christina stared out the window as the truck drove down the lane toward the training barn. In every direction she could see lush bluegrass pastures, white board fence, and sleek horses. Ponds and woods dotted the farm, and most of the pastures and barns were surrounded by trees to provide cool shade.

As Brad drove, he named each horse in the field and explained the history behind every building or feature. For the first time Christina understood why Brad was always so upset that Parker didn't pay any attention to the family farm. It was a gorgeous place—and would one day be his.

Brad parked and they went into the building that housed the swimming pool. The pool was about fifty feet long and oval-shaped. A ramp covered with rubber matting sloped into one end. A groom walked along-side the edge of the pool holding a longe line. In the greenish blue water, a horse swam to the far end, his front and hind legs thrusting vigorously.

Christina watched in amazement. The only thing sticking out of the water were the horse's ears, eyes, and nose. Moist air blew from its nostrils as if it were a dragon.

"How's Gullivar doing?" Brad called to the groom, who gave him a thumbs-up sign.

"He's decided he likes it," the groom called back.

"Gullivar bowed a tendon about two months ago," Brad told Christina. "The swimming has kept him in super shape while the leg is healing. Ready to go back to the training barn?" he asked as they went back out-side.

"I can't wait," Christina said, and climbed into the truck. "What exactly will I be doing with Star?" she asked excitedly.

"You'll start out as Star's groom," Brad said. "Right now that means working with him about an hour every day, grooming, tacking up, teaching him to stand in crossties, longeing him in the training ring, loading him on a trailer—everything you do at Whitebrook. Matt, his regular groom, will fill you in on what he's been doing. And Star's about ready to start in long lines. Would you like to help with that?"

"Yes, please." Christina nodded. "I want to do *everything* with him." Brad parked the truck in front of the training barn. Turning in the seat, he gave her a probing look. "I'd like to ask you a question."

"Okay," Christina said warily.

"Why are you so interested in working with Star? Whitebrook has a lot of nice colts and fillies. Besides, I thought you and Parker were only interested in that eventing business."

"We are. But Star's special. When Wonder died, my mom was so upset, she wanted nothing to do with him. I took over and kind of became his mom." Christina flushed. "I'm sure that sounds silly to a professional horseman like you."

He shook his head. "No. It sounds just like someone we both know very well. She was younger than you when she fell in love with Wonder, but she was just as obsessed."

"My mom, right?" Christina asked.

"Right. I never had any idea what she saw in that crippled foal." Brad snorted. "I was pretty certain Wonder wouldn't amount to anything, and boy, was I wrong. Obviously I'm not going to make that mistake again."

Suddenly he frowned and pointed a finger at her. "Wonder's Star is going to be Townsend Acres' next

82

champion," he said in a low voice. "And no one is going to mess with that, especially not you."

Christina's eyes widened. "Wh-what do you mean?" she stammered, taken aback by Brad's sudden change in tone. In a split second he'd turned from genial tour guide to ruthless estate owner.

"As long as you follow my rules, we'll get along fine and you can work with Star as long as you want," Brad continued, his eyes cold. "But start questioning me the way you did the other day, and you're out of here—no matter what your parents have to say about it. Understand?"

Christina nodded dumbly, her heart racing. She could tell from Brad's tone and expression that he was serious. Brad was used to wheeling and dealing with rich and powerful people. He didn't care about her.

"Come on, I'll introduce you to the other grooms," Brad said, and stepped into the barn. Christina followed him nervously. Was she doing the right thing or just asking for trouble?

When they reached the third stall, Christina reflexively called out, "Hey, Star, it's me, boy."

The handsome chestnut colt came to the door of his stall and nickered, his ears pricked forward.

Christina rushed over and stuck her fingers through the wire mesh. Star snorted warily and then sniffed her fingertips.

"And one more thing," Brad said sternly from behind her. "We don't coddle our horses here."

Just seeing Star once more was enough to convince Christina that she was making the right choice. But if she wanted to work with Star, she would have to do it on Brad's terms.

And she'd have to watch every step.

9

"I'M HERE NOW," CHRISTINA SAID, BURYING HER NOSE IN Star's mane. He turned his head, his ears pinned angrily. She ignored his look. If she could maintain her cool after Brad's threat, she could handle a cranky yearling. Especially one she loved more than anything and who loved her, too.

Christina thought back to Brad's cold words. It was almost as if he hoped she would mess up so he could get rid of her as soon as possible.

But she wasn't going to mess up. She wouldn't give him the satisfaction. More important, she couldn't let Star down—not when he needed her as much as he did.

Tears filled Christina's eyes. *Don't lose it now*, she chided herself. She wiped her eyes on the sleeve of her T-shirt.

Voices rang down the aisle, buckets clunked, hooves clomped, and doors slammed. The training barn was bustling with activity. Even though she was upset, Christina had managed to keep her composure as Brad showed her through the facility. There were twenty-five yearlings and five grooms. Brad had introduced her to Matt Chambers, Star's regular groom, and Christina had instantly recognized the nervous guy who had yelled at her and Melanie when they'd visited Star.

"When Matt gets done with that colt, he'll fill you in on the rules and routine," Brad had said before leaving. "I'm sure you have a *lot* to learn," he'd added with such emphasis that Christina wanted to stick her tongue out at him. It was clear that he didn't think living at Whitebrook had taught her anything.

Sighing, Christina stroked Star's neck. "First we'll clean you up," she told him. "I'm going to brush you until you're so shiny I can see my face in your coat."

"Rule one, we're not supposed to make pets out of the horses," a voice said from behind her.

Startled, she whirled around. Matt stood in the open doorway. "Rule two, if you're in the stall with a yearling, always secure him with a lead." He held one out to her. His face was shadowed by the brim of his cap, but Christina could tell his expression was serious.

Like everyone around here, Christina thought, suddenly missing Melanie's constant clowning around at Whitebrook. *Does anyone ever laugh or joke at Townsend Acres?*

"I've broken two rules already?" she asked as she took the lead.

"Yup."

She snapped the rope to the halter ring, then stroked Star's shoulder. His ears were still back, but he didn't look quite so nasty. "How many to go before I've broken them all?" she asked.

"Twenty. I should know—I've broken all of them at least once myself," Matt said, lightening his tone.

Maybe Matt isn't so bad without Brad around, Christina thought. "How long have you been working here?" she asked.

"About a month. Long enough to know that this place is run like the military."

"I kind of guessed that when I saw all the equipment in the stallion barn lined up and saluting Brad."

Matt cracked a grin, then glanced over his shoulder, as if feeling guilty that he'd smiled. "I've only got fifteen minutes. What do you want to know about Star?"

"Why were you acting so nervous and bossy the day my cousin and I came here?"

"That's easy. I'd only been here a couple of weeks, and Dunkirk was on my back every second. I couldn't do anything right. Plus he's a real stickler when it comes to uninvited guests coming into the barn. Then—" His gaze darted to Star and his mouth tightened. The colt had kept his ears pinned ever since Matt came over to the stall.

"You were assigned Star and you didn't get along?" Christina guessed.

"At first we got along fine," Matt said. "Like a typical colt, he was full of himself, but I can handle that. It was only after Dunkirk starting working with him that he changed. Any tiny misstep Star made, Dunkirk would punish him by slapping him with the lead shank or yanking the halter. He told me that's what I should do. I didn't have any choice. After about two days Star was like a different horse."

Frowning, Christina scratched under the colt's mane. "He turned into a mean old brat."

"To tell you the truth, I'm kind of afraid of him. He's smart and quick. One day he got me cornered in the stall. If someone hadn't come along, I think he would have struck me with his front hooves." Matt nodded in the colt's direction. "That's when they isolated him."

Christina glanced sharply at Matt. "That's why he was by himself that day?"

"Right. It's the Townsend Acres technique for 'breaking' horses of aggressive behavior. You isolate them from other horses, then make them rely totally on you—a human—for food and companionship."

"But that's terrible—especially for Star." Christina explained to Matt how Star had grown up an orphan. "Being alone is probably his worst fear."

"I guess that explains why Star acted the way he did," Matt said. "Plus he didn't really deserve that kind of treatment. But Mr. Townsend doesn't like anything—

a person, a horse, or a method—that doesn't conform to the way he likes things done. And Star has not been going along with the program."

Christina grimaced. "That's my fault. Well, mine and Nana's."

"Nana's?"

"Nana was the goat we borrowed to keep Star company. She didn't exactly teach him how to behave, though." Christina sighed worriedly. "I hope I can help him. I hope it's not too late."

"Me too," Matt said. He smiled fondly at Star. "You can tell just by looking at him that he's got a lot of potential."

"Chambers!" a voice hollered down the aisle.

Matt stiffened. "Dunkirk," he said in a low voice, adding loudly, "Rule number four: Grooming is always done in crossties. Only five horses in the aisle at a time—"

Dunkirk's face appeared over Matt's shoulder. "He filling you in?"

"Yes," Christina answered curtly.

"Good." He nodded once. Matt stepped aside so Dunkirk could enter the stall. When Star saw the trainer, he stepped nervously away. Christina stood protectively in front of the colt, reaching up to put a reassuring hand on his neck.

"There's a list of rules and a schedule on the bulletin board," Dunkirk said. "The schedule is important to maximize use of the paddocks, walkers, and so on.

Feeding times and amounts are also strictly scheduled. No treats or extras. Understood?"

"Yes, sir." Christina felt as though she should raise her arm in a salute.

He passed her a white sheet of paper. "Since you're under eighteen, your parents have to sign this waiver. The rules are on the back. Study them tonight. Be here at six sharp every morning. Can you do that with your school commitments?"

"I'll do it somehow, sir," Christina answered nervously.

"Good." Dunkirk glanced at Matt. "Hurry up and finish here, Chambers. You and Alpha are in the training ring in five minutes."

When he left, Christina exhaled loudly. "Whew. How do you stand it all day?" she asked Matt.

Matt shrugged. "I keep telling myself it's only for six months or so. Then I'll move on. Townsend Acres is considered one of the most successful training and breeding farms in Kentucky," he explained. "It'll look great on my work references. And I *am* learning a lot, even though I disagree with some of Townsend and Dunkirk's methods." He checked his watch. "I have to get busy. Why don't you just groom Star today? According to the schedule, you can use the crossties for the next half hour."

"Right. I'll get him cleaned up, and then spend the rest of the morning memorizing the rules," she said jokingly. But Matt didn't smile.

"Thanks," she said when Matt turned to leave, and he waved at her over his shoulder.

"Well, at least I made one friend," she told Star. Ever since Dunkirk had entered the stall, the colt had been standing in the corner, his expression wary—even after the head trainer had gone. Christina walked to his head, and the colt pinned his ears in alarm. "But it obviously wasn't you," she added wistfully. She clipped the lead shank on Star's halter and reached up to rub the soft white star between his eyes. "You and I are going to be friends again, even if I have to break a million rules."

Christina spent Saturday night memorizing the Townsend Acres rules list. Melanie had laughed uproariously as Christina read them out loud. Christina thought they were funny, too, especially rule number four: Always begin grooming a horse from the left side first. Work quickly in this order: curry, brush, soft brush, comb. Christina could picture the grooms at Townsend Acres, standing to the left of their horses all lined up in crossties, grooming in unison as though it were an army drill. But after she'd read through all the rules, she decided that except for the ones about not babying horses and feeding them treats, they mostly made sense.

Sunday morning Christina showed up bright and early at Townsend Acres. Fortunately, it had worked out that one of Whitebrook's night-shift grooms could drop her off most mornings on his way home.

When she arrived at the farm, Matt was standing in the doorway, washing out a bucket. "I see you didn't read rule number twelve," he said when he glanced over at her.

"Rule twelve?"

"Yeah, about not feeding the horses treats."

Christina flushed. Her back pockets were bulging with carrots. "How'd you know?" she asked in a low voice.

He grinned as he turned on the hose. "All girls give their horses treats. It must be a girl thing."

Laughing, Christina shook her head as she went to report to Dunkirk. She was hoping to impress him by reciting Star's schedule and her list of responsibilities. But first she had to hide the treats. She emptied her pockets into a small bucket and hid it under a pile of saddle pads in the tack room.

"Sounds like you can handle it," Dunkirk said after she told him what she was going to do with Star that morning. Then he turned away and strode down the aisle. "Carmine, don't let him get away with that!" Dunkirk barked at another groom.

Christina didn't want to stick around while Dunkirk yelled at Carmine, whoever he was. She went back to the tack room to retrieve her carrots and hurried down the aisle to Star's stall.

"Morning, Star!" Christina greeted the colt cheerily. The colt looked up from the last of his breakfast hay.

Christina took his halter and lead line off the hook on the outside wall. When she went in the stall, Star immediately flattened his ears.

She ignored him. Leaning her back against the wall, she pulled a carrot from her pocket and took a bite. "Mmm," she said, smacking her lips. "This is delicious."

One ear flicked forward.

She took another bite, crunching loudly. "Yum. Wow. You don't know what you're missing."

The second ear went forward. Turning his head, he snorted curiously in her direction. Christina continued to ignore him, focusing all her attention on the carrot. "This is not only delicious," she said, taking a third bite, "it's good for you, too."

After what seemed like forever, Star took one step toward her. Hesitantly he stretched out his neck. His nose touched her hand, and he blew softly.

"Oh, hello there. Did you want a bite?" she asked. He bobbed his head. "Then you're going to have to ask politely."

Star's lip wiggled against her hand. Christina tried not to laugh. Slowly she straightened and moved to his side. She fed him the carrot, and while he chewed, she slipped on the halter, buckled it, and snapped on the lead line.

"There. You're captured." She scratched under his forelock. "Was that so bad?"

She led him into the aisle and hooked him to crossties. He danced forward, and when the ties grew taut, he pawed the floor and fidgeted, leaving a pile of manure on the aisle floor.

"You're all right," Christina assured him. She had memorized all the Townsend Acres rules and schedules, but she also knew what horses needed the most—trust. Star needed to learn that Christina wasn't going to slap him or yank on his head when he made the slightest move. No matter what he did, she would carry on, working calmly. Eventually Star wouldn't feel so threatened.

Christina began to curry the colt's left side, humming a made-up tune, and soon the colt lowered his head and stretched his neck out in pleasure.

Matt came down the aisle brandishing a pitchfork. "Rule number eight: Never leave manure in the aisles," he said.

"I was going to clean that up when I finished grooming him. I've only done the left side—I couldn't just stop!" she joked.

"Well, now you don't have to," Matt said, scooping up Star's mess and tossing it into a red muck bucket.

"Thanks," Christina said.

"Hey, he's a lot quieter for you than he was for me." Matt said, smiling appreciatively at Star.

Christina shrugged. "He knows me," she said. "I think I might try his tack on today, too, just to see how he is."

"Do you want help?"

She shook her head. "Thanks, but I think it's better

if I do it. The fewer people around, the better he seems to be."

"Okay, but yell if you need something."

When he left, Christina carried on brushing Star and humming. When she was done with the soft brush and had combed his mane and tail, she wiped away the last particles of dust from his gleaming coat with a soft towel. Then she stood back to admire her work. Star's coat seemed to be bathed in a golden glow. His muscles rippled on his long neck and powerful hindquarters. He had yet to be ridden, but to Christina he looked every inch a champion.

"Has my dad gotten to you yet?" a voice asked. It was Parker, walking up behind her. He was wearing beige breeches and a blue polo shirt, and his hair was still wet from the shower.

"He's all right, as long as you stick to the rules," Christina answered.

"I'll say," Parker scoffed. "Anyway, Star looks happy. And you do, too," he added earnestly.

"Thanks." Christina didn't know what else to say.

"Hey, I have a lesson later, but when you're done here, why don't we hang out in my room? We could watch a movie or something," Parker offered.

Christina hesitated. Once she was done with Star, she had to go back to Whitebrook, exercise-ride two of the three-year-olds, and ride Sterling. Plus she was going to have to get up early the next day and do it all over again. *I don't have time to hang out*, she thought.

"Sorry, I can't," she said. "I'm just too busy." Even though she saw Parker's face fall, she couldn't help feeling relieved. More than anything else, she didn't want to think about whether she and Parker were turning into something more than friends. From now on she would just stick to horses.

"All right," Parker said dejectedly. "I'll see you later." He turned and strode down the aisle and out the barn door. *Please don't be mad*, Christina pleaded silently, watching him go.

She put Star back in his stall and walked down the aisle to the tack room. On the brass hooks marked with Star's name, she found a light exercise saddle and a bridle with a thick rubber snaffle bit.

Star snorted warily when Christina entered the stall carrying the tack. He pressed himself against the wall as if he wanted to disappear through it.

"You're all right, boy," Christina soothed. "We won't do anything you don't want to do."

She put the saddle on the ground and let the bridle dangle from her left hand, down by her legs. Then she held her right hand out, palm up, and walked toward Star. The chestnut colt looked at her hand, snorted, and then pricked his ears.

"That's right," Christina told him. "I won't hurt you, Star." *Ever*, she added to herself.

When she was close enough, she rubbed his soft nose, working her way up his finely sculpted head to his pointed ears and back down again. She wanted to get him used to the feel of friction on his face. While she rubbed, she lifted the bridle up until the leather was in sniffing distance. Star didn't seemed to notice—he just went on enjoying his massage. Christina slipped her index finger in the corner of Star's mouth, just as she'd done when she'd introduced him to a bottle when he was a tiny orphaned foal. Star loosened his jaw and lowered his head.

"Good boy," Christina praised. She removed her finger and reached up to rub behind his ears.

With her left hand she raised the bridle up a few more inches. Star sniffed it and then snorted, his ears flicking back and forth. Christina held the bridle still— she didn't want the colt to feel that it was being forced on him. She rubbed Star's nose again with her free hand, sliding her index finger into his mouth once more. Star dropped his poll and his jaw opened slightly. Slowly Christina eased the bridle toward him, wiggling her finger inside Star's mouth so he'd concentrate on that rather than on the bridle. When the bit reached Star's teeth Christina pressed it into his open mouth and pulled her finger free. Star bobbed his head, chewing furiously on the thick black rubber bit. Christina stood on tiptoe and pulled the leather straps over his ears.

"Good boy!" Christina called. "Good, good boy!" She gazed up at Star lovingly. He looked handsome in his bridle—like a real racehorse. His mouth was beginning to foam up from chewing at the bit, but she had managed to put his bridle on without a fight.

Christina led Star around his stall a few times to get the feel for the bit in his mouth. Then she removed the bridle and fed him a carrot.

"That's enough for today, Star," she said. "We can do the saddle some other time."

Star sucked in his breath and snorted loudly, showering her with foam from his mouth. Christina laughed and patted his shiny neck.

She carried the tack back to the tack room, ducking under crossties and dodging horses. The barn bustled with activity, but she saw no sign of Brad. Dunkirk was outside watching a yearling being longed, and the other grooms were so busy with their own yearlings that they didn't pay much attention to her.

That's fine with me, Christina thought. She didn't want anybody spying on her, telling her what to do, or yelling at her to hurry up. It was going to take a lot of patience to undo all the damage that had been done. But what Star really needed most was love.

And she was planning to give him lots of it.

10

"EASY, GIRL," CHRISTINA CROONED AS STERLING CANTERED up the hill to an angled platform called a ski jump.

"Keep her steady," Samantha called. Samantha was mounted on Blueberry, one of her lesson horses, shouting instructions as Christina schooled Sterling over Whisperwood's cross-country course.

Easter vacation was long over. It was a Wednesday afternoon in mid-April, and this was the last time they would practice cross-country before the Meadowlark event on Saturday.

So far Sterling had been jumping beautifully. She was soft and round at the gallop, and she leaped over the obstacles as if they weren't even there. They'd schooled over Whisperwood's course hundreds of times, but Christina was beginning to feel more confident about Meadowlark.

As they neared the ski jump, Christina rode a half halt to collect Sterling, then squeezed her calves against the mare's sides to signal the take-off. Sterling flew over the jump, landed smoothly, and then charged downhill toward a row of tractor tires. As they drew closer, Sterling seemed to plummet down the steep hill, her balance tipping to her forehand.

Leaning back, Christina propped her hands on the mare's withers, trying to keep Sterling balanced. If they reached the four-foot fence all strung out, Sterling would never have the impulsion to clear it.

"Circle, circle," Samantha hollered. "Get her collected."

Christina hesitated. She thought she *was* collecting Sterling. Then Sterling bobbled slightly, her weight shifting to the forehand once again, and Christina had to grab her mane with one hand to keep from pitching over her neck.

Using a pulley rein with the other hand, Christina turned Sterling in a large circle and slowed her to a canter. It was warm, and the mare's neck was bathed in sweat. Flecks of foam flew from her mouth, and her nostrils were flared.

"Get her settled before taking the tires," Samantha called.

Christina cantered in a circle until Sterling was settled and balanced, then steered her toward the tires. The mare flew over them, but when Christina turned her to go up the hill toward the bank, she could feel the usually game mare falter.

"Pull her up!" Samantha ordered.

Circling Sterling toward Blueberry, Christina stared at her instructor. They still had four more fences to go. "Why?" she asked.

"She's had it," Samantha answered.

Before Christina even gave the signal, Sterling slowed to a jerky trot. Christina could feel the mare's sides heaving like bellows. "It must be the heat," she said.

Samantha shook her head as she rode Blueberry closer. "She's just not as fit as she should be. That's why she was having so much trouble going downhill." Samantha shrugged. "Sometimes it's harder to muscle up a mare."

"But Foxy's fit," Christina pointed out.

"Parker's been really working on building her up."

"And I haven't?" Christina retorted.

Samantha's gaze was cool under the brim of her riding helmet. "I'll let you answer that yourself. Now take her for a long walk to cool her out. I have to watch Foxy and Parker."

Disheartened, Christina walked Sterling away from Samantha. "I'm sure you're fit," she muttered to the mare. Sterling answered by blowing noisily through her nostrils.

The mare was still puffing, but her gait was long and springy.

Samantha's wrong, Christina thought. *Sterling is fit. It's just too hot out.*

They'd been working almost every day after school: up hills, down hills, along the roads, and on the trails. Sterling *had* to be fit.

Christina gnawed her lip, her confidence slipping. Deep down she knew Samantha was right. She hadn't worked Sterling as much as Parker had worked Foxy. She'd been too busy with Star.

Every morning for the past week and a half, she'd arrived at Townsend Acres bright and early to groom and work with Star. By the time the school day was over, she didn't have much energy left for Sterling. The payoff was that Star was turning back into his confident, mischievous self. And Christina wouldn't have traded her time with the colt each day for anything.

Christina laced her fingers in Sterling's mane. "I'm sorry," she apologized to the mare. "It's my fault you're not ready."

The sun was setting and the evening breeze had dried the sweat on her cheeks. Bending, she felt Sterling's neck. It was damp but cool. "I'd better give you a bath."

As they headed toward the barn, the sound of hooves on the packed earth made Christina look to the left. Parker was cantering down the hill toward the tires. He had Foxy rated and balanced perfectly. They met the fence just right, sailed over it, and continued up the hill to the Picnic Table. Foxy jumped the huge obstacle cleanly, then disappeared over the hill.

Christina sighed. "That's how it's supposed to be done," she told Sterling. *Why can't I focus the way Sam wants me to?* she wondered.

That night, Christina vowed to herself, she'd go home and read all her books on eventing. She'd practice her dressage test on foot and count strides when she walked. Sterling deserved only the best rider, and Christina knew that recently she had been only half there for the horse.

When she reached the barn, she untacked Sterling, bathed her with warm water, then put on her light-weight cooler. They walked back toward the cross-county course. Samantha and Parker were coming toward her, riding side by side, talking so intently they didn't even notice Christina. Even from a distance, Samantha could tell that Foxy hadn't gotten nearly as sweaty and winded as Sterling.

"She looked great!" Christina called when they came within earshot. Parker glanced up and smiled, but Samantha kept talking. Christina could hear snatches of what she was saying: "Bold over the water jump. Cleared the oxer by a foot. Nice pace"—all things Christina would have liked to hear.

Turning Sterling, Christina led her back to the barn. Tor, Samantha's husband, was riding out of the shed on a tractor with a manure spreader hooked behind. She waved as the tractor clanked past and into one of the fields. Sterling didn't even look at the noisy vehicle.

"You *must* be pooped." Christina felt under the mare's blanket. She was still damp.

Parker halted Foxy next to them and dismounted. "If you two do that well this weekend, you'll clean up," Christina said.

"You guys did okay," Parker said as he loosened the girth.

"Okay won't get us a ribbon," Christina replied.

For the past few weeks their conversations had stuck safely to horses. Christina had to admit she wasn't exactly happy about it, but it was all she could handle for the moment. It was hard to know what Parker felt about it, or if he even noticed.

"Meadowlark is only your first event of the season," Parker pointed out. "Even if you have just a halfway decent ride, you have all summer to get better."

"Yeah, I guess," Christina mumbled. Parker took a step toward her. "What's wrong?" he asked.

"I'm just worried about this weekend."

"Why? Because you have to leave Star? Or are you afraid you'll miss something at Townsend Acres?"

Christina clearly heard the sarcasm in Parker's words. "What's that supposed to mean?"

Parker went to Foxy's other side to run up the stirrups. "It means that all you've talked about for the last week and a half is Star and the farm. I'm surprised you even remembered we were going to an event this weekend."

So he has noticed, Christina thought. *And he is mad*. "I

thought you'd be interested. Besides, Townsend Acres does belong to your family."

Parker looked at her across the top of his saddle. "If I were interested, I would hang around the farm myself, not wait for a news update from someone totally enamored of my father."

"I'm not enamored. And I've hardly seen your father since the first day he gave me the tour."

Parker came around the other side. "Oh, right, the *grand* tour," he said sarcastically.

"Yes, the *grand* tour. Your family's farm is, like, the nicest in the state, Parker, or haven't you noticed?"

"I don't have to notice. My father reminds me every day how stupid I am to be at Whisperwood instead of Townsend Acres." Angrily he pulled the reins over Foxy's head and led her into the barn.

Christina followed with Sterling. "Maybe that's because you never gave Townsend Acres a chance," she countered.

Parker shot her a get-real look over his shoulder. "I should have known," he said, stopping Foxy in the aisle and facing Christina.

"Known what?"

"That you'd get sucked into my father's web."

"That's not fair. There are a lot of people at Townsend Acres working hard to raise and train great racehorses. And your dad, well . . . he does have a lot of strict rules, but he's been letting me handle Star exactly the way I want."

Parker shook his head in disbelief. "That's what you think. My father knows everything that goes on at that farm. *Everything*. If he's left you alone, it's because you're following his plans—whether you know it or not. But watch out, Chris. Because the day will come when you will want to do things differently, and then you'll find out what he's really like."

Clucking to Foxy, Parker led her down the aisle. Christina stared after him openmouthed. She knew Parker and his father didn't get along. But Parker made his father sound like a monster. Brad couldn't be that bad, could he?

"Come on, Sterling," she said as she turned in the other direction. She wanted to stay out of the barn until Parker left. "Let's go eat some nice long grass."

For the past few days Christina had been lightly longeing Star while he wore his bridle and saddle. He'd gotten used to the stirrups rapping against his sides and the tug of the reins on his mouth. He was a quick learner, and soon he'd learned to walk, trot, and halt when Christina called out the commands.

Now it was Friday morning, and he was ready for the long reins. Christina had never worked a horse in long reins before, so she'd read everything she could on the subject and watched Matt and the other grooms until she was sure she knew every step.

"Need help?" Matt asked when Christina came out

of the tack room with a pair of long reins in hand.

"I think I'll be okay."

He looked dubiously at her. "We usually buddy up for the first time. It's a lot easier if someone's guiding the horse's head while you walk alongside with the reins."

"I know," Christina said. She also knew how nervous Star was around the other grooms. "I'll try it today by myself and see how it goes. But could you do me a favor? I'm riding in an event tomorrow—will you keep an eye on him for me? Dunkirk knows about it, so I'm sure he'll ask you to take care of him, anyway."

"Don't worry," Matt assured her. Bending closer, he whispered, "I'll even give him a carrot for you. Just don't tell the guys. They'll think I'm getting girly."

Christina socked him on the arm, then went down the aisle to where Star waited, already tacked up in crossties. She hesitated for a second, admiring the colt.

He'd really changed in the last couple of weeks. His chestnut coat shone bright and coppery, he'd grown at least an inch, and his muscles were beginning to fill out. But best of all, his sour expression was gone.

As soon as Star saw Christina, he gave a throaty whinny and stepped forward to nuzzle her arm. She held up the coiled long reins, and he sniffed them curiously.

"I hope you're ready for this," Christina said. "Because I'm not."

Hooking a lead line to the bit, she led him from the

stall. When the two reached the round training ring, she closed the gate. Facing Star, she scratched his chest. For this first lesson, they wouldn't do much, but Christina was still nervous. Star pawed the ground, eager to run.

"All right. Be patient," she said as she unhooked the lead. She hooked a long rein to his right bit ring and passed it through the stirrup and over the saddle to the left side. Next she hooked the other rein to the left bit ring. That day she would keep the long lines coiled in her hands and walk beside him. Later she would slowly let the lines out so he would get the feel of them against his sides and flanks. Eventually she would walk behind him and steer, like the driver of a cart, but without the cart. The point was to get the horse used to having pressure on both sides of his mouth, learning to bend and change direction depending on the pressure.

When the lines were attached, Christina took a deep breath. "Walk," she said, and Star strode right off, Christina walking next to the stirrup instead of by his head. When she asked him to whoa, she pulled back on the reins. He stopped dead.

"Good boy." They tried it a few more times, with Christina walking on both sides. Star was listening perfectly. She was so pleased, she decided to turn and cut across the ring. Halfway across, the loud noise of a truck backfiring made Star jump in the air, pulling Christina off balance. When he landed, his shoulder knocked into her and she fell face first in the soft footing.

Star stared at her lying at his feet, startled. Christina

tried to get up, but the long lines had tangled around her legs. Eyes rolling, Star backed up to avoid stepping on her. But the reins tightened, and the bit dug into his mouth. Throwing his head back, he tensed his muscles for flight.

Christina panicked as the long lines tightened around her legs. "Whoa, Star!" she cried, her voice breaking as the fear of being dragged overcame her. Star froze, his eyes white with fear. "Whoa, Star," Christina repeated—more softly this time, though her heart was racing. Slowly Christina inched forward in the dirt, trying to release the pressure of the reins on his bit. Finally she was able to swing her legs around and the long lines sagged.

Star lowered his head, still gawking at her as if she were some sort of strange creature. "It's just me, boy," she crooned as she reached forward and untangled the lines from around her ankles. When her legs were free, she sighed with relief. She was okay—shaken, but okay. Now she had to make sure Star didn't tangle himself up in the reins.

"Chris?" Matt threw open the gate. Immediately Christina put her hand up to stop him. "Don't come in," she warned. "I don't want him to panic and get the lines wrapped around his legs."

Matt nodded and stood by the gate. Christina reached for the reins. One lay across Star's back. The other hung down from the stirrup to the ground. If he took off running, it would be a disaster.

"Good boy." She continued to talk soothingly. Slowly she got to her knees and began to coil the lines. When they were rolled up and secure in her hands, she stood up. Star rotated his ears nervously as if to ask, *What happened?*

When Christina reached his head, she was light-headed with relief. Star's chest and neck were lathered with nervous sweat, and his nostrils flared in and out with fright, but he wasn't hurt.

"Are you all right?" Matt asked. He took off his cap and wiped the sweat from his forehead.

Christina sagged against Star's shoulder. "Yeah, I'm fine. I think." She turned her hands over to look at her palms. She'd landed on her hands, and they were grazed and dirty. She was lucky.

"For a second there, I thought I thought you were going for a nasty ride," Matt said. He pointed around the ring. "What happened?"

"It wasn't Star's fault," Christina said quickly. "I tripped and the reins got tangled and . . ." Tears filled her eyes.

"Oh, wow, don't cry," Matt said awkwardly. "I mean, I don't even have a tissue."

"That's okay," Christina said, wiping her nose on her shirt. Embarrassed, she glanced around. As far as she could tell, no one else had witnessed the near fiasco.

"Sure you're all right?" Matt asked again, as if afraid to leave her.

"Yeah. Thanks for coming to rescue me."

"I didn't exactly rescue you. Though I would have," he murmured under his breath. Christina looked over at him. He was smiling sheepishly. She smiled back, noticing for the first time how cute he was.

"Well, I'd better get back to work," Matt said, turning to go.

"Me too." She checked her watch, gasping. "Oh, no. I was supposed to get the bus home already! By the time I get Star cleaned up, I'll never make my school bus!"

"How about if I take you home?" Matt suggested. "I'll tell Dunkirk it's an emergency."

Christina was already leading Star toward the gate. "That would be great. And it is an emergency. I have a geometry quiz first period."

She led Star out of the training ring. Out of the corner of her eye she spotted Brad Townsend's new pickup truck. It was cruising slowly down the drive. She sucked in her breath, remembering Parker's words: *He knows everything that happens around the farm.*

Had Brad witnessed her fall? Would he yell at her? Or, even worse, would he tell her she could no longer work there?

She couldn't worry about it now. Quickly Christina bathed Star and turned him out in a paddock to graze. When she was ready to go, Matt zoomed up on a motorcycle.

A shiver of excitement raced up her arms as she clipped on the extra motor cycle helmet, climbed on behind Matt, and slid her arms around his narrow waist.

"Hold tight," he said, and gunned the engine.

The wind whistled past Christina's ears as they roared down the drive. She closed her eyes, enjoying the blast of air against her skin. The houses, barns, and fields that lined the roads flashed past until, all too soon, they were flying up Whitebrook's drive. Matt slowed to a stop in front of the house, the motor rumbling.

"Thanks. That was great!" Christina said over the roar. When she climbed off, she could see Matt's grin reflected in the side mirror.

"We'll have to do it again sometime," he said. "See you Monday." Christina watched as he rolled forward and then roared back down the driveway.

Melanie came running from the house. "Who was that?"

Racing past her cousin, Christina leaped up the porch steps. "I'll tell you on the bus. I have to hurry— I'm late!"

"But what about Parker?" Melanie demanded. They were on the bus, and Christina was explaining who Matt was and how sweet he'd been since she started working at Townsend Acres.

"We haven't been getting along too well," Christina admitted. "Last time we were together we had a fight."

"Does it have something to do with Matt?" Melanie teased.

Christina shook her head. "No. Our problems started

way before that." She told Melanie about their race and the stakes being a "date." "But then Parker didn't say anything else about it. I guess he didn't want to go."

Melanie stared at Christina and shook her head incredulously. "You can be so dense sometimes."

"What do you mean?"

"Did you ever notice that all the girls at Henry Clay swoon whenever they see Parker coming down the hallway?"

"Uh—no."

"But that the only one he spends any time with is you?"

Christina shrugged. "That's because we ride together."

Melanie threw up her hands. "You're useless!"

"What?" Christina asked.

"When it comes to Parker, you are totally useless."

Christina's mouth fell open. "I am not."

"Then how come you can't see that Parker is totally in love with you?"

"But—but—he isn't," Christina said, blushing red. "He didn't even want to go on a date with me."

Melanie poked her in the chest with one finger. "He wanted to, but you made it sound as if *you* didn't want to go out with *him*."

"Because I thought he only wanted to be friends," Christina explained. "Why didn't he say anything?"

"Because guys are clueless when it comes to stuff like this. Besides, Parker's too proud."

"I think it's a Townsend trait. So what should I do, O Wise One?" Christina joked.

"I have no idea." Melanie grinned devilishly. "Come on, we're here."

Christina stood up, hitching her backpack up on her shoulder as she followed her cousin off the bus. Maybe she'd find time to talk to Parker at the event the next day, though she was supposed to focus on her riding, not chase Parker down and ask him out.

But at school that day she was planning to avoid him at all costs.

11

CHRISTINA WALKED STERLING INTO THE MEADOWLARK warm-up area. Her dressage test was in fifteen minutes. Christina was nervous, but she was glad she had evented at Meadowlark before—Sterling wasn't spooking at every noise and tiny flutter on the ground. Sam couldn't be there to coach Christina and make her concentrate, since she was riding a younger horse in training level. *Focus, focus,* Christina repeated to herself. But she knew her mind and heart were not on the task at hand. She kept worrying about Star—was Matt taking good care of him in her absence? And she kept looking for Parker.

As Christina walked Sterling around, letting her get used to everything, she spotted Parker leading Foxy and walking next to his grandfather, Clay. Parker was taller than his grandfather, but the two looked very similar, with thick hair and intense blue eyes. They even walked alike.

Christina waved, but they were talking so intently, they didn't notice her. Then Sterling shied at a paper cup skittering in the breeze, and Christina turned her attention back to her horse and her dressage test.

Focus, focus, Christina silently chanted again. She had to push thoughts of Parker and Star out of her head. She had to remember why she was at Meadowlark. She squeezed Sterling into a trot and dropped her stirrups, concentrating on sitting deep to the trot.

Christina rode into the dressage ring, confident and relaxed, and halted, saluting to the judges. Preliminary level didn't have any advanced movements, but the judges looked for a horse to be responsive and move correctly at a working trot and canter. Christina and Sterling had always communicated well, and they worked hard. Sterling anticipated every command and executed it perfectly, floating through the test. By the time Christina gave her final salute, she couldn't wipe the pleased grin from her face. As she left the arena, she saw Clay Townsend grinning at her from the sidelines. Parker was beside him, his expression blank.

"Congratulations, ladies," Clay said to Christina and Sterling. "That was a very nice test."

Christina slid off and gave Sterling a big hug. "Thank you," she said to Mr. Townsend, and stole a sideways glance at Parker. He was looking down, avoiding her gaze. "I hear you had a nice test, too," she told him. "Sorry I didn't see it."

Parker only nodded in response. Christina was glad Mr. Townsend was there to break the awkward silence.

"Your mare is filling out nicely," Clay said as he walked around Sterling, studying her. "You made a good choice—what was it—three years ago?"

Christina nodded, surprised that Mr. Townsend remembered.

"But I hear you have good instincts about horses," he added.

"What's Parker been saying about me?" she asked. She kept her tone light, hoping Parker would react. But he only looked at Clay curiously.

Mr. Townsend arched his gray brows. "It wasn't Parker." Startled, Christina's gaze darted from Parker to his grandfather. Had Brad been reporting on her to Clay?

"I'd better go get ready for cross-country," Parker interrupted. He turned to go and then paused. "You coming?" he asked Christina.

But Christina's curiosity was piqued. She shook her head, ignoring Parker's annoyed glance as he stalked off.

"Have you seen Star?" she asked Mr. Townsend. "Do you think he can be a champion like Wonder?"

Clay laughed. "You sound just like Ashleigh! Don't tell me you've become as obsessed with racing as she is."

"No," Christina said quickly. "But I love Star and I want him to have the best chance possible."

"Well, Star's got the bloodlines and conformation to be a winner," Clay said. "But he also has to have it up here." He tapped his temple.

"But he's fine, it's just—" Christina faltered, wondering how much she should confide in Clay. Should she tell him she was worried Brad was going to work the colt too hard, too fast?

Side by side they started walking toward the Whitebrook van, with Sterling walking behind them. Christina unsnapped her helmet strap.

"Star is different—he's nervous. I know Mr. Townsend and Mr. Dunkirk know what they're doing, but . . . so far Star only really trusts me. So what I'd like to do, if it's all right . . ." She hesitated, afraid he would think she was overstepping her bounds.

"Go on," Clay Townsend encouraged.

"I'd like to work with him slowly, the way I have been, all summer, and wait until the fall to back him. And I want to be the first one to ride him," Christina rushed on before she chickened out.

"Have you discussed this with Brad?"

She shook her head. "I'm afraid he'll say no."

Stopping, Mr. Townsend reached out and patted her shoulder. "I'll talk to him. Brad does get a little overzealous sometimes, but he's a good trainer." Then his expression turned stern. "But I have some advice for you, too, young lady. If you want Star to be a winner, you're going to have to fight for him all the way."

Christina swallowed hard, then nodded.

"Well, then, good luck with everything," Mr. Townsend said. With a wave, he walked away, his stride jaunty.

Pulling off her helmet, Christina ran her fingers through her damp bangs. She glanced at Sterling, who was pulling on the reins, attempting to drag Christina over to a tasty patch of grass just out of reach. *How am I supposed to fight for Star when I'm here with Sterling?* Christina wondered.

She just had to try to do it all.

Bending down, Christina adjusted the Velcro on Sterling's red splint boots. "Whoa," she said firmly when Sterling cocked her hind foot and switched her tail.

It was after lunch, and as soon as Christina had put the boots on the mare, Sterling knew it was time for jumping. Already her neck was lathered in anticipation.

"She's getting pretty keyed up," Melanie said from Sterling's head. She was holding the mare's halter while Christina put on the boots.

"I'm getting keyed up, too," Christina said. "I've only jumped Meadowlark's cross-country course at training level. These jumps will be higher, and they've added some new ones. We have to jump over a hay wagon."

Melanie's eyes opened wide. "Full of hay?" she asked.

"It's empty, but it's still big and wide and scary," Christina said.

"I'd much rather gallop a thousand-pound horse forty miles an hour down a dirt track any day," Melanie replied. "Jumping is scary."

Standing up, Christina went over to the tack trunk to get her safety vest while Melanie started to tack up Sterling. The mare was fidgety, whinnying at every horse that walked by. "Stand up!" Christina heard Melanie say sharply. Then, "Ouch, that was my foot!"

Christina started to giggle.

"I really don't think a squashed toe is that funny," Melanie fumed.

"It's not. I'm sorry," Christina apologized, still laughing. "I'm just so nervous, I'm feeling punchy."

"Have you talked to Parker yet?" Melanie asked.

"No. He's ignoring me." Christina giggled, as if it were the funniest thing in the world.

Just then Sterling squealed and kicked out. Christina doubled over with laughter.

"You two are pathetic," Melanie said, shaking her head. "I'll be amazed if you even get out of the starting box."

"What's going on?" Samantha asked as she came around the front of the van. She was dressed like a kid, in a baseball cap and jeans, but her expression was serious.

Straightening, Christina choked down the last of her

laughter. "I'm having a nervous breakdown," she answered.

Samantha chuckled and pulled Christina's saddle off a bale of hay. "As long as you have it before cross-country and not during."

"Right," Christina said, buckling her safety vest and tying on her number pinny.

Samantha tightened the girth, and Sterling squealed and kicked out once again. "She's going to need a good warm-up today," she advised. "Do you want me to watch you school over the warm-up jumps?"

"No, we'll be all right," Christina replied. She knew that having Samantha watch her would only make her more nervous.

When everything was ready, Christina mounted and trotted Sterling over to the cross-country warm-up area. Riders were cantering their horses in circles, popping back over a large oxer, and Christina had to be careful not to get run over. She brought Sterling down to a walk, asking her to bend and flex her neck before squeezing her into a round, ground-eating canter. Sitting lightly, Christina concentrated on getting them both relaxed and settled.

The preliminary course consisted of twenty obstacles ranging from a solid stack of logs to a jump down a bank into deep water. Since Christina had ridden preliminary in the fall, she knew what to expect. Still, her heart seemed to pound especially hard under her safety vest.

To do well, she had to concentrate. But her mind kept straying back to her conversation with Clay. If he meant what he said, would Christina actually have a chance to ride Star?

Goose bumps of excitement made her arms tingle. If Star really did have Wonder's heart and speed, he might be a famous racehorse one day—and she would be a part of it!

Taking a deep breath, Christina forced her thoughts away from Star and back to the cross-country course. It was timed, so pacing was especially important. She and Sterling had to get over all the obstacles with no time penalties in order to be in the ribbons.

"Number fourteen, you're on deck," the steward called.

"That's us, Sterling," Christina said. Holding the reins in one hand, she stroked the mare's neck.

As they approached the starting box, the roar of a motorcycle made her twist in the saddle. It was Matt, riding up the hill while an event official ran after him, hollering, "Stop—you can't go through there!"

Excited by the noise, Sterling pranced sideways. Christina turned the mare toward Matt, who stopped a safe distance away, jumped off his motorcycle, and ran toward them.

"What's wrong?" Christina asked, her heart leaping into her throat when Matt pulled off his helmet. His face was anxious and worried. Instantly Christina knew there was something wrong with Star.

Christina steered Sterling toward Matt.

"What's wrong?" she demanded.

"They're backing him today," Matt said breathlessly.

Christina was so stunned, she wasn't sure if she had heard Matt correctly. "What?" she asked.

"They're backing Star. I heard Brad tell Dunkirk this morning."

"But why—who—?" Christina stopped, bewildered.

"Julio's backing him. He's the one Brad always uses to start the yearlings."

"But why didn't Brad ask me? Why didn't he say anything to me?"

Matt shook his head. "He doesn't have to, Christina. He's the boss."

"I can't believe it." Anger raced through Christina. She clenched and unclenched her fists on the reins. Brad must have planned it all along, waiting until he knew she wasn't going to be around. How could he do this to her, and to Star?

Whinnying loudly, Sterling swung her hindquarters around. Just in time, Matt jumped out of the way. "I'm sorry I interrupted you in the middle of your ride," Matt said. "I should have waited, but I thought you'd want to know."

"No, I'm glad you told me. Can you take me over to Townsend Acres?"

"Sure. But you'd better get off your horse first."

Christina had completely forgotten she was even riding Sterling. The mare was jigging nervously. "Whoa," Christina said as she dismounted. *Poor Sterling,* she thought distractedly. *I had her all excited for cross-country, and now I'm getting off.*

"And I'll have to drop you off at the end of the driveway," Matt went on. "I took a chance coming here. I told Dunkirk I had to go to the bank. If they knew I rode over here to tell you about Star, I'd be fired for sure."

"Fired! But why would they fire you for talking to me?"

"Don't you know by now?"

"I know Brad has rules and schedules and certain ways of doing things. But he's not a dictator."

Matt cocked his head as if to say, *Oh, really?* and Christina closed her mouth. She'd been so naive. Why hadn't she listened to Parker?

"Number fourteen!" a voice said sharply. The steward strode up, clipboard in hand. "Everyone's waiting, number fourteen. Either you get on your horse and get in the starting box now, or be eliminated."

Christina stared at the steward. Riding in the event just didn't seem that important anymore.

"I'm dropping out," Christina said without hesitation. "My mare . . . um . . ." She pointed to Sterling's front leg. "I think she's lame."

"All right, then," the woman said, and scribbled on her clipboard. "I'll notify the event officials."

Sterling nudged Christina with her nose as if to ask what was going on. Just then Melanie ran up. She glanced curiously at Matt, then focused on Christina. "What are you doing?" she demanded. "You were supposed to go a few minutes ago."

Christina thrust the reins into her cousin's hands. "Dropping out. I'm going with Matt to Townsend Acres. Brad's backing Star—now! I have to stop him!"

"But what about the event? What'll I tell Sam and your parents and Parker?"

"Tell everyone I'm sorry," Christina said as she started after Matt. "Star's more important!"

12

WHAT AM I GOING TO SAY TO BRAD? CHRISTINA WONDERED furiously. She held tight to Matt's waist as they zoomed down the two-lane road toward Townsend Acres. The wind buffeted her cheeks, and her eyes streamed with tears.

Confronting Brad head-on would be foolish, she knew. He would laugh in her face, then order her off the farm. She had to persuade him to change his mind. Clay had understood her logic. Maybe Brad would, too.

Matt slowed the motorcycle, and when Christina looked over his shoulder, she saw that they were already at the gates of Townsend Acres. "I'll drop you off here," he said as he pulled over onto the side of the drive.

"Thanks," Christina said, feeling dizzy and uncertain.

Matt tilted up his visor. "Are you going to be okay?" he asked.

Unsnapping her riding helmet, she pulled it off and nodded. "Yeah, thanks. I owe you one," she said.

Matt grinned. "You'd better see how it goes first. Star might be fine, and you might get into trouble for just being here."

Christina shook her head. "I want to be here no matter what happens." *I promised Star I wouldn't leave him,* she added to herself.

"Good luck," Matt said. Dropping his visor back into place, he roared up the drive.

Christina stood rooted to the spot. When the motorcycle was out of sight, she inhaled deeply, squared her shoulders, and marched up the drive. By the time she reached the barn, she was soaked with nervous sweat, but determined to convince Brad that she should be the one to get on Star first. And she wanted to *wait*.

Brad and Dunkirk were in the aisle looking over a horse held by T.J., one of the grooms. Brad nodded when he saw Christina, a hint of surprise in his eyes, but he didn't stop talking. Christina walked over to Star's stall. It was empty.

She whirled around and approached the group in the aisle, a smile plastered on her face. As usual, Brad was smartly dressed—there wasn't a speck of dirt or horsehair on him.

"Hello, Christina," Brad greeted her politely, any trace of surprise carefully erased. "What are you doing here? I thought you were at the event with Parker."

"I was, but Sterling threw a shoe and I had to drop out," Christina replied, wondering how many lies she was going to have to tell before the day was over. "Is Star outside?"

"Yeah," Dunkirk said, his cheek bulging with a wad of chewing tobacco. "Angie's bringing him in, though."

"Really?" Christina said brightly, though her heart began thumping faster.

"Yup. We're going to back him today," Dunkirk said. "Julio's been working with all the yearlings. Star's next on the list."

"Um . . ." Christina shifted her gaze to Brad, who was brushing an imaginary piece of lint from his pant leg. "I thought you were going to wait," she said, directing her words at him.

Dunkirk spit a wad of juice on the floor. "We did wait."

"That's right, Christina," Brad agreed. "We left him until last. You've had several weeks to work with him, and you've done a terrific job. But now it's time for him to get with the Townsend program."

"Well, I'm sure the program is perfect for all the other horses." Christina tried to keep the sarcasm out of her voice. "But Star's not ready. And he's really anxious around the other grooms. I'm certain some stranger getting on his back will scare him to death."

Dunkirk snorted. "That's because you baby him too

much. It's time he got treated like a horse instead of—"

Brad silenced Dunkirk with a wave of his hand. "Christina, we appreciate the work you've put into Star. Now it's time to make him a racehorse. That's what we do here at Townsend Acres. And we do it well."

Christian locked gazes with him. She could tell by the hard glint in his eyes that he wasn't going to budge. "Okay, then let me be the first to get on him. I'm the only one he knows and trusts."

Brad shook his head. "Too risky. You're not even a real employee."

"Then at least let me hold him!" Christina insisted.

Brad exchanged glances with Dunkirk, deliberating. "All right," he said. "But you must do *exactly* as I say."

She nodded, willing to agree to anything just so she could be there with Star.

The thud of hooves on tanbark made her turn. Angie was leading Star in from outside. When he saw her, he whinnied a greeting.

"Groom him and tack him up," Brad ordered her. "Julio will be ready in fifteen minutes."

Christina tried to stay calm as she brushed Star, but her palms were so sweaty, she kept dropping the curry comb. Worried that Star would pick up on her nervousness, she began to hum a familiar tune.

By the time the colt was saddled and bridled, she'd run through the song five times. Her mouth was dry, her throat raw, but Star was calm.

"I'll be right beside you, every second," Christina assured him as she unhooked him from the crossties. "I promise."

Matt was coming out of the tack room. When he saw no one was looking, he gave her a thumbs-up sign. *Thanks*, Christina mouthed. *For everything*, she wanted to add. She couldn't imagine what would have happened if Matt hadn't warned her. But the hard part wasn't over yet.

Julio was walking up the aisle toward them. He was smaller than Christina, with bowed legs and fingers gnarled from having broken them so many times in falls. He'd retired as a jockey several years ago and made his living by traveling around the local farms helping to break yearlings.

Christina knew he was a fine rider, but he also got paid by the horse. That meant he couldn't take his time getting to know the colt or filly he was working with.

Dunkirk came up with a chain lead shank. "Put this over his nose."

"No." Christina shook her head. "It'll just upset him." She felt bad enough having to hook the lead line onto the bit.

Dunkirk rolled his eyes. "He's not a little baby,"

"All yearlings are babies," Christina replied. "In any other sport, colts and fillies wouldn't be backed until they were a year older!"

"This isn't any other sport." Dunkirk spat a wad at her feet. "This is racing. And yearlings are babies that are all muscle and weigh eight hundred pounds. I'm not putting Julio in danger because some kid—"

"That's okay." Julio slapped Dunkirk's shoulder. "I trust her." He smiled at Christina, his teeth crooked.

Christina led Star to the round training ring where Julio would get on him. She walked the colt around, explaining to him what would happen. "It's no big deal. Julio's just going to lie across your back."

Star pranced sideways, showing off. He chewed the bit and tossed his head playfully. Christina was relieved to see he wasn't nervous. Then Julio came into the ring, snapping on his helmet. Star halted. Head up, he eyed the ex-jockey.

Leading the colt in a circle, Christina stroked his neck. "It's okay. I know you're not used to him. But he's a friend, sort of."

Out of the corner of her eye, she saw a blue pickup truck drive up to the barn and stop. Parker got out of the driver's side. Just then Brad and Matt walked up to the ring.

"Let's go," Brad said, leaning his arms on the fence. "We've got three more horses to get done. Matt, go on in and give Julio a leg."

Christina focused her attention back on Star. She took several deep breaths, steadying herself. Then she halted him in the center of the ring.

As soon as Julio and Matt approached, she knew the whole situation was a mistake. Star tensed every muscle. He threw up his head and his eyes rolled. "Julio,"

Christina said in a low voice, "this isn't going to work."

Julio waved dismissively. "I get on a hundred horses a week," he said. "They all react differently. I can handle it."

"But *Star* can't," Christina insisted. "He isn't ready." Already the colt was retreating from Julio. Switching his tail, he swung his hindquarters away. Christina held tight to the lead but moved with him, trying not to jerk his head and get him more worked up.

Julio snorted. "None of the youngsters think they're ready. They want to eat grass in the field all day. Come on. I have others to do," he added impatiently.

Christina glanced at Matt, but he only shook his head helplessly. "Mr. Townsend," she tried once again, "this isn't going to work. Star's too scared. He's—"

"Enough," Brad snapped, cutting her off. "If you aren't capable of holding the colt, then let Dunkirk have him."

"No, I can handle him," Christina said quickly, choking back the emotion that filled her. She was going to have to stand idly by while they ruined her horse!

Suddenly Parker was at his father's side. "Look, Dad—"

"Stay out of this, Parker," Brad said curtly. "You wanted nothing to do with this farm, as I recall."

Parker flushed angrily, and Christina's heart went out to him. He was risking a fight with his father for her sake.

Star began to back up, and Christina had to turn back to him. "Easy, boy," she crooned.

"Hold him steady," Julio instructed. He held on to the saddle while Matt boosted him over. For a second Star stood still as Julio lay across the saddle like a sack. Christina could see that every muscle in the colt's body was trembling and taut. The colt began to prance in place, his steps awkward and unbalanced. His ears were pinned and his eyes rolled back in his head, trying to get a look at the thing on his back.

Christina stroked Star's neck and scratched under his forelock. "You're doing great," she soothed. "Then I'll give you a treat, and you'll see—it's no big deal."

But suddenly Julio swung his right leg over Star's back and sat up in the saddle. Christina stared up at him, horrified. The most frightening moment for any horse was when he saw a person looming over his head and neck for the first time. When they backed a horse at Whitebrook, the rider never sat all the way up unless the horse was dead calm.

And Star was anything but calm.

The colt froze. His eyes rolled back in his head. Then he reared up on his hind legs, jerking the lead from Christina's grasp. His front legs flailed in the air. Julio leaned forward on Star's neck, but his weight had unbalanced the immature colt. Star flipped over, landing on his back, with Julio beneath him.

"Star!" Christina screamed. Star flopped heavily

over on his side, trying to get all four legs beneath him. Then he scrambled to his feet, shaking from head to toe. Julio lay on the ground under the colt's belly. His eyes were closed.

Christina grabbed the dangling lead line. "Whoa," she said, her voice shaking. If Star moved, he'd trample Julio!

Star stood still, but his ears flicked nervously back and forth. "Easy. You're fine," Christina crooned. "Just don't move."

Glancing uneasily at Star, Matt walked across the ring and bent down to grab Julio's arms and slide him from under the colt's feet. As soon as Julio was free, Christina exhaled in relief. She led Star into the corner and ran her hands over each of his legs, checking to make sure he was okay. The colt seemed unharmed, but the damage the experience had done was immeasurable.

Pushing past his father, Parker threw open the gate and hurried over to Christina. As soon as Christina saw his worried expression, she began to cry. Parker wrapped one arm around her shoulder, and she pressed her forehead against his chest.

"Is Julio going to be all right?" she asked, glancing over Parker's shoulder. The ex-jockey lay in the dirt, his eyes still closed. Brad and Dunkirk had come into the ring and were hunched over him.

"I don't know. Matt ran up to call nine-one-one," Parker said.

"I told them Star wasn't ready," Christina said, choking on her tears.

Parker hugged her closer. "I know. I heard you. It wasn't your fault. My father should have listened to you," he declared, his voice filled with anger.

Suddenly someone jerked the lead line from Christina's fingers. It was Dunkirk. "I'll take him," he said brusquely. "I should have been holding him in the first place."

"No, you shouldn't have," Christina said, quickly clamping her fingers on Star's halter.

Straightening, Brad came toward them. She swung to face him. "I should never have let you back him," she said. "It's *your* fault he flipped and hurt Julio. Star wasn't ready!"

"No, he was ready all right. My mistake was letting you hold him." Brad narrowed his eyes. "Don't ever speak to me like that again, Christina," he said, his jaw muscles tight. "This is my farm. You have no idea what you're talking about."

"You're wrong." Parker stepped from behind Christina. "Christina does know what she's talking about. You should have listened to her. The colt *wasn't* ready. Not every animal fits into your rules and regulations, you know."

"Including you, right, Parker?" Brad asked, his tone cool.

"Including me." Parker met his father's gaze straight on.

Christina held her breath. Keeping his eyes on his son, Brad folded his arms across his chest. "Then I suggest you leave," he said calmly.

Parker raised his brows, as if surprised by his father's reaction.

"And I mean leave. Your mother and I will arrange for you to finish your junior year at the Windsor-Huntington School in Connecticut. I'm sure that with a generous donation, they'll still take you."

Parker's face flushed angrily. "I won't go."

"No?" Brad countered.

"No. I'm not letting you and Mother arrange my life anymore. I'm out of here. I'll get my things and wait for you in the truck, Christina." Without a backward glance, Parker strode from the round ring.

Brad watched his son leave, then turned to Christina. "Give Star's lead to Dunkirk. You've done enough damage for one day."

"Me?" Christina's shoulders shook with anger. "You're the one who wouldn't listen," she accused. "And now you've driven away your son."

"Get off my farm, Christina," Brad said without a flicker of emotion. "You're no longer welcome here. You're no longer Star's groom."

His last words cut through Christina like a knife. Slowly she released her hold on Star's halter.

"P-Please take good care of Star," she stammered, running from the round ring before Brad had the satisfaction of seeing her burst into tears.

13

CHRISTINA RACED ACROSS THE LAWN TO PARKER'S TRUCK, parked in front of the Townsend Acres mansion. The door to the house was open and Parker came out, his arms loaded with clothes. His mother, Lavinia, was right behind him. She wore a crisp white blouse with a dove gray straight skirt and high heels. She was a beautiful woman, but as she followed Parker out of the house, lines of anger were etched on her face.

"Where do you think you're going?" Lavinia demanded as Parker threw the clothes in the bed of his truck. "What are you doing with your clothes?"

"I'm leaving," Parker said, glaring at his mother. "And don't worry, I didn't take anything that doesn't belong to me."

When he saw Christina standing next to his truck,

Parker stopped in his tracks. His eyes probed hers worriedly. "Are you okay?"

"I'm all right," she whispered softly. But it was a lie. She was close to tears, and she didn't dare look in the direction of the training ring. Star was more than likely being punished for something that wasn't his fault, and once again Christina had broken her promise and left him alone.

"Get in the truck and I'll take you home," Parker said.

"Don't you leave, Parker Jamison Townsend," Lavinia said from the front steps, her tone imperious. "Don't you dare walk out. Not until your father hears about this!"

Parker shook his head bitterly. "He already knows," he said, and climbed into the truck.

Lavinia's mouth opened and then closed. Abruptly she whirled on her high heels and flew inside, slamming the door.

Not until they were down the drive and on the main road did Christina let out her breath. Closing her eyes, she laid her head against the back of the seat. "I'm so sorry, Parker. I didn't want you to get in the middle of this."

"Hey, you were the one who got dragged into the middle of the latest Townsend family feud." He laughed sharply. "Did you see my mother's face? I thought she was going to ruin her latest eye-lift."

"At least she was upset that you were leaving. Your father . . ." Christina pictured Brad's hard expression when he'd ordered first Parker, then her off the farm.

"Dad's not exactly in touch with his emotions," Parker joked.

An ambulance zoomed past them and turned up the Townsend Acres driveway, its siren blaring. Christina choked back a sob. *What if Julio is dead and they blame Star?*

"He'll be all right," Parker assured her, as if he'd read her mind. "I bet that guy's taken worse falls before. The ground was pretty soft."

Christina wiped her cheeks and glanced at Parker. "What are you doing here, anyway? You're suppose to be at Meadowlark, winning the event."

"I finished cross-county, and I should be able to make stadium jumping," Parker said, not sounding at all concerned. "When Melanie told me what was happening, I couldn't let you face my dad alone. So what happened after I stormed off?"

Christina grimaced. "He told me to leave Townsend Acres and never come back."

"Sounds like we're both outcasts."

"At least I have a home to go to. What are you going to do?"

Parker shrugged, as if not having a place to sleep was no big deal. "I'm just glad I'm out of there. If I stayed any longer, I might become *one of them*," Parker said in his best horror-movie voice.

Christina smiled. "Don't you ever get nervous or worry about anything?"

He shrugged again, his face suddenly serious. For a few miles they drove in silence. Parker turned on the radio and fiddled with the tuner, then turned it off.

"Yeah, I worry about things," he said suddenly. "Like you going out with someone like Matt."

"Matt?" Turning in the truck seat, Christina stared at him in surprise.

"Yeah, Matt. You know, the guy who works at Townsend Acres? The one who drove you home yesterday on his motorcycle?"

"How'd you know about that?"

Parker's smile was sarcastic. "How do you think?"

"Your father?"

"I told you, he knows everything."

"Did he tell you that I fell down and Star almost got tangled in the long lines? Not that it matters anymore."

"If he did mention it, I didn't notice. I was too busy wondering about you and Matt."

"There's nothing between me and Matt. I was late for school and he helped me out." Christina stared at him. "Are you jealous, Parker?" she asked before she could stop herself.

"No." He sounded surprised. "What makes you say that?"

"Well, a while ago you blew up at me because you said I was spending too much time with Star. And now you're mad about Matt. It made me wonder."

"Wonder what?"

Christina exhaled loudly. "Is this some kind of quiz

show? Or a contest to see who will admit it first?"

"Admit what?"

"Admit . . . admit . . ." Christina waved her arm around, unable to say it. She hoped Melanie was right about Parker and her, because she was about to put everything on the line.

"Admit that you like me?" Parker finished her sentence before she had a chance to.

"No," Christina said, taken aback. "I was going to say 'admit that *you* like *me.*'"

"Huh." He gripped the steering wheel so hard, his knuckles were white. Flipping on the turn signal, he slowed and pulled into Whitebrook's drive.

Christina slid down the seat, totally mortified by what she'd said. *I dropped out of the event, I've lost Star, and now I'm losing Parker.* More than anything, she wished she could start the day over, or just forget it ever happened.

Parker stopped the car. "Aren't you getting out?" he asked.

Christina looked up at her house. It was quiet. Of course—everyone was at Meadowlark. "Do you mind driving me back to the event?" she asked sheepishly.

Parker put the truck in gear and eased it down the driveway. Christina tried to think of something to say to break the awkward silence, but Parker spoke first.

"While I was riding cross-country we went by that jump—where I fell, remember?"

Christina nodded. How could she forget? It was an

old hay barn that had been converted into a jump. The wide double doors had been removed on both ends, so the horse jumped up into the building, cantered through, and jumped out the other side. Since the barn had been built into a steep bank, the second part of the jump was an eight-foot drop over a hay manger.

Christina's stomach twisted as she thought back to the last time they'd ridden at Meadowlark. It had been almost three years before, when she'd just met Parker. The barn was an advanced jump and not part of the preliminary course. But Parker had recklessly and illegally taken Foxy through it. Foxy had somersaulted over the manger, throwing Parker and landing on top of him.

Parker had come out of it with a broken arm and a concussion. Foxy had had a hematoma and a chipped hock.

Suddenly the truck stopped. Parker had pulled over to the side of the road.

"Parker, what are you doing?" Christina demanded, confused.

Parker turned toward her, his intense blue eyes boring into hers. "Do you remember that day?" Parker asked.

Christina glanced at him incredulously. "The day you fell? Of course I do. It was pretty scary."

"After Foxy went down, I don't remember much," Parker said. "But I do remember one thing—hearing your voice."

Christina flushed and looked into her lap. "But you

had a concussion," she reminded him. "You were out cold. How could you hear me?" For a second the image of Parker trapped under Foxy's body swam into her mind. While they'd waited for the ambulance, she'd kneeled on Foxy's neck with one knee, keeping her down. If the mare had scrambled to her feet, she would have trampled Parker.

"I could hear you," Parker insisted. "You kept talking to me. I think you were afraid I might stop breathing or die. You said stuff like, 'You and Foxy aren't afraid of anything, are you? You're such a great team, I bet you'll beat us to the Olympics. Your parents will be so proud. Even your mom will be glad you kept riding.'"

Christina's mouth dropped open. "How do you remember what I said?"

"I just do. Because that's when I realized you were . . . special." His voice lowered. "You were scared and crying, but you kept talking to me." He reached up and brushed a strand of hair off her cheek.

"That was nearly three years ago," Christina whispered. Parker was so close, she had to tilt her head to look into his eyes.

"I know. And after all that time I still think you're special. Really special." Bending down, his arm stole around her waist.

Christina felt her insides quiver as she reached up to clasp her hands behind Parker's neck.

She'd kissed a few boys before, but Parker Townsend's kiss was definitely the best.

14

"MAYBE I COULD STAY AT SAM AND TOR'S," PARKER SAID AS they drove along toward Meadowlark. "I practically live there, anyway. And they're always talking about needing more help."

Reaching up to where his hand lay on her shoulder, Christina laced her fingers with his. "That's a great idea. They have that room over the garage—you could live there."

"But how do I bring it up? I don't want to just barge in and say, 'Gee, Sam, Tor, can I live with you?'"

"I'm sure they'll offer when they hear what happened. And if they don't, I'll ask them. I'll be so smooth and diplomatic, they'll think it was their idea."

Parker raised his eyebrows. "Aren't you the same girl that just got kicked off Townsend Acres for opening her big mouth?" he teased, his fingers squeezing hers.

Christina frowned, and Parker glanced at her apologetically.

"I'm sorry. I know how worried you are about Star," he said.

Christina nodded. "Do you think your grandfather would talk to Brad? He seemed to be on my side when I told him about Star this morning."

"We can talk to him, but he's not around much anymore."

"And you won't be there, either." *Who will keep an eye on Star?* Christina wondered desperately. Then she thought about her conversation with Clay. *If you want Star to be a champion,* he'd told her, *you're going to have to fight for him every step of the way.* Christina pressed her lips together. She knew what she needed to do. It was time to bring Star home.

"What happened?" Ashleigh asked when Christina and Parker arrived at Meadowlark. Ashleigh and Mike were pacing in front of the horse van, while Samantha stood by the cab, her arms crossed. Christina had never seen her mother look quite so worried. "Melanie told us you'd gone to the Townsends'," Ashleigh said, opening the truck door.

As Christina climbed out, her dad came over. He put a hand on each shoulder and stared into her eyes. "Something must really be bothering you to run off in the middle of an event like this. Is it about Star?"

Fresh tears started to flow as Christina nodded. She glanced over at Samantha. "I'm sorry, Sam," she apologized. "I let you and Sterling down."

Samantha smiled. "It's all right. I know you wouldn't have gone off unless it was really important."

A familiar whinny rang from the van. "Is Sterling okay?" Christina asked anxiously.

"Melanie took good care of her," Sam assured her.

Just then Kevin and Melanie came around the corner of the van, Foxy in tow. The mare was all tacked up. Her hooves were polished and her coat shone. "Your steed is ready for stadium jumping, Mr. Townsend," Kevin announced, bowing from the waist. "You'd better get her warmed up!"

"Thanks, Kev." Parker gave Christina's hand a squeeze before striding over to Foxy to mount up.

"Good luck," Christina said softly. "I'll be watching."

"Not until you tell us what's going on," Ashleigh said, but her tone was gentle.

"Uh, we'll go find a spot along the rail so we can watch Parker," Melanie said, as if she knew the three of them needed to be alone.

When Melanie, Samantha, and Kevin had left, Christina faced her parents. "It may not seem like a big deal to you, but to me—" Her voice cracked. Tears spilling from her eyes, she looked at her mother. "Mom, Star is just as important to me as Wonder was to you. When I heard Brad was backing him today without

146

telling me, I was terrified, because I knew in my heart Star wasn't ready. And I was right."

Christina told them how Star had grown more and more anxious. "I warned Brad and Julio, but neither of them listened to me. Star reared up and flipped. And now Julio's unconscious. Brad ordered me off the farm—he told me I can never work with Star again." Covering her eyes, Christina started to sob. Ashleigh wrapped her arms around her and held her close.

"Oh, Christina, I had no idea," her mother said, her own voice choking.

"We didn't realize Brad was being so stubborn about Star's training," Mike said. "You know the colt best—Brad should have listened to you."

"I meant I didn't really believe how attached you'd become to Star," Ashleigh clarified in a whisper.

Christina nodded, her cheek rubbing against the front of her mother's shirt. "I know he's just a horse, Mom. But it's as if I know what's going on in his head—and his heart."

"I understand perfectly," Ashleigh said, and Christina knew her mother finally did understand. "I just wish I had understood earlier. You were always so adamant about eventing, Chris. I thought you were being stubborn about wanting Star at Whitebrook so you could turn him into an event horse."

Christina pulled back. "An event horse? I never said that. I've always known Star would become a race-horse."

"You never told *us* that," her father said.

"I guess I never really said it to anyone—except Star. He knows he's going to be a champion." Christina looked back and forth from Mike to Ashleigh and took a deep breath. "Brad Townsend is going to ruin Star if he stays there. I know it. We have to get him back."

Ashleigh sighed. "I should have listened to you earlier, Chris. It's just that the memories of Wonder kept getting in the way. Will you forgive me?"

Christina gave her mother a hug. "As long as you promise to let Star come home."

"Uh, I hate to break up this touching scene, but if we're going to bring Star home, we'd better do it," Mike said.

"Now?" Christina gasped.

"Brad's not going to like it now or later," Mike said, his tone serious.

"That's for sure," Ashleigh agreed. "Let's watch Parker ride, then head over to the Townsends to bring Star home."

Christina's heart swelled when she heard her mother say those magic words.

And this time I won't be alone. We'll face Brad together.

Christina held her breath as Parker took Foxy over the last jump, sailing over it with a foot to spare. When they cantered between the two flags of the finish line, the crowd burst into applause.

148

"All right, Parker!" Christina, Melanie, and Kevin whooped while Ashleigh and Mike and Sam clapped noisily.

"With that round, he should get first in preliminary!" Samantha cried, beaming.

"At least one of your students made it," Christina joked.

"You'll get there," Samantha assured her. "Though now that Parker's going to be living at Whisperwood, he may have an advantage."

Christina looked at Samantha. "He told you?"

Samantha nodded slightly.

"And it's all right if he stays with you?"

"More than all right. We can use the help!"

When Parker rode from the ring, Christina ran up to him. "You were terrific! Listen, I can't stay. My mom and dad are going with me to Townsend Acres."

"I'm coming with you," Parker said.

"No way. You're in enough trouble with your dad already."

Parker grinned. "Then I can't get into any worse trouble, right?"

"Right." Christina laughed. "But what about our horses?"

"Kevin and I are willing to take care of them for you, if you would be so kind as to buy us pizza this evening," Melanie piped up.

Parker grinned. "It's a deal."

"Definitely," Christina agreed.

"All right, Chris. You go with Parker. We'll meet you at the Townsends'," Mike said. "First we need to stop at Whitebrook and pick up the horse trailer. Don't do anything until we get there," he cautioned them.

Fifteen minutes later Parker drove up the lane to Townsend Acres. Christina's stomach was twisted into a knot. The day had been so crazy, she was feeling dizzy. *What if Brad says no? What if he refuses to let us take Star?*

Stopping the truck in front of the barn, Parker killed the engine. Since it was late afternoon, the place was quiet. Christina opened the door of the truck. "Hey!" Parker put his hand on her arm. "Your parents said to wait."

"But I have to make sure Star is okay," Christina said. "I'll check on him and come right out. Promise." Flashing Parker a grin, she ran into the barn and over to Star's stall. But he wasn't there.

Christina's heart flew into her throat. Had they isolated him again? She raced down the aisle to the far end, her boot heels tapping the cement aisle.

"Star!" she called when she reached the last stall. Throwing open the door, she stepped inside—and clasped her hands to her mouth to hold back a sob.

Star was huddled in the far corner. There was no food or water. His neck was crusted with sweat from that afternoon, and they'd left him completely tacked up. Christina stared in horror as she realized they hadn't even taken off the longe line. It was wrapped around his legs in tight tangles.

"I can't believe Brad did this to you!" Christina moaned. She had to get him out of there. She couldn't leave him at Townsend Acres one more second.

Furious, she raced back to the tack room and grabbed his halter and a pair of trimming scissors. When she hurried into the stall, Star didn't lift his head to look at her. Then she realized why. The longe line was so tight, they'd forced his muzzle almost against his chest.

Christina unsnapped the line from the bit, then laid a soothing hand on his neck. "It's okay, boy. I know I broke my promise not to leave you. But it won't ever happen again."

Quickly she got to work, cutting through the webbing as fast as she could. When his legs were free, she untacked him.

As the saddle and bridle came off, Star slowly came back to life. By the time she'd put on his halter and snapped a lead to it, his ears were pricked. And when she brought him a half bucket of water, he drank greedily.

"What are you doing?" a voice demanded.

Christina jumped, sloshing water on her boots. Brad was standing in the doorway.

"I thought you understood you weren't allowed on this farm," Brad said, glowering at her.

"Uh . . ." Christina backed nervously away from his angry expression, bumping into Star's side. "We're taking Star home."

Brad cocked his head. "*We?*"

"My mom and dad. They should be here any minute with the horse trailer."

Brad gave a short bark. "You're bluffing, Christina. Now give me that horse and get off my property, or I'm calling the police. Right now you're only trespassing, but if you take Star from the stall, I'll charge you with stealing."

Stealing! She could tell from the hard line of Brad's mouth that he *wasn't* bluffing. Still, her fingers gripped the lead tighter. "No. I'm taking Star out of here."

"Give me that horse." Brad's voice was low and threatening. Christina held his gaze. She knew he was used to everyone jumping at his command. But this time she wasn't going to jump.

Brad clenched his jaw. Reaching out, he grabbed Christina's wrist in one hand. With the other hand he jerked the lead line out of her grasp.

"No!" Christina cried, lunging for the lead shank, but Brad knocked her away. Star pinned his ears. Snaking his head around, he came at Brad, his teeth bared. Brad threw up his arm to shield his face, dropping the lead.

Snatching up the lead, Christina gave it a tug. "Star, no!" With a toss of his head, the colt backed up.

Dropping his arm, Brad glared at Star and then at Christina. "That horse is dangerous!" he declared. "We're just lucky Julio's all right, or I'd threaten to sell the monster."

"If he's such a monster, then you won't mind if we take him off your hands," Ashleigh's voice rang out.

Christina looked over Brad's shoulder. Ashleigh stood in the doorway, with Parker behind her.

Red-faced, Brad glared at Ashleigh. Christina had never seen him so angry. "He's not leaving Townsend Acres."

Ashleigh lifted her chin defiantly. "I don't want to argue with you, Brad. Our families have had too many disagreements. Let us take Star back to Whitebrook. You know that's where he belongs."

"If he stays here," Parker chimed in, "you'll kill his spirit, just like you tried to kill mine."

"By trying to knock some sense into your stubborn skull?" Brad shot back.

Ashleigh raised her hand to silence them. Christina held her breath, afraid that if Brad felt backed into a corner, he would refuse to let them take Star.

"Mr. Townsend," Christina said, her voice quavering, "please. I love Star and he loves me. I know that's hard for you to understand—" Her voice broke. Star nudged her with his nose, pushing her forward. "But it means he belongs with me."

Brad gazed down at her, then over at Star, who stood docilely beside her, and Christina thought she saw his hard expression soften for a moment.

Abruptly Brad swung toward Ashleigh. "She's your daughter, all right," he said, as if it were an insult. "Go ahead, take him." He jabbed his index finger at

Ashleigh. "But if Whitebrook doesn't make him a champion, then I will. That colt had better win big in his first or second race, or he comes back to Townsend Acres. Agreed?"

"Agreed," Ashleigh said without hesitating.

Brad nodded once. Ashleigh and Parker stepped back. As he passed by, Brad stopped in front of his son. "I'm sorry about this morning," he said stiffly, and then turned to walk away.

Christina felt as if a huge weight had been lifted from her shoulders—and her heart. Turning, she flung her arms around Star's neck. "I can't believe it's over!"

Ashleigh came into the stall, smiling with relief. "Come on, let's get Star out of here before Brad changes his mind. Your dad's outside in the trailer."

"I'll go put the ramp down," Parker said, and Christina flashed him a grateful smile.

"So this is the colt that's going to be our next champion," Ashleigh commented as they led Star down the aisle.

Christina stopped abruptly as the impact of what Ashleigh had agreed to sunk in. "What if Star doesn't win his races and Brad takes him back?"

"He's Wonder's colt. He'll be a winner," Ashleigh stated with confidence. "We're going to make sure of it."

"We?"

"I think it's about time I paid some attention to this colt myself," Ashleigh explained.

"You mean you'll help me train him?" Christina asked, her eyes shining.

"Of course," Ashleigh assured her. "I can hardly wait."

Christina wasn't sure how such a horrible day could turn itself around completely and become so perfect. Suddenly she felt like the luckiest girl in the world.

She put both hands on Star's halter and planted a kiss on his soft muzzle. "Come on, Wonder's Star. Let's go home."

ALICE LEONHARDT has been horse-crazy since she was five years old. Her first pony was a pinto named Ted. When she got older, she joined Pony Club and rode in shows and rallies. Now she just rides her Quarter Horse, April, for fun. The author of more than thirty books for children, she still finds time to take care of two horses, two cats, two dogs, and two children, as well as teach at a community college.

THOROUGHBRED

◆◆

If you enjoyed this book, then you'll love reading all the books in the THOROUGHBRED series!

◆◆

◆◆

THOROUGHBRED

All books are
$4.50 U.S./$5.50 Canadian